About

Jeff Deaver is the bestselling author of a number of powerful suspense novels. He was a lawyer before quitting work to become a full-time writer. He divides his time between Washington, DC and California. *The Bone Collector* is now a major film starring Denzel Washington and Angelina Jolie.

The Lesson of Her Death

Speaking in Tongues

Jeffery Deaver

CORONET BOOKS
Hodder & Stoughton

The Lesson of Her Death
first published in Great Britain in 1993
by Hodder and Stoughton

Speaking in Tongues
first published in Great Britain in 1999
by Hodder and Stoughton

This paperback omnibus edition published in 2000
by Hodder and Stoughton
A division of Hodder Headline

A Coronet Paperback

10 9 8 7 6 5 4 3 2 1

ISBN 0 340 79464 X

Printed and bound in Great Britain by
Clays Ltd, St Ives plc

Hodder and Stoughton
A division of Hodder Headline
338 Euston Road
London NW1 3BH

THE LESSON OF HER DEATH

For Carla Norton

AUTHOR'S NOTE

I would like to express my grateful appreciation to Jerry Cowdrey, Laguna Niguel, California, for her insights into the plight and the potential of learning disabled children. Similarly, my thanks to my sister and fellow author Julie Reece Deaver, Pacific Grove, California, and special thanks to Karen Cowdrey of Los Angeles, whose insights into psychotherapy and the human mind have proved invaluable in many, many ways. Also, my appreciation to my editor, Kate Miciak, among whose uncanny talents are the abilities to inspire, to instruct, and – not the least – to instill in an author the same enthusiasm she feels for the written word. And finally, my heartfelt thanks to my agent and friend, Deborah Schneider.

JWD, *New York City*, 1993

PART ONE

Profile

1

With every passing mile her heart fled a little more.

The girl, nine years old, sat slumped in the front seat, rubbing her finger along the worn beige armrest. The slipstream from the open window laid a strip of blond hair across her face. She brushed it away and looked up at the unsmiling, gray-haired man of about forty. He drove carefully, with his eyes fixed beyond the long white nose of the car.

'Please,' the girl said.

'No.'

She put her hands into her lap.

Maybe when he stopped at a red light she would jump out.

Maybe if he slowed down just enough . . .

Would it hurt, she wondered, to leap from the car into the tall grass beside the road? She pictured herself tumbling through the green blades, feeling the cold sprinkle of dew on her face and hands.

But then what? Where would she run to?

The first click of the turn signal interrupted these thoughts and the girl jumped as if a gun had fired. The car slowed and rocked as it pulled into the driveway, aiming toward a low brick building. She realized that her last hope was gone.

The car eased to a stop, brakes squealing like a sob.

'Give me a kiss,' the man said, reaching over and

pushing the buckle release. The seat belt retracted. She held on to the nylon like a lifeline.

'I don't want to. Please.'

'Sarah.'

'Just for today? Please.'

'No.'

'Don't leave me.'

'Out you go.'

'I'm not ready!'

'Do the best you can.'

'I'm scared.'

'There's nothing to be—'

'Don't leave me!'

'Look—' His voice grew stony. 'I'm going to be right nearby. Just over at Blackfoot Pond. That's hardly a mile away.'

Her inventory of excuses was depleted. Sarah opened the car door but remained sitting.

'Give me a kiss.'

She leaned over and kissed her father quickly on his cheek then climbed out of the car, standing in the cool spring air heavily scented with bus exhaust. She took three steps toward the building, watching the car pull out of the driveway. She thought suddenly about the Garfield toy stuck to the back window of the family station wagon. Sarah remembered when she'd placed it there, licking the cups before squeezing them against the glass. For some reason this memory made her want to cry.

Maybe he would catch a glimpse of her in the mirror, change his mind and return.

The car vanished behind a hill.

Sarah turned and entered the building. Clutching her lunch box to her chest she shuffled through the corridors. Although she was as tall as any of the children swarming around her she felt younger than them all.

Tinier. Weaker.

At the fourth-grade classroom she stopped. Sarah looked inside. Her nostrils flared and she felt her skin prickle with a rash of fear. She hesitated only for a moment then turned and walked resolutely from the building, buffeted and jostled as she forced her way through the oncoming stream of shouting, calling, laughing children.

Not thirty feet from where they had found the body last night, he saw the note.

The piece of paper, pierced by a wild rose stem the shade of dried blood, fluttered in the moist wind, sending out a Morse code in the low morning sunlight.

Bill Corde pressed toward the paper through a tangle of juniper and maple saplings and stubborn runners of forsythia.

Had they missed it? How could they?

He barked his shin on a hidden stump and swore softly but continued toward the scrap.

Corde was six foot two and his short hair was Persian-cat gray, which because he was just about to turn forty made him maybe seven-eighths premature. His skin was pale, the month being April and Corde having been fishing only twice so far that season. He looked lean from a distance but his belt curled outward more than he would have liked; Corde's most strenuous sport these days was gentlemen's softball. This morning as always his New Lebanon Sheriff's Department shirt was clean and stiff as a sheet of new balsa wood and his beige slacks had razor creases.

Corde was by rank a lieutenant and by specialty a detective.

He remembered this place not twelve hours before – last night, lit only by the deputies' flashlights and the edgy illumination of a half-moon. He had sent his men to scour the ground. They were young and austere (the ones trained in the military) or young and arrogant (state police academy grads) but they were all earnest.

Although they were virtuosos at DUI arrests and joyridings and domestics, what the deputies knew about murder they had learned mostly from pulp thrillers and

TV, just like they knew about guns from stubbly autumn fields, not from the state pistol range up in Higgins. Still they had been ordered to search the crime scene and they had, doggedly and with fervor.

But not one of them had found the piece of paper toward which Bill Corde now struggled through thick brush.

Oh, you poor girl . . .

. . . who lies at the foot of a ten-foot-high earth dam.

. . . who lies in this chill wet dish of mud and low grass and blue flowers.

. . . whose dark hair is side-parted, whose face is long, whose throat thick. Her round lips curl prominently. Each ear holds three wire-thin gold rings. Her toes are lanky and their nails dark with burgundy polish.

. . . who lies on her back, arms folded over her breasts, as if the mortician had already done her up. The pink floral blouse is buttoned high. Her skirt extends so modestly below her knees, tucked beneath her thighs.

'We got her name. Here we go. It's Jennie Gebben. She's a student.'

Last night Bill Corde had crouched down beside the body, his knee popping, and put his face next to hers. The pearlish half-moon was reflected in her dead but still unglazed hazel eyes. He had smelled grass, mud, methane, transmission fluid, mint from her lips and perfume like pie spices rising from her cold skin.

He had stood and climbed to the top of the dam, which held back the murky waters of Blackfoot Pond. He had turned and looked down at her. The moonlight was otherworldly, pale, special-effects light. In it, Jennie Gebben seemed to move. Not living, human movement but shrinking and curling as if she were melting into the mud. Corde had whispered a few words to her, or to whatever remained of her, then helped the men search the ground.

Now, in the morning brilliance, he pushed his way through a final tangle of forsythia and stepped up to the rosebush. With his hand inside a small plastic bag,

6

Corde pulled the paper from the russet thorns.

Jim Slocum called, 'The whole shebang?'

Corde did not answer him. The boys from the department had not been careless last night. They could not have found this scrap of paper then because it was a clipping from the morning's *Register*.

Slocum asked again, 'The whole, uhm, place?'

Corde looked up and said. 'The whole thing. Yeah.'

Slocum grunted and continued unwinding yellow police-line tape around the circle of wet earth where the girl's body had been found. Slocum, after Corde, was the next senior New Lebanon town deputy. He was a muscular man with a round head and long ears. He'd picked up a razor-cut hairstyle in 1974, complete with sideburns, and had kept it ever since. Except for theme parks, hunting trips, and Christmas at the in-laws', Slocum rarely left the county. Today he whistled a generic tune as he strung the tape.

A small group of reporters stood by the road. Corde would give nothing away but these were rural news hounds and well behaved; they looked all filled up with reporters' zeal but they left the two officers pretty much alone, content to shoot snaps and study the crime scene. Corde figured they were sponging up atmosphere for tomorrow's articles, which would brim with adjectives and menace.

Corde lowered the newspaper clipping, now wrapped in the plastic bag, and looked around him. From the dam, off to his right, the ground rose to a vast forest split by Route 302, a highway that led to the mall then to a dozen other county roads and to a half-dozen state highways and to two expressways and eventually to forty-nine other states and two foreign countries where a fugitive killer might hide till the end of his days.

Pacing, Corde looked over the forest, his lips pressed tightly together. He and Slocum had arrived five minutes before, at eight-thirty. The *Register* started hitting stores and porches at about seven-fifteen. Whoever had left the clipping had done so in the past hour.

7

Listening to the hum of wind over a strand of taut barbed wire, he scanned the ground beneath the rosebush. It was indented by what seemed like two footprints though they were too smeared to help in identification. He kicked over a log that appeared newly fallen. A swarm of insects like tiny armadillos scurried away. Striding to the top of the dam, he placed his hands on green metal pipes sunk into the dirt as a railing.

He squinted deep furrows into his forehead as he looked through the morning sunlight that crackled off the wind-roughed water of the pond. The woods stretched away from him, endless acres encased in a piercing glare.

Listen . . .

He cocked his head and pointed his ear at the stream of light.

Footsteps!

He gazed once again into the heart of the forest. He lifted his hand to his eyebrows to shade the sun yet still the light dazzled. It stung his eyes. He could see everything, and he could see nothing.

Where?

When he lowered his palm it came to rest on the grip of his service revolver.

She ran most of the way.

The route from New Lebanon Grade School to Blackfoot Pond was three miles along 302 (which she was forbidden to walk on) but only a half-hour through the forest, and that was the path she took.

Sarah avoided the marshy areas, not because of any danger – she knew every trail through every forest around New Lebanon – but because she was afraid of getting mud on the shoes her father had polished the night before, shiny as a bird's wings, and on her rose-print knee socks, a Christmas present from her grandmother. She stayed to the path that wound through oak trees and juniper and pine beds of fern. Far off a bird called. *Ah-hoo-eeeee.* Sarah stopped to look for it. She was warm and took off her jacket, then rolled up the sleeves of her white blouse and unbuttoned the collar. She ran on.

As she approached Blackfoot Pond she saw her father standing with Mr Slocum at the far end of the water, two or three hundred feet away through the thickest part of the forest. Their heads were down. It looked as if they were searching for a lost ball. Sarah started toward them but as she stepped out from behind a maple tree she stopped. She had walked right into a shaft of sunlight so bright it blinded her. The light was magical – golden yellow and filled with dust and steam and dots of spring insects that glowed in the river of radiant light. But this was not what made her hesitate. In a thicket of plants beside the path she saw – she *thought* she saw – someone bending forward watching her father. With the light in her eyes she couldn't tell whether it was a man or woman, young or adult.

Maybe it was just a bunch of leaves and branches.

No. She saw movement. It *was* somebody.

Her curiosity suddenly gave way to uneasiness and Sarah turned away, off the path, starting downhill to the pond where she could follow the shoreline to the dam. Her cautious eyes remained on the figure nearby and when she stepped forward her gleaming black shoe slipped on a folded newspaper hidden under a pile of dry leaves.

A short scream burst from her mouth and she reached out in panic. Her tiny fingers found only strands of tall grass, which popped easily from the ground and followed her like streamers as she slid toward the water.

Corde called to Slocum, 'You hear anybody over that way?'

'Thought I might have.' Slocum lifted off his Smokey the Bear hat and wiped his forehead. 'Some footsteps or rustling.'

'Anything now?'

'Nope.'

9

Corde waited four or five minutes then walked down to the base of the dam and asked, 'You through?'

'Yessiree,' Slocum said. 'We head back now?'

'I'll be taking a Midwest puddle jumper over to St Louis to talk with the girl's father. Should be back by three or so. I want us all to meet about the case at four, four-thirty at the office. You stay here until the Crime Scene boys show up.'

'You want me just to wait, not do anything?'

'They're due here now. Shouldn't be long.'

'But you know the county. Could be an hour.' Slocum's way of protesting was to feed you bits of information like this.

'We gotta keep it sealed, Jim.'

'You want.' Slocum didn't look pleased but Corde wasn't going to leave a crime scene unattended, especially with a gaggle of reporters on hand.

'I just don't want to get into a situation where I'm sitting here all day.'

'I don't think it'll—'

A crackle of brush, footsteps coming toward them.

The officers spun around to face the forest. Corde's hand again fell to his revolver. Slocum dropped the tape, which hit the ground and rolled, leaving a long thick yellow tail behind it. He too reached for his pistol.

The noise was louder. They couldn't see the source but it was coming from the general direction of the rosebush that had held the clipping.

'Daddy!'

She ran breathlessly toward him, her hair awash in the air around her, beads of sweat on her dirty face. One of her knee socks had slipped almost to her ankle and there was a thick streak of mud along a leg and arm.

'Sarrie!'

My sweet Lord! His own daughter. He'd had his hand on his gun and he'd been five seconds away from drawing on her!

'Oh, Sarah! What are you doing here?'

'I'm sorry, Daddy. I felt all funny. I got to school and

I thought I was going to be sick.' Rehearsed, the words stumbled out in a monotone.

Jesus Lord . . .

Corde crouched down to her. He smelled the scent of the shampoo she had received in her Easter basket not long ago. Violets. 'You should never, *never* be where Daddy's working. You understand that? Never! Unless I bring you.'

Her face looked puffy with contrition. She glanced at her leg then held up her dirty forearm. 'I fell.'

Corde took out his sharp-ironed handkerchief and wiped the mud off her limbs. He saw there were no cuts or scrapes and looked back into her eyes. There was still anger in his voice when he demanded, 'Did you see anyone there? Were you talking to anybody in the woods?'

The fall had not bought the sympathy she'd expected. She was frightened by her father's reaction.

He repeated, 'Answer me!'

What was the safest answer? She shook her head.

'You didn't see *anyone?*'

She hesitated then swallowed. 'I got sick at school.'

Corde studied her pale eyes for a moment. 'Honey, we talked about this. You don't get sick. You just *feel* sick.'

A young reporter lifted a camera and shot a picture of them, Corde stroking a slash of blond hair out of her eyes. Corde glared at him.

'It's like I have pitchforks in my tummy.'

'You have to go to school.'

'I don't want to! I hate school!' Her shrill voice filled the clearing. Corde glanced at the reporters, who watched the exchange with varying degrees of interest and sympathy.

'Come on. Get in the car.'

'No!' she squealed. 'I'm not going! You can't make me.'

Corde wanted to shout with frustration. 'Young lady, get in that car. I'm not going to tell you again.'

'Please?' Her face filled with enormous disappointment.

11

'Now.'

When Sarah saw her plan wasn't going to work she walked toward Corde's squad car. Corde watched, half expecting her to bolt into the forest. She paused and scanned the woods intently.

'Sarah?'

She didn't turn her head. She climbed into the car and slammed the door.

'Kids,' Corde muttered.

'Find yourself something?' Slocum asked.

Corde was tying a chain of custody card to the bag containing the newspaper clipping he had found. He signed his name and passed it to Slocum. The brief article was about last night's killing. The editor had been able to fit only five paragraphs of story into the newspaper before deadline. The clipping had been cut from the paper with eerie precision. The slices were perfectly even, as if made by a razor knife.

Auden Co-ed Raped, Murdered was the headline.

The picture accompanying the story had not been a photo of the crime scene but was a lift from a feature story the *Register* had run several months ago about a church picnic that Corde had attended with his family. The cut line read, 'Detective William Corde, chief investigator in the case, shown here last March with his wife, Diane, and children, Jamie, 15, and Sarah, 9.'

'Damn, Bill.'

Slocum was referring to the words crudely written in red ink next to the photograph.

They read: JENNIE HAD TO DIE. IT COULD HAPPEN TO THEM.

2

They climbed the stairs slowly, one man feeling the luxurious carpet under his boots, the other not feeling a single thing at all.

Outside the wind howled. A spring storm enveloped this lush suburb, though inside the elegant house the temperature was warm and the wind and rain seemed distant. Bill Corde, hat in hand, boots carefully wiped, watched the man pause in the dim hallway then reach quickly for a door knob. He hesitated once again then pushed the door inward and slapped the light switch on.

'You don't have to be here,' Corde said gently.

Richard Gebben did not answer but walked into the middle of the pink carpeted room where his daughter had grown up.

'She's going to be all right,' Gebben said in a faint voice. Corde had no idea whether he meant his wife, who was in the downstairs bedroom drowsy from sedatives, or his daughter, lying at the moment on a sensuously rounded enamel coroner's table two hundred miles away.

Going to be all right.

Richard Gebben was a crew-cut businessman with a face troubled by acne when young. He was Midwestern and he was middle-aged and he was rich. For men like Gebben, life moves by justice not fate. Corde suspected the man's essential struggle right now was in trying to understand the reason for his daughter's death.

'You drove all the way here yourself,' Gebben said.

'No, sir, took a commuter flight. Midwest Air.'

Gebben rubbed the face of his Rolex compulsively across his pocked cheek. He touched his eyes in an odd way and he seemed to be wondering why he was not crying.

Corde nodded toward her dresser and asked, 'May I?'

'I remember when she left for school the last time she was home, Thanksgiving . . . I'm sorry?'

'Her dresser. I'd like to look through it.'

Gebben gestured absently. Corde walked to the bureau but did not yet open it. 'Thanksgiving. She'd left the bedclothes all piled up. In a heap. After she'd gone to the airport, Jennie's mother came up here and made the bed and arranged it just like that . . .' Corde looked at the three pink-and-white gingham pillows on top of the comforter, a plush dog with black button eyes sticking his head out from under them. 'My wife, she took a long time to arrange the dog.'

Gebben took several deep breaths to calm himself. 'She . . . The thing about Jennie was, she loved . . .'

What was he going to say? Loved *life?* Loved *people?* Loved *flowers kittens poetry charities?* Gebben fell silent, perhaps troubled that he could at this moment think only of the cheapest clichés. Death, Corde knew, makes us feel so foolish.

He turned away from Gebben to Jennie's dresser. He was aware of a mix of scents. She had a dozen bottles of perfume on the mirrored dressing table. The L'Air du Temps was full, a bottle of generic cologne nearly empty. He lifted it, looked at the label and set it down. His hand would retain for days the sharp spicy smell, which he recalled from the pond last night.

The bureau contained nothing but clothes. Above it a hundred postcards and snapshots were pinned to a corkboard. Jennie's arm twined around the waists of dozens of boys, faces different, poses similar. Her dark hair seemed to be darker in summer though that might be a trick of Kodak convenience photography. She often wore it pinned back. Her sport was volleyball and a dozen pictures revealed her playing the game with lusty determination on her face. Corde asked if he could have one of these, a close-up of Jennie, pretty face glossy with sweat. Gebben shrugged. How Corde hated this part of the job, walking straight into the heart of people's anguish.

Corde touched several recent snapshots of the girl with friends. Gebben confirmed that all of them were away at other schools – all except Emily Rossiter, who was Jennie's current roommate at Auden. Corde saw: her high school ID card. Ticket stubs from a Cowboy Junkies concert, a Bon Jovi concert, a Billy Joel concert, a Paula Poundstone show. A greeting card with a silly cartoon rabbit on the front offered her congratulations on passing her driving test.

Corde pulled the chair away from her desk and sat. He surveyed the worn desktop in front of him, nicked, scratched, marked with her doodlings. He saw a bottle of India ink. A framed picture of Jennie with a scruffy cocker spaniel. A snapshot of her coming out of church one recent spring, maybe at Easter, blue crocuses at her feet.

She died on a bed of milky blue hyacinths.

In a lopsided clay cup was a chewed yellow pencil, its eraser worn away. Corde lifted it, feeling beneath the thick pads of his fingers the rough indentations and the negative space of Jennie Gebben's mouth. He rubbed the wood, thinking that it had once been damp from her. He replaced the pencil.

He went through her desk, which held high school assignments, squares of wrapping paper, old birthday cards.

'No diaries or letters?'

Gebben focused on the detective. 'I don't know. That's where they'd be.' He nodded toward the desk.

Corde again looked carefully. No threatening letters, no notes from spurned boyfriends. No personal

15

correspondence of any kind. He examined the closet, swinging aside the wealth of clothes and checking the shelves. He found nothing helpful and closed the double doors.

Corde stood in the middle of the room, hands on his hips, looking around him.

'Was she engaged? Have a steady boyfriend here?'

Gebben was hesitating. 'She had a lot of friends. Nobody'd hurt her. Everybody loved her.'

'Did she break up with anybody recently?'

'No,' Gebben said and shrugged in such a way that Corde understood the man had no idea what he was saying.

'Anybody have a crush on her?

'Nobody who knew Jennie would hurt her,' Gebben said slowly. Then he added, 'You know what I was thinking? Since I got the call I haven't told anybody. I've been working up courage. For all those people – her grandparents, her friends, my brother's family – Jennie's still alive. For all they know she's sitting in the library studying.'

'I'll leave you now, sir. If you can think of anything that might help us I'd appreciate a call. And if you find any letters or a diary please send them to me as soon as you can. They'd be very important.' He handed Gebben one of his cheap business cards.

Gebben studied the card. He looked up, sloe-eyed and earnest. 'It's going to be all right.'

He said this with such intensity that it seemed as if his sole purpose at the moment was to comfort Bill Corde.

Wynton Kresge sat in his office in the main administration building of Auden University. The room – high-ceilinged, paneled in oak – was carpeted in navy blue, pretty much the same color as that in his Cutlass Supreme though this pile was twice as thick. His desk was a large mahogany piece. Occasionally when he was on the phone listening to someone he had no desire to be listening to (which was pretty often), Kresge would imagine ways to get the desk out of the office without knocking a hole in the wall. On particularly slow days he actually considered trying to remove it. He would have been a good candidate for this project: Kresge was six foot four and weighed two hundred and sixty pounds. His upper arms measured fifteen inches around, his thighs were twenty-four, and only a minor percentage of those dimensions was fat. (He had never lifted a barbell in his life but had retained much of the muscle he cultivated when he was a college linebacker for the Tigers not the Missouri Tigers the *Dan Devine* Tigers.)

The top of the desk held one telephone with two lines, one brass lamp, one blotter, one leather desk calendar opened to this week, one framed photo of an attractive woman, seven framed photos of children, and one piece of paper.

The paper, held down by Kresge's massive hand as if he were afraid it would blow away, contained the following words: *Jennie Gebben. Tuesday ten p.m. Blackfoot Pond. McReynolds dorm. Lovers, students, teachers, robbery? rape? other motive? Susan Biagotti?* Beneath this was an awkward diagram of the campus and the pond and the road around it. Kresge touched his earlobe with the butt of his Schaeffer sterling silver ballpoint pen, which he had polished just the night before, and considered what he'd written.

Kresge drew additional lines on the paper, crossing off words, and adding others. He was drawing a dotted line from the campus to the pond when a knock on the closed door made him jump. By the time his secretary walked into the room without announcing herself further the piece of paper was wadded up and slam-dunked into Kresge's wastebasket.

'She wants to see you,' said the secretary, a pretty woman in her late thirties.

'She does.'

The secretary paused then said, 'You're holed up in here.'

17

'I beg your pardon?'

She said, 'I used to think that that phrase was "hauled up." Like they hauled somebody up in a tower so he could escape from the police or something.'

'The police?' Kresge asked.

'But then I found out it was "holed up." Like, go into a hole.'

'I don't really know. Now?'

'She said now.'

Kresge nodded. He unlocked his top drawer and from it took out a dark gray Taurus 9mm semiautomatic pistol. He looked to make certain there was a full clip in the grip of the gun then slipped it in a belt holster. He left the room with what the secretary sensed, though Kresge himself did not, was a look of intense, almost theatrical, determination on his face.

This was how she would build the house: She would find some land – there, that beautiful field with the gold and white flowers in it, there through the window, surrounded by green-silver trees. She could see, from her cell, the tall grass waving in a breeze soft as a kitten's lazy tail. Then she would call her friends the animals and—

'Sarah, are you with us?'

Her head snapped away from the window and she found thirty-two children and one adult staring at her. Her breath escaped in a soft snap then stopped completely. Sarah looked at their eyes and felt her heart shudder then start to beat at a fast gallop.

'I called on you. Come up here.'

Sarah sat still and felt the pure heat from her face flood into her arms and chest.

Mrs Beiderson smiled, her face as sweet as Sarah's grandmother's. Mrs Beiderson smiled a lot. She never raised her voice at Sarah, never shouted at her, never took her hand and walked her to the principal's office like she did the boys that drew pictures on their desks or fought. Mrs Beiderson always spoke to Sarah in a voice like a pussy willow.

Sarah hated her more than anyone in the world.

'Sarah, now come along. This is just practice. You're not being graded.'

The girl looked at her desk. Inside was the pill her mother had given her. But it wasn't time to take it yet.

'Now, Sarah.'

Sarah stood, her hands at her sides, too heavy to lift. She walked to the front of the dungeon and turned to face the class. She felt Mrs Beiderson's smile pelt the back of her neck like a whip of snakes. She glanced at the trees outside the window. Oh, the freedom of the trees! She could smell the bark, she could feel the fuzz on the bottom of an elf cap growing up through ivy, she could see the doorway to the secret tunnel in her house.

Looking out over her classmates' faces, she saw Priscilla Witlock laughing, Dennis Morgan twisting up his fat lips into a mean grin, Brad Mibbock rolling his eyes. Laughter roaring so loud it struck her face and stung. She saw boys holding fists above their you-knows and moving them up and down, she saw girls with long red fingernails and dangling bracelets, girls her age but with round perfect breasts and sleek makeup and high heels, girls taunting her . . .

And Mrs. Beiderson, who saw only the bored faces of her class and heard nothing but Sarah's whimpering, said, 'Sarah, your word is "clarify."'

The sound hit Sarah with the jolt of a schoolyard punch. Her daddy had helped her with this word. But she knew it had several up-down letters, which were very hard for her. She began to cry.

'You've done it before,' smiling Mrs Beiderson said in her soft lying, cheating, snaky voice. 'You're not trying, Sarah. We all have to try.' Mrs Beiderson touched the rose cameo at her throat. '"Clarify" is on the list. Didn't you study the list?'

Sarah nodded.

'If you studied the list then there's nothing to cry about.'

Now *everyone* would know she was crying, even the students in the back.

'I can't.'

'You don't want us to think you're being difficult, do you? "Clarify."'

Between sobs, Sarah said, 'C.'

'Very good.' The snake smiled.

Her knees quivered. 'I don't know. I don't.' More tears.

'What's the next letter?'

'I don't know.'

'Try.'

'C-A . . .'

Mrs Beiderson exhaled a sigh. 'All right, Sarah. Sit—'

'I could do it at home—'

'—Down. Anyone else?'

And Priscilla Witlock didn't even rise from her seat but was staring right at Sarah, slinging out the letters, C, then L, then A, then R, spelling the word in the time it took Sarah to take a huge gulp of air to try to quench her fear.

And then she felt it. First a trickle. Then a flood, as her panties grew wet and she put her hand down-there to stop herself but knowing it was too late, the flowing warm moisture running around her leg and Mrs Beiderson saying, 'Oh dear oh dear,' and some of the class looking away, which was as bad as the rest of the class staring, as bad as knowing the story would be all over town and everybody would know even her grandfather up in heaven would know . . .

Sarah threw her arms around herself and ran to the door, pushing it open with her shoulder. The glass burst into a spiderweb of cracks. She leapt down the stairs two at a time and ran blindly down the corridor to the front door of the school, leaving on the linoleum the swirls and drips of her shame, like fragments of the letters that had beaten her once again.

* * *

The woman said, 'Whatever has to be done and I mean it.'

Dean Catherine Larraby was fifty-five and, if you squinted, looked like Margaret Thatcher. Gray hair, round face, stocky. Reassuring jowls. Eyes tired but severe. A coolness around the edges that Bill Corde thought was permanent and had not arisen with the killing. She had not applied her makeup well and the powder had accumulated in the creases around her mouth and on her forehead.

He breathed deeply. He was still queasy from the bumpy flight back from St Louis and more so from the frantic drive from the county airport to make this meeting.

Through the windows of her breezy office Corde saw the manicured grass of the quadrangle, bordered with luminous green trees. Students walked along the sidewalks and paths; it seemed to Corde that they moved in slow motion. He remembered college as much more frantic. He was constantly hurrying, walking briskly into class, sweating, unprepared.

A man appeared in the doorway, a tall, heavyset black man.

'Ah,' the dean said, 'Detective Corde. Wynton Kresge, head of campus security.' Corde shook his callused wad of hand and did a double take when Kresge's expensive suit coat swung open, revealing the no-nonsense automatic pistol.

The dean looked at Kresge but when she spoke it was to the sixteen thousand parents of her eight thousand wards. 'We've got to catch this man. We're *going* to catch him.'

Corde said, 'I'd like to start interviewing Jennie's friends and professors as soon as possible.'

The dean's stubby fingers aligned a pen three times. 'Of course,' she said after a moment. 'Is that necessary?'

Corde took out a stack of blank three-by-five cards. 'I'd like to ask some preliminary questions. I have an address for her. McReynolds Hall. That's correct?'

'Right. She was GDI,' Kresge answered; the dean frowned.

Corde began to write. He printed his notes and used only capital letters, which with their many curved strokes gave a vaguely oriental appearance to his handwriting. 'GDI? That's a sorority?'

'No,' Kresge explained, 'GDI is what the dormies call themselves. People who aren't in frat or sorority houses. It means God Damn Independents.' The dean kept staring at him and Kresge said, 'Well, that's what they say.'

The dean said, 'There are so many implications.'

Corde said, 'I beg your pardon.'

'We may get sued,' she said. 'When I talked to her father last night he said he may sue the university. I told him it didn't happen on campus.'

'It didn't,' Kresge said. 'Happen on campus, I mean.'

Corde waited a respectful time for either of them to make some point then continued, 'I'd like a list of all the residents and employees, handymen and so on, in that hall—'

'It's a very large dorm,' the dean said. 'That might cause, I don't know, panic.'

'—and also her professors and students in all her classes.' Corde noticed Dean Larraby wasn't writing any of this down. He heard rustling next to him. Kresge was jotting notes with a silver pen in a soft leather diary.

Corde asked, 'I'd like to know if she was seeing a therapist or counselor. And I'd like a list of any employees of the school convicted of violent crimes.'

As icily as a deposed prime minister, Dean Larraby said, 'I'm sure we don't have any.'

'You'd be surprised,' Corde said.

'I'll find out,' Kresge said.

'I'll guarantee you that we have no criminals on our staff.'

'Probably not,' Corde said agreeably. He turned to Kresge. 'You're going to be my contact here?'

'Sure.'

Corde shuffled his index cards. He said to Kresge, 'If you could get this info to me ASAP?'

'No problem, Detective,' Kresge said. 'And I'd be happy to interview some of the students for you, or the professors. I know a lot of them personally and . . .'

Corde found he'd been ignoring Kresge. He looked up and smiled. 'Sorry?'

When Kresge repeated his offer Corde said, 'Not necessary, thanks.'

'I'm just saying if you need a hand.'

Corde turned to the dean. 'I'd like a room of some kind.'

Dean Larraby asked, 'Room?'

'For the interviews. We'd prefer to do it on campus.'

Kresge said, 'The Student Union's got a lot of activity rooms.'

Corde marked a note on one of his cards. 'Book one for me, would you?'

There was a slight lapse before Kresge said, 'Will do.'

'Detective . . .' The dean's voice contained an element of desperation. Both men looked at her. She put her hands flat on the desk as if she were about to rise and lecture. Her fingers touched the wood with twin clicks and Corde noticed rings – a thick purple stone on her left hand, an even larger yellow one on her right. *Presents to herself,* Corde thought. 'We have a contradictory problem here,' she said. 'You read the *Register,* you must know this school's in the midst of a fiscal crisis. Our enrollment is the lowest it's been in twenty-three years.' She smiled humorlessly. 'The baby boomers have come and gone.'

Corde did read the *Register*. He had no idea what shape the finances of Auden University were in.

'It's of course in our interest to find the man who did this as fast as possible. But we don't want it to appear that we're panicked. I've already gotten a call from one of the school's benefactors. He's quite concerned about what happened.' Corde looked at her blankly. 'When benefactors get concerned, Detective, I get concerned.'

Kresge said, 'We've beefed up security patrols in the evening.'

Corde said that was good.

The dean continued as if neither had spoken. 'We're getting applications now for the fall term and they're running much lower than we'd expected.' She caressed her cheek with her little finger and missed an uneven streak of prime minister makeup by a millimeter. 'Isn't it most likely, Detective, that it was a drifter or somebody like that? Somebody not related to the school?'

Kresge said, 'We can't assume anything, Dean.'

The dean was ignoring Kresge too. She was his boss and could do a better job of it than Corde.

Corde said, 'We just don't know anything at this point.'

Kresge said, 'One thing I wanted to mention. The Biagotti killing.'

The dean clucked. 'Wynton, Susan lived off-campus. She was killed in a robbery attempt. Isn't that what happened, Detective?'

'Susan Biagotti? It seemed to be a robbery, I recall.'

The dean continued, 'The school had nothing to do with it. So—'

'It was never solved, Dean,' Kresge's baritone droned. 'I was just speculating.'

'—why bring it up?'

Corde said to both of them, 'I don't think there's any connection. But I'll look into it.'

'There was no connection,' the dean said sourly.

'Yes, ma'am. I'm sure that's the case. Now the sooner I get back to work, the sooner we'll catch this fellow. You'll get that information, William?'

'Wynton.'

'Sorry.'

'Uhn, Detective, I wanted to ask you something. About motives for this type of crime. I—'

Corde said, 'I'm sorry. I'm running pretty late. If you could just get me as much of that information as you can

24

in the next hour or so I'd appreciate it. And the room. Don't forget the room.'

Kresge's spacious unsmiling face nodded slowly. 'You'll get it when you want it.'

Diane Corde pressed the phone tight against her ear. She still held a grocery bag in one muscular arm.

'Oh, no . . .' She listened for a moment longer then lifted the phone away from her mouth. She called, 'Sarah? Sarah are you home?'

Silence, broken only by the click and whir of the refrigerator.

'No. She hasn't come back yet. When she's upset sometimes she hides in the woods.'

Diane cocked her head as she listened to Sarah's teacher explain how concerned they all were. Mrs Beiderson also added delicately that the girl had been daydreaming all morning before the practice test. 'I sympathize, Mrs Corde, I really do. But she simply *must* try harder. She's bringing a lot of these problems on herself.' Diane nodded at the phone. Finally she said the words that seemed to end so many of these conversations: 'We'll talk to her about it. We'll talk to her.'

They hung up.

Diane Corde wore blue jeans and a burgundy cotton blouse. With her high school graduation cross gold and glistening at her throat she looked like a pretty, born-again country-western singer. Her husband said she had thisaway hair because she wore it moussed up and brushed back. Wide-shouldered and thin-hipped, Diane had a figure that had pretty much withstood two children and forty-three years of gravity. On her forehead was a small scar like a crescent moon, which mimicked by half the end of the iron pipe she'd run hard into when she was four.

Diane set the groceries on the counter and returned to the back door to get her keys from the lock.

No keys.

She tried to recall – she had hurried inside from the

25

car when she heard the phone ringing. She looked on hooks, on counters, at the bottom of her purse, in the freezer (it had happened more than once). On the off chance that she'd left them in the station wagon she walked outside and ducked her head through the open window. They hung from the ignition. She shook her head at her absentmindedness and plucked them out. She started back to the kitchen. She stopped cold, one foot on the doorstep.

How had she gotten inside without the keys?

The back door had been open.

The dead bolt was the only lock on the door and it could be secured only with a key. Diane clearly remembered locking it when she left for the A&P. Somebody had entered the house and left without bothering to relock the door.

Bill had been a cop for twelve years and had made his share of enemies; he'd instructed the children a thousand times always to lock the door when they left.

But Sarah of course could ignore a thousand stern warnings.

The girl had probably returned home to wash up after the incident at school then run outside to hide in her magic woods, forgetting to lock the door. *I'll have another talk with her* ... But then Diane decided, no, the girl had been through enough. No scoldings today. She returned to the kitchen, dropped the keys into her purse, and began to think about supper.

She sits in the woods, hugging herself, knees up to her lowered chin, in the circle of magic stones. Sarah Corde is now breathing slowly. It has taken hours to calm down. By the time she got here, running the entire two miles from the school, her dress and underpants were dry but still she feels dirty – as if a sorcerer had thrown a potion on her.

She is no longer crying.

Sarah lies back in the grass that she pulled out of the nearby field and spread in the circle like a bed. She lifts the hem of her dress up to her waist as if the sunlight will clean the poison completely away and she closes her eyes. Sarah is sleepy. Her head grows heavy as a stone and she feels that she is floating in the moat of an old castle. *Beiderbug Castle* . . .

Sarah looks up at the clouds.

A huge dog with wings big as the county, a chariot pulled by a flying fish, and there, there – a towering thunderhead – is a god carrying a fierce club. He wears golden sandals, magic shoes that carry him high above this terrible place, the earth . . .

As she falls asleep she pictures the god turning into a wizard.

When she wakes, an hour or more has passed. The chariot is gone, the flying fish is gone, the god with his club is gone.

But Sarah finds that she has had a visitor.

She sits up, pulling her skirt down, then reaches forward cautiously and picks up Redford T. Redford the world's smartest bear, who sits beside her, the shaggy face staring at her with humorous, glassy eyes. She left him that morning propped on her bed after she hugged him a tearful good-bye and left for school. How he got here she has no idea. In the ribbon around his collar is a piece of paper. Sarah unfolds it, panicking for a moment as she sees that it contains words she must now read. But then she relaxes and takes one word at a time. After fifteen minutes of agonizing work she manages to read the entire note.

She is shocked and terrified by its message. Suspicious of words, she decides she must have read it wrong. She tries again and finds that, no, she read it correctly.

Her first thought is that she could never do what the awkwardly printed letters suggest.

But as the girl looks around her at the dense woods, where she has hidden so often after fleeing from school, the woods in which she feels more at home than in her own living room, that fear slowly fades.

And eventually becomes joyous anticipation.

Sarah rises to her feet, thinking that one part of the note certainly is true. There really *is* nothing left for her to do.

3

The New Lebanon Sheriff's Department was a small place. Four private offices – for the sheriff, for Detectives Corde and Slocum and for Emma, the radio dispatcher/secretary. The central room contained eight gray GI desks for the deputies. To the side was a long corridor that led to the two cells of the lockup. On the wall was a rack containing three shotguns and five black AR-15s. The room was filled with enough unread and unfiled paper to go head to head with any small-town law enforcement office in the country.

Jim Slocum – fresh back from the pond – looked up from his desk, where he was reclining in a spring-broken chair and reading the Register. Sheriff Steve Ribbon stood above him. Ribbon, solid and sunburnt red as the flesh of a grilled salmon, was slapping his ample thigh with a book. *What's the Pocket Fisherman want now?* Slocum raised an eyebrow. 'Damn mess.' He held up the paper like a crossing guard with a portable Stop sign. It was folded to the article on the Gebben murder.

Ribbon crooked his head to say, yeah, yeah, I read it. 'Come on into my den, would you, Jim?'

Slocum followed the sheriff five feet into his office. Ribbon sat, Slocum stood in the doorway.

This's right clever, we just reversed positions.

'Bill here?' Ribbon asked.

29

'He flew over to St Louis this morning to talk to the girl's father—'

'He did *what?*'

'Flew up to St Louis. To talk to the girl's—'

Ribbon said, 'The girl was killed? That girl? Why'd he do that for? He think we're made of money?'

Slocum chose not to answer for Bill Corde and said only, 'He said he wants us all to meet about the case. At four, I think it was.'

'We gotta watch our pennies, I hope he knows that. Anyway, I wanted to kick something around with you. This killing's got me bothered. I hear it wasn't a robbery.'

'Doesn't seem to be.'

'I was noticing there were some parallels between what happened and a couple other cases I'd read about. It occurred to me that we might have a cult killer problem here.'

'Cult?' Slocum asked carefully.

The book dropped onto the desk. A paperback, fanned from bathtub or hammock reading. *Bloody Rites.* On the cover were three black-and-white photos of pretty girls over a color photo of a blood-spattered pack of tarot cards. 'Whatsis?' Slocum picked it up.

'I want you to read it. I want you to think about it. It's about this Satanist down in Arizona a couple years ago. A true story. There are a lot of similarities between what happened here and that fellow.'

Slocum flipped to the pictures of the crime scenes. 'You don't think it's the same guy?'

'Naw, they caught him. He's doing life in Tempe but there are . . . similarities.' Ribbon stretched out the word. 'It's kind of scary.'

'Damn, they were good-looking.' Slocum gazed at the page of the book showing the victims' high school graduation pictures.

Ribbon absently stroked his black polyester tie and said softly, 'What I'd like you to do is get yourself up to Higgins. The state police have a psychology division up there. Follow up with them on it.'

'You think?' Slocum read a passage where the writer described what the Arizona killer had done to one co-ed. He reluctantly lowered the book and said, 'I'll mention it to Bill.'

'Naw, you don't have to. Just call up the boys in Higgins and get an appointment.'

Slocum grinned. 'Okay. I won't fly.'

'What?'

'I won't fly up there.'

'Why would you? – Oh, yeah, haw.' The sheriff added, 'We gotta make sure word gets around about this.'

'How's that?'

Ribbon said, 'Well, we should make sure the girls in town are warned about it.'

'Wouldn't that kind of tip our hand?'

'It's our job to *save* lives too.'

Slocum flipped through the pictures again. Ribbon leaned forward and tapped the book. 'Hang on to that. You'll enjoy it. It's a real, what do they say, page-turner.'

The Incorporated Town of New Lebanon reluctantly owned up to its mouthful of a name. By the time the village was chartered in the 1840s all the good names – the European capitals and harmonious-sounding biblical locales – had been taken. The final debate had pitted the New Lebanonites against New Luxemburgians. Because the former had a respectful ring of Old Testament, the vote was predictable.

The town was in Harrison County, named after William Henry, not because of his thirty-day term as president but for his tenure as Indiana Territory governor during which he decimated native Indian tribes (Tippecanoe, of campaign-slogan fame) and allowed counties like this his namesake to congeal into what they were today: mostly white, mostly Protestant, mostly rural. New Lebanon's economy floated on milk, corn, and soybeans, though it had a few small factories and one big printing plant that did a lot of work for Chicago and St Louis and New York publishers (including the ever-scandalous and -anticipated *Mon Cher* magazine, scrap bin copies of which flooded the town monthly thick as shucked cobs at harvest).

Also located in New Lebanon was the only four-year college for a hundred miles. Auden University goosed the town population up to fourteen thousand from August to May and gave locals the chance to sit through performances of second-tier orchestras and avant-garde theater companies, which they boasted about being able to attend but rarely did. The NCAA was about the only real contact between Auden and the natives, virtually none of whom could afford the seventeen-thousand-dollar tuition, which bought you, times four, just a liberal arts degree and what the hell good was that?

The residents had ambivalent feelings towards the students. The school was a bounty, no denying: thousands of young people with nothing to do but eat out, go to movies and redecorate their dorm rooms, and what's more there was a new brood of them every year just like hogs and veal calves. And some locals even felt a nebulous pride when Auden University Economics Professor Andrew Schoen appeared on *Meet the Press* or a book by English professor John Stanley Harrod was favorably reviewed in the *New York Times,* to which a grand total of forty-seven New Lebanonites subscribed.

On the other hand Auden was a burden. These money-shedding young people got drunk and puked and sneered and teepeed trees with toilet paper and broke plate glass. They shamelessly bought Trojans and Ramses in front of grade-school children. They walked around looking important as bankers. They burned effigies of politicians and occasionally a flag. They were gay and lesbian. They were Jewish and Catholic. They were Eastern.

Bill Corde was not a product of Auden though he was of New Lebanon. Born and reared here, he'd ventured away only for four years of service (standing guard with his M-16 over missiles in West Germany) and a few years in Missouri as a patrolman then detective in the St Louis Police Department. He returned to New Lebanon and after six months of feed and grain, teaching Sunday school and thinking about starting a contracting business, he applied for a job at the town Sheriff's Department. His experience made him a godsend to Steve Ribbon, whose closest approximation to police training had been the Air Force (he and *his* rifle had protected B-52s in Kansas). After a year as the department's oldest rookie Corde was promoted to detective and became the town's chief felony investigator.

On the neat wall above his neat desk in the hundred-and-four-year-old town building were some framed documents: a diploma from Southwestern State University and certificates from the ICMA's Police Business Administration Institute of Training in Chicago as well as one from the Southern Police Institute in Louisville. The proof was absent but he had also taken various FBI training seminars and courses in law and visual investigation analysis. He had just returned from Sacramento and a week-long session at the California Department of Justice.

The certificates he had proudly tacked up were simple vouchers of completion; Corde was a bad student. He collected words that described himself. He was *persistent*, he was *industrious*, he had *sticktoitiveness*. But Bill Corde was born C-plus material and that didn't change whether the subject was one he hated (English, social studies) or loved (criminal psychology or link-analysis-charting techniques). He wrote slowly and produced leaden meat-and-potato reports, and although as detective his official hours were pretty much eight to six he would often stay late into the night muscling through an article in *Forensics Today* or the *Journal of Criminal Justice,* or comparing the profiles of suspects in his cases with those in the NASPD's *Felony Warrants Outstanding Bulletin.*

Some people in town – that is to say, the people who worked for him – thought Corde took his job too seriously, New Lebanon being a place where the State Penal

Code's thousand-dollar threshold between petty and grand larceny was not often crossed, and four of last year's six deaths by gunshot were from failing to open a bolt or breach when climbing over a fallen tree. On the other hand Corde's arrest-per-felony rate was a pleasure to behold – ninety-four percent – and his conviction-to-arrest ratio was 8.7:10. Corde kept these statistics in a thirdhand IBM XT computer, the department's major concession to technology.

He now finished reviewing the coroner's preliminary report on Jennie Gebben and stood up from his desk. He left the sheriff's office and strode across the hall to the lunchroom. As he walked a quarter materialized in his hand and he rolled it over the back of one finger to the next and so on, around and around, smooth as a poolhall hustler. His father had taught him this trick. Corde Senior made the boy practice it with his hand extended over an old well on the back of the family property. If he dropped a coin, *plop,* that was that. And his father had made him use his own two bits. Corde had seen a lot on TV recently about men's relations with their fathers and he thought there was something significant about the way his father had taught him this skill. He had learned a few other things from his old man: His posture. A loathing of second mortgages. An early love of hunting and fishing and a more recent fear of the mind's wasting before the body. That was about all.

Corde was real good at the coin trick.

He entered the lunchroom, which was the only meeting place in the town building large enough to hold five brawny men sitting – aside from the main meeting room, which was currently occupied by the New Lebanon Sesquicentennial Celebration Committee.

He nodded to the men around the chipped fiberboard table: Jim Slocum, T.T. Ebbans – the lean, ex-Marine felony investigator from the Harrison County Sheriff's Department – and New Lebanon Deputy Lance Miller. At the far end of the table, surrounded by two empty chairs, was Wynton Kresge. Corde thought, *Antsy as a*

34

tethered retriever on the first day of season.

He dropped the quarter into his pants pocket and stood in front of a row of vending machines. He was about to speak when Steve Ribbon walked in. Corde nodded to him and leaned back against the Coke machine.

'Howdy, Bill. Just want to say a few words to the troops about this case, you don't mind.' The sheriff's ruddy face looked out over the men as if he were addressing a crowd of a thousand. Ribbon scrutinized Wynton Kresge who represented two oddities in this office – he was black and he wore a suit. Kresge took the look for a moment, realized he was being asked a question then said, 'I'm from the college.'

'Oh. Well.' Ribbon's voice enlarged to encompass everyone. 'I just want to put my two cents in. You all are the task force on this thing. Now Bill's in charge.' He looked at Ebbans. 'Which I think is what Sheriff Ellison's agreeable to.'

'Yessir,' said Ebbans. 'I'm just a hired hand here.'

'Now between all of you,' Ribbon continued, 'you got a flatbed full of investigating experience.' His burdened gray eyes rose to Corde's. 'And I'm busier'n a dog in a fire hydrant factory . . .'

Corde nodded sympathetically. *Trout're running and there's an election come November.*

'So I can't get as involved in the case as I'd like. But keep remembering, people're going to be watching us. They're going to be real curious how we do on this one so I want us to be pretty, you know, aggressive. Now I've been doing some research and I'm pretty bothered by this cult business.'

Corde was silent. It was Ebbans who asked, 'Cult?'

'What I want you to do is first come up with a profile of our killer.'

Jim Slocum said, 'In these situations that's what you always have to do.'

Wynton Kresge wrote this down.

'Absolutely,' Ribbon said. 'I know we haven't had any of these kinds of killers here in New Lebanon before but

I think it's important for us to get up to speed. What you have to do with cult murderers is peg them. Find out what makes them tick.'

Kresge scribbled rapidly. Corde glared at him and he stopped writing.

Ribbon continued, 'Now a profile should include two things. The physical description of our man, one, and what's going on in his mind, two. Stuff like is he sexually repressed, does he hate his mother, does he have trouble, you know, getting it up, was he beaten as a child . . .'

Corde, who had a well-used NCAVC criminal profiling flowchart tacked up on his wall, nodded solemnly and let the embarrassment for his boss trickle off.

'Sounds important,' Miller said, and brushed his hand over his excessively short crew cut.

'Absolutely,' Ribbon said. 'I've been reading up on investigations like this. One thing that's troubling is this moon business. Think about it. She was killed on the night of the quarter moon. That could be lunar fixation for you. And this one's particularly troubling, you know why? Because we've got two quarters and a full and a new. So that's four potential strike windows—'

'What's that?' Wynton Kresge asked the question that Corde had been about to.

Ribbon said patiently, 'That's the entire period when our man's likely to kill again. In this case I'd say it's from thirty-six hours in front of the full moon till thirty-six hours after.'

Corde and Ebbans, who'd worked together on investigations for four years, got to play the eye-rolling game.

'Ah,' Kresge said, and wrote.

Corde and Ebbans played the game again.

'Well, that's my two cents. I'll let you boys be. Do me proud and go catch this sickie.' Ribbon left the room.

Corde took center stage. He searched for something politic to say. 'All right, I suppose we might be looking at the possibility of a serial killing here but I wouldn't go spreading that around. We don't want to give anybody

36

any ideas.' Slocum seemed about to speak but remained silent and Corde continued, 'Now I'm going to give us ten days to get a suspect under. And I want an ID within two or three.' From his St Louis days Corde remembered the forty-eight/four rule in homicide investigations: If you don't identify the perp within forty-eight hours of a killing, the odds are it will take at least four weeks to find him.

'Also,' Slocum said, 'the full moon's coming up in seven days or so.' He was scanning a *Farmer's Almanac*.

Corde said delicately, 'I think Steve's got a good point. We've got to be aware of this moon business but we don't want to drop other leads because of it. It'll be something to consider, is all.' Corde opened the envelope Kresge had brought and pulled out several sheets. 'Wynton here was good enough to bring us some dope on the victim and I want to go over it now.'

Corde also opened an envelope of his own. He shook out the glossy photograph of Jennie Gebben on the volleyball court. It showed clear eyes, a competitive smile, patches of sweat soaking her T-shirt, more throat than a girl that age would want. He noticed in the photo two metal hoops in each ear. When had the third hold been added? he wondered.

Corde handed the photo around. Miller glanced quickly then passed it on.

'No,' Corde said solemnly. 'Take a good look. Remember what she looked like.'

Miller was flustered for a moment then did what he'd been told.

When the picture had made the rounds Corde said, 'I flew over to see her father this morning and he wasn't much help. There were no diaries or letters I could find but he's going to keep looking. He says he doesn't know of anybody who might've wanted to hurt her but I put the bug in his ear and he might not know it but he's going to be looking at people at the funeral, who's there and who isn't. Maybe he'll remember a boyfriend or somebody who had a grudge against her.'

Kresge said, 'That's why you went this soon to see him? I was wondering why you did that.'

'You were?' Corde asked absently. He turned to the files that Kresge had brought. 'Jennie Gebben was twenty. She was a junior at Auden. No loans or scholarships, so I guess Daddy paid for most of it. She was an English lit major. GPA two point nine seven. Say, I'd like you to take notes on this.' Slocum and Miller picked up pens. Corde continued, 'Treasurer of the Folklore Club. Meals on Wheels volunteer once a week early in the semester but she gave that up after a couple months. Worked three days a week in the office of the dean of financial aid.

'Her classes this semester were French Reading III. Her professor was Dominique LeFevre. The Civil War to the Centennial taught by Randolph Sayles. Contemporary Literary Criticism, by Elaine Adler-Blum. Chaucer, by Robert . . . Ostopowiscz. Well, that's a mouthful. And here's another one: The Relation Between Psychology and Literature: The Nineteenth and Twentieth Centuries. Her teacher there, I mean, her professor was Leon Gilchrist. And a seminar group of that same class taught by Brian Okun. Finally The Roots of Naturalism, Charles Gorney.'

Corde wondered momentarily what the courses were about. Corde had graduated in the top half of his class because his school had plenty of engineering courses. He shuffled through the file Kresge had brought him then stapled the class roster sheets together. He set them aside.

Kresge said, 'Excuse me.'

Corde glanced up. 'Yes?'

'Just wanted to tell you, I checked with the clinic. She wasn't seeing a therapist and had only one visit this year. It was to get antibiotics for bronchitis.'

'No therapist,' Corde repeated. The fact was recorded neatly on a three-by-five card. He did not notice Slocum and Miller play a round of eye rolling.

'Also,' the security chief added, 'Personnel has a

38

policy of never hiring ex-felons. So if there are any on staff they lied about it on their résumés.'

Ebbans asked, 'Was she ever up before the UDB?'

University Disciplinary Board. Kresge said she wasn't.

'Now,' Corde said, jotting down these facts, 'as for the murder: At around ten o'clock on Tuesday night she was raped and strangled, possibly by someone she knew.'

'How could you tell that?' Kresge asked and Corde glanced at him with irritation.

'Look—' Corde began.

Ebbans answered Kresge. 'Because she didn't run and because he got close enough to subdue her before she fought back.'

'How do you know that?'

'If she'd fought there'd be tissue under her nails.'

'Kleenex?'

Slocum laughed. Ebbans said, 'Skin. The man's skin.'

'Oh.' Kresge added, 'But then if she knew him, he probably wasn't a, you know, cult killer.'

Slocum lectured, 'Not so, Chief. A good percentage of sacrifice killers know their victims.'

'Oh. I didn't know that.'

The meeting was meandering away from Corde. He said emphatically, 'We have a lot of unknowns here. Maybe robbery wasn't a motive. But maybe it was. Maybe he got scared before he could take her valuables.'

Slocum laughed. 'Bill, she had a diamond necklace. When he was through doing it to her he could've snatched it, just like that.' He illustrated ripping a chain off his own neck. 'Wouldn't take more than two seconds.'

Ebbans said, 'What's the coroner say about COD?'

'Just what it looked like. Traumatic asphyxiation. Pinpoint hemorrhages in the eyes. Fractured hyoid. Our man used his hands at first then he finished with a wire or rope. We didn't find any weapons. The coroner said the man was a foot or so taller than her. He wasn't so strong. He had to rearrange his grip on her neck several times. He did it from the front. Oh and the coroner guessed he wasn't married. Or he had a bad sex life with his wife.'

'Why's that?' Miller asked.

'Quantity of the semen. Probably hadn't had sex for four, five weeks.'

Jim Slocum said, 'Then you mean he had a *good* sex life with his wife.' Miller laughed out loud; the others except Corde snickered.

Corde looked at his cards, fanned some out. 'Now what I want to do is focus on four areas. First, on the mall and on drivers along 302. I'd like you to handle that, Jim. It's a tall order. But that's a real busy road and we probably had some people coming home from the mall around ten that night,' Corde jotted a note on an index card. 'Oh, and check out if anybody picked up any hitchhikers.

'Now, second, T.T., I was thinking maybe you could hit the houses around the pond.'

Ebbans nodded and Corde said, 'Third, Lance and I'll set up shop at the school and start talking to students and employees.'

'Yessir.' Even sitting, Miller seemed to be at attention. He reminded Corde of a color guard Marine. 'What exactly—'

'We'll go over it later. I also want you to talk to the phone company and find out what calls went out from the phones in the dorm from last Saturday through Tuesday night.'

Miller whistled softly. 'Must be a lot of students making a lot of calls, wouldn't you think?'

'You would,' Corde said. 'And we need a warrant for the dorm room. It'll be pro forma but you've gotta do the paperwork.'

'Right.'

'And finally I want all the prints on everything we found at the scene matched against known sex offenders in the county. T.T., if you could coordinate that with your office?'

'Will do. I'll order the printout.'

'Wynton, I don't suppose you folk fingerprint students and professors?'

'Been my dream and desire but no we don't.'

Corde referred to his notes again and started to say something to Kresge then paused. He scanned everyone's face. 'One thing Steve said is right. The *Register* and WRAL are going to be looking at this thing real close. No talking to reporters. Refer everyone to me or Steve or Sheriff Ellison.'

Echoes of 'yup' or 'uh-huh' filled the room.

Corde turned back to the security chief. 'You get us a room, William? Uh, Wynton, I mean.'

'In the Student Union. Off the cafeteria. Room 121. You got it all week, next too if you let me know by Friday.'

'Preciate it.'

Kresge cleared his large throat with a snapping sound. 'One thing I thought I should mention. I was driving past the pond on my way to work this morning. I just took a stroll around.'

'What time?' Corde noticed something challenging in his own voice. He wished he'd used more of it.

'Six-thirty. I left about seven.'

'You see anybody there?'

'Yessir,' Kresge said enthusiastically. 'A Con Ed tent up the road forty yards past the dam. You know, the kind they use for emergency repairs and—'

Corde said, 'They weren't there last night. They set up at five a.m. Branch took down a line. I already checked.'

'Oh,' Kresge said with disappointment.

'You see anybody else?'

'No.' He consulted his supple leather notebook. 'There's a whole 'nother thing I wanted to bring up. What you and I and the dean were talking about. Susan Biagotti.'

Corde and Ebbans exchanged looks but this time there was no eye rolling.

'Who's that?' Miller asked. 'Rings a bell.'

'Auden student killed last year.'

'Ah, right.'

Corde had been away on a joint county-state task

41

force in Fredericksberg for a month. The case had landed in Ribbon's lap and by the time Corde returned to New Lebanon, many leads had gone cold. They had never even ID'd a suspect, let alone made a case.

'It's my intention to look into it,' Corde said abruptly. 'Like I told the dean.'

'I've got my own file on the case,' Kresge said. 'You want, you can have a copy of it.'

Corde smiled in a meaningless way. 'I'll let you know if we need it.'

As he rearranged his papers the plastic bag containing the clipping he had found that morning at the pond fell to the floor. He stooped and picked it up. He stood. His knee didn't pop. Thirty-nine years of knee, five of it popping. He wondered if he'd gone and cured himself. He passed the clipping around the table. 'This is another thing we have to consider.'

The deputies frowned with suitable concern as they read.

'I'm sending it up to Higgins for analysis today. Unless we find prints though or the rest of the paper it came from in somebody's back pocket I don't think it'll help. But you might want to keep an eye on yourselves and your families. You know most threats like this are just cranks but you never can tell.'

'Most threats?' Kresge asked. 'You mean this happens a lot?'

Corde hesitate then said, 'Actually it's never happened.'

Ebbans looked up from the note then slid it back to Corde. 'I know something else about this guy,' he announced.

'What's that?' Jim Slocum asked.

'Well, you could nearly see the girl from the road even if you weren't looking. Why didn't he drag her behind the truck at least? Then he came back in the morning to leave that note? It was like he didn't care if anybody saw him. That says to me he's a real gutsy fellow.'

Corde lifted the plastic bag away from Miller. 'Gutsy,' he said. 'Or crazy. Either way's a problem.'

4

By the time she approached her house, Sarah had memorized the note, which now rested in her skirt pocket, along with the five twenty-dollar bills that had been wrapped in it.

> *Dear Sarah—*
>   *I heard you fighting with your daddy today, about school. I know he'll keep making you go back. I want to help. I'm just like you, we both hate school. You have to leave. Get away! Go to Chicago or, St Louis. There's nothing left for you to do. You'll be safe. I'll look out for you.*
> *   —Your friend*

This idea is not new to her. Sarah had thought of running away a dozen times. Last March, the week before the arithmetic test, she had spent an hour at the Greyhound station, working up courage to buy a ticket to Grandma's place, before her courage broke and in tearful frustration she returned home.

Running away . . .

Sarah paused at the front doorstep. On tiptoe she saw her mother in the living room. She ducked. The motion made the paper in her pocket crinkle. While she waited for her mother to leave the room she pulled out the money and studied the bills, cautiously rubbing them as

43

if they were pages from a book of witch's spells. She folded them tight again and put them back into her pocket.

Sarah Corde, nine years old, cared nothing for school, hopscotch, Simon Says, housework, Nintendo, sewing, cooking, cartoons on TV. But she believed fervently in magic and wizards, and she believed that this message was from a particular wizard who had been watching out for her for years. He was all-knowing and he was kind, and – with all the money – he was pretty darn rich too, it seemed.

Sarah was nobody's fool. She was going to do exactly what the wizard suggested. She also noted to her vast joy that although she would probably take this advice and go to Chicago, he had given her enough money to surely take her halfway around the world.

The front door slammed and the feet were up the six stairs in three fast *thuds* before Diane could get to the front hall.

She dried her hands as she continued to the stairs, pausing beside the coat rack and a wooden plaque of a goose wearing a blue bonnet and scarf. She straightened it absently and called, 'Honey! Sarrie?'

There was no answer.

A moments later: 'Honey, come on down here.'

A weak voice said, 'I'm taking a bath, Mommy. I'll be down before supper.'

'Honey, Mrs Beiderson called.'

Silence.

'Sarah—'

'I want to take my *bath,* Mommy. Can we talk about it, you know, later? Like, *please?*'

'Come on out. She told me what happened at school.'

They continued this tug-of-war for a few minutes, Diane slowly edging up the stairs toward the girl's room. There was no lock on the door but Diane was reluctant to invade her children's territory. 'Come on, honey. You can help me make dinner.'

'I don't *want* to!' Sarah answered shrilly.

In these words Diane heard reason start to shatter. This was the time to back down. *No hysteria, please. Not that.* Sarah's attacks nailed her mother with tearful pity. And they also made her seethe; unable to distinguish between the moments Sarah was truly panicked and the times she was faking, Diane invariably backed down.

Coward . . .

The phone began ringing.

She glanced at it. 'All right, Sarah, we'll talk later.'

As she walked into the kitchen Diane noticed that it was five p.m. She knew who the caller would be.

She was married to him.

Bill would ask about the kids and how Diane's day had gone and then he'd get suddenly sheepish and tell her he had to work late. Again. Every other day for the past month he skidded home just as supper was landing on the table and on more than a few occasions he had missed the evening meal altogether.

And worse news: he now had a murder case.

She remembered seeing the thick black type of the headline in the *Register* and reading the scant words about that poor dead student and feeling a wave of utter regret – for herself as well as for the poor parents of the murdered girl. She knew she was going to see even less of Bill until the man was caught.

She picked up the beige phone.

It was not her husband.

She heard odd sounds in the background, like eerie electronic rock music, the sort she chided Jamie for listening to. She assumed it was one of his friends.

'Corde residence,' she said, wholly polite.

'This's Mrs Corde?' The voice was tenor-pitched but it seemed smoother than an adolescent's, more confident. She knew all of Jamie's friends and this didn't sound like any of them.

'Yes, this is she. Who is this? Say, could you please turn that music down?'

The volume of the music diminished. 'You're Jamie's mother?'

'You want to speak to Jamie?'

'I'm calling from New Lebanon High? I'm the senior advisor of the freshman section of the yearbook and — this is really a hassle — but we lost a bunch of the bio sheets of some of the students, you know. We're way past the deadline and I'm calling people and filling in the forms over the phone.'

'Well, Jamie won't be home for another couple hours.'

'Could you just give me some information about him?'

'Well, I don't know . . .' Diane said. She knew the risks mothers ran making decisions for their teenage boys.

'Today's the last day we can get anything typeset.'

'What do you want to know?'

'Who's his homeroom teacher?'

This seemed harmless enough. She said, 'That'd be Mr Jessup.'

'And is he on any teams?' the advisor asked.

'Wrestling. He also does gymnastics but he doesn't compete. And he's going to do the triathlon next year.'

'Triathlon. So he's a bicyclist?'

'You can't hardly keep him off it. He'd ride it to the dinner table if we let him.'

The boy laughed overloud at what he must have thought was a stupid joke. He then asked, 'What kind of bike does he have?'

'It's Italian. A fifteen-speed. I don't remember the name. Is it important?'

'No, I guess not. What clubs is he in?'

'Science Club and Latin Club. He was in Photo Club for a while but he quit that to spend more time working out. Say, will he have a chance to look this over?'

'Not really, no. We're going to press tomorrow. But he wouldn't want just a blank space under his picture, would he?'

'I guess not.'

'What's his favorite music video?'

'I have no idea.'

46

'His favorite movie?'

'I couldn't say.'

'How about his favorite groups?'

'Groups?'

'Music groups?'

Diane was disturbed to find how little of this she knew. She said abruptly, 'Can you wait a moment?' then set the phone down and fled into his room. She picked up several handfuls of tape cassettes and hurried back to the kitchen. She read the labels into the phone. 'Tom Petty . . . Uhm, Paul McCartney – well, I remember him of course.'

'Ha.'

'Then U2 and Metallica and Ice Cube and Run DMC, whatever that is. And he's got three tapes of this group Geiger. I guess they're from Germany.'

'Everyone knows Geiger.'

Well, excuse me . . .

She continued, 'I don't know if those are his favorites. He's got a lot of tapes.'

'Could you make up a quote for him?'

No way. 'I think that'll have to be blank.'

'I guess that's okay. You've been a big help, Mrs Corde.'

'When is the yearbook coming out?'

'Won't be long. Maybe I'll bring Jamie's by myself.' The voice lowered a few tones. 'I'd like to meet you.'

Diane laughed but silently; she understood fragile adolescent pride. 'Well, that would be very nice.'

Hit on by a high schooler! Maybe you've got some of the old allure after all – even if it's just in your voice.

When he got the note he'd been saying:

'The phrase that some soldiers used was "horizontal refreshment." Medical records tell us that at the height of the war, nearly ten percent of Union troops suffered from some form of VD . . .'

Associate Dean Randolph Rutherford Sayles took the slip of paper from the teaching assistant. He recognized

47

Dean Larraby's elegant scrawl, as distinctive as her ubiquitously disquieting choice of words summoning him immediately to her office.

Silence rose. He found he was looking past the paper, staring at the whorls and lines of the lectern, at an ink stain.

'. . . In Washington, D.C., the south side of Pennsylvania Avenue contained dozens of houses of prostitution – a locale where I believe a number of lobbyists now maintain offices . . .'

Sayles was in his trademarked posture: standing, both hands on the lectern, hunched forward. Sayles nurtured a classic professorial vogue, unkempt and preoccupied and tweedy, flaunting this style in the face of Brooks Brothers chic (passé on Wall Street but au courant in Cambridge, Hyde Park and Ann Arbor). He had sandy hair that he kept unruly and would grin like the absentminded scholar he had never been when it flopped into his face.

'. . . And more astonishing, there are hundreds of documented cases of women disguising themselves as soldiers and circulating among the men to provide sexual favors for a profit. Perhaps this is where the phrase "military service" arose . . .'

These tidbits sounded frivolous but the students, who had waited in line since six a.m. on registration day to sign up for The Civil War to the Centennial, loved them. Sayles had worked hard at perfecting his lecturing skills. Nothing was more important to him than bestowing knowledge. He was tenured at thirty, two years after his doctoral thesis was published and one year after his book, the *Economics of Freedom,* garnered a favorable *Times* review and started its record six-month run as number one on the National Association of Historians' recommended list.

'As the war, which both Yanks and Rebs truly believed would last no more than six months, stretched on and on, the moral thread of the resoundingly Protestant and predominantly evangelical armies frayed . . .'

More problematic was Sayles's second job as an associate dean, which he did not enjoy at all. But he was sophisticated enough to know that he could not survive forever without the yoke of administrative duties and he had struggled to master the perversity of collegiate infighting. Besides, his bailiwick was the Civil War and what better metaphor could there be for a college campus? He was like Grant, marshaling forces and riding herd over a bunch of brilliant feisty generals – that is, students – who drank too much, whored too much (or who railed loud against drinking and whoring), while he somehow managed to fight a war. And like Grant, Sayles had happened to rise to this position at the most difficult time in the history of his institution.

'. . . But it wasn't until after the Dynamic Duo of Defeat – Gettysburg and Vicksburg – that the Southern troops embraced fundamentalist revivalism with a gusto . . .'

A warm spring breeze eased through the auditorium's huge windows, so high they could be locked and unlocked only with a twelve-foot-long pole. The class was half empty. Sayles considered the reason why attendance was poor and his eyes fell on a particular empty seat, surrounded by a blossom of other vacancies.

Ah, yes, the memorial service.

He had not had the strength to attend. The only place he could possibly be was here.

The bell – not an electronic wail but an old-fashioned clapper on steel – rang and Sayles dismissed the class. He stood at the lectern while the class departed then he reread the dean's note. He too left the room and walked along a broad sidewalk, campus buildings on one side, the five-acre quadrangle on the other, to the university's administration building.

On the second floor he entered a large anteroom. He walked past the room's only occupant, a secretary with whom he had long ago had an affair, a mousy woman with a bony face. He vaguely remembered breasts like fat pancakes.

'Oh, did you hear? Professor? A student was—'

Without answering he nodded and walked past her into the large inner office. He closed the door and sat in one of the oxblood leather chairs across from the dean's desk.

'Randy,' she said, 'we have a real problem.'

He noticed her hand was resting on that morning's *Register*. The article about the murder was circled and above the headline was written: *Dean Larraby. FYI.* He looked at Bill Corde's picture then back to the dean. Sayles said, 'She was in my class.'

Dean Larraby nodded without expecting any further response. She closed whatever massive work she had been reading – it appeared more legal than scholarly – and pushed it to the corner of her desk. Her fingers caressed the edges of the purple stone on her left hand.

Sayles said, 'Have you talked to the police?'

'What?'

'The police?'

She responded querulously, 'Yes, there was a detective here. This man, in fact.' She nodded at the paper. 'He wanted to know all about the Gebben girl.'

The Gebben girl.

Sayles, whose brilliance like that of many professors was in large part memory, recollected perfectly how the dean had greeted him a few moments ago and asked, 'What kind of problem? What else did the police say?'

The Gebben girl. Student number 144691.

'The police? That's not what I'm talking about,' she said. 'This is serious. I've finished meeting with the Price Waterhouse people. There are no funds to move into the loans accounts.'

'What do you mean?' Shock pummeled Sayles. The image of Jennie Gebben fell from his thoughts.

'None.'

'But there was going to be an operating surplus this term,' he whispered. 'I thought we'd worked that out.'

'Well,' she said testily, 'there isn't.'

Oh, how he hated her. She'd told him, she'd *promised*

him, there would be money. The shock yielded to a maelstrom of anger. He swallowed and looked out the window at the grassy quad whose sidewalks he had crossed perhaps ten thousand times.

'The fact is the money isn't there.'

'What are we going to do?' His voice rose with panic. 'Can we cover it up?'

'Cover it up? We're long past that point.' She smiled but cruelly and he thought her face looked like a malicious tortoise's. 'Randy, without that money, the school is going to close.'

'What *happened* to it? We were supposed to have two and a half million.'

She tossed her head at a question he himself knew the answer to. Why does a college lose money? Auden University had been skimming the surface of insolvency for ten years. Competition from cheaper state and trade schools, decreasing college-age population, escalating salary demands and costs . . .

'This murder, it's going to focus a lot of attention on the school and its problems. That's the last thing we need. Not now. We can't afford people pulling their children out. And for God's sake we don't need profiles of the school in the press.' She did not look at the *Register* but her fingers absently tapped the grim headline.

Sayles said coldly, 'Her death was most inopportune.'

The dean missed his irony. She asked, 'Does anybody know about our arrangement?'

Long dark hair. It often dipped down over one eye. Which? Her right eye. She would keen with passion. The Gebben girl. Student number 144691. She would cry at the scent of a forest filling with stiff fall leaves.

'Does anybody know?' he mused. *Nope, not anymore she doesn't.* Sayles shook his head.

The dean stood and walked to the window. Her back was to him. She had a solid figure, rubbery and strong; this was appealing – the severity and solemnity one wants in airline pilots and surgeons. A large, stern

51

woman, hair going a little wiry, eyes puffy from wrestling with an injustice only partially of her own making.

Jennie Gebben. Who would grip his cock with her prominent teeth and rasp up and down along his swollen skin.

Who could not without prompting analyze European motives behind Civil War foreign relations but who had the far more enduring gift of pressing her knees into Sayles's midriff and with a stone-buffed heel square against his asshole force his pelvis against hers.

Student number 144691.

'Randy, we can expect an audit by mid-June. If you don't raise three million six hundred thousand dollars in cash by then—'

'How am I supposed to get that much money?' He heard his voice rise to a strident whine, which he detested but could not avoid.

'You?' she asked. Dean Larraby polished the purple stone against the fabric of her skirt then looked up at Sayles. 'I think it's pretty clear, Randy. You, better than anybody, know what's at stake if you don't find that money.'

She got the idea from a made-for-TV movie.

It had been a film about a thirteen-year-old girl, and her mother and stepfather *hated* her. Once, they locked her in the house while they went away to gamble and the girl ran away from home by jumping out a window then grabbing onto a freight train that went to New York City.

Sarah shut off the water running in the bathtub, which though it *was* filled with steamy water and fragrant violet bubble bath did not – as she had told her mother – contain her. She had run upstairs and taken a fast shower then dressed quickly. Now, wearing a T-shirt, overalls, Nikes and a nylon windbreaker – her traveling clothes – she listened to her mother fixing dinner downstairs.

In the film, when the girl ended up in New York she

lived in the alley and had to eat bread somebody had thrown out and she smoked a cigarette and just before this big guy was going to take her up into his apartment and do something for her Sarah didn't know what, the girl's mom showed up and hugged her and brought her home and dumped the stepfather. And they showed an 800 number you could call if you knew any runaways.

What a stupid movie – about as real and interesting as a cereal commercial. But it solved a big problem for Sarah because it showed her how to save all of the wizard's money and still get to Chicago.

She was thinking of the railroad train.

There were no railroads in New Lebanon. But there *was* a truck. It was a big one that looked sort of like a train and it passed the house every afternoon. The truck had a platform on the back that she thought she could hold on to, and it went past the house real slow. She could catch the truck easily and then climb onto the back and sit there. When he stopped for the night she could ask the driver where to find another truck going to Chicago.

Sarah packed her Barbie backpack. She took Mr Jupiter her shooting star bank, pairs of Levi's and sweatshirts and socks and underpants, her toothbrush and toothpaste, and a skirt and a blouse, her Walkman and a dozen books on tape. Of course Redford T. Redford the world's smartest bear would be traveling with her. And she took some things from her mother's dresser. Lipstick, mascara, fingernail polish and panty hose.

It was now five-thirty. The truck usually went past the house about six. Sarah walked around her room. She suddenly realized she'd miss her father. She started to cry. She'd miss her brother some. She thought she'd miss her mother but she wasn't sure. Then she thought of the wizard telling her, 'I'll look out for you,' and she thought about school.

Sarah stopped crying.

She lifted the window, which opened onto the backyard of their house. She tossed the backpack out, hearing the coins in Mr Jupiter ring loudly. She climbed out, hanging from the ledge, her cheek pressed hard against the yellow siding, then she let go and dropped the few feet to the soft ground.

5

When he hung up the phone Brian Okun recognized a contradiction that would have made a tidy little philosophical riddle. As the black receiver started downward he thought, *He's got no right to talk to me that way.* As it settled in its cradle: *He's got every right to talk to me that way.*

Okun was lanky as a cowboy and his face was obscured by the strands of black beard that weaseled unevenly out of his wan skin. Inky Brillo hair hung over his ears like a floppy beret. He sat in his tiny cubicle overlooking the quad, his tensed hand still clutching the telephone, and developed his thought: *He has no right because as a human being I'm entitled to a mutual measure of dignity. John Locke. He has every right because he's in charge and he can do what he fucking well pleases. Niccolò Machiavelli cum Brian Okun.*

The man he was thinking of was Leon Gilchrist, the professor for whom Okun worked. When Gilchrist joined Auden two years before, the horde of eager PhD candidates seeking jobs as graduate assistants largely bypassed him. His reputation preceded him from the East – a recluse, a foul temper, no interest whatsoever in campus sports, politics or administration. While this put off most grad students it merely upped the ante for Okun, who was as intrigued by Gilchrist's personality as he was impressed by his mind.

Any doubts that remained about the professor were obliterated when Okun read Gilchrist's *The Id and Literature*. The book changed Okun's life. He stayed up all night, zipping through the dense work as if it were an *Illustrated Classics* comic book. He finished it at exactly three-ten in the afternoon and by four was sitting in Gilchrist's office, being obnoxious, insisting that Gilchrist hire him to teach the seminar sessions of his famous Psych & Lit course.

Gilchrist asked a few innocuous questions about the subject matter then grew bored with Okun's answers and silenced the grad student by hiring him on the spot.

Okun, almost as quickly, regretted the decision. The professor turned out to be more reclusive and odd and aggressively prickish than rumoured. Narcissistic and anal expulsive, Okun observed (he too, like Gilchrist, was dual-degreed: psychology and English lit). He gave the man wide berth and had to improvise his professor-handling techniques like a doctor developing new antibiotics to meet particularly virulent strains of bacteria.

Gilchrist was impossible to outflank. Okun was not surprised to learn that he was more savvy than he seemed and had pegged Okun early as having designs on his job. But by now, after two semesters of continual jockeying if not outright combat, Brian Okun, chic, moody, himself brilliant, an enfant terrible of the Modern Language Association, Brian Okun had nothing but wounds to show from the run-ins with his scholastic Wellington.

Today, for instance – the phone call.

The professor had left for San Francisco last week to read a paper at the Berkeley Poetry Conference and had been expected back tonight, in time for tomorrow's lecture. Gilchrist had called however to say he would be staying another week to do research at San Francisco State. He abruptly told Okun to have another professor prepare and deliver his lecture tomorrow.

The session was entitled 'John Berryman: Self-Harm

and Suicide Through the Poet's Eye.' Okun considered himself a Berryman scholar and fervently wanted to deliver that lecture. But Gilchrist was on to him. He ordered Okun, with a tinny insulting laugh, to find a full professor. He used that phrase. *Full professor,* a painful reminder of what Okun was not. Okun agreed, extending his middle finger to the telephone as he did so. Then he hung up and the interesting philosophical dilemma occurred to him.

Okun now paced – to the extent he was able to do so in a cluttered eight-by-eight room. As his mind leapt backward, zigzagging through time, he found he was picturing vague scenes of Victorian tragedy (Charles Dickens had given a lecture in this very building as part of his US tour in the 1860s, a fact Okun had collected and cherished) but the image that he arrived at was not from one of Dickens's books; it was of a girl wearing a white layered nightgown, her long hair spilling like dark water on the pillow. A girl with a pallid face. Mouth curling outward. Eyes closed. Her name was Jennie Gebben and she was dead.

At only one point since his graduation from Yale had Brian Okun ever doubted that he would be a Nobel Prize winner. There was some question as to whether he would win for nonfiction writing – some quantum-leaping analysis of, say, the relation between Yeats's haywire obsession with Maud Gonne and his art. Or whether he would produce a series of showy, anxious quote Updike Coomer Ford quote *New Yorker* novels ridden with quirky characters and heavy with the filigree of imagery and dialect-laden talk. Either was fine. Only twenty-seven, on the verge of doctorhood, Brian Okun felt mastery of his scholarly self.

He also believed however that his right brain needed more life experience. And like many graduate students he believed that life experience was synonymous with fucking. He intended to fill the next five years with as many female students as he had the stamina to bed and the patience to endure afterward. Eventually he would marry – a woman who was brilliant and homely enough to remain utterly devoted to him. The nuptials would have happened by the time the Swedish girls, hair glowing under the blaze of the burning candle wreaths, woke him up in Stockholm on the morning of the award presentation.

But these dreams were disrupted by a particular individual.

Jennie Gebben had been a curious creature. When he'd first read her name in class he'd paused. His mind had tricked him and he misread it. He thought he'd seen *Jennie Gerhardt,* one of Theodore Dreiser's tragic heroines and a character that Professor Gilchrist discussed at length in his famous paper in which he psychoanalyzed Dreiser. Okun had looked at Jennie across the U-shaped classroom table and held her eyes for a moment. He knew how to look at women. After a moment he commented on the name error. Several people in class nodded in self-indulgent agreement to impress him with their familiarity with Naturalistic writing.

Jennie gave a bored glance at Okun and responded brashly that she'd never heard of her near namesake.

He asked her out three days later, a record in self-restraint.

At a university like Auden, located in a two-cinema, four-screen town, inappropriate liaisons cannot proceed as they would in an anonymous city. Okun and Jennie spent their time walking in the woods or driving out to the quarry. Or spending nights in her room or his apartment.

He brooded to the point of fetish. Why this fierce attraction? Jennie wasn't gifted artistically. She wasn't brilliant, she was a B-minus student with a solid Midwestern artistic sensibility (this meant that she had to be told what was valid and what was not). He was stung by these limitations of hers. When he inventoried what he loved about her he came up with shrinkage: the way she covered her mouth with her delicate hand at scenes of violence in movies, the way she let slip little murmurs from her throat as she looked at a chill spring wash of stars above them, the way she could drop her shoulder and dislodge a satin bra strap without using her fingers.

Of course some aspects of Jennie Gebben he loved intensely: her suggestions when they were making love that he might like to try 'something different.' Did he enjoy pain? Would he please bury his finger in her, no no not in my cunt, please, yeah, there all the way . . . Did he like the feel of silk, of women's nylons? And she would bind a black seamed stocking tight around his balls and stroke his glans until he came, forceful and hurting, on the thick junction of her chin and throat.

Several times she dressed him in one of her nightgowns and on those occasions he emptied himself inside her within seconds of fierce penetration.

These were the bearings of their relationship and as impassioned as Okun felt, he knew they could not be trusted. Not when your lover was Jennie Gebben. The murmurs and whimpers had taken on too great a significance for him. Out of control he crashed.

It occurred when one night he had blurted a marriage proposal to her. And she, less intelligent, a common person, had suddenly encircled him in her arms in a terrifying maternal way. She shook her head and said, 'No, honey. That's not what you want.'

Honey. She called him honey! It broke his heart.

He raged. Jennie *was* what he wanted. His tongue made a foray into the crevice of his lips and he tasted her. That was proof, that was the metaphor: *he hungered for her.* He cried in front of her while she looked on maturely, head cocked with affection. He blurted a shameful stream: he was willing to do whatever she wanted, get a job in the private sector, work for a commercial magazine, edit . . . He had purged himself with all the hokey melodrama of mid-list literature.

Brian Okun, radiant scholar of the esoteric grafting of psychology and literature, recognized this obsessive effluence for what it was. So he was not surprised when, in an instant, love became hate. She had seen him vulnerable, she had comforted him – this, the only woman who had ever rejected him – and he detested her.

Even now, months after this incident, a day after her murder, Okun felt an uncontrollable surge of anger at her, for her simpering patronizing *Mutterheit*. He was back on the Nobel path, yes. But she had shaken something very basic in his nature. He had lost control, and his passions had skidded violently like a car on glazed snow. He hated her for that.

Ah Jennie, what have you done to me?

Brian Okun pushed his hands together and waited for the trembling to stop. It did not. He breathed deeply and hoped for his heart to calm. It did not. He thought that if only Jennie Gebben had accepted his proposal, his life would be so unequivocally different.

The smell of the halls suggested something temporary: Pasty, cheap paint. Sawdust. Air fresheners and incense covering stale linens. Like a barracks for refugees in transit. The color of the walls was green and the linoleum flecked stone gray.

Bill Corde knocked on the door. There was no answer.

'Ms Rossiter? I'm from the Sheriff's Department.'

Another knock.

Maybe she'd gone to St Louis for the funeral.

He glanced behind him. The corridor was empty. He tried the knob and pushed the open door.

A smell wafted out and surrounded him. Jennie Gebben's spicy perfume. Corde recognized it immediately. He lifted his hand and smelled the same scent – residue from the bottle on her dressing table at home.

Corde hesitated. This was not a crime scene and students in dormitories retained rights of privacy and due process. He needed a warrant in hand to even step into the room.

'Ms Rossiter?' Corde called. When there was no answer he walked inside.

The room Jennie and Emily shared had a feeble symmetry. Bookcases and mirrors bolted to opposite walls. The beds parallel to each other but the desks turned at different angles – looking up from a textbook, one girl would look out the small window at the parking lot; the other would gaze at a bulletin board. On one bed rested a stuffed rabbit.

Corde examined Jennie's side of the room. A cursory look revealed nothing helpful. Books, notebooks, school supplies, posters, souvenirs, photos of family members (Corde noticing that the young Jennie bore a striking resemblance to Sarah), makeup, hair curlers, clothes, scraps of paper, packages of junk desserts, shampoos, lotions. Sheer pastel underwear hung on a white string to dry. A U2 poster, stacks of cassettes, a stereo set with a cracked plastic front. A large box of condoms (latex, he noted, not the lambskin found at the crime scene). Thousands of dollars' worth of clothes. Jennie was a meticulous housekeeper. She kept her shoes in little green body bags.

Corde noticed a picture of two girls: Jennie and a brown-haired girl of delicate beauty. Emily? Was it the same girl in one of the pictures on Jennie's wall at home? Corde could not remember. They had their arms around each other and were mugging for the camera. Their black and brown hair entwined between them and made a single shade.

A clattering of laughter from the floor above reminded him that he was here without permission. He set the picture down and turned toward Jennie's desk.

He crested the rise on 302 just in front of his house.

Corde had ticketed drivers a dozen times for sprinting along this strip at close to sixty. It was a straightaway, posted at twenty-five after a long stretch of fifty, so you couldn't blame them for speeding, Corde supposed. But it was a straightaway in front of *his* house where *his* kids played. When he wasn't in the mood to ticket he took to leaving the squad car parked nose out in the drive, which slowed the hot-rodders down considerably and put a slew of brake marks on the asphalt just over the crown on the rise like a grouping of bullet tracks in a trap.

Setting a good example, Corde braked hard then signaled and made the turn into his driveway. He parked the cruiser next to his Ford pickup, which was fourthhand but clocked in at only sixty-seven thousand miles. He stepped out into the low sun and waved to Jamie, who was in the garage, lifting his bike up onto pegs in the exposed two-by-fours. In Jamie's hands, the bike seemed to weigh only a pound or two.

The boy was fair-skinned and slight but he was strong as sinew. He worked out constantly, concentrating on many reps of lighter weight rather than going for bulk. He waved back to his father and headed toward the backyard, where he would pitch a tennis ball onto the crest of the roof and snag the fly with all sorts of fancy catches. The expression on his face was the same one that Corde had puzzled over for over a year until he finally recognized it as a look of Diane's – contentment, Corde liked to think, though also caution and consideration. He was proud of his son – quiet and easygoing, a devoted member of the freshman wrestling team, a B-plus student without trying, good in Latin and biology and math, the secretary of the Science Club.

Corde believed his boy would grow up to be Gary Cooper.

Detouring through the Rototilled earth of the side yard, Corde turned on the sprinkler, which began to saturate the patch of mud that the seed package had promised four weeks ago would be luxurious green in six. Corde watched the wave sweep back and forth for a minute, then walked toward the split-level house, aluminum-sided bright yellow. Corde had an acre of land, all of it grass (or soon to be, Ortho assured him), punctuated with juniper bushes and saplings that in fifty years would be respectable oaks. The property bordered the panhandle of a working dairy farm to the north, beyond which was a forest. Surrounding houses, all modest split-levels or colonials, sat on similar plots along Route 302.

He heard a chug of a diesel engine. Up the road the driver of a White semi, hauling a Maersk Line container, started shifting down through his many gears as the truck rolled over the crest of the highway probably right on the posted speed. Corde watched the majestic truck for a moment then started toward the house.

A motion caught his eye and smiling still he glanced to the corner of his yard. Something nosing out of the bushes toward the road. A dog?

No!

'Sarah!'

His daughter stood up and looked at him in panic – a deer spotting a hunter. She turned and ran at top speed toward the truck, whose driver was oblivious to the girl.

'Sarah, stop!' Corde shouted in astonishment. 'No!' He ran after her.

She was squealing with terror, running ahead of herself, tripping as her feet windmilled, her arms flailing in panic. She was aiming right for the truck's massive rear wheels, which were as tall as she was.

'Oh, honey, stop! Please!' he gasped, and ran flat out, the Mace canister and a Speedloader falling from his Sam Browne belt, handcuffs thwacking his back.

'Leave me alone!' Sarah wailed, and plunged ahead toward the truck's tires.

She dropped the backpack and made a frantic spring for the truck. It seemed like she was going to leap right for the huge thundering disks of tires, firing pebbles into the air behind the trailer.

Sarah was three feet from the wheels when Corde tackled her. They landed, skidding, in a pile on the messy shoulder as the truck rumbled past them, the stack burping as the engine revved and the driver upshifted, unaware of the struggle he left behind.

63

Sarah squealed and kicked. Panicked, Corde rolled to his knees and shook her by the shoulders. His hand rose, palm flat. She squealed in terror. He screamed, 'What are you *doing*, what are you *doing?*' Corde, who had spanked Jamie only once and Sarah not at all in their collective twenty-four years on earth, lowered his hand. 'Tell me!'

'Leave me alone!'

Diane was running toward them. 'What happened? What happened?'

Corde stood. The panic was gone but it had left in its place the sting of betrayal. He stepped back. Diane dropped to her knees and held the child's face in her hands. She took a breath to start the tirade then paused, seeing the despair in her little girl's face. 'Sarah, you were running away? Running away from home?'

Sarah wiped her tears and nose with her sleeves. She didn't respond. Diane repeated the question. Sarah nodded.

'Why?' her father demanded.

'Because.'

'Sarah—' Corde began sternly.

The little girl seemed to wince. 'It's not my fault. The wizard *told* me to.'

'The wizard?'

'The Sunshine Man . . .'

This was one of the imaginary friends that Sarah played with. Corde remembered Sarah had created him after the family attended the funeral of Corde's father and the minister had lifted his arms to the sun, speaking about 'souls rising into heaven.' It was Sarah's first experience with death and Corde and Diane had been reluctant to dislodge the apparently friendly spirit she created. But in the past year, to the parents' increasing irritation, the girl referred to him more and more frequently.

'He made Redford T. Redford fly out to the forest and he told me—'

Diane's voice cut through the yard. 'No more of this

magic crap, do you hear me, young lady? What were you doing?'

'Leave me alone.' The tiny mouth tightened ominously.

Corde said, 'It's going to be okay, honey. Don't worry.'

'I'm *not* going back to school.'

Diane whispered in a low, menacing voice, 'Don't you ever do that again, Sarrie, do you understand me? You could've been killed.'

'I don't care!'

'Don't say that. Don't ever say that!' Mother's and daughter's strident tones were different only in pitch.

Corde touched his wife's arm and shook his head. To Sarah he said, 'It's okay, honey. We'll talk about it later.'

Sarah bent down and picked up her knapsack and walked toward the house. With boundless regret on her face, she looked back – not however at the ashen faces of her parents but toward the road down which the silver truck was hurrying away without her.

They stood in the kitchen awkwardly, like lovers who must suddenly discuss business. Unable to look at him, Diane told him about Sarah's incident at school that day.

Corde said contritely, 'She didn't want to go today. I drove her back this morning and made her. I guess I shouldn't have.'

'Of course you should have. You can't let her get away with this stuff, Bill. She uses us.'

'What're we going to do? She's taking the pills?'

'Every day. But I don't think they're doing any good. They just seem to make her stomach upset.' She waved vaguely toward the front yard. 'Can you imagine she did that? Oh, my.'

Corde thought: *Why now? With this case and everything, why now?* He looked out the window at Sarah's bike, standing upright on training wheels, a low pastel green Schwinn, with rainbow streamers hanging pathetically from the rubber handle grips. He thought of Jamie and his high racing bike that he zipped along on fast and daring as a motocross competitor. Sarah still couldn't ride her tiny bike without the trainers. It embarrassed Corde when the family pedaled to town together. Corde tried to avoid the inevitable comparison between his children. He wished whatever God had dished out for them had been more evenly divided. It was difficult but Corde made a special effort to limit the pride he expressed for Jamie, always aware of Sarah's eyes on him, begging for approval even as she was stung by her own limits.

A more frightening concern: some man offering a confused little girl a ride home. Corde and Diane had talked to her about this and she'd responded with infuriating laughter, saying that a wizard or a magic dog would protect her or that she would just fly away and hide behind the moon. Corde would grow stern, Diane would threaten to spank her, the girl's face became somber. But her parents could see that the belief in supernatural protectors had not been dislodged.

Oh, Sarrie . . .

Although Bill Corde still went to church regularly he had stopped praying. He'd stopped exactly nine years ago. He thought if it would do anything for Sarah he'd start up again.

He said, 'It's like she's emotionally dis—'

Diane turned on him. 'Don't say that! She has a high IQ. Beiderson herself told me. She's faking. She wants to get attention. And, brother, you give her plenty . . .'

Corde lifted an eyebrow at this.

Diane conceded, 'Okay, and so do I.'

Corde was testy. 'Well, we've got to do something. We can't let that happen again.' He waved toward the yard, like Diane reluctant to mention his daughter's mortality.

'She's got her end-of-term tests in two weeks.'

'We can't take her out of school now,' Corde said. 'We can't hold her back another grade.' He looked out the window. Why did the sight of a bicycle standing upright bother him so?

It encouraged him that she could read some books by herself.

It encouraged him that she had made and kept a few friends.

It encouraged him that she was pretty.

It destroyed him that she wasn't like Jamie.

'There's something I ought to tell you,' Corde said, hesitating, not knowing how she'd respond.

He pointed to the *Register,* which rested with odd prominence on top of four cans of tomatoes in the middle of the table. It was open to the article about the murder.

'Somebody left a copy of that story at the crime scene. It was saying that maybe we shouldn't be investigating this case too hard. Now it could be a prank and even if the killer left it I don't take it all that serious. But I'm going to have a deputy here at the house.'

This however seemed to be just another small burden on his wife's shoulders. Diane said matter-of-factly, 'We shouldn't let Sarah play by herself then.'

'Not outside the yard, no. We'll have to tell her somehow. But we don't want to scare her. She spooks so easy.'

Diane said, 'You keep babying her. She's never going to grow up if you keep treating her that way.'

'I just think we have to be careful is all.' Corde lifted his eyes to the post-and-rail fence two hundred feet away and saw a Hereford grazing in the field beyond. It reminded him of a picture Sarah had once tried to draw of a dalmatian. The drawing had been pathetic – an infant's scrawl. 'It comes close to breaking my heart,' he said. 'It's like she's . . .'

'She *isn't* retarded,' Diane hissed.

'I didn't say that.'

'My daughter is not retarded.' She turned her attention to the refrigerator. 'I don't want to talk about it anymore.'

6

*Rockets rising from grass from mud no no not mud servo
rockets Dathar man he's great muscles ripping them all
apart shooting with xasers . . .*

Their bodies falling . . . Falling into flowers.

Falling. Into. Mud . . .

Philip Halpern sat behind the two-bedroom house,
under the six-by-six back porch, which was for him at
this moment the control room of his Dimensioncruiser.
He listened. He heard footsteps from the house. They
receded. *Falling in mud, in flowers. No no no . . .*

Philip was blond, five feet eight, and he weighed two
hundred and forty-five pounds. He was the second heaviest person in his freshman high school class. Tonight, in
size forty-four Levi's and a dark green shirt, he sat in a
pile of leaves that had drifted under the porch. The boy
lowered his head and stared at the bag at his feet. It was
small, a sandwich bag, the sort that would contain
lunch, when his mother made his lunch, of bologna
sandwiches smeared with Hellmann's and potato chips
and bananas and Oreos and eighty cents in dull-clinking
coins for chocolate milk. Although what the bag contained
tonight was small his hand moved slowly when he
picked it up, as though the contents were very heavy.

'Phathar!' a nearby voice whispered.

Philip jumped then answered, 'Jano, that you?' He
squinted and saw a boy his age crawling through a

secret gate they had built together in the chicken-wire fence that surrounded the Halpern property. 'Jano, shit, be quiet.'

Between themselves, Philip and his friend had taken the names of characters in a recent science fiction film they'd seen four times. It was like a code, a secret that bound them together in this alien world.

'Phathar, I've like called you ten times.' Jano's voice was agitated.

Phathar whispered harshly, 'Just chill, will you? Shut up.'

Jano – full name Jano-IV of the Lost Dimension – climbed through the lattice gate of the porch. He said, 'Why didn't you call me back? I thought you'd been arrested or something. Man, I almost puked this morning. I mean, like really.'

'Chill . . . out. Okay?' Although Phathar-VII, also a warrior from the Lost Dimension, was calm and in control, Philip Halpern, young and overweight, was close enough to panic without his friend's adding to it. He said, 'So what is there to do?'

'I don't know. I almost puked,' Jano repeated, looking as if he had. His mouth was wet and his eyes red and though it was too early in the season for serious freckles, the brown dots stood out on his face in sickly contrast to his pale skin.

Phathar said, 'How can they even find us?'

'Oh, Jesus.'

'You're like a total pussy.'

'I am not!' Jano's eyes blazed.

Philip, whom Jano could have pounded to the dirt floor with a single fist, backed off. 'All right, dude, all right.'

Jano said, 'We've got to destruct the files.'

'You know how long it took us to make those up?'

Jano said, 'We've got the names of half the girls in class on them. All the codes, all the pictures.'

'I've got them in a secret file. If anybody tries—'

'But the pictures—' Jano whined in a voice that

wasn't at all the voice of a Dimensional warrior.

'No, listen,' Phathar said. 'If anybody tries to open the drawer everything self-destructs. It's automatic.'

Jano gazed into the night. 'Oh, man, I wish we hadn't done it.'

'Stop talking that way,' Phathar whispered ruthlessly. A fleck of saliva shot onto Jano's arm. The boy's revulsion showed in his face but he didn't brush the dot away. Phathar continued, 'We *did* do it! We. Did. It. We can't bring her back to life.'

'Dathar could,' Jano sniveled.

'Well, we can't so quit like crying about it.'

'I almost puked.'

Above them: A squeak of opening door. A low voice snapped, 'Phil!' Both boys froze. 'Phil-lip!' His father's voice stabbed through the night like a Dimensioncruiser's engine kicking into antimatter mode. 'The fuck are you? You got school tomorrow.'

Philip wondered if he himself was going to puke. Even Phathar was trembling.

'You can hear me, you got ten minutes. I have to come looking for you it'll be with the handy man.'

When the screen door slammed Phathar said, 'You gotta leave. He finds you here he'll whip me.'

Jano stared at the underside of the porch above them then said, 'Tomorrow.' He left silently. To his shadowy, receding form, Phathar lifted his arm and closed his fingers in a Dimensional warrior salute.

Oh, she struggled. She wrote the words a dozen times, careful always to tear up the ruined note and drop it into a garbage can. She'd failed him once. She wasn't going to make it worse by letting her mother and dad find out about him.

Sitting at her desk she hunched over the tricky letters, willing her pen to move one way then watching it move the other. She would tell it to go up to make the top of a b and instead it went down and became a p. Left instead of right.

Is how an S goes? No. Yes.

Sarah Corde hated S's.

She heard the crickets playing their tiny squeak-fiddles outside in the cool night, she heard the wind brushing the trees. Neck and back cramped with tension she wrote for another half hour then looked at her work.

Im sorry. I cant' go awya, they wont let me anb a police man is ~~coomign~~ comming in the mourning to watch us. Can you help me? You can have yor mony back. You are the Sunshine Man arent' you? Can I see you?

She signed her name carefully.

She felt a moment of panic, worrying that the Sunshine Man might not be able to read the note. Then she decided that because he was a wizard he could probably figure most of it out.

Sarah folded the paper and wrote his name on the outside. She put on her jacket then she paused. She opened the note and added some words at the bottom.

Im sorry I dont' spell good. Im realy sorry.

Then she snuck out the back door into the windy night and ran all the way to the circle of rocks.

The deputy showed up at eight-thirty almost to the second. He was young pink-scrubbed beefy eager and he wore on his hip a combat-gripped .357 Colt Python with a six-inch vented barrel. He was, in short, everything a husband could want to protect his wife and kids.

'Morning, Tom.' Corde picked up the *Register* from the driveway and held the screen door open for the deputy.

'Howdy, Detective. Nice house you got here.'

Corde introduced him to the family. Diane offered him some coffee. He declined regretfully as if this were a slap at her cooking.

The deputy retreated to the comfort of his Dodge watchtower parked in the driveway and the family sat down to breakfast. Jamie and Diane were talking about something, animated, near to an argument. Sarah sat quietly but was overjoyed at the news that she could stay home from school today. ('Only today, mind you, one day, just one, but no more absences for the rest of the year, you understand, young lady?' – Oh, yes, and how many times had they said the same thing?)

Corde wasn't listening to his wife and son and he wasn't observing his daughter's elation because he was reading a short article in the *Register* and he was shocked.

Cult Suspected in Auden Co-ed Murder

He set his coffee on the table and knocked the syrup over. He didn't notice it fall. Diane glanced at him, frowning, and righted the bottle.

. . . Sheriff's Department investigators are looking into the possibility that a cult or religious killer may be stalking the town of New Lebanon . . .

His eyes jumped through the article.

. . . and robbery was not a motive. Because she was killed on the night of the first quarter of the moon, there has been speculation that Miss Gebben may have been a sacrifice victim, possibly one in a chain of such killings. Sources close to the Sheriff's Department also disclosed that death threats have been made against its personnel . . .

Threats plural?

. . . Sheriff Steve Ribbon stated emphatically, however, that they would in no way impede the investigation. 'We aren't going to be bullied by these people, whoever they are, however sick they might be,' Ribbon said. 'We have some strong leads and we're pursuing them real hard.'

'Damn,' Corde muttered, bringing an end to breakfast table arguments and meditations on freedom. He looked over the paper to find his family staring at him.

'What is it, hon?'

He handed Diane the article and told the children it was nothing. Jamie glanced over his mother's shoulder as she read.

'A cult?' he asked.

Diane finished the article. Jamie picked it up and continued to read.

73

His wife asked him, 'What's wrong with the story? I don't get it.'

'Too much publicity,' he muttered. 'I think it's best to play cases like this close to your chest.'

'I suppose,' she said, and began clearing away dishes.

Corde stood to fetch his gunbelt but before he left the kitchen he glanced at his wife. She was intent on dishes and seemed to have missed what was so troubling to him – that this story was a huge sign for the killer, which said, in the vernacular of Steve Ribbon, *You may've threatened Corde but no matter. He's going ahead full steam and he don't give a good goddamn about your threats. You do your worst, you aren't stopping our boy Bill.*

They wouldn't go so far as to blurt out, 'I was at a frat party', or 'I was on a date the night it happened' or 'You can ask anyone, I didn't even *see* her that night', even though that's what they wanted to blurt. But they were defensive and they were scared. Dodging Corde's cool green eyes, the boys glanced from his face to his gun, the girls to the floor. Some of them seemed inconvenienced, some were near tears. Often they did cry.

Room 121 in the Student Union had never been put to such a sorrowful purpose.

The room was worse than any interrogation cubicle at the New Lebanon Sheriff's Department. It was painted beige and smelled of adolescent perfume and after-shave lotion, chalk, poster paints, bitter bad coffee and food cooking in grease. Corde sat at a lightweight metal desk he could lift with his knees by flexing his toes and he felt ridiculous. Lance Miller was in the opposite corner of the room.

Throughout the morning students and staff workers of the school gave Corde their version of the essay 'The Jennie Gebben That I Knew.' They put their words to many uses – exonerating themselves, pressing the wound of loss, putting their names into the public record.

Some even tried to help him catch a killer.

74

In the morning alone Corde filled two packs of three-by-five cards. At one p.m. they took a break. Corde opened his briefcase to get a new pack of cards. As he cracked the cellophane wrapping, Miller glanced into the briefcase and noticed Corde staring at a photo taped to the inside. It was the one of Jennie Gebben, face shiny with sweat. Corde was aware of Miller's watching him and closed the lid. Miller went to the cafeteria to buy sandwiches.

After lunch Miller looked out the window and said, 'Oh, boy, here he comes again.' Corde looked up and saw Wynton Kresge coming up the sidewalk. 'What's that man want?' Corde asked.

The security chief entered the small room, carrying an envelope.

'Hiya, Wynton,' Corde said. 'What can we do you for?' Kresge set an envelope on Corde's desk. 'What'd this be?' the detective asked.

'I don't know. I was over to Town Hall and I saw Detective Slocum there. I mentioned I was going to be nearby the Student Union and he asked me if I'd mind dropping this off and I said I'd be happy to.' He stopped abruptly, looking pleased he'd given the explanation so smooth. On the outside was stamped: *Forensic Lab Interoffice Use Only – Fredericksberg*. Kresge asked him, 'They have a division in the state that looks for clues?'

'This's the county lab. Jim Slocum was in the office? He's supposed to be checking out the roads and the mall,' Corde snapped.

Kresge asked, 'You want me to check out anything at the mall? I'd be happy to.'

'No.' Corde was miffed. He walked out of Room 121 to a phone booth disfigured with innocuous messages. Kresge remained in the activity room for a moment looking awkwardly at the blackboard. Then he left, walking past Corde and waving good-bye. Corde, the phone crooked under his neck, nodded and watched his broad trapezoidal back disappear down the corridor. A deputy in the office said that Slocum wasn't there. Did Corde want him to call in? Corde answered, 'No,' and hung up angrily. He returned to the room and looked inside the envelope Kresge had brought.

'Oh, no.'

Miller looked at him.

'We missed ourselves a knife.'

'At the crime scene?'

'Yup.' Corde was looking at a bad photocopy. The technician had merely laid the weapon on the copier platen. The edges were out of focus and the background was smudged black. It was a short folding stiletto with a dark handle and a thin blade, which looked about four inches long – two shorter than the state limit for concealed weapons. There was a design on the handle – an insignia of some kind – in the shape of crossed lightning bolts. It looked vaguely like a Nazi insignia, Corde thought.

He read the brief report from the Harrison County Crime Scene Division. The knife had been found in the flowers beneath where Jennie Gebben had lain, the blade closed. It had not been used on her – there were no traces of blood tissue on the blade – though it might have been used to cut the rope the killer strangled her with.

Steve Ribbon had added a handwritten note. *Bill – Offering? Sacrifice? More evidence of Cult action. You should follow up.*

'Stupid of us, Lance. Damn stupid, missing something like this. And I went over the site twice. Slocum and I both.' Corde's skin felt hot from this lapse. He pulled another report from the envelope – about the newspaper clipping and its threatening message. There had been no fingerprints. The red ink, in which were found several marker fibers, was from a Flair pen, sold in millions of stores around the country.

On the Analysis Request form he had filled out to accompany the threat Corde had asked, *What was used to cut the clipping out of the paper?*

A technician had replied, *Something sharp.*

Finally the envelope contained the warrant permitting them to search Jennie's half of the dorm room. He handed it to Miller and told him to get over there with a crime scene unit. As he did so he happened to glance at Miller's notes and he realized he should have been paying more attention to what the young deputy was doing. 'You wrote down the score of the homecoming game she went to.'

'Shouldn't I've?'

'No.'

'Oh. I thought you wanted specifics.'

Corde said, 'And you're supposed to be asking the girls in her dorm when Jennie had her period.'

'You can't go asking somebody that.'

'Ask.'

Miller turned fire red. 'Can't we look it up somewhere?'

'Ask,' Corde barked.

'Okay, okay.'

Corde read one of Miller's notes: *Roommate and JG just before dinner on Tuesday night. They had discussion – 'Serious' (Fight?) Couldn't tell what was said. JG unhappy as she left. Roommate: Emily Rossiter.*

Corde tapped it. 'That's interesting, I want to talk to Emily. Get over there now and have her come in.'

7

Bill Corde was irritated at the fluorescent tube that flickered frantically above his head and he was exhausted from sifting for hours through the goofy and theatrical attitudes of young people on their own for the first time. He was thinking of closing up for the day and returning to the office when a young man appeared at the door. He was in his mid-twenties. A squat mass of black crinkly hair was tied in a ponytail. His face was very narrow and he had high ridges of cheekbones, under which was a dark beard. He wore blue jeans and a black T-shirt. 'You Detective Corde?'

'That's me. Come on in.'

'I got a message that you wanted to see me.'

'What's your name? Here, sit down.'

'Brian Okun. Is this about Jennie Gebben?'

'That's right.' Corde was flipping through the index cards. Slowly, card by card, reviewing his boxy handwriting. It took a long time. He looked up. 'Now, how exactly did you know her?'

'She was in Professor Gilchrist's class. Psychology and Literature. He lectures. I teach the discussion section she was in.'

'You're on the faculty?'

'I'm a graduate student. Ph.D. candidate.'

'And what did you do in your section?'

'They're discussion groups, as I said.'

'What do you discuss?'

Okun laughed, puzzled. 'Do you really care?'

'I'm curious.'

'The question last week was: "How would John Crowe Ransom and the school of New Criticism approach the poetry written by someone diagnosed with bipolar depression?" Do you know what the New Criticism movement was all about, Officer?'

'No, I don't,' Corde answered. 'Do you know if Jennie was going with anybody?'

'"Going with." What does that mean? That's a vague term.'

'Was she seeing anyone?'

Okun asked in a voice crisp with irony, '"Seeing anyone"? Do you mean dating?'

It seemed to Corde that the boy wasn't hostile. He looked genuinely perplexed – as if the detective were asking questions that could not be answered in plain English. 'I'd like to know about anyone Jennie may have had more than a passing friendship with.'

Okun's eyes ricocheted off Corde's cards. 'I suppose you know I took her out a few times.'

Corde, who did not know this, answered, 'I was going to ask you about that – do you usually date students?'

'This's a college town. Who else is there to ask out?' Okun's eyes met Corde's.

'Isn't it unusual for a professor to ask out his students?'

'I'm not a professor. I told you that. I'm a doctoral candidate. Therefore we were both students.'

Corde rubbed his finger across a Styrofoam cup of cold coffee. He shuddered at the squeaky sound. 'I'd appreciate you answering my questions in a straightforward way. This is a pretty serious matter. How long were you seeing her?'

'We broke up several months ago. We'd dated for three months off and on.'

'Why did you break up?'

'It's not your concern.'

'It may be, son.'

80

'Look, Sheriff, we went out five or six times. I never spent the night with her. She was sweet but she wasn't my type.'

Corde began to ask a question.

Okun said, 'I don't feel like telling you what my type is.'

'What were the circumstances of you breaking up?'

Okun twitched a shoulder. 'You can't really call it breaking up. There was nothing between us, nothing serious. And neither of us saw any point in going on with it.'

'Do you know who Jennie began seeing after you?'

'I know she went out. I don't know with whom.'

Corde fanned through his three-by-fives. 'That's interesting. Several of her other friends also told me they aren't sure who she was dating recently.'

Okun's eyes narrowed and his tongue touched a stray wire of beard. 'So, a mystery man.'

Corde asked, 'What kind of student was she?'

'Slightly above average but her heart wasn't in studying. She didn't feel passion for literature.'

He pronounced it *lit'rature.* Corde asked, 'Was there anybody in class she was particularly close to? Other than you?'

'I don't know.'

'Did you see her personally in the last month?'

Okun blinked. *'Personally?'* he asked the ceiling. 'I suppose I'd have to see her *personally,* wouldn't you think? How else can one see anyone? Do you mean did I see her *intimately?* Or do you mean *socially?'*

Corde thought of the time he managed to cuff and hogtie George Kallowoski after the man had spent ten minutes swinging a four-by-four, trying in his drunken haze to cave in Corde's skull. He thought a lot better of Kallowoski than he did of this boy. 'Outside of class, I meant.'

'I hadn't seen her socially for a month. I assume you remember that I told you I didn't see her intimately at all.'

'Do you know if there was anybody who had a gripe with her? Anybody she'd fought with recently?'

'No.'

'Did she get along well with her roommate?'

'I guess. I don't know Emily that well.'

'But you knew Jennie well enough to know that Emily was her roommate.'

Okun smiled. 'Ah, ratiocination! Does this mean you've trapped me?'

Corde fanned his cards like a Las Vegas blackjack player. 'Now, Emily . . .' He looked up, frowning. 'I thought you told me you never stayed overnight in Jennie's room?'

Okun, observing the interrogation from a different plane, sighed. He descended to say, 'Emily has a big mouth . . . I was being euphemistic when I mentioned spending the night.'

'Euphemistic?'

Okun said, 'It means I was not being literal. I was being metaphoric.'

'I know what euphemistic means,' said Corde, who did not.

'I mean I didn't have sexual relations with her. We stayed up late discussing literature. That was all. Officer, it seems to me like this is some kind of personal vendetta.'

'I don't believe you're right about that.'

Okun looked out of the small window as if he were stargazing then said, 'I don't know whether you went to college or not but I imagine you don't have a lot of respect for what I do.'

Corde didn't say anything.

'I may look like a, what would you call it? Hippie? That's your era. I may look like a hippie. But it's people like me who teach half this illiterate world to communicate. I think that's a rather important thing to do. So I resent being treated like one of your local felons.'

Corde asked, 'Will you submit a blood sample?'

'Blood?'

'For a genetic market test. To compare with the semen found in Jennie Gebben's body?'

Brian Okun said, 'Fuck you.' Then he stood up and walked out of the room.

Do You Drive Your Man Crazy?

Diane Corde sat in the paneled office and flipped through a *Redbook*.

Question 1. What is the wildest thing you and your mate are capable of doing?

A. Taking skydiving lessons together.

B. Making love outdoors.

C. Going skinny-dipping

D. Taking ballroom dancing classes.

Diane didn't like the place. It reminded her too much of the office of the vet who spayed their puppies and dispensed worm drops. It was nothing but a cheap paneled waiting room and a sliding glass window, behind which was a gum-chewing receptionist, who seemed about to ask, 'Time for Fluffy's distemper shot, is it?'

Diane swallowed, dry-mouthed, and returned to the magazine.

Question 7. How surprised would your mate be if you called him up one afternoon and told him to meet you after work in a ritzy hotel room, where you would have champagne and caviar waiting for him?

A. Not surprised at all.

B. Somewhat surprised.

C. Very surprised.

D. Astonished.

Corde and Diane had met at a Methodist church singles supper sixteen years before, held in the boathouse on Seever Lake. Corde had shown up with only bags of potato chips, getting mileage out of a bad joke ('Sure I know it's a pot luck supper – y'all're lucky I didn't bring a pot'). Corde then spotted Diane Claudia Willmot arranging pickles in a Tupperware bowl and asked her if she'd like to go for a walk. She said she would, only wait a minute she wanted to get her purse, which she did, and they wandered around in the park until, thank you Lord, a roaring cloudburst forced them into a little shack and while the other pot-luckers were eating beans and franks and making forty-days-and-forty-nights jokes, Corde and Diane kissed, wet and hot, and she decided she was going to marry him.

She was four years older than Corde, which is a big difference between people at only one age – their mid-twenties, which is where the two of them happened to be. Crying, Diane asked him, 'What are you going to do when I turn thirty? You'll still be young.' And Bill Corde, who was in fact worried about the age difference (but because he thought *she* might leave him for an older man), told her something that turned out to be completely true: that he didn't think she'd go too ripe before he himself went gray.

One problem he hadn't counted on, though. Diane was divorced, married two years to a salesman up in Fredericksberg. They'd split up before Corde met her and when she'd confessed the marriage, nervous about the response, he'd smeared on the nonchalance real thick. But later he got to thinking about Diane and Stuart together and he claimed it turned his stomach into a cloverleaf. Diane was tolerant at first but then Corde's insecurity began to wear on her. She didn't know how to placate him. It didn't even seem to make him feel better when she repeated over and over the partial truth that she and Stu hadn't had a good sex life. Although she didn't dwell on it she assumed that Corde had had his share of women and hoped it was true so that he had sowed all the wild grains he had in him. But it wasn't the sex that tormented Corde; it was something trickier – jealousy that the woman he wanted to marry had confessed secrets to another man, that she had cried in front of him, that she had comforted him. Corde could not be allayed, looking sheepish and sorrowful at this retroactive betrayal. 'But it was before I even *knew* you,' Diane snapped, and he got a look at her spirited side, as she'd intended. Corde brooded plenty and finally Diane called the bluff. 'You gonna mope like that, go find yourself a virgin you think is worth all this heartache you're making for yourself.'

Their wedding, the following month, was appropriately punctuated by an inundation to match that of the day they'd met. They both took this as a good omen, which had proved to be pretty accurate. Sixteen years of marriage and when they called each other darling, they more often than not meant it. Diane said the secret to their success was that they had faulty memory circuits and tended to forget rather than forgive the transgressions. The closest either of them had come to an affair were unpure thoughts – along the lines of those about Susan Sarandon and Kevin Costner when Corde and Diane made love the night they'd rented *Bull Durham*.

They had weathered a near-bankruptcy, the deaths of Diane's father and Corde's mother, a stroke that made Corde's father forever a stranger and then the old man's death, and some bad problems when the family was living in St Louis.

Lately Corde was spending more and more time on cases, away from home. Yet oddly the brooding sense of threat she felt did not come from his long hours or moody obsession with his work. Rather, Diane Corde felt that for some reason it was the trouble with Sarah that was driving them apart. She did not understand this at all but she sensed the momentum of the rift and sensed too, in her darker moments, its inevitability.

She looked at her watch, felt a burst of irritation at having been kept waiting then looked at the receptionist, who moved the gum around in her mouth until she found it a comfy home and continued addressing bills.

Question 11. Does your husband . . .

The door to the inner office opened and a woman in her late thirties stepped out. She wore a beautiful pink suit, radiant, vibrating. Diane studied the dress before she even glanced at the woman's face. *That is a tart's color.* A formal smile on her lips, the woman said, 'Hello, I'm Dr Parker. Would you like to come in?'

Ohmagod, she's a fake! Here she is just a Mary K rep who won the Buick and is on to better things. As she stood, Diane thought hard how to escape. Vet's office, pink suit and the woman's only references had been the yellow pages. But despite the misgivings Diane continued into the office. She sat in a comfortable armchair. Dr Parker closed the door behind them. The room was small, painted yellow and – another glitch – contained no couch. All psychiatrists' offices had couches. That much Diane knew. This office was furnished with two armchairs across from a virtually empty desk, two answering machines, a lamp and a clean ashtray on a pedestal. A cube box of Kleenex.

The doctor's thick gold bracelet clanked on the desktop as she uncapped a pen and took a notebook from the desk.

On the other hand, the doctor passed the wall test. One side of the room was filled with somber, stout books like *Psychodynamics in the Treatment of Near-Functioning Individuals* and *Principles of Psychopharmacology*. On the facing wall were the diplomas. Dr Parker had graduated from the University of Illinois, cum laude, from Northwestern Medical School and from the American College of Psychiatrists. Three schools! Diane, who had limboed out of McCullough Teachers' College with a B-minus average, looked at the squirrelly proclamations full of Latin or Greek phrases and seals and stamps then turned back to find the doctor gazing expectantly at her.

'Well,' Diane said, and folded her sweating hands in her lap. She felt the wave of tears slosh inside her. She opened her mouth to tell the doctor about Sarah and said instead, 'Are you new in town?'

'I opened my practice a year ago.'

'A year,' Diane said. 'New Lebanon a little quiet for you?'

'I like small towns.'

'Small towns.' Diane nodded. A long moment of silence. 'Well, it is a small town. That's true.'

Dr Parker said, 'When you called you mentioned your daughter. Why don't you tell me about her.'

Diane's mind froze. 'Well.'

The doctor's pen hovered, ready to scoot along the paper, dragging the eighteen-karat bracelet behind.

Diane blurted, 'Our Sarah's been having some problems in school.'

'How old is she?'

'Nine.'

'And how many months?'

'Uh, six.'

'That's fifth grade?'

'Fourth. We held her back a year.'

'Tell me about her problem.'

'She's a smart girl. She really is. Some of the things that come out of her mouth ...' Examples vanished from Diane's mind. 'But she has this attitude ... And she's lazy. She doesn't try. She won't do her homework. She fails her tests. I was reading this book? *Your Hidden Child.*' She paused, waiting for Dr Parker to approve the paperback. The doctor lifted her eyebrows quizzically, which gave Diane the impression she didn't think much of the book. 'It said that children sometimes behave badly because they want attention.'

'You said she's smart. Do you know her IQ?'

'I don't remember,' Diane said, flinching. This was something she should have looked up. 'I'm sorry. I—'

'It doesn't matter. We can get it from the school.'

'But she acts hostile, she acts stupid, she has temper tantrums. And you know what happens? She *gets* attention. I think that's a lot of why she seems to be slow. We have another child – Sarah's the second – so we think that she feels jealous. Which is crazy because we spend lots of time with her. Much more than we do with Jamie. I don't let her get away with it. I don't put up with any nonsense from her. But she doesn't listen to me anymore. It's like she tunes me out. So what I'd like you to do is talk to her. If *you* tell her—'

'Has she ever seen a therapist or counselor about this?'

'Just a counselor at her school. The New Lebanon Grade School. He recommended that book to me. Then I talked to our pediatrician about it. Dr Sloving? He's an expert with children?'

Dr Parker apparently did not engage in the practice of confirming parents' opinions. She looked at Diane pleasantly and said nothing.

'Anyway we went to Dr Sloving and he prescribed Ritalin for her.'

'For attention deficit?'

This gave Diane a burst of relief, thinking that at least dottering old Sloving had diagnosed the problem correctly.

Dr Parker continued. 'Was she behaving in an unruly way, overly active? Any compulsive behavior – like washing her hands frequently?'

'Oh, she's restless a lot. Jittery. Always running around. Nervous. She drives me to distraction.'

'Did Dr Sloving give her any psychological testing?'

'No. He took a blood sample.' Diane was blushing and looked away from the doctor. 'But he's known her all her life . . . I mean, he *seemed* to think it was the best form of treatment.'

'Well,' said stern Dr Parker, 'if attention deficit is the diagnosis what brings you to see me?'

'I think the medicine's working.' Diane hesitated. 'But not too well. In fact sometimes I don't think it does any good, to be honest with you. It makes her very, I don't know, spacy at times. And it upsets her stomach and seems to make her more jittery. She says it gives her the tummy squabbles.' She looked down at her hands and found to her astonishment her knuckles were white as ivory. 'The truth is she seems to be getting worse. Her grades are still terrible. Yesterday she tried to run away. She's never done that before. And her temper tantrums are more violent too. She talks back more than she ever did. She also talks to herself.'

'Let me ask you a few things . . .'

An avalanche of questions followed. Diane tried to understand where the doctor was headed. But it was useless; just when Diane would think she understood what the doctor had in mind, she would throw a curve.

'Does she watch much TV?'

'Two hours in the evening, only when her homework's done. Actually she likes movies more. She thinks most sitcoms and commercials are stupid. She calls them yucky.'

A miniature smile made a reappearance. 'I'm inclined to agree. Go on.'

'She pretends she doesn't learn things quickly . . . I know she's, I don't want to say, faking . . .' Diane realized she just had. 'Well, she picks up some things so fast that when she acts stupid, it rings false.'

'What's easy for her?'

'Remembering movies and stories we've read to her. And the characters in them. She can act out scenes perfectly. She can remember dialogue. Oh and guessing the ending of movies. Dressing up in costumes. She loves costumes. But it's all things like that – pretend things. Anything having to do with real life – school, cooking, gym, bike riding, games, sports, sewing . . . All that seems beyond her.' Diane looked away from the doctor's eyes. 'The other day she wet her pants in front of the class.'

Dr Parker's mouth tightened and she shook her head. Diane watched her record in a tiny, cold notation a fact that would probably dog her daughter for the rest of her life. Diane took a Kleenex and pretended to blow her nose then twined the paper between her strong fingers and slowly shredded it into confetti.

More questions. This was hard. Diane tried, oh she did, but her way was to keep family flaws hidden like her mother's jewelry – anything real, anything diamond, anything gold was to be trotted out only on rare, vital occasions. It took all her strength to give this sleek, chic-suited stranger these facts – about Bill, about Jamie, about the grandparents, about Sarah's shyness and her wily manipulation. Dr Parker glanced at her watch. *Is she bored?*

The doctor asked, 'When you were pregnant did you drink or take any kind of medication?'

'I didn't drink, no. Occasionally I took a Tylenol. But only a couple of times. I knew it wasn't good.'

'How is your relationship with your husband?'

'Excellent. Good.'

'Do you quarrel openly? Have you ever talked about divorce?'

'No. Never.'

'Do either of you drink now or take drugs?'

'We drink socially is all,' an offended Diane said. 'We never do drugs. We go to church.'

There was a pause while the doctor's hand sped along the page. Diane said. 'So we were thinking that if somebody like you, a doctor, told her she should cut out this nonsense and get down to work, well, then . . .' Her voice tapered off.

The doctor chewed her thin lower lip, lifting off a fleck of lipstick. The expensive pen got capped. The teeth released the lip and the doctor leaned back in her leather chair. 'I've worked with learning disabled children before—'

'But she's not disabled,' Diane said quickly. 'I told you, her IQ —'

Dr Parker said, 'A learning disability isn't a function of IQ. It's —'

'Doctor,' Diane explained patiently. 'Sarah is a smart, shy little girl. She's learned a . . .' Diane remembered a phrase from the *Hidden Child* book. '. . . pattern of behavior to get attention from my husband and me and her teachers. We've played into her hand. Now we need an expert like you to tell her to buckle down and get to work. She's gotten away with too much from us. She'll listen to you. That's why I'm here.'

Dr Parker waited a moment then spoke. 'I want to say

something to you and you can think about it and talk it over with your husband. First, I should tell you – based on what you've told me – I'm not sure your daughter suffers from attention deficit disorder. Some psychiatrists feel that ADD is a condition different from hyperactivity. From my own research I think they're intertwined. If I understand correctly, Sarah doesn't show general overactivity – what we call hyperkinetic behavior. Her restlessness may be secondary; she has other problems and they in turn make her jittery and anxious. Ritalin is a temporary measure at best.'

'But Dr Sloving said it would help her to learn now and that she'd retain what she did learn.'

'I understand and there's something to be said for that. But with all respect for your internist, I feel doctors are prescribing Ritalin a little too quickly. Many parents prefer a diagnosis of ADD because they'd rather see a physical than a psychological explanation for their children's troubles.'

'Sarah is not crazy,' Diane said icily.

'Absolutely not,' the doctor said emphatically. 'A developmental disability is a common and treatable problem. In our days it translated as stupid or lazy or recalcitrant. Professionals don't think of it that way anymore. But a lot of people do.'

Diane felt the sting of criticism coming from the doctor's placid face. She said abruptly, 'Why, how can you say that? You should see all the work Bill does with her. And every day I march her downstairs and make her do her homework. Sometimes I spend an hour before breakfast with her.'

The doctor said in a soothing voice, 'I'm sure it's been very difficult for you and your husband. But it's important to put aside our thoughts that she's lazy or stupid or just ornery.'

'It was very hard to come here in the first place,' Diane blurted angrily. 'I just want you to tell her to buckle down, to—'

Dr Parker smiled. 'I know this is difficult for you, Mrs

Corde. You'd like a quick fix for your daughter's troubles. But I don't think we're going to find one. If she has a developmental problem, as I think she does, then the treatment requires the parents to expect *less* from the child, not more. We want to reduce the stress and pressure on her.'

'But that's just what *she* wants.'

Dr Parker lifted her hands and although she was smiling Diane believed the gesture meant the doctor had won this round. She boiled at this woman, who was making the meeting into a contest over her daughter's fate. She didn't grow any calmer when the doctor said, 'First, I'll do a series of tests to determine exactly what the problems are.'

Oh, I can psyche you out, honey. The dollar signs are looming.

'Then I'll have her come in for regular sessions and we'll treat her – probably in conjunction with learning specialists.'

'Well,' Diane said coldly, still stupefied by what she saw was a dressing-down.

Dr Parker asked, 'Shall we schedule an appointment?'

Diane summoned sufficient etiquette to say politely, 'I think I should talk it over with Bill.'

She stood up and watched the pink-suited bitch also rise, smile warmly and extend her hand, saying, 'I look forward to hearing from you. It's been a pleasure.'

For you maybe. Unsmiling, Diane shook the doctor's hand, then walked out the door.

Outside the office, in the parking lot, she tore the doctor's card in four pieces and smiled them into the breeze.

Corde and T.T. Ebbans stood over a desk in the main room of the Sheriff's Department, poring over the computer printout that Ebbans had ordered from the county data base. It was headed: *Known Sex Offenders, Convicted, By Offense.*

In the past three years the district attorney had

prosecuted or pled out eleven rapists, four aggravated sexual assaulters, three child molesters, three exhibitionists ('Hell, flashers, you mean . . .'), a couple of peepers, and three excessively embarrassed residents whose offenses involved livestock.

'We got ourselves a relatively unperverse community,' Ebbans commented, noting that these numbers – except for the sheep – were considerably lower than the state average per thousand residents.

Corde and Ebbans had just learned that every one of the rapists and the assaulters was accounted for. Ebbans said he'd do an informal check of the exhibitionists and peepers. He was not enthusiastic about the prospect.

'It'll be a waste, I know,' Corde said. 'But we gotta do it.'

Ribbon had come up and was tugging at an earlobe as he looked over the list and chuckled. Lance Miller walked into the office, just returned from the dorm. Corde noticed that he was vastly uncomfortable.

'Whatcha got, Lance?'

The young man plunked his hat onto a rack beside the door and buffed his crewcut with his pink fingers. He walked to the cluster of senior officers. His eyes fished around the office. 'Well, Bill, I went over there to that McReynolds place, the dorm, with the Crime Scene fellows. Like you asked.'

Corde motioned impatiently with his hand. 'She coming in to be interviewed? Emily?'

'Well, I just talked to her for a minute. She's real pretty.'

'Who's that?' Ribbon asked.

Corde said, 'Jennie's roommate.'

'She was damn upset,' Miller continued. 'She said it seems somebody broke into the dorm and stole all of Jennie's letters. She—'

'Well, well, well . . .' the sheriff said. 'That's interesting.'

'She went to a memorial service they had for Jennie over at one of the churches yesterday and left the door unlocked. When she got back somebody'd stolen this folder with all Jennie's letters and important papers.'

Corde was nodding.

'I asked around but almost everybody was at the service and nobody had any leads on the break-in.'

'Members of the cult maybe,' Ribbon offered, looking eyebrows-up at Corde.

Miller said, 'There's something else too.' His eyes had fallen to the desk and had focused on the phrase that said in green computer type, *Incidents of forcible sodomy to date.*

'Emily gave me a few things that this guy hadn't stolen.'

'Good,' said Corde.

'One of them was a calendar from last year.' Miller cleared his throat.

'And?' Ribbon said.

'A pocket calendar thing? It was in Emily's desk and that's why it wasn't stolen.'

'What about it, Lance?' Corde was growing impatient.

Miller seemed relieved that he could now rely on visual aids. He flipped the battered gray booklet open to the prior year, January. Written in the square for a Saturday night toward the end of the month were the words: *Bill Corde. Nine p.m. My place.*

8

'I interviewed her.'

'Part of a case?'

'The Biagotti case,' Corde said. His eyes were on the rumpled page of Jennie's calendar for the last week in January. On Thursday she had to pick up her dry cleaning. On Friday she was going to the drugstore for shampoo, Tampax and Sudafed.

On Saturday she'd seen Bill Corde. Nine p.m. Her place.

Neither Ebbans, with his affection for Corde, nor Miller, with his inexperience on the job, wanted any part of this.

Ribbon's eyes looked into Corde's, which were two uneasy pools of green.

The sheriff squinted memories back into his thoughts and said, 'That was after you got back from the task force, sure. It would've been around the end of January.' He seemed measurelessly relieved at this. 'You didn't know her otherwise?'

'No.'

Then Ribbon's face clouded again and his eyes fell to the calendar. 'She called you Bill. What do you make of that?'

Ebbans wandered away to his temporary desk and sat down to make a phone call, real or imaginary.

Corde said calmly, 'When I called Jennie up to see

when I could interview her about the Biagotti case, she and I got to talking and it turned out we'd lived near each other in St Louis. We, you know, chatted for a while about that. By the end of the conversation I called her Jennie. I guess she wrote down Bill.'

'You knew each other in St Louis?'

'What exactly are you getting at?'

'Nothing, Bill. I'm not suggesting a single damn thing. I just have to keep an eye out for this sort of situation.'

'What sort of situation?'

'I just want everything on the table.'

'Everything is *on* the table.'

'Good. But while your dander's up I'm just gonna ask one more question and then we'll say good-bye to it. In the Biagotti file you've got a record of that conversation you had with Jennie?'

'No.'

'Why not?'

'I didn't write anything down. I stopped by the dorm that Saturday. Nine o'clock. Jennie and I talked about fifteen minutes. She knew the Biagotti girl a little but that was it. Jennie was one of maybe fifty students I talked to about the case.'

'You didn't talk to fifty of them on Saturday night.'

'But I talked to a lot of them then. And on Sunday morning too. And on Sunday night. And—'

'That's a good answer.'

'That's the true answer,' Corde shot back.

'Okay, Bill, don't get riled. If I don't ask, somebody else might. Let's forget the whole thing.'

Ribbon tapped the sex offender printout. 'This was a good idea, this sex stuff. I'd also check out, you know, occult bookstores and that sort of thing. I think there's one of them not far from the campus on Waverly Street or Stinson. They've got a bulletin board in the doorway. See if they have announcements for cult . . . What do cults have? Services or meetings or something?'

'Probably services,' Miller said helpfully. 'Being religious, I mean.'

'Well, I'd check that out. Absolutely.' Ribbon returned to his office. The floor wheezed under his solid footsteps.

Corde found Ebbans and Miller staring at him. Ebbans punched a number into the phone. Corde handed Jennie's calendar to Miller. 'Log that into evidence, Deputy. And let's get back to work.'

For a time after he'd met with Dean Larraby he felt like General George Thomas who in 1863 earned his nickname the Rock of Chickamauga by preventing Braxton Bragg's counterattack from becoming a total rout of the Union forces. Faced with overwhelming odds and bowed under losses but infinitely confident and strong.

By now though Professor and Associate Dean Randolph Rutherford Sayles is pierced with a despair as sharp as any triangular musket bayonet. He sits where he has sat for the past three hours, smoking his thirteenth cigarette of the afternoon, in the Holiday Inn on the Business Loop with four Auden University trustees from the East Coast. Their transcripts he is not familiar with, but this he has finally concluded about them: they are men who view Auden as a trade school. Two are lawyers, one is the director of a large nonprofit philanthropic organization and one is a doctor. Their interest in the school derives from the Poli Sci Department, the business school, the Biology Department.

They never glean of course that Sayles holds them in patient contempt for their philistine perspective on education. He can't afford for them to catch on; either personally or through their fund-raising efforts these four are responsible for close to eleven million dollars a year of funding for the school. Sayles the history professor thinks they are rich fools; Sayles the associate dean of financial aid, immersed presently in hot fucking water, charms them effusively as they indulge in dishes of bad

97

fruit salad in the Riverside dining room.

Occasionally they seem to grow tired of Professor Sayles and their eyes dip toward a five-page document, which the professor prepared earlier in the day and which he views the way FAA inspectors might study the jagged remains of a 747.

'Gentlemen, Auden University is a qualifying not-for-profit corporation, which exempts the institution under the Internal Revenue Code Section 503(c) from paying federal income tax and from a parallel section in the state revenue code from paying state tax. Being a not-for-profit corporation, however, does not mean that it can lose money with impunity.' Ha ha ha. He catches each of their eyes seriatim. 'So while the terms red and black don't have the same meaning they might for, say, GM, or IBM, we are seriously considering changing the school's colors from black and gold to crimson . . .'

He is passionate and funny, teasing his audience in the manner of a toastmaster, a serendipitous skill he has learned from years of lecturing to twenty-year-olds with attitudes. Yet these Easterners are immune and actually seem embarrassed for Sayles. One says, 'We've got to start thinking more global on this. Let's start a law school or hang some balls on the MBA program. Move up into the Wharton frame of mind.'

'Hmm. High capital expense for that,' Sayles offers. *Try fifty million minimum.*

'Maybe a noncredit continuing education program?'

Sayles nods gravely, considering. *You stupid prick. Farmers and Kmart checkers aren't going to pay good money to study Heidegger at night.* 'Hmm. Small market for that,' he says.

One trustee, a trim, golf-playing lawyer, who turned down even the fruit cup as too caloric, says, 'I don't think we should be too fast to give up on Section 42(f) aid.' Under the state education law private colleges can qualify for grants if they admit a large number of minority students, regardless of their academic record.

The others gaze at him in puzzlement. At least here Sayles has allies. The lawyer says, 'It was just a thought.'

'Three point six million,' Sayles says slowly, and the discussion goes round and round again. Sayles begins to understand something. These men court clients and patients and chief executive officers who routinely write them checks of ten twenty a hundred thousand dollars. They live with streaked-haired, face-lifted wives and are limoed to art museums and restaurants and offices. Aside from semiyearly meetings at Auden, Palm Springs and Aspen, they are never seen west of Amish country. He decides their interest in their alma mater is just that – an *interest*, nothing more. He is sickened by their suggestions, which are paltry and, worse, obvious; they are student responses to the assignment 'How to Save Auden University.'

By the time the last dots of syrup have been sucked out of the fruit cups, Randy Sayles senses with a feeling of terrible waste that he is alone in this struggle to keep the school afloat. The school. And his own career. And perhaps his freedom.

The Easterners promise to keep their thinking caps on. They promise to increase their personal pledges. They promise to mount a campaign among their peers in the East. Then they shake Sayles's hand and climb into the limo (university-financed, fifty-six dollars an hour) for the ride to Harrison County Airport.

Sayles is in terrible despair. He returns to his office and, with the help of one of the school's lawyers, fills out a Section 34 form requesting emergency state aid for private educational institutions. Too little. At best, Auden might receive six hundred thousand. But Sayles urges the lawyer to file the application anyway and to do so by fax. In a daze he watches the gray-suited lawyer leave his office and he has a vivid image from one of his own lectures – not of George H. Thomas rallying his troops to a bloody defiant stand but rather of Union General Irvin McDowell at Manassas Junction, watching in confused despair the spirits of his many men fly to heaven under the shocking clatter of Jackson's guns.

Special to the Register – The carcass of a recently killed and skinned goat was found in a fourth-grade classroom in the New Lebanon Grade School yesterday.

The carcass was discovered by a janitor at six a.m. and had apparently been left after the school was closed at midnight. The vandal gained access to the school by breaking through a ground-floor washroom window. No one was in the building at the time.

A large quantity of blood – believed to have come from the animal – was smeared on the walls of the classroom.

The room will be closed for cleaning for several days. Fourth-grade students will attend class in the school's recreation room.

Investigators feel this incident may be related to the rape and murder of an Auden University co-ed by the so-called 'Moon Killer' on the night of April 20. School officials reported that the vandal wrote the word 'Lunatic' on the classroom wall in blood.

This word comes from the Latin 'Luna,' meaning moon.

Board of Education officials approved emergency funds to hire a security guard who will be at the school during school hours through the end of the term.

Meanwhile, the teachers' union and officials of the PTA have contacted the office of John Treadle, Harrison County Supervisor, with a request for a town curfew and for additional police to help investigate the crime. One PTA official, who insisted on anonymity, said that if the killer is not found within the next few days, parents should consider keeping children home from school.

*The next full moon will occur five days from
now, on the night of Wednesday, April 28.*

'This is getting out of hand,' Bill Corde said.

Steve Ribbon brushed the newspaper delicately. He
seemed to decide not to reply to Corde's tight-lipped
comment. The sheriff instead asked, 'A goat?'

'This kind of stuff . . .' Corde shook his head. 'I mean,
people *read* this. People believe it . . .'

'We can't control the press, Bill. You know that. What
was the handwriting like? On the classroom wall?'

'What was it like? I don't know. You want to get a
graphoanalyst—'

'"Lunatic." It's Latin for—'

'This moon thing is making people crazy,' Corde
protested. 'There's some no-fooling hysteria out there.'

'Can't deny the facts.'

'Steve, it was kids.'

'Kids?'

'A prank or something. High school kids.'

'I don't know, Bill.'

'Even if it *was* Jennie's killer, all he did was leave
some showy clues making it look like this was related to
the moon somehow.'

'Well, if the shoe fits . . .'

'Naw,' Corde said. 'He'd do it to throw us off. I mean,
why kill a goat? Why not another victim?'

'Not killing anybody don't mean anything. Maybe the
strike window was narrower than I guessed.'

Corde debated for a moment. 'Well, Steve, isn't it
possible that this wouldn't've happened if the guy hadn't
read that story in the *Register* about cults?'

'*My* interview the other day, you're saying.'

Corde could think of no response. He shrugged. 'We
didn't find any evidence of cult or Satanic stuff around
Jennie's body.'

'The knife. You're forgetting the knife.'

Corde pulled at his lip for a moment. 'I don't know
what to make of the knife, that's true.'

He could see no reason to pursue this line of talk with Ribbon. He said, 'Another thing I want to do – I want to take out an ad and ask for witnesses. Tell them everything'll be confidential.'

The sheriff said, 'What'll it cost?'

'The *Beacon* won't be much but we'll have to do it in the *Register* too, I think. It'll be about four hundred for the week. We get a discount.'

'We haven't got that in our budget. It's already dented from you taking that flight to St Louis.'

Corde said, 'I think we've got to. Nobody's come forward. We need some help.'

'Do the *Beacon* but I can't afford the *Register*,' Ribbon said. 'I've got another idea though. You ought to ask all the county shrinks about their patients. And all releases for the past month from Gunderson. That's an approach a lot of investigators take in serial killings.'

'A low-security mental hospital, two hundred miles away?' Corde asked.

'A lot of crazies go through Gunderson.'

'And every one of them shrinks is going to plead privilege.'

'I don't much care about that. At least it'd be on record that we asked and we'd keep ourselves covered pretty damn good.'

'We don't have the manpower to do what we're doing now let alone send somebody around to every therapist in the county.'

The men looked at each other for a lengthy moment and finally Corde said firmly, 'I'll take responsibility for the way I'm handling the case.'

Ribbon stroked his bulbous red cheek with a raw knuckle. 'No need to have words over it, Bill.' He smiled. 'You're absolutely right. It's *your* case. And *your* responsibility. You do what you think you ought.'

The low late afternoon sun fell on her desk and onto the piece of paper she had in front of her. Sarah reached forward and the square beam of light seemed to warm her hand. Specks of dust floated along the beam and Sarah had this image: If she were no bigger than a bit of dust she could float away, sail right through the open window and outside. Nobody would see her. Nobody would know.

She hunched over and smoothed the paper, which was all crinkly and limp. She felt some slight disappointment; it looked just like red ink on typewriter paper. She was hoping that he'd leave messages in stone or on a big sheet of brown burnt paper.

A comma of tongue touched the dimple in her upper lip and she leaned forward in concentration. Sarah found reading harder than writing because even though she had a terrible time remembering spelling and how the letters were supposed to go, at least *she* decided which words to use. Reading was the opposite. You had to look at words somebody *else* had picked and then figure out what they were.

This was torture.

She sighed, lost her place and started over. Finally after twenty minutes she finished. A wave of happiness swept over her – not just because she managed to complete the note but at what the words themselves said.

Sarah:
   I got your note. I was real glad to get it. Don't worry about your spelling. It doesn't matter to me how well you spell. I'm watching you, I'll come visit very soon. I'll leave a surprise for you in the garage.
   And yes I am -

                    The Sunshine Man

Happy, yes, although she felt a bit of disappointment – he had left the note while her mother had been out, Tom the deputy had been reading on the front porch and Sarah herself had been watching an afternoon movie.

103

Why, she wondered, hadn't the Sunshine Man waited for her and given her this message in person, instead of leaving the note where she found it – under the pillow of her bed?

Whoa . . .

Diane Corde paced through the kitchen.

'She was a four-star, flaming you know what.'

'Whoa,' Corde said. 'Hold on here.' He opened his first of two after-work beers. This one was his favorite and he really enjoyed the sound of the tab cracking. Today the ritual wasn't giving him any pleasure.

Diane tore open the freezer door, pulled out a four-pound pack of ground round and tossed it loud into the sink. Frost flew like shrapnel. Corde stepped back. He said, 'I just asked how it went.'

'How it went is it cost us a hundred and ten dollars – one hundred and ten! – for this woman, you should've seen, a doctor wearing a pink dress, no you shouldn't've seen, for this woman to tell me about my own daughter. Honestly!'

'Simmer down now and tell me what she said.'

'I was perfectly civil with her. I was polite. I tried to make a few friendly jokes.' Diane turned to her husband. 'I think she's from the East.'

'Tell me what she said,' Corde repeated patiently.

'She insulted Dr Sloving and she talked to me like I was keeping Sarrie from getting help because I was afraid people'd say she was crazy.'

Corde squinted, trying to work this out.

'I mean, what she wants to do is for us to pay her a hundred and ten dollars – my *word*, a hundred and ten dollars – an hour just—'

'I got my insurance.'

'. . . to give Sarah some tests . . .' She crossed her arms and paced some more. 'I mean, she was practically looking me in the eye and saying she's got learning disabilities.'

'Does she?' Corde asked. Diane stared at him. He

added, 'Have learning disabilities, I mean?'

'Oh, okay!' Diane thundered. 'You're taking her side? Fine.'

Corde sighed. 'I'm not taking sides.' He retreated. 'You'd think a hundred ten dollars'd buy you more than that.'

'I'd say you would.' Two potatoes crashed into the sink.

Sarah appeared in the doorway and Diane's pacing slowed. The little girl watched her and said cautiously. 'Mommy, it's time for my pill.'

Two more potato hand grenades were lobbed into the sink. 'No,' Diane said. 'You're not taking them anymore. Give me the bottle.'

'I'm not?'

Corde asked, 'She's not?'

'No.'

'Good, I don't like them. They taste pukey and they give me tummy squabbles.'

'Now you and your father are going to work on your spelling for the test next week and—'

'I'm not going to take—'

'You'll do as you're told, young lady!' Diane pulled onions out of the refrigerator. *Thunk*, into the sink. 'And on Saturday I'm taking you to see Dr Parker. She's a nice lady and she's going to help you in school.'

'Okay.' Sarah caved, fear of tests having a heavier specific gravity than fear of an angry mother.

'Honey,' Corde told her, 'you run into the den. I'll be there in a minute.' When she left, Corde cocked his head and said to his wife, 'Excuse me?'

Diane looked exasperated. 'Excuse me what?'

'I thought . __ I mean, what you just said. I thought you weren't going to take Sarah to see her.'

'Meat loaf?' Diane asked.

'Uhm, sure.'

'Of *course* I'm taking her.' Diane aimed a bunch of carrots at him and whispered harshly, 'That woman is a bitch and she's a fashion plate and if she doesn't help my daughter then heaven help *her*.'

Philip Halpern nervously carried the paper bag as he wound through the cluttered backyard to a greasy stone barbecue pit piled high with cinders and burnt steak and chicken bones. The boy set the bag in a cone of ashes and dug through pockets compressed by his fat body. Finally he took a book of matches from his shirt pocket. He did this with the reverence of someone who's afraid not of the fire itself but of unguessed risks that he's been warned fire holds. The match ignited with a burst of pungent sulfur. He lit the bag. It began to burn. Philip wondered if the smoke would be poisonous. He wished he had asked his friend Jano to do this—

Oh no . . .

Philip heard the footsteps. He looked up and in the dusk he saw the vague form of his father, a heavy man with a crew cut, wearing blue jeans and a T-shirt. The only distinct thing about the lumbering shape was the red dot of his cigarette held between his fingers at his side. Philip felt his heart freeze.

'Whatcha doing, son?' asked the benign voice.

'Nothing.'

'You ask me if you could burn something?'

'No, sir.'

'You lit the matches yourself?'

'I was just fooling around.'

'Fooling around with matches?'

'It's in the barbecue,' Philip said, trying to keep his voice steady.

'I can *see* it's in the barbecue. Did you ask me if you could light a match?'

'No, sir.'

'What'd it be?'

'Huh?'

'What'd I say about answering me that way? You forget the rules?'

'I'm sorry,' Philip said quickly.

'So what is it? That you're burning?'

106

'Just some paper I found.'

'More of those magazines?'

'No, sir.' *Please, please, please. Just leave me be. Please.* Philip felt tears dribbling down his cheek. He was thankful for the darkness; the surest way to get smacked was to cry. 'Just some paper.'

'Where d'you get those magazines?'

'It wasn't magazines.'

The bag flared suddenly as the contents caught fire. Philip believed he sensed a terrible smell. A human smell. He had an image of a small space creature enveloped in swirls of flames. He swallowed. In the flickering light he saw his father's face, a frown etched into the matte skin.

'You were out Tuesday night,' the man said. 'I looked in your room and you were out.'

Philip's voice clogged. His heart beat like a roaring car engine and shoved all the blood out of his chest and into his face and temples.

'Weren't you?'

Philip nodded.

His father said, 'A man answers, a girl nods.'

'Yessir, I was out.'

'Where?'

'Just went for a walk.'

'Uhm,' his father said. 'All right. Handy man.'

'Please, Dad . . .'

'Don't whine.'

'I just . . . I'm sorry. I was just . . .'

Just what? Philip didn't know what he could say. He couldn't tell the truth about the bag. He wanted it to burn to silent ash, he wanted his father to die, he wanted to be thin. He wanted to stop thinking about breasts about girls about mud . . .

'Please.'

'Hold out your hand.'

'Please.' But even as he was saying this, his hand rose. He found that it hurt less when he looked and he now stared at his own knuckles.

107

'You get one for the matches, one for the magazines, one for lying.'

'I'm not—'

'Two for lying.'

His father raised his fist and brought down his knuckles hard on the back of Philip's hand. The boy wheezed in pain.

Philip knew how he would kill his father. It wouldn't be strangulation, the way the Honons had killed Princess Nanya. It would be with some kind of gun. He wanted to pierce his father's body. He fantasized on this as the man's thick knuckles rose and fell, bone like iron, bone like xaser torpedoes.

Again, the searing pain. Philip pictured his father lying by the roadside, blood easing from deep wounds.

The flames in the barbecue flickered in the cool breeze. The radiation of heat ceased. His father's hand rose a final time.

Philip pictured his father lying by the roadside.

He pictured his father dying in a bed of blue flowers, dying in a patch of mud.

Bill Corde shudders once and wakes. It is two a.m.

He is a man whose dreams are anchored in logic, a man with a solid belief that images in sleep are replays of the week's events as sensible and sure as spark plugs firing according to the electricity sent to them by a new-scraped distributor. Dreams are not omens from wily gods, they are not inky-dark desires long ago snuffed.

Tonight however Bill Corde lies awake with trembling heart and legs so wet that he wonders for a horrid moment if he let go of his control as did his father every night of the last two months of his life. He reaches down and feels with meager reassurance the sweat along his thigh.

The dream was this:

Corde was sitting on a porch, the one he remembers from childhood. Only he was now an adult full grown and gray as the paint on the split oak of the floorboards.

There had been a terrible mistake, a misunderstanding so shocking that Corde was crying with agony. 'I know,' he answered the unseen person inside the house who had just told him the news, 'I know I know I know . . . But I thought different all these years. I *believed* different . . .'

Oh no, oh no . . .

How could he have been wrong?

What the bodiless voice had told him and what Corde finally and tragically acknowledged was that although he believed that he had two children, he in fact has but one – the other being just a bundle of cut grass hunched up in the backyard of his house.

In his dream he sobbed and then he woke.

Now, lying in his damp pajamas, listening to the tick of Diane's breath, he feels the slam of his heart. He supposed the dream itself lasted no more than five or ten seconds. Yet he thinks he will carry with him for the rest of his life the memory of those dream tears he cried for his lost child – and for himself, because half his joy all these long years with his family has been false.

The burgundy Cadillac Eldorado pulled into the parking lot and eased into a slot painted in black letters: *Mr Gebben.*

The driver of the car looked at the sign for a moment and thought of the parking space he had just left – one at the Stolokowski Funeral Home up the road. The sign there, which read *Families and Guests,* had been painted not in black but in bright blue. Richard Gebben thought there was sad irony in this; the blue of the sign at the funeral home was the exact shade of his company's corporate logo.

He climbed out of the car and, slouching, walked into the low pebble-walled building. An airliner's roar filled the sky for a moment and a jumbo jet began its takeoff roll at nearby Lambert Field. As the thick glass door swung shut behind him, the sound diminished to a whisper. 'Oh,' the receptionist said, and looked at him with a surprised stare. Neither spoke as he walked past.

In his outer office Gebben accepted the hug of his tearful secretary.

'You didn't . . .' she began. 'I mean you didn't need to come in today, Mr Gebben.'

He said softly, 'Yes I did.' And then escaped into his own sanctum. He sat in a swivel chair and looked out over a weedy lot surrounded by razor-wire-topped chain link and an abandoned siding.

Gebben – this stocky bull of a man, a Midwesterner with a pocked face, founder from scratch of Gebben Pre-Formed Inc., a simple man able to make whip-crack decisions – today felt paralyzed. He needed help, he had prayed for it.

He now spun slowly in his chair and watched the man who was going to provide that help walk up to his office door. A man who was cautious and respectful but unafraid, a man who had an immense physical presence even among big men. This man stood in Gebben's doorway, patient, his own huge shoulders slumped. This was the only man in the world Gebben would leave his daughter's wake to meet. The man entered the office and, when invited to, sat in an old upholstered chair across the desk.

'I'm very sorry, Mr Gebben.'

Though Gebben did not doubt the sincerity of those words they fell leaden from the man's chapped lips.

'Thank you, Charlie.'

Charles Mahoney, forty-one years old, was six three and he weighed two hundred and eighty pounds. He had been a Chicago policeman for thirteen years. Five years ago a handcuffed felony-murder suspect in Mahoney's custody had died when two of the man's ribs broke and pierced his lung. A perfect imprint of the butt of a police service revolver had been found on the suspect's chest. Mahoney couldn't offer any suggestions as to how this freak accident occurred and he chose to resign from the force rather than risk letting a Cook County grand jury arrive at one very reasonable explanation.

Mahoney was now head of Gebben Pre-Formed's Security Department. He liked this job better than being a cop. When people were found inside the chain link or in the warehouse or in the parking lot and they got impressions put on their chests and their ribs broken, nobody gave a shit. Except the people with the broken ribs and Mahoney could tell them point blank to shut up and be happy that their ribs were the only things broken. They were rarely happy. But they did shut up.

Richard Gebben, who by fluke of age had missed military service, knew the Chicago story about Mahoney because the security chief was Gebben's surrogate platoon buddy. They drank together on occasion and told war stories and travel stories, though most of them involved Mahoney talking and Gebben saying, 'It must've been a fucking great time,' or 'I've really gotta do that.' Gebben always picked up the check.

Gebben now held Mahoney's eyes for a moment. 'I'm going to ask you to do something for me, Charlie.'

'Sure, I'd—'

'Let me finish, Charlie.'

Mahoney's eyes were on a toy truck that Gebben's Human Resources Department passed out at Christmas. On the side of the trailer was the blue company logo. Mahoney didn't have any kids so he'd never been given a truck. This irked him in a minor way.

'If you agree to help me I'll pay you ten thousand dollars cash. Provided—'

'Ten thousand?'

'Provided that what I'm about to tell you never leaves this room.'

9

She put the words one right after another in her mind. She said them aloud. '"As virtuous men pass mildly away / And whisper to their souls to go . . ."'

The girl lay in the single bed, on top of a university-issue yellow blanket, under a comforter her mother had bought at Neiman-Marcus. The room lamps were out and light filtered through the curtains, light blue like the oil smoke of truck exhaust. Tears escaped from her eyes, saliva dripped onto the blanket beneath her head.

She remembered the last thing Jennie Gebben had said to her. *'Ah, kiddo. See you soon.'*

Emily Rossiter spoke in a frantic whisper. '"Whilst some of their sad friends do say, / The breath goes now and some say no."'

They weren't working. The words were powerless. She rested the book on her forehead for a moment then dropped it on the floor. Emily, who was twenty years old and intensely beautiful, had a large mass of curly dark hair, which she now twined compulsively around her fingers. She recited the poem again.

At the knock on the door she inhaled in shock.

'Emily Rossiter?' A man's voice was speaking. The doors were thin. She felt the knocking resonate upon her heart. 'It's Deputy Miller? I was by before? We were wondering if you could come in and speak to Detective Corde for a bit? He's pretty anxious to see you.'

A woman's voice, that of the housemother, asked, 'Emily? Are you there? This gentleman wants to talk with you.'

'I'll drive you over.'

She heard their voices speaking to one another. She couldn't make out the words. She—

Oh no. The key! The housemother has a key. Emily flipped off the covers. She scooted off the bed and stood in the middle of the room like a child, knees together, panicked. Another knock.

Emily stepped into her closet and sat on the floor, which was strewn with fallen hangers and dust balls and tissue from the dry cleaner's. She quietly pulled several of her winter coats off the hooks above her and covered herself entirely.

'Emily?'

Breathe slowly, breathe slowly. They can't get you here . . . You're safe with me, kiddo.

But there were no keys in the door. After a moment she heard footsteps walking away, the jangle of the awful police equipment receding. It would be safe to climb out but there was something so comforting about lying under satin and cashmere so hidden that she was compelled to stay. '"Such wilt thou be to me, who must / Like the other fool obliquely run . . ."'

She wrapped the coats tighter about her.

They took Jennie away.

They took her letters away.

And now they want me too . . .

Ah, kiddo . . . Emily lay her head on the thick hump of a suede jacket.

'"Thy firmness makes my circle just, / And makes me end where I begun."'

The green Schwinn bicycle sat in the garage, standing upright. Twined around and around the small bike were little lights, a string of Christmas lights from the indoor tree. Wound around the handlebars, the fenders, the training wheels. The lights were on and the bike glowed like a city seen from an airplane landing.

They glowed too in reflection on the surface of the puddle of water on the garage floor.

Sarah stood in the doorway and looked at the spectacle in awe. It made her think of the movie *E.T.*, which she'd seen five times, the scene where the creature makes the bikes fly through the sky.

She walked around it, studying the lights with fascination. This bicycle had terrified her when she'd received it two years ago. At her mother's insistence she had tried riding it several times without the training wheels and nearly fell headlong onto the concrete of the driveway. She'd leapt off and run into the house screaming in panic. Even with the wheels on she avoided riding it when other children or Jamie, who rode his tall fifteen-speed so fast, might see her.

But what she was looking at now didn't scare her. It was a bike but it was also something else. Something more. Something pretty and something mysterious. With the cord plugged into the wall socket to light the bulbs she couldn't ride it of course. But she could sit on it and pretend she was pedaling – riding through the sky.

She could fly to the Sunshine Man's cottage and thank him . . .

She could be the queen of the sky, as if the dots of yellow lights were the stars in her own constellation . . .

Stepping forward into the puddle of still water, she reached for the handlebar.

'Sarrie, like what *are* you doing?'

Jamie stood in the doorway, pulling on his brown leather biking gloves. He slipped off his Styrofoam helmet and set it on a shelf. He stood with his hands on his hips for a moment then walked toward the bike.

'Nothing.' She stepped away, looking down.

'Did you do that?'

She didn't answer.

'That's like totally stupid.'

'I'm not stupid,' she said meekly.

He walked to the outlet and yanked the plug out of the wall then began unwinding the lights.

'No, don't!'

He shouted, 'Look! Look at this!' He held up a portion of wire that had been wound around the frame of the bike. The plastic insulation was missing and several inches of copper wire were exposed and wrapped around the foot pedal. He pointed at the floor beneath the bike. 'And there's water spilled there.'

'Don't yell at me!'

'If you do stupid things you're gonna get yelled at.'

'Stop it! Stop it!'

'Don't lay one of your effing tantrums on me! It won't work,' he shot back.

He wound the electrician's tape around the exposed wire, then carefully rolled the wire into a circle and replaced it in the box marked *X-mas Lights*.

She muttered ominously, 'You shouldn't've done that.'

Diane appeared in the doorway. '*What* is going on out here? I heard you all the way in the bedroom.'

Jamie said, 'Sarah was playing with the Christmas lights.'

'Sarah, were you?'

The little girl puckered her lips into an angry pout. 'He called me stupid.'

Diane turned on him. 'Jamie?'

'Well, she was *being* stupid. She could've like electrocuted herself or something.'

'It was pretty and he *ruined* it.'

'Mom,' he said, utterly exasperated.

Diane turned to her daughter. 'You know to leave the decorations alone. If you broke any it'll come out of your allowance.'

'I didn't do anything!' Sarah shrieked then stormed out of the garage.

Jamie pulled his bike off the pegs stuck in the garage wall and lifted it down. Diane walked over to him and spoke in a menacing whisper, 'How many times have I told you not to call her stupid.'

'She was playing with—'

'I don't care what she was doing. It's the worst thing in the world for her. Don't do it.'

'Mom.'

'Just don't do it.'

'You don't under—'

'Did you hear me?'

His strong hands squeezed the brake levers on his bike. Diane repeated her question. 'Yes,' he grumbled formally.

Diane's voice softened. 'If you see her doing something like that again come tell me. Your sister's going through a very rough time right now. Little things are really hard on her.'

'I said all right.'

He angrily wheeled his bicycle back and forth.

Diane wiped her hands on her skirt. 'I'm sorry I lost my temper.'

'Okay,' he muttered. 'No problem.'

'You have the match tonight, right?'

'Yeah.'

'We'll be there.'

'You and Sarah.'

'Your father's going to be working. It's a very important case.'

He leapt on the high bike and rolled down the driveway.

'I wish you'd let the deputy take you to school. Your father doesn't want you two going places alone.'

He shrugged.

'Jamie,' she shouted, looking on the shelf beside the door. 'Wait! Your helmet . . .'

But the boy seemed not to hear and leaned sharply into the turn as he sped out of the driveway and into the road.

He thought it was a skull but he couldn't be sure.

'You Watkins?'

'That I am.'

Naw, couldn't be. Jim Slocum walked into a small, windowless office in the State Building in Higgins. He introduced himself. He wasn't impressed; his own office in the New Lebanon Sheriff's Department was bigger and had a window to boot. This room smelled of onions and was filled with books and telexes and photocopies of memos. He glanced at some and thought how boring they must be. *Justice Department Monthly Homicide Demographics Report. Intrafamily Violence Review – Midwest Edition.*

Slocum squinted at the glass-enclosed bookcase behind Watkins. No, it was a grapefruit the guy had put in there and forgotten about. Maybe an ostrich egg.

Earl Watkins was short and round and wore a tight blue button-down dress shirt. Round metal-rimmed glasses hung on his nose. His mouth was a squooshed O above a deep cleft chin. 'Take a pew.'

Slocum settled onto the hard oak chair. 'Say, what is that?'

He followed the deputy's finger. 'That? It's a skull. See the bullet hole?' Watkins, a huge Capitol rotunda of a man, with flags of sweat under his arms, was a special agent, Violent Crime Division, State Police.

Slocum said, 'We're hoping you could shed some light on this situation we've got ourselves. Help us out with a profile of the killer. I'll tell you, there's some spooky stuff involved.'

Watkins asked slowly, 'Spooky stuff?'

Slocum gave him a summary of the Gebben murder then added, 'Happened on the night of the half-moon and underneath her was this cult knife.' He handed Watkins a photocopy.

The large man looked at it briefly, without emotion. 'Uh-huh. When was her birthday?'

Slocum blinked. He opened his near-empty briefcase and looked into then closed it, remembering the exact spot where he'd left the rest of the file on his desk. 'Uhm, I've got somebody compiling all that stuff. I'll get you a copy.'

Watkins then asked, 'Multiple perpetrators?'

'Don't know. Were a lot of footprints around. Mostly men's. I had pictures taken of them. I'll get you copies if you want.'

'Naw.' Watkins studied the photocopy of the knife. 'Uh-huh, uh-huh. Did he cut her?'

'No. Strangled.'

Watkins said, 'I don't know what this insignia is. You have any idea?'

'They look sort of German. Like the Nazis, you know.'

'It's not a swastika.'

'No,' Slocum said. 'I don't mean that. I saw this TV movie. The Gestapo had these insignias—'

'Not the Gestapo. The SS. The *Schutzstaffel*.'

'That's it, yeah. Lightning bolts.'

'Only those were parallel. These are crossed.' Watkins waved the sheet. 'Knife have any manufacturer?'

'No. Just "Korea" stamped into the end.'

'The hasp,' Watkins said. 'When the guy raped her, how much come was there?'

Slocum sought the answer in the ceiling of the office. He thought that Watkins asked this too eagerly and he wondered if Watkins, who wore no wedding ring, was gay. 'The ME estimated three ounces.'

'Uh-huh,' Watkins said. He linked his fingers and cradled the back of his head. He asked Slocum dozens of questions: whether restraints were used, if the killer found the victim or kidnapped her, if there was evidence of alcohol, how Jennie's body had been arranged in the flowers, whether foreign objects had been inserted into her anus or vagina, how attractive she was, if there were lip marks or other evidence that the killer had drunk her blood or urine.

'That's pretty damn gross,' Slocum said, offended at the question.

'Any fingerprints?'

'On the knife, yeah. Then a mess of 'em other places too. I'm having somebody check those against known sex offenders.'

'That's a good place to start.'

'I'm making damn sure this situation isn't gonna happen again,' Slocum said with relentless sincerity.

'Are you now?' The state detective seemed amused. He scratched at the photocopy then gazed absently at the black toner that came off on his thumb. Watkins interrupted Slocum's account of the goat found in the grade school by saying, 'Tell me about number two.'

'Only one goat I heard about.'

'The other *victim?*'

'We've got no other victim. Just the Gebben girl.'

'When you called,' Watkins said, examining a slip of paper, 'you said *killings.*'

'Did I? There's only one now. But we're worried that we'll have a repeat in the next week. With the full moon, you know.'

'Steve Ribbon's your sheriff, right?'

'Yep, sure is.'

'And Hammerback Ellison, he's Harrison County sheriff? They're both up for reelection next fall.'

The dividing line between what he should say and what he shouldn't had always been blurry for Jim Slocum. 'Yep. I believe so. I'm not sure they're running.'

Watkins wiped a wave of sweat off his forehead. That was the smell, Slocum recognized. Sweat. Not onions. Watkins grinned. 'Lotta folk say Steven Ribbon's bubble's a little off-plumb.'

Slocum's eyes weaseled away from Watkins's and he studied the spine of *Modern Sociopathology*. 'I don't know about that.'

'Naw, I suppose you wouldn't.' Watkins smiled like he'd hit a hole in one. 'Well, you want to make this more'n what it is—'

'Hey—'

'That's your all's business.' Then the smile left his face and he said, 'With only one killing and on these facts it's way too early to know what you've got. You need more information.'

120

'Can't you give us some idea, going on the assumption it's a cult?'

'I can give you the textbook profile for a classic cult killer if you want. But don't take it to the bank. I've got no idea whether it applies or not.'

'I understand that. Sure.'

'That said, you want me to go ahead?'

'Shoot.' Slocum straightened up and flipped his notebook open. As he did so he glanced at the skull and had a passing thought. *Where could a man get himself one of those?*

'Dogit,' Amos Trout said. 'Why'd it have to happen just now?'

'Always the way. You oughta—'

'Can't afford a new one. You gotta patch her.'

Trout stood with the mechanic in the left bay of the Oakwood Mall's Car-Care Centre, looking down at the tub of water so grimy it might have come from Higgins Creek downstream of the old paper mill. In the tub was a Goodyear tire and out of its side was escaping a steady stream of greasy bubbles.

Trout, forty-four, was wearing dark slacks and a short-sleeved white shirt. He had thinning hair, cut short and combed back. In his plastic pocket protector were three pens, a tiny calculator and a sales tax chart. Trout sold carpeting at Floors for All. He looked sadly at the bubbles. 'What'll it cost for a patch?'

'Five seventy-five.'

'I could do it myself, I was home,' Trout said.

'You ain't home.'

'Looks to be a pretty slow leak and she got me all the way here this morning. I could just pump her up and take my chances.'

'You could. You wouldn't want to do that, without you had yourself a good spare. That's my opinion.'

Trout wouldn't have been so concerned about the tire if after he closed up tonight he and the wife weren't driving up to Minnesota to catch big lazy muskies and

121

sit in lawn chairs while they drank cocktails out of the back of their beige accordion Travel-All. And it was going to be four weeks before he got back to thirteen-ninety-five acrylic pile your choice of colors pad included free if you buy today.

'Plug her,' he said. 'And do a good job. I'm about to put some road under that Buick.'

Four blessed weeks thank you Lord though I'm sorry about the wife part.

The tire man went to work. After a moment he held up a piece of glass like a Dodge City doctor who'd just extracted a bullet from a gun-slinger's arm. 'There she be. You had steel belteds it wouldn't even've dented 'em.'

Trout studied the glass. 'I knew I picked up something. Tuesday night I was coming back late on 302. And you know that curve by the dam? Blackfoot Pond? Where everybody fishes?'

The mechanic slicked a plug with glue and began driving it into the puncture. 'Uhn.'

'Well, I went around the curve and this fellow comes running up right into my lane.'

'Maybe your lights're on the blink. I could check—'

'They're fine except one high beam's out of whack.'

'I can just—'

'That's okay. And so I went off the road so's not to hit him. Wham bam just like that. He froze. I went over a beer bottle. You know it's those fishermen, they leave all kinds of crapola around. They don't do that in Minnesota.'

'They don't?'

Trout said, 'Scared the living you know what out of me, seeing that fellow. He looked scared as I was.'

'Don't blame him. I wouldn't wanta be Buick feed myself.'

'Yessir.' Trout looked at his watch. It was two o'clock. He paid for the plug. 'You sell propane?'

'You got a tank, you can fill it.'

'No, I mean for a Coleman.'

'Naw, gotta go to the Outdoor Store for that.'

122

'Guess I better. Long lunch hour today. But, hell with it, I'm almost on vacation.'

The sound of the gears buzzing was just audible over the wind that hissed past his ears.

Jamie Corde upshifted as he came to the crest of the hill on Old Farm Road. Below him, a hazy mile away, the school sat in a field – tar-topped brick buildings squatting in a couple of acres of parking lots and lime-green grass.

This was his favorite stretch of road – a sharp decline of smooth asphalt, which if you caught it at the right time of day was pretty much traffic free. Although he now rode a fifteen-speed Italian racing bike, the boy often surged down this road on his old three-speed Schwinn, which was mounted with a speedometer. On a summer day with tires fat from the heat inflation he could hit fifty miles per hour before he had to brake for the stop light where Old Farm crossed Route 116.

He started downhill.

Jamie Corde loved to run and he was a ragingly fast runner, but he knew that nothing could beat the feeling of speed not of your own making – flying down a mountain of snow in Colorado or racing down a slope like this one, effortlessly, the gears ratcheting beneath your toe-clipped feet. As if the powers of nature were taking you someplace you couldn't find by yourself.

The bike was steady under his strong arms as the dotted centerline became a single gray blur. He leaned forward to cut the drag and concentrated on nothing but steering around patches of pebbles. He did not think of his mother or his sister, he did not think of his father. With the exception of a few images of Greg LeMond in the Tour de France, Jamie Corde thought of speed and speed only.

Halfway down the incline, to his enormous delight, he passed a car. True, it was an old Volkswagen diesel and it was being driven by someone who resembled Mrs Keening, his antiquated Latin teacher. But it was nonetheless a car and he had outraced it, feeling with

123

utter ecstasy the motion of the driver's head as she glanced at him with disapproving awe.

A half mile ahead at the foot of the hill lay the intersection. He noticed with disappointment that he had timed his assault on the slope wrong. If he had waited three or four minutes at the top and started his descent just as the stoplight had turned red, he might have arrived when it was green and he would have swept smoothly through. But the light was now changing to yellow. Route 116 was heavily trafficked and was favored by this particular light, which kept drivers on Old Farm Road waiting impatiently for long minutes.

He slowly squeezed the rear brake lever. *Thonk*. A sudden sensation. Something had struck his right calf. He believed he had hit a small animal – a field mouse or chipmunk – and it had been flung up against his leg by the hissing wheel. Almost simultaneously his hand on the brake lever began to cramp. He glanced at the handlebars and noticed that the lever was all the way to the metal.

Jamie looked down at the rear wheel. What had struck his leg had not been an animal. It was the rubber pad of the rear brake shooting from its housing. The metal seemed slightly bent and he realized with horror that when he had lifted the bike onto the pegs in the garage last night, he must have hit the steel jacket that held the pad, loosening it. His father had warned him a dozen times to be careful when he placed the bike on the wall; he continually ignored the advice.

He was two hundred yards from the intersection and still accelerating, approaching forty-five or fifty. The bike began to vibrate. He gripped the handlebars with trembling fists as he swept over stones and branches; he was going too fast to maneuver around them. Sweat of panic burst from his neck and under his arms. He felt the icy chill as the moisture evaporated in the slipstream. Jamie gently squeezed the front brake. No effect. He squeezed harder and the rear end of the bike rose suddenly, nearly sending him tumbling head-forward over the front wheel. He was now a hundred yards from the intersection. He kept as much pressure on the front brake as he dared but still the bike continued to speed up.

A stand of tall oaks flashed into his vision and vanished. A roadside truck, some fence posts. The shoulder here was narrow. Paralleling his mad course was a barbed wire fence that would lacerate him if he were to set the bike down in the gravel beside the road.

Jamie Corde, an A-minus science student, knows that terminal velocity in earth atmosphere is approximately one hundred and thirty miles an hour, he knows that human organs cannot withstand instant deceleration from any speed about fifty. He glances up at the cross-traffic along Route 116, trucks and cars whizzing past. Tears – from the wind, from his panic – streak from his squinting burning eyes and disappear into his hair. He sits up to increase wind resistance. He remembers a prayer from Sunday school. He drags his feet on the asphalt but shreds the running shoes' nylon toes quickly. He lifts his feet to the pedals and the bike hurtles forward once again.

10

Seventy-five yards . . .

The hill had bottomed out but the bicycle tore along the road at close to sixty, the noise of the wheels and gears wholly obscured by the howl of the slipstream. Several bugs died against his face with sharp stings. The lightweight frame of the bike shuddered painfully with every stone.

Jamie eased onto the centerline of Old Farm Road where there was less debris. A fragment of bottle or a smear of grease could kill him.

Fifty yards from the intersection . . .

He believed he heard a horn behind him, maybe the Volkswagen driver trying to warn him.

Forty yards . . .

The man in a car waiting at the light glanced in his rearview mirror and Jamie saw astonishment in the glossy rectangle that reflected the man's eyes.

Thirty . . .

Two Japanese imports and a Buick dashed through the intersection on 116 going north. A tanker truck rumbled south.

And Jamie Corde began to pedal.

He couldn't stop in time. That was clear. Either he was going to dart between cars or he was going to get nailed. He lowered himself into his best aerodynamic huddle, clicked into his highest gear, released the front brake lever and pedaled as he never had before. He felt a warm sense of calm envelop him. The cars were on a different plane. The wind, the barbed wire, the road too. The bike itself. The fear vanished. He was above all of these things. The blue-haired woman piloting the Volkswagen, the driver whose eyes gaped in the mirror, the trees, the birds startled and fleeing from Jamie's own speed – nothing was of the least importance. He smiled and struggled to pedal fast enough to keep up with his trilling wheels, propelling himself faster and faster.

Fifteen yards . . .

The car waiting for the green light was a Nissan and its license plate number was DRT 345.

Ten . . .

An old skid mark in the shape of a sine curve crossed both lanes.

Pedal pedal pedal pedal! . . .

A wooden crate that had contained Rock Island peaches lay shattered by the roadside, wads of blue tissue paper bleeding into the ground.

. . . faster than light . . .

The southbound Taurus station wagon, doing about sixty-five, began its skid thirty feet from where the bike was entering the intersection. The gray vehicle's end drifted to the left as the frozen wheels howled. The driver steered into the skid expertly, which had the effect of moving the car into the oncoming lane and aiming the grille precisely at where the speeding bicycle would cross the highway.

The front-seat passenger lowered her face below the dashboard.

The baritone Detroit horn blared.

The driver flung an arm over his eyes.

Ping.

Jamie Corde had an impression of fingers snapping beside his head as he passed in front of the station wagon. The bumper missed his rear tire by no more than six inches. Their combined speed was close to one hundred ten miles an hour.

His ears filled with the horn and the endless scream of the locked wheels. Then he was past Route 116, dancing over what was otherwise a risky patch of pebbles and transmission fluid as confidently as if the road were a smooth, banked racetrack. He relaxed his numb legs and coasted. Horns shrieked behind him and he knew he was getting cussed out by at least one station wagon full of people.

But what could he do except keep going, leaving them far far behind?

Jamie Corde continued to pedal – furiously to keep his speed up. As he approached the school he stood high on the pedals. He gazed up into the sky and breathed in hot oily air, waving a fist above his head, laughing and howling like a desert-loco cowboy.

Jim Slocum opened the candy bar and took a bite, pressing the candy up against the roof of his mouth. He dropped a dollar on the counter.

'Be right with you, Officer,' the young woman behind the counter said.

'Take your time.'

Slocum leaned against the counter in the Sweets 'n' Things shop at the Oakwood Mall. He took another bite of Milky Way, which was still his favorite candy bar. Always had been, always would be. The door to the candy store opened and Slocum watched a teenage boy enter. Fat. Wearing grimy clothes. Blond hair long and stiff with spray or grease. Slocum recognized him as Philip Halpern. The boy glanced at Slocum in unconcealed surprise. He walked to the wall of glass canisters of penny candy and began to fill a bag.

Slocum was put off. He felt angry at the boy for his weight and his lack of willpower. He wanted to say, 'You keep eating like that you're gonna stroke out by the time you're twenty, son.' He kept these thoughts to himself though. Like all New Lebanon deputies Slocum had answered domestic violence calls at Creth Halpern's shabby bungalow. The father could be frightening – his eerily confused eyes as much as his temper. The ex-sailor would slouch on the couch picking at a flap of skin from his right-hook knuckle and smiling at the bloody streaks on the dented front of the Kelvinator.

His wife, pungent with gin, holding ice to her pretty face, would look up with a drunk's sincerity and say, 'We was fooling around is all.' Philip, himself sometimes bruised, usually hid in the bedroom. There was a daughter too. Slocum bet she'd be knocked up and Remington-married by the time she was sixteen.

Boy, you stay that fat, they won't let you join the Army and what're you gonna do then? Jim Slocum was convinced that all emotional troubles could be cured by varsity football or basic training.

The clerk's customer left the store.

'Miss,' Slocum said to her, 'I'm asking all the merchants here in the mall if they were open late on Tuesday night.'

'This have to do with the student girl who got killed?'

'Yep, sure does.'

'Is this fellow, you know . . .' Two furrows of concern appeared on the young woman's brow.

'How's that?'

She touched her heavily moussed brown hair. 'What I heard was, Debbie Lipp told me, who's ever behind that killing? He's looking for brunets. I bought some Clairol yesterday. I mean, I had my colors done and going blond would throw it all off but . . .'

Slocum watched a tear center in her eye and roll over the edge of the eyelined lid.

'I wouldn't go doing that, miss. He's not looking for brunets that we know about. Your hair looks real nice just the way it is.' He smiled. 'Sexy too.'

'I'm *scared*, Officer.' Her brittle voice cracked. 'I gotta drive home at night and Earl he's my husband's shift's not over till eleven. Sitting there in the trailer for three hours! By myself . . . I can't watch TV, for the noises outside. I can't read. I just sit. I'm too addled to even knit

130

and I'm going to miss my niece's birthday with the vest I promised her.' She cried, grim and silent, for a moment.

'We're doing everything in our power to get this son of a gun. Now I was asking about Tuesday?'

'I can't help you, I'm afraid. We close at seven on Tuesday.'

Well, there you have it. Dead end. 'Tell you what, give me a quarter pound of those jelly beans. What flavor'd they be?'

'The watermelon ones?'

'Yeah.' Slocum paid. He took the change and smiled a flirt at her. 'I get by here on occasion. I'll look in on you and see how you're doing.'

She swallowed and lifted away a tear with a corner of her sleeve. 'I'd rather you was out *catching* him.'

'Well, we're doing that too,' he said stonily and took the candy, walking to the door. He glanced at the Halpern boy. 'You want a snack, eat apples,' he snapped.

Slocum ambled through the recession-battered wasteland of the mall until he came to the last store on his list. Floors for All. Inside a young man with trim hair sat at a desk, carefully writing in an order book. 'Afternoon,' Slocum said.

'Howdy, Officer, what kind of carpet you interested in today? We got a special—'

'This place here open late on Tuesday?'

'Yessir. Lot of carpet stores close down weeknights but we're number one with carpet, number one with service. Nights're important. We get men come in after work to check out the carpet their little ladies've chose earlier in the day.'

'You working this last Tuesday?'

'No sir, that'd be Mr Trout. Amos Trout.'

'Will he be coming in today?'

'Oh, he's in. He's not here right now because he got car problems. He took a late lunch. Should be back any time.'

'I'll stop back later.'

Slocum left the store and halfway to the exit nearly

walked into Adeline Kraskow. 'Well, well, well.' Slocum circled her.

'Hey, Jim,' she said in her husky voice. She was young and might have been pretty if she'd forced her salt-and-pepper hair into staying put. The strands reminded him of BX cable. She also needed to move some of the boob weight down to her toothpick legs (a rearrangement Slocum never thought he'd recommend to any woman). Addie had dry skin and high cheekbones and she wore little makeup. This made Slocum think that she was desperate for a man.

He asked, 'What's happening?'

'Doing a story on how this cult murder thing is affecting business.'

'Bad?'

'Yep. People're scared. Staying home and not spending money. What are you doing here?'

'I can't really talk about it.'

They stood for a minute, silent. Slocum had a fast series of thoughts: that he'd been promising to bring the wife to the mall, that he could do that on Sunday and that while she did her shopping he could talk to this guy Amos Trout at the carpet store. He asked, 'I'm taking kind of a break. You interested in getting a drink?'

Adeline Kraskow said, 'Sure. I guess.' And she stuffed her notebook into her huge purse and together they strolled through the mall.

They had known each other for exactly one year, ever since she started covering the police beat for the Harrison County *Register*. The top-heavy Ms Kraskow didn't know that Slocum regularly had acrobatic sexual intercourse with her and had been fellated by her dozens of times – each instance of course in his Technicolor imagination while he was engaged in considerably more mundane sexual activity with his wife of eleven years, or with his right hand. He supposed that if in real life Addie had ever stubbed out one of her chain-smoked cigarettes and unzipped his fly he'd have gone limp as month-old rhubarb but still he liked to sit with his knee pressed accidentally on purpose up against her thigh while she asked her reporter's ever-serious questions. Now he maneuvered her into a dark corner booth of the mall's only full-fledged restaurant, T.K. Hoolihan's.

'You're on duty?' she asked.

'I'm undercover. I can drink.'

'You're wearing a uniform. How can you be undercover?'

'Well, I'm wearing Jockey shorts. No, that's under*wear* not undercover.' He laughed to show it was a joke. Addie smiled with flirtatious contempt. They ordered neat scotches and he paid.

'Thank'y.' She lit a cigarette, inhaled and shot out a stream of smoke at the plastic Tiffany lampshade decorated with robins. 'So, you got any leads yet?'

'I told you—'

'Is there a connection with the Susan Biagotti killing?'

'Bill wouldn't want me talking on that.'

'I'm sure he wouldn't. But I can't ask only questions people want me to ask. The Biagotti killing never got solved. Here Steve Ribbon's revving up for reelection and he flubbed that case bad. Now there's a second girl dead.'

'Addie.'

She said, 'You don't know how persistent I am. Tell me *something*. Anything. I promise your name won't appear anywhere in the story.'

Slocum sighed.

Addie leaned forward, strategically, and whispered, 'Cross my heart.'

The warmth she denied the parents she spent on the children.

Diane Corde could at least say that for the woman.

'Hello, Sarah,' the woman said ebulliently. 'I'm Dr Parker. How are you today?'

In the silence that followed, the three of them standing

133

in the veterinarian waiting room, Diane said, 'Honey, you know how to answer.'

'I'm not going to take the spelling test,' Sarah said in a dour, snappy voice. 'And I'm not going back to school.'

'Well, now Sarah,' the doctor said cheerfully, 'we've got some other things to talk about. Let's not think about your spelling test today, all right?'

'Sarah,' Diane barked, 'I won't have you behaving this way.'

Dr Parker didn't intrude between mother and daughter; she simply kept the smile and extended her hand. Sarah shook it abruptly then stood back, looking, Diane thought sadly, like the little brat she'd become.

'Come on inside,' the doctor said. 'I've got some things I'd like to show you.' She motioned the girl into her office. Diane looked through the door and noticed a number of dark green boxes on her desk. The letters WISC-R were stamped into them.

She then glanced at Dr Parker to appraise today's fashion choice. A close-fitting red silk dress. With *dark* stockings. In New Lebanon! Didn't some famous gangster's moll wear a red dress when she turned him in?

Diane stepped forward after Sarah. But Dr Parker shook her head and nodded to the couch in the waiting room. 'Just Sarah and me today.'

'Oh. Sure.'

Diane, feeling chastised, retreated to the couch and watched the receptionist open a pack of Trident and slip a piece into her mouth. The woman noticed Diane staring at her and held up the package.

'I don't chew gum, thank you.'

As the doctor's door closed Diane caught a glimpse of her daughter's face staring fearfully down at the boxes. The door latch clicked. Diane sighed and aimlessly picked through a basket of wilted magazines. She lifted one to her lap with substantial effort and turned the pages.

A few minutes later Diane closed the unread magazine and slumped on this rec room couch, awash with defeat.

Defeated by her husband, in whose presence Sarah relaxed and laughed – her husband who could speak Sarah's flawed, tricky language while Diane could not.

Defeated by Sarah herself with her wily tactics of tears and panic.

By this harlot of a shrink, who was taking their scarce money so eagerly.

And by her own guilt.

Diane Corde gazes with unseeing eyes at a glossy magazine peppered with giddy photos of models while her legs shake with the terrible anguish of retribution. Diane Corde, fairly good Methodist, has been taught to believe in divine justice, taught to believe that revenge is fair and cleansing. But it is not. Because the person who is paying the exacted price for the sins is not the mother who committed them but the daughter.

Did you drink while you were pregnant?

No. Of course not.

What a question! No one drank when they were pregnant. No one took sleeping pills. No one took aspirin. All you had to do was read the science and health section of the *Post-Dispatch* or *Register* or even *Reader's Digest*, for heaven's sake, and you knew how to behave when you were pregnant.

Drinking liquor? No sane pregnant woman would drink.

Unless, unless . . .

Unless, for instance, someone you loved had perhaps done something very bad. Your husband maybe. And after word got out – in the newspapers – the neighbors would look at you funny or not look at you at all. And people would call late at night and just listen for a moment before hanging up as if they were curious to hear if your breathing was more monstrous than theirs.

Unless that person, your husband maybe, kept doing nothing and saying nothing nothing nothing until the money ran out and the only solution was to move from

135

a nice shipshape suburb to a small, tired rural town and start life over again.

His life.

And yours, in the process.

So even if you were pregnant wasn't that reason enough to take a drink now and then? Just to kill the silence of a man doing nothing, the heaviest silence that there is? A pill now and then. A few more drinks. And a few more ... To break the mournful web surrounding the seven a.m. breakfast table? To help you sleep, even if you woke up with a dogjaw pressure in the back of your head every other morning? Nobody drinks when they're pregnant.

Oh, Sarah ...

Diane Corde looked at the cheap door separating herself from her injured daughter and focused on the magazine again. She read every word of an article about a boat trip down the Loire as if she were going to be tested on the subject in the morning.

'I don't like her,' Sarah announced in the car on the way home.

'Why not?'

'She gave me all this stupid stuff to do. Drawing pictures and answering questions. I did it at school already.'

'Wasn't she nice to you?'

'Mrs Beiderbug—'

'Beiderson.'

'Mrs Beiderson's nice to me and *she* makes me feel all yucky. I felt yucky when I did those tests in Dr Parker's office.'

'She's trying to help you.'

'I hate her!'

'Sarah, don't talk that way.'

'She's going to make me take the spelling test at school. I saw you talking with her after. That's what she told you, isn't it?'

Yes, it was. Diane hesitated then said, 'Dr Parker

wants you to keep studying. Next time you see her she's going to give you some tricks to help you take tests.'

'I'm *not* going back to school.'

Diane's patience had just about evaporated and she said nothing.

'I hate it. I feel stupid in school. The Sunshine Man . . .' Her voice faded.

'We all hated school. That's what your father and I keep telling you. Everybody does.' This was spoken through firmly clenched teeth. 'You remember what a good job you did on your story this spring? About the birds.'

Sarah got a C plus, her highest grade ever in English, and had written a single page. Other students had filled four or five.

Sarah whined, 'I don't want to take the tests. Don't make me!'

'I'm going to work with you on the words tonight. Then we're going to Jamie's match.'

'No,' she announced. 'I want Daddy to help me.'

'Your father's working late.' Diane pulled the car into the driveway. She waved at the deputy in the cruiser parked in front of the house. He nodded back and returned to the newspaper. Diane braked to an angry stop.

Sarah said, 'He's always working.'

They got out of the car and walked through the garage to the back door.

'No, he isn't. He spends a lot of time with you. He's missing Jamie's match too tonight.'

'Wrestling's stupid.'

'Don't criticize your brother! He's doing just fine in school . . .' Diane was horrified at these words. She glanced at Sarah surreptitiously but the girl hadn't notice the unintended slight. 'Mommy, look, there's something on the back steps.'

Diane saw a small white envelope. Sarah scooped it up eagerly and looked at it. She frowned then handed it to her mother. They continued into the house. Diane paused in the hallway, the sunlight pouring through the open door. It fell on her hands, turning them blood red. 'Go on upstairs and get your books.' The little girl gave an extended sigh and clomped the stairs.

The envelope was addressed to *Officer Corde*. Red ink, sloppy handwriting. Diane tore it open, lifted out the contents.

'What is it?' Sarah yelled.

Diane jumped. 'Nothing, honey.'

She dropped the glossy square Polaroid back into the envelope, which she shoved into her pocket. She called the Sheriff's Department. She got the dispatcher. 'Emma, it's Diane Corde. Find him and tell him to get home. Tell him we're okay but I need him and I need him now.'

She hung up and started toward the front door to summon the deputy. She got only as far as the living room before she paused, leaned against the wall and surrendered to her tears.

11

Bill Corde crouched casually in front of Sarah. He measured his words then said, 'Honey, I have to ask you something and you'll tell me the as-you-love-me truth?'

'Sure, Daddy.' The girl returned his gaze cautiously. 'Did I do something wrong? I'm sorry.'

'No, no, honey.' Corde's heart cried as he looked into her penitent eyes. 'I'm just curious to know something. Has anybody maybe taken your picture in the last couple days?'

'My picture? No.'

'Or maybe just asked if he could take your picture? Some stranger on the way home from school?'

'No.'

'You're sure?'

'Did I do something wrong?' She seemed about to cry.

'No, nothing. It's okay. You didn't do anything wrong. I was just curious. You run get washed up for dinner.'

Corde returned to Steve Ribbon and Tom, who were walking in slow paces around the fence behind Corde's property. 'Nothing, Bill,' Ribbon said. 'Not a footstep.'

'Dry grass. What do you expect?'

The deputy said, 'I was here all afternoon.' He was defensive. 'I can't be both at the front and the back at the same time.'

'I'm not blaming you, Tom.'

Ribbon shielded his eyes like a Plains warrior's and

gazed off into the forest. 'Anybody live thataway?'

Corde leaned on a cockeyed, termite-chewed fence post, squinting against the sunset light. 'Five hundred acres of forest, mostly private. A few houses. Beyond that's the river and the other way's the preserve and the university and downtown beyond that. He could've come from anyplace. He could've parked on 302 by the bridge and walked. None of the neighbors saw anything.'

Corde examined the photograph again, through the plastic bag in which it now rested. It was of a girl about Sarah's age – the face wasn't visible – lying in grass. Her skirt was pulled up to her waist and the V of white underwear filled the center of the shot.

On the back was printed in red marker: YOU'RE WORKING TOO HARD, DETECTIVE

'Hell.' He winced as if the message brought him physical pain. 'I don't think it's her. She says nobody took her picture recently and I know she wouldn't lie to me. But goddamn . . .'

The deputy said, 'We should get a handwriting analysis. The newspaper clipping at the pond and this.'

'I'm sure they're the same,' Corde said. 'Even *I* can see the similarity.'

'Nobody saw nothing? Your son?'

'Nope. Nobody was here.'

'Brother, I'm sorry about all this, Bill,' Ribbon offered.

'*You're* sorry?' Corde muttered, walking inside.

Diane was sitting on the couch, her hands together. Corde sat beside her and cradled her hands in his. 'This could be just a prank, maybe it has nothing to do with the case.'

'A prank? It was *our* daughter!' she whispered violently.

'We don't know that for sure. It could be anybody. She tells me nobody took her picture.'

'She *tells* you? Oh, Bill, you know Sarah. Half the time she's off in her own world.'

'He's trying to spook me is all. Look, if that *was* Sarah

140

in the picture and he'd wanted to hurt her, why didn't he?'

She pressed her eyes closed. Wrinkles blossomed into her face and for a moment she seemed ten years older than she was.

'If anybody's at risk, it's me,' Corde said.

'That sure makes me feel damn better,' she shot back at him.

'Honey, this fellow isn't stupid. Murdering a law enforcement officer's a capital crime.'

'Does *he* know that?' she blurted.

'Diane.'

She stormed into the kitchen.

There was nothing more to do. Corde went back outside to talk to Ribbon. Ten minutes later Diane poked her head out the door and told him in an ominous monotone that dinner was ready. Corde asked Steve Ribbon and the deputy if they wanted to stay but they couldn't or more likely didn't want to. They left. Corde walked into the dining room, then Jamie and Sarah joined their parents and the family sat down to dinner.

Corde told the children with gentle words that there might be some people who weren't real happy with what he was doing to solve this case, so not to go anywhere by themselves and to stay close to home. Don't talk to strangers. Then Corde somehow found the strength to turn the conversation funny and talked about a sports blooper tape he'd seen recently. The only time a pall filled the room was when Corde realized he had stopped talking in mid sentence and was staring out the black window at the backyard. He stood up fast and closed the drapes. Everybody looked at him. Then he sat down and ate a huge third helping of string beans even though he didn't want them but it seemed like a comic thing to do and the evening returned more or less to normal.

T.T. Ebbans's practice was to question people at home at night. He'd try not to conduct interviews during business hours at offices, where guards are up and minds instinctively think up lies and excuses – for bosses, for fellow workers, for clients, for creditors.

Ebbans also happened to enjoy the evening. It reminded him of a wholly different era of his life, years before. The oily smell of night, the stillness, the bleaching to monotone of the deep colors of the day and the feel of his heartbeat quickening – a prelude to the five-man search-and-destroy night missions that were both the peak and the valley of his life.

At ten-thirty he came to the last house, a colonial on one acre sloping down to Blackfoot Pond. This hour was usually postbedtime in New Lebanon for anybody under fifteen and over thirty. But lights shone in the windows of this house. He thunked the brass lion's-head knocker once and the door swung open almost immediately. He found the couple waiting for him. Communication was good among Blackfoot Pond homeowners.

They all introduced themselves church-social formal. Tall, paunchy, bushy-haired Hank said, 'Come on in, Officer. Get you anything?'

'Maybe if I could trouble you for a glass of water.'

'Surely.' Lisa, still in her real estate broker's white blouse and trim red skirt, vanished like a spooked mouse.

Hank motioned Ebbans into a living room spotless as an operating theater. Plush white carpet, a cream-color sofa covered with clear plastic. The furniture was antiqued white and gold. Lisa walked into the room and handed the water to the deputy. They both stared at him as he drank it all down. He wasn't so thirsty as this but he didn't know where to set down the glass. He handed it to her. 'Thank you.' She returned a moment later. They sat. Plastic crinkled loudly.

Hank said, 'You're here about the murder.'

'I'm asking everyone in the area if they saw or heard anything around the time of the killing. That would be ten o'clock.'

'That was Tuesday, right?' Lisa asked, gesturing,

moving her fingers in a circular motion to count back on an invisible calendar.

'Nothing,' Hank said. 'We didn't see anything.'

'No,' Lisa echoed. 'Not a thing. Sorry we can't be more help.' Hank said he wished they could but, well, Ebbans knew how it was.

The deputy let them stew in a lengthy silence then asked Lisa, 'But do I understand that you saw something another night?'

Lisa's busy hands spread apart for a moment. Ebbans noticed they had left sweat stains on her crimson skirt. 'Pardon?'

Hank said, 'We didn't see—'

Ebbans said to his wife, 'You asked if it was Tuesday. I was just wondering if that meant you saw something some night other than Tuesday.'

She stared for a minute then gave a fast burst of a laugh. 'Oh, I see what you mean. No. The only reason I asked if it was Tuesday was to, you know, orient myself. Because of Sean. He . . .' She blinked. Hank's head turned slowly to her. Ebbans figured they had debated all evening about keeping their secret. Lisa began to tremble. Ebbans wondered how loud the discussion between these two would be after he left.

'Sean is . . .?' Ebbans asked.

'Our son,' Hank muttered.

Lisa said, 'He *was* here on Tuesday. That's right. I'd forgotten.' She swallowed hard and Ebbans wondered if she was going to cry. 'Sean got home from a Rifle Club practice late.'

'What time would that have been?'

She looked at her husband and decided not to lie. 'About ten.'

Ebbans asked, 'Is Sean here now?'

'Well, he is,' Hank conceded. 'But I doubt he can help you.'

Lisa said, 'It was pretty dark. I don't think he saw much.'

'Anything you tell me is confidential. Nobody'll

know he gave us any information.'

Hank walked to the stairs and called his son. A tall boy in jeans and a T-shirt appeared in a minute, looking assured, smiling, staring Ebbans right back in the eyes. Ebbans, who had two daughters and had never for one minute regretted that, thought he would love to have a son like Sean. 'You heard about the girl was killed over by the dam.'

'Yessir. We heard the next day.'

'I understand you got home about ten. From the Rifle Club. What kind of gun you shoot?'

'Winchester 75. With a target barrel.'

'That's a good gun. What's your rank?'

'Sharpshooter. All positions.'

Ebbans jutted out his jaw, impressed, and asked, 'You were outside about ten on Tuesday?'

'After I dumped the garbage bags in the bin I saw this raccoon and I chased him off, down toward the lake. I saw two people sitting on the other side of the dam.'

'What were they doing?'

Lisa said, 'Don't be afraid to say you don't know, if you don't.'

'Looked like they had tackle but it might just have been gym bags or something. They weren't fishing.'

'Can you describe them?'

'Sorry, sir. Not too good.' He nodded vaguely toward where the dam must have been. 'It's a ways. All I could see was their, you know, outlines. Silhouettes.'

Ebbans said, 'Could you tell if they were men or women, boys? White or black?'

'Well, I got the feeling they were guys. Kids from school, I mean.' He added formally, 'I don't believe they were African-Americans.'

'What did you see them do?'

'After a couple minutes they stood up and picked up whatever they were carrying and walked to the dam. There was this flash from one of their hands. I thought it was a knife. The way he held it.'

Ebbans said, 'Might it have been a bottle or a soda can?'

'Yessir, could've been. They sat on the dam for a while then I saw one of them point and they ducked down and ran off into the bushes. I thought they might be hatters so—'

'Hatters?'

'You know, like geeks or something. So I put the bikes in the garage.'

'And you didn't see them again?'

'Nosir. But I did see someone who walked by close to them. An old guy. He was fishing. He was about sixty, I'd guess. About my grandpa's age. He was casting spoons but he had a fly fisherman's hat on. A red one.'

'You haven't seen him since?'

'Nosir. You want me to keep an eye out for him, I'll be happy to do that.'

'No, honey,' Lisa said. 'I mean, you've done plenty.'

With the authoritative voice of a middle manager, Hank said, 'That's not our job, son.'

'You won't use his name, will you?' Lisa asked. 'You won't talk to reporters?'

'All names are confidential. I promise you that.' Ebbans looked at his watch and said he had to be going and thanked Lisa for the water and Hank for the time. He said to the boy, 'I sure appreciate your help. It was a brave thing to do. And I'd appreciate anything else you can do for us.'

At the door, the only hand he shook was Sean's.

In the dark they talked.

Brian Okun said, 'Think about what you're saying. What you're calling melancholia was cynicism.'

The young woman considered this then said, 'No, I don't think so.'

'How much of Wallace Stevens have you read?'

They were in Okun's apartment in downtown New Lebanon, a half mile from the quadrangle. This was the town's sole urban tenement neighborhood, which consisted of one block of three-story walk-ups, eighty years old.

'Enough to know that he was sad,' Dahlia answered.

'Sad men don't write poetry like his. Skeptics do. There's a power about him.'

'What about "Sunday Morning"?' she asked. 'You call that power? The woman has no energy. She's almost paralyzed at the thought that there's no God.'

'"Sunday Morning" is the most . . .' Okun found a word that conveyed contempt. '. . . accessible poem. It doesn't count. But since you've brought it up I maintain that only a cynic would create that imagery in the first place.'

Dahlia was from Wichita but was of Eastern Indian ancestry. She was short and voluptuous (Okun called her 'plump' – another nod to Dickens). He wished she knew more about the Modern poets. He said, 'You forget Stevens was a lawyer for an insurance company. A businessman. Wait! Wait . . .'

Okun, who was lying naked between Dahlia's dark smooth thighs, tensed for a moment, slipped his penis out of her and came generously on her black fur of pubic hair. He squeezed against her and lay still for a moment.

He kissed her breast and said, 'Are you okay?'

By which he meant did she have an orgasm. When she said a hesitant 'I'm fine,' he rolled off her and began reciting from memory the Stevens poem 'Notes Toward a Supreme Fiction.'

They had been dating off and on for a year when Okun fell in love with Jennie Gebben. After the breakup with Jennie, Okun and Dahlia continued to see each other on occasion and more rarely to have lethargic sex. Not a word was ever spoken about marriage, monogamy or even vaguer commitments.

Although he was more frank with her than with anyone else at Auden, tonight she was unknowingly taking part in an experiment Okun was just about to commence.

He turned on the overhead light and lit a cigarette. He stared at a flap of paint on the ceiling, a flap that for some reason always made him think of the severed portion of Vincent van Gogh's ear. 'I was in Leon Gilchrist's office today.'

'He's off someplace, isn't he?'

'San Francisco. Poetry conference at Berkeley.'

'He doesn't seem like the UCB sort.'

'I have no idea what sort he is. The strange sort.'

Dahlia said, 'He's brilliant.'

'Stating the obvious diminishes you,' Okun said, a homemade aphorism he used often.

'He's cute,' she said.

'Cute? Bullshit.'

'Well, I don't know. Maybe not. He's intense. I have trouble picturing him. He's nondescript.'

'Oxymoron. How can he be intense and nondescript at the same time?'

She blotted her sable groin with his sheet. 'I don't know.'

'He had a draft of my evaluation for the faculty committee in his desk.'

'You went through his desk?'

'Do you know what he wrote on it?'

She asked, 'How could you burgle his desk?'

'He said he did not want to work with me next semester. And he recommended that my advisor look long and hard at my dissertation.'

She was shocked. 'He *what?*'

'He said I was arrogant and lacked sufficient depth to be a talented professor. He said if the school insisted on hiring me after conferring the degree, it should be as a librarian.'

This was all true. When Okun had first read the words on Gilchrist's evaluation form he had felt physically ill. He now had some distance, but reciting the professor's scathing critique made his hands quiver with rage.

'Brian! Why did he say that?'

'He's a vengeful prick is why. I'm as smart as he, I

have more social skills and I want his job. He's figured that out.'

'Why were you going through his desk?'

Okun barked, 'I'm his graduate assistant. If I can't have access to his desk, who can?' He then added coyly, 'Can you keep a secret?'

'Brian.'

'It's something I've been wrestling with. I've got to confide in somebody. It's about him. Gilchrist.'

'You're dying to tell me.'

'I shouldn't.'

'Tell me.'

'Did you know that he and Jennie Gebben had an affair?'

'The girl who was killed? Ohmagod!'

'From almost the first week in September.'

'No!'

'He's into S and M.'

'I knew that,' Dahlia said, surprising Okun, who had fabricated this detail – as he had the fact of the affair itself. He asked where she'd heard this. She shook her head. 'Don't know.'

Okun continued, 'He used to tie her up and whip her tits. Oh and he'd piss on her. I think she pissed on him too.'

'God.'

Her wide-eyed expression of shock was delicious. Okun smiled then chuckled silently. Dahlia frowned across the pillow at him then grimaced and slapped his arm. 'You're making this up, you fuck.'

He laughed hard. 'I doubt Gilchrist knew Jennie from, excuse the expression, a hole in the wall. But you swallowed it raw.'

'Prick. So you going to start a rumor, are you?'

Okun said, 'He's not going to crater me with a bad evaluation. He's dumped on the wrong person.'

'But he could be arrested!'

'Divorce yourself from simplicity, darling . . . He was in San Francisco when she was killed. They'll find that out soon enough. I don't want him to go to jail. I just want to make him sweat.'

'You know what I think?'

'I'm vindictive and petty?' he asked, curious.

'I think you should cut out the part about getting pissed on. That's too sick for words. Nobody around here'd buy that.'

'Good point,' Okun said, always willing to take good advice. 'A little paraphilia goes a long way. Kiss me.'

'No.'

'Why not?'

'Because you scare me, Brian.'

'Me?'

'Yes, you.'

'Kiss me.'

'No.'

'Yes,' he commanded. And she did.

The security guard led Corde and Ebbans through the garbage room of Jennie's dorm to an emergency exit.

It was early the next morning and the air was humid and filled with smell of lilac, dogwoods and hot tar from roofers forty feet above their heads.

Corde and Ebbans had returned to the dorm to see if they could find Emily. Corde thought they might catch her before she left the dorm. She wasn't there although her bed had been slept in and the bar of Camay in the cream-color soap dish was wet. The detectives had waited in her room for nearly twenty minutes but she never returned. Just as the antsy guard seemed about to complain, Corde glanced out the window into the parking lot.

'Huhn.'

He'd written a note to Emily on one of his business cards and had left it on her desk. He then had said to Ebbans, 'Follow me.'

Ebbans did, trailed by the guard, a man with a huge swelling of latticed nose, who hadn't smiled at the men all morning.

Bill Corde pushed the stained bar on the gray fire door and stepped into the parking lot behind the dorm. The three men walked along a small grassy strip that separated the building from the parking lot. Grass and weeds. And oil drums painted green and white. Corde asked the guard, 'Are those the school colors?'

'Nope. They'd be black and gold.'

'Ugly,' Ebbans said.

'You salute it, you don't wear it,' the guard grumbled. 'Least, I don't.'

They saw however that not all the oil drums were green and white.

One was black.

'Fire?' Corde asked now as he walked up to the drum.

'Pranks.' The guard rubbed his great crosshatched nose and muttered, 'That the way they be. Think they own the world, the students, you know what I'm saying? Be spoiling stuff for everybody.'

Corde peered into the drum.

'Let's get it over. But slow.'

Together they eased the heavy drum to the ground. A small avalanche of ash puffed up gray cloud. Corde and Ebbans went onto their knees and probed carefully, trying not to shatter the thin pieces of ash. There were two blackened wire spirals that had been the spines of notebooks. The rest was a mostly unrecognizable mound of ash and wads of melted plastic.

Corde found several fragments of unburnt white paper. There was no writing on them. He eased them aside. He then found half a scrap of green accounting printout paper filled with numbers.

'What's this?'

Ebbans shrugged. 'I don't do brainy crimes.'

Corde put the scrap in a plastic bag.

Ebbans plucked a small pair of tweezers from the butt of a Swiss Army knife and reached forward. He gently lifted a bit of crinkly purple paper. All that remained was the upper lefthand corner.

March 14, 1
Jennie Ge
McReyn
Aude
New

'Her letters,' Ebbans said. There was triumph in his voice. 'There you go, Bill.'

'A pile of ash is all they are.'

Ebbans often worked like a dog on scent. 'Maybe, maybe not. Let's keep going and see what we can find.'

Together the men crouched down and began their search again. When they finished, an hour later, they had nothing to show for their effort but the scraps of paper they had found right off, and two uniforms filthied, it seemed, beyond saving.

Even from the distance he sees fear in their eyes, in their posture, in their cautious gait.

Driving along Cress Street, a shortcut to the Sheriff's Department, Bill Corde watches people on the sidewalks of New Lebanon. Shades are drawn. More than the usual number of stores had not yet opened this morning although it is a glorious spring day in a town that has wakened early for a hundred and fifty years.

The people are skittish. *Like cattle in thunder.* Corde drums the steering wheel and wishes he hadn't compared his good citizens to fed-out slaughter animals.

Ace Hardware, Lamston's, Long's Variety, Webb's Lingerie and Foundations . . . Stores or the descendants of stores identical to them that have been here forever. Stores he has walked past for years, stores he has shopped in and answered 911 calls at, stores whose owners he sees at PTA meetings. But today, as he cruises slowly in and out of elongated morning shadows, Corde hardly recognizes the street and its occupants. He feels what a soldier feels in an occupied foreign city. He thinks of his own time in uniform – when he once got lost in an old quarter of Berlin.

151

Corde stops his cruiser at the Main Street light.

A sudden crack on the window makes him jump.

Gail Lynn Holcomb – a high school class mate of his – knocks again with red knuckles. He cranks the glass down and looks up at her frowning overly powdered face.

'Bill, how's this thing *going?*' There is no need to be more specific. She continues, 'Should I keep Courtney out of school? I'm thinking I ought to.'

He smiles to reassure her and says she doesn't have to worry.

But he sees that the words are pointless. She *is* worried. Oh, she's terrified.

And as he tells her that he thinks the Gebben killing is an isolated incident he observes something else too. He sees that she resents him.

Corde has been a small-town deputy for nine years, which is about eight years longer than it takes to understand the ambiguous status of cops in towns like New Lebanon. People here respect him because they've been taught to, and what small-town people are taught when young stays with them forever. People knock on his windows with fat, nervous hands and ask his advice and invite him to Rotary Club lunches and buy peanuts from him at the PTA fall fund-raiser. They josh and nod and shake his hand and cry against his solid shoulder.

But there's a distance that's real and it's big and it never shrinks. Because if Bill Corde stands for anything it's that the long arm of malice can reach into the center of this safe little town, where it ought not to be; New Lebanon doesn't deserve the same fate as East St Louis or the South Side of Chicago or the Bronx, and Bill Corde is uniformed proof that its fate is different in degree only, not kind.

What Corde sees now in this agitated blond bundle of Gail Lynn, gone heavy on potato chips and cola and cello-wrapped cookies, unskilled with the makeup brush, but a good mother and a good wife, is this very rancor.

Oh, how she resents him!

Because she now must fight daily, amid the noise of soap operas and sitcoms, with her husband and daughter about locking doors and latching windows and chaperoning dates and which routes to take to and from jobs and shopping centers and schools . . .

Because tomorrow morning Courtney with her thick wrists and bright blue eye shadow might walk uncautiously into a Middle School girls' room, where a man waits in a stall, holding a narrow wire destined for a young girl's throat . . .

Because life for Gail Lynn Holcomb is already a relentless series of burdens, and she surely doesn't need this one too: this murmur of utter fear that grows louder and louder each day that Bill Corde, sitting calmly in his safe and secure black-and-white Dodge, fails to catch this lunatic.

'We're doing everything we can,' Corde concludes.

The light changes.

'Don't you worry now,' he adds, and pulls into the intersection. She does not respond beyond pressing her flecked lips together and staring at the car as it turns onto Main Street.

12

Special to the Register – *Investigators from the New Lebanon and Harrison County Sheriffs Departments have developed a profile of the so-called 'Moon Killer,' who raped and murdered a 20-year-old Auden University co-ed on April 20, the* Register *has learned.*

Criminal behavior experts have reported that the man, whose motive may have been to sacrifice the victim as part of a cult ritual, is probably in his late teens or early twenties and white, and he lives within ten miles of the murder site.

The man might be obsessed with occult literature, much of which will be pornographic in nature. He may have a history of sexual problems and may himself have been abused as a young child.

He may come from a broken home, and at least one parent was a hostile disciplinarian. He is a loner.

There is no known religion or cult in which human sacrifice to the moon is or was practiced. This means that the 'Moon Killer' might have created his own 'religion,' as did Charles Manson or Jim Jones. The moon may be significant because in mythology and certain religions it represents the female. It is women that the killer fears and hates.

Investigators are considering the possibility that

the recent murder is related to the beating to death
last year of another Auden co-ed, Susan Biagotti,
21, a resident of Indianapolis.

It is believed that the killer may act again on the
night of the next full moon, Wednesday, April 28.
Deputies and Auden campus security police have
intensified patrol efforts and are urging young
women to avoid going outside alone.

Corde dropped the *Register* on Jim Slocum's desk and
said, 'How'd this happen?'

Slocum rubbed his cheek. 'You got me. Steve had an
idea to have me go up to Higgins and talk to the state
boys. Just a spur-of-the-moment thing.'

'Didn't you check out the roads and the mall, like I
asked?'

'Did that too. Put nearly two hundred miles on the
cruiser. Didn't find diddly.'

'Well, did you talk to a reporter?'

'Why would I talk to a reporter?' He frowned and
slapped the newspaper with his hand. 'Where I was
maybe a little careless was I wrote up a memo after I
talked to the State Police and circulated it to everybody
on the case. It's in your in basket. Didn't you see it? You
know what I'll bet happened is something got leaked
from the state.'

Corde was angry. He shouted throughout the office,
'No reporters! Nothing goes to the press without clearing
it with me. Understood?' Four deputies nodded, stiff-
faced with unjust accusation.

'But Bill,' Slocum said, 'there's a lot that adds up.
Look at this moon thing. The "lunatic" message, the
knife—'

Corde snapped, 'Damned coincidence.'

'Everybody knows about the full moon. Remember Ed
Wembkie?'

Corde said, 'This is not some guy got foreclosed out of
his farm and went crazy.'

'Ed killed that banker on the night of the full moon.'

'Was also the day the marshal tacked up the auction notice. And what's this talk about Biagotti? Who brought that up?'

Slocum shrugged. 'We *are* looking into it. Or at least you said you were going to.'

'Jim, I don't care that it's *accurate*,' Corde said in a low voice. 'I care that it's being talked about in the press.' He punched the newspaper. 'There's nothing we can do about it now. But in the future—'

'In the future I won't trust them state boys,' Slocum said earnestly. 'That's for damn sure.'

Corde stared at the article for a moment. He clicked his tongue. 'Okay, what's done's done. Now, I'd like you to get out to the truck stops and along 116, put up some fliers asking for witnesses. That route's a feeder for the interstate if you're coming from Hallburton.'

'That town's mostly dead, Bill. I doubt there'd be any truck traffic.'

'Do it just the same. Fast-Copy's delivering them this afternoon.'

'Uhn,' Slocum said.

Corde continued into his office. He cracked open the window. Before he could sit down T.T. Ebbans walked up to his desk, carrying his own *Register*.

Ebbans said angrily, 'We've got ourselves a leak, looks like.'

Corde snorted and swung his door shut. 'It's not a leak if the sheriff doesn't mind.' He dug into his in box and found Slocum's memo. It presented most of the same information that was in the article. Across the top Slocum had scrawled: *Something to think about.* Corde handed the memo to Ebbans, who read it and said, 'Watkins knows what he's about but it's too darn early for this sort of profile. He should know better.'

Corde nodded toward Ribbon's office. 'You know something, T.T.,' he whispered. 'Steve'd look like a genius, he stops a cult killer in his tracks, don't you think? Especially if he could tie the Biagotti killing to this guy.'

'I guess,' Ebbans said, 'but he wouldn't, you know, hurt the case just to do something like that.'

Corde shrugged. 'We catch this guy, five'll get you ten Ribbon mentions Biagotti at the same press conference. Also with this Moon Killer poop he's taking a lot of focus off the school, which is where he doesn't want the focus to be.'

'Why not?'

'You don't live in New Lebanon, T.T. Hell, the school damn near pays our salaries. If Auden goes, what've we got? Precious little. Farms. A few dealerships. Insurance.'

Corde tossed the *Register* into the trash. He began pacing slowly and then stopped abruptly. 'You know, I can't let that go.'

Ebbans looked at him quizzically.

'Woman came up to me today and she was mighty spooked, like she had the killer on her trail. Some paperboy or milkman comes to somebody's front door and he's going to get himself shot. Who's going to come forward with evidence if they think they're going to get gutted by a werewolf or something?'

Ebbans said, 'The stories've run already, Bill. There's nothing you can do about it.'

'Yeah there is.'

Corde picked up the phone. He called the *Register* and then WRAL, the local TV station in Higgins. He asked them about deadlines and if they'd be interested in a statement about the Auden co-ed case by the chief investigator. He took down some information then hung up. After Corde hung up Ebbans glanced toward Ribbon's office and raised an eyebrow. He sang, 'He ain't gonna like it.'

Corde shrugged and proceeded to spend an agonizing half hour composing a release. After a dozen rewrites he slipped it over to Ebbans.

New Lebanon Sheriff's Department investigators are following several leads in the rape and murder of an Auden University co-ed. Although it has been

*suggested that the murder was cult or sacrifitial,
investigators have said that this is only one
possibility and, they are also exploring the
possibility that a friend or acquaintance of the
victim's from Auden University may have been
somehow involved. Anyone with any information
is urged to immediately contact the New Lebanon
Sheriff's Department in complete confidentiality.*

'You spelled sacrificial wrong and also it doesn't
sound like a newspaper story. They write things
different. Smoother or something.'

'Well, I don't care about that. They'll doll it up. What
do you think about *what* it says?'

Ebbans read it again. He shrugged. 'I think you
hedged pretty good – at least so's Ribbon won't get too
bent out of shape. But you know one thing, Bill. If we
keep playing it up that we're after a cult killer the real
perp might be, you know, lulled into thinking he's safe.
He won't be as likely to carry out those threats against
you. You run this, well, he may come looking for you.'

Corde had not considered this. He smoothed the copy
of his release in front of him. 'It's a risk, true. But it's *my*
risk and I think I have to take it. We've got to get
ourselves some witnesses.'

Returning to work from lunch Corde parked in the
Town Hall lot and saw Steve Ribbon climbing out of his
cruiser.

The sheriff grinned a vacuous smile and motioned to
him. Corde walked over to the car. They leaned butt-
first against the fender.

'Howdy, Steve.'

The sheriff nodded.

The sunlight hit Ribbon's face and revealed a speckle
of red on his cheeks. It reminded Corde that Ribbon
volunteered every Christmas to play a Jaycee's Santa
and slogged around in the snow and mud on New
Lebanon's east side, visiting trailers and maimed

159

bungalows occupied mostly by single parents and their kids.

Whenever he formed opinions about Steve Ribbon, like the one he'd shared with T.T. Ebbans that morning, Corde tried to temper them with the memory of how the man spent December 24.

'Say, Bill, there's a situation I've got to let you know about.' The *Register* was tucked under Ribbon's solid arm.

'Shoot.'

'I was just over at County. Hammerback's office. Last night he got a call from Dean Larraby over at Auden. You know her, right?'

Corde grunted affirmatively.

'Well, here's the scoop.' Ribbon cleared his throat. 'I seen that report on the burnt-up letters. The Gebben girl's letters?'

'Yup.'

Ribbon exhaled long through closed teeth, stopping his breath with his tongue every second or so. *Thup thup thup* . . . When his lungs emptied he took another breath and said, 'Somebody saw you coming out of her room the day they were stolen.'

Corde looked down at the pebbly asphalt.

'Wednesday afternoon,' Ribbon said. 'The day after she was killed.'

'Wednesday. I was there, yeah. I wanted to talk to Jennie's roommate.'

'Well, you didn't *say* anything about it. When Lance told us the letters were missing and—'

'Steve, I was there without a warrant. The door was unlocked and people knew the girl was dead. I was afraid evidence would start to disappear. I took a fast look around the room and that was it.'

'Did you see—'

'The letters weren't there, no.'

'Well, Jesus, Bill.' Ribbon chose not to mention the most serious offense, the one that would be filling an uneasy ninety percent of his thoughts – that Corde had

160

destroyed the letters himself. Instead he said, 'Anything you'd picked up wouldn't've been admissible. That would've thrown the case all catercorner.'

'If I'd found anything I would've phoned in for a warrant then just baby-sat until Lance or T.T. showed up with it. All I was worried about was evidence disappearing.'

'Which is just what happened anyway.'

'Yes, it did.'

Ribbon's eyes swung like slow pendulums from Town Hall to a Chevy pickup and back. 'I don't think this's a problem. Not yet. Hammerback's got more important things to worry about and the dean didn't know diddly about warrants or anything. She just had her tit in a wringer 'cause she doesn't like the way we're going after the school and not letting her know what we're about. But for Pete's sake, Bill, there's stuff about this case that could bite us in the ass we aren't careful.'

Corde held Ribbon's eye. 'I didn't burn those letters, Steve.'

'Absolutely. I know you didn't. The thought never crossed my mind. I'm just telling you what some people who don't know you as good as me might think. Just, sort of, be on your guard, you know what I'm saying? Good. Now how 'bout we get back to the salt mines?'

The front door of the Sheriff's Department office swung open and into the office strode Wynton Kresge. Corde had a permanent image of Kresge, walking into a room just this way, swaggering and carrying a manila folder. It was becoming a cliché. Kresge, dropping the envelope on a desk and standing like a proud retriever that'd set a shot quail one inch from a hunter's boot.

'Thankya, Wynton.' Corde sat in a chair at an unoccupied desk, opening the envelope. Still stewing about what Ribbon had told him, he added dismissingly, 'That's all.'

Kresge went from hangtail to a pit bull in less than a second. Ebbans saw it coming and winced. Corde was caught completely off guard.

'I'm just curious 'bout something, Detective,' Kresge said loudly in a James Earl Jones baritone.

Corde looked up. 'I beg your pardon?'

'What would you like me to call myself?'

'How's that?'

'I was just hoping you could provide some *en*-lightenment. Should I call myself Messenger?'

'Oh, boy,' Ebbans muttered.

Kresge said, 'Maybe Step-'n'-fetch-it?'

Ebbans said again, 'Oh, boy.'

Corde blinked. 'What're you talking about?'

'I'm talking about I don't work for you. I don't get a damn penny of town money, so everything I do for you's gravy and you treat me like I'm delivering pizza.'

Corde looked at Ebbans for help but the county deputy's face was a mask. Corde asked Kresge, 'What are—'

'This girl gets herself killed and I say, "Let me help you interview people." I say, "Let me help you look for clues." I say, "Let me help you put up fliers." And you treat me like a busboy. You say—'

'I didn't—'

Kresge shouted, 'You say, "No, Wynton, no thanks, you're a *black* man! I don't need your help."'

'Oh, boy,' Ebbans said.

'You're crazy!' Corde yelled.

'I don't see so many deputies working for you. I don't see so goddamn many suspects lined up you can cart 'em off in a bus. I offer you some help and what do you say? You say, "That's all. Run 'long now. I'll call you when I need some im-poh-tant pay-pahs."' Menace was deep on his brow.

Work throughout the department had stopped. Even the 911 dispatcher had walked into the doorway of her office, leaning sideways, her head held captive by the plugged-in headset.

Corde stood up, red-faced. 'I don't have to listen to this.'

162

'I'm just curious what you've got against me?'

'I don't have anything against you.'

'You don't want my help 'cause I'm black.'

Corde waved his arm angrily. 'I don't want your help 'cause you don't know what you're doing.'

'How would you know? You never tried me out.'

'You never asked me if you could help.'

'Hell I didn't!' Kresge looked at Ebbans. 'Did I ask to help? Did I volunteer?'

Ebbans said to Corde, 'He did ask, Bill.'

Corde glared.

Kresge said, 'I wish you lots of luck, *de*-tective. You need any more help from the university Security Department, you talk to one of the guards. They wear uniforms. They make seven twenty-five an hour. They'll be happy to pick up things for you. You can even tip, you want.'

Ebbans and Corde both squinted, waiting for the rippled glass window in the door to explode inward from the concussion of Kresge's slam. Instead, he closed it delicately and stomped off down the serpentine path to the driveway.

Ebbans started laughing. Corde, his face red with anger, turned on him. 'This isn't goddamn funny.'

'Sure it is.'

'What's with him? What did I do?'

Ebbans said, 'Don't they teach community relations in these here parts?'

'That's not funny.' They heard a car squeal away from the curb outside. Corde said. 'God*damn!* I don't understand what I did.'

Ebbans said, 'He could be helpful. Why don't you apologize?'

'Apologize?' he roared. 'For what?'

'You weren't taking him seriously.'

'He's a *security guard.*'

'You still weren't taking him seriously.'

Corde said, 'I don't care if he's black. Where did he get that idea?'

'Don't get so riled.'

'Son of a bitch.'

Ebbans said, 'He might sue you. Discrimination.'

It took Corde a minute to realize that Ebbans was joking. 'Go to hell.'

'You take everything else seriously. Just not him.'

Corde shook his head in anger then stood. He walked to the coffee vending machine and returned a minute later, sipping the burnt-tasting liquid. He grabbed the envelope Kresge had delivered. Without seeing them he looked at the half dozen résumés it contained for a few minutes then said, 'I hope he does sue. I'd like the chance to say a few things to him in court.'

Ebbans said, 'Bill, simmer down.'

Corde started reading the résumés. He looked up a moment later, was about to speak, then closed his mouth and went back to reading. A half hour later he'd calmed down. He asked Ebbans, 'These things say CV on them. What does that mean?'

'I don't know. Where?'

'At the top. Oh, wait, here's one it's spelled out. *Curriculum Vitae*. What's that?'

'Maybe it's Greek for résumé.'

Corde said, 'Professors . . .' And went back to reading.

After he finished he read them again and then said to Ebbans, 'May have something here. Interesting.'

'What's that?'

Corde handed Ebbans a copy of Randolph Sayles's CV. 'What's this tell you?'

Ebbans read carefully. 'Got me.'

'He's one of Jennie's professors. Over the last twelve years he's been a visiting professor at three other schools. Two of them were for one-year terms. But at that one, Loyola, in Ohio, he left after three months.'

'So?'

'After Loyola, it says, he spent the next nine months researching and writing a book before he came back to Auden. Nine months. That's the rest of the one-year period, after you subtract the three.'

Ebbans said, 'Well, these professors travel around a lot, don't they? Maybe he took time off.'

'But he hasn't published any books since he's been back from Loyola. That was four years ago.'

'Maybe it's about to come out.'

'Well, let's speculate. Doesn't it seem possible, let's just say, he got dumped from Loyola and didn't want to come back here right away. It would look strange. He'd have to explain why he got kicked out.'

'That's a reach, Bill.'

Corde picked up the telephone. He dialed long-distance directory assistance, then the number he'd been given. As he did, Ebbans continued, 'I don't know. Getting fired's pretty thin grounds to make him a suspect, isn't it?'

Not if he was fired because he slept with a student then assaulted her when she threatened to report it.

The dean at Loyola College outside of Columbus, Ohio, took some convincing before he would tell Corde this and even then he did so only after he'd patched in the school's lawyer, on an extension, to tell the dean what questions to answer, which turned out to be all of them.

After he hung up Corde said to Ebbans, 'The assault charges were dropped. Nothing ever came of them but Sayles agreed to resign. What do you think now?'

'I think there's something else.' Ebbans pointed at the résumé. 'Randy Sayles is the associate dean in charge of financial aid.'

'Rings a bell.'

'Jennie Gebben worked for him.'

They were outside in the yard, lapped by bands of cool air then hot. As Corde and Diane sat pressed together on the picnic blanket, he remembered this phenomenon from his teenage days. They called it *hotcolds*. Waves of warm breeze alternating with waves of cold, drifting through fields around the New Lebanon High School at dusk. A schoolmate had an explanation: when a man and a woman did it, the air around them got real hot and stayed that way for hours; what the boys felt was proof that somewhere upwind a dozen girls had just gotten laid.

Corde and Diane had come outside to watch what was advertised as a meteorite shower. After the threatening photo he had made an extra effort to get home early and once there stay put for the evening. He'd noticed the story about the meteorites and, after Sarah and Jamie were in bed, asked his surprised wife if she'd like to have a date in the backyard. Diane had spread the blanket down and with half a bottle of wine beside them they sat close together, fingers twined, listening to crickets and owls and feeling the hotcolds wash over them.

The sky was clear and dominated by the near-full moon. They'd seen only one meteorite in fifteen minutes, though it had been spectacular – a long pure white streak covering half the sky. The afterimage remained in their vision long after the burning rock disintegrated.

'Do you wish on 'em?' Diane asked.

'I think you can. I don't know.'

'I don't know what to wish for.'

'If you decide,' Corde said, 'don't say it out loud. Meteors're probably like birthday candles and wishbones.'

She kissed him, gripping his lip with her teeth. They lay on the dew-moist blanket, kissing hard, sometimes brutally, for almost five minutes. His hand slipped up under her sweater and into her bra. He felt her stiffen as her nipple went instantly hard.

'Passion,' he whispered, grinning.

'Cold,' she said, exhaling a laugh. 'I know a place where it's warmer.'

'So do I.' His hand started toward her jeans.

Diane grabbed it with both of hers. 'Follow me.' She stood up and pulled him towards the house.

'Does this have anything to do with your wish?' he asked.

* * *

They lay in the same pose as in the yard. Now though they were naked and atop a hex-pattern quilt Diane's mother had begun the year of the Iran embassy takeover and finished the year of the *Challenger* explosion. The three-way light was on dim and Corde had licked off the last bit of her lipstick. He rolled her over on her back.

'Wait a minute,' she said, bounding up. 'Let me put it in.'

The promised minute passed. Then several others. He heard running water. He heard a toothbrush. He rolled over on his back, gripping himself and squeezing to keep hard.

He heard the toilet flush. He squeezed harder.

He heard the medicine cabinet opening and closing. He stopped squeezing; he was firm as a teenager.

For about ten seconds.

'Ohhhh, Bill . . .'

The heartsick cry, the alto moan of Diane's voice, was pitiful. A scream would have been less harrowing. Corde was on his feet and running into the bathroom, thinking only when he arrived that he should have taken the time to unlock the bedside table and pull his pistol from the drawer.

The blue diaphragm case lay at her feet. The rubber disk itself rested like a pale yellow blister on the sink.

Diane was sobbing, her arms around herself, covering her nakedness even from her husband.

Bill saw a small white square on the floor at her feet. He picked it up while Diane pulled her red terrycloth bathrobe off the back of the door and slipped it on, tying the belt tightly around her. 'It was inside,' she whispered, spinning a stream of toilet paper off the roll and using it to pick up the diaphragm. She carried it like a crushed wasp to the wastebasket and dropped it in. She did the same with the plastic case, then began scrubbing her hands with soap and hot water.

This Polaroid had been taken at the same time as the one left on the back steps. The scene was of Sarah, or whoever the girl might be, lying in the grass, her skirt still up to her waist. The angle was about the same, so was the lighting. There were in fact only two differences. The photographer was now much near – only several feet from the girl.

And the message in red marker on the back was different. It said: GETTING CLOSER

13

Corde unlocked the gun rack and lifted out his long, battered Remington. He slipped three shells into the tube and from a desk drawer took a cylindrical chrome lock. He separated it and fitted the two parts on either side of the trigger guard. He squeezed them together with a soft ratchety sound. He put one key on his keychain and carried the other key and the gun itself into the living room, where Diane sat staring at the floor. Her mouth was a thin line.

'How is he *doing* this?' Diane's voice broke in frustration.

'I don't know, honey.'

'How does he get past the deputy?'

'I think he might've left that note the same time he left the other one. He's probably long gone by now.'

'*Might've . . . probably . . .* Doesn't anybody *know* anything about this man?'

Corde kneaded the key absently. *No, we don't. We don't know a damn thing at all.*

After a moment he said, 'I'll talk to Tom tomorrow. Have him make trips around the house and into the woods.'

Corde set the gun in the corner. 'I didn't chamber a round. You'll have to pump it once. The safety's off. Just pump and pull. You know how to do it. Aim low.' He handed her the key and she stood up and put it in her purse. She seemed calmer now, seeing the gun, having some control.

'Wait a minute,' Corde said. He took the key out of her bag and walked into their bedroom. He returned a moment later with a thick golden necklace. He slipped the key over the end and then clasped it behind her neck. He kissed her on the forehead.

She said, 'This's the chain you gave me when you gave me your class ring.'

'Figured that was the right length to let everybody know to keep their hands off.' The key rested at the shadow of her cleavage.

She smiled and hugged him and cried some more.

Corde said, 'It's plate, you know. The chain.'

'Isn't a girl alive can't recognize plate from solid. But it was the ring I was most interested in.'

Corde held her face. 'We're going to get through this just fine. Nothing's going to happen to you or the kids. He's just doing this to rattle me. I promise.'

Diane dried her eyes and walked toward the bedroom. She said, 'God give me strength.'

At first no one in town paid much attention; it was mostly little things. Like when the *Register* came out, more people than usual bought it. And what they turned to first was the almanac page, which showed the phases of the moon for the next thirty days.

Sales of shotgun shells and rifle ammunition were running twice what they usually did this time of year (being nowhere close to season yet). The sporting goods section of Sears, which normally sold tons of Ted Williams baseball gear this month, was doing most of its dollar volume in low-cost .22s, .30-'06s, and even Crossman CO_2 air pistols.

Business at the quad and HoJo's and Baskin-Robbins fell to nothing as parents refused to let their daughters go on dates after dark. Exam grades at Auden went up as students who would normally be outside groping under clothing or pledging fidelity over the long summer months stayed home and broke the spines of books. A number of students were taking incompletes and returning home three weeks early.

A lot of town dogs were kept hungry.

Corde's awkwardly phrased press statement, meant to reassure the people of New Lebanon, in short, had no effect on the hysteria.

Bob Siebert came home late to his trailer on Route 302. He opened the door and in the dark kitchen found himself staring at his five-year-old son, who was aiming Siebert's Ruger .225 deer rifle more or less at his father's heart. Standing silhouetted in the moonlight, afraid to speak, Siebert froze. It was only after the short click of the firing pin that he began to breathe again. He lifted the gun away, laughing madly and thanking the Lord that his son had not known how to chamber a round. His smile faded when he opened the rifle's bolt and the misfired shell spiraled out. Siebert's legs went slack, his pants went wet and he dropped sobbing to the floor. The boy said, 'I thought you was the Moon Man, Daddy.'

And on Tuesday, one day before the full moon, the first graffiti went up.

No one saw who'd done it and in fact hardly anyone recognized the drawings at first. Clara and Harry Botwell were returning home in their 1976 Buick Electra from the Shrimp 'n' Salad Night at the Wrangler, Clara driving, being the less impaired. Harry pointed to the wall of the First Bank of New Lebanon and said, look, somebody had painted a big gumdrop on the side of the bank, and Clara studied the wall and asked, why was it on its side and anyway why would anybody paint a gumdrop?

'Sweet Mary,' she said, 'that's no gumdrop, it's a half-moon.' In panic she gunned the big engine and shot through a red light, broadsiding a Celica. The couple escaped unhurt, though the driver of the Toyota went to Memorial with a broken arm.

The bank wasn't the only site of a half-moon. Three hundred citizens punched in 911 that night (most of

them for the first time in their lives) to report a half
dozen of the graffiti moons. The callers were all pretty
shaken up; the paint the artist had used was blood.

This evening, Randolph Sayles, professor and dean,
student of Union economics and apologist for the noble
Confederate States of America, sat in his backyard
smoking a cigarette and staring at the evening sky
bright with moonlight. He held a drooping fax in his
hand. Sayles tapped an ash to the ground in front of him
and looked at it. Beside his muddy boots a tree root had
grown out of the earth and then, only a few inches away,
had returned underground as if even this short excursion
into the world was intolerable. He heard footsteps. He
recognized them.

Joan Sayles was an angular woman with short-
cropped blond hair and abrupt hips and long breasts.
Tonight she wore a white blouse, tied in the front à la
Lana Turner, and skimpy, baggy shorts. She sat beside
her husband. Dimpled bands of white flesh hung from
her upper legs.

A full professor of sociology at Auden, she was one
year older than Sayles and had an IQ two points higher
than his, though they both fell in the ninety-ninth
percentile. When they met, their last year of
undergraduate school (on this same campus), one of
them had been a virgin and it hadn't been Joan. Even as
a grad assistant she had professorial drive and an
instinctive grasp of institutional politics. He appreciated
these talents in her although he realized too late that
she used these to pursue not only tenure but Sayles
himself. She was successful on both fronts; they were
married the day after he sat for his doctoral orals. And
if he'd never felt a moment of resounding passion for her
– nothing close in fact to what he felt when he stood at
the lectern – that was all right. He loved her (he
believed). Anyway he needed a wife (he was pretty
sure), stability and a brainy spouse being Doric columns
of Midwest university success.

'What are you doing out here?' she asked, squinting in the violet moonlight. The gesture pulled the corners of her mouth up in a wet grotesque smile that Randy Sayles did not want to look at. She noticed a small muddy shovel next to him and her eyes dipped to his boots. 'Moonlight gardening?'

He imagined that her question, which sounded simply curious, was in fact laced with mockery.

He thought: *What does she know?*

'Taking in the air,' he answered. 'You had a meeting tonight?'

'Completed.' She was holding a batch of white, stapled papers rubber-banded together. She had made many notes and marks on the first page of the top paper. He noticed C/C+. She was a bitch of a grader.

'What are you doing?' she repeated. When he did not respond she asked, 'Are you ignoring me for a reason?'

He apologized with a sincerity that surprised them both, then handed her the fax. The state had rejected Auden's application for an emergency loan.

'Ah.' She handed it back and lit a cigarette. It hung from the side of her lips and this made her mouth even sloppier and more lopsided. Joan inhaled then lifted a long finger to her tongue and touched away a fleck of something. 'I'm sorry.'

Sayles squeezed her knee in response. She said, 'Do you know what one of my students wrote? The issue was whether a population center like New Lebanon had an inner city. He wrote that it didn't. Rather, he said, it had a wrong side of the tracks. I gave him an A minus, solely for that.'

Sayles said, 'Clever.'

'You know, if I had it to do all over again I'd pick something frivolous. Romance languages or art appreciation. No, I know. Russian literature.'

She touched the side of her tongue again, probing, as if she wanted to make sure it wasn't numb.

He said, 'The police want to see me.'

'About that girl in your class? The one who was killed?'

Sayles nodded.

'You were sleeping with her?'

This was not truly a question. *So she does know.*

His silence was an answer she could read. 'Did you enjoy it?' she asked.

'On occasion.'

'They don't think you had anything to do with it, do they?'

'Of course not.'

How does she know?

Joan finished her cigarette and dropped it on the ground. She did not step on it. After a moment she shuffled the papers in her hand and said, 'You know, I'm astonished at how college sophomores cannot put sentences together,' and walked back to the house along a narrow patch stained red and purple by droppings from a row of mulberry trees.

Where T.T. Ebbans wanted to be: standing in the exact position of the man he was talking to, the man leaning on the bent branch beside the muddy Des Plaines and connected to a hook sunk in murky water by twenty feet of fishing line via a Sears rod and reel. The man in the red hat.

'Those're some flies,' Ebbans said, nodding at the hat.

'Yessir.'

Ebbans leaned over and looked into the Rubbermaid bucket where three pale catfish floated motionless. 'A fly fisherman doesn't get bored feeding stinkballs to suckers?'

'I don't fly. S'only the hat. Was a present from my wife.' A moment later he added, 'I got a license. Only I left her at home.'

'Uh-huh,' Ebbans said. 'You by any chance fishing on Tuesday evening down at Blackfoot Pond?'

'This *is* my evening.'

'How's that?' Ebbans asked.

174

'I work owl at the container plant. Get off at seven in the a.m. Go to bed. Eat. Fish. Go to work. That's my life. Your evening's my day.'

'Some fella there saw someone fits your description.'

He grunted.

Ebbans said, 'We had a girl killed over there on Tuesday.'

'That was there? Shitabrick. I didn't know. Yeah, I was there on Tuesday.'

'When did you leave?'

'Must've been nine-thirty or ten. Got off to a late start because of the storm.'

'You see anybody else?'

'When I was leaving I seen two kids come up. They had tackle but they weren't fishing. I figured they maybe had a Delco or a hand-crank and were just going to jolt up some worms.'

'They were kids?'

'Looked to be teenagers.'

'You know them?'

'Didn't see 'em up close. They were down at the foot of the dam, walking up to the pond. One of them was fat so they were going slow. The fat one was wearing something dark. The other one was thin and was wearing a jacket may've been gray.'

'How old?'

'High school. I dunno.'

'Both white?' Ebbans asked.

'What else 'round here?'

'I'd like to have a talk with those boys or one of them. You see them I'd appreciate your letting us know.'

'You bet.'

'You do that I'll forget to tell Fish and Game about the license you left at home.'

'I've been meaning to get me one,' he said. 'You know how it is. One thing after another.'

The First Methodist Church of New Lebanon announced today that Sunday school classes will be canceled until

175

further notice following the vandalism of the school by the man authorities are calling the 'Moon Killer.'

'Authorities' are calling?

A painting of a half-moon in blood was found on the door of the first-floor girls' room in the Sunday school building, located at 223 Maple Street, adjacent to the church.

The blood matched that from a goat whose carcass was found several days ago in the New Lebanon Grade School.

How do they know that? I didn't know that.

Attendance at the town's schools has fallen dramatically since the Moon Killer began stalking the streets of New Lebanon . . .

'Stalking' the streets?

Tonight will be the first full moon since the murder of the Auden co-ed . . .

Jennie. Her name is Jennie Gebben.

. . . and residents are urged to stay home from sunset to sunrise . . .

Bill Corde, sitting in Room 121 of the Auden Student Union, stared at that morning's *Register* for five minutes before pitching it out. He opened an envelope he had picked up at the office on the way over here. It contained a report from the county lab about the match between the carcass blood and the graffiti blood.

How did they know? I didn't.

A man appeared in the doorway. Corde looked up at him.

'Excuse me. I'm Professor Sayles. You wanted to see me?'

'Come on in. Sit down.' Corde shoved aside the lab report and motioned with his palm toward the chair across from his miniature desk.

Sayles sat, folding his long legs slowly. He scooted the seat back. 'This has to do with the Jennifer Gebben murder?'

Corde asked, 'She was in your class?'

'Yes, she was.' Sayles looked at his watch. A wrinkled,

frayed shirt cuff appeared outside his blue blazer and stayed there. 'And she worked part-time for me. In the Financial Aid Department.'

'Did you know her well?'

'I try to know all my students.'

'But you knew her better than the others,' Corde said.

'The class she was in is large. The Civil War Centennial course is very popular. I try to know as many students as I can. I think it's important. Any personal attention in class can be very inspiring. Don't you remember?'

Corde, who had spent most of his school years trying to avoid the attention of teachers, said, 'Why was she working for you? I assume she didn't need the money.'

'Why do you assume that?' Sayles asked dourly.

'She wasn't in the work-study program and didn't have any student loans or scholarships. Seems she would've followed those routes before she'd get a part-time job paying five-ten an hour.'

'There's something altruistic about disbursing money to needy students. Jennie helped organize last year's AIDS walkathon. And she was also a Meals on Wheels volunteer.'

'For a month or two,' Corde said.

'For a month or two.'

'But how did she come to work for *you*?'

'We got to talking about how curious it was that I – a history professor – ended up in charge of financial aid and she asked if she could assist me.'

'What were the circumstances of this conversation?'

'Officer.' Sayles was riled. 'I hardly recall.'

'Was there anybody in class she was particularly friendly with?'

'I never paid any attention.'

'Did you ever see her with anyone who wasn't a student?'

Sayles shrugged. 'No.'

'How often did you work together?'

'Several times a week.'

'You see her socially?'

'No, not socially. We'd have dinner after work sometimes. Often with other people. That was all.'

'You don't consider that social?'

'No, I don't.'

Corde watched the man's dark eyes, which in turn studied three dirty fingernails on his right hand.

'Professor, were you asked by Loyola College to stop teaching there?'

Sayles started to reach for his red-and-blue striped tie. He stopped and tilted his head slightly, adjusting the needle valve on his indignation. 'I was, yes.'

'That was because you'd been involved with a student?'

'Involved with? Yes.'

'And you assaulted her?'

'I did not. We had an affair. I broke it off. She wasn't happy about that and called the police to report that I'd assaulted her. It was a lie.'

'Were you having an affair with Jennie Gebben?'

'No. And I believe I resent your asking me that.'

'I have my job to do,' Corde said wearily.

'And if you think anyone from the university had something to do with her death . . .' Sayles's voice grew harsh. '. . . you're badly mistaken. There are enough unfounded rumors about the murder already. It's hard enough running a school and raising money for it without spooking parents and benefactors. Read the paper. *Your* department said it was a demonic killing.'

'We have to look at all possibilities.'

The watch was again gravely consulted. 'I have a class in five minutes.'

'Where were you on the night she was killed, Professor?'

He laughed. 'Are you serious?' Corde lifted an eyebrow and Sayles said, 'I was home.'

'Is there anyone who can verify that?' Corde glanced at the narrow gold ring. 'Your wife maybe?'

His voice grew soft in anger. 'I was by myself. My wife was doing research at the library until midnight.'

'I understand that Brian Okun was seeing Jennie?'

178

'Seeing her? I'd say he was seeing her. He was sleeping with her.'

In his Chinese handwriting Corde made a small notation on a three-by-five card. 'Could you tell me who you heard that from?'

'I can't recall.'

'What's your opinion of him?'

'Of Brian? You can't suspect Brian of hurting Jennie.'

'Your opinion?'

'He's brilliant. He needs to temper his intelligence somewhat. He's a little arrogant for his own good. But he'd never hurt Jennie.' Sayles watched Corde slowly write. 'May I go now?'

Corde completed the card and looked up. 'I—'

'Look, I can't help you. I have nothing more to say.' Sayles stood and his grim surliness was at a high pitch now.

This anger seemed out of proportion to the circumstances of the questioning. At first this reinforced Corde's suspicion of the man. But one look into Sayles's face told another story. The source of the professor's indignation was contempt. Contempt at himself for loving Jennie Gebben. Whatever her talents in bed, which Corde guessed were pretty damn plentiful if both Sayles and Okun had risked their jobs to have her, Jennie was still nothing more than an average student, a suburban girl, fat at the throat, the daughter of a small-business man, a Meals on Wheels volunteer, a very ordinary young woman.

And here was Randolph Sayles, PhD, just blistered with humiliation for the love he'd spent on this common girl.

So Corde released him. And like a squirming cat escaping at last from his master's arms the professor stalked out of Room 121 neither dallying nor fast, absorbed with forgetting the prior moments of troubling captivity.

Returning to the office Corde found on Slocum's desk

the stack of fliers from Fast-Copy, which were supposed to be tacked up thick as litter along Route 116. Slocum was out, he learned, looking into reports of missing goats.

The difficult night at home had now caught up with him – the second photo, his guilt at missing another of Jamie's wrestling matches tonight, a tempestuous dream that woke him at one. Unable to sleep he had sat for two hours in the back bathroom with the shotgun on his lap, scanning the forest for any sign of the intruder. Once, he was sure he'd seen a face looking at the house and had gone so far as to chamber a shell and walk outside, hands shaking in anticipation as much as from the pre-dawn chill. But as he stood shoeless on the slab back porch the image became a moonlit tangle of trees and leaves.

He'd turned to walk back into the house and Sarah had scared the utter hell out of him, bounding forward from the stairs. They stared at each other – Corde, shocked, the girl more disappointed than anything. She was headed for the back door and he'd thought for an instant that she was sleepwalking. But, no, she was only after a glass of water. 'What's wrong with your bathroom?' Corde asked as his heart's gallop slowed. She had drunk the water, staring out the window, until he impatiently shooed her off to bed.

He did not get to sleep till five.

Then there'd been a fight at breakfast. Sarah had shrilly refused her mother's demand that she study before going to school. Corde had had to both comfort his wife and calm his daughter. He tried not to take sides and they both ended up mad at him.

Now, in his office, the door closed, Corde sat at his desk for ten minutes, arranging and rearranging the tall stacks of his three-by-five cards, fat and limber from all the shuffling. He spread them out until they covered his desk.

A dull bicentennial quarter appears in his hand and begins flopping over the backs of his fingers. He stares at the cards and after a few minutes Bill Corde is no longer in the Sheriff's Department but is on the Auden University campus and the day isn't today but is Tuesday, April 20. It is four-thirty p.m.

Corde pictures Jennie Gebben leaving Professor Sayles's lecture hall and walking to the university bookstore three blocks away to cash a check for thirty-five dollars. Her picture is taken by the cashier's security camera and the film shows her wearing a white blouse with a button-down collar. Her dark hair is straight, a thick strand sloping over her forehead. The shutter catches her with eyelids half closed. The time on the film is 16:43:03. Jennie continues to the dorm and arrives there at about five. She and Emily Rossiter remain in their room with the door closed for about an hour. The girls on the floor can detect the roommates having what seems to be an argument though no one hears enough to know the substance of their discussion.

Lance Miller's report on the phones shows that during the hours Jennie was at the dorm today, there have been no outgoing long-distance calls and most local calls are to innocent recipients. The only local call whose recipient can't be ascertained is to the Auden School of Arts and Sciences; which of the sixty-four extensions the call is transferred to cannot be determined. Both Randy Sayles's and Brian Okun's numbers are among those sixty-four, as is Emily's; she works as an assistant in the Sociology Department.

At about six-fifteen Jennie takes a shower and with hair still damp walks with three other girls to the cafeteria. They have asked Emily to join them but she moodily declines. The four eat dinner and talk. Jennie eats quickly and leaves early. She too is moody. Her dinner companions return to the dorm at seven-thirty and watch a TV game show for a half hour. Jennie enters the lounge and watches TV for a few minutes then looks at her watch. She seems distracted, edgy. At about eight-fifteen she leaves the lounge and tells one of the girls that she'll be back by midnight.

The next time Jennie Gebben is accounted for, it is ten-fifty-eight. She has been raped and strangled to death and her body is lying in a bed of blue hyacinths at the muddy base of Blackfoot Pond dam.

At the site of her death: Nineteen shoe and boot prints around the body, most of them men's or teenage boys' sizes. The Ford pickup, covered with 530 partial and 140 full fingerprints. Scraps of standard, virtually untraceable typing paper. Cellophane wrappers from several snack foods sold by Wise and Frito-Lay and Nabisco. Cigarette butts, beer and soda bottles and cans, a condom, the semen in which doesn't match that found in the victim.

And the knife (whose source even the FBI has not been able to identify, despite the assistance of the Seoul Prefecture of Police and faxed inquiries to twelve professors of religion, criminology and parapsychology around the country).

None of the fingerprints found at the crime scene matches those on file in Harrison County. The prints are now in Higgins and in Washington, D.C., for similar cross-checking in state and federal files. Fingerprinting the dorm room netted 184 partial and whole prints, sixty-two of which belonged to Jennie and other students on the floor. The others are as yet unmatched.

After reporting the theft of Jennie's letters Emily Rossiter has turned uncooperative. She still has not appeared at Room 121 and she has not returned his calls.

Corde has looked carefully through the file on the Biagotti case – the case that introduced him to Jennie Gebben. On January 15 of the previous year, Susan Biagotti was in her off-campus apartment when she was beaten to death with a hammer during a robbery. As Corde told Ribbon, Jennie could offer no insights into the crime. The girls did know each other but only casually. Susan lived two buildings away from Brian Okun's apartment but Corde can find no other connection between the two of them. The phase of the moon on

January 15 was three days after new.

The burnt scraps found in the oil drum behind Jennie's dorm include three types of paper. Hammermill long-grain recycled white typing paper, Crane's laid stationery, tinted violet, and sprocketed green-and-white-striped computer paper whose manufacturer has not been determined. Ninhydrin analysis has revealed two partial fingerprints on the Crane's stationery and one complete print on the computer printout. All three are Jennie's. The county lab reports that the amount of ash in the drum would be equal to about fifty to seventy-five sheets of eight-and-a-half-by-eleven-inch paper. The ash was so badly destroyed that no latent watermarks, writing or fingerprints are detectable.

The printing on the computer paper is of dollar amounts ranging from $2,670 to $6,800. The printer was a nine-pin dot matrix. The extreme faintness of the type suggests it was printed in the machine's highspeed mode or that the ribbon was old. Both county and State Bureau of Investigation technicians report that the papers and ink are too common to provide further leads unless matching samples are recovered.

Jennie died of traumatic asphyxia. The killer strangled her with his hands then used a rope or cord to make sure she was dead. The speed with which she died makes an erotic asphyxia interlude unlikely. She did not die standing up; the backs of her shoes kicked deep impressions into the mud before they flew off, and the soles of her feet were clean. The semen in and on her body is from a single individual and was serum-typed B positive. There is evidence of both vaginal and anal intercourse.

No one has found the murder rope though a technician noticed a fresh cut on a short piece of plastic-coated clothesline dangling from a tie-down cleat in the abandoned truck. The medical examiner said the injury to her neck was consistent with that type of rope. The cult knife contains no particle residue from the cord but that is not conclusive. Moreover, the blade of the knife is razor sharp and the county forensic lab reports that the clothesline on the Ford was cut with a sharp instrument. A particle of cotton fiber, matching Jennie's panties, was found on the stiletto.

Of Jennie Gebben, Corde knows this:

She dated frequently though these were not typical Burger-King-and-a-movie events. She simply vanished in the evenings, sometimes for the entire weekend. She rarely talked about her companions on these outings though what she did share caused considerable stir. Sex was Jennie's favorite topic. Not boys or dates or engagement rings. *Sex.* Jennie had been found masturbating in the dorm bathroom a number of times and she didn't mind being watched. She got pleasure from blunt talk (*'One time Jennie and I we're in the study room, okay? And it's all quiet and she like looks up and goes, "You ever take it up the ass?" and I'm like, "Oh my God, did you really say that?"'*).

Her reluctance to discuss her lovers fueled the rumors that she slept with professors. Last year she supposedly went out with one professor for much of the spring term. They kept it intensely secret though it was believed that he was in the Education School and that they had contemplated marriage.

A number of girls call Jennie's sexual behavior disgraceful but when they do, the disdain is transparent and there is envy beneath.

Many students say that they considered her a searcher, unsettled, unhappy. Several give similar versions of the same incident: Late one night Jennie was in the stairwell of the dorm by herself. She was crying and the echoes of her voice on the concrete walls made a terrible, mournful moan. 'I'm so *lonely* . . .' one student believes she was saying. Another, on the floor below, heard, 'If only I had him . . .'

She was not religious and had never attended a church in New Lebanon. She had some tapes by New Age musicians and several crystal necklaces but little interest in spiritualism or the occult. Students have given conflicting reports about her relationship with her parents. Jennie was cool toward her mother. Her connection with her father, on the other hand, was turbulent. On the phone she sometimes told him in oddly passionate terms that she missed and loved him. Other times she slammed the phone down and announced about him, 'What a prick.'

Bill Corde drops his quarter on the table and scoops up his index cards, considering all these facts, and he tries to picture the killer. But he sees woefully little. Far, far less than the profile in the *Register* (which infuriated him partly because he doubted he himself could ever create such a vivid image of a criminal). Corde's own profiling technique, that of the National Center for the Analysis of Violent Crime, is charted on the yellowed sheet of paper pinned on the corkboard behind his desk. It is a lengthy process of inputting voluminous facts, arranging them into models, assessing the crime and finally creating then fine-tuning the criminal profile. (He knows that the NCAVC procedure includes an optimistic sixth and final step: apprehension of the killer – a stage that seems despairingly unattainable at this moment, eight long days after Jennie Gebben's demure body was found in a bed of muddied hyacinths beside that gloomy, still pond.)

Corde knows many details about Jennie Gebben. He knows that Brian Okun has lied to him and that Professor Sayles might have. He knows that two boys were near the dam shortly before her death and one of them may have had a knife. The trail is cooling and there is so much more to learn. More interviews, more facts to unearth . . . Though he secretly wonders: Is he merely stalling, hoping for a picture of the killer to flutter down from heaven, a picture as clear as the portrait of Jennie taped inside his briefcase?

Bill Corde riffles the index cards.

He believes much and he knows little. A mass of information is in his hands but the truth is somewhere between the facts themselves, in the gaps of his knowledge, like the shadows between the flipping cardboard. For now, Corde sees only darkness as dense as the water in Blackfoot Pond. He sees no deeper than the reflection of double moons in the facets of a dead girl's necklace.

Corde hopes for startling illumination and yet he fears it will be a long, long time coming.

14

Her trouble came with the first asymmetrical block.

Resa Parker flipped through the green booklet, its cover printed with the large black letters *VMI, Developmental Test of Visual-Motor Integration*, and noted the exact point where Sarah Corde's abilities failed her: trying to copy a line drawing of an uneven rectangle.

Setting this aside the psychiatrist reviewed the *Wechsler Intelligence Scale for Children – Revised*, examining the snaky plot of the verbal and performance tests in the WISC-R profile blocks. The *Revised Gray Oral Reading Test*, which was strictly timed, showed Sarah – a fourth grader – reading at a first-grade level. Without the stress of a clock she was slightly better.

The scores were worse than the doctor had expected.

Sarah now sat in front of her, struggling through the last of the diagnostic tests – the *Informal Test of Written Language Expression*. Dr Parker saw the anxious behavior, the darting eyes, the quivering knees, the frosting of sweat. The psychiatrist, who had at one time been in daily analysis for six years, continually confronted her own anger and insecurity and the coldness with which they were manifest; she struggled to instill serenity in the child. 'Take your time, Sarah.' Big smile. 'There's no rush.'

She noted the process of internalizing. Sarah didn't

sound out unknown or difficult words. She stared at them without lip movement until she applied whatever phonetic skills she could muster and then wrote the words slowly in crude letters. Sarah leaned forward, an intense frown on her brow as she tried to conjure up the words. In her eyes the agony of repeatedly slamming into her limitations was clear.

Children of policemen have a higher incidence of learning disabilities than those of other parents and Dr Parker noticed in herself a kernel of resentment toward Bill Corde. It was a rancor that she would never reveal but that he would have to go a long way in rebutting. Diane Corde refined much of what she said through a very complex series of filters and Dr Parker wondered just how much the man actually helped his daughter, in contrast to how much Diane believed, or wished, he did.

The doctor also knew something else – how little the girl would ultimately improve and the immense effort and expense even that limited progress would require.

'I'm afraid your time's up,' Dr Parker said, and took the notebook from the girl, who was sweating and nearly breathless. She examined the girl's sad attempt to write a story about a simple illustration in the test booklet – a boy with a baseball. Sarah had started: *His naem was Freddie. And he watnted to play* ~~bsebale,~~ *baseball, only* . . . The handwriting was abysmal. The story continued for a half page; an average child could easily fill three of four pages in that time. 'All right, Sarah, very good. That's the last of our tests.'

Sarah looked mournfully as the written language test was slipped into the file. 'Did I pass?'

'You don't pass these tests. They're just to tell me about you so I can help you do better in school.'

'I don't want to go back to school.'

'I understand, Sarah, but it's not a good idea for you to stay back another year. You don't want all your classmates to advance a grade while you're left behind, do you?'

'Yes,' Sarah answered without hesitation, 'I'd like that.'

Dr Parker laughed. 'Well, how about if I call Mrs Beiderson and have her agree that you can take your tests out loud? Would that be all right?'

'So I wouldn't have to write out the answers?'

'Right.'

'Would she do that?'

'I'm sure she would.' The call had already been made.

'What about the spelling test? I'm ascared of spelling.' The voice grew meek. Manipulatively meek, the doctor noted. Sarah had tried this technique before, with success.

'I'd like you to take it. Would you do it for me?'

'I'll be up in front of everybody. They'll laugh at me.'

'No, you can do it by yourself. You and Mrs Beiderson. That's all.'

The child's instinctive sense of negotiation caught on that this was the best she could do. She looked at Dr Parker and nodded uneasily. 'I guess.'

'Good. Now—'

'Can I finish the story at home?'

'The story?'

'Freddie and the baseball.' She nodded at the booklet.

'I'm sorry, Sarah, that's all we had time for.'

The girl's face twisted with enormous disappointment. 'But I didn't get to write down the neat part!'

'No?' Dr Parker asked. 'What's the neat part?'

Sarah looked up at the same diplomas the doctor had watched Diane Corde scrutinize so desperately the previous week. The girl turned back, looked into the doctor's eyes and said, 'What happens is Freddie hits the baseball into the street and it goes rolling down the sidewalk and into a drugstore. And there's Mr Pillsit ...' Sarah's eyes widened. 'And he used to play for the Chicago Eagles. That was a ball team that had real eagles that would swoop down and grab the baseball and sail out over the grandstand and they won every game there was. And Mr Pillsit says to Freddie—'

Dr Parker held up her hand. 'Sarah, did you read this story someplace?'

She shook her head. 'No, I just made it up, like I was supposed to. I *thought* I was supposed to. I'm sorry . . .' The eyes lowered theatrically. 'Did I do something wrong?'

'No, not at all. Keep going.'

'And Mr Pillsit, he says to Freddie, "If you really want to play baseball, I can make you the best player that ever was, only you have to go find the tallest tree in the eagles' forest and climb up to the top. Are you brave enough to do that?"'

Freddie was of course up to the job, and Sarah enthusiastically continued with his adventures, not noticing the psychiatrist's braceletted hand reach forward and nonchalantly lift her gold pen, recording in rapid, oblique symbols of speed writing Freddie's quest for the magic baseball – fighting Hugo the Claw, the worst eagle that ever was, building a new clubhouse for the team after their original one burned down, running away from home and living in a big nest with a family of beautiful golden eagles. Freddie never returned home though he did become a famous baseball player. By the time Sarah finished, Dr Parker had filled ten pages of steno paper. 'That is a very interesting story, Sarah.'

'No,' Sarah said, sounding like a TV film reviewer. 'But the picture was of Freddie and a baseball so I couldn't think of anything else.'

The doctor flipped through her notebook slowly then said, 'All right, I've got to look over all the work you've done for me and you've got to go study for your tests.'

'I want my daddy to help me.'

After a moment the doctor looked up. 'I'm sorry, Sarah. What did you say?'

'I want Daddy to help me study. Is that okay?'

'That'll be fine,' Resa Parker spoke absently. Her mind was wholly occupied by a boy and a baseball and a talking eagle.

* * *

190

'This is my federal firearm permit and this is my Missouri private investigator's license.'

Sheriff Steve Ribbon studied the squares of laminated plastic in the man's wallet. He'd never seen a federal firearm permit. Or a Missouri private eye's license.

He said, 'Looks in order.'

Charlie Mahoney put the wallet back in his pocket. He wore a businessman's suit – in a fine, faint plaid that looked gray but up close was tiny lines of pink and blue. Ribbon liked that suit a whole lot. Ribbon nodded him toward a chair, observing that the man had two types of self-assurance: the institutional authority of a long-time cop. And the still confidence of a man who has killed another man.

Mahoney tossed an expensive, heavy tan raincoat onto an empty chair and sat down across the desk from Ribbon. He talked without condescension or interest about the beautiful spring weather, about the difficulty of getting to New Lebanon by air, about the ruralness of the town. He then fell silent and looked behind Ribbon, studying a huge topographical map of the county. During this moment Ribbon grew extremely uncomfortable. He said, 'Now what exactly can I do for you?'

'I'm here as a consultant.'

'Consultant.'

'I'm representing the estate of Jennie Gebben. I was a homicide detective in Chicago and I have a lot of investigatory experience. And I'm offering my services to you. Free of charge.'

'The thing is—'

'I've apprehended or assisted in the apprehension of more than two hundred homicide suspects.'

'Well, what I was going to say was, the thing is, you're a, you know, civilian.'

'True,' Mahoney conceded. 'I'll be frank. I can't tell you how upset Mr Gebben is that this has happened. This has nothing to do with your ability to collar the perpetrator, Sheriff. Sending me here was just something he felt he had to do. Jennie was his only child.'

Ribbon winced and felt genuine sorrow in his heart. 'I appreciate what he must be going through. I've got kids myself. But you know how it is, regulations. You must've had those in Chicago.'

'Sure, plenty.' Mahoney studied the great blossom of Ribbon's face and added some shitkick to his voice as he said, 'Can't hurt just to do a little talking. That can't hurt nothing now, can it?'

'No, I suppose not.'

'You're in charge of the case?'

'Well, ultimately,' Ribbon said. 'But we got a senior detective here who's doing most of the legwork. Bill Corde. Good man.'

'Bill Corde. Been doing this sort of thing for a few years?'

'Yessir, he has.'

'What approach is he taking?'

'Well, he's thinking that it was somebody who knew her. Most likely somebody at the school.'

Mahoney was nodding in a way that said to Ribbon he was troubled. 'Playing the odds.'

'Beg your pardon?'

'He's taking the cautious approach. Statistically most people are killed by somebody—'

'—they know.'

'Exactly. But from what I've read about this case it's a little stranger than most. Some twists and turns, you know what I'm saying?'

'I hear you.' Ribbon's voice lowered. 'I've got a load of trouble with what's happening here. There are some, you know, cult overtones to the whole thing.'

'Cult.' Mahoney was nodding again, this time agreeably. 'Like she was a sacrifice victim or whatever. Right. Those goats and that blood. The moon and everything. Whoever picked up on that idea was doing some good law enforcement work.'

Ribbon's caution was on the ebb but he said, 'I still have some trouble with you getting involved, Mr Mahoney. I—'

'Charlie,' Mahoney chided. 'Charlie.' He lifted his thick hands, with their yellow-stained index fingers, heavenward. 'At least do yourself a favor and let me tell you about the reward.'

'Reward.'

'Mr Gebben is a very wealthy man. He's offering twenty-five thousand dollars for apprehension of the killer.'

Ribbon chewed on his cheek to keep the rampaging grin at bay. 'Well, my, that's generous . . . Of course you can imagine that rewards like that generate a mess of bounty hunting. We got a lot of people in this county own guns and can carry them legally.'

Mahoney frowned as he corrected himself. 'Should've said: the reward is for professionals only. For law enforcers. That way there's no risk of people who don't know what they're doing getting hurt.'

'Mr Mahoney.'

'I'm a cop, you're a cop . . .'

'*Charlie*. Charlie, it might not look good for . . . Well, politically is what I'm saying, to have an outsider here. It might look like we don't know what we're doing.'

'It might also look like you thought so highly of the community that you had the foresight to call in some special help.' Mahoney took a leisurely moment to study his watch. 'Well. There you have it. Now, you can kick my ass out of here tomorrow if you want. But I'm stuck in town for the night at least and don't know a soul. How 'bout you and me get a drink and trade war stories. There's not much else to do in this town, is there?'

Ribbon almost made a comment about one pastime being raping co-eds by moonlight but caught himself. 'Well, there are,' he said, 'but 'cept for fishing none of 'em's as fun as drinking.'

She lifted the card off her desk with a trembling hand and stared at it, the little white rectangle. It was stiff and the corners were very sharp. One pressed painfully into her nail-chewed thumb, which left a bloody smear on the card.

Emily Rossiter started to sit on the bed but then thought that *they* might have sat here. They'd probably looked between the mattress and the springs. They'd felt the pillow. They'd run their hands along the same sheets where she and her lover had lain. She dropped the card and saw, as it flipped over and over, the words *Please call me . . . Det. William Corde* flash on and off then disappear as the card landed in the wastebasket. She wondered if even the trash had been violated. Emily walked into the hall then into the telephone alcove.

She made a call and stiffened slightly when someone answered. 'It's Emily . . . I have to see you. No, now.' She listened for a moment to vehement protests then answered defiantly. 'It's about Jennie.' The voice on the other end of the line went silent.

'So I go like you are too much why don't you just sit on it and then Donna's like he is too totally much it's like you know like his eyes have this total hard-on and I go . . .'

Philip Halpern thought: *Shut. Up.*

In the room he and his sister shared there was one telephone. His sister, fourteen, used it most of the time.

The cool breeze of an April evening flowed through the window, rippling the green sheet that separated Philip's side from his sister's. Taped on the poorly painted walls were dozens of creased posters, the sort that come stapled in the centerfold of teen magazines. The wind momentarily lifted aside the Kmart sheet, studded with tiny red flowers, and for a brief moment Luke Perry and Madonna faced off against the Road Warrior and Schwarzenegger's Terminator.

In Philip's half of the stale-scented space: stacks of comic books, science fiction novels, drawing tablets, plastic figures of comic book heroes and villains. Hundreds of magazines, *Fangoria, CineGore, Heavy Metal*, many missing their covers; unable to afford them, Philip regularly swiped the unsold, stripped copies from trash bins behind New Lebanon News. On his dresser and desk rested elaborate plastic models of space ships perfectly assembled but coated with grime. In the corner, a hatrack project for shop class, partially completed, hid a massive dustball.

Dominating the room was a huge hand-printed sign. In oddly elaborate script it read: *Entry Forbidden*, the message surrounded by dozens of letters from the runic alphabet and tiny sketches of gargoyles and dragons.

Philip lay in his sagging bed on a mattress now dry but marred with a hundred old urine stains. He had told his parents that he had to study for a test and went into the bedroom. His father had seemed pleasantly surprised at this news then turned on *Wheel of Fortune*. Philip did not however study. He read Heinlein, he read Asimov, he read Philip K. Dick (he believed at times he was possessed by Dick's spirit), he lay on the bed, staring at flowers and mentally designing a laser, until his sister came into the room and made the phone call to her girlfriend.

Shut. The. Fuck. Up.

Their father opened the bedroom door abruptly and said, 'Off the phone. Lights out. Now.' His hand swept the light switch down. The door closed.

'. . . naw, my old man . . . gotta go. Yeah, tomorrow.'

Philip turned the laser onto the afterimage of his father to see if it would work. It did, spectacularly. Philip invented very efficient weapons.

His voice hissed as he fired it again.

Rosy said, 'Asshole.'

'Say that to him.'

'I'm talking to you,' she said. He heard the zipper of her jeans. He wondered what she was going to wear to bed.

Philip said, 'You're a 'ho.'

She said, 'You wish.'

'Bitch.'

'Fag.'

The springs of her mattress squeaked as she flopped into bed. Philip lay unmoving for ten minutes – until he heard her steady breathing. Fully dressed, he sat up, feeling the cool air from the open window wash over him. He climbed through the window and as he fell to the spongy ground he slipped into the Lost Dimension; it was Phathar the warrior who staggered briefly then righted himself and strode confidently out of the moonlight-flooded backyard.

15

Professor Randolph Sayles wondered why there were no crickets or cicadas here. He listened. It was late April. Was it too early for them? He didn't know entomology. He'd struggled through life sciences, biology being the one course that had deprived him of a four-point grade average in undergraduate school. Twenty-six years later he still resented this.

He stood in the Veterans Memorial Park for ten minutes before she appeared. He thought Emily Rossiter was one of the most beautiful young women he'd ever seen. She had curly brown hair, surrounding a round face of Italian or Greek features, very pale. On her beauty alone he could have lived forever with her, sufficiently happy, sufficiently in love.

Yet as she approached him now – under a trestle of budding maples, the defiantly glaring moonlight silver against the riffling underside of the young leaves – what he saw shocked him. She was like a homeless woman, disheveled, her face puffy, her hair in tangles and unclean, her mouth slack, clothes dirty. Her eyes unfocused, her weak smile mad.

Yet despite her crazed demeanor, despite his anger toward her, despite his fear of her, Randy Sayles wanted nothing so much as to make love to her. Here, immediately, on the grass, on the dirt, hot flesh on flesh in a sea of cool spring air . . . He wanted to force her down and press on her, harder harder . . . He wanted to sample her vulnerability. He wanted her salty, unwashed flesh between his teeth . . .

He had once tried to seduce her, an incident that ended unconsummated and dangerously close to rape. She had finally repelled him with a slap, drawing blood. He had apologized and never approached her again. Curiously this scalding memory exponentially increased his hunger for her now.

He stood slouching, hands pocketed, as she stopped two feet away from him. They stood under a streetlight that seemed duller and more eerie than the light from the full moon. 'Emily.'

'You know what happened to her, don't you?' The words seemed to stumble from her mouth.

'What is it you want?'

'To Jennie. You know what happened to her?'

She began to walk, suddenly, as if she just remembered an appointment. Sayles followed, slightly behind. They moved this way, together, for five minutes then turned north along a path that led to a circle of brick surrounded by concrete benches and behind them a tall boxwood hedge. They would have three of four minutes' warning in case somebody walked toward them.

When speaking with female students Sayles automatically considered escape routes.

'Where are you staying,' he asked, 'in the room?'

'Ah, kiddo,' Emily whispered to no one.

'You should think about going home. Take incompletes. I'll arrange it if you like.'

'Kiddo.'

'What were you trying to say on the phone? You didn't sound very coherent.'

'I didn't know it would be this hard. It's so hard without her.'

'What do you want?'

The moonlight shone on her cheeks in two streaks leading from her eyes to her mouth. Sayles stood with his hands still in his pockets, Emily with her arms crossed over breasts he had never seen. She asked, 'You saw her the night she died, didn't you?' She spoke from some brink whose nature he couldn't fathom; was it resolution or resignation?

Sayles said, 'No.'

'I don't believe you.'

They were in the small park off the quad, a place where lovers over the years had unzipped and unbuttoned all manners of fashions as they lay struggling on fragrant Midwest grass. Tonight the park was, or appeared to be, deserted. Emily said, 'You know what happened to her, don't you?'

After a moment Sayles asked, 'Why are you asking me?'

'Ah, kiddo,' Emily muttered. 'Ah kiddo kiddo kiddo . . .'

Sayles asked in a furious whisper, 'What are you saying? What do you know?' He was engulfed with emotion and couldn't will his strong hands to stop as they grabbed her shoulders.

She seemed to waken suddenly and stood back, shaking her head. crying. 'You're hurting me . . .'

'Hey, anybody there?' a gruff voice called. Footsteps behind them. Someone walking in the woods nearby, separated from view by the boxwood hedge. Emily broke away. Sayles started toward her. She waved her hand wildly, as if brushing away a riled bee.

'Tell me!' Sayles whispered viciously.

Emily walked quickly down the path. He started after her but the intruder, a security guard, shone his light in their direction. They both dodged it. Emily ran.

Sayles whispered, 'Wait!' Then he stepped through the bushes, out of sight of the guard. He hurried through the darkness in the direction he believed she had gone.

Phathar jogged slowly down the path, gasping for breath. It reminded him of dreaded PE class tomorrow; the students were going to run the 880 – the purest form of Honon torture for him. He pictured himself plodding along, fat bouncing, as the others – who'd all finished – hooted and laughed. *'Way to go, Phil. Hustle, Phil. Hustle!'* His bowel churned.

He came out of the woods and walked for fifty feet before he smelled the water and the mud. He found himself at the foot of Blackfoot Pond dam. Phathar felt a stirring in his groin, and he painfully admitted to himself that despite the horror of last Tuesday night Phathar wished in his Dimensional soul he could relive the half hour he had spent here.

Lights. The sound of a speeding car. He crouched and ran to a low hemlock. The lights swept over his head like searchlights in a prison camp and the car disappeared with a hiss of tires, loud in the damp air. Phathar walked into the dish of mud and began his search for the knife that he had discovered to his horror had been lost that night. He was stung by this carelessness, not worthy of Phathar at all (but typical of a fat clumsy high school freshman). Back and forth, using a small penlight he'd wrapped with black construction paper to mask the light, he searched.

Phathar slowly grew serene. Smelling the mud and water, hearing the groan of bullfrogs reminded him of biology class – his best course. He remembered the time he had helped the teacher collect frogs from the banks of the Des Plaines one night and the man had thanked Philip in front of the class the next day. Philip's face had burned with rare pride at the compliment. He had felt bold enough to volunteer to pith frogs for anyone who didn't want to. He jabbed a probe into the heads of a dozen frogs that day. One girl thanked him and said he was brave. Philip had stared at her, dumbstruck.

After a half hour of futilely scanning the muck for the knife, he gave up. He couldn't stay any longer; his father might make an unexpected raid on the bedroom. He started for the path. Then: footsteps. The boy froze, sweat bursting on his forehead, his neck bristling with panic. He retreated to the hemlock. The steps grew closer and he cowered beneath the muffling boughs. He leaned out and looked.

A girl!

Philip calmed immediately and a thrill rippled through his plentiful body.

Another college girl, it seemed. About the same age as the first one. Only prettier. Not so horsey. He felt the stirring in his groin again. Almost a burning vibration. She was alone. He wondered what her tits looked like, hidden under the thick sweater. Her skirt was loose and flowing. Philip felt a painful erection. The girl walked right past the hemlock. She stood in the center of the clearing.

Pacing back and forth she stared at the ground until she came to a bed of blue flowers. She dropped to her knees, smearing her skirt with mud. She leaned forward. He couldn't see what she was doing. He heard her muttering to herself.

'Emily!' A man's breathless voice called from the road.

Philip's erection vanished and he crouched beneath the tree. The girl dropped lower and melted into the flowers. Ten yards away the man jogged along Route 302. He stopped and looked out over the pond. The moonlight was in his eyes and Philip could see him squinting. He was looking right at where the girl was hiding but didn't see her. He called once more then started back along the road. Soon he was gone.

The girl sat up. Philip heard a rustle of the leaves as she stood. He heard an owl close by. Philip pulled a branch down to see her better. He wondered what her ass was like. He wondered if her breasts smelled the way the other girl's had – like pumpkin pie spices. He wondered if she had blond hair or brown between her legs. The erection returned and pressed roughly against his taut jeans.

Slowly the beautiful girl stood and walked along the path. Philip saw she'd forgotten her purse. He let go of the branch. It snapped up and cut off his view of her. He stepped away from the tree and walked into the clearing, where he picked up the purse and without opening it, lifted it to his face. He smelled the scent of lemon perfume and leather and makeup. He slipped it inside his shirt and followed her.

The full moon is high above New Lebanon.

Most of the men are nearly invisible in their camouflaged hunting gear though you can see occasional glints off class rings and glossy blue-black barrels and receivers. They hide behind stands of bushes, dodging pricklers and feeling colder than they think they ought to, it being nearly May. They walk in clusters of two or three along trimmed streets. They cruise in cars. Some, veterans, have blackened their cheekbones and are consumed by a lust they have not felt for twenty-five years.

A number of men pad through fields where they figure there's not much chance of finding any killers but where, if they do, the spotlight of a moon will illuminate their target. Their guns are loaded with rock salt or buckshot or deer slugs and some of the hunters have tapped the bullets and filled the holes with mercury then waxed them over again to make sure that even if they just wing the killer he's not getting up ever ever again.

Some go out with beer and fried chicken and make a campfire, hoping their presence alone will deter the man. Some take the job of guardian more seriously and believe that the entire future of a wholesome New Lebanon depends on their vigilance. And their aim. Jim Slocum and Lance Miller, stripped of their indicia of police authority, are out with one such group.

There are no gunshots until eight p.m., almost exactly as Bill Corde turns onto Route 302, heading home. The first shooting is, not surprisingly, one of the hunters putting a load of buckshot into another one. Fortunately the shooter had his choke wide and the victim got stung by only five or six pellets. The second victim is a cat and the third is a movie poster of Tom Cruise, which may or

202

may not have been an accident.

It isn't until nearly nine that Waylon Sinks, juggling a thirty-two-ounce bottle of Budweiser and a Browning 16-gauge, forgets to put the safety on as he goes over a fence and kills himself unpleasantly. The New Lebanon Sheriff's Department, as well as the county sheriff's dispatcher and 911 for most of Harrison County, have been taking dozens of calls. Mostly they are sightings of the Moon Killer, who is sometimes spotted carrying a long knife, sometimes a rope. Usually he's standing in backyards and looking in windows though sometimes he is climbing walls or scampering over roofs. There isn't much the deputies can do. Officers make their rounds, and under their spotlights the offending shadows vanish completely.

The moonlight beats down on the town of New Lebanon.

It beats down so hard you can nearly hear a buzz like a high-watt bulb or like the humming of blood in your ears when you hold your breath in fear. The moonlight beats down and throughout the town you can see uneasy faces in windows and you can hear dogs howling – though what they bay at isn't the white eye of the moon but the incessant forms of the prowling vigilantes, bleached yet black in the eerie wash of illumination.

Corde arrived home at eight-thirty. He sent Tom the deputy back to his uneasy wife and children. Diane and Jamie were at a wrestling match at the high school, where Corde himself oh-so wanted to be. He walked into the house, half wondering if he should have tipped Tom something; the cheerful young man had been more a baby-sitter than a guard these past few days.

Corde pulled off his muddy shoes and hugged Sarah. He washed his hands and face in the kitchen sink then poured a Diet Coke for her and a seltzer for himself. Only the Warner Brothers glasses were clean and he kept the Road Runner glass for himself. He handed Sarah Porky Pig.

They got to work.

She was particularly edgy tonight. The study session went badly from the start. She panicked often and began talking nonsense, joking and giddy. This put Corde in a bad mood because Diane had told him that Mrs Beiderson was making special arrangements for Sarah's tests and he thought the silliness measured up to ingratitude.

They were in the living room, on the couch, surrounded by a mass of papers. Sarah looked so small and overwhelmed by the mess that Corde picked up the papers and organized them into a single stack. They were Sarah's attempts at the practice spelling test. So far, twelve tries, her best score had been twenty-two out of fifty. Thirty-three was passing.

Corde had that day written a check to Dr Parker for $880, which was exactly twice what it cost him to insulate the entire attic.

'Let's try again,' he said.

'Daddy, I don't want to take the test. Please! I don't feel good.'

'Honey, we've got to work on a few more words. We're only up to the M's.'

'I'm tired.'

Tired was the one thing his souped-up little daughter was not. At battle stations again, they sat with the spelling list between them.

'Okay, the M words.' He joked, 'The M for "mouthful" words.'

'I don't want to take the damn test,' Sarah said sullenly.

'Don't cuss.'

'It's a shitty test! I don't want—'

'Young lady, don't you use that word again.'

'—to take it! I hate Dr Parker.'

'Just the M words.'

'I'm tired,' she whined.

'Sarah. Spell "marble."'

Eyes squinting, lip between teeth, back erect. She said, 'M-A-R-B-L-E.'

'Very good, honey. Wonderful.' Corde was impressed.

'Marble' went on the plus side, joined by 'make,' 'mark,' 'miss' and 'milk.' Sarah wasn't as lucky with 'middle,' 'missile,' 'makeshift,' 'messenger,' 'melon' and 'mixer.' Dr Parker hadn't suggested it but Corde took to drawing pictures of the objects next to the words. This seemed clever but didn't help.

Sarah's mood was getting progressively worse. Her leg bounced. Her tiny fingers wound together frantically.

'Now spell "mother."'

Sarah started to cry.

Corde was sweating. He'd been through this so many times and her defeats were always his. He wanted to shake her. He wanted to grab her by the shoulders and point her at Jamie and say, *You've got the same blood. There's no difference between you. Can't you understand that? Just work hard! Work hard! Why won't you do that?* He wanted to call up the psychiatrist and tell her to get her fashion-plate ass over here this minute. In a tired voice: 'You're doing fine. A lot better than when we started tonight.'

'No, I'm not!' she said. She stood up.

'Sit down, young lady. You've done the word before. Try it again. "Mother."'

'M-O- . . .'

Corde heard her hyperventilating and thought momentarily of Diane's long labor when the girl was born. Breathe, breathe, breathe . . .

'It's E-R. No, wait, M-O-T . . . I got lost. Wait, wait . . .'

Corde set the piece of paper on the table with the other failed tests and picked up a blank sheet. He began to write, 'M-O-T-H . . .'

'No!' she screamed.

Corde blinked at the volume of the wail and the terror it contained. 'Sarah!'

'I don't know it! I don't know it!' She was howling. Corde – standing up, sending a chair flying – believed she was having a seizure.

'Sarah!' he shouted again. His neck bristled in panic. Corde took her by the shoulders. 'Sarah, stop it!'

She screamed again and tipped into hysteria.

He shook her hard, her hair flying around her head like golden smoke. The glass tumbled over, a flood of brown soda poured onto the carpeting. She broke away from him and raced up the stairs to her room. Sheetrock throughout the house shook as her door slammed.

Corde, hands shaking, was mopping up the spilled soda with wads of napkins when the doorbell rang.

'Oh, Lord, now what?'

Steve Ribbon leaned on the doorpost, looking out over the lawn. 'Talk to you for a minute, Bill?'

Corde looked toward Sarah's bedroom then back to Ribbon. 'Come on in.'

Ribbon didn't move. 'Your family home?'

'Just Sarah. Jamie and Diane are at a meet. Should be home anytime.'

The sheriff didn't speak for a minute. 'Why don't you step outside here?'

Corde shook his head. 'I don't want to go too far. Sarah's not feeling well.' He stepped onto the porch. Ribbon closed the door behind him. Corde flicked spilled soda off his fingers. The sheriff's squad car was parked in the driveway. Jim Slocum was driving. In the back was a blond man, heavy, craggy-faced, eyes fixed on the headrest in front of him.

Ribbon's eyes scanned the moonlit ground, studying the perfectly trimmed grass. He said, 'Bill, I've got to talk to you. They found Jennie's roommate. Emily Rossiter.'

Corde crossed his arms.

They found . . . Not *we* found. Corde understood the difference.

It was his turn to stare at the neatly edged front lawn. From where he stood it was in some geometric shape whose name he couldn't recall – a rectangle pushed to one side.

'Somebody hit her over the head then threw her in Blackfoot Pond right by the dam. She drowned. And there's some pretty unpleasant stuff he did to her.' Ribbon paused. 'There's a tentative match between shoeprints nearby her and those found by the dam the night Jennie Gebben was killed. I know your opinion, Bill, but it looks like there probably was a cult killer all along.'

PART TWO

Physical Evidence

1

The medical examiner was in a prickly mood. For the second time in two weeks, he stood in mud, at night, beside this dark pond. His usual demeanor – that of a cheerful TV doctor – was absent.

Streaks on her face, hair muddy and plastered around her head the way a bald man hides scalp, still-beautiful Emily Rossiter lay on a blanket, faceup. A black hideous wound marred her temple. A large fishhook was embedded deep in her groin in the center of a slick patch of dark pubic hair. The hook was attached to a long piece of twenty-pound test line, which had pulled her skirt up between her legs.

A crowd of locals and reporters stood on the fringe of the crime scene – a sloping grassy backyard that bordered Blackfoot Pond.

The ME, a thin man of fifty, said to T.T. Ebbans, 'Blow to the right temple with a rough, irregular object. Death by drowning.'

'Rape?'

'Not this time.'

'What about the hook?' Ebbans asked. 'After she was dead?'

'Dollars to doughnuts.'

Jim Slocum said to Ebbans, 'There, you've got your postmortem piercing. That's common in sacrificial murders.'

Ebbans pushed past the reporters, telling them that Sheriff Ribbon would be holding a press conference in ten minutes. He joined Bill Corde up by the road.

'Detective Corde!' Addie Kraskow waved frantically, her laminated *Register* press pass bouncing on her chest. 'You didn't think a serial killer was involved. You feel differently now?'

Corde ignored her, and Ebbans repeated. 'Ten minutes. Press conference.'

Addie didn't pursue the question anyway; she noticed a photo opportunity and sent her photographer to shoot the body being zippered up and carried toward the ambulance that stood in the driveway of a house, next to a child's pink-and-white tricycle. The cameramen were scrambling like panicked roaches to get the tricycle and the body bag in the same shot.

The County Rescue Squad scuba divers arrived and suited up. One of them looked at the pond and muttered, 'Whore's pussy.'

Corde sternly told the man to act professionally.

On the periphery of the action Wynton Kresge leaned against an old, beige Dodge Aspen crowned by a blue revolving light. On the door was the Auden University seal, printed with the school name and the words *Veritas et Integritas*. Ebbans nodded in his direction. Corde and Kresge ignored each other.

'I step into a mantrap on this one, or what?' Corde asked Ebbans.

'You play it like you see it, Bill. That's all you can ever do.'

'Crime Scene have a chance before everybody started padding around?'

'It was virgin. We didn't find much other than the boot prints but it was a virgin.'

Corde glanced at the cluster of policemen beside the pond. One was the blond man he had seen in the back of Ribbon's car.

Ebbans followed his eyes. 'Charlie Mahoney.'

'What's he doing here?'

'Representative of the family.'

'Uhn. What family?'

'Works for Jennie's father.'

'And?'

'Don't ask me.'

'Well, let's see what we've got.' Corde started down to the water.

'Wait up a minute, Bill.'

He stopped. Ebbans stepped beside him and when he spoke his voice was a whisper. Corde lowered his ear toward the man. 'I just wanted you to know,' Ebbans began then hesitated. 'Well, it's bullshit is what it is . . .'

Corde was astonished. He had never known Ebbans to cuss. 'What, T.T.?'

Their eyes were on an indentation in the grass – a wheel tread left by the gurney that had carried Emily's body to the ambulance.

'Was there any connection between you and Jennie?'

Corde looked up and kept his eye on the mesmerizing lights atop the ambulance. 'Go on. What are you saying?'

'There's some talk at County – just talk – that you burnt those letters because you were, you know . . .'

'I was what?'

'"Seeing her" is what somebody said. And because of that maybe you wanted to deep-six the evidence. I don't believe—'

'I didn't do that, T.T.'

'*I* know that. I'm just telling you what I heard. It's just a rumor but it's one of those rumors that won't go away.'

Corde had been in town government long enough to know there are two reasons rumors don't go away. Either because somebody doesn't want them to go away.

Or because they're true.

'Who's behind it?' Corde asked.

'Don't know. Hammerback seems to be on your side. But with the election he's paying out his support real slow and if you turn out to be a liability he'll burn you in a second. Who else it could be I just don't know.'

At Corde's feet drops of dew caught the flashing lights

213

and flickered like a hundred miniature Christmas bulbs. "Preciate your telling me, T.T.'

Ebbans walked to the ambulance and Corde headed down to the pond, whose turgid surface was filled with bubbles from the divers as they searched for clues to the death of this beautiful young woman – whose story and whose secrets were now lost forever and would never be transcribed on one of Bill Corde's neatly ordered index cards.

He stood for a long time, with his feet apart in a patch of firm mud, looking over the water, and found himself thinking not at all of fingerprints or weapons or footprints or fiber traces but meditating on the lives of the two girls murdered in this dismal place and wondering what the lesson of those deaths would ultimately be.

'She's calm now.' Diane Corde was speaking to Dr Parker in her office. 'I've never seen her have an attack like that. Bill said he asked her to spell a word and she just freaked out.'

Mother. That was what Sarah was supposed to spell. Diane didn't tell the prim doctor this. Neither did she say how much she resented Corde's callousness in telling her which word so panicked Sarah.

Dr Parker said, 'I wish you'd called me. I could have given her a tranquilizer. She had a panic attack. They're very dangerous in children.'

Although the doctor's words were spoken softly Diane felt the lash of criticism again. She said in a spiny tone, 'I was out and my husband had just got some bad news. We couldn't deal with it all at once.'

'That's what I'm here for.'

'I'm sorry,' Diane said. Then she was angry with herself. *Why should I feel guilty?* 'I've kept her out of—'

'I know,' Dr Parker said. 'I called the school after you called me.'

'You did?' Diane asked.

'Of course I did. Sarah's my patient. This incident is my responsibility.' The blunt admission surprised Diane but she sensed the doctor wasn't apologizing; she was simply observing. 'I misjudged her strength. She puts on a good facade of resilience. I thought she'd be better able to deal with the stress. I was wrong. I don't want her back in school this term. We have to stabilize her emotionally.'

The doctor's suit today was dark green and high-necked. Diane had noticed it favorably when she walked into the office and was even thinking of complimenting her. She changed her mind.

Dr Parker opened a thick file. Inside were a half dozen booklets, on some of which Sarah's stubby handwriting was evident. 'Now I've finished my diagnosis and I'd like to talk to you about it. First, I was right to take her off Ritalin.'

I'm sure you're always right.

'She doesn't display any general hyperkinetic activity and she's very even-tempered when not confronted with stress. What I observed about her restlessness and her inattentiveness was that they're symptomatic of her primary disability.'

'You said that might be the case,' Diane said.

'Yes, I did.'

But of course.

'I've given her the Wechsler Intelligence Scale for Children, the Gray Oral Reading Test, Bender Gestalt, Wide Range Achievement Test and the Informal Test of Written Language Expression. The results show your daughter suffers from severe reading retardation—'

'I don't care what you say,' Diane blurted, 'Sarah is not retarded.'

'That doesn't mean that *she's* retarded, Mrs Corde. Primary reading retardation. It's also called developmental dyslexia.'

'Dyslexia? That's where you turn letters round.'

'That's part of it. Dyslexics have trouble with word attack – that's how we approach a word we've never seen before – and with putting together words or sentences. They have trouble with handwriting and show an intolerance for drill. Sarah also suffers from dysorthographia, or spelling deficit.'

Come on, Diplomas, cut out the big words and do what I'm paying you to do.

'She has some of dyslexia's mathematical counterpart – developmental dyscalculia. But her problem is primarily reading and spelling. Her combined verbal and performance IQ is in the superior range. In fact she's functioning in the top five percent of the population. Her score, by the way, is higher than that of the average medical student.'

'Sarah?' Diane whispered.

'It's also six points higher than your son's. I checked with the school.'

Diane frowned. This could not be. The doctor's credentials were suddenly suspect again.

'She's reading about three years behind her chronological age and it usually happens that the gap will widen. Without special education, by the time she's fifteen, Sarah's writing age would be maybe eleven and her spelling age nine or ten.'

'What can we do?'

'Tutoring and special education. Immediately. Dyslexia is troubling with any student but it's an extremely serious problem for someone with Sarah's intelligence and creativity—'

'Creativity?' Diane could not suppress the laugh. Why, the doctor had mixed up her daughter's file with another patient's. 'She's not the *least* creative. She's never painted anything. She can't carry a tune. She can't even strum a guitar. Obviously she can't write . . .'

'Mrs Corde, Sarah is one of the most creative patients I've ever had. She can probably do all of those things you just mentioned. She's been too inhibited to try because the mechanics overwhelm her. She's been conditioned to fail. Her self-esteem is very low.'

'But we always encourage her.'

'Mrs Corde, parents often encourage their disabled children to do what other students can do easily. Sarah is not like other children. Encouragement like that is just another way of helping her fail.'

'Well,' Diane said stiffly. 'You sure don't hesitate to call it the way you see it, Doctor.'

Dr Parker smiled a smile that meant nothing at all to Diane, who was for once relieved that the psychiatrist had set a frigid atmosphere for these sessions. She had no problem saying bluntly, 'That's very well and good, Doctor, but how the hell are you going to help my little girl?'

'I want you to find a tutor. They're expensive but you need one and you need a good one. I recommend that you check with the Auden lab school.'

'Why can't we help her? Bill and me?'

'Sarah needs a specialist.'

'But—'

'It's important that she see someone who knows what they're doing.'

Diane thought it was remarkable that you could both admire and detest someone at the same time.

'Second, I'd like to work with her myself. Until we build up her confidence in herself she's never going to improve. Her self-esteem has been very badly damaged.'

'What can you do that we haven't? All right, maybe the way we tried to teach her was wrong. But you keep forgetting that we've always supported her. We always tell her how good she is. How talented.'

'But she doesn't *believe* you. And how can she? You push her to work harder and it does no good. You tell her she's doing well but she isn't, she's failing her classes. You tell her she's smart but by all the outward manifestations she isn't. Mrs Corde, you've acted for the best motives but your efforts have been counterproductive. We need to encourage Sarah to do the things she's genuinely good at.'

'But haven't you heard what I've told you? She isn't good at anything. She doesn't even like to help me cook or sew. All she does is play games by herself, go to movies and watch TV.'

'Ah. Precisely.' Dr Parker smiled like a chess player calling checkmate.

Diane blinked. *What'd I say?*

'I'd like to see Sarah as soon as possible. If you could make the appointment with Ruth.' The cryptic eyes, so talented at dismissals, glanced at another file.

'Okay, sure.' Diane stood.

Then she hesitated.

She sat down again. 'Say, Doctor . . .'

'Yes?'

Diane blurted, 'Where does it come from? Dyslexia?'

'I'm sorry, I should have discussed that with you.' She closed the second file and turned full attention to Diane. 'We don't know exactly. It used to be that a lot of doctors attributed it to physical problems – like memory confusion between the two hemispheres of the brain. That's been discredited now though vision and hearing problems can be major factors. My belief is that like many developmental problems dyslexia has both a nature and nurture component. It's largely genetic and the prenatal period is very critical. But how parents and teachers respond to the child is important too.'

'Prenatal?' Diane asked, then casually added, 'So could it be that someone who had maybe smoked or drank or took drugs during pregnancy might cause dyslexia in their children?'

'To some extent though usually there's a correspondent decrease in IQ . . .' Dr Parker squinted and flipped through her notes. 'Anyway I thought you said you largely abstained while you were pregnant.'

'Oh, that's right,' Diane said. 'I was just curious . . . You know, when someone you love has a problem you want to know all about it.' Diane stood up. She sensed Dr Parker studying her. 'Well, I'll make that appointment.'

'Wait a minute, please.' Dr Parker capped her pen. 'You know, Mrs Corde, one of the underlying themes of my approach to therapy is that we really *are* our parents.' She was smiling, Diane believed, in a heartfelt way for the first time since they had begun working

218

together. 'I call parents the quote primary providers and not just in a positive sense. What they give us and what they do for us – and *to* us – include some unfortunate things. But it can include a lot of good things too.'

Diane looked back at her and tried to keep her face an unemotional mask. She managed pretty well, even when the doctor said, 'I've seen a lot of parents in here and I've seen a lot of people in here because of their parents. Whatever's troubling you, Mrs Corde, don't be too hard on yourself. My opinion is that Sarah is a very lucky girl.'

Technically this was trespassing. But boundaries in the country aren't what they are in the city. You could walk, hunt, fish on almost anybody's land for miles around. As long as you left it in good shape, as long as the feeling was reciprocal, nobody made an issue.

Corde ducked under the wire fence, and slipped into the scruffy forest behind his property. He continued for a ways then broke out into a clearing in the center of which was a huge rock some glacier had left behind, twenty feet high and smooth as a trout's skin. Corde clambered onto the rock and sat in one of the indentations on the west side.

She wears a turquoise sweater high at the neck, half obscuring her fleshy throat.

To the south he could just see a charcoal gray roof, which seemed attached to a stand of adolescent pines though in fact it covered his own house. He noticed the discolored patch near the chimney where he had replaced the shingles last summer.

'You used to live in St Louis, didn't you?' Jennie Gebben asks.

Oh, she is pretty! Hair straight and long. Abundant breasts under the soft cloth. Sheer white stockings under the black jeans. She wears no shoes and he sees through the thin nylon red-nailed toes exceptionally long.

'Well, I did,' he answers. 'As a matter of fact.' He

clears his throat. He feels the closeness of the dormitory room. He smells incense. He smells spicy perfume.

'Eight, nine years ago? I was little then but weren't you in the news or something?'

'All cops get on the air at one time or another. Press conferences or something. Drug bust.'

Saturday night, January a year ago, branches click outside the dormitory window. Bill Corde sits on a chair and Jennie Gebben tucks her white-stockinged feet under her legs and lies back on the bed.

'It seems it was something more than that,' she says. 'More than a press conference. Wait. I remember. It was . . .'

She stops speaking.

Bill Corde, sitting now on the flesh-smooth rock in the quiet town of New Lebanon, watched the sun grow longer to the horizon through a high tangle of brush and hemlock and young oaks soon to die from light starvation.

Shots fired! Shots fired! Ten-thirty-three. Unit to respond . . .

Each inch the sun fell, each thousand miles the earth turned away from it, he sensed the forest waking. Smells grew: loam, moss, leaves from last fall decomposing, bitter bark, musk, animal droppings.

. . . this session of the St Louis Police Department Shooting Review Board. Incident number 84-403. Detective Sergeant William Corde, assigned to St Louis County Grand Larceny, currently suspended from duty pending the outcome of this hearing . . .

Corde thought he'd be happy just being a hunter. He would have liked to live in the 1800s. Oh, there was a lot that amused and appealed to him about the Midwest at the end of the twentieth century. Like pickup trucks and televised Cardinals and Cubs games and pizza and computers and noncorrosive gunpowder. But if you asked him to be honest he'd say that he'd forgo it all to wake up one morning and walk downstairs to find Diane in front of a huge fireplace making johnnycakes in the beehive oven, then he and Jamie would go out to trap or

220

hunt all day long among the miles and miles of forests just like this one.

A. *Well, sir, the perpetrators . . .*

Q. *You knew them to be armed with assault rifles?*

A. *Not with assault rifles, no, though we knew they were armed . . . The perpetrators had taken the cash and jewelry and were still inside the store. I ordered my men into the alley behind the store. It was my intention to enter through a side door and take them by surprise.*

Corde listened to the snapping of some invisible animal making its way through the woods. He thought how odd it was that a creature was moving past him, probably no more than ten feet away, yet he sensed no danger. He felt if anything the indifference of the surroundings, as if he had been discounted by nature as something insignificant and not worth harming.

Q. *Sergeant Corde, could you tell us then what happened?*

A. *Yes, sir. There were a number of exit doors leading from the stores into the alley. I had inadvertently told the men to enter through door 143.*

Q. *Inadvertently?*

A. *That was a mistake. The door that opened onto the jewelry store was number 134. I—*

Q. *You mixed up the numbers?*

A. *Yes, sir. In speaking with the fire inspector, he had told me the correct number of the door. I had written it down. But when I radioed to the men which door to enter, I read it backwards.*

Q. *So the men entered the mall through the wrong door.*

A. *No, they tried to. But that door was locked. As they were trying to get it open, thinking it was the correct door, the perpetrators ran into the alley and fired on the policemen. Their backs—*

Q. *Whose backs?*

A. *The policemen's backs were to the perpetrators. Two police officers were killed and two were wounded.*

Q. *Have the perpetrators been apprehended?*

A. To date, one has. The rest have not.

He'd been suspended with half pay for six months but he quit the force a week before reinstatement. He sat around in his suburban home, thinking about the men who'd died, thinking of the kind of jobs he ought to get, replaying the incident a hundred times then a thousand times. He stopped going to church and didn't even have the inclination to turn a bar or the bottle into his personal chapel. He spent his time with the TV, doing some security jobs, some construction work. Finally the mortgage payments on the trim suburban split-level outran their savings and with Sarah on the way they'd no choice but to come back to New Lebanon.

Feed and grain, planning and sawing, teaching . . . Long, long days. Then he's seen the ad in the paper for a deputy and he'd applied.

After Bill and Diane had moved back to New Lebanon he had five years with his father before the stroke. Five full years of opportunities to talk about what happened at the Fairway Mall. But what the two men spent those years on was pheasant loads and movies and carburetors and memories of their wife and mother.

One day, a month before the blood clot swapped a clear, complicated mind for one that was infinitely simple, Corde was crouched down, sharpening a mower blade in his father's garage. He heard the footsteps and he looked up to see the old man standing hunched and pale, licking the top of a Dannon yogurt container. His father said, ''Bout time to deal with St Louis, wouldn't you say?' Corde stood, his knee popping and pushing him oh-so-slowly upward. He turned to face his father and cleared his throat. The elder Corde said solemnly, 'Ten bucks says they'll cave to New York.' Corde rolled grass flecks off his hands and dug into his pocket for a bill. 'You're on,' he said. His father wandered into the yard while Corde turned back to the iron blade in complete remorse.

Q. If someone else had read the number of the door to the policemen in the alley, the mishap might not have happened. Or if you had taken your time and read the number slowly?

A. (garbled)

Q. *Could you repeat that please.*

A. *The mishap probably would not have happened, no.*

He'd never told anyone in New Lebanon. The facts were there, somewhere in his file in St Louis. If Steve Ribbon or Hammerback Ellison or Jim Slocum or Addie Kraskow of the *Register* wanted to go to the trouble to look it up, they would find everything. But the New Lebanon Sheriff's Department simply glanced at his résumé and believed the truthful statement that the reason for termination from his last job was that he'd quit. They believed too his explanation that he had grown tired of fighting city riverfront crime and had wanted to move back to his peaceful home town. After all, he had a six-year-old son and a baby on the way.

Who'd think to look beyond that?

Another snap, nearby. Corde turned. The animal materialized. A buck. He saw two does not far off. He loved watching them. They were elegant in motion but when they stopped – always as if they were late for something vitally important and had time to give you just a brief look – they were completely regal. Corde wished he was a poet. He wanted badly to put into words what he felt at this moment: The knowledge in the deer's eyes.

The melting sun.

The unseen movement of the woods at dusk.

The total sorrow when you fall short of the mark that you know God's set for you.

With a single crack of wet wood, the deer were gone. Bill Corde scooted off the rock and slowly made his way to his twentieth-century home, with his pickup truck and television, and his family.

2

*Special to the Register – Two days after the slaying
of a second Auden University co-ed by the man
known as the 'Moon Killer,' John Treadle, Harrison
County Supervisor, ordered Sheriff's Department
deputies to step up nighttime patrols around New
Lebanon.*

*'But,' he said, 'I can't emphasize enough that
girls shouldn't travel by themselves after dark
until we catch this man.'*

*The body of the student, Emily Rossiter, a resident
of St Louis, was found floating in Blackfoot pond
on the night of the full moon. She had been struck
on the head and left to drown. The body was
reportedly mutilated.*

*'We're devoting a hundred and ten percent of
our time to solving these cult murders,' Steven
Ribbon, Sheriff of New Lebanon, said last night.
He added that he had taken the unusual step of
asking an outside consultant to assist in the
investigation.*

*'This man has a number of years of homicide
investigation experience with a big city police
department and he's already provided some real
helpful insights into the workings of this killer's
mind.'*

Citing security, Sheriff Ribbon would give no

details on this consultant's identity or exact role in the case.

The Chamber of Commerce estimates that the series of murders has cost the town one million dollars in lost revenues.

Her biggest fear is that somehow her father has scared off the Sunshine Man.

It is now a couple of days in a row that her daddy has gotten up late, had breakfast with them and then been home before supper. But worse than that he had gone for long walks in the woods behind the house, the woods where the Sunshine Man lived. Sarah considers herself an expert on wizards and she knows that they resent people who don't believe in them. Her father's certainly a person like that.

Although she's questioned Redford T. Redford at length about the wizard the bear has remained silent. She has left several presents and painstakingly written notes for the Sunshine Man in the magic circle. He has not picked them up or responded.

She has thought about running away again. But because her mother has agreed with Dr Parker to keep her out of school for a while, Sarah is willing to postpone her escape plans. She listens to her books on tape, she looks at her picture books, she watches television, she plays with her stuffed animals.

At night Sarah sits and stares out the window. Once, when the waning moon is bright, she thinks she sees the form of a man walking through the woods. She flashes her bedside light and waves. Whoever it might be stops and looks at the house but does not respond. He seems to vanish. She stares after him until the trees begin to sway and the night sky opens up in great cartwheeling streaks of stars and planets and giants and animals, then she crawls under the blankets. She holds tight to her piece of magic quartz and, knowing the Sunshine Man may be out there, sends him a message in her thoughts.

226

Sarah wishes her father would start working late again. And sure enough, after just two days, she gets this wish. He's up and gone before breakfast, and home long after she's gone to bed. One morning, when he hadn't seen her for two days, her father left a note at the breakfast table for her; it sounded all stiff. Sarah sadly thinks the Sunshine Man is much smarter than her father.

She hopes the wizard will come back and make her smart. She believes he can do it. She also knows though that this will be a very hard wish to grant so she tells herself to be patient. She knows she'll have to wait just a little while longer.

Philip closed his bedroom door and immediately they were warriors once again, tall and dignified and ever correct, struggling to understand this strange dimension.

Jano looked around the room. 'Your sister here?'

'Nope.'

The boys who knew Philip's sister, and that was a lot of boys, did not call her 'Rose' or 'Rosy'; they called her 'Halpern,' which seemed to Philip to say everything there was to say about her.

Jano whispered urgently, 'Well?'

'What?' Phathar shoved a dripping handful of popcorn from a half-gallon bag into his mouth.

He whispered, 'Did you do it?' Jano's eyes were red and it looked like there was a streak of dried snot under his nose. Phathar wondered if his friend had been crying (Phathar assumed *he* was the only freshman boy who still cried).

Jano repeated, 'The girl at the pond. Emily something. Did you?'

He ate another mouthful. 'Nope.'

Jano whispered, 'I don't believe you.'

'I didn't do it, dude.'

'You wanted to fuck her so you killed her.'

'I did not.' With a pudgy finger Phathar worked a hull out from between an incisor and his gum.

'I am like totally freaked. What are we going to do?'

'Have some popcorn.'

'You are like too much, man. She's dead too and you're like—'

'So what? You saw the way the Honons mowed down the Valanies. They just like went in with the xasers and totally mowed them down. The women and the kids, everyone.'

'That's a movie.'

Phathar repeated patiently, 'I didn't like kill her.'

'Did you find the knife?'

'I might have if I hadn't been alone.'

'I couldn't make it. I told you. Maybe you didn't lose it.'

'I lost it.'

Jano said, 'Man, we've got to get rid of everything.'

'I told you, I put a destructor on the files. It's great. Here look.' Phathar walked to a locked metal file cabinet. He unlocked it and pulled a drawer open. Inside were stacks of charts and drawings and files. Resting on top of them was a coil from a space heater. 'Look, this is a lock switch that I got from *Popular Mechanics*. It's great. If you open the cabinet without shutting off the switch . . .' He reached inside the cabinet and pointed to two pieces of wood wound with wires pressing against each other, like a large clothespin. '. . . Somebody opens the drawer and it closes the circuit. The coil gets red hot in like seconds and torches everything.'

'Totally excellent,' Jano said with admiration. 'What if it burns the house down?'

Phathar did not respond. Through the closed door, they heard Philip's father singing some old song. 'Strangers in the Night.'

Jano looked in the bottom drawer of the file cabinet. 'What's that?' He picked up the brown purse, smeared with mud.

Phathar froze. He was in a delicate position. This was his only friend in high school; he couldn't do what he wanted to – which was to scream to him to put it

228

back. He said simply, 'It's hers.'

Jano clicked it open. 'The girl's? The second one! You *did* do it!'

Phathar reached out and closed it. 'Would you just chill? I saw her but—'

'I don't see why you're denying it, man.'

'—I *didn't* kill her.'

'Why'd you keep it?'

'I don't know.' Phathar in fact had wondered that a number of times. 'It smells nice.'

'You get over with her too?' Jano had stopped looking shocked and was curious.

'Are you deaf? Like are you totally deaf?'

'Come on, Phathar, I tell you everything. What was it like?'

'You're a fucking hatter. I followed her for a while but then I took off. There was some dude wandering around.'

'Who?'

'I don't know.'

'They found her in the pond. Yuck. If you did it with her your dick'll probably fall off, with that water. What's in the purse?'

'I don't know. I didn't open it.' Phathar stood up and took the purse away from his friend. He put it in the file cabinet and laid another heater coil on top of it. He closed the drawer.

'I don't think that's a good place for it,' Jano said.

'How come?'

'Even with the destructor it'd take a while for the leather to catch fire.'

Phathar decided this might be true. He retrieved the purse. He held it out to Jano. 'You take it. Throw it someplace.'

'No way. I don't want to get caught with it. Why don't you burn it?'

'I can't. My dad'd whack me again. Maybe I'll hide it under the porch and some night when he's playing cards I'll burn it.'

The terrible, glass-splintering crash came from the

living room. The boys each stared at the dirt-smeared wall through which the sound had come. Philip dropped the purse into the empty popcorn bag and wadded it, along with some trash, into a green plastic garbage bag, which sat in the corner of this room. They stepped into the hall.

Philip's mother was on the floor, on all fours, her knees spread out, skirt up to her trim waist. The eyes in her pretty face were nearly closed and her head lolled as the muscles in her smooth arms tried to keep her shoulders from dropping to the ground. Mr Halpern stood above her, his hands gripping the stained orange blouse, saying desperately, 'It'll be all right, it'll be all right. No, no, it'll be all right.'

And she was repeating louder and in a shrill soprano, 'Lemmealone, lemmealone!' In her hand was a white wad of cloth. On the stained carpet was a fresher stain of vomit. The smell of sour gin was thick in the air. Philip started to cry.

'Mrs Halpern,' Jano whispered.

Philip's father looked up. 'Get the fuck out of here, both of you.'

Jano said, 'But she's sick.'

Whimpering, Philip said, 'She's not sick.'

'Get the fuck out!' his father shouted. 'Both of you. Out out out!' He stamped his foot as if he were spooking dogs.

Philip said to Jano, 'Please.'

'But—'

'Please,' Philip said. His friend fled outside. Staring out the front window Philip heard the scuffling of his mother's shoes. His father had lifted her into an armchair and was whispering to her. Philip walked past his parents and out the back door then he slipped under the porch.

Philip hid the bag containing the purse under a mound of soft black dirt. He rocked back and forth in the crisp dusty leaves.

Oh, he was tired.

He was tired of so much. His father wore torn T-shirts and made the handy man visit. His mother packed him greasy sandwiches for lunch – when she made his lunch – and forgot to wash the clothes. There were enemies everywhere, everywhere you looked. His sister was a 'ho, he was fat. She was *Halpern*, he was *Philip*. Phil-lip. He got a D in phys ed and a B in biology and, while another glass shattered somewhere in the house above him, a single thought centered in his head – an image of a shy young girl leaning on a lab table and telling him how brave he was while Philip stuck a needle way deep into a frog's brain then slit its belly open and watched the slick lump of a heart continue to beat on and on and on.

Bill Corde was sitting in infamous Room 121 of the Student Union. He was alone, surrounded by the now familiar scents of fatty meat, bitter paper and burnt coffee.

More students, more three-by-five cards. Today's questions were similar to last week's but they were not identical.

Today he was asking about *two* victims.

Corde took notes, jotting down the boxy oriental letters, but the hours were unproductive; he heard variations on what he had already learned or pointless, obscure details. 'Emily wore this yoked dress a lot then one day it got stolen from the laundry room. That was just before she was killed. I mean, like the *day* before.' Corde nodded and recorded this fact, unsure what it might mean or what he would ever do with it but afraid to let the item get away. He had this feeling often.

Many thoughts intruded on the interviews, not the least of which was a vague disquiet about Charlie Mahoney, the mysterious consultant. Ribbon had introduced them but the man had said little to Corde and been in a hurry to leave the office. Corde had not seen him since.

When Corde asked Ribbon what 'real helpful insights'

Mahoney had provided, picking up the sheriff's phrase from the *Register*, he'd been as elusive as Corde expected. 'Mahoney's here as an observer is all. What I said was mostly for public relations. Trying to calm people down a little.'

Well, who the hell got 'em un-calm in the first place, with all this talk of a Moon Killer?

'I don't want a civilian working on this case,' Corde said.

'I know *you* don't,' Ribbon had answered cryptically and returned to his office.

Now, in Room 121, Corde looked at his watch. Four p.m. He wandered out to the cafeteria and bought an iced coffee. He finished it in three swallows. He was eager to go home. He nearly did so but his resolve broke – or discipline won – and he stepped to the door and waved a final student inside then told the others to come back tomorrow.

It was just as well that he did not leave. This last student was the one who told him Jennie Gebben's secret.

She was round and had thick wrists and was worried about a double chin because she kept her head high throughout the interview. With that posture and the expensive flowered dress she seemed like an indulged East Coast princess.

The lazy Southern drawl disposed of that impression quickly. 'I do hope I can help you, officer. It's a terrible thing that happened.'

Did she know either of the murdered girls? Just Jennie. How long had she known her? Two years. Yes, they shared some classes. No, they had never double-dated.

'Do you know either Professor Sayles or Brian Okun?'

'Sorry.'

'Do you know who Jennie might have been going out with?'

The fleshy neck was touched.

It reminded him compellingly of Jennie's throat.

Corde looked from the white flesh back to the paler white of his three-by-five cards.

'Well, would you be speaking of men she went out with?'

'Students, professors, anyone.'

'. . . or girls?'

The tip of Corde's pen lowered to a card.

'Please go on.'

The girl played tensely with the elaborate lace tulle on the cuff of her dress. 'Well, you know 'bout Jennie's affair with that girl, don'tcha?'

After a pause he wrote 'Bisexual?' in precise boxy letters and asked her to continue.

The girl touched her round pink lip with her tongue and made a circuit of Corde's face. 'Just rumors. Y'all know how it is.' The plump mouth closed.

'Please.'

Finally she said, 'One time, the story goes, some girls were in a dorm across campus and saw Jennie in bed with another girl.'

The flesh was no longer pale but glowed with fire.

'Who was this other girl?'

'I was led to believe their . . . position in bed made it a little difficult to see her. If you understand what I'm saying.'

'Who were these girls who saw it?'

'I don't know. I assumed you knew all about this.' The frown produced not a single wrinkle in her perfect skin. 'You know of course about the fight she had?'

'Tell me.'

'The Sunday before she died. Jennie was on the phone for a long time. It was late and she was whispering a lot but I got the impression she was talking to somebody she'd dumped. You know that tone? Like where you have to get meaner than you want to because they're not taking no for an answer. They all were carrying on and my room is right near the phone and I was going to go out and tell her to hush when I heard her say, "Well, I love her and I don't love you and that's all there is to it."

Then crash bang she hung up.'

'Loved "her"?'

'Right. I'm sure about that.'

'The call, did she make it or receive it?'

'She received it.'

No way to trace. 'Man or woman?'

'She sounded like she was talking to a man but maybe I'm projecting my own values. With her, I guess it could've been either. That's all I know.'

'Nobody else has said anything about it.'

She shrugged. 'Well, did y'all ask?'

'No.'

'Then that pretty much explains it, would'n you say?'

When she had gone Corde bundled his cards together and tossed them into his briefcase. He noticed that the phone booth up the hall was free and he walked quickly to it. As he stood waiting for someone to answer his call, two young men walked past lost in loud debate. 'You're not listening to me. I'm saying there's perception and there's reality. They're *both* valid. I'll prove it to you. Like, see that cop over there? . . .' But at that moment T.T. Ebbans said hello and Corde never heard the end of the discussion.

He lusted for her.

What a phenomenon! He was actually salivating, his nostrils flaring as if he could smell her and he wanted more than anything to pull open her white blouse and slip a high-rider breast into his mouth.

Brian Okun said to Victoria Feinstein, 'I'm thinking of doing a seminar on gender identity in the Romantic era. Would you be interested in being on the panel?'

'Interesting idea,' she said, and crossed legs encased in tight black jeans.

They were sitting in the Arts and Sciences cafeteria, coffee before them. Victoria was Okun's most brilliant student. She had stormed onto campus from Central Park West and Seventy-second Street. He had read her first paper of the semester, 'Gynocriticism and the Old

New Left,' and bolstered by her self-rising breasts and hard buttocks decided she was everything that Jennie Gebben was and considerably more.

Alas this proved too literally true however and he found with bitterness that certain aspects of her knowledge – semiotics, for instance, and South American writers (currently chic topics in the MLA) – vastly outweighed his, a discrepancy she gleefully flaunted. Okun's hampered hope vaporized one day when he saw Victoria Feinstein kiss a woman on the lips outside his classroom. Still Okun admired her immensely and spoke to her often.

It troubled him to use such a brilliant mind in this cheap way.

She said, 'Why Romantic? Why not Classic?'

'Been done,' he dismissed.

'Maybe,' she pondered, 'you could do it interstitially – the Augustan era interposed against the Romantic. You know Latin, don't you?'

'I do, *mirabile dictu*. But I've already outlined the program. I hope you'll think about it. I'd like the panel to be straight, gay, transvestite and transsexual.'

Victoria said, 'Ah, you want a *cross*-section?'

He laughed hard. *Why oh why don't you want to sit on my cock and scrunch around?*

She was courteous enough to ask the question before he had to steer her there. 'Is this for Gilchrist's class?'

'Leon's? No, it's my own idea. He's out in San Francisco. Won't be back for a couple of days.' Gilchrist had in fact called Okun the night before to tell him that he would be arriving in three days and had ordered Okun to prepare a draft of a final exam. Okun noted that the son of a bitch called at exactly the moment a substitute professor was delivering Gilchrist's lecture; he wanted to make certain that Okun hadn't been standing before *his* class.

'What's he doing out there?' she asked.

'Healing the wounds, I guess.'

'How's that?' she asked.

'You know. The girl.'

235

'The girl?'

He looked confused. '*You* told me, didn't you?'

'I don't know what you mean.'

'What was her name? The first one who was killed. Jennie something. I thought you told me. About the two of them?'

She asked in astonishment, 'Gilchrist and Jennie Gebben, they were fucking?'

'It wasn't you who told me?'

'No.'

'Who was it?' He looked at the ceiling. 'Don't recall. Well, anyway, I heard they were a unit.'

'Poor girl,' Victoria said, frowning. 'Gilchrist, huh? I wouldn't have guessed Jennie and him. I heard he was an S and M pup.'

Okun nodded knowingly, quelling resentment that this was the second person who seemed to know for a fact something about his own professor that he had not been aware of.

She continued, 'I'm surprised at the leather. My opinion was that Gilchrist would be more of your classic postwar British pederast. You know, I think they should castrate rapists.'

Okun thought for a moment. 'That might make another seminar. "Mutilation and Castration as Metaphor in Western Literature."'

Victoria's eyes brightened. 'Now there's an idea for you.'

3

She wasn't sure what the vibration was. Alignment maybe. Or a soft tire.

Driving home from Auden University, Diane Corde noticed that the steering wheel seemed to shake; her engagement ring bobbled noisily on tan GM Plastic. Then she realized the station wagon was fine; it was her hand that shook so fiercely – the first time in her life that a reference to money had made her fingers tremble.

Diane was returning from a meeting with the admissions director at the Auden lab school. The woman, who looked sharp and professional (no sultry pink, no clattering bracelets, no hussy makeup), had explained the procedures. Sarah's file, which Dr Parker had already forwarded to the school, would be reviewed by the school's special education admissions board. They would make a recommendation about placing Sarah in one of the classes or arranging for private tutoring.

'I'm sure,' the woman said, 'your daughter will be accepted.'

Diane was grateful to tears at this news.

Then the director had consulted a sheet of paper. 'Let's see . . . Tuition for a special education class at Sarah's level is eight thousand four hundred. Now we—'

'A year?' Diane had interrupted breathlessly.

The woman had smiled. 'Oh, don't worry. That's not per semester. That's for the entire year.'

Oh don't worry.

Eight thousand four hundred.

Which exceeded Diane's annual salary when she'd been receptionist for Dr Bullen, the oldest living gynecologist in New Lebanon. 'Does insurance ever cover it?'

'Medical insurance? No.'

'That's a little steep.'

'Auden's lab school is one of the best in the country.'

'We just bought a new Frigidaire.'

'Well.'

Diane broke the silence. 'Dr Parker mentioned a private tutor is an option. Three times a week, she said. How much would that be?'

The woman had cheerfully parried that the total fee for a tutor would be two hundred seventy dollars a week.

Oh don't worry.

Diane had smoothed her navy blue skirt and studied a cleft of wrinkle in the cloth. She felt totally numb; maybe bad news was an anesthetic.

'So you see,' the admissions director had said, smiling, 'the school is in fact the better bargain.'

Well, Diane Corde didn't see that at all. Bargain? What she saw was everybody taking advantage of her little girl's problem – all of them, Dr Parker the harlot and this pert *L.A. Law* admissions director and the prissy tutors who weren't going to do anything but get Sarah's brain back up to the level where God intended it to be all along.

'Well, I'll have to talk to my husband about it.'

'Just let me say, Mrs Corde, that I think we can be of real help to your daughter. Sarah has the sort of deficit that responds very well to our method of education.'

Well, now, miss, hearing that makes me feel just jim-dandy.

'Shall I start Sarah's application? There's no fee to apply.'

Oh, a freebie!

'Why not?' she had asked, wholly discouraged.

Pulling now into the driveway of her house Diane waved to Tom, standing scrubbed and ruddy beside his Harrison County Sheriff's Department cruiser. After the two threatening Polaroids and the second murder, he had taken to marching a regular line around the backyard at various times throughout the day. He was also armed with his wife's opera glasses, which, he explained, she bought for when they went to Plymouth Playhouse Dinner Theater. With these he'd often scan the forest for hostile eyes. He looked silly, a beefy red-cheeked young man holding the delicate plastic mother-of-pearl glasses, but Diane was grateful for the effort. There had been no more threats and the sense of violation had almost vanished.

'Coffee, Tom?'

He declined, gosh-thanks, and turned back to the woods.

Jamie walked outside, slipping a T-shirt on over his thin muscular body. He was the epitome of grace and she enjoyed watching him climb on his bike and balance while he pulled on his fingerless riding gloves.

'Where're you off to?'

'Practice.'

'When's the match?'

'Saturday.'

'How's your arm?'

'It's like fine. No problem.'

'Garage looks nice.'

'Thanks. I did the windows. They were totally gross.'

'You did the *windows?*' she asked in mock astonishment.

'Very funny. And I found the old Frisbee.'

'We'll play tonight, you and me.'

'Yeah, okay. We oughta get a glow-in-the-dark one. Gotta go.' He pushed the bike forward without using his hands and coasted down the driveway as he closed the Velcro fasteners on his gloves. She watched him lean forward and his muscular legs start to pedal. *He's going to be a heartbreaker.*

Inside the house Sarah was playing with a stuffed animal. After Diane had delivered the news that the school was over for the year, the girl glowed with Christmas-morning happiness. This bothered Diane, who saw in the girl's face the look of a spoiled child who finally got her way.

'The Sunshine Man . . . He came back.'

'Did he now?' Diane asked absently.

'He saved me from Mrs Beiderbug.'

'Sarah. I've told you about that.'

'Mrs Beider*son*.' She sprang up and ran into the kitchen.

Diane hung up her jacket. 'Who's the Sunshine Man again? Which one's he?'

'Mommy.' She was exasperated. 'He's the wizard who lives in the woods. I saw him again today. I thought he'd gone away but he came back. He cast a spell on Mrs Beider—' She grinned with coy nastiness. '—Beider*son*. And I don't have to go back to school.'

'Just for the term. Not forever.'

Although the girl's insistence that magical characters were real frequently irritated Diane, at the moment she wished that she herself had a Sunshine Man to watch over her shoulder. Or at least to cast a spell and cough up some big bucks for special ed tuition. As she looked through the mail she asked, 'Your father call?'

'Naw.'

Diane went into the kitchen and took four large pork chops from the refrigerator. She chopped mushrooms and sauteed them with oregano and bread crumbs then let the filling cool while she cut pockets in the pork.

'You sure your father didn't call? Maybe Jamie took a message.'

'Mom. Like *there's* the board. Do you see any messages?'

'You can answer me decently,' Diane snapped.

'Well, he didn't call.'

Diane carefully cut a slit in the last pork chop.

'I'm not going back to school ever again,' Sarah announced.

'Sarah, I *told* you, it's just for—'

The girl walked upstairs, singing cheerfully to herself, 'Never ever again . . . The Sunshine Man, the Sunshine Man . . .'

Children. Sometimes . . .

The young woman said, 'I believe it was Leon Gilchrist.'

Cynthia Abrams was a thin sophomore, smart and reasonable and unpretentious. Corde liked her. She had long shimmering dark hair, confident eyes, earrings in the shape of African idols. She was a class officer and the campus director of ACT-UP. She was sitting forward, elbows on the low desk in the Student Union, holding a cigarette courteously away from him while she answered his questions.

Corde glanced down and found the professor's name on a card. A note said that Leon Gilchrist had been in San Francisco at the time of the first killing and had not returned as of three days ago. He put a question mark next to the name.

'And you think they had an affair?'

'I don't know for sure. I heard several rumors that she'd gone out with professors over the past couple of years. One or two she was pretty serious about. Then I recently heard Professor Gilchrist's name mentioned.'

'Who did you hear this from? About Gilchrist?'

'I don't remember.'

'Do you know if there was any bad feelings between them?'

'No. I don't really *know* anything at all. I'm just telling you what I heard.'

Corde glanced at his open briefcase and saw the picture of Jennie Gebben. 'Do you know of *anyone* who would have wanted to hurt Jennie or her roommate?'

'No, I sure don't. But I want to say something else. You seem like a reasonable man and I hope I can speak frankly to you.'

'Go right ahead.'

'The gay community at Auden is not popular in New Lebanon.'

This was hardly news to Bill Corde, who had been on a panel to recommend to the state legislature that consensual homosexual activity be removed from the penal code as a sexual crime – both because he thought it was nobody's business but the participants' and because criminalizing it skewed statistics and confused investigations. He had never heard such vicious words as those fired back and forth in the Harrison County Building public meeting room during the panel discussions.

She asked, 'You know Jennie was bisexual?'

'Yes, I do.'

'That fact hasn't come out in the press yet but if it does I'm concerned it will get mixed up with, you know, cult or Satanic aspects of the murders. I abhor the linking of homosexuality and violence.'

'I don't see why that connection would be made,' Corde said. 'It certainly won't come from my department . . .'

Somewhere in Corde's mind was a soft tap as a thought rose to the surface.

'Was Emily . . .' What was the proper terminology? He felt on some eggshells here. 'Was she a lesbian?'

'I don't know. I didn't know her very well.'

'You think Jennie might have been targeted *because* she was bisexual?'

'A bias-related crime?'

'We don't have those laws on the books here.'

She lifted a coy eyebrow. 'I graduate in two years. I hope that will have changed by then.'

'I'm thinking more in terms of helping me with a motive.'

'I suppose. There's always the possibility of antigay violence in areas that are less . . .' Now *she* trod lightly. '. . . enlightened than some.'

Corde considered this motive but he couldn't carry it

very far. He wanted all of his cards in front of him. He wanted to read what other students and professors had told him. He wanted more information about Emily.

He said, 'This has been very helpful. Anything else you can think of?'

'There is one thing I'd like to say.'

'What's that?'

'My roommate, Victoria, and I were having this discussion last night?'

'Yes?'

'She brought up the idea of surgically castrating rapists. Would you be interested in signing a petition to send to the state legislature?'

Corde said. 'I better not. In the Sheriff's Department, we're not supposed to be too, you know, political.'

He couldn't recall the last time he felt so unwelcome.

'Detective, I think it's pretty clear that you're dealing with some kind of crazy person. Some psychopath. He is not a student, it is clearly not a professor. Everyone on this faculty has the highest credentials and the most impeccable background. Your rumormongering is despicable.'

'Yes'm,' Corde said to Dean Catherine Larraby. 'I was asking about Leon Gilchrist? You didn't really answer my question.'

'You're not suggesting that he had anything to do with the deaths of these two girls?'

'Has he ever been in any trouble with students? Here or at another school?'

The dean whispered, 'I'm not even going to dignify that with an answer. Leon Gilchrist is a brilliant scholar. We're lucky to have him on staff and—'

'I've heard from a number of sources that Jennie had relations with at least one professor. One person I interviewed thinks Gilchrist might be him.'

'Professors at Auden are forbidden to date students. Doing so is grounds for dismissal. Who told you?'

'I told her I'd respect her confidence.'

243

She looked for a way to pry this information out of him. Not finding one she said, 'Impossible. It's a vicious rumor. Leon isn't well liked—'

'No?' A tiny note went onto a stiff white card.

'Don't make anything out of that,' she snapped. 'Professors can be like children. Leon has an infantile streak in him, which he has trouble controlling. He makes enemies. People as brilliant as he breed rumors. You didn't answer my question. Is he a suspect?'

'No.'

'He was reading a paper at the Berkeley Poetry Conference at the time of the killings,' she said.

'Did you know that before or afterward?'

'I beg your pardon?' she asked cautiously.

'I'm curious if after Jennie was killed you suspected something about Professor Gilchrist and checked on his whereabouts at that time.'

The eyes went to steel cold. 'I have nothing further to say to you, Detective.'

'If you could—'

'She was killed by a psycho!' The dean's shrill voice tore through the room. 'The same one who vandalized the grade school and churches. The same one who murdered Emily. If you'd taken this psychopath seriously, instead of digging into banal college gossip, Emily would still be alive today.'

'We have to explore all angles, Dean.'

'I'll guarantee you that Leon did not have relations with Jennie and he didn't have anything to do with her death or Emily's. Now if you'll excuse me I'm in the midst of emergency funding meetings, which by the way are necessary largely because you people haven't caught this madman.'

When Corde had left the office Dean Larraby snatched up the phone and snapped to her secretary, 'Is Gilchrist back from the Coast? When's he expected? . . . Who's his teaching assistant?' Her foot tapped in anger while she waited. 'Who, Okun? Give him a call and tell him I want to see him. Tell him it's urgent.'

* * *

Charlie Mahoney was pretty tired of New Lebanon. The incident that had cemented this opinion was a bad meal at Ewell's Diner – particularly bad meat loaf (gristle), extraordinarily bad mashed potatoes (paste) and moderately bad bourbon (oily). This cuisine was followed by an early evening in the motel room where he was now lounging in front of a small TV that was not hooked up to cable. The exact instant when boredom became loathing occurred during a Channel 7 commercial break – four straight minutes of grating ads for products like hog feed and cultivators and used cars and kerosene.

Who the fuck buys kerosene from a TV ad?

He lay on the sagging bed and looked up at the stucco ceiling. Stucco. *Who invented stucco? And why would anybody put it on a ceiling where you had to look at it all night long because there was nothing else to do? How many college sluts had lain here on this bed with their legs in the air and stared at this ceiling thinking stucco who the fuck invented stucco Jesus when is this son of bitch going to finish?* . . .

When Mahoney's thoughts got tired of Midwest decor they ambled over to Richard Gebben.

Mahoney, not a man with much heart to spare for anyone, least of all an employer, had sat with perplexed but genuine sympathy as he watched Richard Gebben absently drive the toy Christmas truck back and forth on his desk, back in St Louis.

Gebben Pre-Formed We Fabricate the World.

'Jennie's mother, I don't know when she's going to come out of it. She may never. She doesn't cry anymore. She doesn't do anything but sometimes she has these, I don't know, bursts of energy, Charlie. She'll be lying in bed then she leaps up and has to polish the silver. The silver, Charlie. For Christsake, we have a *maid*.'

A jet had begun its takeoff run and the tenor roar filled the beige office. The DC-10 was well over Illinois before Gebben spoke again.

245

'Jennie,' he had said, addressing Mahoney, not the spirit of his daughter.

He had proceeded to speak about *reputation*. About the *media*, about *misunderstandings*. He had spoken about *troubling discoveries*. Then he paused and the truck stopped rolling and as he stared out the window at a tall gray McDonnell Douglas hangar Richard Gebben spoke about his daughter the whore.

To Mahoney – a man who had seen evidence of just about every sexual act humankind could think of – the fact that Jennie slept with women as well as men was unremarkable. What was a little boggling, at least in the age of AIDS, was the sheer volume of both men and women she'd had between her legs.

'Charlie, I don't care what you have to do. This fellow Corde is going to be taking her life apart. He's already been looking for diaries and letters. I can't let that happen, Charlie. You know what happens in investigations like this. They look at every little detail of somebody's life. They make up stories about people. The newspapers just love that crap. *You* know, Charlie. It happens all the time. You saw it happen.'

No, Mahoney had never seen it happen. What he saw happen was Ismalah R dissed Devon Jefferies who went home to his crib on South Halsted, picked up his MAC-10 then came a'calling to spray Ismalah R with forty or fifty rounds and the asshole just died where he stood and nobody made up a single fucking thing about him at all.

That was what Mahoney had seen.

And what he saw now was a pathetic Richard Gebben with his pitted face and moist eyes, trying to save what little remained of his daughter.

Well, that was how Gebben had explained Mahoney's mission to New Lebanon, and ten thousand dollars had bought Mahoney's unwavering acceptance of it along with a generous number of encouraging nods and mutterings of sympathy thrown in.

But Mahoney knew there was more.

Gebben had taken many business trips to places that

had a light market share of the Gebben Pre-Formed steel sheeting business, if any at all. Unnecessary trips. To Acapulco, Aspen, Puerto Vallarta, Palm Beach. And he was always accompanied by a sultry blond secretary or young marketing assistant or steno typist. This was the role model he had been for his daughter. It was a lesson she had learned, and learned well, and maybe it had killed her.

And, who knew? Maybe Gebben himself had even come to visit Jennie late at night, Mommy fast asleep . . .

As a cop Mahoney had seen a good deal of emotional pain. He remembered walking up three flights of shit-stinking stairs in a tenement, knocking on the door to deliver some news to a young woman. She listened, nodding vigorously as she held her daughter, who had little plastic toys tied into her hair where pigtails sprouted from her scalp – tiny trains, soda bottles, dogs, dolls. The woman saying, 'I unnerstand, I unnerstand,' and Mahoney thinking, *Understand? You poor bitch. There's nothing* complicated *here. Your old man just got blown away in a drug deal . . .*

But Mahoney knew of course that it *was* complicated.

So complicated she would never *unnerstand* it. As complicated as Gebben's reasons for wanting his daughter's secrets to stay hidden forever. Reasons that Charlie Mahoney, lying on a lumpy bed in front of a flickering Ralston Purina commercial, would never completely figure out.

Not that he needed to. He had his ten thousand dollars and he had a specific job.

Which arrived at that moment in the form of Steve Ribbon, who knocked and called, 'Hey, Charlie? I'm a little late, sorry. You in there, Charlie?'

'Right with you.'

Mahoney let him wait for a full minute then stretched and stood and opened the door.

Ribbon grinned shyly like a police cadet on graduation day. The sheriff, who had ten years on Mahoney, looked

247

like a youngster and Mahoney thought, Damn if these small towns didn't preserve you real well.

'Steve,' he said ebulliently, 'how you doing?'

They shook hands. Ribbon walked in, saying, 'I like that. The way you kept your hand in your jacket when you opened the door.'

'Habit.'

'You looked pretty smooth. Cabrini projects, you were telling me the other night. War zone. Brung a present. You want a drink?'

'Sure.'

Ribbon poured John Begg scotch into squooshy plastic hotel cups. They tapped them together and sipped. Ribbon was in uniform and when Mahoney glanced at the top of the sheriff's head Ribbon took off his Smokey hat and dropped it down on the dresser.

'You're not getting tired of our little town, are you?'

'Tired?' Mahoney grunted. 'It's heaven on earth.' He slipped off his jacket. He hung it up and poured more scotch.

Ribbon's eyes slipped to the large dark gray automatic pistol riding high on Mahoney's right hip.

'Steve, I happened to have a talk with Deputy Ebbans, Jim Slocum and some of the other boys on the case today. I sounded them out about how the investigation's going.' Mahoney's eyes tunneled into Ribbon's, which danced a little, looked briefly back then danced away again. This was fun. It was the way Mahoney used to look at perps and he missed doing it. 'There're a couple of things I've got to talk to you about.'

Ribbon responded exactly the same way the perps had – fiercely studying the scenery behind Mahoney as if memorizing the wall or window or front door.

'But first off. Good news. I just talked to Mr Gebben.'

'Did you now?'

'And you know that reward I was talking about?'

'Reward?' Ribbon frowned. Then he nodded. 'Right, yeah, I recall you mentioning that.'

'Well, he's authorized me to release some of it now.'

'We haven't caught anybody yet, Charlie.' Ribbon snorted a laugh.

'Well, I've told him you're doing a good job and he wants to show his support.'

'That's real kind of him, Charlie.'

'He's a generous man. But I'm afraid we've got to talk about something. Kind of an unpleasant situation.'

'Unpleasant.'

Ribbon licked the rim of his cup and Mahoney let him fret for a delectable minute before he said, 'Again, I don't want to be imposing myself. You're the boss here, Steve.'

'I value your opinion. You're surely more of an expert than any of us.' Ribbon seemed at sea and took refuge in the scotch. He drank long and busied himself with pouring another glass.

'I hate to say anything.'

'Naw, go ahead, Charlie.'

'Well, it's about this Bill Corde.'

Corde pulled into the Town Hall driveway and saw three deputies standing in front of a new Nissan Pathfinder 4X4. It was a beauty. Corde admired it. He saw nothing wrong with buying foreign as long as the quality was better than American. He had a little problem *paying* foreign, having testdriven a Pathfinder himself; he knew he was looking at over twenty thousand dollars worth of transport.

Corde turned his attention away from the truck and back to the lardy figure of Dodd Humphries he was helping out of the squad car and through the parking lot. As he passed the truck Corde said to the men, 'Who's the proud father?'

'Steve bought her.'

Corde laughed in genuine surprise. 'Steve Ribbon?'

'Surely did. Walked right into the dealership and drove out this morning.'

'Hell you say. He was gonna drive that Dodge till it dropped.' Corde looked at the shimmering chrome and metallic-flecked burgundy paint and he said to Lance

Miller, 'He's gone and set a bad precedent. Now everybody's gonna want their trucks with all cylinders running.'

They entered the Sheriff's Department wing. Half the complement was out inspecting the sheriff's new wheels. Jim Slocum was looking at a handful of letters. Corde assumed they were more of the worthless confessions and tip letters that accompany any publicized investigation.

'Dodd, you can't keep doing this,' Corde said to his prisoner.

'Doing what?' the man asked drowsily.

The man's Toyota pickup had sheared a leg off the Purina feed billboard on 116 and dropped a painted sixty-foot Hereford on her black-and-white rump. Miller took him into the lockup in the back of the office. When he returned Corde looked up from the arrest report. 'Two point four. He's more than legally drunk. I do believe he's legally dead.'

Miller said, 'Well, he's legally barfing and he's got bits of windshield falling out of his skivvies. It's all over the floor.'

Corde said, 'Give him some paper towels and make him clean it up. Nobody should be drinking like that on a weekday morning.'

'He'll lose his license this time,' Miller said.

'Hardly matters,' Corde answered. 'That was his last truck.'

Steve Ribbon appeared in the doorway and looked at Corde. 'Talk to you for a minute, Bill.'

Corde followed him into his office and the sheriff shut the door. Ribbon sat down and expanded his cheeks like a blowfish's body and started to bounce a Ticonderoga number two off the drum of his skin. Corde decided it might be a long conversation and sat down in the chair opposite the sheriff's desk.

'Bill . . .' The pencil stopped being a drumstick and became a Flash Gordon rocket crash-landing on the desk. 'Damn this bureaucracy, Bill.'

Corde waited.

'County and state and everybody.'

'Okay, what's up, Steve?'

'I got a call from Ellison.'

'Uh-huh.'

'Bill, this is a damn difficult thing to say to you.'

Corde laughed without humor. 'Then spit it out fast.'

Ribbon said, 'The county's taking over the Gebben and Rossiter cases.'

It took several seconds for the fire to burn across Corde's cheek. 'The county.'

'T.T.'s going to be heading her up.'

'Well, Steve, legally, I suppose, the county can take over any murder investigation it wants to. But the point is it's never—'

'Bill.'

'The point is it's never happened before. All right. I'm a little angry. That's what you're hearing. I don't think we've done anything to make Ellison feel this way.'

'It was the situation at the dorm.'

'*What* situation?'

Ribbon surveyed the rocket pencil's crash site. 'They think you burned her letters and her diary, Bill.'

Corde said nothing.

'They're thinking it was curious you flew to St Louis so fast after the killing. When you didn't find anything there you went to her dorm room and took them and burned it all up. Don't look that way, Bill. They think you were trying to cover up something between you and her. There'll be an inquest next month and you're off the case till it's over.'

4

Wynton Kresge's great-great-great-grandfather, whose name was Charles Monroe, had been a slave, one of two, on a small farm near Fort Henry, Tennessee. The story goes that when the Emancipation Proclamation took effect on New Year's Day in 1863 Monroe went to his master and said, 'I am sorry to tell you this, Mr Walker, but there is a new law that says you can't own slaves anymore, including us.'

Walker said, 'They did that in Nashville?'

Monroe answered, 'No, sir, they did that in the capital, that is to say, Washington, D.C.'

'Blazes,' Walker said, and added that he'd have to look into it. Because both he and his wife were illiterate they had to ask someone to tell them more about this law. Their charming innocence was demonstrated by their choice of Abigail, the Walkers' second slave, to confirm the news. She did so by reading from an outspoken abolitionist penny sheet, which printed the text of the Proclamation while avoiding an inconvenient discussion of Lincoln's jurisdiction to free slaves located in the Confederacy.

'Damnation, he's right,' Walker said. Then he wished Monroe luck and said by any chance you be interested in staying on for pay and Monroe said he'd be happy to and they negotiated a wage and room and board and Monroe kept on working on the Walker farm until he married Abigail. The Walkers gave them their wedding and Monroe named his first son Walker.

Family history.

And probably as embellished and half-true as any. But what Wynton Kresge thought was most interesting was how his children responded to the story. His eldest son, Darryl, eighteen, was horrified that he had been descended from slaves and never wanted the fact mentioned. Kresge felt bad the boy was so ashamed and grumbled that since he was black and had grown up in the United States and not on the Ivory Coast, how come that was such a shock?

Kresge's eldest daughter, Sephana, sixteen, on the other hand often talked about Monroe's plight. Which was how she referred to it. *Plight*. She hated Monroe for going back to work for Walker. She hated him for not putting a Minié ball in his master's head and torching the farm. Sephana had posters of Spike Lee and Wesley Snipes on her wall. She was beautiful. Kresge had put all serious talks with his daughter on hold for a few years.

Kresge's fifth child, named after the ancestor in question, was eight and he loved the story. Charles often wanted to act it out, insisting that Kresge take the role of Mr Walker, while Charles did an impersonation of someone probably not unlike his namesake. Kresge wondered what his youngest son, Nelson, aged two, would say about their ancestor when he learned the story.

These were the thoughts that kept intruding into Kresge's mind as he sat trying to read in the massive bun-buster swivel chair. He felt all stifled and bouncy with nervous energy so he stood up and walked to the window in the far corner of his office. He reached out and rested his hands on the windowsill and did half a dozen lazy-boy push-ups then twelve more and twelve more after that until he smelled sweat through his shirt.

The window overlooked not the quad but a strip of commercial New Lebanon, storefronts and flashing trailer signs and a chunk of the satellite dish on the Tavern. He was anxious and his muscles quivered from using them the wrong way, in a soft office, in a soft university, a soft white university, where you had to keep your temper and give reasons and all the suspects were good students and were trying hard and were just out for some fooling 'round.

He sat on the windowsill, his huge shoulders slumped.

Thinking of his ancestor (perhaps because Walker had ultimately gotten *his* freedom) had put Wynton Kresge in mind of his essential problem – he was not what he wanted to be.

Which was a cop.

He would be a cop in Des Moines. He would be a cop in Cape Girardeau, Missouri. In Sandwich, Illinois. He'd be a cop taking tolls on the interstate if they let him spend a good portion of the time cruising around in a souped-up four-barrel Dodge, tagging speeders and hunting down child molesters and stopping DUIs.

What was ironic – no, what was bitterly mean – was that every day Kresge got résumés from cops all over the country. From real COPS! They wanted to work for him. *Dear Sir: As a law enforcement officer of ten years standing, I am seeking a position in private security services and would like to be considered for any position you might have open . . .*

Knock me upside the head. I mean, this is too much!

Kresge would have dropped down on his massive, linebacker knees to kiss the police academy graduation ring of any one of those applicants and trade jobs in a minute. Gold shields, GLA supervisors, Ops-Coordinators, portable patrolmen, CS technicians. They all wanted to sit in Kresge's cracked leather chair and swivel back and forth and spend the three hours between start of business and lunch deciding how to allocate guards for the homecoming game.

And what did Wynton Kresge want to do but walk a beat?

He wanted to drive an RMP (remote mobile patrol, a squad car to everybody else; Kresge had learned this), he wanted to kick in doors of murder suspects, he wanted to pin drug dealers up against jagged brick walls and scream at them: *WHERE'S THE STASH?* (Was that what they called it? He'd learned a lot but there was much he had not learned.)

He had a very real problem however, Wynton Kresge's first goal in life was to be a cop. But his other goal was to make sure his salary exceeded his age. He now made fifty-three thousand dollars a year (being forty-two he was proud of this accomplishment). He was therefore in the Loop. Hooked. Hung up. Wynton Kresge received a salary not unattainable by senior detectives or police administrators in large cities but a complete rainbow for a rookie. It'd be back to school at no pay then a grunt pulling twenty, twenty-five even with overtime. Kresge alone would be able to cope with a career change of that magnitude. Kresge married might be able to.

But not Wynton Kresge father of seven. He loved cops but he also loved being a good father. He thought about reeducating them. He thought about having a family conference and telling them they were going to have to buckle down. Dad was about to take a fifty percent cut in salary and become a cop. (Man, he could *taste* the silence in the living room after dropping that news.)

So he watched *Miami Vice* reruns and led his men in drills for dealing with students who'd gone ED (the cop word for emotionally disturbed) and with demonstrators who might try to burn down the stadium (none so far) and he kept his thirteen-shot 9mm automatic loaded and ready on his hip waiting for the chance to draw down on a crazed assault-rifle-wielding sniper (none of them either), picking him off from fifty yards on the knoll of the quad.

This was all Wynton Kresge had for police work.

This, and thinking a lot about the murders of Jennie Gebben and Emily Rossiter, which is what he had been doing most of this hot afternoon. He now walked to his desk and balanced a book on his hand then flipped it lightly in the air as if he were tossing a coin to help him make a choice. That was in fact exactly what he was doing and when he caught the book, cover up, Kresge walked abruptly out of his office.

She died two weeks ago tonight. It took me all of fourteen days to lose the case.

Corde spent five minutes looking for change in front of the vending machines, waiting for the jolts of anger that never came. He dropped in thirty-five cents and pushed *coffee milk and sugar*. The steaming liquid poured in a loud stream into a fragile cardboard cup. It sounded exactly like a man taking a leak.

T.T. Ebbans walked up next to him, digging in his pockets. Corde held out a handful of change. Ebbans picked out some and bought himself a Reese's Peanut Butter Cup. 'I'm sorry, Bill.'

Corde sipped the coffee. It tasted salty. The machine's spigot dispensed both coffee and chicken bouillon.

'This's real bushwah. I don't know what's going on. What'd Ribbon say?'

'I'm off the case. He's going to fight the inquest. But I hardly believe him. He didn't fight worth diddly to keep me from getting the boot.'

'The burnt letters?'

'Yup.'

'Did anybody *see* you take them? They have a witness? Any fingerprints? What's their probable cause?'

Corde said, 'We're at the witch-hunt stage now, T.T. The due process comes later – *after* my name's been drug through the dirt.'

After they find out about St Louis. When it'll be too late.

When Ebbans spoke again, after a pause, the flinch in his voice was unmistakable. 'Hammerback ordered me to look into every escape and recent release from the hospital at Gunderson.'

'I've heard this before.' Corde shook his head.

Ebbans continued. 'Yep and then talk to school counselors and psychiatrists in town here and see if they had any patients with, you know, dangerous tendencies.'

'They won't say anything. It's all privileged. Hammerback oughta know that.'

'There was some mention of it in a book that Ribbon keeps loaning to people.'

Corde pointed in the general direction of Blackfoot Pond. 'Well, Emily was Jennie's *roommate*. It's pretty damn odd for a cult killer to pick her for the second victim, wouldn't you say?'

'I just tell what I been told.'

'I know that, T.T.'

Ebbans took a long time staring at the copy of the *Register* sitting in the lunchroom. The front page had a headline: *Terror Continues with Stapleton Girl Cult Threat.*

'What's that?' he asked, pointing to the story.

'Turned out to be the boyfriend she dumped. But the paper had to, you know, put it in terms of the Moon Killer. Damn. Good God damn. . . . Well, the case's yours now, T.T. I told you what I found most recent, about Jennie having that girlfriend and a fight with somebody who wasn't too happy about it. And about them maybe getting killed because they were gay. Oh, and don't forget Gilchrist. He could tell us some good stuff about Jennie.'

'I don't know. Word is we gotta concentrate a hundred percent on the cult thing. Forget the university connection, forget her personal life. Those're orders.'

Corde closed his eyes for a moment, rubbed them. 'Son of a gun, this's great. First I lose the investigation. Then it's forget the school. Then they don't want to hear that the victim might've had a girlfriend . . . I don't know what's going on, T.T. The biggest problem in this case isn't the *killer*, it's us. It's the good guys.'

'Seems that way.'

Corde poured the coffee out then said, 'You know, I was thinking. You're in a tough spot.'

'How's that?'

'Let's say it's what you and me think, that it's not a psycho. That'll mean a lot of wasted time and a lot of panic and news stories about the department's going in the wrong direction. You're walking point on this whole case.'

'Well that's true, Bill. I hope you won't be offended if I tell you that if it turns out right—'

'You'll be in the catbird's seat, and more power to you. But with Ellison and Ribbon right beside you especially come November.'

'I hear what you're saying. But I just want to get that guy, whoever he is. That's all I care about. I'm no good at this politics stuff. It's like people're using those girls' deaths for themselves. They're twisting things around. Makes me sick.'

Ebbans finished his candy and rolled the wrapper into a tiny wad, pitched it out. He looked around and said in a low voice, 'I know you're off the case and everything and you'll be doing a bang-up job keeping the roads free of gin-drunk felons but since you're giving me all your notes and leads it's only fair I give you something in return.'

'What's that?'

'I told you somebody put the kibosh on the school side of the case? The order came from Ribbon and Hammerback. But you know where *they* got the word?'

'Sure, yeah, I know.' Corde grimaced. 'Dean Larraby.'

'Nope,' Ebbans said. 'It was a friend of yours. Randy Sayles.'

Corde considered this. 'Well, well, well. That's nice to know . . . But you didn't hear me say that.'

Ebbans touched his ear. 'Deaf as a mounted trout.'

As he walked out of the vending room Bill Corde stepped right into the broad form of Wynton Kresge. 'Oh, sorry,' Corde said pleasantly, and smiled before he remembered he was mad at the security chief.

Kresge blinked and started to smile back before he recalled *he* too was mad. He ignored Corde and turned back to where he'd been, standing in Jim Slocum's doorway, holding a book open and pointing to a passage.

'Yessir, Chief,' Slocum was saying to Kresge. 'We've pretty much got it under control. But I appreciate your concern.'

'What I'm saying is, you ought to read this . . .' Kresge sounded like he was arguing with a belligerent waitress.

Slocum said formally, 'We've got ourselves a pretty demanding situation, Chief, as you can well imagine . . .'

Corde left the office. He got into his squad car and started the engine. Wynton Kresge came out and walked towards his Olds, which was parked two empty spaces from Corde's cruiser. Kresge's was nice-looking, new. Everybody seemed to have a new car but Corde. Kresge flung the book into the front seat then opened the door. He got in and started the engine. The two men sat twenty feet apart in their cars, staring straight ahead as their engines idled.

A very strained Bill Corde shut off the engine, paused a moment then walked over to Kresge. 'Talk to you?'

Kresge shut off his engine and got out. He stood up, taller than Corde, many pounds heavier. Corde said, 'About last week . . . What I want to say is I'm sorry. At first I didn't think you were right and I'll tell you it didn't have anything to do with you being who you are or anything like that but maybe I was the way you said and if I was I apologize.'

There was a moment of fierce silence and Corde couldn't think of anything to do but stick out his hand. Kresge looked down and seemed boxed into a corner. He took the hand and shook it firmly then released it. 'I'm bad-tempered sometimes.'

'I get kind of caught up in these cases. They can be frustrating.'

'I understand that.' He nodded with a grimace toward the Sheriff's Department.

'What were you doing there?'

Kresge fished the book out of the front seat. 'Finished this today. I'm not saying I'm an expert but I think you're looking for the wrong guy.'

Corde looked at the spine. *Psychotic Functioning*

Individuals: Volume Three. Criminal Behavior.

'Listen up.' Kresge opened the book, found an underlined paragraph, and read: '"In a study of psychopathic and sociopathic (here used synonymously) homicides in England, Scotland and Northern Ireland conducted from 1956 to 1971, we (Irvine & Harrington 1972) concluded that the number of homicides that are in fact astrologically or astronomically driven are exceedingly rare. Of the eighty-nine psychopathic murderers convicted of their crimes, only one was in fact motivated to commit murder on the night of the full moon. In extensive interviews and examinations of records in the man's hometown of Manchester, it was learned that he had been killing animals and human victims indiscriminately, as often as five times a year for the past fifteen years, always on the night of the full moon. He had no sexual contact with his victims and indeed found such thoughts abhorrent. On the other hand, Scotland Yard reported that for the years 1961 through the present, the only years for which such data are available, as many as ten murders per year are committed on the nights of full moons, under the guise of psychopathic episodes when the criminal's true motives for the killing are revenge, robbery, rape and organized-crime expediency."'

'You just read them that?' Corde nodded toward the office.

'Tried. They weren't interested.'

'You mind if I borrow it? Make a copy of some of it? It's kind of a jawful and I'd like to read it slow.'

'It'll be overdue day after tomorrow.'

'I'll do it myself. Tonight.' After a moment Corde asked, 'If you don't think it's a psycho, who would you be looking for?'

'Nobody's been much interested in my opinion.'

'Tell me. Just for the hell of it.'

Kresge said, 'At first I was pretty sure it was the girl's lover. A professor or a student. You should see all of what goes on here on campus. Young people on their own. Doing whatever they want. Fair game for the

261

professors – men *and* women, I ought to tell you. So that was my original thought. But that was before . . .' Kresge's hand rose in a straight-arm salute then closed into a fist. He looked at Corde expectantly.

'I'm sorry?'

Kresge said, 'You know, the knife. So now I figure it was a kid, maybe some punk.'

'Uh-huh.' Corde nodded absently then said, 'What knife?'

'"I come in peace."' Kresge's hand rose and closed again. '"From a land that is here and yet not here."'

'Uh-huh. What are you talking about?'

'Didn't you see *The Lost Dimension*?'

Corde said he hadn't.

'The movie. It was at the Duplex a couple months ago.'

'I don't remember.' Corde was thinking of some film with creatures that had red eyes. 'Oh, wait, was that the one with these snake things?'

'Yeah. The Honons. They were battling the Naryans in the Lost Dimension.'

'But what's . . .' He lifted his hand and closed his fist.

'It's the Naryan salute.' Kresge snorted a baritone laugh. 'Don't you remember?'

'Nup.'

'You mean you guys don't know? . . . About the knife? Back there in that bag.'

The cult knife.

'I saw it on the deputy's desk . . .' Kresge pointed.

'That symbol on the knife. It's from the *movie*?'

'You really didn't know, did you?'

Corde lifted his fingers to his eyes. 'I don't believe it!' He turned toward the department. 'Hell, I gotta tell 'em.'

But he stopped abruptly. Staring at the ancient Town Hall he sucked on the inside of his cheek for a moment. 'Wynton, you want to go for a ride?'

'I guess. Can we go in the squad car?'

'Sure. Only I can't use the siren.'

'That's okay.'

5

They arrived at the toy store just as it was closing.
Together the two large men strode to the door. Kresge
stood awkwardly with his hands on his hips while Corde
knocked. After a moment the owner appeared.

'Can you open up, Owen? Important.'

'I'm closed, Bill. It's suppertime.'

'Open her up. We gotta talk to you. Business.'

'Couldn't you call me—'

'Official, Owen.'

The heavyset, mustachioed man in a plaid shirt and
blue jeans opened the door. The store was dim. Costumes
and helmets and monster masks lining the wall made
the place seem as eerie as a wax museum at night. Some
toy at the far end of the store gave off red dots of light.
Corde looked around and flicked on a light. He squinted
and walked to a rack he spotted just behind Owen. He
stared at thirty stilettos just like the one found under
Jennie Gebben.

'What are these?'

'What do you think they are?' As if Corde had asked
who was George Washington.

'Owen.'

He said, 'They're Naryan Lost Dimension survival
knives.'

'What's that symbol?'

Owen sighed. 'That's the insignia of the Naryan

263

Empire.' He extended his hand the way Kresge had done. "'I come in peace, from—'"

Corde said, 'Yeah, yeah, I know. The movie company makes 'em?'

'They license somebody in China or Korea to make them. They sell all kinds of things. Helmets, xaser guns, Dimensional cloaks, scarves . . . All that stuff in the movie.'

Kresge said, 'He doesn't remember the movie.'

'He doesn't?' Owen asked. 'Like Ninja Turtles a few years ago. T-shirts. Toys. Tie-ins they're called.'

'How many of these knives have you sold?'

'They're a best-seller.'

Corde glanced at Kresge and said, 'I somehow figured they might be. How many?'

Owen said, 'That's I think my third merch rack. Why?'

'Has to do with an investigation.'

'Oh.'

Corde pulled out a pen and handed it and a stack of blank three-by-five cards to Owen. He asked, 'Could you give me the names of everybody you've sold one of those knives to?'

'You're kidding.' Owen laughed, then looked at Kresge. 'He's kidding.'

Kresge said, 'No, I don't think he's kidding.'

Owen's smile faded. 'Practically every kid in New Lebanon bought one. It'd take me an hour to remember half of them.'

'Then you better get started.'

'Aw, Bill. It's suppertime.'

'The sooner you write the sooner you eat, Owen.'

Bill Corde parked the squad car in the lot next to the five-foot-high logo of the Fredericksberg *Register* – the name in the elaborate hundred-year-old typeface as it appeared on the paper's masthead. He and Wynton Kresge got out of the car and walked into the advertising office. The girl behind the counter snapped her gum once and hid it somewhere in her mouth. 'Hi, gentlemen. Help you?'

Corde said, 'Last week I called about running an ad as part of an investigation down in New Lebanon.'

'Oh, that girl that was killed. I heard there was another one too.'

'Did I talk to you?'

'No, that'd be my boss, Juliette Frink. She's left for the day. But I can take the order. How long you want it run?'

'A week, I think.'

'What size?'

Corde looked at samples of ads under a faded Plexiglas sheet covering the counter. 'What do you think, Wynton?'

Kresge said, 'May as well go pretty big, wouldn't you think?'

Corde pointed to one. 'I guess that size.'

She looked. 'That's two columns by seventy-five agates.' She wrote it down. 'What section of the paper would you like?'

'Oh. I hadn't thought. Front page?'

'We don't have ads on the front page.'

'Well, I don't know. What's the best-read section?'

'Comics first then sports.'

Corde said, 'I don't think we can run an ad like this on the comic pages.'

Kresge said, 'But sports, you might lose women, you know.'

The clerk said, 'I read the sports page.'

'How about the same page as the movie ads?' Kresge said.

'That sounds good,' Corde said.

She wrote it up. 'Juliette said you get a public-service discount. That'll be four hundred eighty-four dollars and seventy cents. Then you want us to typeset it for you that'll be another twenty-five dollars. You have cuts?'

'Cuts?' Corde blinked. He was thinking of the thin

slash the rope had made on Jennifer Gebben's throat, the fishhook embedded in Emily Rossiter.

'Pictures, I mean.'

'Oh. No. Just words.' He wrote out copy for the ad. Corde pulled out his wallet and handed her his Visa card. She took it and stepped away to approve the charge.

'What is it,' Kresge said. 'You pay then get reimbursed?'

Corde snickered. 'I guess you oughta know, I was just relieved of duty.'

Kresge frowned severe creases into his wide face. 'Man, they fired you?'

'Suspended.'

'Why?'

'They claim I took some letters out of Jennie's room.'

'Did you?' Kresge asked, but so innocently that Corde laughed.

'No,' he said.

'Hardly seems fair,' he said. 'You mean, you're paying for this ad yourself?'

'Yup.'

He wasn't though, it turned out. The clerk, embarrassed, returned. 'Sorry, Officer . . . They kind of said you're over the limit. They wouldn't approve it.' She handed the card back to him.

Corde felt the immediate need to explain. But that would involve telling her a long story about two children – one with primary reading retardation – and a psychiatrist and a new Frigidaire and roll after roll of Owens-Corning attic insulation and a boy coming up on college in a few years. 'Uh . . .' He looked for a solution in the back of the cluttered Advertising Department.

Kresge said, 'Miss, Auden has an account here, right?'

'The university? Yessir. The student affairs office. Ads for plays and sports. I was to the homecoming game last fall. That third quarter! I'll remember that all my life.'

'Yes'm, that was a game and a half,' Kresge said. 'Can you put these on the school account?'

'You work for the school?'

'Yes, ma'am,' Kresge said. 'I do.' He pulled out his identification card. 'I'll authorize it. This's official school business.'

She rummaged under the counter and pulled out a form. 'Just sign this requisition here. Fourth and twelve on the Ohio State forty. Did Ladowski punt? No sir. And it wasn't even a bomb but a hand-off to Flemming. Ran all the way, zippity-zip.'

'While I'm about it,' Kresge said, 'run that ad for *two* weeks and put a border around it like that one there.'

'You got it.'

'That's real good of you, Wynton,' Corde said. 'I do appreciate it.'

'People keep forgetting,' Kresge said quietly, 'they were my girls too.'

Corde spent the evening talking to the parents of boys who'd bought Naryan Dimensional stilettos. He was easygoing and jokey and careful to put them at ease. No, no, we don't suspect Todd Sammie Billie Albert not hardly why he's in Science Club with Jamie . . .

'I'm just,' he would tell them, 'getting information.'

They nodded gravely and answered all his questions and smiled at his jokes.

But they were scared.

Men and women alike, they were scared.

The second killing had proved the cult theory. The words that Corde had spoken to chubby Gail Lynn Holcomb had been proved utterly false. They *did* have something to be scared of. As far as the good citizens of New Lebanon were concerned, Satan himself had arrived, with two murders to his name and more on his mind.

Corde went from house to house and listened to parents, without exception, account for every minute of each boy's whereabouts on the night of April 20 – a feat possible, Corde knew as a father, only if every man and woman he talked to had turned psychic.

He saw through much of the smoke of course but still found no leads.

Long about midnight Corde noticed a dusty drawer somewhere in his mind. It seemed to contain Sheriff's Department regulations and he believed, when he peered into it, that he saw something about officers who continue to engage in police work when suspended being guilty of impersonating sheriff's deputies. He peered further and saw the word 'misdemeanor' though his mind was often very dark and the word might actually have been 'felony.'

Corde felt suddenly pummeled by fatigue. He returned home.

A county deputy, Tom's replacement for the evening, sat in the driveway. Corde thanked him and sent him home and then went into the house. His children were asleep in their rooms. His wife too. Corde was grateful for that. He wasn't looking forward to telling Diane that he'd been suspended.

The next morning he was up early. He kissed Diane, dodged a chance to give her the hard news and slipped out for a secret meeting with T.T. Ebbans. They rendezvoused outside the Sheriff's Department on the hard-packed dirt the deputies sometimes used for impromptu basketball games. They both felt like spies or undercover narcs, padding around out of sight of the department's grimy windows.

Corde told him about the knife and Ebbans slapped his head. 'Doggone, I saw that movie.'

'So'd I, T.T., and I'll bet every deputy in there did too. Hell,' he said in a whisper, 'I'll bet Ribbon's even got the comic book. I talked to maybe thirty people last night. Here's the list and my notes. Nothing real helpful.'

Ebbans took the sheet. 'Watch yourself, Bill.'

Corde tapped his holster.

'I don't mean that. You forget you're suspended?'

'This thing's too important to leave to Ribbon. You got what I asked you for?'

Ebbans handed Corde a plastic bag containing the green computerized accounting ledger that they'd found in the burnt oil drum. 'Don't lose it, Bill. I'm taking a chance as it is.'

'I think I've found me an expert who can help.'

'I also looked into the Gilchrist angle. Forget about it. He flew out to San Francisco to read some paper on Saturday before Jennie was murdered and he was still out there when Emily was killed. I don't think he's back even yet.'

'You might want to talk to him though. He might know some of Jennie's boyfriends. Or girlfriends.'

'Maybe I'll ask him on the sly.' Ebbans added, 'We've pulled up with a stitch on this mental-patient stuff. And the occult bookstore leads are going nowhere. This whole cult thing is looking thin as October ice. I think we oughta tell Hammerback and Ribbon.'

'Hold up a while,' Corde said gravely. 'Next thing you know you'll be off the case too and Jim Slocum'll be our new investigator in charge.'

'Hey now,' said Ebbans brightly, 'that'd give us a chance to read Miranda to werewolves and vampires.'

'Mrs Corde? Hello. My name is Ben Breck.'

Diane held the phone warily. From the man's cheerful voice, she suspected a salesman. 'Yes?'

'I'm from the Auden University lab school. You were speaking to the admissions department about a tutor?'

It turned out that he *was* a salesman of sorts but Diane listened anyway. Breck was selling something pretty interesting.

'I'm a visiting professor from the University of Chicago. I noticed your daughter's application for admission to the Special Education Department.'

And how much are you going to cost, Doctor Visiting Professor from the Big City? A hundred an hour? Two?

'Our daughter's seeing Resa Parker, a psychiatrist in

town. She recommended we find a special ed tutor.'

'I know of Dr Parker.' Breck then added, 'I've done a lot of tutoring and I thought I might be able to help you.'

'Dr Breck, I appreciate your call but—'

'Money.'

'Beg pardon?'

'You're worried about the fees at Auden. And I don't blame you one bit. They're outrageous. I wouldn't pay them myself.'

My, my, a doctor with a sense of humor. How refreshing.

'It is one of my considerations,' Diane admitted.

'Well, I think you'll find me fairly reasonable. I charge twenty dollars an hour.'

Breck named a figure that two weeks earlier would have paled Diane; now she felt as if she'd pocketed found money. 'That's all?'

'I do ask to use the results of your daughter's progress in my research. Anonymously, of course. I'm scheduled to publish my findings in the *American Journal of Psychology*. And I'm doing a book to help teachers recognize the problems of learning disabled children.'

'Well, I don't know . . .'

'I hope you'll think about it, Mrs Corde. From the application it looks like your Sarah has a lot of potential.'

Diane said, 'You've worked with students like Sarah before?'

'Hundreds. In the majority of cases we've cut the gap between reading and chronological age by fifty percent. Sometimes more.'

'What are these techniques?'

'Feedback, monitoring, behavioral techniques. Nothing revolutionary. No drugs or medical treatment . . .'

'Sarah doesn't do well with medicine. She's had some bad reactions to Ritalin.'

'I don't do any of that.'

'Well,' Diane said, 'I'll discuss it with my husband.'

'I hope to hear from you. I think Sarah and I can help each other a great deal.'

* * *

> Seven days till the half-moon.
> Do you know where your .357 is?

T.T. Ebbans walked into the New Lebanon Sheriff's Department, glancing at the sign, and asked, 'Who put that up?'

Jim Slocum looked up from that day's copy of the *Register* and said, 'I did.'

'Could you please take it down?'

'Sure. Didn't mean anything. Just thought it'd be kind of a reminder. For morale, you know.'

Ebbans sat down at his desk. On it were fifteen letters from people who claimed they knew who the killer was because they had dreamed about it (eight of them) or had psychic visions of his identity (four) or had been contacted in a seance by the victims (two). The remaining correspondence was from a man who explained that in a former life he had known Jack the Ripper, whose spirit had materialized in a condominium development outside of Higgins. There were also twenty-nine phone messages about the case. The first two calls Ebbans returned were to disconnected phones and the third was a man's recorded voice describing how much he loved sucking cock. Ebbans hung up and gave the rest of the messages to Slocum and told him to check them out.

Corde's news about the knife had both elated and depressed him. It had cheered him up because it was a solid lead and like any cop he'd take a single piece of hard evidence any day over a dozen psychics or a week's worth of the most clever speculation. The news had also depressed Ebbans because it meant the line of the investigation he had inherited was looking pretty abysmal. Corde's warning about Ebbans walking point, which he'd discounted at first, came back to him. Ribbon wasn't pleased with the *Register* story that morning. *"Cult" Weapon in Auden Death Is Movie Toy*. The sheriff had said coolly, 'Guess your boys should've checked that out to start.'

My boys.

Ebbans returned to a stack of discharge reports from a mental hospital in Higgins. Ten minutes later the door swung open and a man in blue jeans and a work shirt stood uneasily in the doorway. Ebbans frowned, trying to place him. It took a minute.

The red hat man, without the hat.

'Detective?'

'Come on in.'

The man said, 'What it is, I just thought you'd like to know. You asked me about those boys I seen the night that girl was killed. The boys by the pond? I was leaving the lake and just now one of them was back. He had his tackle but he wasn't fishing, he was just walking around, looking at things. Would he be the Moon Killer?'

Ebbans stood up and said, 'He out there now?'

'Was when I left.'

'Miller, come on, you and me're taking a ride.'

So like what's the reason?

Why is this guy your friend?

Jano didn't have any answers. Philip was a freak. He was fat and had bad skin – not zits, which everybody had, even Steve Snelling, who could have any girl he wanted. It was more that Philip's skin was dirty. Behind his ear it was always gray. And his clothes were hardly ever clean. He smelled bad. And forget about sports. No way could he even play softball let along gymnastics. Jano remembered how his friend had strained to get up on the parallel bars and he had watched horrified as the wood rods sagged almost to breaking point under the weight.

Why were they friends?

This afternoon Jano was walking around Blackfoot Pond, holding the gray chipped tackle box and the rod and reel. Tracing steps, trying not to think about that terrible night of April 20. He felt bad. Not depressed but fearful, almost panicked. He felt as if a screaming Honon warrior in an invisible Dimensional cloak was racing toward him from behind, preparing to leap, closer closer closer, to tear him apart. Jano's heart galloped in his chest, heating his blood as it pumped and he felt terror spatter him like a spray of hot water. Like a spray of come.

He pictured the girl lying in the mud, her white fingers curled, her eyes mostly open, her bare feet with their long toes . . .

No no no! She's not an actress in a movie, thirty feet high on the screen in the mall. She is exactly what she is: pretty, heavy, smelling of mint, smelling of grass and spicy flowers. She is still. She does not breathe. She is dead.

Jano shuddered, feeling the Honon troops circling around him, and found he was staring at the crushed muddy blue flowers at his feet. He thought of Philip drowning the other girl, holding her down. And what was he, Jano, going to do now? Who could he talk to? Nobody . . . The panic crested and he sucked in air frantically.

Eventually he calmed.

Why is he your friend?

Well, he and Phathar *did* talk about sci fi a lot. And movies. And girls. For a guy who never dated, Philip was an expert on sex. A walking dictionary of terms that every fifteen-year-old should know. He told Jano how gay guys shoved their fists up each other's asses and how you could tell whether a girl was a virgin by the way she bent over to tie her shoes.

But Jano decided that their most common bond was how much they hated their fathers. Phathar was scared of his and that made plenty of sense because the old man was a total hatter. (One Halloween, Philip's dad had come into the yard, sneaking up behind trick-or-treaters, carrying bloody cow's intestines in his arms. He'd just stood staring at the totally freaked kids). But Jano's father was worse. He was like a Honon warrior hiding in a Dimensional cloak, passing through the house as if Jano didn't exist. Sneaking past, looking at his son oddly, then vanishing.

... The dimensional warp swelling out out out finally bursting into the now, the here, all that purple energy of the Naryan realm flooding onto the earth ...

The movie had had a happy ending. Jano didn't think this life would. He climbed to the top of the dam and then dropped onto his knees. He leaned forward looking at his gray reflection in the still water. He didn't like water that was so still. It made him look like death. His thin face. He lowered his head to the water. He wondered what it was like to breathe water instead of air.

Look at that, Jano. You ever touched a girl there? You ever tasted a girl?

He stared at the water. He could smell its oily sourness.

You ever fucked a girl, Jano?

By lowering his head another two inches he could taste the water. He could lick it. The same way that Phathar gave him the opportunity to taste the girl's cold mouth, her tongue, her cunt. He could swallow the water, he could swallow her, hide in her forever. A princess—

'Excuse me, young man.' The voice was like a chill downpour on his back. He leapt up. 'I talk to you for a minute?' The deputy was tall and very thin.

Jano's mouth was dry as summer pavement. He swung his tongue back and forth between his sticky teeth and didn't say anything.

'What's your name?'

'I didn't do anything.'

'I'd just like to talk to you.' The deputy was smiling but Jano'd seen that smile before and didn't believe it. A lying smile. The same smile his father kept on his face. 'I understand you and a friend were fishing here at night about ten days ago.'

Jano couldn't speak. He found his skin was contracting with terror and he imagined that his bowl of thick hair was vibrating visibly. Other footsteps sounded behind him. He turned.

Lance Miller grinned and said to him, 'Hey, how you doing?'

Jano didn't answer.

The other cop looked at Miller and said, 'You know him?'

'Sure, T.T.,' Miller said. 'This's Bill Corde's son. Didn't you introduce yourself, Jamie?'

6

With panic in his voice Randy Sayles said, 'I have a lecture.'

'He said it's now'r never.'

'A LECTURE!'

'Professor,' the departmental secretary said, 'I'm only reporting to you what he said.'

'Shit.'

'Professor. There's no need to be vulgar.'

He sat at his desk at nine o'clock in the morning, gripping the telephone receiver in his hand as if he were trying to squeeze out an answer to the dilemma. Sayles's last lecture of the year was scheduled to begin in one hour. It was set against the centennial celebrations throughout the US in 1876. The climax was a spellbinding account (his students', not his, review) of the Custer massacre. For him to miss this particular class was obscene. This fucko fund-raising crap had totally disrupted his teaching and he was torrid with rage.

He said, 'Tell him to hold.' He dialed the dean. Her secretary said she was out.

'Shit.'

Yes, no, yes, no? Sayles said into the receiver. 'Okay, I'll see him. Get Darby to take over for me.'

'The students will be disappointed.'

'*You're* the one who told me it was now or never!'

She said, 'I was only—'

'Get Darby.' Sayles banged the phone down and ran from his office, hurrying to his car. As he roared out of the professors' parking lot, he laid down two streaks of simmering rubber as if he were a sixteen-year-old in a stolen 'Vette.

He paced across the gold carpet, staring down at the stain made by the cola Sarah spilled the night Emily was murdered.

'Oh, Bill.'

'It doesn't mean I'm fired. I still draw pay.'

'What were these letters?'

'Who knows? We found ash. We found scraps.'

He looked up at his wife. Before Diane did something she dreaded, her eyes grew very wide. Astonishingly wide and dark as night. This happened now.

Bill Corde waited a moment, as if taking his temperature. The sense of betrayal never arrived and he said finally, 'I didn't take them.'

'No.'

He couldn't tell how she meant the word. Was she agreeing? Or disputing him?

She asked, 'They don't know about St Louis, do they?'

'I never told them.' He did not tell her that Jennie Gebben had known.

She nodded. 'I should see about a job.'

'I told you I'm not fired. I—'

'I'm just thinking out loud. This is something—'

'Well, there's nothing wrong with that.'

'This is something we have to talk about,' she continued.

But they didn't talk about it. Not then at any rate. Because at that moment a squad car pulled into the driveway.

Corde leaned against the glass. He smelled ammonia. After a long moment the front door of the car opened. 'It's T.T. He's got somebody with him, in the back. What's he doing, transporting a prisoner?'

Ebbans climbed out of the squad car and unlocked the back door. Jamie slowly stepped out.

Halbert Strumm, who lived in an unincorporated enclave of Harrison County known as Millfield Creek, had made his fortune in animal by-products, turning bone and organ into house plant supplements marked up a thousand times. Strumm would say with sincerity and drama that it brightened some stiff gelding's last walk up the ramp to know he was going to be sprinkled lovingly on a tame philodendron overlooking Park Avenue in New York City. It was comments like this that kept Strumm held in contempt or ridicule by all the people who worked for him and most of the people who knew him.

Although he had not attended Auden University, Strumm and his wife Bettye had embraced the school as their adoptive charity. Their generosity however was largely conditional and they invariably looked for an element of bargain in their giving. Off shot a check for a thousand dollars *if* they got subscription seats to the concert series. Five hundred, a stadium box. Five thousand, a trip to the Sudan on a dig with archeology students made wildly uncomfortable by the couple's rollicking presence.

Now Randy Sayles, pulling into the Strumms' driveway, was not sure if the couple was going to like the deal he was about to propose. Strumm, a huge man, bald and broad, with massive hands, led Sayles into his greenhouse, and there they stood amid a thousand plants that seemed no healthier than those in Sayles's own backyard garden, which did *not* gobble down the earthly remains of elderly animals. There was an injustice in this that depressed Sayles immensely.

'Hal, we have a problem and we need your help.'

'Money, that's why you've come. It's why you always come.'

'You're right.' Sayles leaned hard into the abuse. 'I'm not going to deny it, Hal. But you understand what

Auden does for this town. We're in danger of losing the school.'

Strumm frowned and nipped off a tendril of green from a viney plant. 'That serious?'

'We've already drafted severance letters to the staff.'

'My word.' *Nip.*

'We need some money and we need your help. You've always been generous in the past.'

'You know, Professor, I'm in a generous mood today.'

Sayles's heart beat with a resounding pressure, he heard the hum of blood speeding through his temple.

'I might just be inclined to help you out. Do I assume you're talking about some serious bucks?'

'I am, that's true.'

'You know I went to a state school.'

Sayles said, 'I didn't know but that's okay.'

'Of course it's fucking okay,' Strumm barked. 'We didn't have a good team. We had a terrible team. I always thought if I had it to do over again I'd go to a school that had a good team.'

'Auden has a pretty good team.'

'It's got a nice stadium.'

Sayles said it did, that was true. 'Modeled on Soldier Field in Chicago.'

'That a fact? I've had a dream in my life,' Strumm said. 'A man gets older and he starts to think about his dreams more and more.'

'Happens to all of us.'

'One of my dreams has been to make a lot of money.'

Well, you certifiably crazy old cocksucker, you sure have done that.

'Another's to give some of it to a school like Auden . . .'

Are you playing with me or is this for real?

'And in exchange . . .'

Spit it out.

'. . . they'd build a football stadium in my honor. You see, I had my chance and I didn't seize it. So the next best thing would be to have a stadium named after me.'

'Well, Hal, we have the stadium already.'

'Named after Barnes. Who was he?'

'One of our graduates in the 1920s. A philanthropist. He set up an endowment that's still in effect.'

'So that means you're not inclined to change the name of the stadium?'

'It's in the terms of the endowment. There's nothing we can do about it.'

Strumm studied a sickly plant and sprinkled on its leaves something out of a package labeled "Strumm's Extra." *Extra what?* Sayles wondered. The businessman said, 'Well, enough said of that. I've had another dream. I've always wanted a reactor named after me.'

'A nuclear reactor?'

'At Champaign-Urbana I think it is, they've got a research reactor named after somebody. I thought that would be almost as good as a stadium.'

'Hal, we don't need a reactor. We don't have a science department to speak of. We're mostly liberal arts.'

What was in the white-and-yellow packages? Old horses? Old pigs? Strumm shit?

'I'd write you boys a check for two hundred thousand dollars if you built a reactor and named it after me.'

Sayles said quietly, 'Hal, we need three and a half million.'

Nip.

'That much, hum? I couldn't come close to that. Been a bad year for the company. Economy's down, people get rid of plants. First thing to go. I'm not recessionproof like everybody says.'

'Auden's going to close.'

'Even if I had a stadium and a reactor both I couldn't come up with much more than a quarter million.'

'We can name a chair after you. A building. We've got a couple buildings. You could have your pick.'

'Three-hundred's the top. Maybe for a vet school I could go up to three-fifty but that'd be the end of it.'

'We don't want a vet school, Hal.'

'Well, there you have it.'

Nip.

281

Sayles drove at seventy miles an hour all the way back to the campus. His car came to rest partially over the curb of the parking lot. He ran through the corridors of the Arts and Sciences Building and stopped in front of the door to his lecture hall, composing himself and listening to Glenn Darby's voice explain about Sayles's absence.

He caught his breath then pushed the doors open and strode confidently down the long aisle to the podium. He was halfway there when the class realized he had returned and broke into applause, which grew ever louder, rolling and rolling, then was joined by whistles and shouts. By the time he was on the podium, clipping on his lavaliere mike, the applause had became a standing ovation and it was five minutes before he was able to quiet the students.

Then – barely holding back tears – Randy Sayles began to speak, resonantly and impassioned, delivering what might very well be his last lecture at Auden. Or, for that matter, his last lecture at any university.

Corde was no longer pacing. He sat on the couch, slouched down and grim, and Diane was sitting in a straight-backed chair nearby. She held her hands in her lap. Jamie Corde sat between his mother and father. He looked shrunken. 'Son, this is pretty serious. I don't need to tell you that.'

'I didn't do anything.'

'T.T. said you told him you were at the pond by yourself the night the Gebben girl was killed.'

'I was. I was just fishing by myself is all.'

Diane said, 'Honey, please.'

Her eyes were on a studded milk-glass candy dish and it was impossible to tell if she was speaking to father or son.

'Jamie, we *want* to believe you. It's just that T.T. talked to a couple of people say they saw *two* boys and you fit the description of one of them.'

'So you don't believe me. You think I'm lying.'

This was a matter-of-fact announcement. He wouldn't hold Corde's eyes, which was okay with Corde because he would sure have trouble looking back into his boy's.

'Son, we need to know what happened. I don't remember where you were that night, I—'

Jamie leaned forward. 'How would you know where I was *any* night?'

Diane said sternly, 'Don't talk to your—'

He continued, 'Where was I *last* night? Two nights ago? How the hell would you have any idea?'

His mother rebuked, 'Young man.' But there was no edge to her words.

The boy was quiet for a moment. Then he said, 'I went fishing. I was there by myself.'

A felony investigator, Corde had a dozen tricks he could try to drag the real story out of the boy. Bluffs and traps and intimidations. He'd learned them from his journals and seminars and bulletins. He'd practiced them in his continuing education courses. He'd tried them out on car thieves and burglars. He couldn't bring himself to use them now; he was crying out for the truth but he wanted it only one way.

'Were you fishing by the dam?'

'Not so close to the dam. Up a ways, in somebody's yard.'

'I've told you you're not to trespass there.'

Jamie didn't answer.

Corde asked, 'Did you see the girl or anyone else that you hadn't recognized before?'

'No. I just fished then I came home.'

'Why didn't you tell me any of this before? You knew I was on the case.'

'Because I was there alone and I didn't see anything. What was there to say?'

'Jamie, please.'

The boy looked away. 'I'm going to my room.'

'Jamie . . .' Corde scooted forward on the couch and touched his son's knee. The boy remained unresponsive.

Corde asked the question he'd been putting off. 'The other night, Wednesday, you weren't home either, were you?'

Diane said, 'Bill, what are you asking?'

Jamie kept his eyes on his father. 'He wants to know my *whereabouts* the night the second girl was killed. That's what he's asking.'

Corde said, 'Wait a minute, son. You can't treat this so light. T.T. and Steve are going to want to talk to you . . .' Jamie walked casually out of the living room. Corde's face went bright red with fury and he stood. Then he sat slowly on the couch again.

Diane said, 'You know he didn't have anything to do with it.'

'I know he was there.' Corde looked at her miserably. 'And I know he's lying to me. That's all I know.'

Dear Sarah . . .

She read the note again but had trouble because of the voices from the other room. Something was going on with Jamie. Her brother scared her some. At times she idolized him. When, for instance, he would include her in what he was doing – like repeating jokes to make sure she got the punch line or taking her along when he went shopping at the mall. But other times he'd look at her like she wasn't even in this world, as if he was looking *through* her. He would get all dark and secretish. In Jamie's dresser Sarah had found magazines filled with pictures of women without any clothes on and a lot of copies of *Fantagore* – movie scenes of monsters, and people being stabbed or cut up.

She guessed her father had found the magazines and that was why they were fighting.

She tried to ignore them now and turned back to her immediate problem.

Which was what should she give to the Sunshine Man?

She wanted him to have something special. Something personal from her. But when she tried to think of a present her mind went blank. Maybe she could—

The sounds from the next room grew louder. Jamie was mad and her parents spoke in grim voices. It was the way they had talked when Grandpa got sick in the middle of the night and went to the hospital and then didn't come home ever again.

Then the voices finally stopped and she heard Jamie go into his room and close the door and she heard music start up, the soundtrack from that science fiction movie he'd seen three or four times.

What would the Sunshine Man like?

When her parents went to parties her mother always took a cake or something like that. But Sarah didn't know how to bake. She looked around the room, surveying her toys, videotapes, a dozen stuffed animals. . . . Ah, that seemed like a good choice – because he had made Redford T. Redford fly out to the circle of stones two weeks ago it was pretty clear that he liked animals and they liked him.

She picked one, a small cinnamon bear that her mother had named Chutney.

She put a pink scarf around Chutney's neck and then carried him to the window and together they looked out over the backyard. She took the note from her pocket. This time she read it out loud so that the bear could hear what the Sunshine Man had written to her.

Dear Sarah, meet me tomorrow at our magic stones. Be there at three o'clock. Don't tell anyone. I'll make sure you never have to go to school ever again.

Dean Larraby said, 'I suspect you have two minds about it.'

Brian Okun said, 'Well, of course . . . What can I say? He's my boss. I've learned more about literature from him than from anyone. I respect him immensely.'

The dean continued, 'He was in San Francisco when the murders were committed. So the rumor that he was involved in the girls' deaths, well, there's no foundation to that.'

'You mean, Leon was a *suspect?*'

'The police, you know how it is. Fools. But I'm not concerned about the deaths. The question is whether Professor Gilchrist was dating either Jennie Gebben or Emily Rossiter. Do you know if he was intimate with either of them?'

'Is that what you asked me here about?'

'You're the one he's closest to.'

Okun shook his head. 'But if he's not a suspect . . .'

The dean's square matronly face turned to Okun. This was her pose of sincerity but she spoke with menace. 'I think the most despicable misuse of power is for a professor to seduce his students.'

'I agree one hundred percent. But I don't believe it for a minute about Professor Gilchrist. In fact the only rumors I heard were about him and Jennie. Nothing about Emily.'

'So you *did* hear something.'

He paused, his eyes evasive with embarrassment. 'But you can't believe campus gossip . . .'

'If he was sleeping with her I'll have him dismissed at once.'

'Of course the temptation's there. He lives alone, you know. He's a recluse.' Okun shook his head. 'No, what am I saying? No, as far as I know he never dated her.' The voice lowered. 'There was some talk, you know, that he was a, well, homosexual.'

The South surfaced in both grimace and inflection. 'That's nearly as bad,' she muttered.

As bay-ad. Okun deliberated for a moment. 'I . . .'

'Yes?'

He shook his head. 'I was going to suggest something. But it doesn't really seem supportable.'

'Please say it.'

'Well . . .' Okun's voice faded and his eyes landed on the dean's diploma. University of Kentucky. *Chahm school . . .*

286

She said, 'I hope you feel your first loyalty is to Auden.'

He sighed. 'Dean, I'm as concerned about this as you are. To be blunt, I've invested a lot of time and effort in Leon. I have nothing but respect for him and I want to see him vindicated. I want the opportunity to prove he's innocent. Let me check around his office, see if I can find something about Jennie. Maybe a note from her. Maybe an entry in his desk calendar. If I can't, well, let's just accept that this was a tragic rumor. If I do I promise I'll show it to you and you can make your own decision.'

'That's very courageous of you.'

'It's not courageous at all. This school's been good to me. I owe Auden a great deal.' Okun paused. 'The only thing is . . .'

'Yes?'

'Well, I'd be taking a big risk. This would be, well, spying.' He extended his palms and laughed at the plebian word. 'Leon would fire me in a minute if he found out I'd looked through his personal things.'

'If he was sleeping with Jennie we'd dismiss him. He'd be no threat to you.'

'But if he *wasn't* sleeping with her . . .' *You stupid bitch.* 'That,' he added delicately, 'is the only time when it would be a risk.'

'Of course.' The dean debated and Okun watched her thoughts stroll to where his were impatiently waiting. She said, 'There would be a simple way of protecting you. You've applied for a teaching position here, haven't you?'

'Subject to the acceptance of my dissertation, of course.'

'I could talk to the Appointments Committee. I couldn't guarantee much of a salary.'

'I'm a scholar,' Okun said. 'Money is irrelevant.'

Through the window came a buzz of an old lawn mower. A breeze was blowing but he could detect no scent of cut grass. Okun looked at the worker moving like a drone. He felt abject pity for the man's unimaginative life, a mass of dull years utterly without the cocaine of intellect.

The dean asked coyly, 'Have we just agreed to something?'

A quote of Nietzsche's came to mind. Okun rewrote it slightly and was pleased with the result. *Man is the only animal that makes promises and fulfills threats.*

7

After a sleepless night Corde drove Jamie to the Sheriff's Department. Red-eyed and ragged with anger and exhaustion, Corde had sat silently in the car. Jamie, however, was talkative, almost flighty, as if the two of them were going fishing. In fact he seemed *happier* than if they were going fishing. It made Corde's anger boil harder.

He remembered the way his son's eyes used to brighten when Corde took him for an unauthorized ride in the squad car, a delight Jamie had had no desire to experience in the last few years. Corde glanced at him then back to the road. Somewhere deep in his son, he eagerly believed, was Corde's own fundamental manner, which is why he felt so often that words were unnecessary between them. And now it hurt, oh it hurt, to see the boy wall this nature up as well as he did, secure as a hogtied prisoner, with this chatter. Corde didn't say a single word all the five-mile drive to the Sheriff's Department.

T.T. Ebbans said, 'Hello, Bill. Hi, Jamie.'

Miller waved uneasily to both of them. Corde looked at the astrological chart on the wall prominently taped above Slocum's desk then nodded to both men. Through the doorway of Ribbon's office Corde saw Ribbon and Charlie Mahoney the Family Representative talking. The sheriff glanced up, saw Jamie then walked over to the others. Mahoney hung in the doorway.

There was a long moment's silence then Corde said, 'Jamie tells me he was alone that evening.'

Ebbans was nodding. He had on his face a smile that meant nothing. 'Well,' he began and fell silent. No one spoke. Ribbon stared intensely at the boy. Corde studied the floor.

'Jamie,' Ebbans finally continued. 'We just want to ask you a few questions. You don't mind, do you?'

'No sir.'

'Why don't we go into the back office?'

The boy looked at his father and started after Ebbans. Corde followed. Ribbon said, 'Bill. Just a minute.' He stopped. Ebbans and Jamie disappeared through the door. Neither looked back.

'Best wait here, Bill.'

'I'd like to be with my boy.'

'He didn't say *anything*?' Ribbon asked in a low voice.

'He says he was alone, didn't see the girl or anybody.'

'Do you think he's lying?'

Corde looked into Ribbon's eyes. 'No. Now if you'll excuse me.'

Ribbon touched his arm. 'We talked about it, Bill. We think it's better if you're not there.'

'He's a minor. I've got a right to be present during . . .'

Corde's voice faded and Ribbon verbalized Corde's sudden thought. 'He's not a suspect, Bill. We're just treating him like a witness.'

'I—'

Ribbon shook his head. 'It's better for the investigation and better for you not to be in there. We want to avoid any, you know, appearances of impropriety.'

Corde turned toward the door. Thinking how easy it would be to lift Ribbon's hand off his arm and walk out of the office and into the room where Jamie was. What he did was to take off his hat and drop it on a nearby desk.

Steve Ribbon stepped away, stood for a minute looking

out the window then said, 'We've got to go fishing one of these days.'

Corde said softly, 'You bet, Steve.'

'You little shit.' Charlie Mahoney walked slowly around Jamie.

Mahoney was impressed the boy wasn't crying. He decided he'd have to try harder. 'You're a fucking *liar*. I know it. Your father knows it. And you know it.'

'I was by myself.' Jamie looked at the door. Deputy Ebbans had left a few minutes ago to get Cokes. Jamie was just now catching on that he wasn't coming back.

'Oh, cut the crap. What do you think this is? Like breaking curfew? You think you're gonna get fucking *grounded* for this? You think they're going to take away your *allowance?* I'm talking *prison!* I'm talking about hard time up in Warwick. You're how old? Sixteen?'

'Fifteen,' Jamie said.

Now the boy's voice was quivering.

'You're fifteen now but by the time you come to trial—'

'Me?' His voice cracked.

'You'll be sixteen and they'll send you into the adult wing. That's it, kid. You're fucked.'

And he was starting to cry.

'I didn't do it. I swear I didn't.'

Mahoney sat and leaned forward. 'You don't know jack shit, you little prick! Jack shit. We've gotta find *somebody*. And 'cause we don't have anybody else, as far as I'm concerned that somebody is you.'

Jamie wiped his face. 'Where's my father?'

'He said he was leaving.'

'No! He said he was going to be here with me.'

'He just said that to get you in here. He told us you're lying.'

Jamie looked at the door. His teeth touched and he breathed hotly. 'He did not.'

'He said you lied to him and you'd lie to us.'

'He didn't say that. He wouldn't.'

'Who the hell were you with? You have a daisy chain going, pulling each other's dicks?'

'I'm not a homo!'

'You're not? Then you wouldn't mind a little pussy. A pretty girl walking by herself. A pretty little *college* girl. Were you the one that came all over her?'

The tears were thick. 'I didn't do anything.'

'How many times did you see the movie?'

'What movie?'

Mahoney leaned forward and screamed, 'Will you cut out this bullshit?! How many times did you see *The Lost Dimension*?'

Jamie looked down and picked at a ragged fingernail. 'A couple. I don't know.'

Mahoney said slowly, 'You know, your father gave us some of your shorts. Ones you'd been wearing while you were beating off. We've got samples of your come. We're going to match it against what we found in the girl.'

'My father . . .' Jamie whispered.

'We know there were two of you. We've—'

'He gave you my underwear?'

'We've got enough now to convict *you*. But we don't want to leave that other asshole wandering around the streets. You give his name to us and you'll walk. I guarantee it.'

Jamie looked desperately at the door.

'I was alone.'

Mahoney waited for a long, long minute then kicked back his chair and stood. 'I gotta crap. People like you make me want to shit. I'll be back in three minutes. Think real hard, kid.'

Mahoney left the room. The door remained open about six inches and through the gap Jamie could see the back door of Town Hall. He gazed through the half window at the parking lot and the thick trees beyond.

Outside, it was a May school day. The sun was brilliant and insects zipping through the light flashed like sparks. Outside, kids were lining up to be picked for softball in PE class, they were jogging, playing soccer

292

and tennis, swatting golf balls.

Outside was an entirely different dimension from that in which Jamie Corde now sat.

The sunlight grew in radiance. No, it had moved closer to him! He was astonished to find himself on his feet, no longer sitting in the hard chair. Now, walking across the interrogation room. Now, pushing into the dark corridor, staring all the while at the back window. In the hallway, pausing. The light began to approach him, slowly at first then picking up speed, rushing toward him, as his heart thudded with a shockingly loud pounding, beating ever faster. The light filled his vision, it illuminated his flushed skin, it grew very close. And Jamie understands that no no the sound is not his heart at all but the drumming of his running shoes on chestnut floorboards. His hands rise palms out fingers splayed, the back door explodes outward and a million splinters of glass precede Jamie Corde into the golden light.

One man jumped at the sound. The other did not.

Mahoney looked at the shocked face of T.T. Ebbans, who ran into the corridor behind the Sheriff's Department and stared as the back door, now lacking most of its glass, swung slowly closed once more.

He stepped across the hall to the interrogation room and looked inside then glanced out the broken door and saw Jamie sprinting away from the station house.

'Deputy, you better—'

Ebbans turned his gaunt face to Mahoney. 'Jamie wouldn't run like that. What'd you say to him?'

Mahoney nodded toward the shattered door. 'You better stay on him. You know where he's going.'

Ebbans said evenly, 'I should tell you, sir, I think you're a real son of a bitch.'

'Deputy, he's getting away.'

'What are you doing here?' Corde asked.

Mahoney, walking through the squad room, glanced at the coffee he sipped. 'Devil's brew.'

'Were you in there with my son?'

'I just looked in on him. He and T.T. were talking.'

Corde stepped into the corridor and saw the empty room. He returned as Mahoney was dumping sugar into his cup. 'Where is he?'

'Your kid? I think T.T. said they were going to the lake and look around. I don't know.'

Corde walked to the front door. 'He should've told me.'

Mahoney noticed the evidence envelopes containing the Polaroids and the messages they carried. 'What's this?'

Ribbon answered tentatively, as if asking for Corde's approval, 'Somebody left them for Bill. He thinks they might be his daughter.'

'You show them to her, ask her about it?'

'She didn't see them, no. My daughter has a learning disability. She's going through a rough time right now. This would upset her.'

'Well,' Mahoney said with an exasperated laugh, 'that'd be a shame, but—'

'I asked her if anybody'd taken her picture recently and she said no.'

'You say she's slow?'

'She's not slow,' Corde said evenly. 'She has an above-average IQ. She has dyslexia and dyscalculia.'

'Does she now? Maybe somebody talked her into posing and warned her not to tell anybody about it. That happens all the time.'

'I know my daughter.'

Mahoney, fingering the photos, said, 'Your son, does he have a Polaroid camera?'

Corde turned to Ribbon. 'Can I see you for a minute, Steve?'

The men walked into the sheriff's office, Corde leading. Ribbon left the door open. Corde reached back and closed it. He hardly ever lost his temper but the problem was he couldn't tell when it was going to happen.

Ribbon said, 'All right, Bill, I understand—'

Corde's teeth pressed together fiercely. 'No more with that guy! I don't want him crossing my path.'

'He's—'

'Let me finish. It may be that Jamie knows a little more than he's saying but you know him as well as any boy in town and he wouldn't take those pictures. I'm not going to listen to this crap anymore!'

'But Mahoney doesn't know Jamie at all and you can't condemn him for asking the question.'

'Hell yes I can! This thing is *way* out of hand. The town's scared out of its mind. We got the paper counting down the days till another moon and we're going to get ten more folk shot.'

'You'll remember it was my thought not Charlie's about the moon.'

'Was he interrogating Jamie?'

Ribbon paused. 'He's been helping out some. Bill . . . Look, he's a famous homicide detective.'

'Oh, Steve, come on.'

'We need all the help we can get. This isn't a frat hazing that got out of hand.'

'Do you know where T.T. took my son?'

'I don't know if he did. Or where.'

Corde opened the door and walked into the squad room.

Mahoney said, 'Hold up, Detective.'

Corde walked toward the door.

'Hey, Detective . . .'

Corde kept going.

The window was open, letting in the scent of lilacs and whatever snatches of breeze might penetrate the staleness of the room. The morning was quiet. Philip's father was at the warehouse. His mother was asleep. She hadn't wakened her children in time for school. Philip lay in bed, eating from a box of graham crackers. Crumbs dusted his chest and stomach. He'd wait until ten, when his PE class was over then wake his mother and have her write him a tardiness excuse.

Outside he heard footsteps. He rolled over and looked out the window. 'Hey, Phil!' The voice was urgent.

Philip looked into the stand of lilac bushes. He saw Jamie Corde, sweating and pale. 'Hey, Jano, what's the matter?'

'I went by the school. What're you doing home?' Before Philip could answer he continued urgently, 'Come on out here. I gotta talk to you.'

Philip rolled out of bed, pulled on jeans and a sweatshirt then walked through the house. His sister was asleep under a mound of pink satin comforter. In his parents' room Philip's mother also lay asleep. Her mouth was open and her lipstick had left wet, red blotches on the pillow around her face, like stains of fresh blood. He continued outside, onto the back porch.

'Hey, man,' Philip called, walking barefoot down the stairs, 'what's—'

'I was just at the police.'

The boy stopped walking. 'What did you tell them?'

'Nothing,' Jamie whined. 'Nothing.'

Shit. The knife. That's what it was. He knew it. He felt sweat break out on his forehead. Philip continued into the bushes and sat down. Jamie sat too.

'What do they know?'

'They know I was there and they know I was there with somebody that night. They've got a sort of description of you.'

'Shit. Like, how did they find that out?' Suspicion filled Philip's round face.

'I didn't say anything. My father . . .' Jamie said. 'He . . .' He couldn't bring himself to say anything else about it. He pictured his father going through the dirty clothes, finding his underwear, putting it in an evidence bag . . . He began to cry. 'They said we're going to *prison!* What are we going to do? Oh, man.'

Jamie's hands were shaking but Philip was calm. In the dimension where he spent much of his time nothing was impossible, nothing was what it seemed. Maple trees were sodium boosters of intergalactic vehicles.

Sidewalks were crystal walkways a thousand feet above the plasma energy core of the planet. Stars weren't stars at all but holes in the paltry three-dimensional world through which the all-powerful, all-brilliant Guardians trillions and trillions of light-years big looked down. In Philip's world fat boys in dirty jeans were sinewy, lithe heros, who could pull on cloaks and disappear from their terrible crimes. 'We have to vanish,' he said softly.

'Vanish?'

'Like, dimensionally.' He added in a whisper, 'Permanently.'

Jamie whispered, 'It was just a *movie*, man.'

Philip continued in his quiet voice, 'We're both fucked. You want to go to prison? Then what? Come back and live at home? With your father?' He smiled in a weary way. 'This dimension sucks, Jano.'

Jamie was silent.

'We took an oath,' Philip said quietly. 'We took an oath—'

'We shouldn't have done it to her.'

'An oath to the death.' Philip looked up at the sky through a cluster of faint purple lilacs. '*That* dimension's real. This one isn't. We took an oath. Are you going back on it?'

Jamie grabbed a black branch dotted with buds and small blossoms. He stripped the sinewy twigs away, like peeling skin off bones, and flung the branch away furiously with a low moan.

Philip said, 'Remember Dathar? The way he leapt off the Governance Building? They thought they had him but he got away.'

'He didn't get away. He died. The Guardians brought him back but he died.'

'It's the same thing,' Philip whispered. 'He got away.'

Jamie said nothing.

The sound of a siren, howling like a dentist's drill, filled the front yard. Philip's smile vanished as the squad car skidded to a stop. He stared at his friend. 'You told them!'

'No!' Jamie scrambled to his feet.

Footsteps sounded. Running, the men spread out. Ebbans and Slocum and Miller and two other deputies.

'You turned me in!' Philip screamed as he began willing his huge body to run, feet pointing outward, stomach and tits bouncing with every step, feeling the sting of his chafed legs and the deeper pain of a struggling heart.

'Whoa, boy, hold up there!'

'Stop him! Slow him up!'

Slocum was chuckling. 'He's doing okay for a big fellow.'

Somebody else laughed and said, 'We need ourselves a lasso.'

The men easily caught up with Philip and pulled him to the ground. They were laughing as if they'd grounded a suckling pig for a barbecue. Handcuffs appeared and were ratcheted on pudgy wrists.

One of the cops asked Jamie a question but the boy missed the words. All he could hear was the sound of Philip's voice, filling the backyard, as he shrieked, 'You turned me in, you turned me in, you turned me in!'

8

Corde paused outside the house.

He saw: a broken lawn mower, termite-chewed stacks of black firewood, a V-6 engine block sweating under a foggy plastic tarp, rusty tools, four bloated trash bags, bald tires, a garbage can filled with brackish water. The lawn was riddled with crabgrass and bare spots of packed mud. Showing through the scabby white clapboard of the house were patches of milky green from an earlier paint job.

Three brilliant bursts of color tempered the grim scene – orange-red geraniums in clay pots.

Inside were T.T. Ebbans, Jim Slocum, Lance Miller and the two county deputies. Charlie Mahoney was not there. On the couch sat Philip and Jamie. Creth Halpern stood over his boy, staring down at him. His arms were crossed and he had an eerie smile on his face. Jane Halpern sat in a chair off to the side of the room. Her eyes were red and her lips were glisteningly wet. Corde didn't know much about her. Only that she'd been a thin, pretty cheerleader in the New Lebanon High School class behind his, and she was now a thin, pretty drunk.

The house smelled bad. Food and mold. He also could smell animal and he vaguely remembered a dog nosing in weeds behind a shed in the backyard. With the door wide open the brilliant outdoor light, which looked unnatural in the dank room, revealed a coat of grime and spheres of dustballs. The windows were mostly shaded. Corde stepped on something hard. He kicked away a small, dried dog turd. He crouched next to Jamie. 'You all right, son?'

The boy looked at him silently with an undiluted hate that made Corde want to weep. He motioned to Ebbans and the two of them stepped outside. 'What happened, T.T.? Did you and Mahoney spook Jamie and follow him here?'

To his credit in Corde's mind Ebbans held the detective's eyes and answered honestly. 'I'm sorry, Bill. That's what happened. He just asked to see him for a few minutes by himself and Steve told me to let him. I didn't know what he had in mind. I swear that.'

Corde said, 'You don't think Philip did it, do you?'

'Take a look at what we found.' Ebbans led him to the squad car. Inside was a foot-high stack of porn magazines and violent comic books, also sketchbooks and notebooks. Corde flipped through the crudely drawn pictures of spaceships and monsters, montages of photos cut out of the school yearbook: girls imprisoned in towers and dungeons, chained to walls while snake creatures circled around them. Much of the material had the Naryan insignia hand-printed on it.

Corde thought of the picture of Sarah, her skirt high over her thighs.

'He had this incendiary thing hooked up. We opened the drawer where he'd hid all this stuff and it started to set fire to the file cabinet. It blew a fuse before it did any damage. Lance went through the backyard. In the barbecue he found some scraps of Jockey shorts the kid'd tried to burn.' Ebbans touched a small plastic bag. 'They were stained and it could be semen. Oh, and we also found some pictures of a naked girl. Polaroids.'

Polaroids.

'Jennie?'

'Can't tell. It's a girl's breasts.'

'It's not . . .' Corde dodged Ebbans's eyes. 'Not a younger girl, is it?'

Ebbans said, 'Not a little girl, no.' He continued. 'And I found a pair of muddy boots. I'm doing casts.'

From the porch Slocum offered, 'It all fits the profile. The smut collection, the home situation, everything.'

Corde ignored this and said to Ebbans, 'You didn't question him by himself, did you? He's got to have his parents present.'

'No. I didn't question him at all. But I'll tell you, his father's not going to be much help to the kid. He's the one sent us out to the barbecue. Told us he saw Philip burning something there the night after the first killing.'

Corde stared at the pile in the back seat of the car. In the center of Corde's bulletin board was a sign that he'd sent off for from *National Law Enforcement Monthly* a couple of years ago. The brittle yellow slip of glossy paper read: *Physical evidence is the cornerstone of a case.* He was looking at physical evidence now. Physical evidence that could put two boys in prison for forty years. And one of them was his son.

Ribbon and Ellison arrived in one of the county's fancy Furies. The slogan on the side said, *If you drink, do us all a favor. Don't drive.* Ebbans told them what they'd found.

Inside Halpern was leaning over his son, who stared straight ahead. 'What the hell was going through your mind?' The boy's eyes were glazed. He didn't speak. His face wasn't particularly sad or frightened. He seemed to be possessed.

Philip played at the Corde house once or twice a week. But was this the boy who'd taken the pictures of Sarah? Who had put the threatening newspaper article on the rosebush? And in Diane's diaphragm case?

Was this the boy who murdered Jennie Gebben and Emily Rossiter?

He looked at Philip's round, soft face, smudged with dirt or chocolate, a face that did not appear so much guilty as bewildered.

Corde said, 'Jamie, come here.'

Slocum's head turned. 'Say, Bill . . . maybe it's not such a good idea. Uh, talking to him in private, I mean.'

Corde squashed his temper and ignored the deputy. He motioned to his son. The boy stood and followed him onto the porch. Ribbon stepped forward.

Corde stopped him with a look. 'Leave me alone with my boy.' The sheriff hesitated only a moment before stepping away.

Jamie leaned against the porch bannister and turned to his father, 'I don't have anything to say to you.'

'Jamie, why are you being this way? I want to help you.'

'Yeah, right.'

'Just tell me what happened.'

'I don't *know* what happened.'

'Son, it's murder we're talking about. They're looking for somebody to send to jail for this.'

'I know *you* are.'

'Me?'

'You want me to make up something about Phil?'

'I want you to tell the truth. I want you to tell it to me right here and now.'

'Bill?' Ribbon came to the doorway. 'You can be present at questioning but—'

'Oh, goddamnit,' Corde exploded. 'Goddamnit! You don't have probable cause to charge him. Call the DA. Ask him!'

Ribbon said delicately, 'We do for conspiracy and obstruction. You'll just make things worse for everybody.'

'Jamie, why?' Corde's eyes begged, his hand reached for his son's arm but stopped short of contact. 'What did I do? Why won't you tell me?'

Eyes downcast, the boy let Ribbon lead him into the filthy house, while his father's desperate questions fell like shot quail, silent and flimsy.

The tall grass waved in the wind and the sunlight flickered off the leaves of thin saplings. Sarah stepped into her circle of stones and sat down. She crossed her legs carefully. From her backpack she took the bear she was going to give to the Sunshine Man and set him next to her.

She looked at her Madonna watch. It said 2:40. She closed her eyes and remembered that this meant twenty minutes to three. She hated numbers. Sometimes you counted to a hundred before they started over, other times you counted to sixty.

Twenty minutes until the Sunshine Man arrived.

She remembered a drill at school – her second-grade teacher would move the hands on a clock and then point to different students and have them tell the time. This exercise socked her with icy terror. She remembered the teacher's bony finger pointing at her. *And, Sarah, what time is it now?* She screamed that she didn't know she couldn't tell don't ask don't ask don't ask . . . She cried all the way home from school. That night her daddy bought her the digital watch she now wore.

A sudden breeze whipped her hair around her face and she lay down, using her backpack as a pillow. Sometimes she took afternoon naps here. Looking around her, wondering where the Sunshine Man would come from, Sarah noticed just above the horizon a sliver of new moon. She imagined that the sky was a huge ocean and that the moon was the fingernail on a giant's hand as he swam just below the surface of the smooth water. Then she wondered how come you can see the moon in the daytime.

She closed her eyes and she thought of the giant as he swam, lifting arms as big as mountains from the water, kicking his mile-long legs and speeding across the sky. Sarah was afraid of the water. When the family went to the park downtown she would still play in the baby pool, which made her ashamed but wasn't as bad as the terror of bouncing on the adult pool floor with the water inches from her nose and thinking she might get swept into the deep part.

She wished she could swim. Strong strokes, like

Jamie. Maybe this was something else she could ask the Sunshine Man to do for her. She looked at her watch. 2:48. She counted on her fingers. Two minutes . . . No! *Twelve* minutes. She closed her eyes and kneaded the grass bunched up at her hips and pretended she was swimming, skimming across the pool like a speedboat, back and forth, saving the lives of children struggling in the deep end and racing past her brother once then again and again . . .

Five minutes later she heard the approaching footsteps.

Sarah Corde's heart began pounding in joyous anticipation, and as she climbed out of her imaginary pool she opened her eyes.

Look at this place. Lord.

Bill Corde couldn't get over the size of Wynton Kresge's office.

'Plush.'

'Yeah, well.' Kresge seemed uncomfortable.

The room was probably a third as big as the entire New Lebanon Sheriff's Department. Corde took pleasure walking over the thick green carpet and wondered why two busy oriental rugs had been laid over the pile.

'That's the biggest desk I've ever seen.'

'Yeah, well.'

Corde sat down in one of the visitor's chairs, which was itself bigger and more comfy than his own Sears armchair at home, and his a recliner at that. He tried to scoot it closer to the desk but it wouldn't move and he had to stand again and lug the chair up to the desk.

Kresge explained, 'Was the office of some dean or another. Academic affairs, something like that. He retired and they needed someplace to put me. I think they like having a black man on this corridor. See, when you come this way from the main stairwell you see me at my big desk. Looks good for the school. Think I'm a big shot. Little do they know. So they caught the kid.'

'They caught him. He was a friend of my son's.'

'Well.' Kresge would be wondering whether he should ask the question about how close a friend but he let it pass.

'The evidence is pretty strong against him. He's a spooky boy and his father's worse.' Corde realized he still had his hat on – it banged into the high back of the chair – and he took it off, pitched it like a Frisbee onto the seat of the other chair. He opened his briefcase. 'I need a favor.'

'Sure,' Kresge said eagerly.

Corde leaned forward and set a plastic bag in front of Kresge. Inside was the burnt scrap of computer paper.

'What's this?'

'A bit of that paper we found behind—'

'No, I mean this.' The security chief pointed at the white card attached to the bag by a red string.

'That? A chain of custody card.'

'It's got your name on it.'

'It's not important, Wynton. The piece of—'

'This's for trial, right?'

'Right. So the prosecutor can trace the physical evidence back to the crime scene.'

'Got it. So that if there's a gap in the chain, the defense attorney can get the evidence thrown out?'

'Right.' Because Corde was here to ask a favor he indulged Kresge, who was examining the COC card closely. Finally Corde continued, 'The piece of paper inside? I'd like to find out where it came from. I've got this idea—'

'You're leaning on it.'

'—it's from the school. What?'

'You're leaning on it.'

'On what?'

Kresge motioned him away. Corde sat back in the chair and Kresge yanked a thick wad of computer printouts from beneath a stack of magazines. Corde had been using the pile as an armrest.

'It's a university Accounting Department printout. They send them around every week to each department.

Mine shows me security expenses, real and budgeted, allocation of overhead. You know, that sort of thing.'

'You know what department this was from?'

Kresge looked at it. 'No idea.'

'Any chance you could find out?'

'Technically I don't have access to the Accounting Department's files.'

Corde asked coyly, 'How 'bout untechnically?'

'I'll see what I can do.' After a pause he asked, 'But if they caught the boy what's the point?'

Corde slowly touched away a fleck of lint from his boot heel and stalled long enough that an attractive woman blustered into the office with an armful of letters for Kresge to sign. The security chief rose and with clumsy formality introduced two people with nothing in common except their lack of desire to meet. Corde, however, was grateful for the curious decorum – it seemed to drive the question from Kresge's mind and after the signing-fest, when their conversation resumed, he did not ask it again.

9

She could sense him nearby, almost as though he was hovering right over her body like a wave of hot sunlight.

She swung her head about, peering into the clearing, into the forest, the tall grass.

More footsteps, leaves rustling, twigs snapping.

(So: He doesn't fly, he doesn't materialize, he doesn't float. He walks. That's okay.)

Sarah looked for the glow of sun as he approached but she could see nothing except trees and branches, leaves, grass, shadows. The footsteps grew closer. Hesitant, uncertain. Then she saw him – a figure in the woods, coming slowly toward her, picking his way through the brush. He seemed less like a wizard than, well, a big man tromping noisily through the forest. *(That's okay too.)*

'I'm over here. Here!' She stood up, waving her arm.

He paused, located her and slowly changed direction, pushing aside branches.

She picked up the stuffed bear and ran toward him. She shouted, 'I'm here!'

A sheet of bright green leaves lifted aside and the deputy stepped out, brushing dust and leaves off his uniform.

'Tom!' she cried, her heart sinking.

'Hey, missie, how'd you get here without getting all messed up?' He picked a leaf out of his hair then swatted his forehead. 'Skeeter.' He examined his palm.

Crestfallen, Sarah stared up at him.

'You're not supposed to be out here, you know. You could get me in a whole mess of trouble. You're supposed to stay close to the house. Anyway, 'nough said. Your mom wants to see you now. You've got an appointment at the doctor's, she says.'

'I can't come right now.' She scanned the forest. *He's leaving! I can tell. The deputy scared him off.*

'Well, I don't know,' Tom said patiently. 'Your mother told me to fetch you.'

'Not now, please? Just a half hour?' She was close to tears.

'That's a cute little fellow you've got there. What's his name?'

'Chutney.'

'How about if you and Chutney come home now and afterward you come back here with me and I'll keep an eye on you? How'd that be?'

When she didn't answer, the deputy said, 'Your mom'll be pretty unhappy with me if I don't bring you right now, like she asked. You don't want her to have words with me, do you?'

It was true. If she didn't come now, if she missed the appointment with Dr Parker, her mother would be furious with the deputy. Sarah couldn't stand the thought of anyone being mad because of her. People hated you when you made them mad, they laughed at you.

She looked around her once more. The Sunshine Man was gone now. He'd fled and was far away.

'Why you looking so sad, little lady?'

'I'm not sad.' Sarah walked through the grass. 'Come this way. It's easier.' She led him out of the tall grass into the strip of land beside the cow pasture and turned toward the house, certain that she and the Sunshine Man would never meet.

Special to the Register – *A freshman at New*

Lebanon High School has been charged in the 'Moon Killer' slayings of two Auden University co-eds, law enforcement authorities announced today.

The fifteen-year-old youth, whose identity has been withheld because of his age, was apprehended by town and county deputies at his parents' home yesterday afternoon.

'He clearly fits the profile that we were working from,' said New Lebanon Sheriff Steve Ribbon. 'He had a collection of deviate photographs and drawings of girls from the high school. It looked like he had a whole series of assaults planned.'

Sheriff Ribbon added that authorities are looking at the possibility that the youth was involved in the slaying last year of another Auden co-ed, Susan Biagotti.

'At the time,' he said, 'it appeared that the girl was killed during a robbery. But the way we're looking at it now, it might have been the first in this series of killings.'

Some residents greeted the news of the arrest with cautious relief. 'Of course, we're glad he's been caught,' said a New Lebanon housewife who refused to give her name, 'but it seems like there's still a lot of questions. Was he doing this alone? Is it safe for my children to go back to school?'

Others were less restrained in their reaction. 'We can breathe again,' said one Main Street shopkeeper, who also insisted on anonymity. 'My business came to a standstill the last couple of weeks. I hope he gets the chair.'

Under state law, a fifteen-year-old can be tried as an adult for murder, but no one under eighteen can be sentenced to death. If the jury convicts the youth of first-degree murder, his sentence could range from thirty-five years to life and he would have to serve at least twenty-five years before he would be eligible for parole.

Diane had found a psychiatrist cartoon in a magazine and cut it out for Dr Parker. It showed a little fish sitting in a chair holding a notebook. Next to him was a huge shark lying down on a couch and the little fish was saying to the shark, 'Oh, no, it's perfectly normal to want to eat your psychiatrist.' Diane kept studying the cartoon and not getting it. But the expression on the face of the shark was so funny she broke out in laughter.

Which wasn't as loud as the laughter that escaped from Dr Parker's mouth when she looked at the clipping. Maybe the woman *did* have a sense of humour after all. Dr Parker pinned the cartoon up on her bulletin board. Diane felt ecstatic, as if she'd been given a gold star at school.

Sarah was in the waiting room. Dr Parker had asked to see Diane first today. By herself. This troubled Diane, who wondered what kind of bad news the woman had to report. But seeing the doctor laugh, she sensed this was no crisis. As Dr Parker rummaged through her desk Diane told her about Ben Breck.

'Breck? I think I've heard of him. Let's look him up.' She spun around in her chair and found a huge book. She opened it and flipped through. 'Ah, here we go. He's forty one . . . Impressive. Summa cum from Yale, ditto an M.A. and Ph.D. in psychology. Ph.D. in education from Chicago. He's taught at a number of Ivy League schools. Currently tenured at Chicago. Published extensively in the journals. Visiting at Auden, is he? Lucky you.'

'So I should take him up on it?'

'Cheap tutoring from an expert. I'd say there isn't much of a choice there.'

'I've already told him I would.'

'I think you'll see some dramatic improvements in Sarah.' The doctor looked at her watch. 'This session will be very short, Mrs Corde. A few minutes with you, a few with Sarah. I'm not going to charge you for the time.'

'My horoscope for this month must've said, "You will

meet two generous therapists."'

Dr Parker's sense of humour had been spent on the cartoon; she ignored the pleasantry and dug again with some irritation into the bottom of her desk drawer. Finally she extracted a small black box.

The doctor said, 'You're going to see Sarah carrying this around with her. Tell your husband and son to leave it alone. Don't touch it, don't listen to it, don't ask her about it. Unless she says something first.'

Diane asked the most innocuous question she could think of. 'Is it a tape recorder?'

'That's right.'

'What's it for?'

'I'm going to reconstruct Sarah's self-esteem.'

'How?'

She answered tersely, 'Sarah's going to write a book.'

Diane smiled, a reflex. Then she decided that the joke was in poor taste and she frowned. Dr Parker pushed the recorder, a blank cassette and an instruction book toward Diane, who scooped them up and held them helplessly. When the doctor said nothing more Diane said, 'You're not joking, are you?'

'Joking?' Dr Parker looked as if Diane were the one making the tasteless comment. 'Mrs Corde, I'd think you'd know by now I rarely joke.'

Diane Corde believed that the perfection of children's fingers was proof that God existed, and she thought of this now watching her daughter hold the tape recorder, examining it with some small suspicion and turning it over in her pale hands. Diane unfolded a tattered copy of the instruction manual and took the recorder back. She set it on the living room coffee table. In her left hand she held two AA batteries and a new cassette.

'I think we should . . .' She examined the instruction sheet.

'Lemme,' Sarah said.

Diane read. 'We have to—'

'Lemme.'

Click, click, click. 'There.'

Diane looked down. Sarah had the machine running and was pressing the Play and Record buttons simultaneously, saying, 'Testing, testing.'

'How did you do that? Did you read the instructions?'

Sarah rewound the tape and pressed another button. Diane's tinny voice repeated, '. . . *read the instructions?'*

'Mom, come on. Like, it's easy.' She looked at the recorder then back up to her mother. 'Dr Parker wants me to make up stories and put them in my book.'

'That's what she said.'

'I don't know what to write about. Maybe Buxter Fabricant?'

'I think Dr Parker would like to hear that story. He's the dog that became president, right?'

'I like Buxter—' Sarah scrunched her nose. '—but I already wrote that story. I could write a story about Mrs Drake Duck . . . No, no, no! I'm going to write a story about Mrs Beiderbug.'

'Sarah. Don't make fun of people's names.'

'It's going to be a good story.' Sarah dropped the recorder in her Barbie backpack.

Jamie appeared in the doorway. He was eating a sandwich and carrying a glass of milk. From the way he was looking at Sarah, Diane knew he wanted to talk about something out of the girl's presence. He turned and walked back into the kitchen. She heard the refrigerator door opening and the shuffle as he pulled out a plastic gallon jug of milk.

Diane stood up and walked into the kitchen. She took a package of chicken from the freezer and set it on a pad of paper towels, taking her time as she cut away the plastic wrapper. Jamie sat at the table and silently stared at his glass of milk, which he then gulped down. He stood, filled the glass again and returned to his chair. She thought it was odd that though Sarah had problems with language, speaking with Jamie was often far more difficult.

She asked, 'Practice today?'

'Yeah. Later.'

'Then you have weight training?'

'Not today.'

There was nothing more she could do with the chicken and she decided to boil potatoes, because that would give her an excuse to stay in the kitchen for as long as he wanted her to be there. She began peeling. The silence was thick as oil smoke. Finally she said, 'We know you didn't have anything to do with it, Jamie.'

The prosecutor hadn't presented the boy to the grand jury but he had warned the Cordes sternly that he would have to testify at Philip's trial. And that there was a chance new evidence might arise implicating him further.

Jamie drank the milk like a man on a bender. He stood and she prayed he was just going to the refrigerator, not leaving the room. He poured another glass and sat down again. He asked, 'Did Dad like look through my room or anything?'

'Did he what?'

When he didn't repeat the question she said, 'Your father wouldn't do that. If there was something bothering him he'd talk to you.'

'Uh-huh.' Her son sat with his head tilted, studying the glass. Diane wanted to tell him how much she loved him, how proud they were of him, how the incident at the pond – whatever had happened – was one of those ambiguous glitches in the complicated history of families that don't touch the core of its love. Yet she was afraid to. She believed that if she did, the words would turn his heart as thick as his sculpted muscles and he would move further away from her.

'Jamie—'

Sarah appeared in the doorway. 'He's here, Mommy! Dr Breck!'

Diane looked toward the living room and saw a car parked in the driveway. 'Okay, I'll be there in a minute.'

Sarah left and Diane said to her son, 'Your father loves you.' She stood and ran a hand through his hair, feeling his neck muscles tense at this. He said nothing.

10

A suspect had been arrested but Tom the pink-cheeked deputy was still taking his job seriously.

Nobody had relieved him of his command yet. Besides, he was hugely aware that somebody had gotten past him at least once and that Sarah had hightailed it into the woods right under his nose; he wasn't letting Ben Breck put a foot on the front porch until he had the Queen's okay.

Diane nodded. 'It's all right. He's expected.' She turned to the man standing on the concrete walk. 'Dr Breck?'

'Call me Ben, please.' He walked past the deputy into the house.

Breck was over six feet tall, with dark, unruly hair laced with gray. Forty-one, she remembered Dr Parker had said. He had boyish qualities – his voice and face, for instance – and you could see exactly what he had looked like when he was twelve. He seemed to be in good shape but he was pale and this gave him the deceptive appearance of weakness. His eyes were dark. He wore black jeans and a tweed sports coat over a dark blue shirt. His hands were small and his fingers almost delicate. He slouched. Diane, accustomed to her husband's military posture, was put off by this initially. Almost immediately though this aversion flipflopped and became pleasantly quirky. He carried a battered briefcase.

Diane motioned him to the couch. He glanced out the window. 'Is there, uhm, something wrong?'

'Oh, the deputy? No, my husband's a detective. He's involved in the case where those girls were killed.'

'The students?'

'That's right. The Sheriff's Department sometimes has a deputy keeping an eye out on the houses of the investigators.'

Sarah bounded down the stairs and halted in the arched doorway to the living room, clutching her pink backpack and gazing at Breck. Diane noted that she had changed clothes and was now wearing her favorite T-shirt, bright blue and emblazoned with a seahorse. The girl brushed a long tail of hair from her face and said nothing.

'Sarah, this is Dr Breck.'

'You're my tutor.'

'That's right. I'm pleased to meet you, Sarah,' Breck said.

To Diane's surprise, the girl shook his hand.

Jamie walked quickly through the living room, wearing his biking shorts and a sweatshirt.

'Oh, Jamie . . .'

He glanced at the three people in the room and didn't say a word. He left by the front door. She saw him leap on his bike and pedal quickly out of the driveway.

'Wrestling practice,' she explained to Breck.

'Ah.' Breck turned to Sarah. 'What've you got there?'

'My backpack.'

'What's in it?'

'Barbie. And Redford T. Redford—'

'That's one of her stuffed bears.' Diane felt a need to translate.

'That's a clever name.'

Sarah announced, 'He's the world's smartest bear. And I have my tape recorder.'

'Tape recorder? Oh-oh, are you recording what I'm saying? Like a spy?'

'No!' Sarah smiled. 'I'm writing stories.'

'Stories?' Breck's eyes went wide. 'I've never known anybody who writes stories.'

'Dr Parker is having me write a book.'

Breck said, 'I write books. But mine are very boring. Students use them in class. I'll bet yours are more interesting than mine. Sarah, why don't you sit over here next to me?'

Diane asked, 'Can I get you anything?'

'A salt shaker,' Breck said.

'Pardon?'

'Actually, the whole carton would be better.'

'Salt.'

Breck said, 'Please.'

Diane walked into the kitchen and Breck turned to Sarah. 'How do you spell "chair"?'

'C-H-A-I-R.'

'Very good.'

Sarah beamed.

'How about "table"?'

She closed her eyes and thought for a minute. She shook her head. Then she said, 'T-A-B-E-L. No, L-E.'

'That's right. How 'bout "tablecloth"?'

The girl went quiet, her mood changed fast as a balloon popping. 'I don't know.' Her face became sullen.

'Tablecloth,' Breck said.

Diane, returning with the blue carton, felt an electric rush across her face – sympathetic fear. *She's getting upset, she's going to be blocked and you're bucking for a tantrum, boy . . .*

Breck opened his briefcase and pulled out a sheet of black paper. Diane handed him the salt. Breck took it and poured a large pile onto the paper then spread it out smoothly. Mother and daughter watched – one with fascination, one with caution. Breck said to Sarah, 'Let's spell it together.'

'I don't know how.' She stared at the salt. Diane stood in the doorway until she saw what she believed was a glance from Breck, requesting privacy. She retreated to the kitchen.

317

'Give me your hand,' Breck said to the girl.

Reluctantly Sarah did. He took her index finger and drew a T in the salt with it. 'You feel it?' he asked. 'You feel what a T is like?'

Sarah nodded. Breck smoothed the salt. 'Do it again.'

She hesitated, then started the letter. It was a clumsy attempt, looking more like a plus sign.

'Let's try an A.'

'I can do that one,' she said and smoothed the salt herself.

For a half hour they made salt letters. A hundred 'table's. A hundred 'cloth's. A hundred of those words put together, making a third word. Even though Sarah struggled fiercely to spell it correctly – and did so the majority of times – Breck did not seem interested in her results. Less a tutor than a sculpting instructor, Breck urged her to feel the shape of the letters. Diane crouched like a peeping Tom, peered through a crack in the kitchen door and watched.

At the end of the session he gave Sarah a tracing notebook, which contained a story Breck read to her. Sarah declared it was 'a pretty darn good story,' even though she guessed the ending halfway through. Breck gave her instructions on tracing the paragraphs. He stood up and left Sarah to her book and tape recorder and mangy stuffed bear.

'Hello?' Breck called. 'Mrs Corde?'

'In here.'

He walked into the kitchen, where Diane had rapidly resumed peeling potatoes.

'You are amazing,' she said. Then confessed, 'I overheard.'

'These are very well-known techniques. Rapport with the child. Multisensory stimulation. Work with her motor skills. Use her given talents to compensate for her deficits.'

'You seem like an artist.'

'I like what I do. That's the optimal motivation for any endeavour.'

318

Optimal? Endeavour?

'You want some coffee?'

He said, 'Sure.'

She poured two cups and chattered about her garden and a PTA bake sale she was chairing. Diane Corde didn't know what to make of her rambling. Apparently neither did Breck, who sat in the kitchen and sipped coffee while he looked close to uncomfortable. He gazed out over the backyard. When she paused he said, 'I like these windows, you can see the whole field there. I have bay windows like these in my town house.'

'Where's that?'

'Chicago. South Side. Only I don't see fields. I see the lake.'

'I wonder if that's why they call them bay windows. Bay, lake.'

He said, 'Or perhaps it's because they're shaped like a bay.'

Diane said that was true and felt like a fool that her joke had missed its mark.

Breck said, 'Sarah's a good candidate for improvement. Dr Parker has her dictating stories to build up self-esteem, I assume?'

'That's right.'

'She has an astonishing imagination.'

'She's always making up things. It drives me nutty sometimes. I don't know what's real and what's fantasy.'

'A plight many of us suffer from.'

Plight.

There was a moment of long silence. Breck was still gazing, though no longer at the cow pasture. Now it was Diane's eyes he was examining.

He asked, 'Do you work?'

'Yep. You just finished with one of my bosses. I got two more. Jamie – you saw him – and a husband. They're all a handful.'

'Ah, your son. The bicyclist. Does he have any learning problems?'

'Nope. Good student, good athlete.'

319

'That's not unusual. Birth order is often a significant factor in dyslexia. And your husband's a policeman?'

'A detective. He works like a maniac, he's away from home so much.' Diane found herself about to blurt, 'And *that's* with a case he's been ordered off of!' But she said only, 'We don't get many murders in New Lebanon.'

'From what I've read it's got the town in quite an uproar.'

'Well, all this talk of Moon Killers and cults and that nonsense . . .'

'Is it nonsense?'

'Well, they've caught that boy. I shouldn't be telling you this but that's why Jamie was a little moody. The one they've indicated was a friend of his.'

'Really?' Breck frowned in sympathy. 'Poor kid.'

'I'm of mixed mind. I didn't want to say anything in front of Sarah but the reason the deputy's out there? Somebody's left some threats.'

'How terrible.'

'To get Bill to stop the investigation.'

'And they think your son's friend did that?'

'Philip's a sorry soul. With parents like his I'm not surprised he turned out bad. He's been abused, I'm sure. And his mother drinks. But threatening my daughter . . . I don't cut him any slack. He gets no sympathy from me.'

'But if they've arrested him, why the guard?'

'That's my Bill. Between you and me and the fence post, he's not sure the boy's guilty. He asked to have the deputy kept on the house for a few days longer. I can't say that upsets me too much.' Diane hesitated. 'I guess I shouldn't . . . I mean, this is pretty much classified stuff I'm telling you.'

Breck acknowledged the discretion with a nod and Diane turned the talk back to the PTA. After ten minutes Breck looked at his watch and stood. 'Thanks for the coffee. I'd like to stay longer,' he said with sincerity, 'but I have a lecture to prepare.'

Diane took his hand and found she was studying

parts of him – his floppy hair, his eyelids, his lips, reaching conclusions about each. This allowed her to avoid conclusions about Breck as a person. Or as a man.

She thought suddenly that this was the first time in years she was having a serious talk alone in her kitchen with a man not related by blood or marriage. She asked, 'Next Tuesday?'

'I'll look forward to it.' Breck added, 'I've enjoyed talking with you. I think we have some good rapport established.'

'Is that important?'

'Indeed.' Breck took her hand again. He continued to hold it, pressing firmly, as he said, 'You'd be surprised how important the tutor's relationship with a parent is.'

MEMO

TO: Files
FROM: Dennis B. Brann, Esq.
DATE: May 8
RE: People v. Halpern, a Minor

Attached are the relevant portions of a transcript of my interview with Philip Halpern, defendant in this case, which interview took place today at the New Lebanon Sheriff's Department, following a bail hearing at which bail was set in the amount of $1 million and was not posted. The Grand Jury of Harrison County has indicted Philip with one count of first-degree murder, one count of first-degree manslaughter, one count of first-degree rape and one count of first-degree sodomy, in connection with the death of Jennifer Gebben, and one count first-degree murder and one count first-degree manslaughter in the death of Emily Rossiter.

DNA genetic marker test results indicate that the semen found in and on the Gebben victim was Philip's (see Attachment 'A').

DBB: Philip, I'd like to talk to you about what happened at the pond. Everything you tell me, even if you tell me that you did what you're accused of, is only between us. The court will never find that out.

PH: Yessir.

DBB: Tell me what happened that night, that Tuesday, April 20.

PH: I was with Jamie—

DBB: That's Jamie Corde?

PH: Yeah and what it was, we'd been fishing, only nothing was biting so we thought since it'd rained during the day there'd be some worms close to the surface, so we thought we'd dig some and we walked over along the dam. It was around ten. Jamie and me were walking along there and we looked down and we seen this white thing and we thought it was, I thought it was one of those, you know, those dolls they sell in the back of magazines sometimes . . .

DBB: Dolls?

PH: You like blow them up and, you know, do things to them.

DBB: Inflatable dolls.

PH: Yeah. So I go, 'Let's go look,' and we go down there and it isn't a doll, it's this girl and she's lying there and she looks dead.

DBB: Where was she?

PH: Next to the truck. The old Ford.

DBB: What position was she in?

PH: Lying on her back. They're not listening in, are they? I mean is there a microphone here or anything?

DBB: No, there isn't. It's okay to talk to me.

PH: She was lying in the mud on her back. Her arm's up over her face and her fingers were all curly. It was like weird. Jamie and me walked down to her and we think she's like asleep but then I think maybe she's dead and I don't want to touch her at first and we just stand around and look at her then we look at each other for a while and we're like, oh, man, what're we going to do? And we can't think of anything. So I finally bend down and feel on her neck like they do on TV for the pulse or whatever, and I'm like I can't feel anything and then I . . .

DBB: Go on.

PH: Then I keep touching her. And Jamie bends down and he touches her leg and she's cold but she's not hard like, you know, with rigid mortis. I . . .

DBB: Go on.

PH: I touch her, you know, her tits. Then I pull up her skirt and Jamie's like, 'Man, this is too much.' He goes, 'Like I'm serious, we gotta call somebody. Let's call my dad.' But I'm still touching her. I can't help myself. I cut her underwear off with the knife.

DBB: Your Naryan knife?

PH: Uh-huh. I cut them off, her underwear, and Jamie was touching her, you know, down there. He stuck his finger in a couple times . . . Then I, you know, I did it. I couldn't stop myself.

DBB: You had intercourse with the corpse?

PH: Yeah, I guess.

DBB: Did you ejaculate?

PH: Uh, yeah.

DBB: Did you have both vaginal and anal intercourse with her? You know what I mean by that, don't you?

PH: (inaudible)

DBB: What was that?

PH: I wasn't sure how it, you know, worked at first.

DBB: What happened then?

PH: I kind of just finished. I asked Jamie if he wanted to. But he didn't. He was like totally freaked. So we went home.

DBB: Did you touch her in any way afterward?

PH: Oh yeah. She didn't look right, lying there.

So I made her look better. I pulled her dress down and folded her arms.

DBB: Why did you do that?

PH: Well, in this movie I saw, *The Lost Dimension?* – it's a really really good movie – the hero brings this princess back to life. The Honons had killed her. They're like totally evil. And Dathar like made her look like that.

DBB: Did you think you could bring her back to life?

PH: I don't know.

DBB: Did you ever see the girl before? When she was alive?

PH: No.

DBB: Could you tell me about those pictures of the girls you had in your file cabinet? The drawings?

PH: Well, it was sort of a game Jamie and me made up. It was like based on the movie—

DBB: *The Lost Dimension?*

PH: Yeah. And we wanted to do a computer game of it and sell it but we don't know programming too good so we made up this board game. We used some of the girls from school as characters. We cut their pictures out of the yearbook.

DBB: Was this like a religion or a cult?

PH: No sir. It was just a game. We were going to sell it to Parker Brothers or Milton Bradley. I was going to make a lot of money and get a house of my own and move out.

DBB: Did you see anyone else around the pond that Tuesday?

PH: We saw some guys fishing but that was at dusk.

DBB: Do you have any idea who killed her?

PH: No.

DBB: Do you recognize this photocopy?

PH: That's my knife.

DBB: Are you sure it's yours? Or does it just look like one you have?

PH: I don't know. It looks like mine.

DBB: You don't have that knife any longer?

PH: I lost it. I think I dropped it at the pond.

DBB: Philip, did you know a Susan Biagotti?

PH: Who?

DBB: A student at Auden University.

PH: I don't know about her. I never heard of her.

DBB: She was killed last year.

PH: I don't know anything about that. Really, Mr Brann.

DBB: Now you went back to the pond on the twenty-eighth? The night of the twenty-eighth?

PH: No. Did Jamie tell you that?

DBB: Nobody told me. The prosecutor thinks you were there.

PH: Well, I wasn't.

DBB: You weren't there at the pond?

PH: I don't know. I don't remember.

DBB: The deputies found some bootmarks near where the Rossiter girl was killed. They seem to match boots you had in your garage.

PH: Well . . . (long pause). I think they planted those boots there.

DBB: Philip, I'm on your side. You have to be honest with me. I know you're scared and a lot is happening to you. But you have to tell me the truth.

PH: I don't know what happened.

DBB: Did you threaten Detective Corde or his family?

PH: No. I never did. Who said I did?

DBB: Calm down, Philip. Is there anything you can tell me that might prove you didn't kill the Rossiter girl?

PH: I don't know.

The dean was on the phone when he walked in. She

looked at Wynton Kresge and motioned him inside then hung up.

'You wanted to see me?' he asked.

The dean stood up and walked across her office. It was a lot plusher than Kresge's but he didn't care for it. Too many scrolly twists of wood and ceramic vases and immense nineteenth-century portraits. She closed the door and returned to her seat.

Kresge was tired so he sat too.

'Wynton,' she began. 'I'd like to talk to you about the incidents.'

'Incidents?'

'The girls' deaths.'

'Right. Sure.'

'I mentioned that it was important for the school not to be too involved. I can't tell you the fallout we've had because of the investigation that Detective Corde was doing. Several of our lenders told Professor Sayles point-blank that they would not refinance their loans to us because they'd heard about lesbian orgies in the dorms. Thank God they've caught that young man.'

'I'm sure Bill didn't say anything about orgies.'

'Well, this is just background, Wynton,' the dean said. 'The reason I called you here is that I'm afraid I'll have to let you go.'

'Go?'

'I've gotten a report from the Finance Committee. Did you authorize the placement of some advertising in the *Register*?'

Ads. The ads that Bill Corde couldn't pay for. 'That's right, I did.'

'You have no authority to approve nonsecurity expenses.'

'I'd say it was pretty much a security expense. It was to find the killer of two of our students.'

'Wynton, you made an unauthorized expense. It's the same as embezzlement.'

'That's slander, Dean,' said Wynton Kresge, who owned more law books than hunting books.

'It's a serious breach of procedures. The Personnel Department will be contacting you about the severance package, which is extremely generous under the circumstances.'

She didn't say anything more. She hunkered down in her chair and waited for the onslaught.

Kresge let her flash through a few EEOC nightmares for a long moment then said calmly, 'That'd be effective today?'

'Yes, Wynton. And I'm sorry.'

'Well, Dean, I hope this's all you have to be sorry about,' he said cryptically, and left the office.

11

Chunk.

Lying on the bottom bunk, looking up at the xaser coils above his face, he heard the sound.

Philip Halpern blinked and felt a low punch in his stomach. He recognized the noise instantly. The door of the family's Chevy station wagon slamming. His palms began sweating. His fingers twitched. He stood up and looked through thick bars and thin glass to see what he knew he'd see: his mother coming to visit. He'd been expecting her—

NO, NO, NO!

Oh, God. He'd found it, the plastic hefty bag with the dead girl's purse inside! His father, not forty feet away, holding the bag Philip had buried under the back porch.

The boy stared at his father talking with Sheriff Ribbon, bleak expressions on both their faces. Ribbon pointed back toward the cell. His father stared for a long moment as if he was trying to decide whether he should visit his son. Then they both turned and walked up the street, away from the jail.

These two men looked like any good old boys in New Lebanon, sitting at a green Formica booth in the drugstore. Their solid shoulders arching over heavy white coffee cups. The kind of men who would stand up quick when they heard the four-bar intro of the 'Star-

Spangled Banner'. The kind of men who'd buy a NAPA carburetor at nine a.m. on Saturday and have it seated by ten-thirty. The kind that talked about the price of propane and what poppers the bass were hitting on.

Right now these two men were talking about murder.

'My boy's got his share of problems,' Creth Halpern said. 'He's got more weight than he ought. It's soft weight. It's girl weight. I don't know where he gets it. His mother's a drinker, you know that. I think maybe that mixed up his chrome zones.'

Steve Ribbon nodded and kept stirring the coffee he had no taste for. He listened. This was a pain and in spades.

'Take them pictures.' Halpern was whispering, as if admitting things he'd never in his life spoken out loud. 'The pictures you boys found. I'd sometimes find these girlie magazines. Not like *Playboy*. It was just plain smut. Pictures of people, you know, humping. I don't know where he got them from. I was ascared it was somebody older. Some man. Phil's a little girlish like I say.' Halpern smiled and looked at a Heinz bottle as he sailed over the second great tragedy of his life. 'But the pictures weren't of queers.'

Ribbon asked, 'What you getting at exactly, Creth?'

'He's not the kind of boy would hurt anybody. I don't want him to go to prison.'

'*You* showed us the shorts. That he tried to burn.'

'I was mad then. I wanted to whup him. I feel different now.'

'Why you talking to me? You hired Dennis Brann.'

'I don't do well by lawyers. I didn't take to Brann or him to me.'

'It doesn't look real good for Philip, Creth.'

'He's not bad. He's a disappointment is what he is. You know what'd happen to him if he went to jail?' Halpern glanced at Ribbon, who was silent but who knew exactly what would happen to Philip in general population at the state prison in Warwick and probably on his first day there.

330

Halpern said, 'I can't say I love the boy. I gave up trying a time ago. But I . . . I don't know.'

'Brann's an all-right shyster. He'll give it a good shot.'

'Well, look here what I found.' Halpern lifted the torn, filthy plastic bag onto the countertop. Crumbs of dirt and popcorn fell into a comma of spilled coffee on the Formica and dissolved. 'I found it in this place where Phil played. Like a hiding place. Under the back porch.'

Ribbon opened up the bag. Inside was a purse, stained with mud. He shook it out on the table. He looked up at Halpern. He whispered harshly, 'This's one of the girls'? Hell, what're you giving it to me for? It'll convict him sure, Creth.'

'No, no.' Halpern shook his head. 'There's something you gotta see.'

They stood outside the one-story yellow-brick building in Higgins, both bent over a piece of computer printout paper.

'Well, we gotta do something with it,' Steve Ribbon said. 'Damn, this is a wrinkle.'

Charlie Mahoney handed the printout back to Ribbon then held up the clear plastic bag with a COC tag attached. He read the handwritten letter that was inside.

Ribbon waved the printout as if he were drying ink. 'It says it's a fifty-fifty chance. I don't think we can ignore it.'

'I don't think so either. Who is he? What're his credentials?'

'A graphoanalyst. Works for the state. It's admissible, Charlie. When Brann gets his hand on it, it'll be back to square one and that's gonna be a son of a bitch for all of us.'

'For all of us,' Mahoney repeated slowly. He glanced at Ribbon with a smile that meant if anything: *Why you fat shitfaced rube.*

Ribbon continued, 'The case goes public again, they'll start talking about Jennie and her girlfriend. And the school. I mean, this'll fuck us both.' He glanced at the paper.

Mahoney said, 'I'll bet his father wrote it to get the kid off.'

'Nup, not the father. You don't know him. He wouldn't help his boy that way. But the kid himself might've written it and hid it knowing we'd find it.'

'Any chance at all it's real we gotta give it to Brann. That's the law.' Mahoney stuck a solid finger at Ribbon. 'And say what you like, *you* had the investigation for two weeks before the county and everybody knows it. Your dick's in the ringer just's far as *all of ours* . . .' He drew out the last words melodically.

Ribbon avoided the man's relentless eyes. 'This don't disprove the case against the boy for the Gebben girl's murder.'

'Damnit, Ribbon, you been harping on this cult serial killing shit since the case started. If the boy didn't kill the second girl then where's that theory of yours go?'

Ribbon said, 'You've seen the kid. All those magazines, the pictures, the porn, all that cult crapola. The knife. He guilty or not?'

Mahoney shrugged. 'Probably.'

'What if we was to get a confession outa him?' Ribbon said, and to Mahoney's relief touched away a web of spit that had formed in the corner of his mouth.

'Confession. Uhm.'

'Could you do that?' Ribbon asked. 'You've gotten confessions before?'

Mahoney snorted.

'It sounds like something you'd be good at, getting confessions.'

'Yeah,' Mahoney said, both pleased by the stroking and feeling utter contempt at Ribbon for resorting to it.

'He's in the lockup right now.'

Mahoney looked at his watch.

Ribbon said, 'I think sooner rather than later'd be best, don't you?'

'What about the other deputies?'

'I can arrange for you to be alone with him.'
'Now?'
'Completely alone.'

He didn't have a fifty-thousand-joule xaser gun.

He didn't even have his father's Ruger .22.

But Philip Halpern had one weapon.

He turned back to his cell and stripped the sheet off his bunk. Philip lifted it to his wet mouth and with his teeth tore four notches in the cheap cloth. He ripped the sheet into strips and tied them together. He pushed the table into the exact centre of the room and after a struggle climbed up on top of it. He took hold of the metal overhead lamp shade. A wispy avalanche of dust fell. He breathed it in, coughing and blinking. He smelled the pungent odor of his sweat mixed with pine-scented Lysol. Philip wrapped the sheet-rope around his neck and then looped it around the electric cord.

He stared up. *Penny-Saver Soft Light Registered Trademark Sixty Watts Made in USA*. The nearness of the cheap bulb began to erode his vision. The words faded, the flecks of dust and the corpses of fried bugs on the metal shade grew indistinct. The room became bright as heaven. Philip Halpern lowered his arms.

They heard the boy's loud moan.

Lance Miller cocked his head and said, 'Sounds like he's not feeling good. Maybe we ought to get him something.'

'Shore,' the county deputy said. 'How 'bout a ice-cold girl.'

Lance Miller looked up from *USA Today*. 'Already had hisself two of them.' He returned to an article about Jay Leno.

'Can you get a dose from a corpse?' the county deputy mused.

'That's dis-gusting,' Miller told him.

Another moan, loud and eerie.

'Should we check on him?'

'You see the pictures of his sister's boobs?' Miller asked.

'Missed 'em.'

'He tried to burn them.'

'Her boobs?'

'No, the pictures,' Miller said.

'What were they like?'

'Close-ups, you know. Polaroids.'

'No, her boobs,' the deputy said.

'Not real big. The picture was dark. He didn't use a flash.'

They heard the moan again and looked at each other. 'He's beating off in there,' the deputy said.

'What if he's really sick?'

'I dunno. How 'bout you look now. I'll look later.'

'If he's puking I'm not cleaning it up.'

'We'll draw straws.'

Lance Miller walked into the lockup area, closed the door and continued down the corridor to Philip's cell.

He saw: the boy, the sheet-rope, the table.

'Oh shit. Oh shit.' He fumbled with his key and swung open the door to the cell and leapt up on the table, reaching for the boy's shoulders.

Which is when Philip started to fall.

Behind him trailed the strip of sheet, which he hadn't tied to the lamp, or to anything at all. It streamed behind him like a tail of Dimensional cloak. Firing his secret weapon at Miller – not fifty-thousand joules, not a xaser, not a Honon whip but his two hundred plus pounds of weight. The deputy, struggling to get his balance, slipped onto the concrete floor and landed on his back. Philip continued downward and landed directly on him. There was a huge snap. Lance Miller groaned once then passed out.

Philip grabbed Miller's keys and his Smith & Wesson and walked out of the cell. He unlatched the back door of the lockup, then slipped into Town Hall and out the back door. Once outside he sprinted away from the town building then out of downtown, his lungs sucking air. As

334

the pain in his chest grew, a momentary thought occurred to him – he felt grateful, ebullient even, that he had been in jail and had missed the anguish of the long-distance run in PE class. Now he put his head down and ran faster than he ever had in school. Faster than he'd ever run in his life. Philip ran, he ran, he ran.

Wait. What is this?

Bill Corde stood in the doorway to the lockup and watched one deputy on his knees, leaning over the other one – wait, it was Lance Miller – kissing him.

Wait. No.

What *is* this?

It was CPR. Lance Miller, white-faced and blotched in sweat, thrashed on the floor. Arms sweeping like he was waving down a rescue copter, legs kicking, whispering in between the county deputy's smacks, 'Gedoff, gedoff, gedoff!' The deputy would pinch his nose then breathe air into his lungs.

Corde said, 'I don't think he needs that.'

'S'all right. I've done this before,' the rescuing deputy said as he put both hands on Miller's chest and pressed down hard. The crack of the breaking rib was audible to Corde. Miller muttered, 'Gedoff me,' and fainted.

'Didn't look like he was having a heart attack,' Corde said.

'Look what I done,' said the rescuer, standing up and looking heart-sick.

Corde knelt and checked Miller's pulse. 'I don't think he's hurt too bad. Why don't you call the ambulance?'

'Yeah, I could do that. The kid escaped.' He stood up and ran past Corde to the phone.

'*What?*'

'What should I call? Nine one one?'

'What do you mean, he escaped?'

Clutching the phone the deputy blurted, 'Ran outa here five minutes ago. Hello, we need a ambulance at the sheriff's office. There's a injured deputy. I was giving him CPR and he didn't take to it.'

Corde ran through the lockup, out the back door, then to the Town Hall exit door, which swung wide into the sunlit parking lot. *Outhouse fulla shit!* There was no sign of the fleeing boy. He trotted back into the office just as the fire siren began its throaty wail.

Corde had the dispatcher call Ebbans in then he picked up the phone and dialed Ribbon's home. 'Hey, Ettie, can you get him down here soon's you can? We got an escape . . . Yeah? Where? Fishing? Hell's bells!'

Jim Slocum ran through the open doorway, passing the county deputy, who kept an intense vigil for the ambulance. 'What's up, Bill? I just heard an ambulance call.'

'The Halpern boy's gone.'

'Gone? Whatdya?—'

'Escaped is what I mean. Beat up Lance bad.'

'No shit.' Slocum grinned. 'Hell of a scrapper for a fat boy.'

'Where's Steve?'

'Saturday afternoon? Where d'ya think? In his new goddamn truck . . . He got a phone in it?'

'Naw,' Slocum said. 'He was gonna put the old CB in but he didn't get around to it.'

Corde said, 'Get out a description but tell them go easy when apprehending.'

'I can say but it don't mean they'll do.' Slocum walked off to the dispatcher's office.

The medics streamed through the door with a low gurney and explored Lance Miller's body carefully. They gave him an injection then got him outside and into the ambulance. He was awake again and cussing colorfully as they closed the door.

Twenty minutes later Ebbans arrived and Mahoney five minutes after him.

'Great, we got a killer out?' Mahoney said after he'd heard the news.

'Oh, I guess I missed the trial,' Corde said, loud.

Mahoney lifted his eyes to the ceiling.

Slocum said happily, 'We got ourselves some proof

now. I mean, why's he escaping if he didn't do it?'

Corde looked at him as if he'd asked where babies come from.

Ebbans said, 'We better call the state and tell them we got one loose.'

'You might want to mention,' the rib-cracking deputy said, 'he's got a gun.'

Outright silence. Every head in the room turned to him.

The deputy blushed then said, 'Forgot to say, what with Lance being down and all. He got Lance's gun. I thought he'd gotten the Speedloaders but they'd fallen under the bunk. Just the gun he got. I was relieved to find the extra shells.'

Corde said, 'Nobody's supposed to go into the cells with a gun! He didn't leave it in the box?'

'Guess he forgot.'

'Sweet Mary,' Corde whispered. 'Get on the horn,' he ordered Slocum. 'Make it APB to county and state. Armed and emotionally disturbed. Tell them that he's scared but he doesn't want to hurt anybody.'

Mahoney asked, 'You sound like you're in charge here, Detective. I seem to recall you're under suspension.'

The others looked at Corde cautiously, waiting for him to blow. He however had not even heard the words. He was in a different place altogether, running through bushes and trees, wheezing and hawking, right next to Philip Halpern. 'The boy's fifteen. So he doesn't have a driver's license. He's probably trying to get out of the county on foot. How would he do that?'

Slocum said, 'I don't know. I don't think we've ever had an escape situation here.'

Ebbans said, 'What about a Greyhound out of Fredericksberg.'

'Maybe,' Corde said slowly. 'How about the state park?'

Slocum said, 'Damn, sure. It'll lead him right to the river and I bet he thinks he'll snatch a canoe or boat and head south.'

337

The door opened and Harrison County Sheriff Hammerback Ellison stepped into the office. He was a solid, heavy man but his face was pointed and delicate and he had very small feet and narrow ankles. 'I just got the call. The boy got away?'

'Sure did.' Ebbans stood up and picked up his hat. 'And he's got a gun. You and me ought to get over to the state park. That okay with you, Bill?' Ebbans asked. His voice was strident; he was challenging anybody to question the shift of authority back to Corde. *Bless you on this, T.T.* Corde nodded and said to Slocum, 'Jim, why don't you take 302. Just on the chance that he's hitching. I'll take 117 down to the river and see if I find him there.'

Slocum looked at Ebbans, who said, 'Do it, Jim.'

Then Corde said to Mahoney, 'Charlie, maybe you ought to check out downtown. He could be trying to outsmart us and hole up till night somewhere around here.'

Mahoney reluctantly said, 'I don't think he's that smart. But it's not a bad idea.'

They all hurried outside to the parking lot. Slocum got into his car and sped off. Ellison and Ebbans vanished in a cloud of dust and tire smoke. Corde hung back. He started the engine then drove slowly out of the parking lot.

He did not however make the right turn onto Cress, which would have taken him directly to Route 117. He turned left then slammed his foot onto the accelerator.

By the power of Your wisdom,
by the strength of Your might,
guide me, O Guardians,
to the Lost Dimension,
from darkness to light.

Philip pauses to smell the deputy's gun. The scents are oil, plastic and metal warmed to 98.6 by the abundant flesh of his stomach. It is a small gun but very heavy.

Systems armed. Xaser torpedoes in launch tubes . . .

Philip is in the woods that border his parents' house. He is surrounded by lean pines and the hot stems of wild sunflowers and long, bowed grass. Within a frame of trees he can see the Chevrolet. He can see the tail of the duct tape that holds the station wagon's grille, which was shattered when his mother went off the road two years ago. He can see the barbecue. He can see the back porch with its lattice door open wide – left that way by his father after digging up the purse. Philip can see the green of the sagging shack in the backyard. Under one eave of the shack is a huge, skin-creepy wasp nest that has weighed on his mind like a fat pimple for a week. After he kills his father and after he kills Jano the Honon traitor he will fire the rest of the bullets into the wasp nest.

Lock on target, entering Dimensional shift now . . .

No, Philip remembers, he will not shoot all the bullets into the nest. He'll save one.

Philip steps out of the woods and starts toward his house.

Faith. To the Lost Dimension. From darkness to light.

12

'Doing that,' Creth Halpern said, 'won't help much at all.'

His wife looked at him curiously – as if he hadn't spoken, as if he were simply standing in front of her, moving his mouth silently. As if the words buzzed around her head like bees in an old cartoon.

They were both surprised at his comment. It had been years since he'd referred to her drinking. His wife emptied the contents of the heavy glass into her throat and swallowed. She poured another and replaced the plastic pitcher in a refrigerator that held Kraft cheese slices, a near-empty box of Post Toasties, a package of grey ground beef, a half quart of milk. She leaned against the wall. Halpern gripped the screwdriver he was using to crack open a paint-frozen window. He dug the blade into the seam and levered upward, crushing the wood of the sill. The window didn't budge. 'Damn.'

His wife sipped the drink and looked out at a blooming lilac bush outside windows bordered with curtains on which were printed tiny brown tepees.

Halpern for the life of him couldn't understand why she looked so good. In the mornings, a little puffy-faced; at night, eyes dead to all who bothered to look. But that was the only real evidence. Last summer one of Philip's friends had hit on her. A skin-and-bones high school kid! Halpern admitted she had a great bod. How could she pour down the Beefeaters faster than any one of the guys down at the Tap and still keep her face clean and her hair all permed up nice? Her nails done? Her legs shaved?

'Our son,' she said by way of announcement, 'in jail.'

'He didn't do it. He'll be out tomorrow.'

'Oh, come on. He did those *things* to her . . .' She didn't even sound drunk. He wondered if he'd just gotten used to it. He tried to remember her voice when he'd met her, when he'd first started hanging out in the New Lebanon Inn, where she was waitressing. He couldn't. This saddened him greatly.

His wife said to a lumber yard calender. 'I can't call my mother. How can I call her? I'd be so ashamed.'

'He did some things to that girl, yeah, and he oughta be whipped and he will be. But he didn't kill anybody. I'll swear to that. What we should do is get some help.'

'Oh, sure. How?'

'There's state help, I guess. Talk to a . . . I don't know. Somebody.'

'Oh, just like that? Sure. If you made money maybe.' Her voice clear as gin.

'I put a roof over his head. I put food in his mouth. And yours too. Food, and that's not all.' Two digs in one day. Halpern was shaken.

'If you made money—'

'I fucking make money. You could make money too.'

'—we could do a few things.'

'I'm stopping you from getting a job?'

'You don't remember. You don't remember anything.'

Halpern said, 'I can't talk to you when you're this way.'

'How come,' she asked curiously, 'you don't fuck me anymore?'

Halpern's temper blazed then died immediately to a simmer. He considered open-handing her cheek but was paralyzed by a bottomless remorse. He joined his wife in gazing out the window. It occurred to him that most of their arguments happened just this way – her drunk, him thinking about other places and people, both of them staring out the window. Wanting to smack her and not having the energy or the type of hate required.

'Oh, go to hell,' his wife said as if giving directions.

Halpern snatched up the screwdriver. He squeezed it a dozen times, feeling the resilience of the rubberized handle spattered in paint. He stepped slowly to the kitchen sink, leaned forward and dug the screwdriver furiously into the seam of the window, cracking chunks out of the soft pine sill.

He heard a clatter of pans behind him.

He heard the sticky sound of the refrigerator door opening.

He heard the sound of pouring liquid.

He heard his wife's voice. 'Philip!'

Halpern turned. The boy had entered through the back door and stood in the center of the kitchen.

'When d'you get out?' his father asked. He felt a horrid urge, a salivating urge, to step forward and bloody the boy's nose. To scream at him. (To scream what? *How could you do that to a poor girl? How could you, you stupid little prick?* To scream: *What'd I do to make you this way? I loved you! I really loved you! I'm so sorry!*)

Creth Halpern stood completely still, the screwdriver sliding from his hand. He stood twenty feet away from his son, whose upper lip glistened with snot and whose face was glossy with sweat, his fat three-dimensional chest heaving.

'How did you?—'

His wife whispered, 'Oh my God.'

Creth Halpern too saw the gun.

'Whatcha got there, boy?' he asked.

Philip's head turned to his mother. The glass fell from her grip, hitting the floor and whipping a tail of liquor against the refrigerator. Her smooth hands, tipped in unchipped red nails, went to her mouth. Philip turned back to his father. The boy's mouth moved but no words came out. It was the mouth of a fish eating water.

Finally, he swallowed then said in a weak voice, 'The handy man's here.'

'Listen up, young man. Put that gun down.'

'The handy man.'

His mother said, 'Philip, don't do this.' She sobbed, 'Please, don't do this.'

'I never did anything to you,' the boy said to his father.

'Son—'

Philip held the gun up and said, 'Handy man. Handyman, handymanhandyman—'

'I only wanted to help you, son.'

'I never did anything to you,' Philip whispered.

'Son, I know you didn't hurt those girls.'

'You were talking to the sheriff. I saw you.'

'I was giving him that purse you hid. The note! The note was inside. You know what I'm talking about! It shows you didn't kill her.'

In a voice more assured and more adult and more frightening than Halpern had ever heard, Philip said, 'I'm sorry, Dad, but the handy man's here.'

'I wanted to help you,' his father said.

Philip said, 'Hold out your hand.'

Bill Corde stepped silently past a drowsy old mutt, chained to the worn railing of the front porch. He slipped through the door and made his way toward the back of the house along the pink carpet runner, stained with dark patches. He smelled dog piss and old food and bleach. He could see Philip in the kitchen, holding the dark gray gun. He could see Halpern nearby. He could see a woman's white arm ending in long polished nails. Corde stopped in the dining room outside the kitchen doorway. He left his revolver holstered then took off his hat and set it on a dusty Sanyo TV. He paused next to the dining room table, which was covered with sticky soiled dishes and scraps of food, crusts from last night's pizza. In the center of the Formica a large paisley spill of ketchup had coagulated darkly.

344

'Hi, Philip,' Corde said softly.

Creth Halpern jumped at the sound. His wife's shocked face appeared in the doorway. Philip looked at the detective, uninterested, then back to his father and said, 'Hold out your hand.'

Halpern said slowly to Corde, 'He's got himself a gun.'

'Hold up your hand!'

Halpern raised his hands above his head.

'No, not up. Handy man is here. Hold *out* your hand! You know how to do it.'

'Phil,' Corde said. The boy looked at him for a minute then back to his father. When Corde moved a step closer to the living room Philip raised the gun to the center of his father's chest.

'Philip,' Corde said, speaking casually. 'Why don't you set the gun down? Would you please?'

His parents looked helplessly at Corde. He saw despair in their faces and he saw that the boy's father wore it the hardest.

'Please honey, please son,' his mother was whimpering.

Philip looked at her. He smiled. He said, 'Open the refrigerator.'

'Please honey . . .'

'OPEN IT!'

She screamed, and tore open the door. Philip held the gun up and fired a ringing, deafening shot into the bottom of the pitcher. The stained beige Rubbermaid exploded in a mist of gin. His mother screamed again. Neither Corde nor Halpern moved. Philip turned back to Corde.

Corde said, 'Nobody's going to hurt you.'

Philip laughed triumphantly. 'You think I don't know about that? That's what they tried with Dathar. They tried to fool him. They lied to him but he didn't believe them.'

'We want to help you, Phil.'

'Jamie turned me in.'

Corde said sternly, 'No, he didn't. I talked—'

'He did.'

'He didn't!' Corde shouted furiously, risking the boy's reaction. 'I talked to him about what happened. Some people at the sheriff's office tricked him. He didn't know they followed him. He was trying to save you. He has a message for you.' Corde held his hand in the Naryan salute.

The gun in Philip's hand wobbled. 'He said that?'

'He sure did.'

Philip nodded and smiled weakly. Then he turned to his father and spoke in a mournful voice. 'You didn't come to see me.'

'They said I couldn't. There was visiting hours. I was coming tonight. Like at the hospital when we went to visit Gram. They said I could only come at four o'clock.'

Philip looked at Corde, who said, 'That's true, Philip. It's the Sheriff's Department rules.'

The boy's eyes swept the floor.

Outside when he heard the gunshot and the scream, Charlie Mahoney put aside the Motorola walkie-talkie on which he'd just called T.T. Ebbans and Hammerback Ellison. He pulled his federally licensed automatic pistol out of his pocket and started up the porch stairs.

After following Corde here he had waited on the front steps considering what to do next. The gunshot ended the debate. Crouching, taking a fast look through the rusted, torn screen, he pulled the door open and crawled onto the porch. The lime green indoor-outdoor carpet was filthy and Mahoney's expensive gray plaid slacks ended up hoof-marked on the knees with dirt.

He watched them talking, Corde and the Halperns, until the two squad cars silently pulled up. He crawled back to the door, opened it and motioned the men forward. Ebbans and Ellison went around back and Slocum and a county deputy held up on the front steps where Mahoney signaled them to stay.

Mahoney crawled into the living room.

'Son, please, there's nothing to be gained by this . . .'

'Philip, your father and mother and I want to help you.'

The boy was crying now. 'He's always hitting me. I don't *do* anything but he hits me.'

'I want you to be strong,' Halpern said. 'That's all. I know you have it in you. It's going to be all right. They'll see the note and you'll be free. Tell him about the letter, Corde.'

Corde asked, 'Letter?'

Halpern said desperately, 'The note! Tell him!'

Mahoney stood then walked along the corridor into the dining room holding his breath not only to keep silent but to keep the stink of the dog piss and rotting food out of his nostrils.

'What note, Halpern?' Corde asked.

'Didn't the sheriff tell you?'

Mahoney eased forward. A board creaked.

Corde spun around and saw him. 'No!'

The boy's silver-dollar eyes saw Mahoney and he raised the gun. Mahoney did the same. Corde lifted his arms, palms out, his back to Philip and stepped in between them. His nerves bristled at the thought of a Smith & Wesson muzzle ten feet behind him and a Browning automatic's the same distance in front. 'Mahoney, what the hell are you doing here?'

'You fucking son of a bitch, Corde, get out of the way! You fucking—'

'Get out of here, you've got no business! . . .' Corde was shouting. Mahoney was dancing in the doorway, jockeying for a target. The boy stood frozen with fear, the muzzle pointed at Corde's spine.

'Philip,' Corde shouted over his shoulder, 'drop the gun! You'll be okay. Just—'

'GET THE FUCK OUT OF THE WAY!' Mahoney shouted.

Philip's hand drooped. His father looked at him and said, 'Put it down, son. Please.'

The gun sank lower.

A shadow flashed across the kitchen floor. Mahoney

shouted, 'Drop it!' And fired two shots into the ceiling.

Ebbans and Ellison leapt into the kitchen. Philip whirling toward them, Ellison screaming in panic, 'He's shooting he's shooting take him out!' The men's hands vanished in ragged flares of muzzle bursts. Mahoney dropped to the carpet. One slug hissed past Corde's left ear as he collapsed on the floor. Philip spun around and around. Then he fell. Corde scrabbled toward him, shouting, 'No, no, no!' Philip's father stood frozen, his right hand outstretched toward his son.

In the enormous silence that followed, Charlie Mahoney stood up and steadied himself on a pink metal table. He knocked off a flower pot, which broke and scattered a wiry geranium along the carpet, a flower as red and dazzling as the artery blood that sprang from Philip's neck and chest and soaked the filthy floor that may at one time have been white.

PART THREE

Close Pursuit

1

HARRISON COUNTY
SHOOTING INCIDENT INQUIRY BOARD
SUMMARY OF FINDINGS

The matter before the Board is the death of a minor, Philip Arthur Halpern, 15 (the 'Suspect'), who was shot and killed by County peace officers after an escape from New Lebanon town jail where the Suspect had been incarcerated following indictment on charges of murder, manslaughter, rape and sodomy.

On the afternoon of May 8 the Suspect was struck by shots fired by Thomas T. Ebbans, Chief Deputy, and Bradford Ellison, Sheriff, Harrison County. It was determined that Deputy Ebbans fired two shots, hitting the Suspect twice in the chest and Sheriff Ellison fired four times, hitting the Suspect once in the neck. All bullets were recovered. The Suspect was pronounced dead at the scene.

The facts surrounding the shooting are not in dispute. When shot, the Suspect was holding a loaded .38-caliber Smith & Wesson pistol which he had taken from a New Lebanon town deputy whom he had severely beaten when he escaped earlier in the day. The Suspect acted in a deranged manner and it apparently was his intention to shoot his father. Also present were the Suspect's mother, New Lebanon Detective William Corde and Charles Mahoney, a licensed and bonded private investigator from Missouri who was acting as consultant to the New Lebanon Sheriff's Department.

As Detective Corde was attempting to talk the Suspect into surrendering, Sheriff Ellison and Deputy Ebbans approached from the rear entrance to the house. Mr Mahoney stated that the Suspect suddenly raised the gun and, according to Mr Mahoney, 'was about to discharge his weapon at Detective Corde and myself, causing me to fear for our safety.' Mr Mahoney fired two shots at the Suspect, missing both times. Sheriff Ellison and Deputy Ebbans heard these shots and assumed the Suspect, who had turned and was pointing his gun at them, had begun firing. They returned gunfire which resulted in the Suspect's death.

It is the conclusion of the Board that the shooting of the Suspect was justifiable and that both Sheriff Ellison and Deputy Ebbans acted within the boundaries of prudent law enforcement. Detective Corde testified that the Suspect had not been about to fire and we agree that Mr Mahoney was perhaps premature in firing the shots that precipitated the killing. However, that was a judgement he made during an extremely stressful confrontation and this Board is prepared to accept that his behavior was justified under the circumstances.

Testimony was given by the Suspect's father that prior to the incident, he delivered to Sheriff Steven Ribbon of the New Lebanon Sheriff's Department a note purporting to be evidence casting doubt on the Suspect's guilt. Sheriff Ribbon testified that he felt the note was of such importance that he personally took it to the state laboratory for forensic analysis and through a miscommunication, none of the law enforcement officers at the scene of the shooting were made aware of the note's existence. However, the existence and authenticity of the note bear solely on the issue of the Suspect's innocence with respect to his prime indictments in one of the murders of which he was accused; they are irrelevant with respect to the escape and the incidents of assault that led to the shooting.

Therefore, THIS BOARD OF INQUIRY CONCLUDES that

1.The death of Philip Arthur Halpern was justifiable.

2.The death shall not be presented for inquest to the Grand Jury of the County of Harrison.

3.No grounds exist to dismiss, suspend, fine or in any way reprimand Sheriff Bradford Ellison or Deputy Thomas T. Ebbans on the basis of the events occurring in the house of Creth A. Halpern on May 8.

Here is Bill Corde.

He writes three parking violations – after turning the thick handles of the meters to make sure that the perpetrators are in fact out of time and didn't just forget to crank in their coins. This is not generosity on Corde's part; nobody argues with cops more vehemently than parking violators.

He stops Trudy Parson's '74 Gremlin to tell her that the blinker in her right turn signal is on the fritz and the left rear is low too.

He tanks up a Plymouth and sits in a speed trap for half the day, catching himself nothing but one salesman from Chicago. He gives the man a ticket – not a warning – because the driver is wearing a fish gray silk suit and a pinkie ring and has a dark tan and here it is just mid May.

Howdy, fellas, that wouldn't be a beer you got in there, would it, reason I ask is neither of you look like you're eighteen, so if it is I sure hope you're going to tell me that you just found those cans in the street and are about to

*dump them out and take them to A&P for the nickel, is
that right?*

Corde has requested a hearing on the charge of
destroying Jennie Gebben's letters. Because he has
been reinstated and the inquest has been canceled the
district attorney tells him a hearing would be moot.
Corde looks up the word 'moot', then he debates for a
time and files another notice seeking the hearing. A day
later he receives a call from the judge's clerk telling him
that the application was rejected and they will be
sending him a notice to that effect by registered mail
return receipt requested.

Corde receives another official communication. This
one is from the Missouri attorney general's office. It
thanks him for his letter and says that someone from the
office will be checking on the propriety of private
investigation and firearm licences issued to one Charles
Mahoney, a resident of St Louis.

The County Sheriff's Department officially closes
both the Gebben and the Rossiter cases. When Corde
asks to see this note or whatever it is that Creth Halpern
gave to Ribbon, Hammerback Ellison himself calls up
Corde at home and reminds him that the cases have
been disposed of. He uses those words. *Disposed of.*
Corde says he understands but could he still see the
note? Ellison says sorry it's been sent to the archive files.

Corde goes to one of Jamie's wrestling matches and
watches the boy lose bad. The family was planning to eat
out afterward but nobody is in the mood after the loss.
Jamie says he's going out with some teammates and
Corde and Diane and Sarah drive home for French toast.

Corde forms mixed feelings about Dr Parker, who has
just depleted exactly three-fifths of the Cordes' savings
account and has turned Sarah into a story-telling fiend.
The girl has used up four tape cassettes with her book.
When Corde asks her how long the book will be, she tells
him a million jillion pages, and Corde says that's pretty
long, how long will it take to read? She answers forever.
One day Corde finds her looking out over the backyard,

354

long-faced. He asks her what's wrong, thinking her studies are troubling her. She says she's afraid that the Sunshine Man her wizard is gone for good. She hasn't seen him for a long time. Corde would like to console her but he does not know what to say. He tells her to get washed up, it's time for dinner, and she sadly complies.

Diane is glad that Sarah is off the Ritalin since she's just joined the Drug-Free America task force of the Sesquicentennial Celebration Committee and will be personally responsible for the Fourth of July *Just Say No!* float. One morning in their bedroom Diane paints on make-your-man-crazy red nail polish and Corde watches the color go on but what he thinks of is the smell, which reminds him of the dope he brushed on the balsawood airplanes as a boy to stiffen the paper wings. This in turn makes him think of Philip Halpern. He doesn't tell his wife this thought but just says my you look nice, oh, yes . . .

Diane is also his source of information about Sarah's tutor, Ben Breck. Corde still hasn't met him though he'd like to. Sarah has improved remarkably since they've been working together. Sarah talks about Breck often but Corde doesn't feel jealous of this displaced attention though he thinks of the months and months of agony he himself has been through as he worked with her and here this fellow turns her around in a couple of weeks. What can you do?

Corde goes fishing with Jamie. They get into their aluminium canoe and push off into the deep reservoir. Their permits are in order and Corde has with him a knotted length of string to make sure that the bass they take are legal. Corde hopes a big needle-nosed pike or musky has come south; he would like to trophy it for Jamie's wall. The boy continues to be morose and uncommunicative. Corde hashes it over with himself then finally asks bluntly if he wants to talk about Philip and Jamie says no he doesn't. Five minutes later though, out of the blue, the boy says he sort of thinks that Philip thought Jamie'd turned him in.

They beach the canoe and sit together on a slab of steel-color rock. Corde explains that he told Philip before he was shot that Jamie didn't turn him in at all, that Jamie got tricked. Philip understood and believed that. Corde puts thirty-nine years of sincerity into this speech. Jamie's expression doesn't change and they silently return to fishing. Five minutes later Jamie asks if Corde will be at the final wrestling match in two weeks and Corde says that nothing – hell or high water or a sale at Sears – will keep him away. The boy's face comes close to a smile and with the nod he gives his father Corde knows they're back on track.

Corde calls Wynton Kresge at his office and is shocked to hear the secretary say that he's no longer with the school. Does that mean he's quit, Corde asks, or been fired? She says it means he's no longer with the school. He calls Kresge at home but he isn't there or he's told his wife to say he isn't. Corde leaves a message.

Here is Bill Corde, driving out to dark Blackfoot Pond the dark dam the dark trees the gray-green mud, getting out of the cruiser, walking through the tangled brush. There's nothing much to see thanks to the sightseers, the fishermen, two power-out rainstorms and one tornado that vaulted over New Lebanon the other day, spraying branches and a million just-born leaves all over the murder scene.

Here is Bill Corde, flipping a dull quarter over his fingers as he walks through the site of paired deaths over ground that for him fairly trembles beneath his feet.

The case is closed but here he walks, here he bends to the ground and kicks at twigs and leaves and the flattened disks of beer cans, here he pauses at times and squints into the deeper forest then moves on.

Here is Bill Corde.

'You know the one I mean?' the man was asking. He was lean, bald and wore a blue suit whose polyester fibres glistened like mica. Down the front of his white shirt a red-and-black striped tie hung stiff as a paint stirrer. 'The plant out on 117?'

'Walt.'

'I want to explain. Let me explain.'

Professor Randy Sayles wasn't feeling well. Although he was tearfully relieved that the Gebben investigation was over and the Halpern boy was buried, he had learned that the financial situation of the university was worse than Dean Larraby had at first let on. She had called the day before to tell him an additional million was needed. To the man in whose office he now sat Sayles said patiently, 'Go ahead. Explain.'

'She was valued at nine, we loaned seven and when we foreclosed the market'd turned and it was worth five. That's a two-hundred-thousand bad loan and we ate up our reserve by February because of a dozen just like her. No, a dozen and a half.'

The office did not much look like a bank president's. It was closer to a Tru-Value manager's. There was some blotchy modern litho up on the wall but Sayles saw a sticker on the side of the frame and knew he wasn't looking at the real article; you don't generally get much in the way of investment art at Walgreen's especially at a two-for-one sale.

Sayles pulled a packet of papers out of his briefcase. 'I wouldn't be here hat in hand if it weren't serious, Walt. We're looking at a shortfall of close to thirteen million this year.'

'Things're tough all over.'

Sayles tried not to sound desperate. He pictured himself up in front of his class. Assured, smiling, humorous. Everything he'd learned in twenty years of teaching he brought to bear on this man. 'We've got benefactor commitments of about seven. We're talking to—'

The banker too was used to theatrics. 'Look out that window, what do you see?'

Sayles counterattacked. 'I see a city that'll suffer to its very heart if Auden University closes.'

Nice try. The banker smiled and shook his head. 'I'm talking about that building not fifty yards up the street. Plainsman's S&L. The RTC's moved in and she's in conservatorship. They're going to sell it off. We're more solid but not a lot. The loan committee, no way'll it approve Auden a penny.' The banker's voice remained a low calm monotone as he twisted his curly eyebrow with his thumb and ring finger. He dressed in pastel plastic cloth, he had yellow teeth and glistening see-through hair and under the veneer desk he kept a casual beat with crinkly black Monkey Ward shoes. Sayles knew however that Wall Street had nothing on this guy.

'Auden closes,' Sayles said, 'it'll be a tragedy.'

'It'll be a tragedy but it'll be more of a tragedy if I write a bad loan and the US attorney up in Higgins indicts me.'

'Oh, come on, Walt, it's not like you're buying yourself a Porsche. They're not going to arrest you for loaning money to a university.'

The banker looked at Sayles and seemed to be taking his pulse. Sayles thought: *I'm just like the farmers he disbursed loans to, loans written on the strength of bad collateral and their desperation facing the loss of two hundred years' worth of family land.* Randy Sayles, associate dean of financial aid, knew that you never saw a person as clearly as when you hand him a large check.

The professor said, 'What if we gave you a piece of the new dorm? It cost twenty-three million.'

'Cost ain't worth. And if we foreclosed it'd be because the school went under. And what good's a dorm without a school to go with it?'

'Land alone'd be worth three million.'

'Not with an empty dorm sitting on it.'

'You got the parking lot right on the highway.'

'I'm sorry.'

These two words lanced Sayles's heart. He stood up and said with a despair that made both men extremely uncomfortable, 'You were my last chance.' Neither said a word for a moment. Sayles picked up his financials and put them into his battered briefcase.

He started out the door.

'Hold up, Professor . . .'

Sayles turned and saw in the man's face a debate. The banker arrived at a disagreeable conclusion. Writing a name and number on a piece of paper, he said, 'I'm not doing this. You didn't get this from me. You don't know me.'

Sayles looked at the scrawl. *Fred Barrett*. Next to the name was a phone number. Area code 312. Chicago.

'Who is he?'

After a pause the banker said, 'I don't know what you're talking about.'

He found it completely by accident.

Because Brian Okun had made up the rumour that Jennie Gebben and Leon Gilchrist were lovers, he had not bothered to do what he had promised the dean – look through the professor's office for evidence. He would have been content to tell her that he had made a futile search and let it go at that. Then when Gilchrist turned in Okun's scathing evaluation Okun would claim that Gilchrist was seeking retribution for his espionage.

A delightful symmetry to the whole matter.

The whole affair, *you might say.*

This was a good plan but he thought of a much better one when, placing a sheet of student grades on Gilchrist's desk, he noticed an envelope addressed in flowery script to the professor. The writer was a young woman student. Okun lifted the crinkly envelope and found to his huge amusement the paper was perfumed. Gilchrist, finally back from San Francisco, was at the moment lecturing his class, and the graduate assistant immediately sat down in the professor's chair and opened the unsealed envelope.

The poem scanned very badly, thought Okun the critic.

When the memory of you / swallows me the way I took / your lovely cock into my mouth . . .

He decided he would have given it a D for form and a C minus for content ('Your thinking is unoriginal, your meter too unvaried and honey is a hopelessly trite metaphor for semen.') This didn't matter however because he believed the poem would have at least one ardent reader.

Okun now sat in Dean Larraby's office, watching her flick the poem with a tough, wrinkled index finger. 'You didn't . . .' She hesitated. 'You didn't get it out of his mailbox?'

It wasn't stamped or postmarked, you stupid fool, how could it have been mailed? Okun said mildly, 'I'd never do anything illegal. It was lying out on his desk.'

'Who's the girl? Doris Cutting?'

'Student of his. I don't know anything about her.'

'Do you know if he took her to San Francisco with him?'

I just said I don't know her. Senile already? Okun frowned. 'I wonder.'

'This is enough for me.'

'It's hard for me to speak against him,' Okun said. 'He's taught me so much. But to sleep with a student . . . It's a very vulnerable time for young people. I used to respect him.' His mouth tightened into a little bundle of disappointment.

'We'll fire him. We have no choice. It's got to be done. We'll wait till the semester's over. His last lecture's when?'

'Two days.'

'I'll tell him afterward, after the students have gone. We'll want to minimize publicity. You'll keep this quiet until then?'

He nodded gravely. 'Whatever you'd like, Dean.' Okun stood and started for the door.

'Oh, Brian?' As he turned she said, 'I just wanted to say, I'm sorry. I know this was difficult for you. To put the school above your personal loyalty. I won't forget it.'

'Sometimes,' Okun said, 'as Immanuel Kant tells us, sacrifices must be made for a higher good.'

2

'You said you'd polish them.'

'I'll polish them.'

'You said today.'

'I'll polish them today,' Amos Trout said, slouching in his lopsided green Naugahyde easy chair. He scooped up the remote control and turned the volume up.

His lean, wattle-skinned wife poured the Swan's Down cake mix into a Pyrex bowl and decided he wasn't going to get away with it. She set down the egg and said, 'When I was to church Ada Kemple looked right down at my feet, there was nothing else for yards around, had to've been my feet, and if that woman didn't have a gleam in her eye when she surfaced I don't know what. I liked to die of embarrassment.'

'I said I'd polish them.'

'Here.' She handed him the navy blue pumps as if she were offering him dueling pistols.

Trout took them then looked at the TV screen. It wouldn't've been so bad if Chicago wasn't playing New York and it wasn't the bottom of the sixth and the score wasn't tied with Mets go-ahead on third and only one out.

But She had spoken. And so Amos Trout turned the sound up again and carried the shoes down to the basement. (*Don't seem so scuffed that the toothless bitch Ada Kemple has anything to snicker about through her smear of cheap pasty makeup.)*

'. . . a grounder to left . . . *snagged* by the shortstop, backhand! What a catch! There'll be a play at home . . . The runner—'

CLICK. The TV went silent. His wife's footsteps sounded above him on their way back to the kitchen.

Ah, it hurts. Sometimes it hurts.

Trout grimaced then snatched a newspaper from the huge stack that had accumulated while they'd been on vacation in Minnesota. He spread it out on the mottled brown linoleum. He stood slowly and got the paraphernalia – the blue polish, the brush, the buffing cloth – and set it all out in front of him. He picked up each shoe and examined the amount of work. He turned one upside down. A broken toenail like a chip of fogged ice fell out. He set the shoe down on the newspaper and as he applied polish he focused past the shoes to the paper itself.

Trout read for a moment then stood up. He tossed the shoes on top of the clothes dryer. One left a long blue streak on the enameled metal. He carried the newspaper into the kitchen where his wife sat cross-legged, chatting on the phone.

'The game was too loud,' she said to him. 'I shut it off.' Then returned to the phone.

He said, 'Hang up.'

Her neck skin quivered at the command. She blinked at him. 'I'm talking to my mother.'

'Hang up.'

She looked at the yellowed rotary dial for an explanation of this madness. 'I'll call you back, Mom.'

He took the receiver from her and pressed the button down to clear the line.

'What are you doing?'

'Making a phone call.'

'Aren't you going to polish my shoes?'

'No,' he said, 'I'm not.' And began to dial.

The Oakwood Mall. How Bill Corde hated malls.

Oh, the stores were clean, the prices reasonable. Sears guaranteed satisfaction and where in the whole of the world did you get that nowadays without more strings attached than you could count? Here you could buy hot egg rolls and tacos and Mrs Field's dense cookies and frozen yogurt. You could slip your arm around your wife, walk her into Victoria's Secret and park her in front of a mannequin wearing red silk panties and bra and a black garter belt then kiss her neck while she squirmed and blushed and let you buy her, well, not that outfit but a nice sexy nightgown.

But malls for Corde meant the Fairway Mall in St Louis, where two policemen had died because of him and that was why he never came here.

He glanced at Toys 'R' Us. In the window a cardboard cutout of Dathar-IV stood over an army of warriors from the Lost Dimension. Corde looked at this for a moment then walked on until he found Floors for All. He wasn't more than ten feet inside before a sports-coated man all of twenty-one pounced. 'I know who you are,' the kid said. 'You're a man with a naked floor.'

'I'm—'

'Floors are just like you and me. We want new threads sometimes, so does your floor. It gets tired of the same old outfit. What's in your closet right now? A double-breasted suit, slacks, Bermudas, Izod shirts, ha, a khaki *uniform* or two, ha, am I right? Think how jealous your floor is.'

'No—'

'You don't know what a difference new carpeting makes. To your peace of mind. To your marriage.' He was a pit bull with a feeble blond mustache. 'Do you want to talk about stress? What color's your carpet now?'

'I'm not really interested—'

'Bare floors? Whoa, let's talk stress.'

'No carpet. Just Amos Trout.'

'You're not here to buy carpet?'

'No.'

363

'Detective?' Trout came out from the back room. They shook hands.

'Hey, Sheriff,' the kid said, 'your police station have carpeting?'

Trout waved him away.

When they were seated by Trout's desk Corde said, 'Eager.'

'Haw. No. Pain in the ass. But he sells carpet. He'll be down at the Nissan dealership in three years and probably selling Boeings by the time he's twenty-eight. I can't keep boys like that long.'

Corde asked, 'You said you saw the ad in the *Register*?'

'The wife and I were to Minnesota on vacation for a while after that murder happened. Just a coincidence but I saw it when I spread out the paper to shine her shoes. You shine your wife's shoes, Officer?'

'They do love it, don't they? Now tell me, you were driving along Route 302 that night. That'd be Tuesday night, April 20?'

'That's right. I was driving home. It was about ten, ten-thirty or so. That Tuesday was our acrylic pile sale and we'd done so well I'd had to stay late to log in the receipts and mark down which're checks, which're charges, which're cash, you get the picture. So I got me a Slurpee and was driving past the pond when this man suddenly runs into the road in front of me. What happened was that my left high beam's out of whack. And I don't think he could see me coming because there was this bush hanging out into the road that the county really oughta take care of.'

'You had a clear view?'

'Sure did. There he was in front of me, leaping like a toad on July asphalt. Then he saw me and just froze and I swerved out of the way and that was that.'

'Was there a car nearby?'

'Yessir. But I didn't see what kind.'

'Was it light or dark?'

'The car? Lighter more'n darker.'

'You recall the plates?'

'Don't even know if it had plates or was a truck or sedan. I just didn't notice, I was so concerned with not running that man over. What was left of the Slurpee went onto the floor and for the first time I was glad I got the maroon interior.'

'He was a man, not a boy?'

'Not a boy, nope. Probably late thirties, early forties.'

'Could you describe him?'

'Solid build but not fat, short hair, not real dark, combed straight back. He was wearing dark pants and a light jacket but the jacket was covered with dirt.'

'White?'

'Pardon?'

'What was his race?'

'Oh. Yeah, he was white.'

'Jewelry, hats, shoes?'

'No, like I say, I swerved past him real fast.'

'If you saw a picture of him would you remember it?'

'Like in a lineup or something? I could try.'

'Anything else you remember?'

'No.'

'Nothing unusual? Try to think back.'

'No, nothing. Well, except I figured he was handy. I mean, he knew about cars. He was going to replace the ignition cable himself. Not everybody can do that. That's why I almost stopped. To help him.'

'Ignition cable?'

'But it was late and the wife gets a bee in her bra I don't get home by eleven, sale or no.'

'He was working on the car?'

'Not exactly, he was carrying that piece of wire over to it.'

'Could you describe it?'

'You know, ignition wire. White, thick. Looked to be wrapped in plastic like from NAPA.'

'Could it've been rope, like clothesline?'

Amos Trout went silent for a moment. 'Could very well've been.'

* * *

Diane walked into the living room and found Ben Breck cutting letters out of sandpaper. Sarah sat on the couch watching him. 'I owe you a new pair of scissors,' he said.

'Beg pardon?'

He said, 'I only had coarse sandpaper. It pretty much ruined the blade.'

'Well now, I wouldn't worry about it,' Diane said. 'What exactly are you doing?'

'"Storage",' Breck said solemnly and handed an E to Sarah. 'Touch it, feel it.' Sarah ran her hand over the letter. 'E,' she said. The letter joined STORAG on the table. Sarah spelled the word out loud, touching each letter. Breck scooped them up and hid them behind his back and would hand her one at a time. Eyes closed, the girl would touch it then tell him which letter it was.

Diane watched, engrossed in the drill. After ten minutes he said, 'That's it for today, Sarah. You did very well but keep working on the b and the d and the q and the p. You get those mixed up.'

'I will, Dr Breck.' Sarah assembled the sandpaper letters and put them into her Barbie backpack, in which she kept her tape recorder, cassettes and exercises she was working on. Diane slipped her arm around her daughter.

Breck said, 'Next Thursday?'

'Fine,' Diane said, 'I'll be home all day.' Then she added, '*We'll* be home, I mean.'

Sarah ran outside. 'I'll be back later, Mom.'

'Stay close to home.'

Breck and Diane walked into the kitchen and Diane poured two cups from a Braun coffee maker without asking if he wanted any. Breck glanced at her red polished nails then his eyes slipped to her blouse, two buttons open at the chest. He seemed to enjoy the route his gaze followed. She reserved judgment on this reaction.

She reserved judgment on her own as well.

Breck spent a long moment studying a picture of Corde in uniform. It was taped to the refrigerator next to an eagle Sarah had cut out of construction paper.

'It must be exciting being married to a policeman.'

'More of an inconvenience, I'd say. We get calls at all hours and our friends are always wanting Bill to do something about P&Z or fixing tickets or something. Ever been married, Ben?'

She had checked his heart finger at their first meeting.

'No. Never have been so lucky.' He sipped the coffee. Diane watched him closely.

'That too strong, there's hot tap water. Our boiler gets it to about one forty-five.'

'It's fine.'

Diane said, 'The thing about Bill is, he's obsessive. He—'

'You probably mean *compulsive*.'

'I do?'

'Compulsive is when you do something repetitively, obsessive is when you think about something repetitively.'

'Oh. Well, then he's both.' They laughed and she continued, 'He just doesn't stop. He's a workaholic. Not that I mind. Keeps him out of my hair and when he's home he's pretty much *home* if you know what I mean. But once he gets his mind set he's like a terrier got hold of a rat. Last night I went to bed and he was still burning the midnight oil. Bill says a case is like building a brick wall. There are always plenty of bricks if you take the trouble to look for them.'

'And he takes the trouble?'

'Whoa, that's true.'

'I've been an expert witness in court a few times, testifying on the psychology of observation. How witnesses can see things that aren't there and miss things that are. The senses are extraordinarily unreliable.'

'All I know is I don't get much involved in his cases. It's so, you know, grim. It's different when you watch it on television.'

So why hasn't he been married?

'I've done research into violence,' Breck said. 'Two

associates of mine have done work with sociopaths—'

'Is that like a psychopath? Like, you know, Tony Curtis in *Psycho*.'

'Tony *Perkins*, I believe.'

'Right, right.' *Forty-one and never married.*

'They've worked with some pretty odious characters—' *Odious.*

'—and their theory is that commercial entertainment does a disservice when it minimizes violence. That it tends to distort mental judgment and leads to situations where individuals act violently because they feel the impact in human terms will be inconsequential. We're seeing—'

Diane's palms moistened as she leaned forward, trying to follow what he said.

'—many cases of blunted affect on the part of young people in response to films and—'

'Uhm. *Af*-fect?'

He saw that he'd lost her and shook his head in apology. '*Affect*. It means emotion. Kids see people getting blown up and murdered on screen and it doesn't move them. They don't feel anything. Or worse, they laugh.'

'I'd rather Jamie didn't watch those movies ... Well, look at his friend. They got caught up in that *Lost Dimension*. Look what happened.'

'That boy who killed the girls?' Breck asked. 'He might have been influenced by the movie.'

The corner of Diane's mouth hardened. 'Well, even with him getting killed and all, Bill still doesn't think the boy did it.'

'He doesn't?' Breck asked with surprise. 'But your bodyguard is gone.'

'Wait till the story hits the news.'

'Story?'

'There's a new witness.' She slung the words bitterly.

'But the papers all said the boy did it.'

'The papers and just about everybody else in town. They were all too happy to close the case. But not my

Bill, oh no. He's still investigating. He doesn't give up. He went charging off this morning after some new lead. He thinks he can prove the boy didn't do it.'

Diane noted the anger in her voice as she gazed outside at the spot where Tom's cruiser had been parked all these long weeks. 'When you're young, when you're Sarah's age, everything's clear, all the endings are tidy. You know who the bad guys are and if they get away at least they're still the bad guys. At our age, who knows anything?'

Breck finished the coffee. 'You have a lovely home here.'

It seemed to Diane that he said it wistfully but before she heard anything that confirmed that impression, he added, 'Know what I'd like?'

'Name it,' she said, smiling, coquettish as a barmaid.

'Let's go for a walk. Show me your property.'

'Well, sure.' She pulled a jacket on and they walked outside.

She showed him her herb garden then the muddy strip of potential lawn then the spots where the bulbs would've come up if the deer hadn't been at them. Breck muttered appreciative comments then strolled toward the back of the lot and its low post-and-rail fence. 'Let's check out the woods.'

'Uh-un,' Diane said, leading him around to the side. 'We have to go the long way.'

'Around that little fence? We can jump it, can't we?' Breck asked.

'Uhm, see those cows?'

'What about them?'

'How expensive are those Shee-caw-go shoes of yours?' she asked.

'Oh,' he said, 'got it.'

They both laughed as they walked around the pasture and into the strip of tall grass and knobby oak saplings that bordered the forest. Diane wasn't the least surprised when, out of view of the house, Breck took her hand. Nor was she surprised that she let him.

'Weren't the boy after all?'

'Uh-uh. They got a new witness.'

Their eyes would make troubled circuits of the room, following the green-gray checkers of linoleum to their conclusion in the dark reaches of the County Building cafeteria. Then they'd turn back to watch the half-moons of ice slowly water their Cokes.

'Necessitates something.' The man speaking was fat. Through a short-sleeved white shirt his belly worked on the elasticity of his Sears waistband. He had white hair, crisp with dried Vitalis, combed back. His name was Jack Treadle and in addition to other jobs he was supervisor of Harrison County. All aspects of his face had jowls – eyes, mouth, chin. He poked his little finger into his cheek to rub a tooth through skin.

'Suppose so,' said the other man. Just as jowly though not so fat. He too wore short-sleeved white and on top of it a camel-tan sports coat. Bull Cooper was a real estate broker and the mayor of New Lebanon. These two were major players in the Oval Office of Harrison County.

'Way it sizes up,' Treadle said, 'the boy—'

Cooper said defensively, 'He had a gun.'

'Well, he may've. But I don't give two turds about the incident report. We shouldn'ta arrested him, we shouldn'ta let him get loose, we shouldn'ta shot him down.'

'Well . . .'

'Hi ho the derry-o, somebody's gonna get fucked for this.'

'Boy got shot bad,' Cooper agreed.

'Got shot dead,' Treadle snorted. Around them, slow-talking small-town lawyers and their clients ate liverwurst sandwiches and plates of $1.59 macaroni and cheese while they waved away excited spring flies. Treadle was a man who did best with ignorant friends and small enemies; he was in his element here and had nodded greetings to half the room during the course of this meal.

370

He said, 'Hammerback and Ribbon were playing cute. I mean, shit, they were playing big-time sheriffs and they wanted press, they wanted a big bust and they wanted to tie that other co-ed killing last year in with all this serial killer, goat skinner fucking crap. Well, they got press, all right, which are now wondering why we let a innocent kid get killed. We got the SBI looking over our shoulder and we probably got some ethics panel up in Higgins about to poke its finger up our ass. We gotta give 'em somebody. I mean, shit.'

'And you're thinking somebody from New Lebanon, I know you are.' Cooper hawked and cleared his mouth with a thick napkin.

'Naw, naw, don't matter to me. If we pick a county man and I make the announcement then it looks good for me. If he's town and you make the announcement it's good for you. You know, like, it hurts us to do it but we're cleaning out our own. No cover-up.'

'I didn't think of that.' Cooper relaxed then added, 'What about that Mahoney?'

'What about him?'

'Corde copied me on this letter he sent the Missouri AG. He wants Mahoney's nuts, Corde does. Whoa, Ribbon's got a feather in his ass over that, I'll tell you.'

'What's the point?'

Cooper said, 'Mahoney shouldn't've even been on the case. He's a civilian.'

'Well.' Treadle guffawed. 'I don't give a shit about Mahoney. What's done's done. Things like Mahoney fall through the cracks and that's the way of the world.'

'What's the options? Who bites the big one?'

'There's Ellison,' Treadle offered casually, stating the obvious. 'Then there's Ribbon. But if it's somebody too high up it'll look bad for us – like you and me weren't enough in charge.'

Cooper said, 'We had a couple county deputies working on the case. And Bill Corde was running the investigation for a while.'

'Corde's a smart guy and he, he . . .' Treadle stammered as he groped for a thought.

'Found this new witness.'

'He found this witness,' Treadle agreed. 'And he . . .'

'He doesn't take any crap,' Cooper offered.

'No, he doesn't take any crap.'

'But,' Cooper said slowly, 'there's the trouble.'

'What trouble?'

'Didn't you hear? He may've accidentally on purpose lost some evidence. There was word he'd been fucking the Gebben girl. She was a regular little c-you-know-what. Anyway, some letters or shit got burnt up that may've connected her with Corde. They dropped the investigation—'

'What investigation?'

'What I'm saying. About Corde, about him eighty-sixing the evidence. But he wasn't ever found *innocent*. They just dropped it.'

Treadle's eyes brightened. 'Think that's something we can use?'

'I suppose that depends,' Cooper said, 'on whether we *want* to use it or not.'

Bill Corde was talking on the pay phone to Diane. It was after dusk and he was in front of Dregg's Variety, perilously close to Route 117. Every sixth or seventh car whipped by so fast he felt his uniform tugged by the slipstream as if the drivers were playing a fun game of cop-grazing.

'Jamie?' Corde asked, 'What's the matter with him?'

'He got home late. He didn't call or anything. I want you to talk to him. It's the second night in a row.'

'Well, I will. But I'm . . .' Corde let the cyclone from a Mack eighteen-wheeler spin past then continued, 'But I'm a little busy right at the moment. This lead on the Gebben case. He's okay?'

Diane said testily, 'Of course he's okay. I just said he's okay.'

'I'm out here on the highway,' Corde said to explain

his distraction. Then he added, 'I'll talk to him tonight.'

'I don't want you to talk to him. I wanted . . .'

'What?'

'Nothing.'

Corde ignored the brittleness and asked, 'How's Sarah?'

'She had a good session with Ben and she said she did two more chapters of her book. The insurance money didn't come again today. I was thinking maybe you should call . . .'

I'm out here in the middle of the highway.

Diane continued, 'It's over two thousand. Mom had her ovaries out for three thousand five. I'm so glad Ben's only twenty an hour. That's a lifesaver.'

'Right.' *Who's Ben? Oh, the tutor.* 'Well,' Corde said, 'that's good. I better go.'

'Wait. One more thing. The team can't get a bus for the match in Higgins. Jamie wants to know if we can drive him and Davey?'

'I guess. Sure.'

'You won't forget? It's the last match of the season.'

'I won't forget.'

Another car was approaching. This one didn't speed past. It stopped. Corde looked up and saw Steve Ribbon and Jack Treadle looking at him. Ribbon was solemn.

Oh, brother.

It was Jack Treadle's car – a bottom-of-the-line Mercedes though it had a big fancy car phone. They pulled in front of Corde's cruiser and parked. The two men got out. He realized Diane was saying something to him. He said, 'Gotta go. Be back around eight.' He hung up.

Treadle stayed in the car. Ribbon walked toward Corde. They nodded greetings. 'How's that lead of yours panning out, Bill?' he asked with no interest.

'Slow but we're making progress.'

Ribbon said, 'How about we walk over that way?' He pointed to a shady spot of new-cut grass beside an enormous oak.

Something familiar here. Haven't we done this before?
Corde walked along under the tree's massive branches, studying Ribbon's expression then focusing on Treadle's. He fished a nickel out of his pocket and did the coin trick.

There were many things to think about but the one concern he settled on was purely practical: how he was going to break the news to Diane that he'd been fired.

3

'We could sell the car.'

Diane Corde had been cleaning out the cupboards. There were cans and boxes covering the counters and tabletop. Corde pulled off his shoes and sat at the kitchen table. A pork-and-beans can rolled toward him. He caught it as it fell off the table. He read the label for a moment then set it down again.

'The car?' he asked.

Diane said, 'You got the axe, ain't the end of the world. We can sell the second car, don't need it anyway, and that'll save us the insurance and upkeep.'

He looked back at the bottle. 'Why you think I got fired?'

'You looking as mournful as you do presently's got something to do with it.'

Bill Corde said, 'They offered me the job of sheriff.'

After all these years of marriage there were still a few times when she couldn't tell when he was joking. She put away two cans of pinto beans, reached for a third then stopped.

Corde said, 'I'm serious.'

'I'm guessing there'd be a little more to it.'

'They bailed Steve Ribbon out. He blew the case bad but he's in tight with Bull Cooper and Jack Treadle so they're moving him up to some plush job with the county. I'm sheriff. Jim Slocum takes over on felony

375

investigations. T.T. got fired. With this new witness, we know that Philip was innocent. They needed somebody to blame for the boy's death. T.T. took the hit.'

'But I thought there was an inquiry?'

'He's not been charged with anything. He's just been fired.'

'That's too bad. I always liked him. He's a good man.'

'He's a damn good man,' Corde said vehemently.

She sat on the kitchen chair that Corde held out for her. They'd refinished these chairs themselves. A memory smell of the sulfury Rock Magic stripper came back to him.

She said, 'And it's T.T.'s the reason you're upset?'

'Partly. And I'd have to give up investigating.'

'So what you're worried about is sitting behind a desk?'

'Yeah,' Corde said. Then figuring he shouldn't be lying to her at least when it was so clear a lie: 'No. What it is is Slocum'd take over the Gebben case.'

'Well?'

Corde laughed. 'Honey, I've worked with Slocum for years. God bless him but Jim could catch a killer liming the body with the victim's wallet in his hip pocket and the murder knife in his teeth and he'd still screw up the case.'

Diane stared at the groceries for a long moment as if looking for something good about the deputy. She said, 'I guess.'

'I'm not inclined to let go of this one.'

Diane said, 'You won't like my question but I suppose they'd be paying you more money.'

'Some.'

'How much?'

'Five.'

'Hundred?'

'Thousand.'

'Ah.' There was enough reverence in her voice to send a bristle of pain all the way through Corde. Diane stood up. The third bean can joined its siblings on the shelf and then she started on the spices. 'You haven't eaten. What should we have for dinner? You interested in burritos?'

'I don't want this fellow to get away.'

'Slocum taking the case doesn't mean he's going to get away. Jim won't be the only one working on it, will he be?'

'There'll be some rookie from the county probably. The case's an embarrassment now. They just want it to go away.'

Diane gave up on the packaged goods. 'Just let me ask you. Say this fellow hadn't left those pictures of Sarrie for us. Would you still be this hot after him?'

'Maybe not.'

'That hadn't happened you'd take the job?'

Corde said, 'I always wanted to be sheriff.'

'Well, he didn't do anything to Sarrie and he's gone now. He's scooted, hasn't he?'

'Maybe. Not necessarily.'

Diane paused for a moment. 'You've wanted this for a long time. Everybody in town thinks more of you than Steve Ribbon. You could get yourself elected as often as you want.'

'I can't tell you I don't want it bad . . . And I better say it: With Steve gone, they need a new sheriff. It'll be either me or Slocum. We're senior.'

Diane said, 'Well, honey, I don't think you should pass it up. You can't be working *for* Jim. I just can't see that at all.'

Corde smiled in frustration. 'It'd be hard to do that to New Lebanon. Believe you me.'

She ripped open a cello pack of beef chuck cubes. They fell out glistening and soft on the cutting board. She picked up a knife and began to slice the cubes smaller. She wished she could talk to Ben Breck about this. Not ask his advice but just tell him what she felt. Without looking at her husband she said, 'I've got to be honest with you, Bill . . .' She rarely used his name. Sometimes in connection with expensive presents he'd just given her, more often in connection with sentences like that one. 'Jamie's coming up on college age in a few years and you know all about Dr Parker's bills.'

'Five thousand'd go a long way,' Corde said.

They were silent for a long time. Diane broke the stillness. 'Okay, I've said what I wanted to. Why don't you go talk to Jamie? He's got to call if he's going to be out past suppertime. He just came back then went into his room without saying hello or anything and he's listening to some gosh-awful rock music that's got screams and howling on it.'

'Well, maybe that means he's feeling better.'

'He could celebrate feeling better by getting home when he's supposed to and listening to the Bee Gees or Sinatra.'

'I'm not in the mood for giving him a talking-to tonight. Maybe tomorrow I will.'

She wiped her hands, full of dust and old flour. Corde was studying the ingredients of Budweiser and didn't see her wrench her lips into a narrow grimace or tighten her hand into a fist.

He doesn't want to do anything at all for those two girls dead by the pond – who wouldn't be dead if they hadn't been where they shouldn't've, campus sluts both of them. No, no, he wants to save those cops he thinks he laid out on the concrete floor of Fairway Mall, laid them out like the broken dolls they seemed to be on the front page of the Post-Dispatch.

Well, it's too late for them, Bill. It's too late.

Diane said to her husband, 'Quit looking so glum. You think about it tonight and whatever you decide we're still going to have my special burritos for dinner. Then we'll watch that Farrah Fawcett movie and I'll let you guess who the killer is. Now go water that new strip of lawn, whatever the birds've left.'

And she turned back to the sink, smiling brightly and scalded with anger at herself for this complete cowardice.

At eight-thirty in the morning Bill Corde walked into

the Sheriff's Department and hung up his blue jacket and his hat. Then he went into Steve Ribbon's office where he saw assembled the whole of the department except for the two deputies on morning patrol. They all nodded to him. He paused in the doorway then sat down among them – across the desk from Jim Slocum who was sitting in Ribbon's old high-backed chair.

Resting on the desk prominently was that morning's *Register*. The headline read: *'Sheriff's Dep't Reopens Auden Slay Case'*. A subhead: *'Youth's Death Termed "Tragic Accident".'*

'Well, gentlemen,' Slocum said, 'welcome. You've all heard the announcement about Steve's move up and we're real happy about that situation. I've asked you here to chew the fat a little and tell you about some of the changes I'm going to institute. And I want to say, if there are any questions, I want you to interrupt me. Will you do that?'

Lance Miller, his volume hampered by the surgical tape around his ribs, said, 'Sure we will.'

'Good. First off nothing I'm going to do is too, you know, radical but I've been thinking about the department and there are some things we can do different that'll be helpful.' He looked down at a sheet of paper. 'Well, number one, we're going to change the radio codes. We're used to a lot of casual talk on the radio and I don't think we should be doing that. You can get yourself into some real unprofessional situations that way. From now on we're going to be using the Associated Public Safety Communications Officers' Codes. That's like you see on TV. Ten-four. Ten-thirteen. All that. There are thirty-four of them and you'll have to learn them all. Oh and I don't want you to say A, B, C, you know. I want Adam, Boy, Charles and so on. We're not going to use the military ones. I know some of you boys learned Alpha, Bravo, Charlie, Delta. We're civilian and there's no reason for us to be ashamed of it.'

Two deputies nodded to show that they weren't ashamed.

God bless you but... Bill Corde shifted his weight and crossed his arms.

Slocum said, 'Ten-four?'

The deputies smiled politely.

'Another thing, I don't want you to worry about calling me by my first name. I've been Jim to you for years, and I don't want you all going grandiose on me and calling me "Sheriff" or especially "sir" or anything. Promise me that?'

'Yessir!' one of the deputies saluted sharply, and they all laughed.

'I've also been seeing about getting you boys walkie-talkies. Mayor Cooper thinks it's a good idea but where the money's going to come from is a whole 'nother thing so you may have to wait a while on those. But I just want you to know they're on our wish list. Now let's get down to brass tacks.'

Over the next ten minutes Corde tried his best to pay attention as Slocum described his plans for dividing New Lebanon into precincts and the special drug task force he was going to establish.

One deputy frowned and said, 'I don't think I ever arrested anybody for real drugs, Jim. Not more'n a little pot. Or coke at Auden.' He turned to another deputy. 'Anybody?'

The other deputies said they rarely had.

'Ain't been don't mean won't be,' Slocum said and held up a *Time* magazine cover about crack in small towns.

It was then that Corde, mentally, left the room.

A half hour later the deputies departed, carrying their photocopies of the new radio codes that they'd be quizzed on next week. Corde scooted his chair closer to the desk.

'Glad you stayed, Bill. There's some things I wanted to talk to you about.'

'Me too.'

Slocum said, 'I've been doing some thinking and I'd like to tell you what I've decided. This is a pretty odd situation, you being senior to me and me getting the job.

So I've come up with something I think you're going to be pretty pleased with.'

'Go ahead.'

'I'm going to create a new job here. It'll be called vice sheriff.' Slocum paused and let Corde taste the full flavor of the words. When he didn't respond Slocum said, 'And guess who's going to be appointed it? . . . You bet.' Slocum beamed. 'Sounds real nice, don't you think?'

'What exactly does it mean?'

'Oh, don't think I'm doing you a favor. No sir. The fact is you're going to work for it. I've been thinking about where your talents are, Bill. And it's pretty easy to see you're a better administrator than me. I'm going to throw a lot of stuff at you. Scheduling, overtime, personnel problems, payroll. So what do you say to that, Mr Vice Sheriff?'

Corde got up and closed the door then returned to the chair. He easily held Slocum's eye. 'Jim, you're the sheriff now and I think you'll probably run the department pretty good. But I'm doing one thing and one thing only and that's tracking down Jennie Gebben's killer. I'm finding him whether he's in New Lebanon or Fredericksberg or Chicago or Mexico City and I'm bringing him back for trial. Now, tell me, what's the budget for deputies?'

'What?' Slocum was too surprised to frown.

'The budget?' Corde asked impatiently. 'Didn't Steve show you the department budget?'

'Yeah, somewhere . . .' He inspected the desk for a moment, looking for something he had no desire to find. 'But, Bill, the thing is I don't know I can have you assigned to just one case. We're down one man already, what with Lance's broken ribs and all. This's a pretty big request. I'll have to think about it.'

'I believe that's it there, that computer printout.'

Slocum pulled it out and opened it up. 'What, is it this column? It says "Personnel".'

Corde said, 'That's actual. I need to know budgeted.'

'What's that?'

'Here, gimme.' Corde scowled. 'That's what I was afraid of. We've hardly got enough left for raises. Not enough for a new man.'

'Raises? Should I give the men raises?'

Corde was making notes on his index cards. He said, 'We've got about five thousand in travel and equipment left for the rest of the year . . . Well, I'd like you to leave that alone. I'm going to need a good portion of it if not everything.'

'Equipment? But I told you I was having trouble getting money for the walkie-talkies. And I was going to buy us all Glocks. They cost over four hundred each.'

'Glocks? Jim, we don't need fifteen-round automatics.'

Slocum didn't speak for a minute then he said quietly, 'I'm the sheriff, Bill. I said I'd consider your request but I can't promise anything.'

Corde dropped the sheet on the desk. 'Okay, Jim, there's no nice way to say what I'm about to.' He paused while he honestly tried to think of one. 'The only thing I'll add to take the sting out of it is that whether it was you or Steve or Jack Treadle himself sitting where you are, I'd say exactly the same thing. Which is: You got yourself a plum job and you know it and I know it and I'm happy for you. But you got appointed because I turned it down. And the price for that is me getting the Gebben case and all of the travel and equipment budget, every penny of it. After this is over I'd be glad to help you with all this administrative stuff and I'll even learn your radio codes but until then what I just said is the way it is.'

Corde looked back at the shock on Slocum's face, which froze slowly to a chill. Corde wondered if this talk might actually do some good, toughening the man's flaccid way.

'You don't have to be like that, Bill.'

The buffoonery was gone and Corde now saw in Slocum's eyes the too-vivid knowledge that he had advanced by default and he saw too the man's depleted hope, which could have very well been Corde's own broken ambition had life moved just a little different. This stung him – for his own sake as well as Slocum's – but he did not apologize. He stood and walked to the door. 'I'm counting on you to leave that money just where it is until I need it.'

What Wynton Kresge owed: $132.80 to GMAC. $78.00 to Visa. $892.30 to Union Bank and Trust (the mortgage). $156.90 to Union Bank and Trust (the bill consolidation loan). $98.13 to Consolidated Edison. $57.82 to Midwestern Bell. $122.78 to Duds 'n' Things for Kids. $120.00 to Corissa Hanley Duke, the housekeeper. $245.47 to American Express. $88.91 to Mobil *(goddamn Texans, goddamn Arabs)*. $34.70 to Sears.

And that was just for the month of May.

He didn't have the heart to tally the numbers up for the year and he didn't dare calculate the brood's budget for makeup, burgers, ninja outfits, skateboards, air pump Nikes, gloves, basketballs, piano lessons, potato chips, Apple software, Spike Lee and Bart Simpson T-shirts, Run DMC tapes Ice-T tapes Janet Jackson Paula Abdul The Winnans tapes gummy bears white cheddar popcorn Diet Pepsi and whatever else got sucked into the black hole of childhood capitalism.

Darla came to the door of his den and told him the plumber had just finished.

'Oh, good,' Kresge said. 'How much?' He opened the checkbook and tore off a check. He left it blank and handed it to her.

'It's a hundred twenty-four, doll.'

'*How* much?'

'You can't take a bath in cold water.' She was gone.

He marked down: *Check 2025. Amount $124. For SOB, MF"ing Plumber.* Why, he wondered, was it that the more you get the more you spend? When he and Darla had first been married they'd lived in a trailer park south of the Business Loop in Columbia, Missouri. He'd been an assistant security director for the university, making nineteen thousand dollars a year.

They'd had a savings account. A real savings account that paid you interest – not very much, true, but something. You could look at the long line of entries and feel that you were getting somewhere in life. Now, zip. Now, debt.

This was too much. Thinking about the bills, about hungry children, about a wife, about his lack of employment, his palms began to sweat and his stomach was doing 180s. He recalled the time he talked a failing student down from the Auden Chancellory Building. Sixty feet above a slate walk. Kresge, calm as could be. No rope. Standing on a ledge fourteen inches wide. Like he was out looking for a couple buddies to shoot pool with. Talking the boy in by inches. Kresge had felt none of the terror that assaulted him now as he lined up the fat white envelopes of bills and pulled toward him his blue-backed plastic checkbook, soon to be emasculated.

The telephone rang. He answered it. He listened then looked at his watch. Wynton Kresge said, 'Well, I don't know.' He listened some more. 'Well, I guess.' He hung up.

4

'Wynton, come on, get the lead out of your cheeks. You look like a walking tombstone.'

Corde spun the squad car around the corner and pressed the accelerator down. The four-barrel engine, factory-goosed so it could catch 'Vettes and Irocs, pushed both men back in the vinyl seat. *Come on Wynton cheer up cheer up cheer up.*

'What you got there?' Kresge looked at the seat under Corde's butt. 'What you're sitting on?'

A backrest of round wooden balls strung together. It looked like a doormat. 'Good for the back,' Corde said. 'It's like it massages you.'

Kresge looked away as if he'd already forgotten he'd asked the question.

'You like to fish?' Corde asked him.

'I don't want to today.'

'You don't what?'

After a moment Kresge resumed the conversation. 'Want to go fishing.'

'We're not going fishing,' Corde said. 'But do you like to?'

'I like to hunt.'

'I like to fish,' Corde said. 'Hunting's good too.'

They drove past the pond where Jennie Gebben and Emily Rossiter had died. Corde didn't slow down and neither of them said a word as they sped on toward the Fredericksberg Highway.

After ten minutes Kresge touched the barrel of the riot gun lock-clamped muzzle-up between them. 'What's this loaded with?'

'Double-ought.'

'I thought maybe it was rock salt or plastic bullets or something.'

'Nope. Lead pellets.'

'You don't have to use steel? I thought with the wetlands and everything you had to use steel.'

Corde said, 'It's not like we shoot that much buckshot at people 'round here.'

'Yeah, I guess not. You ever used it?'

'Drew a target a couple times. Never pulled the trigger, I'm mighty pleased to say. You got a pretty wife.'

'Yep.'

'How many kids you got, all told?'

'Seven. Where we going?'

'Fredericksberg.'

'Oh. How come?'

'Because,' Corde said.

'Oh.'

Twenty minutes later they pulled into a large parking lot and walked into the County Building. They passed the County Sheriff's Department. Corde noticed an empty office being painted. It was T.T.'s old one. There was no name on the plate next to the door. He could picture a nameplate that said *S.A. Ribbon*. Corde and Kresge continued on, to the office at the end of the hall. Painted in gold on rippled glass a sign read, *County Clerk*.

Kresge stopped to study a *Wanted* poster in the hall. He said to Corde, 'You got business, Detective, I can wait out here.'

'Naw, naw, come on in.'

Corde walked through a swinging gate and into a dark, woody old office presided over by a dusty oil painting of a judge who looked like he'd spent the entire portrait session thinking up cruel and unusual punishments.

From a desk under the window, a grizzled bald man, wearing a wrinkled white shirt, bow tie and suspenders, waved them over.

'Rest your bones, gentlemen.' The county clerk dug through the stacks of papers on his desk. 'What've we got here, what've we got here . . . Okay. Here we go.' He found a couple of sheets of paper, dense with tiny type. He set them in front of him. 'You're a crazy son of a bitch, Corde, to pass up that chance.'

Corde said, 'I probably am.'

'They were good and pissed, I'll tell you. Nobody wanted it this way.'

'Uh-huh.'

'In case you hadn't guessed.'

'I had.'

'What's he mean?' Kresge asked Corde.

The clerk added loudly, as if he hoped to be overheard, 'And nobody here is real happy we inherited you know who.'

Corde supposed he meant Ribbon. 'You can't pin that on me.'

The county clerk grew solemn then spread the papers out in front of him. He flipped through a three-ring binder. He stopped at one page and began speaking rapid-fire toward the book. 'Okay raise your right hand by the power vested in me . . .'

Corde was looking at the sour portrait above their heads. Kresge followed his eyes. The clerk stopped reading and looked at Kresge. 'You gonna raise your hand or what?'

'Me?' Kresge said.

'*You're* the one being deputized.'

'Me?' The man's baritone rose nearly to a tenor.

'Raise your hand, Wynton,' Corde said. Kresge did.

'By the power vested in me by the County of Harrison, you, Wynton Washington Kresge, are hereby appointed as special deputy pursuant to Revised State Code Title 12 Section 131.13. Repeat after me. "I, Wynton Washington Kresge . . ."'

Kresge cleared his throat, looking with astonishment at Corde. 'What is this?'

Corde said, 'Do what the man's telling you.'

'I, Wynton Washington Kresge, do swear to uphold the laws of this state and to tirelessly and faithfully serve and protect the citizens of the County of Harrison and the municipalities located therein . . .'

'If you don't want to say "so help me God," the clerk concluded, 'you can say, "upon my solemn oath".'

Kresge said, 'So help me God.'

Corde shook his hand. The clerk gave him three pieces of paper to sign.

'You didn't tell me.' Kresge whispered this to Corde.

'I need you, Wynton. I figured if I just drove you here you'd be less inclined to say no and go looking for a cushy office job someplace else.'

'Look, Detective, I'm grateful. I really am. But there's no way I can afford to do this.'

Corde smiled cryptically. 'You can't afford not to. Talk to that pretty wife of yours. You'll find some way to work it out.'

The clerk was impatient. 'You two talk about this later, will you?' He finished the paperwork and folded a couple of sheets like a subpoena. He handed one to Kresge. 'Go over to County Central Booking and get fingerprinted on the same form and have a picture ID taken in Personnel. The same building. Bill'll tell you where it is. Have both these copies notarized. Lucy can do it if she's not at lunch, and if she is go to Farmer's Bank. Ask for Sally Anne. Bring me back one copy.'

'But I haven't even thought about it.'

'You're a special deputy, which sounds good but don't let it go to your head, it's the lowest rank we've got. You have a pistol permit?'

'Yes, I do. I did the small-arms course at Higgins. My score—'

'You have to buy your own weapon but you can get reimbursed up to two hundred. Automatics are okay but you can only use accepted loads, the ones on here.' He handed Kresge a badly photocopied sheet of paper. 'Don't get caught with anything heavier. And if you file the trigger it can't be easier than a nine-pound pull.'

Kresge nodded and Corde noticed that he'd stopped arguing.

The clerk continued, 'Your pay is twenty-nine-five annual, prorated for however long you're with us. You'll be assigned to Bill for whatever he needs you for. Ha, ha, big guess. You folks finish up the Gebben case and get this sicko under, we can find a permanent place for you here at the county if you get certified by the state police academy.

'Now, you get benefits as long as you work more than twenty-five hours a week but you gotta take a physical. And for the family you gotta pay something. You got a wife and kids?'

'Seven.'

Corde added, 'That's the kids. He's only got one wife.'

'Oh, one more thing . . .' He tossed Kresge a plastic-wrapped green vinyl notebook about six by nine inches, three hundred or so pages thick. 'That's the state penal code and the *Deputy's Procedural Guide*. Read 'em. Learn 'em.'

'Yessir.' Kresge was lit up with modest pride. 'Do I salute?'

'It's all in there.' The clerk tapped the Guide.

Jennie—
You wanted someone to teach you about love, and all you found was someone to teach you how to die.
Why did you go that night? You said it was over.
Do I believe you or not?
Not knowing is almost as hard as life without you.
Why, kiddo, why?

Till we meet soon,
Em

'It was where?'

'In Emily's purse the night she drowned.'

Wynton Kresge said, 'They thought the Halpern boy wrote that? A fifteen-year-old kid?'

Corde said, 'Uhn.'

Sitting in the New Lebanon's Sheriff's Department, wearing a uniform as spotless and pressed as Corde's, Kresge dropped Emily's plastic-encased note on Corde's desk while Corde read the report aloud. '"Graphoanalysis of Subject Document. My professional opinion is that there is no more than a 50 percent probability that the handwriting is that of Subject Emily Rossiter. Significant similarities are five-degree backslant and short ascenders and descenders and looped capital letters. Deviation from samples submitted are significant but may be attributable to inebriation, drug use, emotional disturbance or unsteadiness of writing surface."'

'Why didn't Philip say anything about it?'

'Maybe he didn't see it. Maybe he saw it and it didn't mean anything to him.' Corde looked at the letter for a long moment then said, 'Let's assume it's really Emily's okay?'

'Okay.'

'Does it tell us anything?'

'Well, it says two things. First, it's a suicide note. So it means—'

'Suggests,' Corde corrected.

'*Suggests* that Emily killed herself. She wasn't murdered.'

'Okay. What's the second thing?'

'That the Halpern boy didn't kill Jennie either. I mean, it *implies* that he didn't.'

'Why?'

'Because the "someone" Emily mentions is probably, well, maybe, the killer. Someone Jennie had an affair with, I'd guess. She sure didn't have an affair with Philip Halpern.'

'Because of where she says she thought it was over?'

'Yeah. Like the affair was over.'

Corde said, 'And look at "go that night". Tuesday

390

night, she might be talking about.' He opened his attaché case. The now-tattered picture of Jennie Gebben fresh off the volleyball court stared down at stacks of plump, dog-eared three-by-five cards. He flipped through one pile and extracted a card.

'That your computer, Bill?'

'Computer, ha. Here we go. Between about five and six on the night Jennie was killed she and Emily had a serious discussion of some kind. Maybe an argument. And Emily was moody that night. She didn't join her friends for supper.'

'So maybe Jennie was going to see her lover, or former lover, and Emily was ticked off.'

'Could be.'

'Wait,' Corde said. He dug through another card. 'The girl who told me that Jennie was bisexual also said that she'd had a fight with somebody the night before she was killed. She said, "I love her, I don't love you." What if she agreed to meet that man—'

'Or woman,' Kresge added.

Corde raised an eyebrow, acknowledging the point. 'Possibly. But Trout, the carpet guy, said he saw a man ... What if she agreed to meet him one last time, and he killed her?'

'That's sounding pretty good.'

'But what about the DNA match? It was Philip's semen found at the scene.'

'Damn, that's right.' Kresge frowned.

'Don't agree with me too fast.'

Kresge considered for a minute and said, 'Maybe the lover killed her. Then the boy actually came along and raped her—'

'Actually, if she was dead first, it wasn't rape. It was violation of human remains. Misdemeanor.'

'Oh.' Kresge looked troubled. 'I've got a hell of a lot to learn.'

Corde mused, 'Well, why didn't Emily come to us and tell us what she knew? Wouldn't she want the killer arrested?'

'Maybe she didn't know his name. If the girls were lovers then somebody Jennie'd had an affair with'd be a sore point between them. Emily maybe didn't want to hear about him.'

'Good point, Wynton. But she could still come in and tell us that *somebody* Jennie had an affair with had killed her.'

Kresge had to agree with that.

Then Corde said, 'Of course look what happened. Emily killed herself. She was pretty crazy with grief, I suppose. She wouldn't be thinking about police. All she knew was her lover was dead.'

Kresge nodded. 'That's good. Yeah, I'll buy that.'

'We got our work cut out for us.' He selected one stack of cards and tossed it to Kresge. 'What we know about Jennie, there're a lot of people who might've had affairs with her.'

'Well, there can't be that many who're professors.'

'Professors?'

Kresge tapped the plastic. 'Well, she's talking about a professor, isn't she?'

Corde stared for the answer in the note. He looked up and shook his head. 'Why do you say that?'

'Well,' Kresge said, 'it says "teach". I just assumed she was talking about one of her professors.'

'Well, Emily could've meant that like in a general sense.'

'Could be,' Kresge conceded. 'But maybe we could save ourselves a lot of time by checking out the professors first.'

Corde picked up the cards and replaced them in his briefcase. He said, '*This* time we get to use the siren, Wynton. *And* the lights.'

You think they care? Oh, you'll learn soon.
You think they want you,
but the way they want you is cold as mother moon . . .

Jamie Corde listened to the lyrics chugging out of his

Walkman headset. He was lying on his back, staring at the setting sun. He wanted to be able to tell the time by looking at where the sun was. But he didn't know how. He wanted to be able to tell directions by the way certain trees grew but he couldn't remember what kind of trees. He wanted to travel into a different dimension. Jamie zipped his jacket up tighter against the cool breeze and slipped down farther in the bowl of short grass to escape from the wind. It was probably close to suppertime but he was not hungry.

He turned the volume up.

> *So just do yourself, do yourself,*
> *do yourself a favor and do yourself . . .*

Jamie was curious where the tape had come from. He'd returned home this afternoon after ditching wrestling practice and found it sitting on his windowsill. Geiger's latest cassette – the tiny cover picture showing five skinny German musicians in leather with long hair streaming behind them, the lead guitarist wearing a noose around his tendony neck.

His parents would never have bought it for him. This particular album was totally fresh; it'd been banned in Florida, Atlanta and Dallas, and most of the record stores in Harrison County refused to carry it. Maybe the last time Philip was over he'd left it. One of the group's songs, from a different, less-controversial album, had been used in The Lost Dimension and the two boys had listened to the soundtrack album frequently.

You think they care?

He held the tape player in both hands, lifted it to his face, pressed it against his cheek.

Do yourself, do yourself, do yourself now . . .

He thought about school, about Science Club, which was meeting right at this moment. They'd maybe look around and ask where's Jamie? And nobody'd know and then somebody might say something about Philip but there wouldn't be much talk about him because this was

393

the end-of-year party and you were supposed to be having fun, drinking Coke and jamming pretzels into your mouth and talking about the summer not about members of the club who were fat and weird and who'd been shot dead by the police.

And also you weren't supposed to talk about boys who cut school the evening of the party to sit next to a grave – friends who when they weren't around you'd joke about being fags so fuck you fuck you fuck you . . .

Just do yourself, do yourself, take a razor take a rope you don't have any hope except to do yourself . . .

Jamie looked at the tombstone and realized he hadn't known Philip's middle name was Arthur. He wondered if that was some relative's name. It seemed weird that his parents would give him a middle name at all because that was something normal parents did and Philip's parents were total hatters.

Jamie sat back and looked at the freckled granite. But this time he saw: *JAMES WILLIAM CORDE*. Jamie imagined his own funeral and he saw his father standing next to the grave. His father didn't seem particularly sad. He was looking off into the distance, thinking about Sarah. Jamie pictured himself sitting alone in front of his own grave tracing the letters of his name. He did not, however, trace his middle name.

They bypassed Supersalesman and walked right into Amos Trout's office. 'Sorry to trouble you again, sir,' Corde said and introduced him to Kresge.

Trout said, 'You in need of wall-to-wall, Deputy?'

Kresge said not just now but he'd discuss it with the wife.

Corde said, 'I wonder if you could go through this book and tell me if you recognize the man you saw in the road that night.'

'Well, like I was telling you I can't recall many details about him. That old Buick moves at a pretty good clip—'

'I've got an Olds corners like nobody's business,' Kresge said. 'GM can put a car together.'

394

'There you go,' said Trout.

'If you could maybe narrow it down to a few men might resemble the fellow you saw it'd make our job a whole lot easier.' Corde handed him a copy of the Auden University yearbook. Trout began to flip through it quickly.

'Take your time,' Corde said.

Corde's heart thudded each time Trout tore off a small piece of paper and marked a page. When he was finished he flipped open to the marked pages and pointed out three men. He said, 'I don't think I'd feel right testifying but it could be any one of these fellows.'

Corde took the book and glanced at the names of the men Trout had marked. He looked up at Kresge, who nodded slowly. Corde thanked Trout and with Kresge in tow left the store, not bothering to jot down the names on his index cards.

Kresge – just back from his first official evidence photographing expedition – had taken the better pictures.

At the crime scene below the dam in April, Jim Slocum had forgotten to override the automatic focus of his 35 mm camera and in the dark he'd sometimes pointed the infrared rangefinder at a bush or hump of rocks. Many of the pictures were out of focus. Several of them were badly overexposed. Kresge had taken his time with the Polaroid.

Sitting in the den that was really Corde's fourth bedroom, surrounded by the debris of two double orders of the Marquette Grill's steam-fried chicken, drinking coffee (Corde) and two-bag Lipton (Kresge) the men leaned close to the photos.

Six eight-by-tens of the footprints by the dam were tacked up on a corkboard next to an ad for a lawn service that guaranteed to make your lawn thick as cat's fur and we mean purrfect. In the center of the board were Kresge's small Polaroid squares.

'I think it's these two,' Kresge said, tapping one of Slocum's pictures and one of his own.

'Why?' Corde asked. 'The tread's similar but look at the size. The crime scene shoe's fatter.'

Kresge said, 'Well, that ground is wetter. By the dam, I mean. I was reading a book on crime scene forensics . . . You know what that word means?'

Corde had forgotten. He thought for a moment, wondering how he could bluff past it and couldn't think of a way. He said, 'What?'

'It means pertaining to criminal or legal proceedings. I used to think it meant medicine, you know. But it doesn't.'

'Hmmm,' Corde said, at least giving himself credit for not looking too impressed.

'Anyway, I was reading this book and it said that prints in mud change shape depending on how close they are to the water source and whether the print would get drier or muddier with time. That dam's got a runoff nearby and it's uphill of where she was found—'

'How'd you know that?'

'I went there and looked.'

'So the print spread. Okay, but how come in the crime scene photo the feet don't point out like in the one you took?'

'I think they do,' Kresge said. 'We just don't have him standing in one place. Look, the heavier indentation's on the right of his right foot and in this one it's on the left of his left. Means the man walks like a penguin.'

'Yessir,' Corde said. 'It sure does.'

'So, I think they're one and the same.'

'I do too, Wynton.' Corde pondered this information. 'I think we're real close to probable cause. But damn I'd love a motive. What else've we got?' He flipped through his cards then lifted out two and read them slowly. He said, 'You remember that scrap of computer paper I showed you, the one I found behind Jennie's dorm? Mostly burned up.'

'I couldn't find out anything about it before I got laid off.'

'Well, in the morning I'd like to check on where it came from.'

Kresge winced. 'Bill, the school's hardly going to let me do that. I got fired. Remember?'

'Wynton, it's not a question of *letting* you. We'll get a search warrant. You've got to start thinking like a cop.'

Kresge nodded, flustered. 'I haven't been on the job too long, you know.'

'That's not an excuse.'

At ten the next morning the men walked up the steps of the dark-brick house and rang the bell.

Wynton Kresge noticed the way Corde stood away from the front of the door as if somebody might shoot through the oak. He doubted anybody was going to do that but he mimicked the detective.

A blond woman in her forties opened the door. Narrow shoulders in a white blouse widening to a dark plaid pleated skirt. She listed to her right under the weight of a large briefcase. She set it down.

Corde looked expectantly at Kresge, who cleared his throat and said, 'Morning, ma'am, would your husband be home?'

She examined them uneasily. 'What would this be about?'

Corde said, 'Is he home, please?'

Kresge decided he wouldn't have said that. He'd have answered her question.

She let them in. 'In his study in the back of the house.'

The men walked past her. She smiled, curious. The motion spread the red lipstick slightly past the boundaries of her lips. 'There.' She pointed to the room then left them. Corde's hand went to the butt of his pistol. Kresge's did too. They knocked on the door and walked in before there was an answer.

The man swiveled slowly in a shabby office chair, bleeding upholstery stuffing. Kresge wondered if he'd found the chair on the street in his poor graduate student days and kept it for sentiment. Kresge's nostrils flared against the old-carpet smell, basement water in wool. He had a strong urge to walk directly to the nearest window and fling it wide open. The papers and books filling every available space added to the stifling closeness as did the jumble of old-time photos stacked against the wall. Everything was covered with thin films of dust.

Randy Sayles put a pencil tick next to his place in the massive volume he was reading, slipped a paperclip between the pages and closed the book.

A jay landed on a bush outside the window and picked at a small blond mulberry.

Bill Corde said, 'Professor Sayles, we're here to arrest you for the murder of Jennifer Gebben.'

Sayles leaned back in the ancient chair. Sorrow was in his face but it seemed a manageable sorrow like that in the eyes of a distant relative at a funeral.

He listened to Corde recite the Miranda rights. Corde unceremoniously took his handcuffs out of the leather case on his belt. Sayles said a single word softly. Corde believed it was 'No.' The professor's tongue caressed his lips. One circuit. Two. He lifted his hands and rested them on his knees; they looked dirty because of the fine dark hairs coating his skin. Corde noticed that his feet pointed outward. He said, 'Will you hold your wrists out, please?'

'Why do you think it's me?' He asked this with unfeigned curiosity. He did not offer his wrists.

'A witness came forward and identified your picture in the yearbook. He saw you by the dam that night. Your hands?'

Sayles nodded and said, 'The man in the car. He almost ran me over.'

Kresge said, 'And your bootprint matches one found at the scene of the killing.' He looked at Corde to see if it was all right to volunteer this kind of information.

'My bootprint?' Sayles looked involuntarily at a muddy corner of the study where presumably a pair of boots had recently lain. 'You took prints of mine from the yard?'

'Yessir,' Kresge said. 'Shot pictures, actually.'

Sayles fidgeted with his hands, his face laced with the regret of a marathoner pulling up cramped a half mile shy of the finish. 'Will you come with me?' Sayles stood up.

'For what?' Corde asked.

'I didn't kill her.' Sayles seemed stricken with apathy.

'You'll have your day in court, sir.'

'I can prove it right now.'

Corde looked at the eyes and what he saw was a load of disappointment – much more than desperation. He motioned with his head toward the door. 'Five minutes. But you wear the cuffs.' He put them on.

As they left the house Kresge whispered, 'So, okay, let me get this straight. If they say they didn't do it we give them a chance to show us some new evidence? I just want to know the rules.'

'Wynton,' Corde said patiently, 'there are no rules.'

The two men followed Sayles outside. They walked to the back of the house – ten feet from the place where Kresge had taken photos of Sayles's footprints. Corde recognized the ruddy box elder root from the Polaroids. Corde glanced toward the front of the house. He believed he smelled cigarette smoke. Corde saw Sayles's wife standing in the kitchen thirty feet away.

Sayles walked to a patch of dug-up earth like two wide tread marks about twenty feet long. Small green shoots were rising from precisely placed intervals along the strips.

'Dig here.' He touched a foot to the ground.

Kresge picked up a rusty spade. Corde now felt contempt in the air. Sayles's eyes were contracted like nipple skin in chill water. The deputy began to dig. A few feet down he uncovered a plastic bag. Kresge dropped the spade on the ground. He pulled the bag out, dusted it off carefully and handed it to Corde. Inside was a length of clothesline.

'That's the murder weapon,' Sayles said.

Corde said to him, 'Do you want to make a statement?'

Sayles said, 'This is the proof.'

'Yessir,' Corde said. 'Do you wish to waive your right to have an attorney present during questioning?'

'He killed Jennie with it. I saw him. It'll have his fingerprints on it.'

'You're saying you didn't kill her?' Kresge asked.

'No, I didn't kill her,' Sayles said. He sighed. 'Jennie and I had an affair last year.'

'Yessir, we figured as much,' Corde said.

In the open window, the blond woman rested her chin in her hand and listened to his words without visible emotion. The cigarette dangled over the sill and from it rose a leisurely tentacle of smoke.

'I was quite taken by her.' He said to Corde, 'You saw her. How could anybody help but be captivated by her?'

Corde remembered the moon, remembered the smell of mint on the dead girl's mouth, remembered the spice of her perfume. He remembered the dull eyes. He remembered two diamonds and he remembered mud. He had no idea how captivating Jennie Gebben was.

Sayles said, 'She went to work for me in the financial aid office.'

'We just came from there. The scrap of paper we found burned behind her dorm matches computer files in your records. You broke into her dorm and stole her letters and papers. You burned them.'

Sayles laughed shortly, the disarmed sound of someone learning that his secrets are not secret at all. He nodded. 'You know the financial condition of the school?'

What was it about educators that made them think their school was exactly the first thing on everyone's mind?

Sayles continued. 'We've been in danger of closing since the mid-eighties. Dean Larraby and I came up with an idea two years ago. As dean of financial aid I started giving out loan money to students who were bad risks. Millions of dollars.'

Corde nodded. 'You gave them the money and they

paid it to the school then they dropped out and defaulted. You kept the money. Who got, uhm, taken in in that deal?'

'It was mostly state and federal money,' Sayles said. 'It's a very common practice at small colleges.' A professor, Sayles was giving them information, not apologizing. 'Times are extremely bad for educational institutions. Auden is being audited in a week or so by the Department of Education. They'll find the loan defaults. I've tried desperately to get some interim financing to put into the loan accounts to cover the deficit but—'

'And Jennie found out about the scam and you killed her,' Kresge said.

'No sir, I did not.' Corde thought something like a Southern military officer's drawl crept into the man's offended voice. 'She knew what was going on. But she didn't care. And I didn't care if she knew. I just arranged for the job for her so we could see each other privately. She took some work home, administrative things. After she died I went to her dorm and burnt those files and her letters. In case she'd mentioned me in them.'

'That's why you urged Steve Ribbon to pull me off the case? So this secret of yours didn't get uncovered?'

'I promised him and Sheriff Ellison they'd have university support in the elections come November.'

Kresge's face blossomed into a large frown at this first glimpse of law enforcement politics. He'd been on the job less than twenty-four hours.

'But I didn't kill her. I swear it.' His voice lowered. 'Our relationship never went past sex. We were lovers. Once or twice I thought about marrying her. But she told me right up front she was in it for the sex and nothing else. I was happy to accommodate. It didn't last long. Jennie was bisexual, you know. She finally patched up her relationship with Emily, her roommate, and she and I drifted apart.'

'Emily's death was a suicide, wasn't it?'

'Yes, I'm sure it was. She called me the night she died. I went to meet her. She was terribly depressed about

Jennie, incoherent. She ran off. I have no doubt she killed herself.'

'Well, Professor, who do you think is the killer?'

'About four months after Jennie and I broke up she said she'd started seeing someone else. We were still close and she told me a few things about her lover. It sounded like a very destructive relationship. Finally she broke it off but the lover was furious. On the day she was killed, after class, Jennie told me she'd agreed to meet for one last time, to say it was over, to leave her alone. I tried to talk her out of it. But that was one thing you just couldn't do with Jennie. You couldn't protect her. She wouldn't stand for it, she wouldn't depend on anybody. I worried about her all evening. Finally, I drove out to the pond, where she'd told me they were going to meet. I found Jennie. With a rope around her neck. That rope. She was dead.'

'She hadn't been raped?' Corde asked.

'No, that must've happened later. The boy that got shot.'

'Why,' Kresge asked, 'did you take the rope?'

'I was going to destroy it. But then I thought for my own sake I should save it – to prove that his fingerprints were on the murder weapon. I wrapped it up in a scrap of plastic and buried it here.'

Kresge was exasperated. 'Destroy the rope? You were trying to cover up the murder? Why?'

'Don't you realize what would happen if word were to get out that a professor murdered one of his students? It would destroy Auden. Enrollment would plummet. It would be the end of the school. Oh, it was hard for me . . . Oh, poor Jennie. But I had to think of the school first.'

'A professor?' Corde asked. 'Who is it?'

'I assume you talked to him when you were interviewing people,' Sayles said. 'His name is Leon Gilchrist.'

Jim Slocum, Lance Miller and a county deputy met

them at the university, in an alleyway behind Jesse Hall.

Corde said, 'He claims it's Gilchrist, one of Jennie's professors.'

Miller said, 'He was in San Francisco at the time of the killing, I thought.'

Corde said to Kresge, 'I checked the flights. Gilchrist flew out on the weekend before the killing. His secretary said he just got back a few days ago.'

Sayles said, 'I swear it, Officer. He was back the Tuesday she was killed.'

Kresge said, 'Maybe if he was planning to kill her he used a different name on the flight.'

Corde nodded then handed Sayles over to Slocum. 'Take him to a cell. Book him for murder one, manslaughter and felony obstruction.'

Corde and Kresge left Sayles's protests behind and walked through the elaborate towering arch, like the doorway in a medieval hall. The sounds of their footsteps resounded off the high concrete walls.

They suddenly heard running water.

'What's that?' Kresge whispered.

As they got closer to the lecture hall they could tell the sound was of applause, which rose in volume and was soon joined by whistles. The noise filled the old stern Gothic corridors. An image came to Corde's mind: gladiatorial battles from an ancient movie.

Doors opened and the halls filled with students in shorts, jeans, sweats, T-shirts. Corde walked into the lecture hall. It did indeed resemble the Colosseum. Steep rows of seats rising from a small semicircular platform, empty except for a chipped lectern. The ceiling of the auditorium was high, hueless, murky with years of grime. The walls were dark oak. The gooseneck lamp on the lectern still burned and in the dimness of the hall cast a pale shadow on the stage.

Corde stopped a crew-cut student. 'Excuse me, this Professor Gilchrist's class?'

'Yessir.'

'Do you know where he is?'

The boy looked around, saw someone and grinned. He continued his scan of the auditorium. 'Nope. Guess he's gone.'

'Was he away from town for a while?'

'Yeah. He was in San Francisco until a few days ago I heard. He came back to give his last lecture.'

'What was the applause about?'

'If you ever heard him you'd know. He's totally, you know, intense.'

Corde and Kresge continued down the corridor until they found Gilchrist's office. The professor was not there and the departmental secretary was gone. Kresge motioned toward her Rolodex, which was turned to the G's. Gilchrist's home address card was gone. The desk drawers were open and although Corde found files on other professors there was none for Gilchrist.

On the way out of the hall they passed the auditorium again.

The lectern light was dark.

The apartment wasn't university property. It was three miles outside of town in a complex of two-story brick buildings, with the doorways on the second floor opening onto a narrow balcony that ran the length of the building. Gilchrist lived in apartment 2D. The complex was surrounded by thick foliage and mature trees. Corde noticed it was only one mile from his own house through the forest. Another brick of evidence for the district attorney – it would have cost Gilchrist merely a pleasant twenty minute walk to get to Corde's house and leave the threatening pictures of Sarah.

Corde drove the cruiser past the entrance to the apartment complex then parked in a clump of hemlock out of sight of the building. Corde unlocked the shotgun and motioned to Kresge to take it. 'You hunt, you told me?'

'Yup.' Kresge took the riot gun and Corde got a moment's pleasure watching the man's thick hands load and lock the gun as if he'd been doing it since he was five. They climbed out and started along the path.

Kresge said, 'I hear something in the woods. Over there.'

Corde looked, squinting through the low light that shattered in the dense woods. 'You see anything?'

'Can't tell. Too much glare.'

'What'd you hear?'

'Footsteps. A dog maybe. Don't hear it anymore.'

'Keep an eye on our backs,' Corde said.

'He's just a professor.'

'Our backs,' Corde repeated.

Crouching, the men walked side by side to the complex's directory. Corde found the super's apartment and rang the bell. No response. He motioned with his head toward the upper balcony. Together they went up the stairs.

Corde whispered, 'You never done this before so we're going in the front door together.'

'Okay with me,' Kresge said sincerely, the last of his words swallowed in a hugely dry throat.

'Let's go.'

Beneath them a horn blared.

Corde and Kresge spun around. Jim Slocum's cruiser – with Randy Sayles handcuffed in the backseat – pulled leisurely into the parking lot. Slocum honked again and waved. 'Hey, Bill,' he called, 'thought you might need some backup.'

'Jesus Lord,' Corde whispered harshly. 'Jim, what're you doing? He's gonna see you.'

Slocum got out of the car and looked around. He shouted, 'What say?'

Corde jumped out of his crouch and ran for the front door of Gilchrist's apartment, shouting to Slocum, 'Watch the back, behind the building! Watch the back.'

Corde and Kresge stood on either side of the door. Kresge said, 'If he's in there he knows he's got company.'

'I hate this,' Corde said.

Kresge said, 'You ever do this before?'

Corde hesitated. 'Not exactly, no.' He knocked on the door. 'Professor Gilchrist. Sheriff's Department. Open the door.'

No response.

'Let me try.' Kresge pounded on the split veneer of the door. 'Police, Professor. I mean, Sheriff's Department. Open the door!'

Nothing.

Corde reached for the doorknob. Both men lifted their guns toward the sky. Corde turned the knob and shouldered it open. They leapt inside.

Jim Slocum turned toward the backseat of the cruiser. He said to Sayles by way of explanation, 'I figured they needed some backup.' And he drove around to the back of the apartment complex.

'Look,' Sayles said, 'I'm not real comfortable here.'

'Minute,' Slocum said, and got out of the car. He unholstered his service revolver and looked around the unkempt yellow lawn.

'You can't leave me here. I'm innocent.'

'Quiet.'

'You can't keep me here!'

'Please, sir, I'd appreciate it if you'd just shut up.'

'Get the goddamn rope fingerprinted. Are you listening to me? Are you listening to me?'

Jim Slocum had been – all the way from the Auden campus – and he was pretty tired of it. He leaned forward. 'Shut . . . your . . . mouth. Got it?'

'You can't keep me here.'

Slocum wandered off to the apartment building's detached workshed. He went up on tiptoes, looked through the window and noted that there was no one inside then he stepped behind it to take a leak.

Breathing stale air Corde and Kresge moved farther into the apartment. On the floor next to them was a wooden coat rack and umbrella stand carved with the bas relief of a hound treeing a bear. Corde glanced at the bear's black glistening mahogany teeth and walked past it.

In the living room the scents were of mildew, moist paper, dust and a sour scent as if a pet had grown old and ill in the room. The light, dimmed by drawn curtains, barely illuminated the space, which seemed uninhabited. The bookcases were filled but the jackets of the volumes all were matte paper imprinted with dull inks, old-style typography. The wooden chairs were coated with dust, the upholstered ones weren't indented. A dust sphere leisurely followed Corde into the living room.

The men danced past each other, stepping into rooms and covering each other – a choreography that Kresge learned quickly. Corde could see he was unnerved and trying to look three directions at once. They secured all the rooms except the kitchen.

They paused outside the closed French doors.

Kresge had his index finger curled around the ribbed trigger of the scattergun. Corde lifted the sizable finger out and straightened it along the guard. He then nodded toward the door and together they pushed inside.

Empty.

Kresge picked up a cup coated with a moldy layer of dry evaporated coffee. He set it down. Stacked on the table were literary magazines, books, dense articles. 'Delmore Schwartz: The Poetry of Obsession.' 'Special Problems in Translating the *Cantos*.' 'The Rebirth of the Poet Warrior' . . .

The feeling first came to Corde as he stood flipping through the blank notepad beside the yellow telephone, which was decorated with a sticker in the shape of a daisy. He paused as the crinkling chill began at the knob of his neck and swept down his spine. His scrotum contracted. One by one he lifted his fingers off his pistol and he felt the pads of his fingers cool from evaporation. He looked around him at the still, pale doorways, out the window at a black gnarled willow trunk.

He's nearby. I can feel it.

Kresge dropped the journal back down on the table.

Corde walked to the stove and touched the top. It burnt his hand. The tea kettle too was hot but then he tapped the metal again cautiously and found that the pilot light was heating the empty pot. He left the kitchen and returned to the second bedroom, which served as Gilchrist's study. He searched the desk. Papers, letters, drafts of articles. Doodles. There were no photos. Nothing gave a clue as to what Leon Gilchrist looked like or where he might be.

A chill again shuddered through Corde's back. Corde had to share this. 'He's nearby.'

'What?'

'I feel him. He's around here someplace.'

Kresge pointed to a coating of dust on the wood floors and the linoleum. Only their footprints showed. 'He hasn't been here for a long time.'

Corde said, 'We'll get the Crime Scene boys to go through it, take some paper samples and fingerprints. Let's get out of here.'

Slocum was walking out from behind the apartment building. He met Corde and Kresge in the parking lot. 'I heard something behind there. I went to check but I didn't see anything. If he had a car it's gone.'

'We should call in a county APB,' Corde said. He walked toward his car. 'DMV license and any tag numbers. Let's get back to the office and fax an ID to the state and the FBI. Get a picture of him from the university.'

'Yessiree, let's move,' Slocum said.

They found though that they had to make a detour.

Which was to drive Randy Sayles to the emergency room at Harrison County Community Hospital. Corde drove, hitting speeds of close to a hundred on the straightaway of 302, while Kresge crouched in the back, applying fierce pressure to the slashes in the man's carotid arteries. Because Sayles's hands were cuffed to the armrest in the backseat of the car, Gilchrist had been free to cut deep and with fearful precision.

409

At the hospital, while Kresge cleaned up as best he could, Corde sat in a blue plastic chair in the lounge. He sat forward, his chin in his hands. The doctor walked out of the ER and after surveying the three cops chose Corde, to whom he said simply, 'I'm sorry.'

Corde nodded and stood up. On the way out of the door he glanced at the sky and believed he saw for a moment a silver crescent of waxing moon before it was obliterated by an oncoming storm.

ber hope the world said the same and with a sense that
would, I made a home to make on my life that much mil-
...
...
...
...
...
...
...
...
...
...
...
...

6

The way Sarah thought of it was that her world suddenly
turned joyous.

For one thing, she woke up without the pitchforks in
her stomach, the way she always felt on school days and
still felt sometimes when she awakened from a dream
about class or about taking a test. This morning, sitting
up in her bed, she felt perfectly free, floating and safe.
It was like she had all the good parts of running away
from home but still had her family and her room and her
magic circle in the forest behind the house.

The day too was perfection itself. The sun was like the
round face of a sky tiger and the wind blew through the
new leaves so crisp and fast you could hear the voices of
the trees calling to each other.

Sarah strolled outside and played a game Dr Breck
had taught her. She looked at the lawn and she said out
loud, 'G-R-A-S-S.' Then came T-R-E-E and C-L-O-U-D.
And she got the giggles when she pointed to Mrs
Clemington next door and spelled, 'T-R-O-L-L.'

She pointed to a cow, ten feet away, separated by the
post-and-rail fence. The animal gazed at her eagerly as
if it was milking time.

She lay down in her circle of stones and took her tape
recorder out of her backpack.

Another good thing about today: she was going to
finish the last chapter of her book. This one was her

favorite story. She'd been working on it for days and hadn't told anyone about it. It filled almost half a cassette and she hadn't even gotten to the climax of the story yet. She'd give the tape to Dr Parker, and her secretary would type out the words and Sarah would get the story back in a few days. Then she would copy it into the notebook and show it to Dr Breck. She wanted desperately to impress him and had worked particularly hard on this story.

Sarah rewound the tape to the start of the chapter to see what she had written so far. She hit the Play button.

Chapter fifteen. The Sunshine Man . . . Once upon a time, deep in the forest, there lived a wizard . . .

The deputies got a kick out of Wynton Kresge – a man who owned more law enforcement books than they knew existed and who could outshoot any of them, either-handed, on the small arms range at Higgins. As far as they could remember there'd never been a black deputy in New Lebanon and it made the office seem like a set on a Hollywood buddy movie.

They were sitting around this evening, debating where Gilchrist might have gone. Prosecutor Dwayne Lovell had gotten a bench warrant issued and faxed to Boston and San Francisco, both cities having been Gilchrist's home at one time, then Corde added Gilchrist's name to the Criminal Warrants Outstanding Bulletin and Database for state and major city law enforcement agencies.

'What will they do?' Kresge asked Corde.

'Boston and San Francisco'll prioritize it. The others? Nothing. But if they happen to pick him up for something else and find his name in the computer they'll give us a call. It's not for sure but we can sleep a little better knowing we've done it.'

'Looking for a tick on a dog,' Kresge muttered as he dialed Boston PD. After a brief conversation, he learned that Gilchrist had no criminal record in Massachusetts.

Earlier that day Corde had granted Kresge's fervent

request that he be allowed to interview Dean Larraby about Gilchrist. It was a long interview and she hadn't been much help though Kresge clearly had enjoyed himself. In searching Gilchrist's office and the other departments at Auden, the men had found that the professor had stolen most of the files containing personal information about himself. The Personnel Department, the Credentials Department, the English and Psych Departments – they had all been raided. Computer files erased. Cabinets emptied.

Kresge and Corde interviewed other professors. None of them knew much about Gilchrist or had snapshots that included him. They could not recall any school functions he had attended.

Brian Okun, Corde learned in a second antagonistic interview, said he knew the professor as well as anyone and could offer no clues as to where Gilchrist might have gone. 'He's resourceful,' Okun said then added with eerie sincerity, 'It's troubling you don't know where he is. The evil we can't see is so much worse than that which we can, don't you think, Detective?'

Corde didn't know about that but one thing he did know: Gilchrist *was* Jennie Gebben's killer. Sayles had been correct; Gilchrist's fingerprints were on the tie-down rope cut from the Ford truck. The rope also contained two of Jennie's partials from trying to fight off the strangulation and one of her hairs. Another strand of her hair was found on a shirt in Gilchrist's closet. He also had several red marking pens whose ink matched those on the newspaper clipping he had left for Corde the morning after Jennie's murder and on the back of the threatening Polaroids. Gilchrist's prints were also found on the back door, window and armrest of Jim Slocum's cruiser. It wasn't necessary to dust for those prints; they had been made with Randy Sayles's blood.

But, as Corde knew and as Wynton Kresge was learning with great disillusionment, finding a criminal's identity is not the same as finding the criminal.

Gilchrist had vanished.

Corde got a deputy to call car rental agencies. No one named Gilchrist had rented a car, the deputy announced, and Corde and Kresge looked at each other, both concluding simultaneously and silently that he wasn't going to be using his real name.

Corde, tapping the butt of his gun with a forefinger, began to say, 'When we got Sayles to the ER—'

Kresge finished the question, 'Did they find his wallet?'

'I don't know,' the deputy said.

Corde continued, 'Find out and if not call back the car companies and ask if someone named Sayles rented a car.'

Kresge didn't wait to find out about the wallet. He got on the horn and called Hertz. A supervisor told him that a Randolph Sayles had rented a car the day before at Lambert Field in St Louis. He'd rented it for two weeks and was paying a drop-off charge to leave the car in Dallas. Kresge got the description and plate number of the car and told them it had been illegally rented. 'Have them notify us as soon as he returns it. Is that right, I mean, the right procedure?'

Corde realized Kresge had looked up from the phone and was speaking to him. Corde, who had never before had a car-renting felon, said, 'Sounds good to me.'

'Okay, it's a green Hertz Pontiac,' Kresge announced, and sang out the license number. Corde had him send that information out over the wire to the county and state.

They checked the Midwest Air commuter flights. No one matching Gilchrist's description had flown from Harrison County Airport to Lambert Field in the past two days and there had been no private charter flights.

State DMV showed a car registered to Gilchrist, a gray Toyota, but no record of a state driver's license. After two hours on the phone, Miller found out that Gilchrist had a Massachusetts license. They'd fax a picture within three days.

'That's the best they can do?'

'And I had to beat them up to get that.'

Kresge said, 'So he drove his car to St Louis, dumped it, rented another one and is going south.'

'Maybe. Maybe he's trying to throw us off. Fax Dallas in any case.' Corde pondered. 'You know, maybe he's flying someplace and just rented the car to cover his tracks. Left it in the airport. Call the airlines, everything that flies out of St Louis. Let's hope he used Sayles's credit card again. And check the airport long-term parking for his own car or the rental.'

Kresge said, 'That's pretty good. How'd you know this stuff?'

'You pick it up as you go along,' Corde said.

'I've got a lot to learn,' Kresge said.

'He's gone over state lines,' Corde said, then added reluctantly, 'We could get the FBI in if we wanted to.'

'How's that?'

'Feddies aren't interested in state crime unless there's interstate flight or you've got a kidnapping, drugs or bank robbery.'

'Why don't we want them in?'

Corde decided it was too early in Kresge's career for this kind of law enforcement education. 'Because,' he answered.

Slocum strolled up. 'Bill, one thing I was thinking.'

'Yup?'

'I'm not so sure this is just a fleeing felon thing.'

Corde wondered what trashy paperbacks he'd been reading.

Slocum continued, 'I was trying to psych him out. I mean, look what he did to Sayles.' When Corde kept staring blankly he added, 'Well, it could've been a revenge situation.'

'Sayles was a witness,' Corde said. 'Gilchrist had to kill him.'

Kresge said, 'But, Bill, we didn't need Sayles to convict him, did we? We had enough other evidence. And Gilchrist would've known that.'

Corde considered and said that was true. 'Go

ahead, Jim, what's your thought?'

'His life's over with. He's never going to teach again, never have a professional job. The best he can do is make it to Canada or Mexico and the first time he runs a red light, zippo, his butt's extradited. I think he's around the bend and wants to get even. He's just killed again. My bet is he rented that car to send us off to Texas but he's staying around here somewhere. He's got some scores to settle.'

Kresge said, 'Maybe we should check out the hotels around the county. Maybe he used Sayles's name there too.'

Slocum said, 'Hotels'd be easy to trace. I was thinking maybe cabins or a month lease somewhere nearby. It's getting near season so nobody'd pay much attention to someone taking a vacation rental.'

Corde said, 'Let's start making some calls.'

It was just a half hour later that Wynton Kresge hung up the phone after a pleasant conversation with Anita Conciliano of Lakeland Real Estate in Bosworth. He jotted some notes on a piece of the recycled newsprint the department used for memos. He handed the sheet to Corde.

The detective read it twice and looked up from the grayish paper. He found he was looking at Jim Slocum, who stood in his office doorway leaning on the frame – the same place and the same way Steve Ribbon used to stand.

'We got him. He's in Lewisboro.' Corde grinned at Slocum. Then he saluted. 'Thanks, Sheriff.'

Bevan's tavern was sixty miles north of New Lebanon in Lewisboro County, edged into a stand of pine and sloppy maples, and just far enough back from Route 128 so you could angle-park a Land Cruiser without too much risk of losing the rear end. Today four men sat in one of the tavern's front booths, drinking iced tea and soda and coffee. A greasy plate that had held onion rings sat in front of them. Lewisboro County Sheriff Stanley Willars said, 'How do you know he's there?'

Bill Corde said, 'Wynton here tracked him down. He called must've been a thousand real estate companies. Gilchrist used Sayles's name and rented it for two months.' Corde wanted more onion rings; he hadn't eaten a meal in eighteen hours. But he counted up that he'd had twelve rings himself so far, with ketchup, and decided not to ask if they wanted another round.

Wynton Kresge said, 'He doesn't have any family that we've been able to find. And no other residences. We think he's there and . . .' Kresge looked at Corde then added, '. . . we want to hit him.'

Corde continued, 'It's your county, Stan, so we need your okay.'

'Never heard of a professor killing anybody before,' said Assistant Sheriff Dudley Franks, who was lean and unsmiling and reminded Corde of T.T. Ebbans. 'You'd think they'd be above that or something.'

Willars said wryly, 'So's Hammerback's providing all the firepower?'

Corde grinned. 'Okay, we'd like some backup too.'

'Uck.'

Corde added, 'Fact of life, Stan.'

Willars said, 'You boys want more rings?' Corde said sure quickly. Willars ordered. He was laughing as he looked out the window at Corde's squad car. 'Look at that Dodge. It brand new?'

Corde said, 'We got 'em this year.'

'You got that damn university down in Harrison. No wonder you got new wheels.' He turned to Franks. 'What year're we driving?'

'Eighty-sevens.'

Kresge said, 'That's pretty old.'

'That damn university,' Willars said. 'Remember those old Grand Furies? The Police Interceptors.'

'That was quite a car,' Corde said.

'Had a four-forty in them, I believe,' Franks offered.

Willars said, 'What I wish is we had one of those

emergency services trucks. You should see the wrecks we get along 607.'

Franks said, 'Sedge Billings near to cut his little finger off with his chain saw trying to get somebody out of a Caprice that went upside down. There aren't but one Jaws of Life in the whole area. Sedge had to use his own Black and Decker.'

The waitress brought the onion rings.

'No,' Willars corrected, 'that wasn't a Chevy, was a Taurus.'

'You're right,' Frank said.

Corde said, 'I don't think Ellison'd have it in his heart or his budget to buy you boys one of those vans. The one they got in Harrison is secondhand. I *know* we don't have the money in New Lebanon.' There was silence as they dug into their rings.

Willars said, 'It's just a shame you couldn't loan it to us from time to time. Like a week we've got it, three weeks you've got it.'

Corde said, 'I don't know the citizens of Harrison'd be too happy to see that. They're the one's paying.'

'True,' Willars said pleasantly, 'but I don't know the citizens of Harrison're real happy about what this Gilchrist fella's done.' With cheer in his voice he added, 'And the fact he's still at large.'

Franks said, 'And the fact that it's election time come November.'

'I'd guess,' Corde said slowly, 'Hammerback'd be willing to work out a sharing arrangement. But only if you're talking a limited period of time. And I've gotta clear it with him.'

Willars said, 'I think of the families of some kid rolls his car off that bend on 607. You ever seen that happen?'

'It's pretty bad?' Kresge asked. 'How come you don't put up guard rails?'

Willars looked mournful. 'Fact is we're a poor county.'

Corde said, 'I think we could work something out.'

Sheriff Willars said, 'That's good enough for me. Let's

pick us up a couple M-16s and go catch ourselves a dangerous professor.'

Warning. No trespassing.

Bill Corde and Wynton Kresge stepped out of a stand of trees and found themselves looking at the summer house Leon Gilchrist had rented in his latest victim's name. A dilapidated two-story frame home on whose south side paint was peeling like colonial-red snake scales. The whole place was settling bad and only the portion near the chimney had good posture. The screen door on the porch was torn and every second window was cracked. A typical vacation house in the lake district of Lewisboro – not a two-week dream rental but a badly built clapboard that had been foreclosed on.

Up next to them walked Willars, Franks and a crew-cut local deputy, a young man bowlegged with muscles. Corde and Kresge had their service pistols drawn and the Lewisboro lawmen held battered dark gray military rifles, muzzle up.

Kresge looked at the machine guns and said, 'Well, well.'

'Peace,' whispered Willars, 'through superior firepower. Your show, Bill. Whatcha wanta do?'

'I'll go in with Wynton and somebody else. I'd like somebody on the front door and the back just in case.'

Willars sent the stocky deputy out back and he took the front door. He said to Franks, 'You be so kind as to accompany our cousins here?'

'Look,' Corde whispered. A light was flashing in an upstairs window. 'He's there . . .' The men crouched down.

Kresge said, 'No, look. It's just the sunlight. A reflection.'

'No, I don't think so,' Franks said with a taut voice. 'I think it's a light.'

'Whatever it is,' Corde said, 'let's go in.'

To his men Willars said, 'Check your pieces. Load and lock. Semiauto fire.' The sharp clicks and snaps of machined metal falling into place filled the clearing then there was silence again. They started forward. A large grackle fluttered past them and a jay screamed. Once out of the brush they ran, crouching, to the front porch and walked up the stairs, keeping low to the steps, smelling old wet wood and decaying paint.

They stood on either side of the door, backs to the house. Near Kresge's head was a sign: *Beware of Dog*. Kresge tested the door. It was locked.

Franks whispered, 'What about the dog?'

'There was one, he'd be barking by now,' Corde said. Kresge said, 'We knock, or not?'

Corde thought of the Polaroid of the girl possibly his daughter. He said, 'No.'

Kresge grunted his agreement like a veteran SWAT team cop and pulled open the screen door for Franks to hold.

'Pit bulls don't bark,' Franks said. 'I saw that on *Current Affair* or something.' He flicked the trigger guard of his rifle with a nervous finger.

Kresge stepped back but Corde touched him by the arm and shook his head then stepped into his place. 'I've got fifteen years' experience on you. Just stay close behind.'

'But I got sixty pounds' weight on you, Detective,' Kresge said and lowered his shoulder and charged into the door. It blew inward, the jamb shattering under his momentum. He slipped on the carpet and went down on his hip as Corde then Franks leapt into the living room after him.

A half dozen mangy pieces of sour overstuffed furniture and a hundred books stared silently back at them.

Franks kept his M-16 up, swiveling from door to door nervously with his head cocked, listening for malevolent growling.

The sunlight was fading fast and throughout the house the colors of rugs and paintings and wallpaper were vanishing. The men walked like soldiers through this monotone. Corde listened for Gilchrist and heard only old boards moaning beneath their feet, the tapping and surges of tiny household motors and valves.

Franks stayed downstairs while Corde and Kresge climbed up to where they had seen the light. They paused at the landing then continued to the second floor. Corde was suddenly aware of the smells: lemon furniture polish, musty cloth, after-shave or perfume.

They swung open the door to the master bedroom. It was empty. Corde smelled the dry after-shave stronger here and he wondered if it was Gilchrist's. It seemed similar to a cologne that he himself had worn, something Sarah had bought him for his birthday. This thought deeply upset him. The sun was low at the horizon, shining into his face. Maybe that *was* the light he'd seen, its reflection in the window. The sun dipped below the trees, and the light grew murkier. Corde reached toward the bedside lamp to pull the switch.

'Damn!'

The bulb was hot.

He told this to Kresge. The two men looked at each other, put their backs together, squinting through the gloom at the half dozen menacing near-human shapes they knew were a coat rack, an armoire, a shadow, a thick pink drape, yet at which each man drew an equivocal target with his pistol.

Kresge reached for the light switch. He laughed nervously. 'Wall's hot too. I think it was the sun. It was falling on the lamp and the wall here.'

Corde didn't respond. He opened his mouth wide and began to take slow breaths. He listened. No footsteps, no motion, no creaks. Walking around the edge of the room where the noise from sprung floorboards would be less, Corde looked in both closets. They were empty. He stepped into the hall and examined the other bedrooms and their closets, filled with musty coats and jackets, faded floral blouses, blankets stinking of camphor.

Kresge said, 'The attic?'

Hell. Going up through a trapdoor into an attic that

was surely packed with furniture and boxes – perfect cover for a gunman . . .

But they were spared that agony. Corde found the trapdoor in the ceiling of the hall. It was padlocked from the bottom.

He exhaled in relief.

On the ground floor again, they moved through the dining room and living room.

Corde thought: *Hell's bells the basement, just like the attic only it's not going to be padlocked at all and that's where Gilchrist is going to be. Has to be. No question.*

'How about the basement?'

'Isn't one,' Franks said.

Thanks, Lord, may be time to reconsider this church business, yessir . . .

Kresge said, 'I'm pretty surely tense in here.' He said it as if he were surprised and Corde and Franks laughed. In the kitchen Corde saw colorful labels that said Heinz and Goya and Campbell's, dented aluminum pans, bottles and chipped canisters, refrigerator magnets of barnyard animals, which had turned dark with years of cooking grime.

Corde said to Kresge, 'Let's keep at it.' He held his pistol with cramping pressure, his finger caressing the ribbed trigger inside the guard where he had told Kresge it should not be. 'I saw something I want to check.'

Franks said, 'There's a room in the back, I listened at it and didn't hear anything. But it's locked from the inside.' He poked a stained yellow drape with the slotted muzzle of his soldier gun.

'Just a second we'll go with you,' Corde called from the living room. He was looking at a pile of ash in the fireplace. He crouched down and sifted through the gray dust. Kresge stood guard over him. In the midst of a pyramid of ash Corde found the scorched cover of a photo album. His hands shook with the excitement of being close to a picture of Gilchrist. But there were none. Almost everything was burnt and the ash dissolved.

But one remained. A Polaroid had fallen through the log rack. Though it was badly blistered from the heat it hadn't burnt completely. The square showed a street in a city, a line of faded row houses, with a few trees in front. Breaking through the Maginot Line of the tops of the residences was a shiny office building five or six stories high.

On the back was written: *Leon, come visit sometime. Love*

Corde wrapped the photo in his handkerchief and put it in his pocket then stood, the familiar pop of his knee resounding through the dark room.

The pop was loud. But not loud enough to cover the crack of Assistant Sheriff Franks breaking through the doorway of the locked room and the thunderclap of the shotgun blast that took off much of his shoulder.

Corde spun fast, dropping into a crouch. Kresge grabbed the convulsing deputy by his leg and dragged him toward the kitchen, along a wall now covered by a constellation of slick blood.

'Okay, okay, okay!' Corde shouted to no one and he rolled forward into the doorway, prone position.

His elbow landed on a bit of sharp bone from the deputy's shoulder. Corde ignored the pain as he fired five staccato shots at the figure inside. Three missed and slammed into the armchair to which was taped the double-barrel Remington wired to the doorknob. Two of Corde's slugs though were aimed perfectly and found their target.

Which wasn't however Professor Leon David Gilchrist but a four-foot-high ceramic owl, which in the dim light resembled not a bird but a laughing man and which under the impact of the unjacketed rounds exploded into a thousand shards of brown and gold porcelain.

7

Bill Corde sat in the Auden University Library.

This was a musty Victorian building, latticed with oak dense as metal and wrought-iron railings that coiled through the balconies and stacks like ivy boughs. The structure might have been imported brick by brick from sooty London and reassembled on this grassy quad within sight of thousands of acres of stalky fields growing a green pelt of corn shoots.

This was the library of a university that Bill Corde would not be admitted to and whose tuition he could not have afforded if he had been.

He had just gotten off the phone with Sheriff Willars in Lewisboro and learned the Dudley Franks was in critical but stable condition. Whatever that meant. Willars had said, 'I'm not a happy camper, Bill, no sir,' and Corde knew there'd be some hefty reparation payments between the two counties.

Gloom had settled on the New Lebanon Sheriff's Department after the shooting. The manhunt that seemed so like a game several days ago had now turned rooty and mean. Gilchrist was both far crazier and far more savage than any of them had guessed and though those two adjectives were rarely if ever found in the vocabulary of modern law enforcement, Corde now felt the full pressure of their meaning.

Gilchrist, Leon David, b. 1951, Cleary, New York. BA

summa cum laude, MA, Northwestern University; PhD English literature, Harvard University; PhD psychology, Harvard University. Assistant Professor and Fellow, Department of English, School of Arts & Sciences, Harvard University. Tenured Professor, Department of English, School of Arts & Sciences, Auden University. Lecturing Professor, Department of Special Education, School of Education, Auden University. Visiting Professor, Vanderbilt University, University of Naples, La Sorbonne Université, College of William & Mary ...

There were two more full paragraphs.

Corde finished his notes then closed the *Directory of Liberal Arts Professors*. It contained no picture of Gilchrist – the main purpose of his visit here. Neither did the three books written by Gilchrist in the library's permanent collection. They were books without author photos, books without jackets, smart-person books. Corde jotted a note on a three-by-five card to call the sheriff in Cleary, New York, to see if there were any Gilchrists still in the area.

He flipped quickly through the *Index to Periodicals*. He was about to close the book when his eye caught the title of an article. He walked to the Periodicals desk and requested the journal the article had been published in. The clerk vanished for a moment and returned with the bound volume of *Psyche: The Journal of Psychology and Literature*.

Corde sat at his place again, read the first paragraph of 'The Poet and the Violent Id' by Leon D. Gilchrist, PhD. He returned to the counter and borrowed a dictionary.

He tried again.

The poet, by which expansive term I am taking the liberty of referring to anyone who creates fictional modes with words, is himself a creation of the society in which he lives. Indeed, it is the obligation of the poet to deliquesce ...

'Deliquesce.'

Corde marked his place in the journal with his elbow

and thumbed through the dictionary. The 'levitate'/
'licentious' page fell out. He stuffed it back between
'repudiate'/'resident' and 'residual'/'response'.

'Deliquesce, v. To melt by absorbing moisture or
humidity contained in the air.'

Okay. Good.

*... obligation of the poet to deliquesce so that he might
permeate all aspects of society ...*

'Permeate.'

Corde lifted the dictionary again.

For ten minutes he fought through the article, his
sweaty hands leaving splendid fingerprints on the torn
jacket of the dictionary, his stomach wound into a knot
– not by what he learned about Gilchrist (which was
hardly anything) but by the slippery obscurity of
meaning. For the first time Corde truly understood his
daughter's predicament.

He paused, saturated by frustration. He breathed
slowly several times and resumed.

*... does not the id of a pulp thriller writer encompass
a lust to travel the countryside, strangling women ...*

Words ...

What did these words say about where Gilchrist was?
What state he would flee to, what country? How he
would try to escape? What kind of weapon he might use?

Letters syllables words sentences ...

What do they say about a beautiful young girl lying
dead in a bed of hyacinths, swabbed with cold mud?
What do they say about the man who closed his hands
around her neck, felt her breasts shaking under his
elbows, felt the slow, bloody give of her throat, felt the
last shiver of her breath on his wrists as she lay down
like a struggling lover and saw for one short moment the
darkening glow of the half-moon?

... the metaphors of violence abound ...

Corde reached forward and ran a finger along
metaphors of violence and seemed to feel heat coming off
the ink.

'Metaphor, n. A figure of speech in which an object,

427

idea or symbol is described by analogy . . .'

WHAT . . .

'Analogy, n. Correspondence between objects generally thought to be dissimilar . . .'

. . . *IS HE TALKING* . . .

'Correspondence, n. A similarity . . .'

. . . *ABOUT?*

Corde leaned forward and pressed his eye sockets into his palms, hearing tiny pops of pressure.

The motives of the poet are the motives of us all. The mind of the poet is the collective mind. But it is the poet – whether his psyche be that of saint or murderer – who perceived the world by the illumination of pure understanding, while others see only in reflected light.

Bill Corde turned to the last page of the article.

Oh Lord . . .

He stopped as if he'd been struck, feeling the throbbing as the blood pumped furiously through his neck. He reached forward and lifted the Polaroid from the binding of the journal.

The snapshot had been taken recently, perhaps when the family had cooked supper outside just two evenings ago. He noticed the garbage can had not been righted after a storm last week. Sarah and Jamie stood around the barbecue looking down at the glowing coals. The picture had been taken from somewhere on the other side of the cow pasture in the forest. Almost the exact spot where Corde believed he had seen someone that night he'd kept his long vigil, shotgun-armed and shivering.

Written across the surface of the photo in smeared red ink were the words: SAY GOOD-BYE, DETECTIVE.

Diane Corde, feeling suddenly sheepish, told Ben Breck that she and the children were going to Wisconsin for several weeks.

'What?' Breck asked, frowning.

Diane lifted her hands to her eyes. Her burgundy nail polish was unchipped and her fingers, often red and leathery from the housework, were soft and fragrant with almond-scented lotion. 'It's the damn case again.'

She explained that there'd been yet another threat by the killer. 'Bill thought it was best if we went to visit my sister.'

He hesitated and then whispered, 'Two weeks?'

She shrugged. 'At least. Or until they catch this crazy man. Or find out he's left town.'

Breck's downcast boyish face and his tone were identical to those of her first husband when she'd told him she had to spend a week with her mother, who'd fallen and broken her hip. It had been the first time they'd be apart and the young man's face had revealed major heartbreak. Breck's eyes now mirrored the poor man's forlorn expression. This troubled and thrilled her.

They heard a voice outside.

In the backyard, Sarah Corde paced, speaking into her tape recorder like a Hollywood producer dictating memos. Tom, the familiar deputy guard, leaned against the fence rail, his head swiveling slowly like a scout's in an old-time Western as he scanned the horizon for marauders.

Breck and Diane stood in the dining room and watched Sarah silently. They stood one foot away from each other. Diane felt him touch her hair, the motion of his hand very gentle, as if he were afraid he might hurt her. She leaned her head against his shoulder then stepped away, both disappointed and grateful to hear him begin to speak suddenly about Sarah. 'She's coming along remarkably well. What a mind! The stories she comes up with are incredible.'

'I've given Dr Parker four tapes already. Her secretary's transcribing the last of them.'

He brushed his salt-and-pepper hair off his forehead in a boyish gesture.

'She's fortunate,' Breck said slowly, his eyes playing over Diane's face. 'She's got a superior auditory processing system. That's how I'm approaching her lessons, and it's working very well.'

Diane had recognized something about him. If he had a choice between a ten-dollar word and a twenty-five-cent word, he picked the big one. 'Fortunate' instead of 'lucky.' 'Auditory processing,' not 'hearing.' 'Onerous.' 'Ensconce.' With anyone else this habit would put her off; in Breck, she found it increased his charm.

No. His 'charisma.'

He continued to speak about Sarah. This was unusual and she sensed he was propelled by nervousness. In most of these after-session get-togethers – usually in the kitchen, occasionally in the woods – they spoke not of phonemes or the Visual Aural Digit Span Test or Sarah's book but of more personal things. The schools he had taught at, his former girlfriends, her first husband, Diane's life as the daughter of a riverboat worker, vacations they hoped to take. Where they wanted to be in ten years, and five. And one.

Yet the nature of these minutes they spent together was ambiguous. Though they talked intimately Breck had not kissed her; though they flirted he seemed bashful. Their contact was plentiful but often seemed accidental: fingers brushing when passing coffee cups, shoulders easing against each other when they stood side by side. She once shamelessly seated her breasts against his arm as she leaned forward to look at an article on learning disabilities. She thought he had returned the pressure but she couldn't be sure. In any event he neither backed away nor prolonged the moment.

She didn't know whether to expect a proposition or not.

A proposition she would, of course, refuse.

She *believed* she would refuse. She wanted him to kiss her. She wanted him to leave. She now touched his arm and he swayed close to her and Diane sensed again the boundary between them that was continually being redefined. They were like teenagers.

Today she believed this barrier was clear and solid. Jamie was only thirty feet away, in his room, and although Bill was at work it wasn't unheard of for him to drop by at this time of day, stay for dinner then return to the office. She and Breck looked at each other for a long moment and she was vastly relieved when he looked at his watch and said, 'Must depart, madame . . .' (She was also pleased that he said this frowning with genuine disappointment.) He gathered his notebooks.

That was when Diane kissed him.

Like a sly college girl, she glanced over her shoulder to make sure Sarah was out of sight then pushed scholarly Breck into the corner of the room and kissed him fast, open-mouthed, then stepped away.

Ohmygod ohmygod . . .

Panic bubbled inside her. Terrified – not that one of her children had seen, not that word would get back to her husband. No, a more chilling fear: what if he hadn't wanted to?

Breck blinked once in surprise. He put his hand on the back of her neck and pulled her quickly to him. As he kissed her hard, his forearm was leveraged against her breast and his hand made one slow sweep along the front of her blouse then wound around to the small of her back. They embraced for a long moment then Diane willed herself to break away. They stood staring at each other, two feet apart, in surprise and embarrassed defiance.

He whispered, 'Can I see you before you go? I have to.'

'I don't know. The deputy'll be watching us like a hawk.'

'I have to see you. Let's get away somewhere.'

She thought. 'I just don't see how.'

'Look, I'd like to tape Sarah taking some tests. If you're not going to be back for a couple weeks I should do it before you leave. Maybe you could come with us to the school. We could have a picnic.'

'I don't know.'

'I want you,' he whispered.

Diane stepped away, rubbed her hands together. She

stared out the window at her daughter prancing about in the grass.

'Did I say something amiss?' Breck asked.

Oh, my. All theses highfalutin' words, all these snappy things he does for Sarah, all the places he's been, and what is at the heart of it all – him being a man and me being a woman.

Do I want this or not? I just can't tell. For the life of me I can't tell . . .

But she said nothing. She kissed him once more, quickly, then led him by the hand to the door. They walked out to his car and she said to him, 'It'll be a couple weeks at the most.' In a whisper intended to convey grave significance she added, 'I think it's for the best anyway, don't you?'

'No,' he said firmly. 'I don't.'

8

The big problem with the My-T-Fine Tap was the dirty plateglass windows. They let in bleak, northern, cool light, which turned the afternoon patrons all pasty and sick.

Also, sitting at a table you could look up under the bar and see the mosaic of twenty years' worth of gum wads.

Corde ordered an Amstel, so tired he wasn't even thinking it was a weekday, and Kresge said, 'I just want to get this right. It's okay to drink *light* beer on duty?'

Corde changed the order to an iced tea.

They sat on stools upholstered in jukebox red vinyl, squinting against the glare. People used to tell Sammie to fill up the window with plants (they died) or blinds (they cost too much). He'd say it's an ugly room who gives a damn anyway. Which it was and nobody did so they all stopped complaining.

Corde asked, 'What are we doing here?'

'Waiting for *her*,' Kresge said, and pointed to the woman in her late fifties, slender, short, with foamy gray hair. She was walking through the door on the arm of an older man, balding and also thin.

'Hey, Wynton,' the woman called. 'How's Darla?'

'Tina, Earl, come on over here for a second.'

The couple walked over and Kresge said to Corde, 'They eat here 'most every day. She and Darla're bridge buddies.' Kresge introduced Corde to Earl and Tina

433

Hess. Earl was a lanky retiree of about sixty. His protruding ears and hook nose were bright with a May sunburn.

'What's that uniform you got yourself, Wynton? The school got you all duded up?'

'Got a new job.'

'Doing what?'

'I'm a deputy.'

'No kidding,' Earl said. 'Like Kojak.'

'He's still got himself some hair left,' Corde said. 'But not a lot.'

'We come for the tuna plates,' Tina said. 'You want to eat with us?'

Corde shook his head and turned the session over to Kresge, who said, 'We've found ourselves a picture and we were thinking maybe you could tell us where it is, Tina.' He turned to Corde. 'Tina worked for Allied Office Supplies.'

'Sales Rep of the Year fifteen years running. My last year I lost to D.K. Potts but only because he got himself the Instant Copy Franchises up in Higgins which are owned by the Japanese and I won't comment on that.'

Kresge continued, 'She's traveled all over the state. Knows every city, bar none.'

'Three years ago I put a hundred thirty-seven thousand miles on my Ford. You ever put that much mileage on a car before she rusted? I should bet not.'

'No, ma'am,' Corde admitted.

'She didn't tell you about the transmissions,' Earl said earnestly.

Kresge said, 'We've got to find the building that's in the picture.'

'That's a sort of tall order,' Tina said. 'Do I have to testify or anything?'

'No.'

'I was hoping I would. You watch *Matlock*?'

'Fraid I don't,' Corde said. Kresge set the photograph on the table.

'Why's it wrapped up?' Earl asked, poking the plastic bag.

'Evidence,' Kresge said.

'Why's it burned?'

'Was in a fireplace,' Corde said. 'You know where that is?'

'Not much to go on.' Tina squinted and studied it. She held it toward her husband and he shrugged. Tina said, 'No idea. Why you so interested?'

'It'd help us in an investigation.'

She handed it back. 'Sorry.'

Kresge, taking the failure personally, said, 'It was a long shot.'

Corde kept the disappointment off his face. 'Thanks anyway.'

'Were you part of that layoff at Auden?' Earl asked Kresge.

'Layoff?'

'They let near to three hundred people go. Professors and staff.'

Kresge whistled. 'Three hundred? No. I left before that happened.'

'After that professor killed that girl,' Earl said, 'a lot of people took their kids out. It was in the *Register*, didn't you read it?'

Tina said, 'I wouldn't send my kids to any school that hired professors like that. I can't blame them.' The couple wandered off to a booth.

As Kresge and Corde stood and dropped bills onto the bar Tina called from across the room, 'Hey, Wynton, got an idea: Why don't you ask somebody in the Fitzberg C of C where that is.'

'Who?'

'The Chamber of Commerce.'

'That's Fitzberg?' Corde asked, pointing at Kresge's breast pocket where the burnt photo now resided.

'Sure, didn't you know?'

Kresge laughed. 'Well, no. You said you didn't recognize it.'

435

'I thought you meant did I know what *street* it was. Of course it's Fitzberg. What do you think that building is in the background? Fireman's Indemnity Plaza. Where else you think they have a building like that?'

Earl said, 'Fitzberg's got a Marshall Field. Best store in the Midwest.'

Dean Catherine Larraby walked in a slow circle around the perimeter of an oriental rug that had been acquired in 1887 by the then chancellor of the school, whose first visitor to tread upon the new carpet happened to be William Dean Howells. The august writer was lecturing at Auden on the contemporary novel. Dean Larraby mentioned this fact as she paced, her eyes on the frayed carpet.

Her visitor this morning wasn't as well known as Howells, at least not among literary circles, though the dean treated him more reverentially than if he had been the ghost of the eminent literatus himself.

She was speaking of Howells, of Dickens, of the school's tradition of academic excellence, of the number of Harvard graduates on the Auden faculty and vice versa, when Fred Barrett, a thick-faced, slick-haired businessman from Chicago, stopped her cold by asking, 'What's with these murders?'

Dean Larraby, heiress to great administrators and greater scholars, overseer of this bastion of Midwest letters, smelled defeat. She stopped pacing, sighed and returned to her chair.

Here he was, another wealthy businessman, able to loan enough money for her to conceal from the Department of Education auditors the bum loans she and Randy Sayles had made, here he sat, a godsend, and yet she would now have to confess that yes a professor had killed a student, and yes that student's lesbian lover killed herself.

And that the professor had then murdered a colleague.

And that yes enrollment had fallen fourteen percent because of the whole damn mess.

He would then gather his London Fog coat and place his jaunty hat on his head and walk away with his five million dollars. And her job and the viability of Auden University would depart with him. The DOE auditors were due in three days. Barrett had been her last chance.

She sighed and said, 'I'm afraid we *have* had some tragedies on the campus this spring. It's unfortunate. But you see why we need the money so desperately. Once we get this all behind us—'

Barrett asked, 'This Professor Sayles is the one who called me. I come all the way from Cicero down here and I find he's dead.' He had an accent that she couldn't place.

'I'm sorry if you wasted your time, Mr Barrett.'

He shook his head. 'Not a waste yet. Let's talk about lending some money.'

Hope glinted. She considered tactics for a moment then said, 'You're familiar with Auden University?'

'Not really. It's like a college?'

The dean thought he might have been joking but she didn't dare risk a smile. She looked around the room for a moment, intuitively grasped that there was no irony in his question and readjusted her sales pitch. 'I think it will be helpful to put the loan in context. Auden is one of the nation's premiere institutions of higher learning—'

'I'm sure it's a great place. How much do you want?'

Don't mince words in Chicago, do you? The dean sought refuge in the high-rise of papers on her desk. 'I know it sounds like a lot. But I can't tell you how important it is to the school that we get this money.'

Barrett cocked an eyebrow, which emphatically repeated his question.

Dean Larraby said softly, 'Five million.'

He shook his head.

'I know it's a great deal,' she pleaded. The nakedness of her voice shocked her and she spoke more slowly. 'But the school is in desperate straits. You have to understand that. Without—'

'It's too *little*. Gotta be ten million minimum or we don't even talk to you.'

Dean Larraby believed she misheard the man. She ran through various permutations of his words. 'You don't loan anything under *ten* million?'

'Not worth our while.'

'But—'

'Not worth our while.'

This was a predicament she had not counted on. 'You couldn't make an exception?'

'I could maybe talk my associates down to eight.'

She wondered if she was being naive when she asked, 'Well, if we were to do business with you, would it be possible to borrow the eight and repay some of it early?'

'Sure. You can borrow it Monday and repay it Tuesday. A lot of my clients do that.'

'They do?' Dean Larraby could find no logical reason for this practice and dropped it from her mind. She regained her stride. She lifted the school's financial statements from her desk and handed one to Barrett. He took it and flipped through the document as if it were printed in Chinese. He handed it back. He shook his head. 'That does me no good. Just tell me, you want the money or no?'

'Don't you want to know about the fiscal strength of the school? Our debt ratio? Our overhead?' Dean Larraby, a liberal arts workhorse from the U of K, was proud of this financial knowledge she'd learned, this *useful* knowledge.

'No,' Barrett said, 'I want to know how much money you want.'

'It sounds like you're just asking me to name a figure.'

Barrett lifted both eyebrows this time.

She stalled. 'Well, what's the interest rate?'

'Prime plus two.'

'You should know there's a collateral problem . . .'

'We're not interested in collateral. We're interested in you paying us back when you're supposed to.'

'We'll do that. We're trimming expenses and we've

already fired three hundred and twelve employees. We've hired a financial advisor and he's cutting—'

Barrett looked at his watch. 'How much?'

The dean inhaled nervously. 'Eight million.'

'Done.' Barrett smiled.

'That's it? You'd write a check to us just like that?'

Barrett snorted a laugh. 'Not a check of course.'

'Eight million dollars in *cash*?' she whispered. He nodded. 'Isn't that . . . risky?'

'It's riskier with checks, believe me.'

'I guess we could put it directly in the bank.'

'No,' Barrett said cautiously, 'that would be inappropriate.' The big word stumbling under his urban drawl. When the dean looked at him quizzically he added, 'What most of my clients do is keep it in their own safe and pay it out in small amounts. If you have to bank it make sure it's in different numbered accounts of less than ten thousand each.'

'That's a rather strange requirement.'

'Yeah, Washington comes up with some funny rules.'

The dean's education was expanding exponentially. 'Your business is headquartered in Chicago?'

Barrett said, 'Among other places.'

'And what line are you? Is it banking?'

'A number of lines.'

Dean Larraby was nodding. 'I don't suppose I should ask where this money comes from.'

'Ask whatever you want.'

'Where?—'

'Various business enterprises.'

The dean was nodding. 'This isn't illegal, is it?'

'Illegal?' Barrett smiled like an insulted maître d'. 'Well, let's look at the broad scenario. I'm lending you money at a fair, negotiated rate based on prime. You pay it back, principal and interest.' His eyes swept up to a portrait of a sideburned former dean. 'That doesn't sound illegal to me.'

'I suppose not,' she said. The dean looked out on the quadrangle then back to the William Dean Howells rug.

439

She wondered if she should ask directly if she had just committed her school to a major money laundering scheme but decided it might be insulting or incriminating and the risk of either was enough to put the kibosh on the question.

She looked out the windows and saw a lilac bush bending in a spring breeze. This reminded her of Whitman's poem about Lincoln's death, and free-associating she recalled that the last time she cried was in college on the wet afternoon of November 22, 1963. She now felt her eyes fill with tears though this time they came from relief and, perhaps, joy.

She said, 'I guess we have a deal.'

Barrett kept a noncommittal, what-a-nice-office-you-got smile on his face. He said, 'You go up to ten million, I'll shave the points to one and three-fourths.'

The dean said, 'Mustn't be greedy now. After all, we have to pay it back.'

'Yes, ma'am, you've got to do that.'

Wynton Kresge said, 'He's checking. He's regular Army. Put some salute in your voice when you talk to him.'

Corde picked up the receiver and listened to the hollowness of a phone on hold. He was in his office and Kresge was at a desk two feet away. Propelled by nervous energy, both stood rather than sat.

After two minutes a crisp voice came on the line. 'Deputy Kresge?'

'Yes sir, I'm here and I have on the line Detective Bill Corde, who's heading the investigation.'

'Detective Corde,' the voice said forcefully, 'Detective Sergeant Franklin Neale up in Fitzberg here. You five by five, sir?'

'Five by five,' Corde said.

'Well, sir, I understand we may have one of your perps down here.'

'That's what Wynton tells me, Detective. What've you got?'

'Well, that Polaroid you sent was a dead end. We

checked deeds and leases for a Gilchrist. Negative that. We knocked on doors of buildings shown in the pics and naturally got negatives there too. But we did some brainstorming and stroked the folks at credit card companies. As best we can tell there's a male perp, cauc, early forties, no distinguishing, using Visa and Amex in the names of Gilchrist comma L. and Sayles comma R.R.'

'It's the same person using both cards?'

'That's what we're reading, sir,' Neale said.

Corde punched the air with a fist. He winked at Kresge.

'You have a hidey-hole for him?' Kresge asked.

'Holiday Inn Eastwood near the river. Checked in as Sayles.'

'He hasn't checked out?'

'No, sir. But we don't know whether he's in or not at the moment.'

'Okay,' Corde said, 'We've got a warrant. Deputy Kresge and I'll be up there in about two hours. You'll keep surveillance on him? I'll fax you the warrant. If he heads out before we get there pick him up, will you?'

'Yessir, it'll be our pleasure. What'd his risk status be?'

'How's that?' Corde asked.

'He armed, dangerous?'

Corde looked at Kresge and said, 'Extremely dangerous.'

9

The hardest part was lying to him.

It wasn't so difficult to tell him that his father couldn't be at the wrestling match after all. And it wasn't so hard to see Jamie take the news with heroic disappointment, just a nod, not even a burst of temper (which she would have preferred, because that's what *she* felt). But making up her husband's words just stabbed her through. Your father said to tell you, Diane embellished, that this killer's on the loose and they've got a real solid chance to catch him. He tried to arrange it different but he's the one's got to go. He's sending all his thoughts with you.

'And,' Diane said, unable to look into her son's eyes, 'he promised he'll make it up to you.'

What in truth happened was that Corde had simply left for Fitzberg and hadn't even bothered to call home or tell Emma to do it for him.

What a long long wait it had been! The time had crept past the hour when Corde was due home. Cars passed but no New Lebanon Sheriff's Department We Serve and Protect cruisers hurried up to the house. The minutes dropping away as Jamie and his teammate Davey sat on the couch fidgeting, joking at first as they talked about whupping Higgins High School's butt then looking out the window anxiously then falling silent. As six-thirty came and went Diane had decided she was going to insist that Corde break procedures and take the boys in the cruiser itself, siren blazing and red light going like a beating heart.

At six-fifty Diane had made the call. It was much shorter than she let on. Emma the dispatcher told her Bill and Deputy Kresge had hurried out the door and would be spending the night in Fitzberg.

Diane thanked her then listened to the dial tone as she continued her fake conversation at a higher volume. 'Oh, Bill, what happened? . . . No, really? You've almost got him . . . Oh be careful, honey . . . Well, Jamie's going to be good and disappointed and here you were already a half hour late . . . Okay . . . Okay . . . I'll tell him . . .'

Then she delivered her improvised monologue and asked the deputy to step inside to baby-sit Sarah.

'Let me get another deputy to go with you, Mrs Corde. Your husband said there's—'

'My husband caused this mess,' she growled. 'And we don't have time to wait.'

Diane and the two boys piled into the station wagon for a frantic ride to the Higgins High School gym. She ran every red light en route and was spoiling for a fight with any uniformed trooper foolish enough to pull her over.

Bill, you and me've gotta talk.

Diane Corde sat on hard bleachers, sipping a watery Coke. She watched the crowds and thought of the smell, the peculiar aroma of school gyms, which a girlfriend had told her years ago came from boys' jockstraps. She wanted to tell this story to someone. She wished Ben Breck were here, sitting next to her.

After ten matches there was a staticky announcement, the only words of which she discerned were 'Jamie Corde.' She set the Coke beside her and finger-whistled at a hundred decibels. The visiting spectators cheered New Lebanon.

Diane watched her son striding out onto the mat, brooding and engrossed and fluid in his step. She whistled again, bringing fingers to the ears of nearby fans. She wailed for New Lebanon and pummeled the bleachers with her feet – the current fad to show support. Jamie was so focused, so single-minded in his efforts. He ran five miles every day, pumped weights every other. He trained and trained. And he had recovered so well from the tragedy of Philip. He was even taking his father's inexcusable neglect tonight in his stride. Diane felt a huge burst of pride for her son, sending it telepathically out to him as he pulled on his head protector and shook his opponent's hand.

Jamie looked up into the bleachers. She waved at him. He acknowledged her in the only way that a competitor could respond to his mother here – by looking at her once, nodding solemnly then turning away. She didn't mind; she knew he was telling her that he had received her psychic message.

Jamie strapped the blue cloth marker on his arm, then reared his head back and breathed deeply.

The whistle blew and the boys exploded into frenzy. Jamie's legs tensed then uncoiled as he leapt at his opponent – a tall blond sophomore – like a striking snake. They gripped arms and necks, heads together. Spinning, spinning, feet snagging the spongy blue mat, inching like grappling crabs. Limbs confused with limbs. Dots of sweat flew. Faces crimson under foam protectors, tendons rising thick from their necks. Furious scrabbling around the mat, hands were claws, gripping at knees and wrists.

Diane shouted, 'Go, go. GO! Come on, JAMIE!!'

A brutal take-down, Jamie lifting the boy off the mat and driving him down onto his back. His head bounced and the boy gazed upward, momentarily stunned. Face glistening, Jamie pressed him hard into the mat furiously, his opponent's arms flailing. Several blows struck Jamie on the back. They were solid strikes but they rebounded without effect.

What was happening?

Diane was frowning, aware suddenly of the quiet of the crowd around her. Then people in the bleachers were on their feet, shouting at the coaches and at the two boys. The blond opponent tried to muscle himself

445

away from Jamie, a centimeter at a time, toward the out-of-bounds line, twisting onto his side, shouting. He'd given up and was bent on pure escape. Several people shot Diane shocked glances as if she were responsible for her son's brutal attack.

She shouted, 'Jamie, stop!'

His opponent's arm was turning blue-gray under Jamie's relentless grip, his legs kicked in despair. The referee's whistle blew shrilly. Jamie didn't let go. He kept driving the boy into the ground and twisting his arm, from which the red marker fluttered like a distress signal.

'Jamie!' she called. 'Honey . . .'

The referee started forward. The sports-coated coaches were on their feet, shouting, red-faced, running toward the mat. The referee dropped to his knees and slapped both hands on Jamie's shoulders. Jamie spun toward him and hit him hard in the chest. Off balance, the referee rolled onto his back.

Diane screamed her son's name.

Jamie rose on one knee. Using all his leverage he bent his opponent's forearm up up up . . . *Thock*. Diane heard the noise of the break all the way up in the bleachers. She froze where she stood and raised her hand to her mouth, watching her son standing, smiling and triumphant, over the unconscious figure of his vanquished enemy. Jamie turned on the coaches and they froze. Then the boy held his arm out straight and high then closed his fingers into a fist. Diane saw him glance toward her as he ran out the open double doors to the football field, his arm still lifted in the macabre salute of victory.

Detective Frank Neale was pretty much what Corde expected. Crew cut, blond, beefy, smooth ruddy skin. Too professional to put an *If we outlaw guns then only outlaws will have guns* sticker on his Fitzberg police cruiser but dollars to doughnuts there'd be one on his (American) 4X4.

But God bless him, he met Corde and Kresge after their frantic two-hour drive with a thermos of the best coffee Corde had ever tasted and four fat roast beef sandwiches. They ate these as they raced through the bleak streets of urban-decaying Fitzberg en route to what Neale described as an MCP in the parking lot across from the Holiday Inn.

'MCP?' Kresge asked.

Neale said, 'Mobile command post.'

'Oh.'

Corde thought it wouldn't be much more than a police car with maybe two radios, which is what an MCP in New Lebanon would have been. But no it was a big air-conditioned Ford van with room for six officers inside. There was a large antenna dish on the roof. Kresge pointed out the bulletproof windows in the front.

'Jesus,' Corde whispered. 'Maybe they got cannons, too.'

No artillery but a rack of laser-sighted M-16s, a gray box containing concussion grenades and rows of radios and computer screens and other imposing electronics. Kresge said, 'All this for one perp?'

Standing as straight as the barrel of a goose-gun, Neale said, 'A lawbreaker's a lawbreaker, Deputy, and a killer's my least favorite kind.'

'Yessir,' said Kresge. 'I'll go along with you there.'

Corde hoped someday soon he could play the eye-rolling game with Kresge. He said to Neale, 'Where's Gilchrist now?'

Neale said, 'TacSurv says he's in the room.'

Kresge asked, 'Tac? . . .'

'Tactical Surveillance. They say he's in the room but we've got a glitch. He's taken in two innocents with him. A couple prostitutes.'

'His profile isn't a lust killing but he's very unstable.'

Neale said, 'We've got a Sensi-Ear on him. He's paid the ladies already and now they're getting down to fun and games. If he goes rogue on us we'll do a kick-in and nail him but if not it's our policy to wait until we're out

447

of hostage situations. Is he the sort who'd take a hostage?'

'He'd do anything,' Corde said emphatically, 'to escape.'

'Okay,' Neale said, 'subject to your go-ahead, sir, we wait.'

The wind swirls into the low bowl of the cemetery and slips inside Jamie's one-piece wrestling uniform.

The boy shivers and stands up. He carefully walks around the portion of the grave in which Philip's body lies and he leaves the cemetery, walking slowly to the Des Plaines River. Here the water's course is narrow and as close to a rapids as a Midwest farmland river ever gets. Upstream a quarter mile it forks and swirls around a small, narrow island filled with brush and dense trees. You can't wade the water but you can reach the island by a thick fallen birch, which he and Philip crossed hundreds of times to reach the Dimensioncruiser that the island so clearly resembles. Jamie crosses the tree now, looking down into the turbulence of the sudsy phosphate-polluted water and once across walks the familiar path past the cruiser's control room, the engine room, the xaser torpedo tubes, the escape vehicle . . .

Jamie stops. He sees on the other side of the island a night fisherman, casting leisurely out into the water. Jamie is bitterly betrayed. Furious. This is their private place, his and Philip's. No one else is allowed here. In the days since Philip died Jamie has come here nearly every day to walk the cruiser's decks. He angrily resents this man's invading the island, taking it over like a Honon warrior. The fisherman turns and looks at the boy in surprise then smiles and waves. Jamie ignores him and walks sullenly back through the island.

Jamie stands under pines crowned with dusty illumination from the lights of Higgins. He pitches stones into the water. In the gurgle of the torrent he imagines he hears the chugging rhythms of Geiger – the searing guitar riffs, the screams from the sweating hatter of a lead singer. He suddenly feels two mosquito stings on his arms. After the insects drink for a moment he smashes them viciously, leaving bloody black spots on his forearms. He listens to the roar of the water.

Do. Yourself.

You gotta do yourself.

You. Got. To. Do. Yourself.

The sky, long past blue, is now the gray color of a xaser torpedo before it detonates. The clouds separate for a moment and Jamie sees the first star of the evening. He feels a cloudburst of agony in his soul, the pain gushing through him. He is gripped with coarse panic and runs to the birch bridge. He steps onto the tree.

Do yourself. You gotta do yourself now!

Jamie walks halfway across then stops. He lifts his arms, like Dathar-IV standing on top of the State Governance Building Bridge, a thousand feet above the solar crystals, Honon troops closing in from either side. Jamie Corde stretches his arms high above his head, two eyes closed, balancing on twenty toes, above a single abyss of racing water.

> *By the power of Your wisdom,*
> *by the strength of Your might,*
> *guide me, O Guardians,*
> *to the Lost Dimension,*
> *from darkness to light . . .*

He drops like a meteorite into the dark rage of water. He feels a scraping pain against his ear as the side of his head smacks the tree on his way down, then a cold colder than he's ever felt envelops his body, squeezing every last bit of breath from his lungs.

Jamie Corde looks up, he sees water, he sees blood and he sees in the tunnel of blackness above him a single star, which he knows is the eye of a Guardian, agreeing to lift him away, safely into a new dimension.

A second thermos of coffee appeared. Neale ran his fingers along his buzz-cut hair and told them of the time one of his snipers picked off a perp at eight hundred yards. 'God held his breath for that one,' Neale said reverently.

On a panel like the dashboard of a 747 a lonely red light began flashing and an electronic beep pulsed. A sergeant picked up a receiver. 'MCP One. This is an unsecured landline. Go ahead.' He listened for a moment. 'Detective Corde, for you.'

'Me?' He took the receiver. 'Corde here.'

'Bill.' The hollowness of Diane's whisper cried a hundred different messages to him.

He said, 'Honey, what is it? Why are you—'

'Bill.'

Corde could hear she'd already cried volumes. He heard noises behind her. Other voices. He hated that sound. They were hospital sounds. He asked, 'Sarah?'

'Jamie.'

'What happened?'

'He's in a coma. He... Oh, Bill, he tried to kill himself. A fisherman found him but—'

'Oh, my Lord.'

He remembered, and the thought was like a wallop in the stomach. 'The wrestling match? I missed it.'

She didn't speak for a moment. 'Come home, Bill. I want you here.'

'Is he going to be okay?'

'They don't know. He almost drowned. He hit his head when he went in. Come home now.'

When they hung up Corde said, 'Wynton, Jamie's hurt. I've got to go.'

'Oh, no, Bill. Was it him?' He nodded toward the hotel.

'No. Something else. Pretty serious. I've got to go. You're in charge here.'

Wynton Kresge had the love for seven children in his voice when he said, 'I'll be thinking of you.' Corde couldn't speak but just rested his hand on the deputy's huge back. In that brief gesture, Kresge felt a huge weight shift and remain on him even after Corde stepped out the door. Kresge said, 'We'll get him, Bill. We'll get him.'

10

'I did this one bad, didn't I?' Corde said.

They sat in the intensive care unit of Community Hospital in a small waiting room separated from their son by a thick blond wood door. The doctors were in with him now. Occasionally the large silver handle of a doorknob would flick and a nurse or doctor would exit silently. This was the purest of punishments.

They held hands but there was minimal returning pressure from Diane's. Corde figured he wasn't entitled to expect otherwise. Other than to tell him that Jamie was in critical condition and still unconscious, Diane hadn't said more than five words since he'd arrived after a perilous drive from Fitzberg through the vast Midwest night. This was her worst anger, a peaceful-eyed, camouflaged fury that seemed almost curiosity.

For the first time in his marriage Corde wondered if he'd lost his wife.

'The case ran off with me.'

He was thinking mostly of the impact on Jamie but he remembered too that he'd turned down the job of sheriff because of Jennie Gebben's death. He supposed Diane also was thinking of this. 'I wish you'd say something.'

'Oh, Bill, how can you figure it all out? Here we spent all our time with Sarah. We just assumed Jamie didn't need us the way she did. And it turns out he was the one that did, and she's doing better without us.'

'This was mostly me,' Corde said. 'I knew about the match. I was even looking forward to it. Then I heard about Gilchrist and I got like a dog, sniffing rabbit.'

She stood up and walked down the hall to a pay phone. Whoever she was calling was not home. She grimaced, hung up, retrieved her coin and sat down in silence.

Their vigil continued. Corde took a quarter from his pocket and started rolling it over his fingers. The coin fell and rang as it spun to a stop. He picked it up and put it back into his pocket. Then the door opened and three doctors walked out. Both husband and wife locked onto their faces and began panning for clues but goddamn they were stone-eyed. One, the chief neurologist, sat in a chair beside Diane. He began to speak.

Corde heard the words. 'Brainstem . . . Minimal . . . Serious concussion . . . No life support . . .' He talked for five minutes and told them all the things they could do for Jamie. They seemed to be good words or at least not bad words but when Corde said, 'When will our boy wake up?' the doctor said, 'I don't have an answer for you.'

'But what do we *do?*'

'Wait.'

Corde nodded. Diane was crying. The doctor asked if they'd like sedatives. They answered, 'No,' simultaneously.

'It wouldn't hurt to get some sleep,' the doctor answered. 'I really don't think he'll take a turn for the worse.'

Corde said, 'Why don't you run home, honey, get some rest.'

'I'm staying with my boy.'

'I'm staying too.'

When the doctor left she curled up in an orange fiberglass chair and it seemed that she was instantly asleep. Corde rose and walked into the room to sit beside his son.

* * *

'Okay, Deputy, home base is clear.'

Wynton Kresge opened his eyes. Franklin Neale stood above him, shaking him awake.

'What time is it?'

'Six-thirty. In the AM. The hookers're gone and home base is clear.'

'Beg pardon?' Kresge asked.

The magic thermos appeared again and coffee was poured. Kresge added three packets of sugar and sipped from the red plastic cup.

Neale said, 'You want to go in after him now or wait till he comes out?'

Kresge was asking Bill Corde silent questions and not a one of them got answered. He looked at Neale, fresh as a recruit on parade. He was clean-shaved. 'What do you think?'

Neale shrugged. 'Well, tactically, it's your classic situation. If we go into his hidey-hole there's a better chance of return fire. If we get him on the street we could lose him or get some civvies casualtied in a firefight.'

Hearing this, the military lingo, made Kresge feel better. He decided he wasn't so much out of his element after all. 'I'd like to go in and get him.'

'Fair enough, Deputy. We've got our SWAT team on standby. You want them to do it?'

Wynton Kresge said, 'I'll go in. I want them as backup.'

And the crew-cut rosy-skin detective was nodding, solemn and eye-righteous, one grunt to another. 'That's the way I'd do it.' Then he looked over Kresge's large frame and said, 'Okay, let's suit you up in body armor. I think we've got something that might fit.'

As he applied the Velcro straps to the Type II vest with the Supershok plate over the heart, Wynton Kresge thought suddenly of an aspect of being a policeman that he had never considered. If the point of being a cop was ultimately to save lives then the flip side was true also – he might have to take a life.

All the while sitting in his Auden U office chair,

feeling the rub of the Taurus automatic pistol on his belt, he had never really considered using the gun. Oh, there'd been his theatrical little fantasies about winging terrorists. But now Kresge felt dread. Not at the real possibility that in five minutes he'd be dodging slugs but at the opposite – that he would have to send bullets hissing through the body of another man. The thought terrified him.

'. . . Deputy?'

Kresge realized the detective was speaking to him. 'Yes?'

Neale opened a diagram of the hotel. 'Look here.'

'Where'd you get that?'

'Our SWAT team has layouts of all the hotels in town. Bus and train stations and most of the office buildings too.'

This seemed like a good idea. Maybe he'd suggest it to Corde.

'Okay, he's in here. Room 258. There's no connecting door. But there's this thing here. What is it?'

One of the other officers said, 'They have a microwave and a little refrigerator there. Pipes. Stainless steel sink. It's probably enough to stop the hollowpoints but we can't use jacketed because of the street on the other side.'

'Deputy?'

Kresge said, 'I don't think we should give him any warning. No gas or grenades. Take the door down and move in fast before he has a chance to set up a fire zone.' He'd seen this in a Mel Gibson movie. He added, 'If that's in accordance with procedures?'

Neale said, 'Sounds good to me, Deputy. Let's get—'

'Sergeant,' the young patrolman at the radio console said, 'he's rabbitting! Left the room and is moving toward Eastwood.' He listened into his headset for a moment then announced to Neale and Kresge, 'TacSurv advising SWAT. They're three blocks away. They'll proceed to deployment.'

'Roger,' the detective said. 'Where's he headed?'

'Toward the river. On foot. Got his suitcase with him. He's moving fast.'

Kresge said, 'Where's that from here?'

'A block.'

'Well, let's go get him.'

Neale pulled on a blue cap that said *POLICE* on the crest.

'TacSurv says he's vanished. He turned before he got to the bridge – into those old warehouses down by the riverfront. He's gone north, they guess.'

The door of the van burst open and Kresge squinted against the blinding light. 'Which way?'

'Follow me.' Neale began running across the street. Past a scabby field overgrown with weeds and strewn with rusted hunks of metal. Kresge could see block after block of one- and two-story warehouses. Most of them dilapidated. Some burnt out.

A perfect hiding place for someone on the run.

A perfect vantage place for a sniper.

An Econoline van screeched to a stop nearby. Five SWAT officers jumped out. Kresge heard: 'Load and lock. Green team, deploy south. Blue, north. Hug the river. Go, go, go!'

Neale pulled up in front of the first building. 'Deputy?'

Kresge looked at him and saw he was motioning to Kresge's pistol, still in its holster.

'Oh.' Kresge unsnapped the thong and drew the gun. He pumped a round into the chamber and slid his right index finger parallel to the barrel. He felt a monumental spurt of energy surge through his chest. Neale pointed to himself then to the right. Kresge nodded and turned the opposite way, toward the river. A minute later Kresge found himself in a long alleyway through which ran rusted narrow-gauge rail lines. It was filled with thousands of black doorways and windows and loading docks.

'Oh, boy,' he sighed, and jumped over a small stone abutment, as he ran into the war zone.

The first five buildings were pure hell. Spinning,

ducking, aiming his pistol at shadows and garbage bags and shutters. Then having gotten this far without being shot, Kresge grew bolder. Gilchrist didn't want to get trapped. *His whole point's to escape. He's not going to back himself into a closed warehouse.*

Though it was in a warehouse that Kresge found him.

The deputy stepped into a huge abandoned space, pillars of jagged sun coming through the broken panes of skylight.

And there was the man he sought. Not fifty feet away, hiding beside an old boiler. He held no weapons, just an old suitcase. He looked benign and small next to the huge tank, a slight man, blond, ashen and nervous. It occurred to Kresge that this was the first time anybody involved in the investigation had actually seen Leon Gilchrist. It wasn't much of a sighting; the light here was dusty and diffuse.

Kresge shouted, 'Freeze.'

The man did, but only in shock and only for a moment. Then very slowly he turned his back to Kresge and started to walk away as if he were reluctantly leaving a lover.

'Stop! I'll shoot.'

Step by step he kept going, never looking back.

Kresge aimed. A clear target. Perfect. Better than on the small arms range at Higgins. His finger slipped into the guard and he started putting poundage on the trigger. About halfway to its eleven pounds of pull he lowered the gun and muttered, 'Shit.' Then took off at a full gallop.

Ahead of him the silhouette became a shadow and then vanished.

One of the patrolmen temporarily assigned to FelAp, the Fitzberg Felony Apprehension Squad, was Tony LaPorda, a great, round chunk of a man, who wore his service revolver high on his belt and his illegal .380 automatic in a soft holster under his pungent armpit. He was a small-city cop – a breed halfway between the calm, slope-shouldered civil servant urban police of, say, New York and the staunch cowboys of Atlanta or San Antonio.

LaPorda wore a leather jacket with a fur collar and dark slacks and a hat with a patent-leather brim and checkered band around the crown. He was typical of the five patrolmen working North Side GLA, who'd been told to volunteer for a couple hours at time and a half to collar some professor from New Lebanon who'd stuck the big one to a student of his.

For this assignment LaPorda was given a special frequency for his Motorola and a flak jacket but not an M-16 (nobody but SWAT had rifles, this Leon Gilchrist not being a terrorist or anything but a fucking professor). LaPorda was not very excited about the project especially when it turned out that the perp was on the move. LaPorda hated running even more than he hated the riverfront.

He trotted lethargically toward one large warehouse where he figured he might sit the whole thing out. He pulled up with a stitch in his side, thinking, *Jesus Christ, this fucking aerobic fucking Jane Fonda crap is what they pay fucking SWAT for.*

He leaned against a warehouse wall, listening to the staticky voices of what a buddy had dubbed the Felony Apprehension Response Team (nobody was faster than cops with this sort of acronym). LaPorda called in too, saying that he'd had no sign of the perp but was on his way to the riverfront for further investigation. Then he dug into his jacket pocket for his Camels. He shook one out and put his lips around it.

He was startled when a polite voice next to him said, 'Need a match?'

When LaPorda turned he didn't see who was speaking. All he saw was a rusty pipe, four inches wide and about four feet long, as it whistled square into his face. The *ponk* echoed off the walls nearby. LaPorda collapsed in a large pile and began to bleed heavily. He did not lose consciousness at first and was aware of hands rifling his shirt. The hands were persistent but delicate; the man they belonged to didn't seem very strong.

Professor's hands, he thought then he passed out.

Wynton Kresge caught him lifting the fallen patrolman's service revolver out of its holster. Kresge wondered if Gilchrist had killed the officer. 'Hold it right there.' He turned and their eyes met. The two were alone. There were no footsteps, no crackles of walkie-talkies. The rest of the teams had passed them by. 'Don't move,' Kresge said. He aimed at the darting, dark eyes then remembered the Deputy's Procedural Guide. Rule 34-6. *The chest, not the head, is the preferred target in an arrest situation.*

Kresge said, 'Drop the gun.'

The sunlight bounced off a high window and illuminated the men in pale light.

'Drop it.'

'Let's talk about this.'

Kresge nodded at the man's gun. 'Now!' It was a double-action revolver. All Gilchrist had to do was aim and pull the trigger. No safety, no slides. Rule 34-2. *Identify suspect's weapon immediately.* 'I'm not going to tell you again.'

'Do you want some money? How much do you want? A thousand? No problem.' He nodded toward the cop. 'That was an accident. He fell. I was trying to help him. You want two thousand?' He gestured casually toward his suitcase, which moved the muzzle of the revolver closer to Kresge.

He remembered the silhouette targets on the Higgins range. He said, 'I'll count to three.'

'Hey, why don't you just count to ten and give me a chance to go away? What could be easier than that? Two thousand dollars cash. I've got it right there in my suitcase.'

'If you don't drop the gun immediately,' Kresge said, 'I am going to shoot you.'

'Oh, I don't think so, Officer.'

11

'He moved. He said something.'

'Detective Corde?' the nurse said.

'I don't know what it was exactly,' he explained.

'Telephone for you, sir.'

Corde said to her, 'He moved. He said something.'

The nurse, who knew all about sleep-deprivation hallucinating, glanced down at Jamie's immobile form. 'That's wonderful.'

'He sat up.'

She had also read Jamie's chart and she knew that he was as likely to fly loop-de-loops through the room as he was to sit up and utter one syllable. 'That's wonderful.'

'Don't you want to tell the doctor?'

She said, 'It's a policeman in Fitzberg on the line. He said it's urgent.'

'Okay.' Corde turned his red eyes to the phone. He walked groggily toward it.

'No, sir, it's out here. We don't put calls through to the ICU.'

'Oh.'

Standing at the nurses' station Corde accepted the phone and said, 'Hello?'

He heard Wynton Kresge ask, 'How's your son?'

'He's asleep now, Wynton. But he sat up and said something to me. I heard him. I don't know what he said but I heard him.'

'That's good. Bill, Gilchrist is dead.'

'Uh-huh. You got him?'

'He was trying to get away. He had Sayles's credit cards in his wallet. Some other people's too. He'd stolen them or bought them. He was going to cover his tracks real well.'

'What happened?'

'Bill, I wanted to talk to you about it. About what I did. He had a gun. He was waving it around. I shot him. Four times.'

'That's good, Wynton.'

'I couldn't stop myself. I kept pulling the trigger. He just fell over and died. I shot him four times.'

'You did fine.'

'But the thing is, Bill, I wasn't sure, I mean, not *really* sure he was going to use his gun. I just couldn't tell.'

'Did they give it to the Fitzberg DA? They're not going to indict you, are they?'

'No. But it's not the law part I'm talking about. I killed him and he might not have been going to shoot me.'

'Wynton, he killed Jennie and he killed Sayles. He was going to draw down on you.'

'But I just don't *know* he was.'

Corde was looking back into the hospital room. All he could see was a mound under the gray sheet that was his Jamie. 'We never really know, Wynton . . .'

'I didn't want to bother you, Bill, but I had to say it, kind of get it off my chest.'

'You get back, you and me'll go hunting. We can talk about it then.' Corde closed his eyes and leaned wearily against the wall.

'I hope Jamie gets better real soon.'

'He talked to me,' Corde said. 'Did I tell you that? He sat up and said something to me. I wish I could remember what.' Corde missed the nurse glancing at him with a sad, straight line of a mouth.

Kresge said, 'Tell him I'm thinking of him.'

'I will, Wynton.'

Corde hung up the telephone and walked back into Jamie's room.

Bill Corde, a tall man now hunched over, with short trimmed hair now mussed, a man in whose heart one grave burden had been eased while another had been accepted. He sat down on a low chair beside his son's bed.

Corde didn't know what a fashion plate was but he decided if Dr Parker was one it was no way an insult. He wished New Lebanon could get a few more of them.

Sitting at the spotless desk, the good doctor was wearing a hot pink dress cut low enough so Corde could have seen a number of freckles on her chest if he was inclined to look, which he was and he did. Her hair was pulled back in a ponytail and she was wearing a thick gold bracelet, which Corde figured he himself might've bought her, what with all the fees. She had matching earrings and he imagined that those too were courtesy of him.

'I'm pleased to meet you at last, Officer.'

On the other hand the way she dabbed her eyes over him he believed she was examining him distrustfully. He wondered if Diane had blown some whistles. 'Well, I sure have heard good things about you, Doctor. Sarah's a whole new girl since she's been seeing you.'

The Dr Parker of reputation emerged. She nodded aside the compliment and asked abruptly, 'Sarah's here, isn't she?'

'She's in the waiting room.'

'Why didn't your wife come? She at the hospital?'

'That's right. Jamie's been in and out of consciousness. They think he's going to be all right. He might have some memory problems, they say. Maybe some other things. A neurologist is going to give him some tests. Dr Weinstein? At Community? Supposed to be the best in the county. That's what we heard.'

Dr Parker gazed at Corde passively and said nothing.

'You know what happened was . . .' Corde's voice suddenly stopped working.

Dr Parker continued, 'He tried to kill himself. Mrs Corde told me.'

'I don't know what it'll be like when he gets home. I don't know what happened exactly or why. But if you'd be available . . .'

'I'd be happy to see both of you,' she said sincerely, but didn't seem to be looking forward to it.

Both of us? Corde nodded. 'I'd appreciate that.'

The doctor opened her drawer and lifted out a thick handful of papers. Corde had a bad moment thinking they were more bills. She slid them across the desk. He glanced at the first one, dense with single-spaced writing and topped by Sarah's byline. Without looking up he said, 'She wrote these?'

'They're her most recent tapes. My secretary's typed them up. She speaks very well, you'll notice. There are only a few places where the words are garbles. And remarkably few places where she goes back to correct herself or misspeaks.'

Corde clipped through the stack. 'There must be a hundred pages here.'

'Close to it.'

He had thought all along that the whole idea was silly. If Sarah was going to do all this work why not make her copy a history book or science book? Something practical? Something that she could use in school. What possible benefit did these stories have? But he kept this to himself. He knew he'd play along with the doctor. She was the expert; besides, Bill Corde was nothing if not a sport.

'Is it really a book?'

'More a collection of short stories with recurrent characters. Like the Winnie the Pooh stories or *Song of the South.* You know, Br'er Fox and Br'er Rabbit.'

'Are they any good?'

'Mr Corde, for a nine-year-old with her history and her problems they are remarkable.'

'What should I do with them?'

'You? Nothing. Dr Breck is using these stories in

Sarah's exercises. Her learning will be exponentially increased if she works with words that she herself has created.'

Exponentially. 'Sure. It's probably a lot of fun too.'

Some blunder here. Dr Parker was frowning. 'It's *mostly* a great deal of work.'

'Sure. I'll bet it is.' Corde riffled the pages again and let the breeze scented with typewriter oil and expensive bond paper blow into his face. He rose and started toward the waiting room, where Sarah was waiting. 'She did this all by herself? Hell, I get sweaty hands every time I have to write out an incident explanation on an MV-204 form.'

'Maybe your daughter can teach you a few things, Mr Corde,' Dr Parker said, and allowed herself an indulgent smile.

Bill Corde doesn't know what to think.

He sits on a folding chair in his den and flips back and forth through Sarah's book. He's read about shape-changing wizards, about dragons and princesses and talking cars, flying loaves of bread, dancing blackbirds and bobcats that sing opera under full moons.

'Why bobcats?'

'Because that's what they are,' Sarah explains.

'Why opera?'

'Because,' she answers with such exasperation that Corde, who asked the question solely because he couldn't think of anything else to say, feels ashamed and therefore doesn't ask why the full moon, which he'd intended to.

'This is what Dr Breck and I are doing,' she explains, touching the typed sheets first then a blank piece of paper in front of her. 'We move all these words over here like they're on a magic train.'

'A train. Ah.'

They sit in the den, Corde with his shoes off, stretched back on the couch feeling like a dog in front of a fire. Sarah is at the wobbly desk. Corde had been by the hospital at seven that morning. He is utterly exhausted though much of that fatigue is held at bay by his daughter's enthusiasm for copying her book. Her leg vibrates with excitement at her task.

It's a mystery to Corde, all these stories of magic otters and flying eagles and trolls and shining wizards. Corde's library contains mostly hunting and fishing nonfiction. The animals he reads about are wolves and grizzles and damn clever trout who elude the most well-placed tufts of fly. They do not wear aviator hats and wetsuits and they do not hold parties in tree trunks or sing any kind of music in the moonlight.

He decides that his daughter would be the kind of film director whose movies he would not go to see.

But he can compliment her on her work, which he does, and watch with fascination as she leans forward, writing with the awkward elegance of a doe on ice.

Corde notices her techniques. With her index finger she writes letters and words on her palm, she traces the letters in a dust of salt on the tabletop, she tears sheets of paper containing a single word into portions of the word and stares at them. Corde himself forgets what the fragments of words are called. *Syllabus?* No. Then he remembers, *syllables*. Although her spelling still needs much work, her self-confidence is bursting. He has never seen her enjoy herself this way. He looks at the first page of the slim stack of sheets Sarah has printed.

MY BOOK
BY SARAH REBECCA CORDE, FOURTH GRADE
DEDICATED TO DR BRECK MY TUTOR

Corde stares at this for a few minutes, wondering if jealousy will surface. It does not.

When she finishes, Corde rises to leave. He watches her for a moment then leans forward and hugs her suddenly and hard. This surprises and pleases her and she hugs back enthusiastically. Corde does not tell his daughter that the complex gratitude he is filled with is only in part for her.

12

An officer in the Fitzberg Police Department's Demographics and Vital Statistics Division made the discovery.

The DemVit man had been cross-checking prints of the bodies of recent DCDS's found at crime scenes against Known Felons (Warrants Open) and was at the tail end of his shift so it took him longer than it normally would have to find the glitch. He marked his conclusion down on an EID form and was about to drop it in the interoffice mail to the Detective Division when he noticed that the body was due for shipping out later that day.

Oh, boy.

Reluctantly he called Mister Master Sergeant Super Detective Franklin Neale.

'Detective? This is Tech Officer Golding in DemVit?'

'Yes, Golding, what's on the agenda?' Neale said.

Hup, two, three four . . .

'There's an EID on that deceased confirmed dead you sent to the morgue two days ago?'

'An erroneous ID?' Neale growled. 'Tell me about it, Officer.'

'We had a tentative ID from personal effects and from some out-of-town deputy?'

'Yes, that's right. The DCDS was the perp in a four-eleven, two counts. Fellow was a real bad operator.'

Tell me, dickhead, do you polish your medals

465

every night? 'Yes-sir,' Golding said, 'well, the prints the coroner sent down match a felon there's a bench warrant out on. Eddie Scavello. Two counts armed, one burglary and ten receiving stolen. Rap sheet full of hot plastic.'

'You're sure?'

'We're talking ninety-eight percent.'

There was silence. Neale said, 'Okay, do me a favor, fax the EID to Harrison County and New Lebanon. Sheriffs' Departments.'

'They have a fax machine in New Lebanon?'

'Officer,' Neale said, 'Consolidated Law Enforcement Agency Guidelines require one in every town—'

It was a joke.

'—over five thousand population.'

'Oh, that's right. I'm glad you reminded me. Whose attention?'

'Wynton Kresge at County, William Corde in New Lebanon. That's *Deputy* Kresge and *Detective* Corde. Write that down and don't get them mixed up.'

'No, sir. I wouldn't.'

'And attach a cover note – mark it urgent – and tell them it looks like their boy Gilchrist is still a loose cannon. My compliments on a job well done, Tech Officer.'

'A pleasure to be of help, Detective.'

Brian Okun celebrated the announcement that Auden University would stay open for another year in what he thought was an appropriate manner: he fucked a student on Leon Gilchrist's desk.

He had another cause for celebration as well. He would, subject to formal acceptance of his PhD thesis this summer, be joining the faculty of the Department of English, College of Arts and Sciences, Auden University.

Okun was now alone. The blond student – ironically, one who had sat next to Jennie Gebben in his seminar session – was gone and he sat naked to the waist in Gilchrist's chair, spinning in slow circles. The blinds were down and since the AC was off (the school being officially closed for two weeks until summer school began) the office was hot as an Ozark swamp in August. Okun looked at spots of moisture on the desktop and wondered whether they were semen or sweat.

Okun had been shocked at the news that Gilchrist was a killer. For a horrible moment he had wondered if the rumor he had started had gotten out of hand. But in reading the *Register* he had understood that Gilchrist and Jennie *had* had an affair. But killing her and Professor Sayles! Astonishing. Okun had suspected that Gilchrist was violent and probably was capable of murder but he had never thought that he *would* kill.

And now the son of bitch was himself dead, shot down by police . . . Okun searched his repertoire for a suitable maxim that might summarize the man. He could think of nothing.

Slipping on his T-shirt, Okun stretched out again, gazing at the old prints, at the hundreds of books that he supposed would go into Gilchrist's estate. An old volume of Freud that might be valuable. More recent books on psychoses and literature. Okun had no claim to them, even as Gilchrist's academic successor, but he figured he could pilfer the choicest ones before the dean raided the office. Musing on these additions to his library, feeling warm and spent, smelling a May breeze and the redolence of sex, Okun closed his eyes.

He was awakened sometime later by a slight stinging on his neck. At first he thought a bee or mosquito had gotten him but as he reached up to the sting he found himself so weak that he could barely lift his hand above his chest.

He looked down and saw that his shirt was soaked with blood. He cried out and forced his hands to his neck. He touched the loose flap of skin where his carotid artery had been severed. Okun tried to stand and fell immediately to the floor. He grabbed at the telephone cord and pulled it off the desk onto the floor beside him.

'Ohgodhelp . . .' The weakness of his voice terrified him.

He pressed 9.

The receiver slipped from his bloody hand. He managed to retrieve it.

He pressed 1.

He stared at the blurring number pad of the phone. He tried to touch the final digit but found his arm would not respond. He heard a hum and a click then a three-part ascending musical tone followed by a woman's electronically-generated voice speaking to him, saying the last words he would ever hear: 'Your call cannot be completed as dialed. Please hang up and try your call again.'

Diane Corde slipped her arms around Ben Breck and hugged him hard.

This seemed a wholly natural thing to do: standing up in her garden as she watched him pull up in the driveway then walking quickly to him, wrapping her arms around him, feeling his around her.

Wholly natural. This frightened her terribly. She said, 'I left a message for you at the library.'

'I've been over at Arts and Sciences. How's Jamie?'

'That's what I called about. He's much better. I just got back from the hospital.'

Diane realized with a shock that they were still embracing. She stepped back quickly. *Oh, God, the neighbors . . . At least he didn't kiss me . . .* She looked around and stepped into the cover of the juniper bushes. Breck followed.

And why didn't he kiss me?

Diane haltingly explained Jamie's diagnosis by rote, not even hearing the words she'd repeated a dozen times that day.

As they talked Breck slipped his hands into his pockets. This added to his boyishness and made him infuriatingly appealing. He wore dark jeans and a thick burgundy sweater with a braided collar. He said, 'You

468

told me on the phone that Wisconsin's out.'

'Surely is. Seems they got that fellow. Got him up in Fitzberg.'

Relief seemed to flood into his face. 'I'm glad you won't be going.'

'Agree with you there. Doris's never outgrown the big sister complex. And it's hardly fair since she only outranks me by thirteen months.'

'I have more selfish reasons for being glad you're not going.' He spoke seductively.

Diane swallowed. 'Say, Ben, I think you and I ought to have a talk.'

'Somewhere alone.' He smiled. 'Private.' A thought seemed to slip spontaneously into his mind. 'How about my place?'

'No,' she whined playfully. 'I'm serious.'

The smile faded. 'Are you saying you don't want to see me?'

'No,' Diane said quickly. 'I'm just saying we have to talk. Before things get... You know. Get too complicated.'

'Fair enough.'

Diane tamped on mounds of moist earth at the base of some newly planted zinnias and asked if he wanted something to drink. She had a recurring image – of her pouring coffee or wine into him in the afternoons. Trying to delay his leaving. All these beverages struck her as funny. She wondered if he ever felt waterlogged on the drive home.

'No, I just better collect Sarah. I've got the video camera reserved for two-thirty.'

'Honey,' Diane shouted, 'Dr Breck's here.'

'Kay,' came the answering shout.

Diane asked, 'These tests you're giving Sarah, what are they?'

'They're the same as Dr Parker gave her. I want to correlate short-term results to sessions of study per week. The first draft of my article for the *New England Journal of Child Psychology* is due tomorrow and I wanted to include her revised results on the Bender-

Gestalt and Gray's Oral. The data are also important for me – they'll give me an idea of where we should go next.'

Data are . . . *Some boys never quit being the show-offs.*

'You think they'll upset her?' Diane asked cautiously.

He shook his head. 'I'll be videotaping her but it's a hidden camera. She'll never know she's being filmed. She'll do fine.'

Sarah's face appeared through the front screen door. 'Dr Breck!'

'Hello, Sarah. Bring your book with you. If we get a chance, we'll do some more work.'

'I've got it here.' She slapped her backpack.

'All of it?'

'Everything. The new pages from Dr Parker too.'

'Good. Let's get a move on.'

She ran to the car. He hesitated, his face clouded. Diane noticed it. 'Something wrong?'

His eyes were distant. He didn't seem to hear her and she repeated the question, touching his arm gently. He blinked and said, 'I was thinking about Jamie.'

'No, no. He's going to be fine. He is.'

Breck's smile returned but Diane saw a glint of something in his eyes – regret or pining, she believed. She considered this. Perhaps what she saw was a childless man approaching middle age, which was one of the saddest things she could imagine. She wanted to wrap her arms around him. She muscled up restraint and laughed. 'That boy's going to be just fine. He's a tough one.'

'I must stop by and visit him sometime. I'll bring him a present. Maybe something about that movie he liked.'

'Come on, Dr Breck!'

Diane said to them both, 'Don't be late,' and stepped back into the tilled dirt of her garden.

When he noticed Tom – the young deputy who had guarded his house – walking toward him, Corde was crouched down, jamming stacks of papers from the Gebben case into file cabinets in the small storeroom off

470

the Sheriff's Department. He paused, a file halfway sunk into a clogged drawer. He froze as he watched the grave face of the approaching deputy.

Jamie!

He knew without a doubt that the hospital had just called and that his son had died. When Corde had last seen him the boy was frighteningly disoriented. His eyes wouldn't stay on his father's face and he blacked out twice.

Propelled by fear Corde rose fast, his knee a resounding gunshot. 'What is it?' he demanded. The desperation in his voice stopped the deputy short.

Tom told him, 'There's a problem on your case, Bill.'
Case?

Corde was confused. He wasn't working on any cases at the moment. The only case he could have meant was the Gebben case. But it was closed. Corde knew this because he had written that word in careful block printing in the 'Status' box on form FI-113, which was this very moment sitting in Sheriff Jim Slocum's in basket.

Corde was wrong.

Tom said, 'We just got a fax. An erroneous identification notice from Fitzberg. The man Wynton Kresge shot wasn't Gilchrist. It was some guy with a rap sheet full of GL arrests, mostly credit card dealing. Prints confirmed it.'

'Oh, no.' Corde closed his eyes as he leaned against the doorjamb. 'Did you tell Wynton?'

'Yessir. And Emma says a call just came in. A grad student was found in Gilchrist's old office a few minutes ago. Murdered, looks like.'

'Okun? Was that the name?'

'Matter of fact, that's it.'

Corde's grim-set mouth didn't come close to the despair he felt. And fear too. Gilchrist had returned to New Lebanon. And Corde knew why.

'Okay, Tom, get over to my house *now* and keep an eye on Diane and Sarah. I think Gilchrist is after them.

And get somebody over to the hospital to stay with Jamie.'

'Will do.'

As he hurried back to the squad room Emma shouted from the dispatcher office, 'Detective Corde? It's Wynton Kresge on the phone for you. He's over at the university.'

Corde sent Tom on his way then trotted to his office and snatched up the phone. 'Wynton, what've we got?'

'Killed just like Sayles, Bill.' Kresge sounded despondent. 'Cut throat. Razor. Witness says a car stopped outside the building, man matching Gilchrist's description got out and went inside for three, four minutes then left, got into the car and drove off. Late-model green sedan, no tag, no make. About forty minutes ago.'

'Any idea where he headed?'

'Just toward the campus exit. They didn't see after that.'

There was a lengthy pause, both men lost in their own vital thoughts. Kresge finally said, 'Looks like I got the wrong man, huh, Bill?'

Corde's squad car moves at seventy, lights whipping around, siren grating. The driving is fast but, in this big taut American cruiser, oddly placid. He is on the outskirts of town, passing small stores and buildings. He sees a vet's office. *Dog 8 Cat Hospital*, the numeral substituting for an ampersand stolen long ago. A long white structure, *TRIBUTION CENT R*, burnt out letters never replaced. He blazed through the town's last stoplight, then the land opens up, there is no traffic and Corde is free to have a discussion with himself. This makes him extremely agitated.

Think, goddamn it. Think.

Leon Gilchrist, who sees by the light of pure brilliance, the Prince of Auden University. Come on, think of something clever, think of something unlikely, think of something he would think of.

Think!

His hands sweat and he feels ill.

I *can't* think!

The newspaper clipping, the scrawled threat.

IT COULD HAPPEN TO THEM.

Corde zooms past Andy Dexter's harvester listing half off the highway as it bobs along at ten miles per hour. The cruiser's slipstream rattles the blades as it passes.

I can't think the way he does . . . He's too smart for me . . .

Corde sees the Polaroid of Sarah and Jamie, looking safe and silly as actors in a commercial. He sees Gilchrist's handwriting:

SAY GOOD-BYE, DETECTIVE.

Corde crests the road by Sutter's farm and is blinded by a sheet of stunning sun. The streaked, bug-dotted windshield goes opaque. He is out of the glare immediately, dropping rollercoaster over the hill and sees before him a three-mile straightaway of cambered gray asphalt. His foot aims for the accelerator then waffles and goes suddenly to the brake.

His skid is as precariously controlled as the ones he practiced for weeks on the State Police course. The Dodge comes to rest dead center in the road, at the head of twin black stripes. The cloud of burnt rubber and dust catches up with the cruiser, encloses it, then passes away intact on an impossibly gentle breeze.

Corde's car sat askew in front of his own house, half on the lawn, engine still running, next to Tom's cruiser, which was parked civilly in the center of the driveway.

Inside Diane looked up at her husband's wide green eyes as he burst through the door. He took her hands and placed her on the couch.

'You're scaring me, Bill.' As if speaking to a stranger. 'Is it Jamie? What's happened?'

Corde sat next to her. His breath was rapid. He didn't

473

let go of her hands. She squirmed. 'What?' she said, then louder: 'What *is* it?'

'I think . . .' He squeezed her cold fingers. 'I think Ben Breck is Leon Gilchrist.'

13

'Oh, God, no . . .' Diane's voice crumbled. 'No, it's not true . . .'

'Gilchrist is a special education lecturer at Auden. Isn't that the department where the tutors work?'

She nodded, her eyes sweeping the floor at her feet.

'He could've read Sarah's file and known all about her problem.'

'No, Bill,' she protested. 'No!'

'What does he look like?'

'No, no, no . . . He wouldn't do that to me. He wouldn't do it! . . .' Her voice vanished in hysterical sobbing.

'Diane,' Corde said harshly, 'you've got to help me on this. Think.'

'Oh, Bill, no!'

He gripped her shoulders. 'Describe him!'

She did, as best she could, her words punctuated with sobs. When she finished she cried, 'Oh, God, it can't be. I know it can't.'

Diane's description was vague but it did depict someone who could resemble Gilchrist. 'Where's he staying?'

'I don't know! Near hear somewhere. He never told me.'

'He never *told* you?' Corde shouted. 'How did you call him?'

'Usually *he* called me. When I called I left messages

475

at the library. I never saw his office.' Every word grew weaker as the evidence mounted.

'What kind of car does he drive?'

'I don't *know*! Quit cross-examining me!'

Corde gripped his wife by her shoulders. 'Think. You must've seen it. Is it green?'

'I don't know. Just a car. American, I think. A four-door of some kind. I don't remember the color. I think it was dark. No ... Oh, and I just saw it! When he picked her up ...' Her hands flew to her face. 'Oh Bill!'

'Sarah?' Corde shouted. 'Sarah's with him now?'

He grabbed the phone and dialed Auden. He heard a click. *You have reached Auden University. The school will be closed until summer session registration on June 10. If you would like to leave a message, press the number of the extension for the department you wish to reach and at the tone leave your message. If you—'*

He slammed the phone down. He paused a moment then picked up the receiver again, intending to dial directory assistance. In his frazzled state of mind he dialed 911 by mistake. He shuddered at the error and pressed the receiver cradle down then released it. The line wouldn't disconnect. He held it again for three seconds. Still no dial tone. Then five seconds. GOD STRIKE THEM DEAD! Finally he heard the tone.

Four. One. One.

'Operator, this is the New Lebanon Sheriff's Department. We have a police emergency. I need the number and address of a man named Breck. In New Lebanon.'

'Breck? First name?'

How many Brecks do you have? 'Ben. Benjamin.'

The wait was a huge black pit. He heard the clattering of keys. He heard pages riffling. He heard a one-sided conversation – another operator saying 'I'll bring 'em home but you have to cook 'em. I won't have time.'

'Sir?'

'Yes?' Corde asked.

'How would you be spelling that?'

'Spell it? How do you think? B-R-E-C-K.'

'There's no listing of Ben, Benjamin or B. Breck in New Lebanon or Fredericksberg. Would he—'

He jammed the button on the phone down again. Shaking his head, he made another call. Dr Parker's receptionist said she was with a patient and Corde said, 'Please tell her this is an emergency.'

The psychiatrist came on the phone and said coolly, 'Yes, Mr Corde?'

He said, 'Do you personally know Dr Breck?'

'Why, what's the problem?'

'Do you *know* him?'

She paused a moment in irritation but must have sensed the urgency. She said, 'No. But I've spoken to him several times about Sarah's course of treatment.'

'But it might not have been Breck you talked to.'

'You mean you think he was an impostor? Oh, I don't think so. He seemed to know a great deal about your daughter. Come to think of it, he knew a great deal about your whole family, Detective.'

'What's your daddy doing today?' Dr Breck asked.

'I don't know. He's at work, I guess.'

'Do you love your daddy?'

'Oh yeah. Sure.'

'Does your mommy love your daddy?'

'Sure. I guess.'

Dr Breck drove quickly. The scenery raced past as if Sarah were riding Cloud-Tipper the eagle. A barn was a red dot in the distance then a red ball then a huge red whale then it vanished behind them like a wish.

Dr Breck slowed and pulled into the driveway of the college. He turned toward a part of the school that was deserted, more trees than buildings. Sarah was able to read at least one sign. *Auden University*. She couldn't understand the word 'university' but she had memorized it because this was where Dr Breck worked and that made it important to her.

'I like these buildings,' Sarah announced. They looked

477

to her like castles – only without gates and drawbridges and the lakes around them. Some even had up-down teeth on the tops like in *Robin Hood* (the old *Robin Hood*, the good one) where the sheriff's soldiers stood and shot crossbow darts at the star, renamed by her 'Arrow Flynn.' Sarah's book contained two stories about castles.

Dr Breck had remained silent as they drove. He seemed lost in thought and she didn't want to trouble him but she tried to read the sign in the front of the building they were passing. She couldn't and she asked him about the words. 'It says "Graduate School of Education,"' he answered. 'Read the other sign there.'

She frowned. '"Arts." Oh oh oh, and "School of." I can read those. And "Sciences."'

'That's good,' he said. '"School of Arts and Sciences."'

'I got back my last story from Dr Parker,' Sarah said. 'Can we read it today?'

'If you'd like.'

'It's my favorite. It's about a wizard I saw over by Blackfoot Pond. He lives in the woods behind my house. He watches the house a lot. It took me forever to write it. I wanted to get it just right. It's got Cloud-Tipper the eagle in it and—'

With sudden curiosity Dr Breck asked, 'This wizard's in your story?'

'Uh-huh. It's called "The Sunshine Man." That's his name.'

'And you saw him by Blackfoot Pond? When?'

'One morning. Last month, I guess. He's been behind the house too.'

'What does he look like?'

'I never saw him up close.' Sarah brushed a strand of hair off her face. 'You know, Dr Breck, I wanted to ask the Sunshine Man to make me smart only I was scared to. But I think he knew. I think he sent you to me.'

'You think so?' Dr Breck pulled the car onto an empty parking lot beside a deserted building. He braked to a stop. She reached for the door handle but before she could pull the lever up Dr Breck's hand touched her arm. 'No, Sarah. Wait just a minute.'

She did as she was told.

Corde ran to the front door. He said to Tom, 'Deputy . . .' His voice shook and he took a deep breath to calm himself before starting again. 'I think that man who's been coming here for the past month, Breck, I think he's Gilchrist.'

'*What?*'

'I'm not going into it now.' He turned to Diane. 'He and Sarah left when?'

Through her tears she said, 'A half hour ago.'

Where are they, where could they go?

Where has he taken my daughter?

'They were going to the school.'

'Which school?'

'Auden. To take some tests. Oh, Bill.' She sobbed and gripped the pillow hysterically. 'He said he was going to *tape* her. He had a camera . . .'

Corde said to the deputy, 'Do an APB. State and federal. Call in a kidnapping-in-progress code and an approach-with-caution. Check Auden first but if he killed Okun this morning—' This brought a moan from Diane. '—I doubt he's anywhere near the campus now.'

'Right, sir.'

'And you tell them that it's *my* daughter he's got.'

'Yessir.'

'If he hostages her *I'm* doing the negotiating, got it? Tell that to Slocum and Ellison and if they have any trouble with that they're to call me. And I want somebody to keep an eye on Wynton Kresge's house. Watch his wife and all the kids.'

Where is she? Where is my daughter? . . .

The deputy asked, 'You gonna stay here, sir? Or you want a couple men on the house?'

'Oh, Bill,' Diane whispered. 'Please God—'

'*All units in the vicinity . . .*'

From outside over the PA system of both squad cars,

as if in stereo, came the radio broadcast.

'All units in the vicinity. Ten-thirty-three in progress. School of Education Building, Auden University. Assault. Man with a knife or razor in late-model sedan. No plates . . .'

Corde and Diane looked at each other.

'Further to that ten-thirty-three. Ambulance is en route. And we have unconfirmed report that a juvenile is involved . . . Make that a female juvenile about ten years of age. Repeat. Ten-thirty-three in progress . . .'

It looked like an auto accident – the driver's door open, the figure lying bloody and still beside the car, one foot up on the driver's seat. Revolving red lights, men and women in uniform.

Diane screamed and flung open the door before Corde had brought his cruiser to a stop in the school parking lot. She sprinted over the cracked asphalt to where the ambulance crew, a cluster of white-coated attendants, was huddled, working feverishly. With her hands over her mouth, Diane looked down, then closed her eyes, muttering indistinct words over and over.

Corde trotted to the car and looked down at the bloody mass at his feet. He took a deep breath and peered over the head of an attendant.

It was not Sarah.

Lying on his back Ben Breck opened his eyes. He squinted and spit blood. He whispered halting yet astonished words: 'Leon Gilchrist! . . . Following us . . .' He held up his arm to examine deep slashes in the palm of his hand with serene curiosity. 'I don't feel any pain.' He looked back at Diane. 'We were in the car . . . he just appeared. Just like that. Had a razor . . .'

'Where's Sarah?' Diane cried.

Corde said to a county deputy, 'Do you know who this man is?'

Diane shouted at her husband, 'It's Ben Breck!'

'She's right, Detective.' The deputy offered Corde a bloody wallet. He opened it. Inside there was an Illinois driver's license with Breck's picture, a University of Chicago faculty picture ID, and an Auden ID, which identified him as a visiting professor.

Visiting professor. So, a temporary address and no directory assistance listing.

Corde crouched. 'Where's Sarah?'

'She ran. I think he's got her,' Breck gasped. 'I don't know what happened. He was . . .' The words dissolved into bloody coughing. 'We'd stopped and he came . . . up behind the car. He was . . . just there. Cutting me, slashing. Grabbing for Sarah . . .'

'Did he hurt her?' Diane asked, choking on tears.

'I don't . . . I couldn't . . . see.'

An attendant finished applying a tourniquet and started bandaging a deep cut.

Corde asked Breck, 'Where did they go? Did you see—'

'There. There.' Breck reached up a bloody hand. At first Corde thought he was pointing out a direction. But no. He saw in the front seat of the car two typed pages. Corde said, 'Those sheets?'

Breck nodded. 'Take them. Read . . . I'm getting very dizzy. My mouth is dry . . .' He closed his eyes.

Corde picked up the sheets. He started to read. His attention flagged and he looked down. Diane took Breck's face in both of her slick, red hands and shouted to him, 'You're going to be all right! You're going to be fine! Do you hear me? Do you hear me?'

She looked up at her husband. Corde put his hand on her shoulder. She picked it up and flung it off then lowered her head to Breck's chest and began to cry.

It wasn't until the ambulance left a minute later, kicking up dust and siren howling, that Corde walked abruptly back to his car and sat in the driver's seat. Finally he began to read.

They stepped over a tangle of brush, between two beech trees that pretty much marked the start of Corde's backyard and entered the forest at the exact spot he had seen, or imagined, the moonlit face staring at the house a month before. They walked on a carpet of spring-dried leaves and low raspy grass, yellow and deer-chewed.

Beside him, dressed in a beige uniform and tan windbreaker, Wynton Kresge was carrying a Remington pump shotgun. The gun had a stiff sling but he did not carry it slung. He held it two-handed like a soldier, index finger pointed forward outside of the trigger guard. The men walked quickly, Corde consulting two sheets of dark-stained typewriter paper as if they were instructions on a scavenger hunt.

The sky was milky. The sun, a white disk low in the sky, was trying to burn off the overcast, but the density of gray meant that it was going to lose. The forest, the cow pasture, the yellow-green carpet in front of him were an opaque watercolor. A coal black grackle flew immediately toward him then turned abruptly away, startling both men.

At an old burnt-down barn that he had forbidden Jamie and Sarah from playing in, they turned right. Beams of the silo rose like charred bones. They walked on, over an old railroad bridge then followed the gravelly roadbed to the Des Plaines. They walked along the bank through more woods until they found the house. Corde folded the sheets of paper and put them in his pocket.

The house was another dilapidated colonial, two stories, narrow and sagging. This one was set in a grim, scruffy clearing, past which you could see storage tanks along the river. A tug towed a rusty barge upstream, its harsh, chugging engine irksome in the heavy air.

In the front yard was parked a green car. A Hertz sticker in the windshield. Corde read the plate.

'It's the one Gilchrist rented.'

Corde crouched and Kresge knelt beside him, under cover of a fallen branch. Corde looked at the ground. He said, 'You stay outside. No matter what you hear. If he comes out alone, stop him. He's the only one who knows where Sarah is. I want him alive.'

Kresge said, 'I'd feel better calling in some backup.

That's what the manual says in cases like this.'

Corde kept studying the house. Lord, it seemed ominous – towery and pale, mean. He said, 'I'm going to get my daughter one way or another. I may need some time with Gilchrist by myself.'

Kresge looked long at Corde, considering these words. He turned back to the house. 'How'd you know this was his place?'

Corde shushed him. Together they closed in on the colonial. Kresge crouched behind the Hertz car and rested the shotgun on the hood. He pointed at the front and back doors, nodding, meaning that he could cover them both. Corde nodded back and, crouching, ran to the front of the house. He paused beside the rotting gray porch. He caught his breath then eased slowly up to the door. He smashed the door in with a vicious kick of his boot and stepped into the rancid-smelling house.

The room was milky, as if illuminated through smoke or mist. Light, already diffused by the clouds, ambled off the silver maple leaves outside and fell ashen in the room. The carpet, walls, plywood furniture, paintings seemed bleached by this weak radiance.

A terrible moment passed. Corde believed the house was empty and Gilchrist had escaped from them again. Then his eyes grew accustomed to the weak light and he saw at the end of the room a pale shape, a sphere that moved. It was mottled with indefinite features like the surface of the moon. Corde saw that it was a man's head and that he was staring back at Corde.

The man slowly rose and stood behind a cluttered desk. About six-two, graying brown hair, trim, gangling arms and long thin hands. He wore a conservative light green tweed sports jacket and tan slacks. His face gave no clue that he was surprised by the intrusion. He examined Corde with brown eyes that were the only dark aspects of his person.

He *looks like me* was the thought that passed involuntarily through Corde's mind.

'Gilchrist,' he said evenly, 'where is my daughter?'

14

Leon Gilchrist walked through a thick beam of dusty light and stopped ten feet from Corde. He folded his arms. A mirthful half smile was on his face. 'Well, I am surprised, Detective Corde.'

'I want to know where she is.' Corde's voice trembled. 'I want to know now.'

'Of course you do.'

'Sarah!' Corde shouted, looking at a stairway that led to the second floor.

'I was just thinking of you,' Gilchrist said mildly. 'You'd be surprised how often you're in my thoughts. About as often as I am in yours, I'd guess.'

Corde stepped forward, raising his revolver to Gilchrist's chest. The professor glanced down at it then slipped his hands into his pockets and studied Corde as if the detective were a bug padding his last circle on the cyanide disk in a kill jar. Then he asked, 'How's your son, Detective?'

An uncertain flicker was in Corde's eyes as they scanned the face of Leon Gilchrist.

'Still enjoy bicycling, does he? Despite the dangers.'

'What are you talking about?'

'And he went for a swim, I heard. The music these young people listen to . . .'

He's trying to get my goat. Calm, stay calm.

'Suicide by drowning. That was uniquely his. The

song, I believe, mentions razors and ropes . . . An alliteration suitable for adolescent lyrics.'

'What did you have to do with that?' Corde's grip on the gun tightened and he was beset by a frightening sense that he was losing control of himself. In his ears he heard a humming of immense pressure. He swung the muzzle toward the professor's face, which tightened microscopically but remained otherwise passive. The barrel stopped short of striking skin. 'I could kill you—'

Gilchrist said slowly, 'I don't imagine you know the writing of Paul Verlaine. The French symbolist poet? No, of course not. I find his poems stunning but I also believe he suffered from the same problem as you do. Stoic on the outside, raging within. He tried to murder his close friend Rimbaud in a fit of passion. He ended up a worthless drunk. But if not for his psychoses the world wouldn't have his astonishing work. The element of compensation is miraculous – compensation, which your little Sarah displays so well.'

Corde's breathing was fierce. He felt himself hyperventilating. He grabbed Gilchrist's collar and pressed the gun muzzle against his ear.

'Ah,' Gilchrist said in a silky voice, 'remember her. Remember Sarah. Our conversation mustn't become so obfuscated by passion that we forget that only I know where she is. *Obfuscated.* Can you deduce what that means, Detective? Can you?'

Corde shoved Gilchrist away and stepped back. He wiped his mouth with the back of his sleeve. He felt that he was the cornered animal and that it was Gilchrist who was playing him.

'Detective, you continually misunderstand whom you're dealing with. I'm not a thug barricaded in a convenience shop. Your concept of intelligence is that it gets you to the bottom row of a category in *Jeopardy!* I'm different in *kind* from people like Jennie Gebben and you and your son and your Sarah and your beautiful Diane.

'I've been studying you and your family since the

486

morning after Jennie died. I saw your daughter at the pond after I'd left my first note to you. Her beautiful hair. The sun was so pretty on her tight, white blouse. Last year's fashions? . . . Had to put off the spring shopping spree at Sears, did we? You know, I've been corresponding with Sarah ever since then. Why the shock, Detective? You would have figured it out eventually. See, that's the problem that concerned me. You're not intelligent but you're dogged – unlike the rest of your colleagues, who are neither intelligent nor persistent.

'Undoubtedly we could put you on the couch and wrench up some reason for this chronic tenacity. You fell asleep at the wheel once or twice when it mattered, didn't you? When was it? Not too formative, I'd guess. Your teenage years? Maybe later. Whatever happened, you'll be paying it off for a long time. I was sure you'd plod along until you stumbled across me.

'Sarah was the perfect distraction. At first I convinced her to run away. When that didn't work I decided I'd infiltrate, throw you off the track. The town wanted a Moon Killer so I skinned a goat and gave them one. "Lunatic." And I did some painting around town with a bit of the leftover blood. *Mezza luna* . . . Oh, I'll bet my frescoes had your boss salivating. But not you, Detective. You kept plodding, ever the pedestrian, getting closer and closer. I needed a more direct attack. I tried threatening you off the case.'

He pointed to a Polaroid camera. 'I'm quite some photog, don't you think? Oh, an aside: I detected that your wife's contraceptive had not been much used of late. Are we in the middle of the sixteen-year itch? Have you noticed any change in her recently? Her pathetically polished fingernails? Her sudden interest in eye shadow? Did you know she and Breck have been for several walks in the forest?'

The professor smiled and lifted his hands like a TV preacher. 'Did you know that while that buffoon of a deputy was supposed to be guarding the old homestead,

I was browsing through your bedroom? I opened your dresser and rearranged Diane's panties. I smelled her pillow. I washed my hands with her cheap L'Air du Lis soap. Oh, I sat on Sarah's bed. I caressed your son's pajamas. It was all so fascinating to me! I lecture – excuse me, I used to lecture – about psychology every day. I've written articles for the most prestigious journals in the field, journals . . .' He cocked an eyebrow with amusement. '. . . that perhaps you've tried to read. But I don't do clinical practice. Toying with your family has amused me greatly. Entwining them in this whole matter. I drew you away from the nest. I sent you to Lewisboro. I sold a handful of credit cards to this polyester thug in a bar in Fitzberg so you'd hightail it over there. Then I circled back. I followed that fool Breck—' Gilchrist sneered the name. '—and I killed him deader than Dreiser's prose. I did all that, Detective, right under your nose and I escaped.'

'But,' Corde said, 'here I am.'

The smile on the professor's face did not diminish. 'But *I* . . . have your daughter.'

'I want to know where she is!' Corde shouted in anguish.

'Stating the obvious,' Gilchrist snorted, 'diminishes you, as a late colleague of mine used to say.'

Sarah, cry for me, baby! Shout, scream . . .

'You son of a bitch!' The menace in Corde's voice rose to the distant smudged ceiling. It seemed to break the shafts of weak light that fell onto the bloodred carpet. Corde pressed his revolver forward and the hammer actually started back. Gilchrist's eyes registered an instant of monumental fear then became calm and conciliatory. He lifted a palm. 'She's all right. I swear it.'

'Where is she?'

Gilchrist's eyes swept over him. The smile had faded. He was now composed and his face was a mask of concern. 'I can't tell you that. I'm sorry.'

'If you've hurt her—' Corde stepped forward, his hand kneading the gun.

'She's fine,' Gilchrist said in a soothing voice. 'Think, Detective. Why would I hurt her? I kidnapped her because I needed some insurance. I couldn't stop you any other way.' He spread his hands out in front of him. 'Look . . . You found out where I was. I had to protect myself.'

'I swear I'll kill you if you don't tell me what you've done with her.' He stifled a spiny urge to fire a bullet into Gilchrist's leg or elbow.

The professor's voice was suavely reassuring. 'I haven't done anything with her. She's safe.' He nodded at his suitcase. 'As long as I get out of here she'll be fine. If you hurt me or arrest me you'll never see her again. It's as simple as that.'

Corde stepped forward and held the gun close to Gilchrist's face. 'Where is she?' he cried.

Gilchrist stepped back. 'Those are my terms. There's no negotiation. My freedom for your daughter. Take it or leave it.'

'You bastard, you damn bastard,' Corde growled.

'That's perhaps true in one context or another but it's irrelevant at this moment.'

The muzzle of the pistol lowered.

Corde's breathing calmed. At least Sarah was alive. At least he had a chance of getting her back home safe. He had a poignant image of the girl sitting in bed, wearing her pajamas and talking to a stuffed bear. Tears saturated his eyes.

'I'll tell you what I'll do,' Gilchrist offered. 'Let's up the ante. In exchange for my head start I'll tell you where your daughter is *and* I'll give you an explanation. I'll tell you exactly how I killed Jennie and why.'

Corde squinted slightly and somewhere in his mind the policeman stepped side by side with the father.

Gilchrist took the uneasy caution in Corde's eyes as an affirmative answer. He sat down in an armchair, launching motes of dust into the sallow light.

'I loved Jennifer Gebben very much. The first time I've ever felt that way about a woman. Ridiculous, when you think about it. She was a simple girl. She wasn't particularly pretty. She vacillated between intense and moody. But when she was with you, in bed, she was completely *with* you. Do you understand what I'm saying? She was the center of the universe. We'd play our games, we'd take our hickory sticks, we'd get out the straps. A lot of women just tolerate it for their man – the remote father problem, of course. But Jennie loved it. She lived for it.'

'Gilchrist—'

'Please. Let me finish. This spring she dropped me cold. She went back to that fucking roommate of hers. "Sorry, it's over with." Well, that wasn't good enough for me. No, sir. I wasn't going to be discarded the way she tossed aside Sayles or Okun. "Sorry, it's over with." Oh, no. I wouldn't tolerate it, not even from a borderline personality. I called her up from San Francisco. She was too pusillanimous to break up – excuse me, Detective. She was too *cowardly* to do it in person. I was in a consuming rage for a full twenty-four hours. I calmed then I flew back.'

'You bought a ticket under a different name. So you intended to kill her.'

Gilchrist paused for a moment and seemed neither surprised nor alarmed that this was public knowledge. 'There's another part. Can you figure it out?'

Corde was nodding. 'You killed Susan Biagotti and Jennie found out about it.'

The professor was, however, overtly disappointed that Corde had made the deduction. Still he continued unemotionally. 'Lying in bed with Jennie . . .' Gilchrist smiled at some memory. 'Or lying in the bathtub with her or on the kitchen floor, I'd tell her things. You did that with her. She was disarming. Well, Susan and I had played some very serious games. I mentioned that one time to Jennie. Stupid of me but I did it.'

'Why did you kill Susan?'

'Accidental. We got carried away and I strangled her.'

Corde winced, uncomprehending. He whispered, 'She was somebody you must've cared about. Yet you hurt her so badly you killed her? Why? Was the sex that good?'

'Not for her it wasn't. Obviously.' He gave Corde a fast chill smile then added, 'I used the hammer to cover up some of the marks and I made it look like a robbery.'

'But you didn't tell Jennie you'd killed her.'

'Of course not.' Gilchrist grimaced at the foolishness of the question. 'But she could link us together. When I called her from San Francisco on Sunday, when she told me she was breaking up with me, we argued. She said she was going back to Emily and if I didn't leave her alone she'd tell the administration about the students I'd slept with. Well, our Virgin Dean has this *thing* – her professors can fuck students' minds all they want but their bodies are off-limits. If Jennie blew the whistle Larraby would find out about Susan and me and I'd have problems. I flew back to New Lebanon and asked Jennie if I could see her. I told her I wanted us to end on a positive note. I said I had a book for her – in memory of our relationship. She agreed. We went for a walk. We ended up at the pond.'

'And you killed her.'

'And I killed her, yes.' Gilchrist seemed to be considering if there was anything else to say about Jennie Gebben and concluded there was not. He added, 'And I killed Sayles and Okun because . . .' He brought his hands together in a concluding way. '. . . they were my enemies.'

'That deputy in Lewisboro got himself shot too.'

'I'm very pleased about that – that it wasn't you, I mean. I was actually feeling somewhat bad thinking that you would be the first one through the door.' He nodded his head slightly.

Corde said, 'I'll give you a one-hour start.'

'Is there anybody outside the house?'

'Just one deputy.'

'So this is an unofficial visit, is it?' Gilchrist glanced

at Corde with a certain level of respect. 'Well, all right. Drop your car keys there.'

'We walked. We didn't drive.'

'Humor me.'

Corde tossed the keys into the middle of the floor. Gilchrist pocketed them.

'She's all right?'

'Of course she's all right. I've tied her hands and feet. That's all. And gagged her.'

People suffocate under gags. An FBI bulletin had just reported on this. Corde had noted the fact in boxy script on a three-by-five index card.

Gilchrist picked up his suitcase. He said, 'The basement.' He walked to the doorway and opened it. He stood at the top of the stairs and flicked a light switch on. Corde shouted, 'Sarah! It's Daddy.'

There was no response. Gilchrist said impatiently, 'The gag. I told you.'

Corde took out his handcuffs and stepped toward Gilchrist. 'Put one on your right wrist and the other on that radiator pipe there.'

'No. We have a deal.'

Corde said, 'I give you my word you get an hour. But I get my daughter first. Or I'll kill you where you stand.'

Gilchrist studied Corde's eyes. 'I think you might, Detective. All right. Follow me. I'll have to show you. It's hard to find.'

'No. You stay here.'

The professor shrugged and said, 'You'll have to turn left at the foot of the stairs then go down a corridor then—'

Corde handed him the cuffs.

'—up a few stairs. You don't have to worry. She's fine. Just fine.' Gilchrist was speaking like a pediatrician who'd nursed a child out of a fever.

Corde smelled the man's scent, sour, old cloth, sweat. He realized suddenly how close they stood.

Gilchrist, reaching for the cuffs, calmly closed his

long fingers around Corde's wrist, the nails dug into flesh, and he threw himself backward down the stairs, dragging Corde with him.

The detective grabbed futilely for the handrail. The gun fired, the bullet sailing into a wall. Together they tumbled down the sharp-edged pine stairs. Snaps and thuds. Corde felt his left wrist pop. The gun flew from his hand. There was a huge reverberation as his head smacked hard into the rickety handrail and he heard another snap of joint that must have come from Gilchrist's arm or leg.

They cartwheeled down and down the wood steps then crashed into the concrete floor and lay still, curled like lovers on a cold winter morning. In the small, dim basement around them were rusted tools, a sprinkling of coal, a half dozen cans of paint. And not another living soul.

Wynton Kresge rested across the trunk of the green Pontiac, in prone firing position. It was the pose of the dressed deer he tied onto his Olds hood when he drove home from hunting. The checkered grip from the Remington had imprinted its design into the pads of his fingers. He smelled gun oil and gasoline and he thought Corde had been inside too damn long.

Then he heard the gunshot. A short crack from inside the house, the ground-floor windows flexing for an instant under the muzzle burst.

Front or back, front or back?

Pick one, damn it.

Kresge stood up, hesitated, then ran over the barren lawn and through the open front door.

'Bill!' he shouted, and in response the poker caught him in the corner of the eye and laid open six inches of cheek. He fell backward hard. The shotgun went off, a chunk of clapboard exploded from the impact of the heavy shot. Hot blood streamed into his eye and mouth and he had a distorted image of Gilchrist limping forward to pick up the fallen shotgun. The professor's right hand was swollen and dark and he too was bloodied about the face.

'Bill!' Kresge called, sputtering through blood.

Gilchrist lifted up the shotgun and pointed it at Kresge's face. The deputy rolled over and tried to scramble away. He heard Gilchrist's grunt as he pulled the trigger and realized that there was a spent round in the chamber. Kresge prayed that he didn't know enough about guns to pump a new shell in.

He heard the double snap of the slide going back and forth and the tap of the old shell falling on the porch.

'No,' Kresge moaned, groping for his automatic. It had fallen from his holster and he could not find it. He crawled another few inches and pressed against the wrought-iron railing. He felt the heavy cold touch of the shotgun barrel on his back.

Then the explosion.

And another and another. Gilchrist reeling over, clutching his chest and stomach, where Corde's bullets had exited. The shotgun fell on Kresge, who grabbed it in his blindness and pointed the muzzle toward the forest. Gilchrist dropped to his knees then fell forward.

Wynton Kresge was surrounded by numb silence, which was broken a moment later by a voice intruding on and finally destroying the deputy's relief: the sound of Bill Corde crying, 'Sarah, what have I done to you, what have I done?'

15

He walked unsteadily, the tufts of grass and wiry roots reaching out and snagging his feet. His voice was hoarse as he cried, 'Sarah, Sarah?' Skittish birds flew up from their ground nests as he stumbled past. Sometimes he heard his own desperate echoes, which fed him momentary false hopes.

He had sprained his wrist in the fall down the stairs but had refused any treatment and hurried outside to search for his daughter.

Or for what he was now beginning to believe with despair: his daughter's body. She had been nowhere in the house or the garage.

Prodded by the horror of loss, his mind in chaos, Bill Corde was combing the five tricky acres around the house – tangled woods, pine needle dunes, a couple deep wells and plenty of dirt soft enough for a shallow grave. Wynton Kresge, stitched and in agony, strode through the same fields. As much as Corde, he dreaded finding a small overturn of earth. Bringing such news about a child to her father was unthinkable to him; still he searched frantically. Other deputies joined in, even Lance Miller, wheezing against the grip of the elastic tape around his ribs. Jim Slocum and two off-duty New Lebanon deputies, entitled to be home with beer, wives and the tube, also combed the scruffy landscape.

Corde staggered through grass and whips of thin

branches. He scrambled and shuddered his way through head-high brush. He fell over a cruelly hidden arc of barbed wire and bloodied his good palm to save his jaw. Every reclining blotch of pink seen through the weeds was a well of agony, every distant yip of a dog or owl's hollow call. Once Corde cried hard as he leapt through tall grass to what turned out to be a beige IGA bag filled with empties.

'Sarah, Sarah?' he called in a whisper and continued across a stand of trees into another field, which was a dozen acres of fresh-plowed dirt.

By seven the sun is low, and narrow shadows of trees stretch out for yard and yards. Bill Corde sits on a hillock of chunky earth covered with dandelions and catnip and stalks of milkweed. His voice is gone, his strength too. He reaches out and affectionately strokes a yellow leaf in a wholly mad way. He thinks he should be searching the fields but he knows it is useless. He can do nothing, nothing but sit and mourn his daughter, and another loss too, for Sarah's death will in an obscure, brutal way also poison the life he shares with Diane, and that with Jamie. The three of them will now be wedged forever apart.

While he searched, hope had been his only instrument and now it too is gone.

He sits for ten minutes in this paralysis then watches as a police cruiser rocks over the uneven ground toward him, Lance Miller cautiously piloting. It stops on an incline. The door opens. Diane gets out.

Then Sarah behind her.

Corde stands uneasily and steps forward. He hugs the girl hard, embracing then wholly encompassing her. 'Honey, honey, honey!' he cries. His intensity begins to confuse her and he forces himself to grow nonchalant. Then a giddiness, which is not faked, sets in. He laughs hard and squeezes her hand.

Diane explains that Sarah came running up the road to their house twenty minutes before. She whispers to Corde, 'She's shaken up bad. She saw Gilchrist attack

Ben and she ran and hid at the school. Then she came home on foot.' Corde cocks an anxious eyebrow and Diane reads the signal. She mouths, 'She's fine. He didn't touch her.'

Diane then nods toward the ambulance parked at the entrance to Gilchrist's driveway. 'They gave her a pill that will keep her relaxed. Didn't they, honey?'

'I feel sleepy, Mommy.'

Although there are a thousand questions he wants to ask, Corde knows not to pursue this conversation with his daughter now. He says, 'Almost suppertime. How about we go home and fire up the barbecue?'

'Okay, Daddy. You hurt your hand.'

'It's nothing.'

They start toward the Dodge in this holiday atmosphere but the weight of the events is suddenly too much for Sarah. She is staring at Gilchrist's house as if gazing at a friend who has betrayed her. Although it is at some distance Corde slowly steps between her and the house on the slim chance that she might see blood. 'He hurt Dr Breck, Daddy. The Sunshine Man hurt Dr Breck. I thought he was my friend.'

'It's all right, honey. You're going to be all right.'

'I feel sleepy. I lost my backpack.'

'We'll get it later, honey.'

'I left it in Dr Breck's car. It has my tape recorder in it. Dr Breck made me run when the Sunshine Man . . .' Her tiny voice fades.

Diane's fingertips rise slowly to her lips but she is determined not to reveal any more horror in front of the girl. She forces a smile onto her face.

Corde asks Diane, 'How's Breck?'

She hesitates. Corde knows she's considering if she should admit the existence of this knowledge. 'I called the hospital,' she whispers. 'He'll live. Hundreds of stitches.'

Sarah looks groggily away. 'I don't like it here. I'm afraid he's going to come back to his house.'

'Who?' Diane asks.

'The Sunshine Man.'

Corde crouches down. 'He's gone away, honey. He'll never come back. I've sent him away.'

Diane looks at the house. She says, 'He lives *there*, your wizard?'

Sarah says, 'I saw him behind the cow pasture a couple times. I wanted him to cast a spell to make me smart so one day I followed him here. But I was ascared to ask so I left.'

'And she wrote a story about it.'

Corde pulls the two stained pages from his breast pocket and reads the words he near to memorized earlier in the day. '"*And the girl climbed onto the back of Cloud-Tipper the eagle and hugged his feather neck. They sailed away from the yellow house. They followed the Sunshine Man home. They flew into the yard then past the cow field and past the old well and the burned-down silo that looked like whale ribs and over the railroad bridge and along the path to the river. Finally, they came to a clearing in the woods. Cloud-Tipper landed gentle. And there was the Sunshine Man's cottage . . ."*'

'You came here by yourself, Sarah?' Diane's eyelids lower at the insolence of tragedy averted by the smallest slip of fate.

'I just wanted him to make me smart, Mommy.'

Diane casually slips her arm around her daughter and they walk toward the squad car. Corde hobbles along behind. Mother and daughter separate for a moment, the girl running ahead.

Corde catches up with his wife, who is now silent, the same wary expression on her face that she'd worn at Jamie's bedside. Corde knows why but doesn't want to consider it now. The pain in his arm is making up for lost time and he's half faint by the time he slides into the backseat of the Dodge, next to Diane. Sarah has claimed the front. Diane brushes her daughter's hair with her fingers.

When Corde sits closer to his wife she shies away from him. Her motion is subtle but is clear.

Miller starts the car and drives slowly over the rough ground, the Dodge sashaying like a canoe in a powerboat's wake. Corde lowers his forehead to his thumb, as if administering Lent ashes, and lets his palm take the whole weight of his head. This is what he thinks: *I am just doing my job the only way I know how. What more is a man supposed to do?* Though Corde suspects that a man must do more and probably a lot more. He knows that when your daughter gets well your son gets sick and when the car is paid off the mortgage goes up and when you decide you love your wife she's gone to another man . . . There's no end to the burdens life lays on you. Oh, there is so much to do and more after that. And more and more and more . . . But it seems to him that this isn't so much the problem as is finding somebody or something that can show you exactly *what* has to be done. This is the lesson. This is what Bill Corde doubts he'll ever get right.

'Everybody buckle up now,' Lance Miller announces and turns the cruiser onto the highway.

Corde got the new FI-113 written up but it was a chore. He was extra careful because he knew it was going to be the basis for Jim Slocum's comments to the press and Hammerback Ellison's as well and he wanted it to be as clear as possible. He tried dictating into Sarah's tape recorder but he kept getting tongue-tied and had to go back to ruled paper and a Bic medium-point.

The *Register* lost its exclusive. The killings had been laid at the feet of a college professor who'd taught at Harvard and had written book reviews for the *New York Times*. The Associated Press and some big-city newspaper reporters came to town, along with a herd of earnest young TV reporters (one from CNN, to the town's delight) with their hair spray and crisp outfits and fancy electronics. One journalist referred to Gilchrist as the 'New Lebanon Cult Killer' but Sheriff Jim Slocum said that 'this didn't appear to be so much a cult situation as a romance-oriented homicide and some follow-up homicides to cover it up.'

Corde had been granted dispensation from learning the radio codes and was now in charge of what Slocum was calling the Felony Desk, something he'd thought up after watching *America's Most Wanted* one night. Things were slow though, the only felon at the moment being Dell Tucker, a New Lebanon farmer who'd turned an AR-15 full-automatic and had been heard testing it on gophers. Corde figured that was mostly a federal offense so why bother? Besides Corde had gopher problems himself.

Wynton Kresge had drawn a tough rotation from Hammerback Ellison. Being new he'd been assigned to a month of speed-trap duty out in the unincorporated portions of Harrison County. Corde told him they couldn't all be glamour assignments.

'S'hardly fair,' Kresge had muttered. Sitting on Corde's desk in the New Lebanon Sheriff's Department he was now looking over the felony investigation report. 'Gilchrist flew back here the day before Jennie was killed . . .' He was speaking to himself, picturing it. 'He bought a new ticket under a different name.'

'We should've checked passengers, IDs and forms of payment. The information was there.'

Kresge said, 'Seems like you can't think of everything.'

Corde thought for a moment. 'True, you can't. But you have to.'

'Flew back all the way from San Francisco?' Kresge mused.

Corde continued, 'And he just stayed in New Lebanon. He rented that house in the woods, the place we found him in. He rented it for a month, laying low. When he called people he just told them he was calling from San Francisco and they believed him.'

'How'd you find that out?'

'I didn't *find* it out. I figured it out. From what he told me. The best source of information on a murder is the perpetrator. Remember that.'

'Well, I will.'

'I think he was going to stay there for a little while then reappear like he'd come back from the conference. But that first morning he must've seen Sarah in the woods. He decided to use her to get to me. Her and Jamie too.'

'How?'

'His threats against Sarah might've stopped me. Or if anything'd happened to the kids, I would've been in no shape to keep going. Remember, everybody else was looking for the Moon Killer. T.T. Ebbans and me – and you too – were looking for somebody like Gilchrist. He knew that. I was the one he had to stop. Hardly Ribbon.'

'Or Werewolf Slocum,' Kresge whispered. 'When you were at the house, where you shot him, he said he had Sarah. Why'd he say that?'

Corde grimaced. 'To do just what he did: get the advantage on me. I didn't play it too smart. It never occurred to me that she'd gotten away. I walked in and asked first off where she was. That gave him something on me and he used it pretty damn well considering he was making it up as he went along. He was playing with me. He got me pretty riled then calmed me down telling me that Sarah was safe and telling me why he killed Jennie. Put me off my guard.'

'Who's this Breck fellow?' Kresge looked at the report. *Now there's a question for you.*

'I just had me a talk with him. He was Sarah's tutor. That's all he was. Breck read part of Sarah's book about this wizard watching our house. He asked her about it and found out she hadn't made that part up. He figured it was the man leaving the threats and that meant he was the killer.'

'Why didn't he tell us before?'

'He just read the damn thing five minutes before Gilchrist gutted him.'

And two days after I read the same story.

'A wrong-time, wrong-place fellow, Breck was,' Kresge offered.

'You could say.'

Although there was a lot more to Breck than this, Corde now understood. But that had nothing to do with Gilchrist or the investigation, and it was going to take a lot of thinking and a lot more talking before Corde figured out what to do about the Ben Breck situation – if there was anything he could do. And the person he had to talk to about it, well, she wasn't much in the mood for conversation.

Who's this Breck fellow?

'Gilchrist,' Kresge said almost reverently. 'He was one step ahead of us the whole time.'

'He always was. And one step behind us too.'

'How'd you know he was in that house, Bill? I've lived in New Lebanon ten years and never even knew there were houses down there by the river.'

'It's tough to explain how the process of deduction works, Wynton.'

'You mean it's something you're born with?'

'No. You can learn. The more you practice the better you are. Remember that.'

'Well, I will.'

Corde stepped out into the backyard of his house and set down his Pabst Blue Ribbon. He inspected the strip of muddy dirt by the dryer exhaust. He shooed off a couple of grackles and bent down low to the ground then went lower, on all fours; it seemed to him the green fuzz hadn't grown a millimeter in the last weeks. He decided it was crazy to try to grow grass here in this sunless rocky gully between two houses populated by hard-running teenage boys who loved shortcuts; he ought to put in gravel and be done with it.

Nevertheless Corde arranged the sprinkler carefully and turned on the water.

He sat down in a plaid lawn chair, the aluminum legs screeching on the slab of concrete he'd laid two years ago and spent two years meaning to enclose. He looked at his watch. Tonight the family was going to visit Jamie in the hospital. They were going to smuggle in a VCR and

Corde was going to hook it up to the TV in the hospital room. They were all going to watch a movie Diane had rented, some cop comedy. But that excursion was planned for after dinner. Now, he wanted to relax for a few minutes. He opened the beer and drank half of it then replaced the can on the concrete while he watched the intermittent rainbow the sprinkler made as it waved a fan of water high enough to catch the last of the sun. He glanced behind him and saw Diane behind the twin Thermopanes, occupied with dinner.

Corde felt a stack of three-by-five cards gig him in the thigh and he took them out of his pocket. Most of them would be filed away in the tall green cabinets he had testily commandeered for his own use down at the Sheriff's Department. One card though, filled with his careful block lettering, he intended to pin up on his bulletin board. He thought he would put it in the space next to his favorite quote – about physical evidence being the cornerstone of a case. This card read:

IT IS THE POET WHO PERCEIVES THE WORLD BY THE ILLUMINATION OF PURE UNDER-STANDING,
WHILE OTHERS SEE ONLY IN REFLECTED LIGHT.

L.D. GILCHRIST

He slipped the card into his pocket then picked up his beer, took several sips and cradled the sweating can on his stomach, listening to the sounds of dusk: cicadas, cricket creaks, an owl waking to his hunger, a dinnertime summons to the neighbor children. Diane banged on the window and shouted, 'Ten minutes.'

Bill Corde said okay. He waited half that time then stood and stretched. He walked to the edge of the concrete deck and leaning outward began to wave the white cards high in the air, shouting 'Whoa, whoa!' at a half dozen shiny grackles, which fled from his muddy patch of frail lawn and vanished into the moonless sky.

SPEAKING IN TONGUES

In the beginning was the Word.
Man acts it out. He is the
act, not the actor.

—Henry Miller

I

The Whispering Bears

1

Crazy Megan parks the car.

Doesn't want to do this. No way.

Doesn't get out, listens to the rain . . .

The engine ticked to silence as she looked down at her clothes. It was her usual outfit: JNCO jeans. A sleeveless white tee under a dark denim work shirt. Combat boots. Wore this all time. But she felt uneasy today, in this stuff. Embarrassed, wished she'd worn a skirt at least. The pants were too baggy. The sleeves dangled to the tips of her black-polished fingernails and her socks were orange as tomato soup. Well, what did it matter? The hour'd be over soon.

Maybe he'd concentrate on her good qualities – her wailing blue eyes and blond hair. Oh, and her boobs too. He *was* a man.

Anyway, the clothes covered up the extra seven . . . well, all right, ten pounds that she carried on her tall frame.

Stalling. Crazy Megan doesn't want to be here one bit.

Rubbing her hand over her upper lip, she looked out the rain-spattered window at the lush trees and bushes of suburbia. This April in northern Virginia had been like June or July and ghosts of mist rose from the asphalt. It was so deserted here. She'd never noticed that before.

3

Crazy Megan whispers, *Just. Say. No. And leave.*

But she couldn't do that. Mega-hassle.

She took off the wooden peace symbol dangling between her breasts and flung it into the back seat. Megan brushed her hair with her fingers, pulled it away from her face. Her ruddy knuckles seemed big as golf balls. A glance in the rear-view mirror. She wiped off the black lipstick, pulled the blond strands into a ponytail secured the hair with a green rubber band.

Okay, let's do it. Get it over with.

A jog through the rain. She hit the intercom and a moment later the door latch buzzed.

Megan McCall walked into the waiting room where she'd spent every Saturday morning for the last seven weeks. Ever since The Incident. She kept waiting for the place to become familiar. It never did.

She hated this. The sessions were bad enough but waiting really killed her. Dr Hanson *always* kept her waiting. Even if she was on time, even if there were no other patients ahead of her, he always started the session five minutes or so late. It pissed her off but she never said anything about it.

Today, though, she found the new doctor standing in the doorway, smiling at her, lifting an eyebrow in greeting.

'You're Megan?' the man said, offering an easy smile. 'I'm Bill Peters.' He was about her father's age, handsome. Full head of hair. Hanson was bald and looked like a shrink. This guy . . . *Maybe a little George Clooney*, Crazy Megan decides. Her wariness fades slightly.

And he doesn't call himself 'Doctor'. Interesting.

'Hi.'

'Come on in.' He gestured. She stepped into the office.

'How's Dr Hanson?' she asked, sitting in the chair across from his desk. 'Somebody in his family's sick?'

'His mother. An accident. I hear she'll be all right. But he had to go to Leesburg for the week.'

'So you're like a substitute teacher?'

He laughed. 'Something like that.'

'I didn't know shr— therapists took over other patients.'

'Some don't. Dr Hanson likes continuity.' He paused, as if he weren't sure she knew what it meant.

Dr Peters – *Bill* Peters – had called yesterday after school to tell her that Hanson had arranged for him to take over his appointments and, if she wanted, she could make her regular session after all. *No way,* Crazy Megan had whispered at first. But after Megan had talked with Peters for a while she decided she'd give it a try. There was something so comforting about his voice. Besides, baldy Hanson wasn't doing diddly for her. What a loser. All she remembered about the sessions was her lame bitching about school and about being lonely and about Amy and Josh and Brittany, and Hanson nodding and saying she had to be friends with herself. Whatever the hell that meant.

'This'll be repeating some things,' Peters now said, 'but if you don't mind, could we go over some of the basics?'

'I guess.'

He asked, 'It's Megan *Collier*?'

'No, Collier's my father's name. I use my mother's. McCall.' She rocked in the stiff-backed chair, crossing her legs. Her tomato socks showed. She planted her feet squarely on the floor.

'You don't like therapy, do you?' he asked suddenly.

Hanson had never asked that. Wouldn't ask anything so blunt. And, unlike this guy, Hanson didn't look into her

5

eyes when he spoke. Staring right back, she said, 'No, I don't.'

He seemed amused. 'You know why you're here?'

Silent as always, Crazy Megan answers first. *Because I'm fucked up, I'm dysfunctional. I'm a nutcase. I'm psycho. I'm loony. And half the school knows and do you have a fucking* clue *how hard it is to walk through those halls with everybody looking at you and thinking, Shrink bait, shrink bait.* Crazy Megan also mentions what just plain Megan would never in a million years tell him – about the fake computerized picture of Megan in a straitjacket that made the rounds of Jefferson High two weeks ago.

But now Megan merely responded, ''Cause if I didn't come to see a therapist they'd send me to Juvenile.'

When she'd been found, drunk, strolling along the catwalk of the municipal water tower two months ago she'd been committing a crime. The county police got involved and it turned messy. But finally everybody agreed that if she saw a counsellor the commonwealth's attorney wouldn't press charges.

'That's true. But it's not the answer.'

She lifted an eyebrow.

'The answer is that you're here so that you can feel better.'

Oh, please, Crazy Megan begins, rolling her crazy eyes.

And, okay, it was way stupid, his words themselves. But . . . but . . . there was something about the *way* Dr Peters said them that, just for a second, less than a second, Megan believed that he really meant them. This guy's in a different universe from Loser Elbow-Patch Hanson.

He opened his briefcase and took out a yellow pad.

A brochure fell out on to the desk. She glanced at it. A picture of San Francisco was on the cover.

'Oh, you're going there?' she asked.

'A conference,' he said, flipping through the brochure. He handed it to her.

'Awesome.'

'I love the city,' he continued. 'I'm a former hippie. Dyed-in-the-wool Deadhead and Jefferson Airplane fan . . . Whole nine yards. 'Course, that was before your time.'

'No way. I'm totally into Janis Joplin and Hendrix.'

'Yeah? You ever been to the Bay area?'

'Not yet. But I'm going someday. Bett doesn't know it. But I am.'

He squinted. 'Hey, you know, there *is* a resemblance – you and Joplin. If you didn't have your hair up it'd be the same as hers.'

Megan wished she hadn't done the cheerleader pert 'n' perky ponytail.

The doctor added, 'You're prettier, of course. And thinner. Can you belt out the blues?'

'Like, I wish . . .'

'But you don't remember hippies.' He chuckled.

'Time out!' she said enthusiastically. 'I've seen *Woodstock*, like, eight times.'

She also wished she'd kept the peace symbol.

'So tell me, did you really try to kill yourself? Cross your heart.'

'And hope to die?' she asked coyly.

He smiled.

She said, 'No.'

'What happened?'

'Okay, what it is is I was drinking a little Southern Comfort. All right, maybe more than a little.'

'Joplin's drink,' he said. 'Too fucking sweet for me.'

Whoa, the *f* word. Cool. She was almost – almost – beginning to like him.

He glanced again at her hair. The fringes on her face. Then back to her eyes. It was like one of Josh's caresses. Somewhere within her she felt a tiny ping – of reassurance and pleasure.

Megan continued her story. 'And somebody I was with said no way they'd climb up to the top and I said I would and I did. That's it.'

'All right, so you got nabbed by the cops on some bullshit charge.'

'That's about it.'

'Not exactly the crime of the century.'

'*I* didn't think so either. But they were so . . . you know.'

'I know,' he said. 'Now tell me about yourself. Your secret history.'

'Well, my parents are divorced. I live with Bett. She has this business? It's really a decorating business is all but she says she's an interior designer 'cause it sounds better. Tate's got this farm in Prince William. He used to be this famous lawyer but now he just does people's wills and sells houses and stuff. He hires people to run the farm for him. Sharecroppers. Sound like slaves, or whatever, but they're just people he hires.'

'And your relationship with the folks? Is the porridge too hot, too cold or just right?'

'Just right.'

He nodded, made a small notation on his pad though he might've been just doodling. Maybe she bored him. Maybe he was writing a grocery list.

Things to buy after my appointment with Crazy Megan.

She told him about growing up, about the deaths of her mother's parents and her father's dad, school, her friends.

Her Aunt Susan – her mother's twin sister. 'She's a nice lady, but she's had a rough time. She's been sick all her life. And she really, really wanted kids but couldn't have them.'

'Ah,' he said.

None of it felt important to her and she guessed it was even less important to him.

'What about friends?'

Count 'em on one hand, Crazy Megan says.

Shhhh.

'I hang with the goth crowd mostly,' she told the doctor.

'As in gothic?'

'Yeah. Only . . .' She decided she could tell him the truth. 'What it is is I kinda stay by myself a lot. I meet people but I end up figuring, why bother? There're a lot of losers out there.'

'Oh, yeah.' He laughed. 'That's why my business is so good.'

She blinked in surprise. Then smiled too.

'What's the boyfriend situation?'

'This'll be short,' she said, laughing ruefully. 'I was going with this guy? Joshua? And he was, like, all right. Only he was older. And he was black. I mean, he wasn't a gangsta or anything. His father's a soldier, like an officer in the Pentagon, and his mother's some big executive. I didn't have a problem with the race thing. But Dr Hanson said I was probably involved with him just to make my parents nuts.'

'Were you?'

'I don't know. I kinda liked him. No, I *did* like him.'

'But you broke up?'

'Sure. Dr Hanson said I ought to dump him.'

9

'He *said* that?'

'Well, not exactly. But I got that impression.'

Crazy Megan thinks Mr Handsome Shrink, Mr *George Clooney* stud, ought to've figured it out. But she explains anyway. *How can a psycho nutcase like me go out with anybody? If I hadn't dumped him – which I cried about for two weeks – if I hadn't left, then everybody at his school be on his case. 'He's the one with the loony girl.' And then his folks would find out – they're the nicest people in the universe and totally in love – and they'd be crushed . . . Well, of course I had to leave . . .*

'Nobody else on the horizon?' he asked.

'Nope.' She shook her head.

'Okay, let's talk about the family some more. Your mother.'

'Bett and I get along great.' She hesitated. 'Only it's funny about her – she's into her business but she also believes in all this New Age stuff crap. I'm, like, just chill, okay? That stuff is so bogus. But she doesn't hassle me about it. Doesn't hassle me about anything really. It's great between us. Really great. The only problem is she's engaged to a geek.'

'Do you two talk, your mom and you? Chew the fat, as my grandmother used to say.'

'Sure. . . . I mean, she's busy a lot. But who isn't, right? Yeah, we talk.' She hoped he didn't ask her about what. She'd have to make up something.

'And how 'bout Dad?'

She shrugged. 'He's nice. He takes me to concerts, shopping. We get along great.'

'Great?'

C.M. points out, *Is that the only word you know, bitch?*

'Yeah,' Megan said. 'Only . . .'

'Only what?'

'Well, it's like we don't have a lot to talk *about*. He wants me to go windsurfing with him but I went once and it's a totally superficial way to spend your time. I'd rather read a book or something.'

'You like to read?'

'Yeah, I read a lot.'

'Who're some of your favorite authors?'

'Oh, I don't know.' Her mind went blank.

Crazy Megan isn't much help. *Yep, he's gonna think you're damaged.*

Quiet! Megan ordered. She remembered the last book she'd read. 'You know Márquez? I'm reading *Autumn of the Patriarch.*'

His eyebrow lifted. 'Oh, I loved it.

'No kidding. I—'

Dr Peters added, '*Love in the Time of Cholera.* Best love story ever written. I've read it three times.'

Another ecstatic ping. 'Me too. Well, I only read it once.' The book was sitting on her bedside table.

'Tell me more,' he continued, 'about your father.'

'Um, he's pretty handsome still – I mean for a guy in his forties. And he's in pretty good shape. He dates a lot but he can't seem to settle down with anybody. He says he wants a family.'

'Does he?'

'Yeah. But if he does then why does he date girls named Bambi? . . . Just kidding. But they look like they're Bambis.' They both laughed.

'Tell me about the divorce.'

'I don't really remember them together. They split up when I was three.'

'Why?'

11

'They got married too young. That's what Bett says. They kind of went different ways. Mom was like real flighty and into that New Age stuff I was telling you about. And Dad was just the opposite.'

'Whose idea was the divorce?'

'I think my dad's.'

He jotted another note then looked up. 'So how mad are you at your parents?'

'I'm not.'

'Really?' he asked, as if he were completely surprised. 'You're sure the porridge isn't too hot?'

'I love 'em. They love me. We get along gre— fine. The porridge is just right. What the fuck is porridge anyway?'

'Don't have a clue,' Peters said quickly. 'Give me an early memory about your mother.'

'What?'

'Quick! Now! *Do it*!' His eyes flashed.

Megan felt a wave of heat crinkle through her face. 'I—'

'Don't hesitate,' he whispered. 'Say what's on your mind!'

She blurted, 'Bett's getting ready for a date, putting on makeup, staring in a mirror and poking at a wrinkle, like she's hoping it'll go away. She always *does* that. Like her face is the most important thing in the world to her. Her looks, you know.'

'And what do you think as you watch her?' His dark eyes were fervent. Her mind froze again. 'No, you're hesitating. *Tell* me!'

'"Slut."'

He nodded. 'Now *that's* great, Megan.'

She felt swollen with pride. Didn't know why. But she did.

12

'Brilliant. Now give me a memory about your father. Fast!'

'Bears.' She gasped and lifted a hand to her mouth. 'No . . . Wait. Let me think.'

But the doctor pounced. 'Bears? At the zoo?'

'No, never mind.'

'Tell me.'

She was shaking her head, no.

'Tell me, Megan,' he insisted.

'It's not important.'

'Oh, it *is* important,' he said. 'Listen. You're with *me* now, Megan. Forget whatever Hanson's done. I don't operate his way, groping around in the dark. I go deep.'

She looked into his eyes and froze – like a deer in headlights.

'Don't worry,' he said softly. 'Trust me. I'm going to change your life for ever.'

2

'They weren't real bears.'

'Toys?'

'Bears in a story.'

'What's so hard about this?' Dr Peters asked.

'I don't know.'

Crazy Megan gives her a good burst of sarcasm. *Oh, good job, loser. You've blown it now. You had to tell him about the book.*

But the other side of her was thinking: Seven weeks of bullshit with Dr Shiny-head Hanson and she hadn't felt a thing but bored. Ten minutes with Dr Peters and she was hooked up to an electric current.

Crazy Megan says, *It's too hard. It hurts too much.*

But Bill couldn't hear her, of course.

'Go on,' he encouraged.

And she went on.

'I was about six, okay? And I was spending the weekend with Tate. He lives in this big house and nobody's around for miles. It's in the middle of his cornfields and it's all quiet and really, really spooky. I was feeling weird, all scared. And I asked him to read me a story. He said he didn't have any children's books. I was really hurt. I started to cry and asked why didn't he have any. He looked all funny and went out to the old barn – where he told me I wasn't ever supposed to go – and he came back with this book. It was called *The Whispering Bears*. Only it turned out it wasn't really a kid's story at all. I found out later it was a book of folk stories from Europe.'

'Do you remember it?'

'Yeah.'

'Tell me.'

'It's stupid.'

'No,' Peters said, leaning forward. 'I'll bet it's anything *but* stupid. Tell me.'

'There was a town by the edge of the woods. And everybody who lived there was happy, you know, like in all fairy stories before the bad shit happens. People walking down the street, singing, going to market, having dinner with their families. Then one day these two big bears walked out of the woods and stood at the edge of town with their heads down and it sounded like they were whispering to each other.

'At first nobody paid any attention then little by little the people stopped what they were doing and tried to hear what the bears were saying. But nobody could. That night the bears went back into the forest. And the townspeople stood around and one woman said she knew what they were whispering about – they were making fun of the people in the village. And then everybody started noticing how everybody else walked funny or talked funny or looked stupid and they all ended up laughing at each other, and everybody got mad and there were all kinds of fights in town.

'Okay, then the next day the bears came out of the forest again and started whispering, blah, blah, blah, you get the picture. Then that night they went back into the woods. And this time some old man said *he* knew what they were talking about. They were gossiping about the people in town. And so everybody figured that everybody else knew all their secrets and so they went home and closed all their windows and doors and they were afraid to go out in public.

'Then – the third day – the bears came out again. And it was the same thing only this time the duke or mayor or somebody said, "*I* know what they're saying! They're making plans to attack the village." And they went to get torches to scare away the bears but they accidentally set a house on fire and the fire spread and the whole town burned down.'

Megan felt a shiver. Her eyes slipped to the top of the desk and she couldn't look up at Dr Peters. She continued, 'Tate only read it to me once but I still remember the last line. It was, "And do you know what the bears were really whispering about? Why, nothing at all. Don't you know? Bears can't talk."'

This is so bogus, Crazy Megan scoffs. *What's he going to think about you now?*

But the doctor calmly asked, 'And the story was upsetting?'

'Yeah.'

'Why?'

'I don't know. Maybe 'cause everybody's lives got ruined for no reason.'

'But there *was* a reason for it.'

Megan shrugged.

He continued, 'The town was destroyed because people projected their own pettiness and jealousy and aggression on some innocents. That's the moral of the story. How people destroy themselves.'

'I guess. But I was just thinking it wasn't much of a kid's story. I guess I wanted *The Lion King* or *A Hundred and One Dalmatians*.' She smiled. But Peters didn't. He looked at her closely. 'What happened after your father finished it?'

Why did he ask that? she wondered. *Why*?

Megan shrugged again. 'That's all. Bett came and picked me up and I went home.'

'This is hard, isn't it, Megan?'

Get a clue.

Quiet!

She looked at Dr Peters. 'Yeah, I guess.'

'Would it be easier to write down your feelings? A lot of my patients do that. There's some paper.'

She took the sheets he nodded toward and rested them on a booklet he pushed forward for her to write on. Reluctantly Megan picked up a pen.

She stared at the paper. 'I don't know what to say.'

'Say what you feel.'

'I don't know how I feel.'

'Yes, you do.' He leaned close. 'I think you're just afraid to admit it.'

'Well—'

'Say whatever comes into your mind. Anything. Say something to your mother first. Write a letter to her. Go!'

Another wave of that scalding heat.

Spotlight on Crazy Megan . . .

He whispered, 'Go deep.'

'I can't think!'

'Pick one thing. Why are you so angry with her?'

'I'm not!'

'Yes, you are!'

She clenched her fist. 'Because . . .'

'*Why?*'

'I don't know. Because she's . . . She goes out with

these young men. It's like she thinks she can cast spells on them.'

'So what?' he challenged her. 'She can date who she wants. She's single. What's *really* pissing you off?'

'I don't know!'

'Yes, you *do!*' he shot back.

'Well, she's just a businesswoman and she's engaged to this dweeb. She's not a fairy princess at all like she'd like to be. She's not a cover girl.'

'But she wears an exotic image? Why does she do that?'

'I guess to make herself happy. She wants to be pretty and young for ever. She thinks this asshole Brad's going to make her happy. But he isn't.'

'She's *greedy*? Is that what you're saying?'

'Yes!' Megan cried. 'That's it! She doesn't care about *me*. The night on the water tower? She was at Brad's and she was supposed to call me. But she didn't.'

'Who? Her fiancé's?'

'Yeah. She went up there, to Baltimore, and she never called. They were *fucking*, I'll bet, and she forgot about me. It was just like when I was little. She'd leave me alone all the time.'

'By yourself?'

'No, with sitters. My uncle mostly.'

'Which uncle?'

'My Aunt Susan's husband. My mom's twin sister. She's been real sick most of her life, I told you. And Bett spent all her time with her in the hospital when I was young. Uncle Harris'd babysit me. He was real nice, but—'

'But you missed your mother?'

'I wanted her to be with *me*. She said it was only for a little while because Aunt Susan was real sick. She said she and Susan were totally close. Nobody was closer to her than her sister.'

He shook his head, seemed horrified. 'She said that to *you*? Her own daughter?'

Megan nodded.

'*You* should have been the person closest to her in the world.'

These words gripped her by the throat. She wiped more tears and struggled for breath. Finally she continued, 'Aunt Susan'd do anything to have kids but she couldn't. Because of her heart. And here Mom got pregnant with me and Susan felt real bad about that. So Mom spent a lot of time with her.'

'There's no excuse for neglecting children. None. Absolutely none.'

Megan snagged a Kleenex and wiped her face.

'And you didn't let yourself be angry? Why not?'

'Because my mother was doing something good. My aunt's a nice lady. She always calls and asks about me and wants me to come visit her. Only I don't 'cause . . .'

'Because you're angry with her. She took your mother away from you.'

A chill. 'Yeah, I guess she did.'

'Come on, Megan. What else? Why the guilt?'

Because my aunt needed my mom more back then. When I was little. See . . .'

Crazy Megan interrupts. *Oh, you can't tell him that!*

Yes, I can. I can tell him anything

'See, Uncle Harris killed himself.'

'He did?'

'I felt so bad for my aunt.'

'Forget it!' he snapped.

Megan blinked.

'You're Bett's *daughter*. You should have been the center of her universe. What she did was inexcusable. Say it. Say it!'

'I . . .'

'*Say it!*'

'It was inexcusable!'

'Good. Now write it to her. Every bit of the anger you feel. Get it out.'

The pen rolled from Megan's lap on to the floor. She bent down and picked it up. It weighed a hundred pounds. The tears ran from her nose and eyes and dripped on the paper.

'Tell her,' the doctor said. 'Tell her she's greedy. She turned her back on her daughter and took care of her sister instead.'

'But,' Megan managed to say, 'that's greedy of *me*.'

'Of *course* it's greedy. You were a child, you're supposed to be greedy. Parents are there to fill *your* needs. That's the whole *point* of parents. *Tell* her what you feel.'

Her head swam – from the electricity in the black eyes boring into hers, from her desire, her fear.

From her anger . . .

In ten seconds, it seemed, she'd filled the entire sheet. She dropped the paper on the floor. It floated like a pale leaf. The doctor ignored it.

'Now. Your father.'

Megan froze, shaking her head. 'Next time. Please.'

'No. Now.'

Her stomach muscles were hard as board. 'Well, I'm mad 'cause why doesn't he want to *see* me? He didn't even fight the custody agreement. I see him every two or three months.'

'Tell him.'

21

'I—'

'Tell him!'

She wrote. Forgetting grammar, spelling, she poured her thoughts out. When the sheet was half full her pen braked to a halt.

'What else is it, Megan? What aren't you telling me?'

'Nothing.'

'Oh, what do I hear?' he said. 'The passion's slipping. Something's wrong. You're holding back. Whispering bears. Something about that story. What?'

'I don't know.'

'Go into the place where it hurts the most. We go deep, remember. That's how I operate. I'm Super-Shrink.'

Crazy Megan can't take it any more. She just wants to curl up into a little crazy ball and disappear.

The doctor moved closer, pulling his chair beside her. Their knees touched. 'Come on. What is it?'

'No. I don't know what it is . . .'

'You want to tell me. You *need* to tell me.' He dropped to his knees, gripped her by the shoulders. 'Touch the most painful part. Touch it! Your father's read you the story. He comes to the last line. "Bears can't talk." He puts the book away. Then what happens?'

She sat forward, shivering, and stared at the floor. 'I go upstairs to pack.'

'Your mother's coming to pick you up.'

Eyes squinting closed painfully. 'She's here. I hear the car in the driveway.'

'She walks inside. You're upstairs and your parents are downstairs. They're talking?'

'Yeah. They're saying things I can't hear at first then I get closer. I sneak down to the landing.'

'You can hear them?'

22

'Yes.'

'What do they say?'

'I don't know. Stuff.'

'What do they *say*?' The doctor's voice filled the room. 'Tell me!'

'They were talking about a funeral.'

'Funeral? Whose?'

'I don't know. But there was something bad about it. Something really bad.'

'There's something else, isn't there, Megan? They say something else.'

'No!' she said desperately. 'Just the funeral.'

'Megan, tell me.'

'I . . .'

'Go on. Touch the place it hurts.'

'Tate said . . .' Megan felt faint. She struggled to control the tears. 'He called me . . . They were talking about me. And my daddy said . . .' She took deep gulps of air, which turned to fire in her lungs and throat. The doctor blinked in surprise as she screamed, 'My daddy shouted, "It would all've been different without *her*, without that damn inconvenient child up there. She ruined everything!"'

Megan lowered her head to her knees and wept. The doctor put his arm around her shoulders. She felt his hand stroke her head.

'And how did you feel when you heard him say that?' He brushed away the stream of her tears.

'I don't know. . . . I cried.'

'Did you want to run away?'

'I guess I did.'

'You wanted to show him, didn't you? If that's what he thinks of me I'll pay him back. I'll leave. That's what you thought, isn't it?'

Another nod.

'You wanted to go someplace where people weren't greedy, where people loved you, where people had children's books for you, where they read and talked to you.'

She sobbed into the wad of Kleenex he offered her.

'Tell him, Megan. Write it down. Get it out so you can look at it.'

She wrote until the tears grew so bad she couldn't see the page. Then she collapsed against the doctor's chest, sobbing.

'Good, Megan,' he announced. 'Very good.'

She gripped him tighter than she'd ever gripped a lover, pressing her head against his neck. For a moment neither of them moved. She was frozen here, embracing him fiercely, desperately. He stiffened and for a moment she believed that he was feeling the same sorrow she was. Megan started to back away so that she could see his kind face and his black eyes but he continued to hold her tightly, so hard that a sudden pain swept through her arm.

A surge of alarming warmth spread through her body. It was almost arousing.

Then they separated. Her smile faded as she saw in his face an odd look.

Of dreadful triumph. His eyes were cold, his smile cruel. He was suddenly a different person.

'What?' she asked. 'What's wrong?'

He said nothing.

She started to repeat herself but the words wouldn't come. Her tongue had grown heavy in her swollen mouth. It fell against her dry teeth. Her vision was crinkling. She tried once again to say something but couldn't.

She watched him stand and open a canvas bag that

was resting on the floor behind his desk. He put away a hypodermic syringe. He was pulling on latex gloves.

'What're you? . . .' she began, then noticed on her arm, where the pain radiated, a small dot of blood.

'No!' She begged him again to tell her what he was doing but the words vanished in comic mumbling. She tried to scream.

A whisper.

He walked to her and crouched, cradling her head, which sagged toward the couch.

Crazy Megan is beyond crazy. She loves him, she's terrified of him, she wants to kill him.

'Go to sleep,' he said in a voice kinder than her father's ever sounded. 'Go to sleep.'

Finally, from the drug, or from the fear, the room went black and she slumped into his arms.

3

One hundred and thirty years ago the Dead Reb had wandered through this field.

Maybe shuffling along the very path this tall, lean man now walked in the hot April rain.

Tate Collier looked over his shoulder and imagined that he saw the legendary ghost staring at him from a cluster of brush fifty yards away. Then he laughed to himself and, crunching through rain-wet corn husks and stalks – the waste from last year's harvest – he continued through the field, inspecting hairline fractures in an irrigation pipe that promised far more water than it had been delivering lately. It'd have to be replaced within the next week, he concluded, and wondered how much the work would cost.

Loping along awkwardly, somewhat stooped, Tate was in a Brooks Brothers pinstripe beneath a yellow sou'wester and outrageous galoshes, having come here straight from his strip mall law office in Fairfax, where he'd just spent an hour explaining to Mattie Howe that suing the Prince William *Advocate* for libel because the paper had accurately reported her drunk-driving arrest was a lawsuit doomed to failure. He'd booted her out good-naturedly and sped back to his two-hundred-acre farm.

He brushed at his unruly black hair, plastered around his face by the rain, and glanced at his watch. A half-hour until Bett and Megan arrived. Again, the uneasy twist of his stomach at the thought.

He glanced once more over his shoulder – toward where he'd seen the wisp of the ghostly soldier gazing at him from the cluster of vines and kudzu and loblolly. Tate returned to the damaged pipe, recalling what his grandfather – born Charles William Collier but known throughout northern Virginia as the Judge – had told him about the Dead Reb.

A young private in the bold experiment of the Confederacy took a musket ball between the eyes at the First Battle of Bull Run. By all laws of mercy and physiology he should have fallen dead by the picket line. But he'd simply dropped his musket, stood up and wandered southeast until he came to the huge woods that bordered the dusty town of Manassas. There he lived for six months, growing dark as a slave, sucking eggs and robbing cradles (the human victuals were legend only, the Judge appended in a verbal footnote). The Dead Reb was personally responsible for the cessation of all foot traffic after dusk through the Centreville woods that fall – until he was found, stark naked and dead indeed, sitting upright in what was the middle of Jackson's Corner, now a prime part of Tate Collier's farm.

Well, no ghosts here now, Tate reflected, only a hundred feet of pipe to be replaced . . .

Straightening up now, he wiped his watch crystal.

Twenty minutes till they were due.

Look, he told himself, relax.

Through the misty rain Tate could see, a mile away, the house he'd built eighteen years ago. It was a miniature Tara, complete with two Doric columns, and was white as a cloud, built in a style that he called John Deere Gothic. This was Tate's only real indulgence in life, paid for with some inheritance and the hope of money that a young prosecutor knows will be showered upon him for his brilliance and flair, despite the fact that a commonwealth's attorney's meager salary is a matter of public record. The six-bedroom house still groaned beneath a hearty mortgage.

When the Judge deeded over the fertile Piedmont land to Tate twenty years ago – skipping Tate's father for reasons never articulated though known to one and all of the Collier clan – the young man decided impulsively he wanted a family home (the Judge's residence wasn't on the farmland itself but was eight miles away in Fairfax). Tate kept a two-acre parcel fallow for one season and built on it the next. The house sat between the two barns – one new, one the original – in the middle of a rough grassy field, punctuated with patches of black-eyed Susans, hop clover and bluestem, a stand of bitternut hickory trees, a beautiful American beech, and eastern white pines.

The eerily balmy wind grabbed his rain slicker and shook hard. He closed two buckles of the coat and happened to be gazing toward the house when he saw a downstairs light go out.

So Megan had arrived. It had to be the girl; Bett didn't have keys to the house. No hope of cancellation now. Well, if you live three miles from a Civil War battlefield, you have to appreciate the persistence of the past.

He glanced once more at the fractured pipe and started toward the house, heavy boots slogging through the untilled fields.

Like the Dead Reb.

No, he reflected, nothing so dramatic. More like the introspective man of forty-four years that he'd become.

An enthymeme is an important rhetorical device used in formal debate.

It's a type of syllogism ('All cats see in the dark. Midnight is a cat. Therefore Midnight sees in the dark'), though the enthymeme is abbreviated. It leaves out one line of logic ('All cats see in the dark; therefore Midnight sees in the dark.'). Experienced debaters and trial lawyers like Tate Collier rely on this device frequently in their debates and courtroom arguments but it works only when there's a common understanding between the advocate and his audience. Everybody's got to understand that the animal in question is a cat; they have to supply the missing information in order for the logic to hold up.

Tate reflected now that he, his ex-wife and Megan had virtually none of this common understanding. The mind of Betty Susan McCall would be as alien to him as his was to her. Except for his ex-wife's startling reappearance seven weeks ago – with the news about Megan's drunken climb up the water tower – he hadn't seen her for nearly two years and their phone conversations were limited to practical issues about the girl and the few residual financial threads between people divorced fifteen years.

And as for Megan – how can anyone know a seventeen-year-old girl? Her mind was a moving target. Her only report on the therapy sessions was: 'Dad, therapy's for, like, losers. Okay?' And the Walkman headset went back on. He didn't expect her to be any more informative – or articulate – today.

As he approached the house he now noticed that *all* of the house lights had been shut off. But when he stepped out of the field he saw that neither Megan's nor Bett's car was in the drive.

He unlocked the door and walked into the house, which echoed with emptiness. He noticed Megan's house keys on the entryway table and dropped his own beside them, looking up the dim hallway. The only light in the cavernous space was from behind him, the bony light from outside, filtering through the entryway.

What's that noise?

He cocked his head. A wet sound, sticky, came from somewhere on the first floor. Repetitive, accompanied by a faint, hungry gasping.

The chill of fear stirred at his neck.

'Megan?'

The noise stopped momentarily. Then, with a guttural snap of breath, it resumed again. There was a desperation about the sound. Tate's stomach began to churn and his skin prickled with sweat.

And that smell . . . Something pungent and ripe.

Blood! he believed. Like the smell of hot rust. Blood and flesh.

'Megan!' he called again. Alarmed now, he walked further into the house.

The noise stopped though the smell was stronger, almost nauseating.

Tate thought of weapons. He had a pistol but it was locked away in the barn and there was no time to get it. He stepped forcefully into the den, seized a letter opener from the desk, flipped on the light.

And laughed out loud.

His two-year-old Dalmatian, her back to him, was flopped down on the floor, chewing intently. Tate set the opener on the bar and approached the dog. His smile faded. What *is* that? Tate squinted.

Suddenly, with a wild, raging snarl, the dog spun and lunged at him. He gasped in shock and leapt back, cracking his elbow on the corner of a table. Just as quickly the dog turned away from him, back to its trophy.

Tate circled the animal then stopped. Between the dog's bloody paws was a bone from which streamed bits of flesh. Tate stepped forward. The dog's head swivelled ominously. The animal's eyes gleamed with jealous hatred. A fierce growl rolled from her sleek throat and the black lips pulled back, revealing bloody teeth.

Jesus . . .

What *is* it? Tate wondered, queasy. Had the dog grabbed some animal that had gotten into the house? It was so badly mauled he couldn't tell what it had been.

'No,' Tate commanded. But the dog continued to defend its prize; a raspy growl rose from her throat.

'Come!'

The dog dropped her head and continued to chew, keeping her malevolent eyes turned sideways toward Tate. The crack of bone was loud.

'Come!'

No response.

Tate lost his temper and stepped around the dog, reaching for its collar. The animal leapt up in a frenzy, snapping at him, baring sharp teeth. Tate pulled back just in time to save his fingers.

He could see the bloody object. A beef knuckle bone. The kennel-owner from whom he'd bought the Dalmatian told him that bones were dangerous treats; he never bought them. He assumed Megan must have been shopping on her way here and picked one up. She sometimes brought chewsticks or rubber toys for the animal.

Tate made a strategic retreat, slipped into the hallway. He'd wait until the animal fell asleep tonight then throw the damn thing out.

He walked to the basement stairs, which led down to the recreation room Tate had built for the family parties and reunions he'd planned on hosting – people clustered around the pool table, lounging on the bar, drinking blender daiquiris and eating barbecued chicken. The parties and reunions never happened but Megan often disappeared down to the dark catacombs when she spent weekends here.

He descended the stairs and made a circuit of the small rooms. Nothing. He paused and cocked his head. From upstairs came the sound of the dog's growl once more. Urgent and ominous.

'Megan, is that you?' his baritone voice echoed powerfully.

He was angry. Megan and Bett were already twenty minutes late. Here he'd gone to the trouble of inviting them over, doing his fatherly duty, and this was what he got in return. . . .

The growling stopped abruptly. Tate listened for footsteps on the ground floor but heard nothing. He climbed the stairs and stepped out into the drizzle once more.

He made his way to the old barn, stepped inside and called Megan's name. No response. He looked around the spooky place in frustration, straightened a stack of old copies of *Wallace's Farmer*, which had fallen over, and glanced at the wall – at a greasy framed plaque containing a saying from Seaman Knapp, the turn-of-the-century civil servant who'd organized the country's agricultural extension services program. Tate's grandfather had copied the epigram, for inspirational purposes, in the same elegant, meticulous lettering with which he filled in the farm's ledgers and wrote legal memos for his secretary to type.

What a man hears, he may doubt. What he sees, he may possibly doubt. But what he does, he cannot doubt.

There you have it, Tate thought, stepping outside once again.

'Megan?' he called.

Then his eye fell on the old picnic bench and he thought of the funeral.

No, he told himself. Don't go thinking about *that*. The funeral was a thousand years ago. It's a memory deader than the Dead Reb and something you'll hate yourself for bringing up.

But of course think about it he did. Pictured it, felt it, tasted the memory. The funeral. The picnic bench, Japanese lanterns, Bett and three-year-old Megan . . .

A cluster of week-old Halloween candy lying in grass, a hot November day long ago. . . .

Until Bett had shown up at his door nearly two months ago with the news of Megan and the water tower he hadn't thought of that day for years.

What he does, he cannot doubt. . . .

The rain began in earnest once again and he hurried back to the house, climbed to the second floor.

'Megan?'

She wasn't there either.

He walked downstairs again. Reached for the phone.

He jumped a mile when, outside, a car door slammed.

Dr Peters – well, Dr Aaron Matthews – sped away from Tate Collier's farm in Megan's Ford Tempo. His hands shook and his breath came fast.

Two close calls.

He didn't know why Collier had returned home this

morning. He *always* kept Saturday hours at his office. Or had every Saturday for the last three months. Ten to four. Clockwork. But not today. When Matthews had driven to Collier's farm – with Megan in the trunk, no less – he'd found, to his shock, that the lawyer had returned. Fortunately he was heading out into the fields. When he was out of sight Matthews had parked in a cul-de-sac of brush beside Collier's driveway, fifty feet from the house, had snuck into the large colonial structure using Megan's keys. He'd tossed the Dalmatian a bone to keep it busy while he did what he'd come for.

He'd managed to escape to the Tempo just as Collier was returning. But as he started to pull out of the bushes into the long driveway Megan's mother's Volvo had streaked past. He braked quickly and she hadn't seen her daughter's car.

Nearly seen a second time! What was going on? Matthews had wondered. Why was *she* here? They couldn't have known what had happened to Megan. Not yet.

Still, it unnerved him. It was bad luck. And although he was a Harvard-trained psychotherapist and did not, professionally, accept the existence of luck, sometimes it took little more than a shadow of superstition like this to drop him into the cauldron of a Mood. Matthews was bipolar – the diagnosis that used to be called manic depression. In order for him to carry out the kidnapping he'd gone off his meds; he couldn't afford the dulling effects of the high doses of Prozac and Wellbutrin he'd been taking. Fortunately, once the medication had evaporated from his bloodstream he found himself in a manic phase and he'd easily been able to spend eighteen hours a day stalking the girl and working on his plan. But as the weeks had worn on he'd begun to worry that he was headed for a fall. And he knew from the past that it took very little to push him over the edge.

But the near miss with Collier and his wife faded now and he remained as buoyant as a happy child. He sped to I-66 and headed east – to the Vienna, Virginia, Metro lot, the huge station for commuters, fifteen miles west of D.C. It was Saturday morning but the lot was filled with the cars of people who'd taken the train downtown to visit the monuments and museums and galleries.

Matthews drove Megan's car to the spot where his gray Mercedes was parked then climbed out and looked around. He saw only one other occupied car – a white sedan, idling several rows away. He couldn't see the driver clearly but the man or woman didn't seem to be looking his way. Matthews quickly bundled Megan out of the Tempo's trunk and slipped her into the trunk of the Mercedes.

He looked down at the girl, curled fetally, unconscious, bound up with rope. She was very pale. He pressed a hand to her chest to make sure that she was still breathing regularly. He was concerned about her; Matthews was no longer licensed in Virginia and couldn't write prescriptions so to knock the girl out he'd stockpiled phenobarb from a veterinarian, claiming that one of his Rottweilers was having seizures. He'd mixed the drug with distilled water but couldn't be sure of the concentration. She was deeply asleep but it seemed that her respiration was fine and when he took her pulse her heart rate was acceptable.

Between the front seats of the Tempo he left the well-thumbed Amtrak timetable that Megan had used as a lap desk to write the letters to her parents and that now bore her fingerprints. He'd circled all the Saturday trains to New York. He'd been very careful – wearing gloves when he'd handled the timetable and the writing paper he'd stolen from Megan's room in Bett McCall's house. He'd spent hours in her room – when the mother was working and Megan was in school. It was there that he'd gotten important insights into her personality: the three Joplin posters, the black light, the Márquez book, notes she'd gotten from classmates laced with words like 'fuck' and 'shit'. (Matthews had written a paper for the APA *Journal* on how adolescents unconsciously raise and lower emotional barriers to their therapist according to the doctors' use of grammar and language; he'd observed, during the session that morning, how the expletives he'd used had opened her psyche like keys.)

He'd been careful to leave no evidence of his break-in at Bett McCall's. Or in Leesburg – where Dr Hanson's mother lived. That had been the biggest problem of his plan: getting Hanson out of the way for the week – without doing something as obvious, though appealing, as running him over with a car. He'd done some research on the therapist and learned that his mother lived in the small town northwest of D.C., Washington, and that she was frail. On Wednesday night Matthews had loosened the top step leading from her back porch to the small yard behind her house. Then he'd called, pretending to be a neighbor, and asked her to check on an injured dog in the back yard. She'd been disoriented and reluctant to go outside after dark but after five minutes he'd convinced her. She'd fallen straight down the stairs onto the sidewalk. The tumble looked serious and for a moment Matthews wondered if Hanson would have to cancel his appointments because of a funeral. But he waited until the paramedics arrived and noted that she'd merely broken bones.

Now, feeling confident, Matthews switched cars –

parking Megan's in the space his Mercedes had occupied – and then sped out of the parking lot.

He took his soul's pulse and found his mood intact. There was no paralysis, no anger, no sorrow dishing up the fishy delusions that had plagued him since he was young. The only hint of neurosis was understandable: Matthews found himself talking with Megan, repeating what he'd told her in the session and what she'd said to him. *Go deep* . . .

Finally, he turned the Mercedes on to the entrance ramp to I-66 and, doing exactly fifty-eight miles an hour, headed toward the distant mountains. Megan's new home.

4

The woman walked inside the house of which she'd been mistress for three years and paused in the gothic, arched hallway as if she'd never before seen the place.

'Bett,' Tate said.

She continued inside slowly, offering her ex-husband a formal smile. She paused again at the den door. The Dalmatian looked up, snarling.

'Oh, my, Tate . . .'

'Megan gave her a bone. She's a little protective about it. Let's go in here.'

He closed the den door and they walked into the living room.

'Did you talk to her?' he asked.

'Megan? No. Where is she? I didn't see her car.'

'She's been here. But she left. I don't know why.'

'She leave a note?'

'No. But her house keys're here.'

'Oh. Well.' Bett fell silent.

Tate crossed his arms and rocked on the carpet for a moment. He walked to the window, looked at the barn through the rain. Returned.

'Coffee?' he asked.

'No, thank you.'

Bett sat on the couch, crossed her thin legs, clad in tight

39

black jeans. She wore a black silky blouse and a complicated silver necklace of purple and black stones. She sat in silence for a few moments then rose and examined the elaborate fireplace Tate'd had built several years ago. She caressed the mortar and with a pale-pink fingernail picked at the stone. Her eyes squinted as she sighted down the mantelpiece. 'Nice,' she said. 'Fieldstone's expensive.'

She sat down again.

Tate examined her from across the room. With her long, pre-Raphaelite face and tangle of witchy red hair, Betty Susan McCall was exotic. Something Virginia rarely offered – an enigmatic Celtic beauty. The South is full of temptresses and lusty cowgirls and it has matriarchs galore but few sorceresses. Bett was a northern Virginia businesswoman now but beneath that façade Tate believed that she remained the enigmatic young woman he'd first seen singing a folk song in a smoky apartment on the outskirts of Charlottesville twenty-three years ago. She'd sung a whaling song *a capella* in a reedy, breathless voice.

It had, however, been many years since any woman had ensnared him that way and he now found himself feeling very wary. A dozen memories from the days when they were getting divorced surfaced murkily.

He wondered how he could keep his distance from her throughout this untidy family business.

Bett's eyes had disposed of the fireplace and the furniture in the living room and were checking out the wallpaper and molding. His eyes dogged after hers and he concluded that she found the place unhomely and stark. It needed more upholstered things, more pillows, more flowers, new curtains, livelier paint. He felt embarrassed.

After several minutes Bett said, 'Well, if her car's gone she probably just went out to get something.'

'That's probably it.'

Two hours later, no messages on either of their phones, Tate called the police.

The first thing Tate noticed was the way Konnie glanced at Bett.

With approval.

As if the lawyer had finally gotten his act together; no more dumb blondes for him. And it was damn well about time. This woman was in her early forties, very pretty. Smooth skin. She had quick eyes and seemed smart. Detective Dimitri Konstantinatis of the Fairfax County Police had commented once, 'Tate, why're all the women you date half your age and, lemme guess, a third your intelligence? If that. Why's that, Counselor?'

Konnie strode into the living room and stuck his hand out toward her. He shook the startled woman's vigorously as Tate introduced them. 'Bett, my ex-wife, this is Konnie. Konnie's an old friend from my prosecuting days.'

'Howdy.' Oh, the cop's disappointed face said, the ex. Giving *her* up was one bad mistake, mister. The detective glanced at Tate. 'So, Counselor, your daughter's up 'n' late for lunch, that right?'

'Been over two hours.'

'You're fretting too much, Tate.' He poked a finger at him and said to Bett, 'This fella? Was the sissiest prosecutor in the commonwealth. We had to walk him to his car at night.'

'At least I could *find* my car,' Tate shot back. One of the reasons Konnie loved Tate was that the lawyer joked about Konnie's drinking; he was now in recovery and hadn't had a drink in four years and not a single soul in the world except Tate Collier would dare poke fun at him about it. But what every other soul in the world didn't know was that what the cop respected most was balls.

Bett smiled uneasily.

Tate and Konnie had worked together frequently when Tate was a commonwealth's attorney. The somber detective had been taciturn and distant for the first six months of their professional relationship, never sharing a single personal fact. Then at midnight of the day a serial rapist-murderer they'd jointly convicted was 'paroled horizontal', as the death row parlance went, Konnie had drunkenly embraced Tate and said that the execution made them blood brothers. 'We're bonded.'

'Bonded? What kind of pinko, Robert Bly crap is that?' an equally drunken Tate had roared.

They'd been tight friends ever since.

Another knock on the front door.

'Maybe that's her,' Bett said eagerly. But when Tate opened it a crew-cut man in a cheap, slope-shouldered gray suit walked inside. He stood very straight and looked Tate in the eye. 'Mr Collier. I'm Detective Ted Beauridge. Fairfax County Police. I'm with Juvenile.'

Tate led him inside and introduced Beauridge to Bett while Konnie clicked the TV's channel selector. He seemed fascinated to find a TV that had no remote control.

Beauridge was polite and efficient but clearly he didn't want to be here. Konnie was the sole reason Megan's disappearance was getting any attention at all. When Tate had called, Konnie'd told him that it was too early for a missing person's report; twenty-four hours' disappearance was required unless the individual was under fifteen, mentally handicapped or endangered. Still,

42

Konnie had somehow accidentally forgotten to get his supervisor's okay and had run a tag check on Megan's car with other agencies for auto accidents. And he'd put in a request for Jane Doe admissions at all the area hospitals.

Tate ushered them into the living room. Bett asked, 'Would you like some coffee or . . . ?' Her voice faded and she laughed in embarrassment, looking at Tate, undoubtedly remembering that this had not been her house for a long, long time.

'Nothing, thanks, ma'am,' Beauridge said for them both.

In the time it had taken Konnie to arrive, Bett had called some friends of Megan's. She'd spent the night at Amy Walker's. Bett had called her first but no one had answered. She left a message on the Walkers' voice mail, then called some of her other friends. Brittany, Kelly and Donna hadn't seen Megan or heard from her today. They didn't know if she had plans except maybe showing up at the mall later. 'To, you know, like, hang out.'

Konnie asked Tate and Bett about the girl's Saturday routine.

'She normally has a therapy session Saturday morning,' Bett explained. 'At nine. But the doctor had to cancel today. His mother was sick or something.'

'Could she just've forgotten about coming here for lunch?'

'When we talked yesterday I reminded her about it.'

'Was she good about keeping appointments?' Beauridge asked.

Tate didn't know. She'd always shown up on time when he took her shopping or to dinner at the Ritz in Tysons. He told them this. Bett said that she was 'semi-good about being prompt'. But she didn't think the girl would miss this lunch. 'The three of us being together and all,' she added with a faint cryptic laugh.

'What about boyfriends?' Konnie asked.

'She didn't—' Tate began.

Then halted at Bett's glance. And he realized he didn't have a clue whether Megan had a boyfriend or not.

Bett continued, 'She did but they broke up last month.'

'*She* the one broke it off?'

'Yes.'

'So is he trouble, you think? This kid?' Konnie tugged at a jowl.

'I don't think so. He seemed very nice. Easy-going.'

So did Ted Bundy, Tate thought.

'What's his name?'

'Joshua LeFevre. He's a senior at George Mason.'

'He's in senior in *college*?' Tate asked.

'Well, yes,' she said.

'Bett, she's only seventeen. I mean—'

'Tate,' Bett said again. 'He was a nice boy. His mother's some executive at EDS, his father's stationed at the Pentagon. And Josh's a championship athlete. He's also head of the Black Students' Association.'

'The *what*?'

'Tate!'

'Well, I'm just surprised. I mean, it doesn't *matter*.'

Bett rolled her eyes.

'It doesn't,' Tate said defensively. 'I'm just—'

'—surprised,' Konnie offered wryly. 'Mr ACLU speaks.'

'You know his number?' Beauridge asked.

Bett didn't but she got it from directory assistance

and called. She apparently got one of his roommates. Joshua was out. She left a message for him to call when he returned.

'So. She's been here and gone. No sign of a struggle?' Konnie looked around the front hall.

'None.'

'What about the alarms?'

'I had them off.'

'There a panic button she could hit if somebody was inside waiting for her?'

'Yep. And she knows about it.'

Bett offered, 'She left the house keys here. She has her car keys with her.'

'Could somebody,' Konnie speculated, 'have stole her purse maybe, got the keys and broken in?'

Tate considered this. 'Maybe. But her license has Bett's address on it. How would a burglar know about this place? Maybe she had something with my address but I don't know what. Besides, nothing's missing that I could see.'

'Don't see much worth stealing,' Konnie said, looking at the paltry entertainment equipment. 'You know, Counselor, they got TVs nowadays bigger'n cereal boxes.'

Tate grunted.

'Okay,' Konnie said, 'how 'bout you show me her room?'

As Tate led him upstairs Beauridge's smooth drawl rolled, 'Sure you got nothing to worry about, Mrs Collier—'

'It's McCall.'

Upstairs, Tate let Konnie into Megan's room then wandered into his own. He'd missed something earlier when he'd made the rounds up here: his dresser drawer was open. He looked inside, frowned, then glanced

45

across the hall as the detective surveyed the girl's room. 'Something funny,' Tate called.

'Hold that thought,' Konnie answered. With surprisingly lithe movements for such a big man he dropped to his knees and went through what must have been the standard teenage hiding places: under desk drawers, beneath dressers, waste baskets, between mattresses, up under box springs, in curtains, pillows and comforters. 'Ah, whatta we got here?' Konnie straightened up and examined two sheets of paper.

He pointed to Megan's open dresser drawers and the closet. 'These're almost empty, these drawers. They normally got clothes in them?'

Tate hesitated, concern on his face. 'Yes, they're usually full.'

'Could you see if there's any luggage missing.'

'Luggage? No . . . Wait. Her old backpack's gone.' Tate considered this for a moment. Why would she take that? he wondered. Looking at the papers, Tate asked the detective, 'What'd you find?'

'Easy, Counselor,' Konnie said, folding up the sheets. 'Let's go downstairs.'

5

What would Sidney Poitier do?

Joshua LeFevre shifted his muscular, trapezoidal body in the skimpy seat of his Toyota and pressed down harder on the gas pedal. The tiny engine complained but slowly edged the car closer to the Mercedes.

Come on, Megan, what the hell're you up to?

He squinted again and leaned forward as if moving eight inches closer to the Merce were going to let him see more clearly through his confusion. He assumed the man, not Megan, was driving though he couldn't be sure. This gave him a sliver of comfort – for some reason the thought of this guy tossing Megan the keys to his big doctor's car and saying 'You drive, honey' riled the young man beyond words. Made him furious.

He nudged the car faster.

Sidney Poitier . . . What would you do?

LeFevre had seen *In the Heat of the Night* when he'd been ten. (On video, of course – when the film had originally come out, in the sixties, the man who would be his father was doing basic training pushups in Fort Dix and his to-be mother was listening to Smokey Robinson and Diana Ross while she worked on her 4.0 average at St Albans.) The film had affected him deeply. The Poitier character, Detective Tibbs, ended up stuck in the small

47

Southern town, butting horns with good-old-boy sheriff Rod Steiger. Moving slow, solving a local murder, step by step. . . . Not getting flustered, not getting pissed off in the face of all the crap everybody in town was giving him.

Sure, the movie didn't have real guts, it was *Hollywood's* idea of race relations, more softball than gritty, but even at age ten Joshua LeFevre understood the film wasn't really about black and white – it was about being a man and being persistent and not taking no when you believed yes.

It choked him up, that flick – the way those movies that give us our role models always do, whether it's the first time we see them or the hundredth.

Oh yes, Joshua Nathan LeFevre – an honors English major at George Mason University, a tall young man with his father's perfect physique and military bearing and with his mother's brains – had a sentimental side to him thick as a mountain. (The week students in his nineteenth-century lit seminar were picking apart a Henry James novel like crows, LeFevre had slunk back to his apartment with a very different book hidden in a brown paper bag. He'd locked his door and read the entire novel in one sitting, crying unashamedly when he came to the last page of *The Bridges of Madison County*.)

Sentimental, a romantic. And, accordingly, Sidney Poitier – rather than Wesley Snipes – appealed to him.

So, what would *Mister* Tibbs do now?

Okay, he was saying to himself, let's analyze it. Step by step. Here's a girl's got a bad home life. None of that talk-show abuse, no, but it's clearly a case of Daddy don't care and Momma don't care. So she drinks more than she ought and hangs with a bad crowd – until she meets LeFevre. And seems to get her act together though she falls off the normal wagon every once in a while. And then one night she climbs up to the top of a water tower (and why didn't she call me, dammit, instead of guzzling Comfort with Donna and Brittany, capital L losers, the Easy Sisters?). And once she's up there, the highest structure in Fairfax, she does a little dance on the scaffolding and the cops and fire department come to get her down.

And she goes to see this shrink . . .

Who tells her she's got to break up with him.

And so she does.

Why? LeFevre had asked her a few weeks ago, as they sat in his car, parked in front of her house on what turned out to be their very last date. '*Why?*'

It's not the differences . . . Meaning the age, meaning the race. It was . . . what the hell was it? He replayed Megan's little speech.

'It's just that I'm not ready for the same kind of relationship you want.'

And what kind is that? I don't remember proposing.

'Oh, Josh, honey, don't cry . . . I need to see things, do things. I feel, I don't know, all tied down or something . . . Living with Bett's like living with a roommate. You know, her date for Saturday's the biggest deal in the world. All she worries about is her skin getting old.'

Old skin? I like your mom. She's pretty, smart, off-beat. I don't get it. What's her skin got to do with breaking up? LeFevre had been very confused as he sat in the car beside the woman he loved.

'Oh, honey, I just need to get away. I want to travel, see things. You know.'

Travel? Where was *this* coming from? I've got a trust fund, Mom and Dad're loaded. I've lived in Jeddah, Cyprus, London and Germany. I speak three languages. I can show you more of the world than the Cunard Line.

'Okay What it is is this therapist. Dr Hanson? See, he thinks it's not a good idea for me to be in a relationship with you right now.'

Then, we'll back off a bit. See each other once a week or so. How's that?

'No, you don't *understand*,' Megan had said brutally, pulling away from him as he tried to take the Southern Comfort bottle out of her hand. And she'd climbed out of the passenger seat and run into her house. LeFevre now leaned over and sniffed the headrest to see if he could smell her perfume. Heartbreakingly, he couldn't.

He pushed the accelerator harder, edging up on the gray Mercedes.

'No, you don't understand.'

No, he hadn't.

Joshua LeFevre had waited a tormented three weeks, then – this morning – woke up on autopilot. He hadn't been able to take the suffocating frustration any more. He'd driven to Hanson's office around the time Megan's appointment would be over. He'd parked up the street, waiting for her to come out. Josh LeFevre could bench-press two hundred and twenty pounds, he could bicycle over a hundred and fifty miles a day. But he wasn't going for intimidation. Oh, no. He was going to Poitier the man, not Snipes him.

Why, he was going to ask the doctor, did you talk her into breaking up with me? Isn't that unethical? Let's talk about it together. The three of us. He had a dozen arguments all prepared. He believed he could talk his way back into her heart.

'No, you don't understand.'

But *now* he did.

God, I'm an idiot.

The doctor had her break up because he wanted to fuck her.

No psychobabble here. No inner child. Nope. The shrink wanted to play the two-backed beast with LeFevre's girlfriend. Simple as a shot in the head.

From where he'd been parked near the office he hadn't been able to see clearly but, suddenly, before the appointment was supposed to be over, Megan's Tempo was pulling out of the lot – with the shrink himself driving, it seemed, and heading north.

He'd followed the car to Manassas – to Megan's dad's farm – where LeFevre'd waited for about twenty minutes. Then, just when he'd been about to pull into the long drive the car had sped out again, and they'd driven to the Vienna Metro parking lot. They'd switched cars – taking his shrinkmobile – and headed west on 66.

What was it all about? Had she picked up some clothes from her father's? Was she going away for the weekend?

LeFevre was crazed. He had to do *something*.

But what would Sidney Poitier do? The script had changed.

Wait till they got to the doctor's house? The inn they were going to? Confront them there?

No, that didn't seem right.

Oh, hell, he should just go home. . . . Forget this crap. Be a man.

His foot eased up on the gas. . . . Good idea, get off at the next exit. Quit acting like a lovesick loser. It's embarrassing. Go home. Read your Melville. You've got a presentation due a week from Monday . . .

The Mercedes pulled ahead.

Oh, yeah, he thought, I'm going to deconstruct motifs

in some fucking story about a big-ass whale while my girlfriend's in bed whispering soft words into her therapist's ear?

He jammed his foot to the floor.

Would Poitier do this?

You bet.

And so LeFevre kept his sweating hands on the wheel of the car, straining forward, and sped after the woman whom he loved and, he believed somewhere in a portion of his sloppy heart, who loved him still.

'She's run away?' Bett whispered.

The four of them were in the living room, like strangers at a cocktail party, knees pointed at one another, sitting upright and waiting to become comfortable. Konnie continued, 'But y'all should consider that good news. The profile is most runaways come back on their own within a month.'

Bett stared out the window at the misty darkness. 'A month,' she announced, as if answering a trivia question. 'No, no. She wouldn't leave. Not without saying anything.'

Konnie glanced at Beauridge. Tate caught the look.

'I'm afraid she did say something.' Konnie handed Bett and Tate what he'd found upstairs. 'Letters to both of you. Under her pillow.'

'Why there?' Bett asked. 'That doesn't make any sense.'

'So you wouldn't find 'em right away,' Konnie explained. 'Give her a head start. I've seen it before.'

Beauridge asked, 'Is that her handwriting?'

Konnie added, 'There's a buddy of mine, FBI document examiner, Parker Kincaid. Lives in Fairfax. We could give him a call.'

But Bett said it was definitely Megan's writing.

'"Bett,"' she read aloud, then looked up. 'She called me Bett. Why would she do that?' She started again and read in a breathless, ghostly voice, '"Bett – I don't care if it hurts you to say this . . . I don't care how *much* it hurts . . ."'

She looked helplessly at her ex-husband then read to herself. She finished, sat back in the couch, and seemed to shrink to the size of a child herself. She whispered, 'She say she hates me. She hates all the time I spent with my sister. I . .' Mystified, hurt, she shook her head and fell silent.

Tate looked down at his note. It was stained. With tears? With rain? He read:

> Tate:
>
> *The only way to say it – I hate you for what you've done to me! You don't listen to me. You talk, talk and talk and Bett calls you the silver-tongued devil and you are but you never listen to me. To what I want. To who I am. You bribe me, you pay me off, and hope I'll go away. I should of run away when I was six like I wanted to. And never come back.*
>
> *I've wanted to do that all along. I still want to. Get away from you. It's what you want anyway, isn't it? To get rid of your inconvenient child?*

His mouth was open, his lips and tongue dry, stinging from the air that whipped in and out of his lungs. He found he was staring at Bett.

'Tate. You okay?' Konnie said.

'Could I see that again, Mrs McCall?' Beauridge asked.

She handed the stiff sheet over.

'You're sure that's her writing paper?'

Bett nodded. 'I gave it to her for Christmas.'

In a low voice Bett answered questions no one had asked. 'My sister was very sick. I left Megan in other people's care a lot. I didn't know she felt so abandoned . . . She never said anything.'

Tate noted Megan's careless handwriting. In several places the tip of the pen had ripped through the paper. In anger, he assumed.

Konnie asked Tate what he'd found in his own room.

It took him a minute to focus on the question. 'She took four hundred dollars from my bedside drawer.'

Bett blurted, 'Nonsense. She wouldn't take . . .'

'It's gone,' Tate said. 'She's the only one who's been here.'

'What about credit cards?' Konnie asked.

'She's on my Visa and MasterCard,' Bett said. 'She'd have them with her.'

'That's good,' Konnie offered. 'It's an easy way to trace runaways. What it is we'll set up a real-time link with the credit card companies. We'll know within ten minutes where she's charged something.'

Beauridge said, 'We'll put her on the runaway wire. She's picked up anywhere, for anything, on the Eastern Seaboard they'll let us know. Let me have a picture, will you?'

Tate realized that they were looking at him.

'Sure,' he said quickly, and began searching the room. He looked through the bookshelves, end-table drawers. He couldn't find any photos.

Beauridge watched Tate uncertainly; Tate guessed that the young officer's wallet and wall were peppered with snapshots of his own youngsters. Konnie himself, Tate remembered from some years ago, kept a picture of his ex-wife and kids in his wallet, tucked away behind his social security card. The lawyer rummaged in the living room and disappeared into the den. He returned some moments later with a snapshot – a photo of Tate and Megan at Virginia Beach two years ago. She stared unsmilingly at the camera. It was the only picture he could find.

'Pretty girl,' Beauridge said.

'Tate,' Konnie said, 'I'll stay on it. But there isn't a lot we can do.'

'Whatever, Konnie. You know it'll be appreciated.'

'Bye, Mrs Coll— McCall.'

But Bett was looking out the window and said nothing.

The white Toyota was staying right behind him. He wondered if it was the same auto he'd seen in the Vienna Metro lot when he was switching cars. He wished he'd paid more attention.

Aaron Matthews believed in coincidence even less than he believed in superstition. There were no accidents, no flukes. We are completely responsible for our behavior and its consequences even if we can't figure out what's motivating us to act.

The car behind him now was not a coincidence.

There was a motive, there was a design.

Matthews couldn't understand it yet. He didn't know how concerned to be. But he *was* concerned.

Maybe he'd cut the driver off and the man was mad. Road Rage.

Maybe it was someone who'd seen him heft a large bundle into the trunk of the Mercedes and was following out of curiosity.

Maybe it was the police.

He slowed to fifty.

The white car did too.

Sped up.

The car stayed with him.

Have to think about this. Have to do something.

Matthews slid into the right lane and continued through the mist toward the mountains in the west. He looked back as often as he looked forward.

As any good therapist will advise his patients to do.

6

The rain had stopped but the atmosphere was thick as hot blood.

In her stylish shoes with the wide, high heels, Bett McCall came to Tate's shoulder. Neither speaking, they stood on the back porch, looking over the back sixty.

The Collier spread was more conservative than most Piedmont farms: five fields rotating between soy one year and corn and rye the next.

'Listen to me, Tate,' the Judge would say.

The boy always did.

'What's a legume?'

'A pea.'

'Only a pea?'

'Well, beans too, I think.'

'Peas, beans, clover, alfalfa, vetches . . . they're all legumes. They help the soil. You plant year after year of cereals, what happens?'

'Don't know, sir.'

'Your soil goes to hell in a hand basket.'

'Why's that, Judge?'

The man had taught the boy never to be afraid to ask questions.

'Because legumes take nitrogen from the air. Cereals take it from the soil.'

'Oh.'

'We'll plant Mammoth Brown and Yellow for silage and Virginia soy too. Wilson and Haerlandts are good for seed and hay. How do you prepare the land?'

'Like you're planting corn,' the boy had responded. 'Sow them broadcast with a wheat drill.'

Out of the blue the Judge might glance at his grandson and ask, 'Do you cuss, Tate?'

'No, sir.'

'Here. Read this.' The man thrust into Tate's hand a withered old bulletin from the Virginia Department of Agriculture and Immigration. A circled chapter bemoaned the rise of young farmers' profanity. *Even some of our girls have taken to this deplorable habit.*

'I'll keep that in mind, Judge,' Tate had said, remembering without guilt how he'd sworn a blue streak at Junior Foote just last Thursday.

Gazing at his fields, the Judge had continued, 'But if you *do* find it necessary to let loose just make sure there're no womenfolk around. Almost time for supper. Let's get on home.'

Tate stayed at his grandparents' house in Fairfax as often as at his parents'. Tate's father was a kind, completely quiet man, best suited to a life as, say, a court reporter – a career he'd never dared pursue, of course, given the risk that he'd be assigned to transcribe one of his father's trials. The Judge had agonized over whether or not to leave the farm to his only son and had concluded the man just didn't have the mettle to handle a spread of this sort. So he deeded it over to Tate while the other kin got money. (Ironically, as Tate learned during one of the few frank conversations he'd ever had with his father, the man had been dreading the day that the Judge would hand over the farm to him.

His main concern seemed to be that running the farm would interfere with his passion of collecting Lionel electric trains.) Tate's timid, ever-tired mother suited her husband perfectly and Tate could remember not a single word of dissension, or passion, between the two. Little conversation either.

Which is why, given his druthers, young Tate would hitch or beg a ride to his grandparents' house and spend as much time as he could with them.

As the Judge presided at the head of the groaning board table on Sunday afternoons Tate's grandmother might offer in a whisper, 'The only day to plant beans is Good Friday.'

'That's a superstition, Grams,' young Tate had said to her, a woman so benign that she took any conversation directed toward her, even in disagreement, as a compliment. 'You can plant soy all the way through June.'

'No, young man. Now listen to me.' She'd looked toward the head of the table, to make sure her husband wasn't listening. 'If you laugh loud while planting corn it's trouble. I mean, serious trouble. And it's good to plant potatoes and onions in the dark of the moon and you better plant beans and corn in the light.'

'That doesn't make any sense, Grams.'

'Does,' she'd responded. 'Root crops grow below ground so you plant them in the dark of the moon. Cereals are above ground so you plant in the light.'

Tate admitted there was a certain logic there.

This was one of three or four simultaneous discussions going on around the dinner table – aunts and uncles and cousins, as well as the inevitable guest or two that the Judge would invite from the ranks of the bench and bar in Prince William and Fairfax counties. One crisp, clear Sunday, young Tate shared an iced tea with one guest who'd arrived early while the Judge was *en route* from the farm. The slim, soft-spoken visitor showed a great interest in Tate's ant farm; it wasn't until a dozen years later that Tate realized the visitor was Supreme Court Justice William Brennan and that he'd probably taken a break from penning his opinion in a decision – maybe a landmark like *Roe v. Wade* – to come to Judge Collier's farm for roast beef, yams and collard greens.

'And,' Grams would continue, scanning the table for the sin of empty serving bowls, 'it's also bad luck to slaughter hogs in the dark of the moon.'

'Sure is for the hogs,' Tate had offered.

The dinner would continue until four or five in the afternoon, Tate sitting and listening to legal war stories and planning and zoning battles and local gossip thick as Grams's mashed potatos.

Now, because his ex-wife stood beside him, gazing out over the acres his grandfather had so lovingly and uncompromisingly nurtured, Tate was keenly aware that those Norman Rockwell times, which he'd hoped to duplicate in his own life, had never materialized.

The vestige of a familial South for Tate hadn't survived long into his adulthood. He, Bett and Megan were no longer a family. Among the multitude of pretty and smart and well-rounded women he'd dated Tate Collier hadn't found a single chance for family.

And so, as concerned as he now was about Megan, the return of these two into his life was fraught with pain.

It brought practical problems too. He was preparing for the biggest case he'd had in years. A corporation was petitioning Prince William County for permission to construct an historical theme park near the Bull Run Battlefield. Liberty Park was going to take on King's Dominion. Tate was representing a group of residents who didn't want the development in their back yard even though the county had granted tentative approval. Last week Tate had won a temporary injunction halting the development for ninety days, which the developer immediately challenged. Next week, on Thursday, the Supreme Court in Richmond would hear the argument and rule whether or not to let the injunction stand. If it did, the delay alone might be enough to put the kibosh on the whole deal.

Overnight Tate Collier had become the most popular – and unpopular – person in Prince William County, depending on whether you opposed or supported the project. The developer of the park and the lenders funding it wanted him to curl up and blow away, of course. But there were hundreds of local businessmen, craftsmen, suppliers and residents who also stood to gain by the park's approval and the ensuing migration of tourists. One editorial, lauding the project, called Tate 'the devil's advocate'. A phrase that certainly resonated in this fervent outpost of the Christian South.

Liberty Park's developer, Jack Sharpe, was one of the richest men in northern Virginia. He came from old money and could trace his Prince William ancestry back to pre-Civil War days. When Tate had brought the action for the injunction Sharpe had hired a well-known local firm to defend. Tate had chopped Sharpe's lawyers into little pieces – hardly even sporting – and the developer had fired them. For the argument in Richmond he'd gone straight to Washington, D.C., to hire a law firm that included two former attorneys general, one former vice-president, and, possibly, a future president.

Tate and Ruth, his secretary/assistant/paralegal, had been working nonstop on the argument and papers for

61

a week, and would continue to do so until, probably, midnight of the day before the argument.

So Bett's reappearance in his life – and Megan's disappearance from it – might have some serious professional repercussions.

Queasy, he thought again of that day when he and Bett had fought so bitterly – fifteen years ago. He thought of the note Megan had written.

That inconvenient child up there . . .

Why had fate brought them back into his life? Why now?

But however he wished otherwise, they *were* back. And there was nothing he could do about it.

Finally Tate asked his ex-wife, 'Think we should call my mother?'

'No,' Bett said. 'Let's give it a few days. I don't want to upset her unnecessarily.'

'What about your sister?'

'Definitely not her.'

'Why not?' Tate wondered aloud. He knew Susan cared very much for Megan. More than most aunts would for a niece. In fact she'd always seemed almost jealous that Bett had a daughter and she didn't.

'Because we don't have any answers yet,' Bett responded. Then, after a few moments, she sighed. 'This isn't like her.' She glanced at the letter in her hand. Then shoved it deep into her purse.

Tate studied his wife's face. Tate Collier had inherited several talents from the Judge. The main gift was, of course, a way with words, and the other, far rarer, was the ability to see the future in someone's face. Now he looked into his ex-wife's remarkable violet eyes, saw them narrow, alight on his and move on, and he knew exactly what was going through her mind. Debate is not just about words, debate is about intuition too. The advocate who can see exactly where his adversary is headed will always have an advantage, whatever rhetorical flourishes the opponent has in his repertoire.

He didn't like what he now saw.

Bett stepped determinedly off the porch and into the back yard, toward the west barn, where her car was parked. He followed and paused on the shaggy lawn, which was badly in need of a mowing. He stared intently at the white streak of the energetic Dalmatian, which had finally forsaken the bone and was zipping through the grass like a greyhound.

Tate glanced at the old barn, alien and yet very familiar. Then his eyes fell on the picnic bench that he and Bett had bought at one of the furniture stores along Route 28. They'd used it only once – for the gathering after the funeral fifteen years ago. He remembered the events with perfect clarity now. It seemed like last week.

He saw Bett looking at the bench too. Wondered what she was thinking.

That had been an unseasonably warm November – just as odd as this April's oppressive heat. He pictured Bett standing on the bench to unhook a Japanese lantern from the dogwood after the last of the guests had left or gone to bed.

Today, Tate paused beside the tree, which was in its expansive, pink bloom.

'Are you busy now?' she asked. 'Your practice?'

'Lot of little things. Only one big case.' He nodded at the house where a paralyzing stack of documents for the Liberty Park argument rested. When they were married the house had been lousy with red-backed legal

63

briefs, forty or fifty pages long. *The Supreme Court of the Commonwealth of Virginia.* Many of them were for death penalty cases Tate was prosecuting. Although he'd been the Fairfax County commonwealth's attorney Tate had often argued down in Richmond on behalf of other counties. 'Have voice, will travel,' his staff had joked. His specialty had become special circumstance murder cases – the euphemism for capital punishment cases.

Bett didn't approve; she was opposed to the death penalty.

Death, Tate reflected, always seemed to lurk behind their relationship. Her sister Susan's continual battle with serious heart disease, and the suicide of Susan's husband, Harris. Then the death of Bett's parents and Tate's father and grandfather, all in the tragically short period of three years.

Tate kicked at piles of corn stalks.

'It's a feeling.' Bett's hands lifted and dropped to her sides. 'Do you understand what I mean?'

No. He didn't. Tate was dogged and smart, but feelings? No, sir. Didn't trust them for a minute. He saw how they got the people he'd prosecuted into deep, deep trouble. When they'd been married Bett lived on feelings. Intuition, sensations, impressions. And sometimes, it seemed, messages from the stars. Drove him crazy.

'Keep going,' he said.

She shrugged. 'I don't believe this.' She tapped her purse. Meaning the letter, he supposed.

'Why do you think that?'

'I was remembering something.'

'Hmm?' he offered noncommittally.

'I found a bag under Megan's bed at home. When

I was cleaning last week. There was a soap dish in it.'

He noticed the tears. He wanted to step close. Tried to remember the last time he'd held her. Not just bussed cheeks but actually put his arms around her, felt her narrow shoulder blade beneath his large hands. No memory came to mind.

'It was a joke between us. I never had a dish in my bathroom. The soap got all yucky, Megan said. So she bought this Victorian soap dish. It was for my birthday. Next week. There was a card too. I mean, she wouldn't buy me a present and a card and then do this.'

Wouldn't she? Tate wondered. Why not? When the pressure builds up the volcano blows – whatever the season, whoever's picnicking on the slopes, trysters or churchgoers. Any lawyer who's done domestic relations work will testify to that.

'You think someone *made* her do this? Or that it's a prank?' Tate asked.

'I don't know. She might've been drinking again. I checked the bottles at home and they didn't look emptier but . . . I don't know.'

'That's not much to go on,' her ex-husband said.

Suddenly she turned to him and spoke. 'It's not a hundred percent thing we've got, Megan and me. There're problems. Of course there are. But our relationship deserves more than that damn letter. More than her running out. . . .' She crossed her arms, gazed into the fields again. She repeated, 'Something's wrong.'

'But what? Exactly? What do you think?'

'I don't *know.*'

'Well, what should we do?'

'I want to go look for her,' Bett said determinedly. 'I want to find her.'

Which is exactly what he'd seen in her purple eyes. What he'd known was coming.

Yet now that he thought about it he was surprised. This didn't sound like Bett McCall at all. Bett the dreamer, Bett the tarot card consulter. Passive, she'd always floated where the breezes took her. Forrest Gump's feather . . . The least likely person imaginable to be a mother. Children needed guidance, direction, models. That wasn't Bett McCall. When he'd heard from Megan that Bett had become engaged last Christmas Tate was surprised only that it had taken her so long to accept what must have been her dozenth proposal since they'd divorced. When they'd been married she'd been charming and flighty and wholly ungrounded, relying on him to provide the foundation she needed. He'd assumed that once they'd split up she'd find someone again quickly.

He wondered if he was standing next to a different Betty Susan McCall than the one he'd been married to (and wondered too if *she* was thinking the same about him).

'Bett,' he said to reassure her, and himself, 'she's fine. She's a mature young woman. She vented some steam and's going out on her own for a few days. I did it myself when I was about her age. Remember?' He doubted that she did but, surprising him, she said, 'You made it all the way to Baltimore.'

'And I called the Judge and he came to get me. A two-day runaway. Look, Megan's had a lot to deal with. I think the soap dish is the key.'

'The dish?'

'You're right – nobody'd buy a present and a card and then not give them to you. She'll be back for your birthday. And know what else?'

'What?'

'There's a positive side to this. She's brought up some things that we can talk about. That *ought* to be talked about.' He too nodded – toward the house, where *his* letter rested like a bloody knife.

Logic. Who could argue with it?

But Bett wasn't convinced.

'There's something else I have to tell you.' She chewed on her narrow lower lip as he'd remembered her doing whenever she'd been troubled. She gripped the porch banister and lowered her head.

Tate Collier, intercollegiate debate champion, national moot court winner, and expert forensic orator, recognized the body language of a confession when he saw one.

'Go ahead,' he said.

'The night before the water tower thing – I was . . . out.'

'Out?'

She sighed. 'I mean, I didn't get home. I was at Brad's in Baltimore. I didn't plan on it; I just fell asleep. Megan was really upset I hadn't called.'

'You apologized?'

'Of course.'

'Well, it was one of those things. An accident. She'd know that.'

Bett shook her head, dismissingly. 'I think maybe that's what started her drinking before she climbed up the tower. And she doesn't like Brad much.'

The girl had described Bett's fiancé as a dweeb who parted his hair too carefully, probably wore sweaters with reindeer on them and spent too much time in front of the TV. Tate didn't share these observation with Bett now.

'Always takes a little while to get used to step-parents. I see it all the time in my practice.'

67

'I held off going over to his place for a while after that. But last night I went there again. I asked her if she minded and she said she didn't. I dropped her at Amy's on my way to Baltimore.'

'So, there.' Tate smiled and caught her eye as she glanced his way.

'What?'

He lifted his palms. 'The worst is it's a little payback. She's over at somebody's house, going to let us sweat a bit.'

So, no need to worry.

You go your way and I'll go mine.

'That may be,' she said, 'But I'll never forgive myself if something happened to her.'

Tate's phone buzzed. He answered it.

'Counselor,' Konnie's gruff voice barked.

'Konnie, what's up?'

'Got good news.'

'You found her?'

Bett's head swivelled.

The detective said, 'She's on her way to New York.'

'How do you know?' Tate asked.

'I put out a DMV notice and a patrol found her car at the Vienna Metro station. On the front seat was an Amtrak schedule. She'd circled Saturday trains to Penn Station. Manhattan. You know anybody up there'd she'd go to visit?'

Tate told this to Bett, who took the news cautiously. He asked about where she might be going.

She shook her head. 'I don't think she knows a soul up there.'

Tate relayed the answer to Konnie.

'Okay, well, at least you know where she's going. I'll call NYPD and have somebody meet the trains and ask around the station. I'll send 'em her picture.'

'Okay. Thanks, Konnie.' He hung up. Looked at his ex-wife. 'Well,' he said. 'That's that.'

But the violet eyes were disagreeing.

'What, Bett?' he asked.

'I'm sorry, Tate. I just don't buy it.'

'What?'

'Her going off to New York.'

'But *why*? You haven't told me anything specific.'

Her palms slapped her hips. 'Well, I don't *have* anything specific. You want evidence, you want proof. I don't have any.' She sighed. 'I'm not like you.'

'Like me?'

'I can't *convince* you. I don't have a way with words. So I'm not even going to try.'

He started to say something more, to cinch his argument. But something she'd said stopped him. He recalled what the Judge had told him after Tate had finished an argument before the Supreme Court in Richmond in a death penalty case, which he later won. His grandfather had been in the audience, proud as a pup that his offspring was handling the case. Later, over whiskies at the ornate Jefferson hotel in Richmond, the somber old man had said, 'Tate, that was wonderful, absolutely wonderful. They'll rule for you. I saw it in their eyes.'

I did too, he'd thought, wondering what else the Judge had in mind. The old man's eyes were dim.

'But I want you to understand something.'

'Okay,' the young man said.

'You've got it in you to be the most manipulative person on earth.'

'What's that?'

'If you were greedy you could be a Rockefeller.

69

If you were evil you could be a Hitler. You can talk your way into somebody's heart and get them to do whatever you want. Judge or jury, you've got that skill. Words, Tate. Words. You can't see them but they're the most dangerous weapons on earth. Remember that. Be careful, son.'

'Sure, sir,' Tate had said, paying no attention to the old man's advice, wondering if the court's decision would be unanimous. It was.

What he does, he cannot doubt.

Bett gazed at him and in a soft voice – sympathetic, almost pitying – she said, 'Tate, don't worry about it. It's not your problem. You go back to your practice. I can handle it.'

She fished in her purse, pulled out her car keys.

He watched her walk away. Then called, 'Come on in here. Please.' She hesitated then followed as he wandered into the barn, the original one – built in the 1920s. It was a grimy place, filled with as much junk as farm tools. He'd played here as a boy, had a ream of memories: horses' tails twitching with muscular jerks on hot summer afternoons, sparks flying as the Judge edged an axe on the old grinding wheel. He'd tried his first cigarette here. And learned much about the world from the moldy stacks of *National Geographic*'s. He also got his first glimpse of naked women – in the *Playboys* the sharecroppers had stashed here.

He slipped off his suit jacket, hanging it up on a pink, padded coat hanger. What was it doing here? he wondered A former girlfriend, he believed, had left it after they'd taken a trip to the Caribbean.

Bett stood near him, holding on to a beam that powder-post beetles had riddled.

Tate rummaged through a box. Bett watched, remained silent.

He didn't find what he was looking for in one box and turned to another. He glanced up at her then continued to rummage. He finally found the old beat-up leather jacket. He pulled it on, took off his tie and unbuttoned the top button of his dress shirt.

Then he righted a battered old cobbler's bench, dropped down on to it and took off his Oxford wingtips and then his socks. He massaged his feet.

His eyes fell again on the picnic bench, visible just outside the door. Thinking again of the night of the funeral. Megan in bed. Bett, unhooking the Japanese lantern, the November night still oddly balmy. She seemed to float like a ghost in the dim air above the bench. He'd come up next to her. Startled her by saying, 'I have something to tell you.'

Now he shoved that hard memory away and pulled on work socks and his comfortable boots.

She looked at him in confusion, shook her head. 'What're you doing?'

'You did it after all,' he said with a faint laugh.

'What?'

'You convinced me.' He laced the boots up tight. 'I think you're right. Something happened to her. And we're going to find out what. You and me.'

II

The Inconvenient Child

7

The rain had started up again.

They were inside now, sitting at the old dining-room table, dark oak and pitted with wormholes.

Tate poured wine, offered it to Bett.

She took the glass, cradled it between both hands the way he remembered her doing when they'd been married. In their first year of marriage, because he was a poor young prosecutor and Bett hadn't yet found her career they couldn't afford to go out to dinner often. But at least once a week they'd try to have lunch at a nice restaurant. They always ordered wine.

She sipped from the glass, set it on the table and watched the sheets of rain roll across the brown fields.

'What do we do, Tate?' she asked. 'Where do we start?'

Prosecutors know as much about police investigations as cops do. But those gears in Tate's mind hadn't been used for a long time. He shrugged. 'I don't know . . . Let's start with her therapist. Maybe she said something about running away, about where she'd go. What's his name?' Tate felt he should have remembered.

'Hanson,' Bett said. She looked up the number in her book and dialed it. 'It's his service,' she whispered to Tate. 'What's your cell number?'

She gave the doctor's answering service both of their mobile numbers and asked him to return the call. She said it was urgent.

'Try that friend again,' Tate suggested. 'Amy. Where she spent the night.' He tried to picture Amy. He'd met her once. He'd counted nine earrings in the girl's left ear but only eight in her right. He'd wondered if the disparity had been intentional or if she'd merely miscounted.

He thought again about her boyfriend. Well, she *was* seventeen. Why shouldn't she go out? But with a college *senior*? Tate's prosecutorial mind thought back to the Virginia provisions on statutory rape.

Bett shifted and cocked the phone closer to her ear. Apparently someone was now home.

'Amy? It's Megan's mother. Honey, we're trying to find her. She didn't show up for lunch. You know where she went this morning after she left you and your mom's?'

Bett nodded as she listened and then asked if Megan had been upset about anything. Her face was grim.

Tate was half listening but mostly he was studying Bett. The tangles of auburn hair, the striking face, the prominent neck bones, the complexion of a woman who looked ten years younger than her age. He tried to remember the last time he'd seen her. Maybe it was Megan's sweet sixteen party. An odd evening . . . For a fleeting moment as he stood beside the girl and her mother, delivering what everyone declared to be a brilliant toast, he'd had a sense of them as a family. He and Bett had shared a momentary smile. Which faded fast, and they'd stepped out of the spotlight and returned to their separate lives. When he'd seen her after that, Tate couldn't remember.

He thought: She's less pretty now but more beautiful.

More confident, more assured, her sunset-sky eyes were narrowed and not flitting around – coy and ethereal – the way they'd habitually done fifteen years ago.

Maybe it's maturity, Tate reflected. And he wondered again what her impression of *him* might be.

Bett put her hand over the receiver and said, 'Amy said Megan left about nine-thirty this morning and wouldn't tell her where she was going. She said she was secretive about it. She left her bookbag there. I thought it might have something in it that'd give us a clue where she went. I said we'd be by to pick it up later.'

'Good.'

Bett listened to Amy again. She frowned in concern. 'Tate . . . She said that Megan told her somebody'd been following her.'

'Following? Who?'

'She doesn't know.'

Okay, hard evidence. The latent prosecutor in Tate Collier awakened a bit more. 'Let me talk to her.'

Tate took the phone. 'Amy? This is Megan's father.'

A pause. 'Um, hi. Is Megan, like, okay?'

'We hope so. We just want to find out where she is. What's this about somebody following her?'

'She was, like, pretty freaked. I mean, her and me, we were sitting around watching this movie, I don't know, on Wednesday, I guess, and it was about a stalker and she goes, "I don't want to watch this." And I'm like, "Why not?" And she's like, "There's this car with some older guy in it and I think he's been following me around." And I go, "No way." But she's like, "Yeah, really."'

'Where?' Tate asked.

'Around the school, I think,' Amy said.

'Any description?'

'Of the guy?'

'Or the car.'

'Naw. She didn't tell me. But I'm like, "Right, somebody following you . . ." And she's like, "I'm not bullsh— I'm not fooling." And she goes, "It was there yesterday. By the field."'

'What field?'

'The sports field behind the school,' Amy answered.

'That was this last Tuesday?'

'Um, yeah.'

'Did you believe her?'

'I guess. She looked pretty freaked. And she says she told some people about it.'

'Who?'

'I don't know. Some guys. She didn't tell me who. Oh, and she told Mr Eckhard too. He's an English teacher at the middle school but he coaches volleyball after school and on the weekends. And he said if he saw it he'd go talk to the driver. And I'm like, 'Wow. This is totally fuck—totally weird.'''

'His name's Eckhard?'

'Something like that. I don't know how to spell it. But if you want to, like, talk to him there's usually volleyball practice on Saturday afternoon, only I don't know when. Volleyball's for losers, you know.'

'Yeah, I know,' Tate said. It had been the only sport he'd played in college.

'You think something, like, happened to her? That's way lame.'

'We'd just feel a little better knowing where she is. Listen, Amy, we'll be around to pick up her bookbag in the next couple of hours. If you hear from her give us a call.'

'I will.'

'Promise?' he asked firmly.

'Yeah, like, I promise.'

As soon as Tate pushed the End button on Bett's phone it buzzed again. He glanced at her and she nodded for him to answer it. He pushed Receive.

'Hello?'

'Um, is this Megan's father?' a man's voice asked.

'That's right.'

'Mr McCall . . .'

'Actually it's Collier.'

'That's right. Sure. Sorry. This is Dr Hanson.'

'Doctor, thanks for calling. . . . I have to tell you, it looks like Megan's run away.'

There was a pause. 'Really?'

Tate tried to read the tone. He heard concern and surprise.

'We got some . . . well, some pretty angry letters from her. Her mother and I both did. And then she vanished. Is there any way we can see you?'

'I'm in Leesburg now. My mother's had an accident.'

'I'm sorry to hear that. But if Bett and I drove up could you spare a half-hour?'

'Well . . .'

'It's important, Doctor. We're really pretty concerned about her.'

'I suppose so. All right.' He gave them directions to the hospital.

Tate looked at his watch. It was noon. 'We'll be there in an hour or so.'

'Actually,' Hanson said slowly, 'I think we *should* talk. There *were* some things she told me that you ought to know.'

'What?' Tate asked.

'I want to think about them a little more. There are

some confidentiality issues . . . But it's funny – I'd expect any number of things from Megan, but running away? No, that seems odd to me.'

Tate thanked him. It was only after hanging up that he felt a disturbing twist in his belly. What were the any number of things Megan was capable of? And were they any worse than her running away?

His precious cargo was in the trunk. But while Aaron Matthews would have liked to meditate on Megan McCall and on what lay ahead for both of them he instead was growing increasingly anxious.

The fucking white car.

He was cruising down Route 66. He'd planned to stop at the house he'd rented last year in Prince William County – only two or three miles from Tate Collier's farm – and pick up some things he wanted to take with him to the mountains.

But he couldn't risk leading anyone to his house and this car was just not going away.

It was raining again, a gray drizzle. In the mist and rain, he couldn't see the driver clearly though he was now certain he was young and black.

And because he followed Matthews so carelessly and obviously he sure wasn't a cop.

But who?

Then Matthews remembered: Megan had a black boyfriend. Josh or Joshua, wasn't it? The boy that Dr Hanson had suggested she leave – if Megan had been telling the truth about that bit of advice, which he suspected she might not have been.

Who was this guy?

As a scientist of the mind Matthews believed in logic. The only time people acted illogically was when they were having seizures, he believed. We might not be able to *perceive* the logic they operated by. It might be illogical to rational observers but that was only because they were not being empathetic. *Once we climb into the minds of our patients,* he wrote in his well-received essay on delusional behavior in bipolars, *once we understand their fears and desires – their own internal system of logic – then we can begin to understand their motives, the reasons behind their actions, and we can help them change . . .*

What was this young man thinking?

Maybe Megan had planned to meet him at the office after the appointment. Maybe he'd just happened to see her car, being driven by a man he didn't recognize, and followed it.

Or maybe – this accorded with Matthews's perceptions on the frightening pathology of love – he'd been waiting at the office to confront the doctor about the break-up. Maybe even attack him.

Thanks for that, Hanson, he thought acerbically. Should have broken *your* hip, not Mom's . . . Rage shook him for a moment. Then he calmed.

Did the boy have a car phone? Had he called the police and reported the Mercedes's license number? It was a stolen plate but it didn't belong to a gray Mercedes and that would be reason enough for the cops to pull him over and look in the trunk.

But no, of course, he hadn't called the cops. They'd be after him by now if he had.

But what if he'd called her *parents*? What did Tate Collier know? Matthews brooded. What was the man thinking? What was he planning to *do*?

Matthews sped on until became to a rest stop then he pulled suddenly into the long driveway, weaving slowly through the trailer tractors and four-by-fours filled with vacationers. He noticed that the white Toyota had made a panicked exit and was pulling into the rest stop after him. Fortunately the rain was heavy again. Which gave Matthews the excuse to hold an obscuring *Washington Post* over his head as he ran to the shelter.

8

They were trotting through the rain to Tate's black Lexus when his cell phone buzzed.

As they dropped into the front seats he answered. 'Hello?'

'Tate Collier, please.' A man's voice.

'Speaking.'

'Mr Collier, I'm special agent William McComb, with the FBI's Child Exploitation and Kidnapping Unit. We've just received an inter-agency notice about your daughter.'

'I'm glad you called.'

'I'm sorry about your girl,' the agent said, speaking in the chunky monotone Tate knew so well from working with the feds. 'Unfortunately, I have to say, sir, based on the facts we've got, there's not a lot we can do. But you made some friends here when you were a commonwealth's attorney and so we're going to open a file and put her name out on our network. There'll be a lot more eyes looking for her.'

'Anything you can do will really be appreciated. My wife and I are pretty upset.'

'I can imagine,' the agent said, registering a splinter of emotion. 'Could you give me some basics about her and the disappearance?'

Tate ran through the physical details, Bett helping on

the specifics. Blonde, blue eyes, five six, a hundred twenty-eight pounds, age seventeen. Then about the letters. Tate asked, 'You heard about her car?'

'Um, no, sir.'

'The Fairfax County police found it at Vienna Metro. It looks like she went to Manhattan.'

'Really? No, I didn't hear that. Well, we'll tell our office in New York about it . . . But do I hear something in your voice, sir? Are you thinking that maybe she *didn't* run away? Are you thinking there was some foul play?'

Tate had to smile. He'd never thought of himself – especially his speech – as transparent. 'As a matter of fact, we've been having some doubts.'

'Interesting.' McComb said in a wooden monotone. 'What specific elements lead you to believe that?'

'A few things. Megan's mother and I are on our way to Leesburg right now to talk to her therapist. See what he can tell us.'

'He's in Leesburg?'

'His mother's in St Mary's hospital. She had an accident.'

'And you think he might be able to tell you something?'

'He said he wanted to talk to us. I don't know what he's got in mind.'

'Any other thoughts?'

'Well, Megan told her girlfriend that there was a car following her over the past few weeks.'

'Car, hm? They get any description?'

'Her girlfriend didn't. But we think a teacher did. Eckhard's his name. Something like that. He's supposed to be at the school later, coaching volleyball. But I'd guess that's only if the rain breaks up.'

'And what's her friend's name?'

He gave the agent Amy Walker's name. 'We're going to talk to her too. And pick up Megan's bookbag from her. We're hoping it might have something in it that'll give us a clue where she's gone.'

'I see. Does Megan have any siblings?'

'No.'

'Is there anyone else who's had much contact with the girl?'

'Well, my wife's fiancé.'

Silence for a moment. 'Oh, you're divorced.'

'That's right. Forgot to mention it.'

'You have his name and number?' McComb asked.

Tate asked Bett, who gave him the information. Into the phone he said, 'His name's Brad Markham. He lives in Baltimore.' Tate gave him Brad's phone number as well.

'Do you think he was in any way involved?' the agent asked Tate.

'I've never met him, but, no, I'm sure not.'

'Okay. You working with anyone particular at the Fairfax County Police?'

'Konnie . . . That'd be Dimitri Konstantinatis.'

'Out of which office?'

'Fair Oaks.'

'Very good, sir. . . . You know, nearly all runaways return on their own. And most of the ones that don't, get picked up and *sent* back home. A little counseling, some family therapy, and things generally work out just fine.'

'Thanks for your thoughts. Appreciate it.'

'Oh, one thing, Mr Collier. I guess you know about the law. About how it could be, let's say, troublesome for you to take matters into your own hands here.'

'I do.'

'Bad for everybody.'

'Understood.'

'Okay. Then enough said.'

'Appreciate *that* too. I'm just going to be asking a few questions.'

'Good luck to both of you.'

They hung up and he told Bett what the agent had said. Her face was troubled.

'What is it?' He felt an urge to append a 'honey' but nipped that one fast.

'Just that it seems so much more serious with the FBI involved.'

How foolish people are, how trusting, how their defenses crumble like sand when they believe they're talking to a friend. And oh how they want to believe that you *are* a friend . . .

Why, no wild animal in the world would be as trusting as a human being. It's amazing we're not extinct.

Aaron Matthews, no longer the stony-voiced FBI agent, protector of the weak, hung up the phone after speaking with Tate Collier. He almost felt guilty – it had been so easy to draw information out of the man.

And what information it was! Oh, Matthews was angry. His mood teetered precariously. All his preparation – such care, such finesse, everything set up to send Collier and his wife into a fit of paralysis and dismay and sit home, brooding about their lost daughter . . . and what were they doing but playing amateur detectives?

Their talking to Hanson could be a real problem. Megan might have said something about loving her parents and never even considering running away. Or, even worse, they might become suspicious of Matthews's whole plan and have the police go through Hanson's office. He'd been careful there but hadn't worn gloves all the time. There were fingerprints – and the window latch in the bathroom where Matthews had snuck in was still broken.

Then there was Amy Walker, Megan's friend. With a bookbag that *probably* didn't have anything compromising but might – maybe a diary or those notes teenage girls are always passing around in school. And this Eckhard, the teacher and coach.

Reports of a car following her . . .

Much of Matthews's reconnaissance had been conducted around the school. If the teacher *had* walked up to the car he might easily have gotten the license number of the Mercedes or even a look at Matthews himself. Mentioned it to school security. And he hadn't changed the license plates to the stolen ones until yesterday. And even if Eckhard didn't *think* he'd seen much, there were probably some prickly little facts locked away in his subconscious; Matthews had done much hypnosis work and knew how many memories and observations were retained in the cobwebby recesses of the mind.

Why the hell was Collier doing this? Why hadn't the letters fooled him? The lawyer was supposed to be *logical*, he was supposed to be *cold*. Why didn't he believe the bald facts in front of him?

A Mood began to settle on Matthews but he struggled to throw it off.

No, I have no time for this now!

(He thought of how many patients he'd wanted to grab by the lapels: Oh, quit your fucking complaining and do something about it! You don't like her, leave. *She* left *you?* Find somebody else. You're a drunk, stop drinking.)

He returned to the phone and called three Walkers

in Fairfax before he got the household that included a teenage Amy.

He spoke with her mother.

'Yes, Amy's my daughter. Who's this?'

'I'm William McComb, with the County. I've gotten a call from Child Protective Services.'

'My God, what's wrong?'

'Nothing to be alarmed at, Mrs Walker. This doesn't involve your daughter. We're investigating a case involving Megan McCall.'

'Oh, no! Is Megan all right? She spent the night here!'

'That's what we understand. It seems she's missing and we've been looking into some allegations about her father.'

There was a moment's pause as if she was here trying to remember, who he was.

'Tate Collier,' Matthews said.

'Oh, right. I don't know him. You think he's involved? You think he did something?'

'We're just looking into a few things now. But I'd appreciate it if you'd tell your daughter she shouldn't have any contact with him.'

'Why would she have any contact with him?' the edgy voice asked. How easily she'd cry, Matthews predicted.

'We don't know. We don't think there'd be any reason for him to hurt or touch her—'

'Oh, God. You don't *think*?'

'We just want to make sure Amy stays safe until we get to the bottom of what happened to Megan.'

'"Happened to Megan"? *Please* tell me what's going on.'

'I can't really say more now. Tell me, where's your daughter now?'

'Upstairs.'

'Would you mind if I spoke to her?'

'No, of course not.'

A moment later a girl's lazy voice: 'Hello?'

'Hi, Amy. This is Mr McComb. I'm with the County. How are you?'

'Okay, I guess. Like, is Megan okay?'

'I'm sure she's fine. Tell me, has Megan's father talked to you recently?'

'Um,' the girl began.

'You answer,' the mother said sternly from the extension.

'Yeah, like, he said she's run away and asked me about it. He was going to come by and get her bookbag.'

'Is there anything in there that might suggest where she's gone?'

'I dunno. I don't think so. Just books and shi – stuff.'

The mother: 'You were going to let him in here? And not tell me?'

The girl snapped, 'Mom, just, like, cut it out, okay? It's Megan's dad.'

Matthews said, 'Amy, don't talk to him. And whatever you do, don't go anywhere with him.'

'I—'

'If he suggests going away, getting into his car, going into his barn . . .'

'God, his *barn*?' her mother gasped. Yep, Matthews could hear soft weeping.

He continued, 'Amy, if he offers you something to drink . . .'

Another gasp.

Oh, my, this was fun. Matthews continued calmly, '. . . just tell him no. If he comes over don't answer the door. Make sure it's locked.'

'Like, why?'

'You don't ask, young lady. You do what the man says.'

'Mom, like, come on . . . What about her bookbag?'

'You just hold on to it until you hear from me or someone at Child Protective Services. Okay?'

'I guess.'

'Should we call the police?' Mrs Walker asked.

'No, it's not a criminal charge yet.'

'Oh, God,' said Amy's mother, the woman of the limited epithets. 'Amy, tell me. Did Megan's father ever touch you? Now, tell the truth.'

'Who? Megan's father? Jeez, Mom. You're such a loser. I never even met him.'

'Mrs Walker?'

'Yes. I'm here.' Her voice cracked.

'I really don't want to alarm you unnecessarily.'

'No, no. We appreciate your calling. What's your number, Mr McComb?'

'I'm going to be in the field for a while. Let me call you later, when I'm back at the office.'

'All right.'

Matthews felt a cheerful little twinge as he heard her crying. Though Amy's silence on the other extension was louder.

He couldn't resist. 'Mrs Walker?'

'Yes?'

'Do you have a gun?'

A choked sob. 'No, we don't. I don't. I've never . . . I wouldn't know how to use one. I guess I could go to Sports Authority. I mean—'

'That's all right,' Matthews said soothingly. 'I'm sure it's not going to come to anything like that.'

'What if Megan's mother, like, calls?' the girl asked.

'Yes,' Mrs Walker echoed, 'what if her mother calls?'

A concerned pause. 'I'd be careful. We're investigating her too. . . . It was a very troubled household, it seems.'

'God,' Mrs Walker muttered.

Matthews hung up.

What a mess this could become. It had seemed so simple in theory. And was so complicated now. Just like the art of psychiatry itself.

Well, there were other things to do. But first things first. He had to get Megan to her new home – with his son Peter – deep in the mountains.

Matthews returned to the Mercedes. He pulled back onto the highway, noting that the white car was still sticking with him like a lamprey to a fish.

9

Amy wasn't home.

Oh, brother. Tate sighed. Looked through a window, saw nothing. Walked back to the front door. Pressed the bell again.

Standing on the concrete stoop of the split-level in suburban Burke, Tate kept his hand on the doorbell for a full minute but neither the girl nor her mother came to the door.

Where'd she gone? Bett had said that they'd stop by soon. Why hadn't Amy stayed? Or at least put the bookbag out on the door stoop?

Was this adolescent friendships nowadays?

'Maybe the bell's broken,' Bett called from the car.

But Tate pounded on the door with his open palm. There was no response. 'Amy!'

'Go round back,' Bett suggested.

Tate pushed through a scratchy holly bush and rapped on the back door.

Still no answer. He decided to slip inside and find the bag; a missing teenager took precedence over a technical charge of trespass (thinking: I could make a good argument for an implied license to enter the premises. Interesting legal concept). But as he reached for the doorknob he believed he heard a click. When he tried to open the latch he found the door was locked.

He peered through the window and thought he saw some motion. But he couldn't be sure.

Tate returned to the car.

'Not there.' He sighed. 'We'll call later.'

'Leesburg?' Bett asked.

'Let's try that teacher first. Eckhard.'

It was only a five-minute drive to the school. The rain had stopped and youngsters were gathering on the schoolyard – boys for baseball, girls for volleyball, both for soccer. Hackeysacks, Frisbees, skateboards. After speaking with several parents and students they learned that Robert Eckhard, the volleyball coach, had put together a practice for three that afternoon. It was now a quarter to two.

Tate flopped down into the passenger seat of the Lexus. He stretched. 'This police work. I don't see how Konnie does it.'

Bett kicked her shoes off and massaged her feet. 'Wish I'd worn boots, like you.' Then she glanced toward the school. 'Look,' she said.

When they'd been married Bett assumed that he knew exactly what she was thinking or talking about. A gesture of her finger, an eyebrow raised like a witch casting a spell – he'd follow her glance and have not a clue as to her meaning. Today, though, he turned his head toward where she was looking and saw the two blue-uniformed security guards, standing in one of the back doorways of the school.

'Good idea,' he said. And they drove around to the door.

By the time they got there the guards had gone inside. Bett and Tate parked and walked inside the school

The halls had that smell of all high schools – sweat, lab gas, disinfectant, paste.

Tate laughed to himself at the instinctive uneasiness he felt being here. Classwork had come easily to him but he'd spent his time and effort on Debate Club in high school and the teachers were forever booting him into detention hall for skipped classes or missing homework. That he would pause at the door on the way out of home room and resonantly quote Cicero or John Calhoun to his teacher didn't help his academic record any, of course.

The security offices in Megan's school were small cubicles of carpeted partitions near the gym.

One guard, a crew-cut boy with half-mast eyelids, wearing a perfectly pressed uniform, listened unemotionally to Tate's story. He adjusted his glistening black billy club.

'Don't know your daughter.' He turned, called out, 'Henry, you know a Megan McCall?'

'Nope,' said his partner, who resembled him to an eerie degree. He stepped into the school proper and disappeared.

'What we're concerned about is this car. A man seemed to be following her.'

'A car. Following her.' The young man was skeptical.

Bett took over. 'Around the schoolyard. This past week.'

Tate: 'We were wondering if anybody might've reported it.'

The man's face eased into that put-upon look security guards are very good at. Maybe they're resentful that they're not full-fledged cops and could carry guns. And use them.

'Are the police involved?' the man asked.

'Somewhat.'

'Hm.' Trying to figure that one out.

'What happens if somebody sees something unusual? Is there any procedure for that?'

'The Bust-er Book,' the guard said.

Bett asked, 'The . . . uh?'

'Bust-er. He's a dog. I mean, a cartoon dog. But it's like "Bust" as in get busted. Then a dash, then E-R. If the kids see something weird they come tell us and we write it down in the Bust-er Book and then there's a record of it, for the police. If anything, you know, happens.'

Tate recalled what Amy'd said. 'It was on Tuesday. Out in the parking lot by the sports field. Could you take a look?'

'Oh, we can't let you see it,' the guard said.

'I'm sorry?'

'Parents don't have, you know, access to it. Only the administration and police. That's the rule.'

'That's it right there?'

The guard turned around and glanced at the blue binder with the words 'Bust-er' on the spine and a cartoon effigy of a dog wearing a Sherlock Holmes deerstalker hat. 'Yessir.'

'If you don't mind . . . See, our daughter's missing. As I was saying.'

'Just have the police give us a call.'

'Well, she's not officially a missing person.'

'Then I guess you don't really need to look at the book.' The guard's lean face crinkled. His still eyes looked Tate up and down and his muscular hand caressed his ebony billy club. He was everything Tate hated about northern Virginia. Snide and sullen. This young man would see nothing wrong with a tap on the wife's chin or a belt on his kids' butts to keep them in line. He was master of the house; everyone else did as told. Dinner on the table at five even if I'm out late drinking, and we're all going to church, and, sure, there are some all-right Negroes but that's as far as I'm going . . . And what're these fucking Orientals doing all over the place here?

A bastard mix of Southern hate and Northern ignorance.

Tate looked at Bett. Her eyebrows were raised as if she were asking: what was the problem? After all, he *was* the silver-tongued devil. He could talk anybody into anything. (Resolved: the Watergate break-in was justifiable as a means to a valid end. Lifelong Democrat, grandson of a lifelong Democrat, Tate had leapt to take that irreverent position. For the pure joy of going up against overwhelming odds. He'd won, to the Judge's shock and permanent amusement.)

'Officer,' Tate began, thinking of the rhetorical tricks in his arsenal, the logic, the skills at persuasion. Ratiocination. He paused, then walked to the door and motioned the guard to follow.

The lean man walked slowly enough to let Tate know that nobody on earth was going to make him do a single thing he didn't want to do.

Tate paused at the front door and looked out over the schoolyard. 'What do you see there?'

The guard hesitated uncertainly. He'd be thinking, what kinda question's that? I see trees, I see cars, I see fences, I see clouds.

Tate waited just the right amount of time and said, 'I see a lot of young people.'

'Um.' Well, what the hell else're you gonna see on a schoolyard? *Course* there're kids.

'And those young people rely on us adults for everything. They rely on us for food, for shelter, for schooling, and you know what else?'

Video games, running shoes, Legos? How'm I supposed to know? What's this Bozo up to?

'They rely on us for their safety. That's what you're doing here, right? It's the reason they hired a big, strong guy like you. A man who's got balls, who's not afraid to mix it up with somebody.'

'I dunno. I guess.'

'Well, my daughter's relying on me for her safety. She needs me to find out where she is. Maybe she's in trouble, maybe she isn't. Hey, let's take an example: you see some tough big kids talking to a little kid. Maybe they're just brothers, fooling around. Or maybe they're trying to sell him some pot or steal his lunch money. You'd go and find out, right?'

'I would. Sure.'

'That's all I'm doing with my daughter. Trying to find out if she's okay. And going through that book would sure be a big help.'

The guard nodded.

'Well?' Tate asked expectantly.

'Nosir. Rules is rules. Can't be done.'

Tate sighed. He glanced at Bett, who said icily, 'Let's go, Tate. Nothing more to be accomplished here.'

As they walked to the car, the guard called, 'Sir?'

Tate turned.

'That was a good try, though. I almost bought it.' With a sneering grin, he picked up a magazine on customized pickup trucks and sat down.

Tate and Bett continued to the car then climbed in and drove out of the lot.

Neither of them could contain the laughter for long.

They both roared. Bett gasped and said, 'That was the biggest load of hogwash I ever heard. "It's the reason they hired a big, strong guy like you."'

Wiping tears from his eyes, Tate controlled his laughing. 'But I kept his attention. That was some pretty good double teaming.'

Bett reached under her blouse and pulled out twenty or thirty sheets of notebook paper. 'I figured I better leave the notebook itself.' She muttered, 'The Bust-er Book? The *Bust-er* Book? Do people really take that stuff seriously?'

Tate drove about three blocks and pulled over to the curb.

'Okay,' she said, 'Tuesday . . . Tuesday.' Flipping through the pages. 'If the stormtrooper back there's the one who keeps the book he's got handwriting like a sissy. Okay, Tuesday . . .' She nodded then read: '"Two students reported a gray car, no school parking permit, parked on Sideburn Road. Single driver. Drove off without picking up student."'

'A gray car. Not much to go on. Anything else?'

'Not then. But Amy said Megan'd been thinking she'd been followed for a while.' Bett flipped back through the pages. Her perfect eyebrow rose in a delicate arc. 'Listen. A week ago. "M. McCall (Green Team)—" That's her class section at school. "—reported gray car appeared to be following her. Security Guard Gibson took report. Did not personally witness incident. Checked but no car seen. Subject did not know tag or make of vehicle." He spelled vehicle wrong,' Bett added. Then looked at her ex-husband. 'Why didn't she tell me about it, Tate? Why?'

Tate had no answer. He asked, 'Any description of the driver?'

'None, no.'

'What kind of car did her boyfriend drive?'

'White . . . I think a Toyota.'

'He could've borrowed one to follow her,' Tate mused.

'Could have, sure.'

More questions than answers.

Tate stared at the turbulent clouds overhead. The sun tried to break through but a line of thick gray rolled over the sky heading eastward. 'Let's go to Leesburg,' he said.

10

Joshua LeFevre glanced down at the odometer. He'd driven another twenty miles along I-66 in his battered old Toyota since the last time he'd checked. Which put him about seventy miles from Fairfax.

Mr Tibbs, the unflappable police detective within him, had figured out where Megan and her therapist lover were going. To the doctor's mountain place. It was now chic for professionals to have vacation homes in the Blue Ridge or in West Virginia, where you could buy a mountaintop for a song.

The rain had stopped and he cranked the sunroof open, listening to the wind hissing through the Yakima bike rack.

It was early afternoon when he broke through the Shenandoahs and saw the hazy Blue Ridge in front of him. Not evocative gunmetal today, the literature major in him thought – the hills were tinted with the green frost of spring growth. Nice place for picnics, he thought, recalling that he and Megan had talked about a bike tour along Skyline Drive later in the spring.

He was lost in this reverie when the Mercedes got away from him.

Never would have happened to Sidney Poitier.

Damn . . .

The Merce had pulled out to pass a semi and he'd followed. But as soon as the big gray car had cleared the cab of the truck the doctor had skidded hard to the right and pulled on to the exit ramp as the truck driver laid on his air horn and braked.

LeFevre's Toyota was caught in the left lane and he couldn't swerve back in time to make the exit.

His head swivelled around and he saw the roof of the Mercedes sink below the level of the highway as it slowed along the ramp.

LeFevre slammed his fists on the wheel. Tantrums were definitely not Poitier's style but he couldn't help it. He thought about making an illegal U over the median but here he was a black kid with knobby dreads driving through the crucible of the Confederacy; the fewer laws he broke, the better.

The next exit was a mile down the highway and by the time he'd followed the Möbius strip of ramps and returned to the exit the Mercedes had taken there was no sign of the big car – only an intersection of three different country roads, any one of which they might have taken.

And, now that he thought about it, the doctor might just have stopped for gas and gotten back on to the interstate, continuing west.

He closed his eyes in frustration and pressed back hard into the headrest.

What the hell'm I doing here?

The stuff love makes you do, he thought.

Hate it, hate it, hate it . . .

LeFevre pulled into the gas station, filled up at the self-service island then walked up to the skinny, sullen attendant with long hair sprouting from under a Valvoline giveaway cap, which was as greasy as the hair. Smiled at him.

'How you doing?' Sidney Poitier asked very politely.

'Okayyourself?' the man muttered.

'Not bad. Not bad.'

The man stared at LeFevre's hair, which was not exactly modeled on Mr Poitier's, circa 1967, but was much closer to a Menace II Society fan's.

'Helpya?'

It occurred to LeFevre that even Officer Tibbs, in suit, tie and polished Oxfords, wouldn't get very far around here asking which way a seventy-thousand-dollar automobile had just gone.

Not without some incentive.

LeFevre opened his wallet and extracted five twenties. Looked down at them.

So did the attendant. 'That's cash.'

'Yes, it is.'

'You charged your gas. I seen you.'

'I did.'

'Well, whatsitfor?'

'It's for you,' LeFevre said in his most carefully crafted Queen's English.

'Uh-huh. Uh-huh. Why's it for me?' The man seemed to sneer.

'I have a little problem.'

The stubbly face asked, Who cares?

'I was driving down sixty-six and this Mercedes cut me off, ran me off the road. Nearly killed me.' (This had happened to Sidney Poitier in *In the Heat of the Night*. More or less.) 'Did it on purpose. The driver, I mean.'

'Don't say.' The man yawned.

'Front end's all screwed up now. And see the bodywork I need?'

Thank goodness, LeFevre thought, he'd never fixed the damage after he'd scraped the side of the car on a barricade when he'd dropped his mother off at Nieman Marcus in Tysons last month.

But the attendant looked at the car without a splinter of interest.

'So you want me to lookit the front end?'

'No, I want the license number of that Mercedes. He came by here five, ten minutes ago.'

This had seemed like a good way to break the ice – asking for the license number. It made things official – as if the police were going to get involved. LeFevre believed this trick was definitely something that Sidney Poitier would do.

'Why'd he run you off the road?' the man asked abruptly.

Which brought LeFevre up cold.

'Um, I don't know.' LeFevre shrugged. Then he asked, 'You know which car I mean?' He remained respectful but decided not to be too polite. Sidney Poitier had glared at Rod Steiger quite a bit.

'Maybe.'

'So he stopped here for gas.'

'Nope.' The scrawny guy looked at the money. Then he shook his head; his slick grin gave LeFevre an unpleasant glimpse of some very bad teeth. 'Fuck. You're shittin' me. You don't want that tag number.'

'Um, I—'

'What you want is to find out where that sumvabitch lives. Am I right?'

'Well . . .'

'An' I'll tell you why you want that.'

'Why?'

''Cause he was drivin' his big old Mercedes and he thunk t'himself, why, here's a black man only he was thinking the N word, driving a little shit Jap car and I can cut him off 'cause he don't mean shit to me.' A faint laugh. 'And you don't want no tag number for State Farm insurance or the poe-leece. Fuck. You wanna find him and you wanna beat the shiny crap outta him.'

So, end of story. Well, it was a nice try. LeFevre was about to put the money away and return to his car – before the man called some real-life Rod Steigers – when the attendant said, 'Now, that frosts me, what he done. Truly does.'

'I'm sorry?' LeFevre asked.

'I mean, I got friends're black. Couple of 'em. And we have a good time together and one of them's wife cooks for me and my girlfriend nearly every week.'

'Well, that right?'

'Fuck, yeah, that's right.' The twenties were suddenly in the man's stained fingers. 'I say, more power to you. Find him and wail on him all you want.'

'How's that?' LeFevre blinked.

'I know that sumvabitch.'

'The man in the Mercedes?'

'Yeah.'

'Dr Hanson, right?'

'I don't know his name. But I seen him off and on for a spell. He comes and goes. Never stops here but I seen him. Pisses me off royal, people like him. Moving everybody down the mountain.'

'What do you mean, "moving down the mountain?"' Sidney Poitier asked politely, smiling now and giving the man plenty of thinking room.

'Any sumvabitch in a Mercedes going into them hills's a real-estate weasel. See, what happened was when folk settled here they moved to the top of the Ridge. Naturally, where else? But they couldn't keep the land, most of 'em. Money troubles, you know. Taxes.

So they kept selling to the government for the Park or to rich folks wanted a weekend place, and families kept moving down the mountain. Now, most everybody's in the valley – most of the honest folk, I mean. Pretty soon there won't be no mountains left 'cept for the rich pricks and the government. 'S what my dad says. Makes sense to me.'

'Where's his place?'

The skinny young man nodded toward one narrow road.

'Up that one there. I don't know where exactly his house is. Only place I know of up there's the hospital. That's what I figure he's turning into condos or something.'

'What hospital?'

'Loony bin. Closed a few years back.'

'How far is it?'

'Five miles, give'r take. At the end of Palmer Road yonder.' He pointed. 'Now, you ain't going to kill him, are you? I'd have some problems with that.'

'No. I really do just want to talk.'

'Uh-huh. Uh-huh.' The man squinted then grinned his bad-tooth grin again. 'You know, you remind me of that actor.'

'I do?'

'Yeah. He's a good one. Don't exactly look like him but you sound like him and sort of hold yourself like him. What's his name? What's his name?'

LeFevre, grinning himself, answered his question.

The man blinked and shook his head. 'Who the hell's Sidney Poitier?'

LeFevre said, 'Maybe he was before your time.'

'What's that guy's name? I can picture him . . . Kicked the shit out of some ninjas in this movie with

106

Sean Connery. Wait! Snipes . . . Wesley Snipes. That's it. That man can *act.*'

LeFevre walked to the edge of the tarmac. The smell of gasoline mixed with the scent of spring growth and clayish earth. Palmer Road vanished into a dark shaft of pine and hemlock, winding up into the mountains.

The young attendant stuffed a strand of slick hair up under his hat. 'He may have a trailer up there. Lotta developers have those Winnebagos or like that. Or maybe he's staying in the hospital itself. Shit, I wouldn't do that for any money. Hear stories about it. People sometimes get attacked. By wild dogs or something.'

Or something?

'Find bloody bones sometimes. And not much else left.'

LeFevre's anger was turning to concern. Megan, what've you gotten yourself into? 'I just follow that road?'

'Right. Five miles, I'd guess. Keeps to the high ground. Then circles back on itself like a snake.'

'A snake,' LeFevre said, absently staring into the murky forest. Thinking of the quote from Dante's *Divine Comedy: Halfway through life's journey I came to myself in a dark woods, where the straight way was lost.* Recalling the story too: How Beatrice took Virgil on a trip to hell.

'Listen,' the attendant said, startling him, 'you stop on your way back, okay? Let me know what happens.'

LeFevre nodded and shook the man's oily hand. He climbed into his car and sped along Palmer Road. In an instant, civilization vanished behind him and the world became black bark, shadows and the waving arms of tattered boughs.

The things we do for love, LeFevre thought. The things we do for love.

*   *   *

Aaron Matthews pulled the Mercedes into a grove of trees beside the asphalt and climbed out, looking back over Palmer Road.

No sign of the white car.

He was sure he'd tricked the boyfriend just fine when he'd sped off the highway beside the truck. The kid was probably in West Virginia by now and even if he managed to figure out which exit they'd taken and backtracked he'd have no way of knowing which way Matthews had gone into the maze of back roads here. Although Matthews had been coming to the deserted hospital for the past year, ever since he'd brought his son here, he'd made a point of never stopping for gas or food at the service station or grocery store at the foot of the exit ramp off Route 66. He was sure the local hicks knew nothing about him.

He climbed back in the car and continued on to the Blue Ridge Mental Health Facility.

Just past the cleft where the road passed between two steep vine-covered hills, the ground opened into the shallow bowl of a valley. Through a picket line of scabby trees a sprawl of low, decrepit buildings was visible.

BRMHF had been the last destination for the hard-core crazies in the commonwealth of Virginia. Schizophrenics, uncontrollable bipolars, borderline personalities, delusionals. Security was high – the patients (i.e., inmates) were locked down at night in restraint (padded) quarters (cells). The eight-foot chain-link fence enclosing the ten-acre grounds was 'designed to provide comforting security to patients and nearby residents alike' (translation: it sported a live current of 500 volts).

The hospital had served its purpose well, until two years ago, when it had been closed down by the state, and the patients were shipped to other facilities and halfway houses.

Matthews was intimately familiar with the place; the patients here had found him a confidant, confessor, judge . . . a virtual father over the course of his four-year tenure. When he thought of home he thought first of this hospital and second the Colonial house in Arlington, Virginia, he'd lived in with Margaret and their son, Peter.

Matthews braked the car to a halt and examined the place carefully for signs of intruders though a break-in would have been very unlikely. The current to the fence had been shut off long ago but the grounds were patrolled by five knob-headed Rottweilers, as raw and brutal as dogs could be, teeth sharp as obsidian; they hunted in packs and one or twice a week killed one of the deer that often strolled through the gate when it was open.

He listened carefully again – no sound of approaching cars – and unlocked the two tempered steel locks securing the gate. He drove inside and parked.

Then he lifted Megan from the trunk and carried her inside, pushing through a door with his shoulder. He'd reversed the locks on the doors – you could simply push in from the outside but couldn't get back out without a key, in effect turning a hospital into a prison.

He stepped into the lobby.

Asylums smell far more visceral than do regular hospitals because even though their province is the mind, the byproduct of that type of pathology is piss, shit, sweat, blood. This was still true of the Blue Ridge Hospital; the air stank of bodily functions and decay.

Through these murky halls Matthews carried his prize in his arms. Feeling every ounce of her weight – though it wasn't the weight of a burden; it was the weight of treasure. Gold or platinum, solid and perfect in his arms.

Matthews carried Megan into the room he'd fixed up for her. He laid her on the bed and undressed her. First the blouse and the bra. Then jeans and panties and socks. His eyes coursed up and down her body. Yet he touched her only once – to make sure her pulse was regular.

Taking her clothes, he left the room, locked her door with a heavy padlock. He thought about stopping to see his son but the boy was in a different part of the hospital and Matthews had no time for that now. He left the building, got into his car and started through the gate. He'd gotten only ten feet before he heard the thump-thump-thump of the flat tire.

Oh, not now! His mood suddenly darkened. And he fought to keep the blackness at bay. He thought of Megan. It buoyed him just enough. Matthews climbed out and walked to the rear of the car.

He took one look at the slash mark in the Michelin and flung the door open, trying to get to the pistol in his glove compartment.

Too late.

'Don't move.' The young man held the rusty machete, left over from the grounds-keeping Matthews had done when he'd brought his son, Peter, here. He gripped the long knife awkwardly but with enough manic determination to make Matthews freeze and raise his hands. The boy's muscles were huge.

He blurted, 'I'll give you my wallet. And there's—'

'I want to know what's going on.'

The young man's voice was astonishing. What a beautiful patois. Carolinian and Caribbean and some succulent English, which tempered the two. This man could fuck any woman he wanted simply by telling her she was beautiful.

'Don't hurt me,' Matthews said desperately.

A flicker of uncertainty in the brown eyes.

'What've you done with Megan?'

Matthews frowned. 'Who *are* you?'

Ah, young man, asked the silent therapist within Matthews, you're not a fighter at all, are you? You're a bit out of your element . . . And why do you feel so guilty, why do you feel so unsure?

The pistol was in the glove compartment only feet away. But his assailant was riding on pure nerves. With his strength it wouldn't take much for the boy to injure Matthews seriously, without even trying. And besides, while he *believed* he wasn't dangerous, Matthews had learned that premature diagnoses can be very risky.

He smiled and lowered his hands. He nodded knowingly. 'Wait, wait. You're not . . . You must be Joshua.'

The boy's face squirreled up into a frown. 'You know me?'

'Sure, I know you,' Matthews said smoothly. 'I was *hoping* we'd get a chance to talk.'

11

'You startled me,' said the soothing voice of Aaron Matthews. 'I didn't mean to react the way I did.'

He glanced at the tire, laughed. 'But then again you did attack my Mercedes with a machete.'

With his voice trembling (love that voice, *love* it), the boy said, 'I thought you'd just brought her here on a date. To show her some of your property or something. Then I saw you carry her inside. What the hell's going on? Tell me!'

'Wait. Carry who inside?' Matthews frowned.

Show her some of your property?

'Megan. I *saw* you two.'

So he's thinking real estate development. Matthews shook his head, glanced toward the hospital. 'You mean just a few minutes ago? Well, I carried in some bags of cleaning supplies. And a tarp. I bought this place and I'm turning it into condos.'

A minuscule lessening of his suspicion. Not believing your own eyes, are you? How often we don't. And you don't do well with embarrassment, do you? A gift from the African-American executive mum, by chance? The one with practiced elocution and the Chanel scarf over the shoulder of the suit she bought at Tysons Galleria?

Matthews noted, however, that the boy continued to

hold the rusty blade firmly in his hand. 'Where is she? What were you doing with her car?'

'Joshua,' Matthews said patiently, 'I just dropped Megan off at my weekend place up the road.' He pointed into the woods. 'A couple miles from here. She wanted to get a head start on making lunch.'

'Why'd you switch cars at Metro?'

'Megan's got a friend. Amy.' He paused.

Joshua said, 'I know Amy.'

'Amy's borrowing her car. We left it at the Metro for her and took the Mercedes.'

The boy frowned. 'I didn't think Amy had a license.'

Matthews laughed. 'Oh? She didn't share that with us. I wondered why she didn't want to borrow her mother's.'

'Good, Matthews told himself, giving his performance high marks.

'But wait . . . I didn't see Megan in your car when I was behind you.'

'You were following us?'

'Yes, I was following you. How did you think I found you?'

'I assumed that Megan told you about me. And that we come up here sometimes.'

Joshua blinked.

Matthews studied the young man for a moment then tilted his head and said with sympathy, 'Look, Joshua, don't do this to yourself.'

'Do what?'

Oh, the desperation Matthews could see in the olive eyes was so sweet. He nearly shivered with pleasure. He whispered, 'You should forget about her.'

'But I love her!'

'Forget about her. For your own good.'

So, Matthews had been right. The man had probably

arrived at Hanson's office toward the end of the session, planning to confront Megan – and presumably the doctor too – about Hanson's advice on breaking up. A little obsessive, are we?

Or just too much testosterone in the blood.

If it weren't for romance we poor psychiatrists would have nothing to do. As Freud said, more or less, Love's a bitch, ain't it?

'You talked her into breaking up with me so you could see her!' Joshua said.

'Megan said that? Well, it's not true. That's completely unethical and I'd never do it.'

Joshua blinked at the vehemence in Matthews's voice. The therapist had deduced that the boy would be a rule-and-regulation victim. Thanks to Dad, of course – the soldier.

The therapist continued, 'She *decided* to break up with you on your own, Joshua. And *then* we started going out.'

'That's not what she said. She said you told her to break up with me.'

'No, Joshua. That's not the way it was at all.'

'But she *told* me!'

'Well, we can't blame her for not being completely honest all the time, now, can we?'

'Blame her?'

'See, Megan has trouble taking responsibility for certain things. Not unusual, not a serious problem. We all suffer from it to varying degrees. It's hard for her to express her inner feelings. Given her parents. . . . You know Tate and Bett?'

Hearing the names, the familiarity in Matthews's voice, the boy's defenses slipped a bit more. But he was still dangerous. Too confused, too much in love, riding on

115

too much emotion. Matthews decided he couldn't win the boy's confidence; he'd have to go in a different direction. 'I've met her mother, not her father.'

'Well, believe me, they're to thank for a lot of her problems. Her lying, for instance. And she'd lose her temper sometimes, wouldn't she?'

'A couple of times. But who doesn't?'

The question told Matthews that the boy was buying the argument. He laughed. 'Joshua, put that thing down and go home. Forget about Megan. This is only going to mean heartache for you.'

'I *love* her.' He was nearly in tears.

By now Matthews had pegged the boy the way a geologist recognizes quartz. An underachiever terrified of his parents, of course. Military dad. Supermother. Who were probably – to use Megan's tired adjective – *great* people. And so Joshua wouldn't let himself be angry with them.

Though the anger was there. It had to be. But where?

Let's find out . . .

'Joshua, you don't understand. You—'

'Then tell me.'

'It's not appropriate—'

Joshua persisted. 'Tell me! What is going on?'

Matthew's eyes went wide, as if he were losing his temper. He said, 'All right! You want to know the truth?'

'Yes!'

Matthews started to speak then, shook his head as if he were struggling to control himself. 'No, no, you don't.'

'Yes I do!' The boy stepped forward, menacingly.

'All right. But don't blame me. The truth is Megan didn't *like* you.'

The young man's face froze into a glossy ebony mask. 'That's not true!'

Matthews's mouth grew tight. 'She told me that the first night we slept together.'

Joshua gasped. 'You're lying.'

'You don't think we're lovers?' Matthews asked viciously, as befit a man no longer fearful but angry.

'No, I don't.'

'Well, then how do I know about that birthmark just below her left nipple?'

Joshua couldn't hold Matthews's cold eyes and he looked down at the moss covering a fallen tree. His hands were shaking.

'What do we think of her pubic hair? Yellow as the hair on her head. And what does she like in bed? She likes men to go down on her all night long. And she loves to get fucked in the ass.'

But not by you apparently. Matthews noted the young man's shocked face.

'Stop it!'

But he continued, 'Our first session she asked me how she could get rid of you.'

'No.'

'Yes!' Matthews spat out, 'You know what she called you? The white nigger.'

The eyes glazed over in pain as the scalpel of his words incised the young man's soul.

'She'd *never* say that.'

'You were the big minority experiment. She wanted a black man to fuck. But not too black. And she thought you were a good compromise. About as white as they come. But then she decided she'd got herself a clunker. She told me she had to drink a half-bottle of Southern Comfort just so she could kiss you!'

'No!'

'She and Amy'd stay up all night making fun of you.

Megan does a great impression of you. She's got you down cold.'

'Go to hell!'

'Joshua, you asked for this!' Matthews shouted. '*You* pushed me, so you're going to hear the truth whether you want it or not. She wanted your pathetic face out of her life. White nigger. You were a toy. She told me again this morning. When we were fucking on the desk in my office.'

It was enough.

The boy erupted. And, while it might have driven someone else to act ruthlessly and efficiently, it drove Joshua manically forward toward Matthews. He dropped the machete and flailed away with his fists. '*She never said that!*' he cried. 'She never said that she never said that she never said that—'

Matthews fell to the ground, covering his head with his left arm. And when he rose a moment later he was holding the machete, which he swung directly into Joshua's throat.

The boy's mournful litany ended in a gurgling scream. Matthews leapt back, away from the boy's swinging fist, and slashed his arm deeply. Then his leg. Joshua fell on to his back, cradling the gash in his throat.

Matthews drew back and plunged the rusty blade into the young man's abdomen. But with astonishing strength Joshua pushed Matthews off, twisted away, and rose to his knees, choking. The blood flowed between the fingers clutching his torn neck. Matthews struck him several times more but Joshua was crawling fast, like an animal, through the gate toward the hospital. Pathetically trying to escape the terrible blade. Matthews didn't bother to pursue him. Joshua got thirty feet into the field surrounding the hospital before collapsing in a stand of Queen Anne's lace, which turned a deep purple under the spray of his blood.

Matthews slowly walked toward him. Then stopped. He heard snarling, growing closer. He backed quickly away from the quivering body.

The Rottweilers charged forward hungrily. Matthews stepped through the gate and swung it closed as the dogs swarmed in a single muscular pack over the body, which had looked so strong and impervious a moment ago and was now just ragged meat.

Matthews leaned against the bars of the gate, enraptured, watching the young man die. Joshua fought – he tried to rise and struggled to hit the dogs. But it was useless. The big male Rottie closed his enormous jaws on the back of Joshua's neck and began to shake. After a moment the body went limp.

The animals dragged him into the ravine for the feast. His body vanished under the mass of snarling, bloody mouths.

Matthews quickly changed the Mercedes's tire and climbed into the car then sped down the rough road. He'd bury what remained of the boy's corpse later. He didn't have time now. Too many things to do. He was thinking that this was just like when he was a practicing therapist. Busy days, busy days. There were people to see, people to talk to.

I'm here to change your life for ever.

Who is he? *Who?*

Megan McCall floated on a dark ocean, that one question the only thing in her thoughts. She opened her eyes and gripped the thin, filthy mattress she lay on. The room swayed and bobbed.

She was dizzy and nauseated. Her mouth painfully

dry, her eyes swollen half closed. She rolled onto her back and examined the small room. There were flaking cushions mounted on all the walls, bars on the windows.

A padded cell.

And the whole place stank so bad she thought she might puke.

She sat up briefly, trying to find a light. There was none. The overhead lamp had been removed and the room was dark. Maybe she—

Suddenly roaring filled her ears. Her vision dissolved into black grains and she collapsed back on the bed, passed out. Sometime later she opened her eyes again, managed to sit up then waited until the dizziness passed and stumbled into the tiny bathroom. The drugs he'd given her . . . still in her system. She'd have to take it slow.

Megan sat down on the toilet, spread her legs and finally worked up the courage to examine herself. No tenderness or pain. No come. He might have groped but he hadn't raped her. She sighed in relief then urinated and washed her hands and face in the basin. She drank a dozen handfuls of icy water. As she stood – careful, careful! Take your time – she caught sight of herself in the metal mirror bolted to the wall. She gasped. Pale and haggard, blond hair knotted and filthy. Eyes red and puffy. She was angry at how frightened she looked and stepped away from the mirror quickly.

She looked for her clothes. Nothing. She couldn't find anything to wrap herself in. No sheets or curtains. This started a crying fit. She huddled in a ball and sobbed.

Wondering how long she'd been unconscious. A week, a day? She wasn't hungry so she guessed it was still Saturday. Maybe Sunday at the latest.

Was anyone looking for her?

Did anyone know she was missing?

Her parents, of course. She'd missed the lunch. Which she'd been going to blow off anyway. Thank God she hadn't called Bett and told her she wasn't coming, the way she'd planned. If that had happened they *still* wouldn't miss her.

And Amy . . .

Should have told her where I was going.

But Crazy Megan was embarrassed. Crazy Megan didn't want anybody to know she's seeing a shrink. Fuck. She should've gone to Juvie after all. Ten days in detention and it'd be over with. But no, she picked the nut doctor.

Who *is* he? she screamed to herself. Was he the man in that car that'd been following her? She'd started to believe that was her imagination.

Standing by the bed, Megan looked out the barred window into a huge field of tall grass and brush. Some trees, many of them cut down and left to rot.

She gasped suddenly as a huge dog trotted past the window and stopped, staring up at her. A bit of bloody flesh dangled from its mouth, red, like a scrap of steak. Its eyes were spooky – too human – and it seemed to recognize her. Then suddenly the dog tensed, wheeled and vanished.

She examined the window. The iron bars were thick and the space between them was far too small for her to get through.

Frustrated, she pounded her palms against the wall.

Who *is* he?

Megan strode to the door, gripped and pulled it hard. It was, of course, locked tight. The tears returned suddenly; they fell on her breasts and her nipples contracted painfully from the sobbing and the dank cold of the dismal room.

Who *is* he?

Why did they make her go to see him?

What'd I do to deserve this? Nothing! I didn't do a thing!

If her mother was going to fuck nerds in Baltimore then for Christ's sake why didn't she call me? Just a three-minute phone call. Sorry honey I'm going to be late call Domino's and use the charge card have Amy over and all right even Brittany too but no boys . . .

If her father was going to spend his life chasing bimbettes why couldn't he at least spend more than one weekend a month with her?

This was *their* fault! Her parents!

I hate you so much! I fucking *hate* you. I—

A sound.

What was it?

A scuttling . . .

It came from the ceiling. Looking up, she saw a number of dark clusters where the wall met the ceiling. She moved closer. Spiders! Huge black ones. And a hundred hundred tiny dots of infants flowed down the wall like black water.

Megan shivered, overwhelmed with disgust, her skin crawling at the sight. She raced toward the door, slamming into it with all her weight, and collapsed on to the splintery floor. She crawled along it, pushing at the baseboards, trying to find a weak spot. Nothing.

She curled up in a ball on the cold floor. Cried for five minutes.

What's that? Crazy Megan asks her alter ego.

This stopped the tears.

Squick, squick.

That sound again. In the ceiling and the walls.

Squirrels, she decided. Then stood and walked to the wall. It was cinder block. How could there be animals in the walls if they were made out of stone?

Then she glanced into the bathroom and squinted. *Those* walls were just plasterboard. And there was a rectangular plate about twelve by eighteen inches mounted on the wall beside the toilet. It had been painted over a dozen times. What did it lead to?

She walked inside, crouched down and ran her finger across the edge of the metal. In the corners she felt three indentations and one screw head. If she could break through the paint she could pull the plate up and bend the metal till it snapped.

But the enamel was thick, like glue, and with her short nails she couldn't get a grip on the edge. She thought of Brittany, with the killer claws, a regular at a local Vietnamese manicure parlor. That was what she needed – slut nails . . .

She searched the bedroom once more but couldn't find anything to use as a tool. Sighing, she returned to the bathroom, lay on the floor and slugged the metal plate. It resounded hollowly, tantalizing with the promise of an empty passageway on the other side. But it didn't move a millimeter. *Keep going*, Crazy Megan says.

Megan slammed her fist into it again and again, until her knuckles began to bruise and swell. She turned around and kicked with her heel. As the center pushed in slightly, a hairline crack formed around the edge and she kicked harder. Her foot felt as if it were going to shatter.

Go! C.M. encourages. *Go for it!*

Megan spun round and tried to grab the side of the plate with her short nails again. They just weren't long enough to get a purchase in the crack and she howled in frustration then lunged forward, bared her teeth and shoved her face against the wall, trying to dig her incisors into the crack.

Her gum tore open on the rough paint and plaster. Her jaw exploded with pain and she tasted blood. Then suddenly, with a snap, her front tooth slipped into the crack and pulled the plate away from the wall a fraction of an inch. Megan leaned away, pressed her hands to her face to ease the pain and spit blood. Then she grabbed the plate and yanked so furiously it gave way at once, ripping the remaining screw from the wall. She fell backwards.

'Jesus,' Crazy Megan says respectfully. *Good job.*

With a gasp of joy she sat up, seeing faint light through the hole. She shoved her head into the opening, looking into another room. The plate had apparently covered an old heating vent. There was a thin grille on the other side about a foot away. She kicked and it fell clattering to the floor. She froze. Quiet! she reminded herself. He could be near by.

Then she started into the opening, head first. Her shoulders were broad but she managed to ease them through. She had to reach down, cramping her arm, and cradle her breasts to keep her nipples from scraping on the sharp bottom edge of the hole. One inch at a time she forced her way through the vent. As she eased through she examined the other room. There were bars on these windows too. But the door was standing open several inches. She could see a dim corridor beyond the doorway.

Another foot, then one more.

Until her hips. They stopped her cold.

Those fucking hips, Crazy Megan mutters. *Hate 'em, hate 'em, hate 'em. You just couldn't lose those ten pounds, could you?*

I don't need any of your crap now, okay? Megan thinks to her alter ego.

The vent on the other side of the wall was slightly smaller than the one in her room. Megan tried wriggling, tightening her muscles, licking her fingers and swabbing her sides with spit but she still remained frozen, exactly halfway into each room, her butt dead center in the wall.

No way, she thought to herself. I'm not getting stuck here! A terrible burst of claustrophobia passed through her. She fought it down, wriggled slightly and moved forward an inch or two before she froze again.

Then she heard the noise. *Squick, squick.*

The scuttling of clawed feet in the wall above. Accompanied by a high-pitch twitter.

Oh, my God, no. The squirrels.

Her heart began to pound.

Squick, squick.

Right above where she was stuck. Two of them, it sounded like. Then more, gathering where the wall met the ceiling.

But . . . what if they weren't squirrels?

Oh, fuck, they're rats! Crazy Megan blurts.

Megan began to sob. The noise of their little feet started coming down the wall. She stifled a scream as something – a bit of insulation or wood – fell on to her skin.

Squick. Squick squick squick. Walking along the ceiling, several of them gathering above her, curious. Maybe hungry. Hundreds of terrible creatures moving toward her stuck body – cautiously but unstoppably.

More rats. *Squick.*

Twitters and scuttling, growing closer still. There seemed to be a dozen now, two dozen. She pictured needle-sharp yellow teeth. Tiny red tongues.

Closer and closer. Curious. Attracted to her smell. There'd been no toilet paper; she hadn't wiped herself after urinating. And she'd just finished her period a day ago. They'd smell the blood. They'd head right for it.

More scuttling.

Oh . . .

She closed her eyes and sobbed in terror. It seemed that the whole wall was alive with them. Dozens, hundreds of rats converging on her. Closer, closer. *Squick squick squick squicksquicksquick . . .*

Megan slapped her palms against the wall and pushed with all her strength, kicking her feet madly. Then, uttering a dentist's-drill squeal, one rat dropped squarely on to her ass. She gasped and felt her heart stutter in terror. She slapped the wall, wriggling furiously. The startled animal climbed off and she felt the snaky tail slip in between her legs as he moved back up the wall.

'Oh,' she choked. 'No . . .'

As she pounded the wall beside her and scrabbled her feet on the bathroom floor, another animal tentatively reached out with a claw and then stepped on to the small of her back. Then she felt four paws. They gripped softly and began to move. A damp whiskered nose tapped on her as the creature sniffed along her skin.

Her arms cramping, she shoved hard. Her foot caught the edge of the toilet in the bathroom behind her and she pushed herself forward two or three inches. It was just enough. She was able to wriggle her hips free. The rat leapt off her and Megan burst into the adjoining room. She crawled frantically into the far corner, as four rats escaped from the wall and vanished through the open door.

She sobbed, gasping for breath, brushing her palms over her skin frantically to make sure none of them clung to her. After five minutes she'd calmed. Slowly she stepped back to the vent and listened. *Squick squick squick*. . . . More scuttling, more twitters. She slammed the grille against the vent opening. The rest of the rats vanished up the wall. An angry hiss sounded from the hole.

God . . .

She found some stacks of newspapers, removed the grille, wadded up the papers and stuffed them inside the wall to keep the creatures trapped inside.

She collapsed back on the floor, trying to push away the horrible memory of the probing little paws, filthy and damp.

Looking into the dim corridor, cold and yellow, windows barred, filthy, she happened to glance up at a sign on the wall.

PATIENTS SHALL BE DE-LOUSED ONCE A WEEK.

The sign – a simple sign – brought the hopelessness home to her.

Don't worry about it, Crazy Megan tries to reassure.

But her alter ego wasn't listening. Megan shivered in fear and disgust and curled up, clutching her knees. Hating this place. Hating her life, her pointless life . . . Her stupid, superficial friends. Her sick obsession with Janis, the Grateful Dead and all the rest of the cheerful, lying fake-ass past.

Hating the man who'd done this to her, whoever he was.

But most of all hating her parents.

Hating them beyond words.

12

The forty-minute drive to Leesburg took Tate and Bett past a few mansions, some redneck bungalows, some new developments with names like Windstone and The Oaks. Cars on blocks, vegetable stands selling – at this time of year – jars of put-up preserves and relishes.

But mostly they passed farmland.

Looking out over just-planted land like this, some people see future homes or shopping malls or townhouses and some see rows of money to be plucked from the ground at harvest time. And some perhaps simply drive past seeing nothing but where their particular journey is taking them.

But Tate Collier saw in these fields what he felt in his own land – a quiet salvation, something he did yet not of his doing, something that would let him survive, if not prosper, graciously: the silence of rooted growth. And if at times that process betrayed him – hail, drought, tumbling markets – Tate could still sleep content in the assurance that there was no malice in the earth's heart. And that, the former criminal prosecutor within him figured, was no small thing.

So even though Tate claimed, as any true advocate would, that it made no nevermind to him whether he was representing the plaintiffs or defendants in the Liberty

Park case, his heart was in fact with the people who wanted to protect the farmland from the concrete and concession stands and traffic.

He felt this even more now, seeing these rolling hills. And he felt too guilt and a pang of impatience that he was distracted from his preparations for the hearing. But a look at Bett's troubled face put this discomfort aside. There'd be time to hone his argument. Right now there were other priorities.

They passed the Oatlands farm and as they did the sun came out. And he sped on toward Leesburg, into old Virginia. Confederate Virginia.

There weren't many towns like this in the northern part of the state; many people in Richmond and Charlottesville didn't really consider most of Northern Virginia to be in the commonwealth at all. Tate and Bett drove through the city limits and slowed to the posted thirty miles per hour. Examining the trim yards, the white clapboard houses, the incongruous biker bar in the middle of downtown, the plentiful churches. They followed the directions Tate had been given to the hospital where Dr Hanson was visiting his mother.

'Can he tell us much?' Bett wondered. 'Legally, I mean.'

She'd be thinking, he guessed, of the patient-doctor privilege, which allowed a doctor to keep silent on the conversations between a patient and his physician. Years ago, when they'd been married, Tate had explained this and other nuances of the law to her. But she often grew offended at these arcane rules. 'You mean if you don't read him his rights, the arrest is no good? Even if he *did* it?' she'd ask, perplexed. Or: 'Excuse me, but why should a mother go to jail if she's shoplifting food for her hungry child? I don't get it.'

He expected that same indignation now when he explained that Hanson didn't *have* to say anything to them. But Bett just nodded, accepting the rules. She smiled coyly and said, 'Then I guess you'll have to be extra persuasive.'

They turned the corner and the white-frame hospital loomed ahead of them.

'Well, busy day,' Bett said, assessing the front of the hospital as she flipped up the car's mirror after refreshing her lipstick. There were three police cars parked in front of the main entrance. The red and white lights atop one of them flashed with urgent brilliance.

'Car wreck?' Bett suggested. Route 15, which led into town, was posted fifty-five but everybody drove it at seventy or eighty.

They parked and walked inside.

Something was wrong, Tate noted. Something serious had happened. Several nurses and orderlies stood in the lobby, looking down a corridor. Their faces were troubled. A receptionist leaned over the main desk, gazing down the same corridor.

'What is it?' Bett whispered.

'Not a clue,' he answered.

'Look, there he is,' somebody said.

'God,' someone else muttered.

Two policemen were leading a tall, balding man down the corridor toward the main entrance. His hands were cuffed behind him. His face was red. He'd been crying. As he passed, Tate heard him say, 'I didn't do it. I *wouldn't* do it! I wasn't even *there!*'

Several of the nurses shook their heads, eying him with cold expressions on their faces.

'I didn't do it!' he shouted.

131

A moment later he was in a squad car. It made a U-turn in the driveway and sped off.

Tate asked the receptionist, 'What's that all about?'

The white-haired woman shook her head, eyes wide, cheeks pale. 'We nearly had our first assisted suicide.' She was very shaken. 'I don't believe it.'

'What happened?'

'We have a patient – an elderly woman with a broken hip. And it looks like he—' She nodded toward where the police car had been. '—comes in and talks to her for a while and next thing we know she's got a syringe in her hands and's trying to kill herself. Can you imagine? Can you just *imagine?*'

'But they saved her?' Tate asked.

'The Lord was watching over her.'

Bett blinked and glanced at the woman.

She continued, 'A nurse just happened by. My goodness. Can you imagine?'

Bett shook her head. Tate recalled that she felt the same about suicide as she did about the death penalty. He thought briefly of her sister's husband's death. Harris. He'd used a shotgun to kill himself. Like Hemingway. Harris had been an artist – a bad one, in Tate's estimation – and he'd shot himself in his studio, his dark blood covering a canvas that he'd been working on for months.

Absently he asked the receptionist, 'That man. Who is he? Somebody like Kevorkian?'

'Who *is* he?' the woman blurted. 'Why, he was her *son!*'

Tate and Bett looked at each other in shock. She said in a whisper, 'Oh, no. It couldn't be.'

Tate asked the woman, 'The patient? Was her name Hanson?'

'Yes, that's the name.' Shaking her head. 'Her own son tried to talk her into killing herself! And I heard he was a therapist too. A doctor! Can you *imagine?*'

Tate and Bett sat in the hospital cafeteria, brooding silence between them. They'd ordered coffee that neither wanted. They were waiting for a call from Konnie Konstantinatis. They'd spoken only ten minutes ago but it seemed like hours.

Tate's phone buzzed. He answered it before it could chirp again.

''Lo.'

'Okay, Counselor, made some calls. But this is all unofficial. There's still no case. *Got* it? Are you *comfortable* with that?'

'Got it, Konnie. Go ahead.'

The detective explained that he had called the Leesburg police and spoken to a detective there.

'Here's what happened. This old lady, Greta Hanson, fell and broke her hip last week. Fell down her back stairs. Serious but not too serious. She's eighty. You know how it is.'

'Right.'

'Okay, today she's tanked up on painkillers, really out of it, and she hears her son. *Your* Dr Hanson. Hears him telling her – well, she *thinks* he's telling her – it looks like the end of the road, they found cancer, she only has a few months left. Yadda, yadda, yadda. The pain's gonna be terrible. Tells her it's best to just finish herself off, it's what everybody wants. Leaves her a syringe of Nembutal. She says she'll do it. She sticks herself but a nurse finds her in time. Anyway, she tells 'em what happened and the administrator calls the cops. They find the son in the gift shop buying a box of candy. Supposedly for her. They collar him. He denies it all. Of course. What else is he going to say? So. End of story.'

'And this all happens fifteen minutes before Bett and I are going to talk to him about Megan? It's no coincidence, Konnie. Come on.'

Silence from Fairfax.

'Konnie. You hear me?'

'I'm telling you the facts, Counselor. I don't comment otherwise.'

'She's sure it was her son who talked to her?'

'She said.'

'Anyway, we can talk to him?'

'Nope. Not till the arraignment on Monday. And he's probably not gonna be in any mood to talk to you even then.'

'All right. Answer me one question. Can you look up what kind of car he drives?'

'Who? Hanson? Yeah, hold on.'

Tate heard typing as he filled in Bett on what Konnie'd said.

'Oh, my,' she said, hand rising to her mouth.

A moment later the detective came back on the line. 'Two cars. A Mazda 929 and a Ford Explorer. Both this year's models.'

'What colors?'

'Mazda's green. The Explorer's black.'

'It was somebody else, Konnie. Somebody was following Megan.'

'Tate, she took the train to New York. She's going to see the Statue of Liberty and hang out in Greenwich Village and do whatever kids do in New York and—'

'You know the Bust-er Book?'

'What the hell is a buster book?' the detective grumbled.

134

'Kids at Jefferson High are supposed to write down anybody who comes up and offers 'em drugs, candy, maybe flashes 'em, you know.'

'Oh, that shit. Right.'

'A friend of Megan's said there'd been a car following her. In the Bust-er Book, some kids reported a gray car parked near the school in the afternoon. And Megan herself reported it last week.'

'Gray car?'

'Right.'

A sigh. 'Tate, lemme ask you. Just how many kids go to that school of hers?'

'I'm not saying it's a *good* lead, Konnie—'

'And just how many parents in gray cars pick 'em up?'

'—but it *is* a lead.'

'Tag number? Make, model, year?'

Tate sighed. 'Nothing.'

'Look, Counselor, get me at least one of the above and we'll talk. . . . So, what're you thinking, somebody snatched her? The Amtrak schedule is bogus?'

'I don't know. It's just fishy.'

'It's not a case, Tate. That's the watchword for today. Look, I better go.'

'One last question, Konnie. *Does* she have cancer? Hanson's mother?'

The detective hesitated. 'No. At least it's not what they're treating for.'

'So somebody talked her into believing she's dying. Talked her into trying to kill herself.'

'Yeah. And that somebody was her son. He could have a hundred motives. Gotta go, Counselor.'

Click.

He relayed to Bett the rest of his conversation with Konnie.

135

'Megan was seeing a therapist who tried to kill his mother? God.'

'I don't know, Bett,' he said. 'You saw his face. Did he look guilty?'

'He looked caught,' she said.

Tate nodded in concession. He glanced at his watch. It was 2.30. 'Let's get back to Fairfax and find that teacher. Eckhard.'

Crazy Megan finally gets a chance to talk.

Listen up, girl. Listen here, kiddo. Biz-nitch, you listening? Good. You need me. You're not sneaking cigarettes in Fair Oaks mall parking lot. You're not flirting with a George Mason junior to get him to buy you a pint of Comfort or Turkey. You're not sitting in Amy's room, snarfing wine, hating it and saying it's great while you're like: 'Sure, I come every time Josh and I fuck. I mean, it's like so easy. It is for everybody, isn't it? I mean . . .'

Leave me alone, Megan thought.

But C.M. won't have any of this *attitude*. She snaps, *You hate the world. Okay. What you want—*

'A family is what I want,' Megan responded. 'That's all I wanted.'

Oh. Well, that's precious, her crazy side offers, nice and sarcastic. *Who the fuck doesn't? You want Mommy and Daddy to wave their magic wand and get you out of here? Uh-huh. Uh-huh. Well, ain't going to happen, girl. So get off your fat ass and get out.*

I can't move, Megan thought.

Up, girl. Up. Look, he—

And who *is* he?

Crazy Megan is in good form today. *What difference does it make? He's the bogy-man, he's Jason, he's Leatherface, he's Freddy Krueger, he's your father—*

All right, stop it. You're like so . . . tedious.

But C.M.'s wound up now. *He's everything bad, he's your mother giving Brad a blow job, he's the barn at your father's farm, he's an inconvenient child, he's a whispering bear—*

'Stop it, stop it, stop it!' Megan screamed out loud.

But nothing stops Crazy Megan when she gets going. *It doesn't matter what he is. Don't you get it? He thinks you're locked up tight in your little padded cell. But you're not. You're out. And you may not have much time. So get your shit together and get the hell out of here.*

I don't have any clothes, Megan pointed out.

That's the girl I love. Oooo. The sarcasm is thick as Noxema. *Sit back and find excuses. Let's see: You're pissed 'cause Mom's off to Baltimore to fuck Mr Rogers and do you say anything about it? No. It rags you that Dad fits you in around his dates with girls who've got inflatable boobs but do you bitch about it? Do you call him on it? No. You go off and get drunk. You have another cigarette. What other distractions can we come up with? Nail polish, CDs, Victoria's Secret Taco Bell the mall the multiplex a boy's fat dick gossip . . .*

I hate you, Megan thought. I really, really hate you. Go away, go back where you came from.

I am where I came from, Crazy Megan responds. *You may have some time to fuck around like this, whining, and you may not. Now, you're buck naked and you don't like it. Well, if that's an issue, go find some clothes. And, no, there's no Contempo Casual around here. Of course I personally would say, Fuck the clothes, find a door and run like hell. But that's up to you.*

Megan rolled to her feet.

She stepped into the corridor.

Cold, painful. Her feet stung from the kicking. She started walking. Looking around, she saw it was a rambling place, one story, and built of concrete blocks. With the padded cell, she figured it was a mental hospital but she couldn't imagine treating patients here. It was way depressing. No one could have gotten better here. All the windows had thick bars on them.

She found a door leading outside and pushed it. It was locked tight. The same with two others. She looked outside for a car, didn't see one in the lot. At least she was alone. Dr Peters must have left.

Keep going, Crazy Megan insists.

'But—'

Keep. Going.

She did.

The place was huge, wing after wing, dozens of corridors, gloomy wards, private rooms, two-bed rooms. But all the doors leading outside were sealed tight and all the windows were barred. Every damn one of them. Two large interior doorways had been bricked off sloppily with cinder blocks and Sakrete – maybe because they led to less restricted wings that didn't have barred windows and doors. Dozens of the large concrete blocks that hadn't been needed lay scattered on the floor. She picked up one and slammed it into a barred window. It didn't even bend the metal rods.

For several hours she made a circuit of the hospital, moving quietly. She was careful; in the dim light she could make out footprints, hundreds of them. She couldn't tell if they'd been left by Dr Peters alone or by him and someone else but she was all too aware that she might not be alone.

By the time she'd made it back to her cell she hadn't found a single door or window that looked promising.

Shit. No way out.

Okay, Crazy Megan offers, chipper as ever. *At least find something you can use to nail his ass with.*

What do you mean?

A weapon, bitch. What do you think?

Megan remembered seeing a kitchen and returned there.

She started going through drawers and cupboards. But there wasn't anything she could use. There were no metal knives or forks, not even dinner knives, only hundreds of packages of plastic utensils. No glasses or ceramic cups. Everything was paper or Styrofoam.

She pulled open a door. It was a pantry full of food. She started to close the door but stopped, looked inside again.

There was enough food for a family to live on for a year. Cherios, condensed milk, Diet Pepsi, Doritos, Lays potato chips, tuna, Hostess cupcakes, Cup-a-soup, Chef Boy-R-Dee . . .

What's funny here?

Jesus. Crazy Megan catches on first.

Megan's hand rose to her mouth and she started to cry.

Jesus, Crazy Megan repeats.

These were exactly the same brands that Megan liked. This was what her mother's cupboards were stocked with. On other shelves were her shampoo, conditioner and soap.

Even the type of tampon that Megan used.

He'd been in her house, he knew what she liked.

He'd bought this all for her!

Don't lose it, babes, don't . . .

But Megan ignored her crazy side and gave in to the crying.

Thinking: if a family of four could live on this for a year, just think how long it would last her by herself.

Twenty minutes later Megan rose from the floor, wiped her face and continued her search. It didn't take her long to find the source of the footprints.

In a far wing of the hospital were two rooms that had been 'homified', as Bett would say when she'd dress up a cold-looking house to make it warmer and more comfortable. One room was an office, filled with thousands of books and files and papers. An armchair and lamp and desk. The other room was a bedroom. It smelled stale, turned her stomach. She looked inside. The bed was unmade and the sheets were stained. Off-white splotches.

Guys're so disgusting, Crazy Megan offers.

Megan agreed; who could argue with that?

This meant that someone else probably lived here – someone young, (she supposed older guys jerked off too but tried to imagine, say, her father doing it and couldn't.)

Way gross thought. From C.M.

Then she saw the closet.

Oh, please! She mentally crossed her fingers as she pulled the door open.

Yes! It was filled with clothes. She pulled on some jeans, which were tight around her hips and too long. She rolled the cuffs up. She found a work shirt – which was tight around her boobs. Didn't matter. She felt a hundred per cent better. There were no shoes but she found a pair of thick, black socks. For some reason, covering her feet gave her more confidence than covering the rest of her body.

She looked through the closet for a knife or gun

but found nothing. She returned to the other room. Rummaged through the desk. Nothing to use as a weapon, except a Bic pen. She took it anyway. Then she poked through the rest of the room, focusing at first on the bookshelves.

Some books were about psychiatry but most were fantasy novels and science fiction. Some were pretty weird. Stacks of comic books too. Japanese, a lot of them. Megan flipped through several. Totally icky – girls being raped by monsters and gargoyles and aliens. R- and X-rated. She shivered in disgust.

The name inside the books and on the front of the comic books was *Pete Matthews*. Sometimes he'd written *Peter M*. It was written very carefully, in big block letters. As if he were a young kid.

Megan looked through the files, most of them filled with psychological mumbo-jumbo she couldn't understand. There were also stacks of the American Psychiatric Association *Journal*. Articles were marked with yellow Post-Its. She noticed they'd been written by a doctor named Aaron Matthews. The boy's father? she wondered. His bio gave long lists of credentials. Dozens of awards and honorary degrees. One newspaper clipping called him the 'Einstein of therapists. He can dissect a psychosis from listening to patient's words for three or four minutes. A master diagnostician.'

In between two file folders was another clipping. Megan lifted it to the light. It showed Dr Peters and a young man in his late teens. But wait . . . The name wasn't Peters. The caption said only, 'Dr Aaron Matthews leaves the funeral home after the memorial service for his wife. He is accompanied by his son, Peter.'

Matthews . . . the one who wrote those articles. So he must have been a doctor here. That's how he knew about the hospital.

Megan studied the picture again, feeling crawly and scared. The son was . . . well, just plain weird. He was a tall boy, lanky, with long arms and huge hands. He had thick floppy hair that looked dirty and his forehead jutted over his dark eye sockets. He had a sick smile on his face.

Leaving his mother's funeral and he's *smiling*?

So the other resident here was the son. Maybe Peters well Matthew's . . . kept the boy locked up here, a prisoner too.

Her eyes fell to an official-looking report. She read the top page.

EMERGENCY INTAKE EVALUATION

Patient Peter A. Matthews presents with symptoms typical of an antisocial and paranoid personality. He is not schizophrenic, under DSM-III criteria, but he has, or claims to have, delusions. More likely these are merely fantasies, which in his case are so overpowering that he chooses not to recognize the borderline between his role playing and reality. These fantasies are generally of a sado-erotic nature, with him playing a non-human entity – stalking and raping females. During our sessions Peter would sometimes portray these entities – right down to odd mannerisms and garbled language. He was often 'in character', and quite consistent in his portrayals of these creatures. However, there was no evidence of fugue states or multiple personalities. He changed personas at his convenience, to achieve the greatest stimulation from his fantasies.

Peter is extremely dangerous. He must be hospitalized in a secure facility until the determination is made for a course of treatment. Recommend immediate psychopharmcological intervention.

Stalking . . . rape.

Megan put the report back on the desk. She found a notebook. Peter's name was written on this too. She read through it. In elaborate passages Peter described himself as a spaceman or an alien stalking women, tying them up, raping them. She dropped the book. There were dozens of others.

Tears again.

Then another thought: Her cell! This Dr Matthews, her kidnapper, had locked her up not only to keep her from getting out but to keep his son from getting *in*. He was—

A creak, a faint squeal. A door closed softly in a far part of the hospital.

Megan shivered in terror.

Move it, girl! Crazy Megan cries, in a silent voice as panicked as uncrazy Megan's. *It's him, it's the kid.*

She grabbed a pile of things to take with her – several of the magazines, file folders about the hospital, letters. Anything that might help her figure out who this Matthews was. Why he'd taken her. How she might get out.

Footsteps . . .

He's coming. He's coming here . . . Move it. Now!

Holding the files and clippings under her arm, Megan fled out the door. She ran down the corridors, getting lost once, pausing often to listen for footsteps. He seemed to be circling her.

Finally she found her way and raced into the room that adjoined hers, the 'ratroom' she thought of it. She rubbed the grate along the edges of the hole in the wall to widen it. She started through and, whimpering, clawed her way forward. Five inches, six, a foot, two feet. Finally she grabbed the toilet in her room and wrenched herself through the hole. She replaced the grate on the far side of the wall and then slammed the metal plate into place in her bathroom.

She ran to the door and pressed her ear against it. The footsteps grew closer and closer. But Peter didn't stop at her door. He kept moving. Maybe he didn't know she was here.

Megan sat on the icy floor with her hands pressing furiously against the plate until they cramped.

Listen, C.M. starts to say. *Maybe you can—*

Shut up, Megan thought furiously.

And for once Crazy Megan does what she's told.

13

The eyes.

The eyes tell it all.

When Aaron Matthews was practicing psychotherapy he learned to read the eyes. They told him so much more than words. Words are tools and weapons and camouflage and shields.

But the eyes tell you the truth.

An hour ago, in Leesburg, he'd looked into the glassy, groggy eyes of a drugged Greta Hanson and knew she was a woman with no reserves of strength. And so he'd leaned close, become her son and spun a tale guaranteed to send her to the very angels that she was babbling on and on about. It's quite a challenge to talk someone into killing herself.

He doubted she'd die from the dosage of Nembutal he'd given her and he doubted that she could find a vein anyway. Besides, it was important for her to remain alive – to blame her son for the Kevorkian number. Poor Doc Hanson. Now either in jail or on the run. In any case, he'd be no help as a witness to Tate Collier and his wife.

Now, as he strolled along the sidewalk near Jefferson High school, Aaron Matthews was looking at another set of eyes.

Robert Eckhard's. Matthews was concluding that the man might or might not have been a good English teacher but he didn't doubt that Eckhard was one hell of a girl's volleyball coach. The diminutive, tweedy man sat with a book on his lap outside the sports field between the grade and high schools.

Wearing a baseball cap and thick-framed reading glasses he'd bought at Safeway – he remembered that Eckhard might have seen him near the school in the Mercedes – Matthews walked slowly past. He studied his subject carefully. The teacher was a middle-aged man, in Dockers and a loose tan shirt. Matthews took all these observations and filed them away but what was helpful were the eyes; they told him everything he needed to know about Mr Eckhard.

Continuing down the sidewalk, Matthews walked into a drug-store and made several purchases. He slipped into the restroom of the store and five minutes later returned to the schoolyard. He sat down on the bench next to Eckhard's and rested the *Washington Post* in his lap. He gazed out at the young girls playing informal games of soccer or jump-rope in the schoolyard.

Once, then twice, Eckhard glanced at him.

The second time Matthews happened to turn his way and saw the teacher look back with a hint of curiosity in his tell-all eyes.

Matthews's face went still with shock. He waited a judicious moment then stood quickly and walked past Eckhard. But as he did, the disposable camera fell from the folds of his newspaper. He stepped forward suddenly to pick it up but accidentally kicked the yellow-and-black box. It went skidding along the sidewalk and hit Eckhard's foot.

Matthews froze. The teacher, his eyes on Matthews's, smiled again. He reached down and picked up the camera, looked at it. Turned it over.

'I—' Matthews began, horrified.

'It's okay,' Eckhard said.

'Okay?' Matthews voice faltered. He looked up and down the sidewalk, faint ill-ease in his face.

'I mean, the camera's okay,' Eckhard said, rattling it. 'It doesn't seem to be broken.'

Matthews began speaking breathlessly, over-explaining, as this script required. 'See, what it was, I was going to D.C. later today. I was going to the zoo. Take some pictures of the animals.'

'The zoo.' Eckhard examined the camera.

Matthews again looked up and down the sidewalk.

'You like photography?' the teacher asked.

After a moment, Matthews said, 'Yes, I do. A hobby.' Smiled awkwardly, summoning a blush. 'Everybody should have a hobby. That's what my father said.' He fell silent.

'It's my hobby too.'

'Really?'

'Been doing it for about fifteen years,' Eckhard said.

'Me too. Little less, I guess.'

'You live around here?' the teacher asked.

'Fairfax.'

'Long time?'

'A couple of years.'

Silence grew between them. Eckhard still held the camera. Matthews crossed his arms, rocked on his feet. Looking out over the schoolyard. Finally he asked, 'You do your own developing and printing?'

'Of course,' Eckhard said.

Of course. The expected answer. Matthews's eyes narrowed and he appeared to relax. 'Harder with color,' he offered. 'But they don't make the throwaways in black and white.'

147

· 'I'm getting a digital camera,' Eckhard said. 'I can just feed the pictures into my computer at home.'

'I've heard about those. They're expensive, aren't they?'

'They are . . . But you know hobbies. If they're important to you you're willing to spend the money.'

'That's my philosophy,' Matthews admitted. He sat down next to Eckhard. They looked out on the playing field, at a cluster of girls around ten or eleven. Eckhard looked through the eyepiece of the camera. 'Lens isn't telephoto.'

'No,' Matthews said. Then after a moment: 'She's cute. That brunette there.'

'Angela.'

'You know her?'

'I'm a teacher at the high school. I'm also a grade school counselor.'

Matthews's eyes flashed enviously. 'Teacher? I work for an insurance company. Actuarial work. Boring. But summers I volunteer at Camp Henry. Maryland. You know it?'

Eckhard shook his head. 'I also coach girls' sports.'

'That's a good job too.' Matthews clicked his tongue.

'Sure is.' Eckhard looked out over the field. 'I know most of these girls.'

'You do portraits?'

'Some.'

'You ever photograph her?'

But Eckhard wouldn't answer. 'So, you take pictures just around the area here?'

Matthews said, 'Here, California. Europe some. I was in Amsterdam a little while ago.'

'Amsterdam. I was there a few years ago. Not as interesting as it used to be.'

'That's what I found.'

'Bangkok's nice, though,' Eckhard volunteered.

'I'm planning on going next year,' Matthews said in a whisper.

'Oh, you have to,' Eckhard encouraged, kneading the yellow box of the camera in his hands. 'It's quite a place.'

Matthews could practically see the synapses firing in Eckhard's mind, wondering furiously if Matthews was a cop with the Child Welfare unit of the Fairfax County Police or an FBI agent. Matthews had treated several pedophiles during his days as a practicing therapist. He recognized the classic characteristics in Eckhard. He was intelligent – an organized offender – and he'd know all about the laws of child molestation and pornography. He could probably just keep the testosterone under control to avoid actually molesting a child but photographing them and collecting child porn was a compulsion that ruled his life.

Matthews offered another conspiratorial smile then glanced at a young girl bending down to pick up a ball. Gave a faint sigh. Eckhard followed his gaze and nodded.

The girl stood up. Eckhard said, 'Nancy. She's nine. Fifth grade.'

'Pretty. You wouldn't happen to have any pictures of her, would you?'

'I do.' Eckhard paused. 'In a nice skirt and blouse, I seem to recall.'

Matthews wrinkled his nose. Shrugged.

He wondered if the man would take the bait.

Snap.

Eckhard whispered, 'Well, not the blouse in all of them.'

149

Matthews exhaled hard. 'You wouldn't happen to have any with you?'

'No. You have any of yours?'

Matthews said, 'I keep all of mine on my computer.'

One of Matthews's patients had seven thousand images of child pornography on computer. He'd collected them while serving time for a molestation charge. The computer they resided on was the warden's at Hammond Falls State Penitentiary in Maryland. The prisoner had written an encryption program to keep the files secret. The FBI cracked it anyway and, despite his willingness to go through therapy, the offense earned him another ten years in prison.

Matthews said, 'I don't have too many in my collection. Only about four thousand.'

Eckhard's eyes turned to Matthews and they were vacuums. He whispered a long, envious 'Well . . .'

Matthews added, 'I've got some videos too. But only about a hundred of them.'

'A *hundred?*'

Eckhard shifted on the bench. Matthews knew the teacher was lost. Completely. He'd be thinking: At worst, it's entrapment. At worst, I can talk my way out of it. At worst, I'll flee the country and move to Thailand . . . As a therapist Matthews was continually astonished at how easily people won completely unwinnable arguments with themselves.

Still, you land a fish with as much care as you hook it.

'You seem worried . . .' Matthews started. 'And I have to say, I don't know you, and I'm a little nervous myself. But I've just got a feeling about you. Maybe we could help each other out . . . Let me show you a couple of samples of what I've got.'

The eyes flickered with lust.

Always the eyes.

'That'd be fine. That'd be good. Please.' Eckhard cleared his excited throat.

Oh, you pathetic thing . . .

'I could give you a computer disk.' Matthews suggested.

'Sure. That'd be great.'

'I only live about three blocks from here. Let me run up to my house and get some samples.'

'Good.'

'Oh,' Matthews said, pausing. A frown. 'I only have girls.'

'Yes, yes. That's fine.' Breathless. A bead of spit rested in the corner of the mouth.

'Age?' Matthews asked, like a clerk inquiring about a customer's shirt size.

Eckhard's eyes moved slowly to a ten-year-old girl skipping rope.

Matthews nodded. 'I've got some good ones I think you'll like.'

Desperately Eckhard said, 'Can you go now?'

'Sure. Be right back.'

'I'll be here.'

Matthews started up the street.

He turned back and saw the teacher, a stupid smile on his face, grinning from ear to ear, looking out over the field of his sad desire, rubbing his thumb over the disposable camera.

In the drug-store once again, Matthews walked up to the pay-phone and called 911.

When dispatch answered, he said urgently, 'Oh, you need somebody down to Markus Avenue right away! The sports field behind Jefferson School.' He described

Eckhard and said, 'He took a little girl into the alley and pulled his, you know, penis out. Then took some pictures. And I heard him ask her to his house. He said he's got lots of pictures of little girls like her on his computer. Pictures of little girls, you know . . . doing it. Oh, it's disgusting. Hurry up! I'm going back and watch him to make sure he doesn't get away.'

He hung up.

Matthews didn't know if snapshots of a fully dressed little girl in a schoolyard next to frames of a man's erect dick (Matthews's own penis, taken in the drug-store restroom twenty minutes ago) were an offense anywhere but once the cops got a search warrant for the man's house Eckhard would be out of commission – and a completely unreliable witness about gray Mercedes or anything else – for a long, long time.

By the time he was back on the street, walking toward his car, Matthews heard the sirens.

Fairfax County took children's well-being very seriously, it seemed.

Tate and Bett arrived at the schoolyard, taking care to avoid the main building, just in case the clean-cut young fascist of a security guard had happened to glance inside the Bust-er Book after Tate and Bett had left and found twenty or so pages missing.

But volleyball practice had been cancelled for today, it seemed. Nobody quite knew why.

In fact the yard was almost deserted, despite the clear skies.

They found two students and asked if they'd seen Eckhard. They said they hadn't. One teenage girl said, 'We were coming here for the practice.'

'Volleyball?'

'Right. And what it was was somebody said it's been canceled and we should all go home. Stay away from here. Totally weird.'

'And you haven't seen Mr Eckhard?'

'Somebody said he had to go someplace. But they didn't tell us where. I don't know. He was here earlier. I don't get it. He's *always* here. I mean, always.'

'Do you know where he lives?'

'Fairfax, someplace. I think.'

'What's his first name?'

'Robert.'

Tate called directory assistance and got his number. He left a message. He had a thought. He asked his ex-wife, 'Where did she hang out?'

'Hang out?' Bett asked absently. He saw her looking into her purse, eyes on the letter containing her daughter's searing words.

'Yeah, with her friends. After school.'

'Just around. You know.'

'But where? We'll go there, ask if anybody's seen her.'

There was a long hesitation. Finally she said, 'I'm not sure.'

'You're not?' Tate asked, surprised. 'You don't know where she goes?'

'No,' Bett answered testily. 'Not all the time. She's a seventeen-year-old girl with a driver's license.'

'Oh. So you don't know where she'd spend her afternoons.'

'Not always, no.' She glanced at him angrily. 'It is not like she hangs out in southeast D.C., Tate.'

'I just—'

'Megan's a responsible girl. She knows where to go and where not to go. I trust her.'

153

They walked in silence back to the car. Bett grabbed her phone again and her address book. She began making calls – to Megan's friends, he gathered. At least she had *their* numbers; still, it irked him that she didn't seem to know basic information like this – important information – about the girl.

When they arrived at the car she folded up the phone. 'Her favorite place was called the Coffee Shop. Up near Route Fifty.' Bett sounded victorious. 'Like Starbuck's. All right? Happy?'

She dropped into the seat and crossed her arms. They drove in silence north along the parkway.

14

Braking to five miles an hour, Tate surveyed the crowded parking lot.

He found a space between a chopped Harley-Davidson and a pickup bumper-stickered with the Reb stars 'n' bars. He navigated the glistening Lexus into this narrow spot.

They surveyed the cycles, the tough, young men and women, all in denim, defiantly holding open bottles, the tattoos, the boots. At the other end of the parking lot was a very different crowd, younger – boys with long hair, girls with crew cuts, layers of baggy clothes, plenty of piercing. Bleary eyes.

Welcome to the Coffee Shop.

'Here?' Bett asked. 'She came *here*?'

Starbuck's, Tate thought. I don't think so.

She glanced at the notes she'd jotted. 'Off Fifty near Walney. This's it. Oh, my.'

Tate glanced at his ex-wife. Her horrified expression didn't diminish his anger. How could she have let Megan come to a place like this? Didn't she check up on her? Most of the parents he knew gave their children pagers. Why hadn't Bett gotten one for her? Or a cell phone?

Her own daughter, for Christ's sake . . .

Tate pushed the door open and started to get out.

Bett popped her seatbelt but he said abruptly, 'Wait here.'

He walked up to the closest cluster – the bikers; they seemed less comatose than the slacker gang at the other end of the lot.

He began asking them about Megan. But no one had heard of her. He was vastly relieved. Maybe it was a misunderstanding. Maybe her friend meant a generic coffee shop someplace.

At the far end of the lot he waded into a grungy sea of plaid shirts, Doc Marten boots, JNCO jeans and bellbottom Levi's. The girls wore tight tank tops over bras in contrasting colors. Their hair was long, parted in the middle, like Megan's. Peace symbols bounced on breasts and there was a lot of tie-dyed couture. The images reminded Tate of his own coming-of-age era, the early '70s.

'Megan? Sure, like I know her,' said a slim girl, smoking a cigarette she was too young to buy.

'Have you seen her lately?'

'She's here a lotta nights. But not in the last week, you know. Like, who're you?'

'I'm her father. She's missing.'

'Wow. That sucks.'

'How'd she get in? She was seventeen.'

'Uhm. I don't know.'

Meaning: a fake ID.

He asked, 'Do you know if anybody's been asking about her? Or been following her?'

'I dunno. But her and me, we weren't, like, real close. Hey, ask him. Sammy! Hey, Sammy.' To Tate she added, 'They'd hang out some.'

A large boy glanced their way, eyed Tate uneasily. He set a paper cup behind a garbage can and walked up to him. He was about the lawyer's height, with a pimply face, and wore a baseball cap backwards. He carried a pager and a cellphone. He eyed Tate cautiously.

'I'm looking for Megan McCall. You know her?'

'Sure.'

'Have you seen her lately?'

'She was here this week.'

'She comes here a lot?' Tate asked.

'Yeah, she, like, hangs here. Her and Donna and Amy. You know.'

'How about her boyfriend?'

'That guy from Mason?' Sammy asked. 'The one she broke up with? Naw, this wasn't his scene. I only saw 'em together once, I think.'

'Was somebody – some man in a gray car – asking about her, following her around?'

Sammy gave a faint laugh. 'Yeah, there was. Last week, Megan and me, we were here and she was like, "What's he want? Him again." And I'm like, you want me to go fuck him up?' And she goes, "Sure." And she goes inside. And I go up to the car but the asshole takes off.'

'Did you get a look at him?'

'Not too close. White guy. Your age, maybe a little older.'

'You get the plate number?'

'No. Didn't even see what state. But it was a Mercedes. I don't know what model. All those fucking numbers. American cars have names. But German cars, just fucking numbers.'

'And you don't have any idea who he was?'

'Well, yeah, I figured. But, you know, Megan doesn't like to talk about it. So I let it go.'

Tate shook his head. 'Talk about what?'

'You know.'

'No, I *don't* know,' Tate said. 'What?'

'Well, just . . .' Sammy lifted his hands. 'What she used to do. I figured he was looking for some more action and had tracked her down here.'

'Action? I don't understand. What are you saying?'

'I figured he and Megan had . . . get it? And he wanted some more.'

'What are you talking about?' Tate persisted.

'What d'you think I'm talking about?' The kid was confused. 'He fucked Megan and liked what he got.'

'Are you saying she had a boyfriend in his forties?'

'Boyfriend?' Sammy laughed. 'No, man. I'm saying she had a *customer*. I don't know how the hell old he was.'

'What?'

'Sure, she—'

The boy probably had twenty or thirty pounds on Tate but farm work keeps you strong and in two seconds Sammy was flat on his back, the wind knocked out of him. Both hands were raised, protecting his face from Tate's lifted fist.

'What the fuck're you saying?' he raged.

Sammy shouting back, 'No, man, no! I didn't do anything. Hey . . .'

'Are you saying she had sex for money?'

'No, I'm not saying nothing! I'm not saying a fucking thing!'

The girl's voice was close to his ear, the blonde he'd first spoken to. 'It's, like, not a big deal. It was a couple years ago.'

'Couple years ago? She's only seventeen *now*, for Christ sake.' Tate lowered his hand. He stood up, brushed the dust off. He looked at the people in front of the bar.

The huge, bearded bouncer was amused. His jurisdiction didn't extend outside the front door, it seemed. Bett was half out of the car, looking at her ex-husband with alarm. He motioned her to stay where she was.

Sammy said, 'Fuck, man, what'd you do that for? I didn't fuck her. She gave it up a while ago. You asked me what I thought and I told you. I figured the guy liked what he had and wanted more. Jesus.'

The girl said, 'Sorry, mister. She had a thing for older men. They were willing to pay. But it was okay, you know.'

'Okay?' Tate asked, numb.

'Sure. She always used rubbers.'

Tate stared at her for a moment then walked back to the car.

Sammy stood up, picked up his beeper, which had fallen off his belt in the struggle. 'Fuck you, man. *Fuck* you! Who're you anyway?'

Turning back, Tate said, 'I'm her father.'

'Father?' the boy asked, frowning.

'Yeah. Her father.'

Sammy looked at the girl, who shrugged. The boy said, 'Megan said she didn't have a father.'

Tate stared at him.

'She said he was a lawyer or something but he ran off and left her when she was six. She hasn't heard from him since.'

In the car Tate asked angrily, 'You didn't know she went there?'

'I told you I didn't. You think I'd *let* her go to a place like that?'

'I just think you might want to know where she was. From time to time.'

'You "just think". You know when people say that?'

'What are you—?' he began.

'They say that when they mean, you damn well *ought* to know where she was.'

'I didn't mean that at all,' Tate snapped.

Though of course he had.

He sped out on to the highway, tires squealing, gravel flying from beneath the tires. Putting the Coffee Shop far behind them.

She finally asked, 'What was that all about?'

He didn't answer.

'Tate? What were you fighting with that boy about?'

'You don't want to know,' he said darkly.

'Tell me!'

He hesitated but then he had to say it. 'He said he thought the guy in the gray car might've been a customer.'

'Customer? At the Coffee Shop?'

'Of Megan's.'

'What? Oh, God. You don't mean—?'

'That's exactly what I mean. That's what the boy said. And that girl too.'

'Vile. You're disgusting . . .'

'Me? *I'm* just telling you what he said.'

Tears coming down her face. 'She wouldn't. There's no way. I believe that in my heart. It's impossible.'

'*They* didn't seem to think it was impossible. They seemed to think she did it pretty often.'

'Tate! How can you say that?'

'And he said it was a couple years ago. When she was *fifteen*.'

'She didn't. I'm certain.'

A wave of fury consumed him. His hands cramped on the steering wheel. 'How could you not know? What were you so busy doing that you didn't notice any condoms in your daughter's purse? Didn't you check who called her? Didn't you notice when she got home? Maybe at midnight? At one? Two?'

'Stop it!' Bett cried. 'Don't attack me. It's not true! It's a misunderstanding. We'll find her and she'll explain it.'

'They seemed to think—'

She screamed, 'It's a lie! It's just gossip. That's all it is! Gossip. Or they're talking about somebody else. Not Megan.'

'Yes, Megan. And you should have—'

'Oh, you're blaming me? It isn't my fault! You know, you *might* have been more involved with her life.'

'Me?' he snapped.

'Okay – sure, your happy family didn't turn out the way you wanted. Well, I'm sorry about that, Tate. But you could have checked on her once in a while.'

'I did. I paid support every month—'

'Oh, for Christ's sake, I don't mean money. You know how often she'd ask me, Why doesn't daddy like me? And I'd say, He does, he's just busy with all his cases. And I'd say, It's hard to be a real daddy when he and Mommy are divorced. And I'd say—'

'I spent Easters with her. And the Fourth of July.'

'Yeah, and you should've heard the debriefings on *those* joyous holidays.' Bett laughed coldly.

'What do you mean? She never complained.'

'You have to *know* somebody before you complain to them. You have to care about them.'

'I took her shopping,' he said. 'I always asked her about school. I—'

'You could've done more. We might've made some accommodation. Might've been a little more of a family.'

'Like hell,' he spat out.

'People've done it. In worse situations.'

'What was I supposed to do? Take up your slack?'

'This isn't about me,' she snapped.

'I think it is. You're her mother. You want somebody else to fix what you've done? Or haven't done?'

'I've done the best I could!' Bett sobbed. 'By myself.'

'But it wasn't you yourself. It was you and the boyfriends.'

'Oh, I was supposed to be celibate?'

'No, but you were supposed to be a mother first. You should've noticed that she had problems.'

Tate couldn't help but think of Bett's sister Susan. The woman had desperately wanted children, while Bett had always been indifferent to the idea. After her husband Harris's death Susan had moved in with a man very briefly – he was abusive and, from what Tate heard, half crazy. But he was a single man – divorced or widowed – with a child. And Susan put up with a lot of crap from him just to have the young boy around; she desperately wanted someone to mother. After they'd broken up, the lover had stalked her for a while but even at the worst moments Susan still seemed to regret the loss of the child in her life. Tate now wished Bett had shown some of that desire for Megan.

'I saw she was unhappy,' Bett said. 'But who the hell isn't? What was I supposed to do? Wave a magic wand?'

His anger wouldn't release the death grip it had on his heart. 'Hell, that's probably exactly your idea of mothering. Sure. Or cast a spell, look up something in the I Ching. Read her tarot.'

'Oh, stop it! I gave up all that shit years ago . . . I tried to be a good mother. I tried.'

'Did you?' he was astonished to find himself saying. 'You sure you weren't out looking for your King Arthur? Easier than changing diapers or helping her with homework or making sure when she was home after school. Making sure she wasn't fucking—'

'I tried . . . I tried . . .' Bett was sobbing, shaking.

Tate realized the car was nudging eighty. He slowed. A deep breath. Another.

Long, long silence. His eyes too welled up with tears. 'Listen, I'm sorry.'

'I tried. I wanted . . . I wanted . . .'

'Bett, please. I'm sorry.'

'I wanted a family too, you know,' she whispered, wiping her face on the sleeve of her blouse. 'I saw the Judge and his wife and you and the rest of the Colliers. I didn't talk about it the way you did but I wanted a family too. But then something happened . . . Everybody died. My mom and dad and your father . . . And you were always in court and you were so distant all the time. So wrapped up in the cases. I was sure you didn't love me . . .'

'I lost my temper. I don't . . . You're right. Those kids back there . . . it was probably just gossip. I'm sure it was.'

But his words were flaccid. And of course they came far too late. The damage had been done. He wondered if they'd separate now and never speak to each other again. He supposed that would happen. He supposed that it would *have* to.

And oddly, he realized how much the idea upset him. No, it terrified him; he had no idea why.

A long moment passed.

Bett spoke first. He was surprised to hear her say, in a calm, reasoned voice, 'Maybe it's true, Tate – what

163

you heard about her. Maybe it is. But you know, people change. They can. They really can.'

They continued on in silence. Bett closed her eyes and leaned her head back on the headrest.

What a man hears, he may doubt.

What he sees, he may possibly doubt.

'Bett? I am sorry.'

What he does . . .

'Bett?'

But she didn't answer.

15

She decided she was safest here, in her cell.

If the father – Aaron Matthews – had wanted to kill her he could have done so easily. He didn't have to sock her away here, he didn't have to buy all the food. No, no, she had this funny sense that though he kidnapped her he didn't want to hurt her.

But the son . . . *He* was the threat. She needed protection from him. She'd stay here locked in Crazy Megan's padded cell until she figured out how to escape.

She opened one of the files she'd taken from Peter's room. In the dim light she scanned the pages, trying to find something that might help her. Maybe the place was near a town. Were there photos or brochures of the hospital and grounds? Maybe she could find a map. If she started a fire, people might see the smoke. Or maybe she'd find ventilation shafts or emergency exits. She remembered a padlocked door marked 'Basement' down one of the corridors near by. If she could break the lock on the door, were there exits down there she might get through? She flipped through the documents, looking for a picture or photo of the hospital – trying to find basement windows or doors she might climb out of.

Damn, that's smart, says an impressed Crazy Megan.

Shhhh . . .

Megan happened to glance at the papers on the top of the pile.

. . . patient Victoria Skelling, 37, paranoid schizophrenic, was found dead in her room at 0620 hours, April 23. COD was asphyxia, from inhalation of mattress fibers. County Police (see annexed report) investigated and declared the death suicide. It appeared patient Skelling gnawed through the canvas ducking of her mattress and pulled out wads of stuffing. She inhaled approximately ten ounces of this material down her throat. The patient had been on Thorazine and Haldol, delusions were minimal. Orderlies described her in 'good spirits' for much of the morning of her death but after spending the day on the grounds with a group of other patients her mood turned darker. She was complaining that the rats were coming to get her. They were going to chew her breasts off (earlier delusions and certain dreams centered around poisoned breast milk and suckling). She calmed again at dinner time and spent the evening in the TV room. She was extremely upset when she went to bed and orderlies considered using restraints. She was given an extra dose of Haldol and locked into her room at 2200 hours. She said, 'It's time to take care of the rats. They win, they win.' She was found the next morning dead. . . .

Gross.

She flipped through more pages.

. . . Patient Matthews (No. 97-4335) was the

last person to see her alive and he reported that she seemed 'all spooky'.

So the boy had been hospitalized here. And after the hospital was closed his father brought him back. Why, she couldn't guess. Maybe he felt at home here. Maybe his father broke him out of another hospital to have him nearby.

She flipped through another report – someone else had committed suicide.

. . . The body of Patient Garber (No. 78-7547) was found behind the main building. The police and coroner had determined that he had swallowed a garden hose and turned the water on full force. The pressure from the water ruptured his stomach and several feet of intestine. He died from internal hemorrhaging and shock. Although several patients were near by when this happened (Matthews (No. 97-4335) and Ketter (No. 91-3212), they could offer no further information. The death was ruled suicide by the medical examiner.

Megan read through several other files. They were all similar – reports of patients killing themselves. One victim was found in the library. He'd apparently spent hours tearing apart books and magazines, looking for a sheet of paper sturdy enough to cut the artery in his neck. He finally succeeded.

She shivered at the thought.

Someone else had leapt out of a tree and broken his neck. He didn't die but was paralyzed for life. When asked about why he'd done it he said, *'He'd been talking to "some patients" and he realized how pointless life was, how he was never going to get better. Death would bring some peace.'*

There were six deaths altogether, the last one about a year ago.

Yet another report stated, *'Patient Matthews was the last person to see victim alive.'* The administrator wondered if he'd been involved and the boy had been interviewed and evaluated but no charges were brought.

Reading more, she found that not long after the last suicide a reporter from the Washington *Times* heard of the deaths and filed an investigative report. The state board of examiners looked into the matter and closed the hospital.

But of course, Megan understood, the deaths weren't suicides at all. How could they have missed it? Peter had killed the other patients and somehow covered up the evidence.

She flipped through the rest of the files and clippings. Nothing she found told her anything helpful. She shoved them under the bed. What can I do? There has to—

Then she heard the footsteps.

Faint at first.

Oh, no . . . Peter was coming up the hall.

Well, he might not know she was here. And if he did, he might not know she was in this room.

But there was a new padlock on it. He'd see that.

Closer, closer. Very soft now, as if trying not make any noise.

She heard his breathing and remembered the picture of the eerie-looking boy – his twisted mouth, the tip of his pale tongue in the corner of his lips. She remembered the stained sheets and wondered if he was walking around, looking for her, masturbating . . .

Megan shivered violently. Started to cry. She eased up to the door, put her head against it, listened.

No sounds from the other side.

Had he—?

A fierce pounding on the door. The recoil knocked her to her knees.

Another crash.

A whispered voice. 'Megan . . .' And in that faint word she heard lust and desperation and hunger. 'Megan . . .'

He knows I'm here . . .

Peter was rattling the lock. A few loud slams of a brick or baseball bat on the padlock.

No, please . . . Why'd Matthews left her alone with him? As much as she hated him, Megan prayed he'd return.

'Megannnnnnn?' It now sounded as if he was laughing.

A sudden crash, into the door itself. Then another. And another. Suddenly a rusty metal rod – like the spears in some of his horrible comic books – cracked the wood and poked through a few inches. Just as Peter pulled the metal back out, Megan leapt into the bathroom, plastered herself against the wall. She heard his breath on the door and she knew he was looking through the hole he'd made.

'Megan . . .'

But from that angle he couldn't see that there was a bathroom; the door was to the side.

For an eternity she listened to his lecherous breathing. Finally he walked off.

She started back into the room. But stopped.

Had he really gone? she wondered.

She decided she couldn't go into the room until dark. Peter might be waiting outside and he'd see her. And if she plugged up the hole he'd know she was there.

She sat on the toilet, lowered her head to her hands and cried.

Come on, girl. Get up.

I can't. No, I can't. I'm scared.

Of course you're scared, Crazy Megan chides. *But what's that got to do with anything? Lookit that. Lookit the bathroom window.*

Megan looked at the bathroom window.

No, it's nuts to think about it.

You know what you've got to do.

I can't do it, Megan thought. I just can't.

Yeah? What choice've you got?

Megan stood and walked to the window, reached through the bars and touched the filthy glass.

I can't.

Yes, you can!

She realized that her crazy side – the angry side, the side that she kept locked up thanks to Southern Comfort and to pot and to fucking old men – that side was dead right. She didn't have any choice at all.

Megan crawled into the room, praying that Peter wasn't outside the door, looking through the peephole he'd made. She reached under the bed, sure she'd come up with a handful of rat. But no, she found only the manila file folder she'd been looking for. She returned to the bathroom and eased up to the window, pressed the folder against the glass. She drew back her fist and slugged the pane. The punch was hard but the glass held. She hit it again and this time a long crack spread from the top to the bottom of the window. Finally, another slug and the glass shattered. She pulled her fist back just in time as the sharp shards fell to the windowsill.

She picked a triangular piece of glass about eight inches long, narrow as a knife. Taking her cue from patient Victoria Skelling's sad end, Megan, using her teeth, ripped a strip off one of the pads on the wall. She wound this around the base of the splinter to make a handle.

Good, C.M. says with approval. Proud of her other self.

No, better than good: *Great.* Fuck you, Dr Matthews. I feel *great*! It reminded her of how she'd felt when she'd written those letters to her parents in Dr Hanson's office. It was scary, it hurt, but it was completely honest.

Good.

Crazy Megan wonders, *So what's next?*

'Fuck him up,' Megan responded out loud. 'Then get his keys and book on out of here.'

Atta girl, C.M. offers. *But what about the dogs?*

They've got claws, *I've* got claws. Megan dramatically held up the knife.

Crazy Megan is impressed as hell.

'There's a van.'

'A van?' Bett asked.

'Following us,' Tate continued, as they drove past the Ski Chalet in Chantilly.

Bett started to turn.

'No, don't,' he said.

She froze. Looked at her hands, fingers tipped in faint purple polish. 'Are you sure?'

'Pretty sure. A white van.'

Tate made a slow circle through the shopping center then exited on Route 50 and sped east. He pulled into Greenbriar strip mall, stopped at the Starbuck's and climbed out. He bought two teas, topped with foamed milk, and returned to the car.

They sipped them for a moment and when a red Ford

171

Explorer cut between his Lexus and the van he hit the gas and took off past the bookstore, streaking onto Majestic Lane and just catching the tail end of the light that put him back on Route 50, heading west this time.

When he settled into the right lane he noticed the white van was still with him.

'How'd he do that?' Tate wondered aloud.

'He's still there?'

'Yep. Hell, he's good.'

They continued west, passing under Route 28, which was the dividing line between civilization here and the farmland that led eventually to the mountains.

'What're we going to do?'

But Tate didn't answer, hardly even heard the question. He was looking at a large sign that said 'Future home of Liberty Land . . .'

He laughed out loud.

This was one of those odd things, noticing the sign at the same time the van was following them. A high-grade coincidence, he would have said. Bett – well, the old Bett – would of course have attributed it to the stars or the spirits or past lives or something. Didn't matter. He'd made the connection. At last he had a solid lead.

'What?' she cried, alarmed, responding more to his outrageous U-turn, skidding 180 degrees over the grassy median, than to the harsh laugh coming from his throat.

'I just figured something out. We're going to my place for a minute. I have to get something.'

'Oh. What?'

'A gun.'

Bett's head turned toward him then away. 'You're serious, aren't you?'

'Oh, yep. Very serious.'

Some years ago, when Tate had been prosecuting

the improbable case of the murder of a Jamaican drug dealer at a Wendy's restaurant in suburban Burke, Konnie Konstantinatis had poked his head into Tate's office.

'Time you got yourself a piece.'

'Of what?'

'Ha. You'll wanta revolver 'cause all you do is point 'n' shoot. You're not a boy to mess with clips and safeties and stuff like that.'

'What's a clip?'

Tate had been joking, of course – every commonwealth's attorney in Virginia was well versed in the lore of firearms – but the fact was he really didn't know guns well. The Judge didn't hold with weapons, didn't see any need for them and believed the countryside would be much more populated without them.

But Konnie wouldn't take no for an answer, and within a week Tate found himself the owner of a very unglamorous Smith & Wesson .38 special, sporting six chambers, only five loaded, the one under the hammer being forever empty, as Konnie always preached.

This gun was locked away where it'd been for the past three or four years – in a trunk in Tate's barn. He sped up his driveway and leapt out, observing that with his manic driving he'd lost the white van without intending to. He ran into the barn, found the key on his chain and after much jiggling managed to open the trunk. The gun, still coated with oil as he'd left it, was in a zip-lock bag. He took it out, wiped it clean and slipped it into his pocket.

In the car Bett asked him timidly, 'You have it?' The way a college girl might ask her boyfriend if he'd brought a condom on a date.

He nodded.

'Is it loaded?'

173

'Oh.' He'd forgotten to look. He took it out and fiddled with the gun until he remembered how to open it. Five silver eyes of bullets stared back from the cylinder.

'Yep.'

He clicked it shut and put the heavy gun in his pocket.

'It's not going to just go off, is it? I mean by itself?'

'No.' He noticed Bett staring at him. 'What?' he asked, starting the engine of the Lexus.

'You're . . . you look scary.'

He laughed. 'I feel scary. Let's go.'

Manassas, Virginia, is this:

Big-wheeled trucks, sullen pick-a-fight teenagers (the description fitting both the boys and the girls), cars on the street and cars on blocks, Confederate stars 'n' bars, strip malls, PCP labs tucked away in the woods, concrete postwar bungalows, quiet mothers and skinny fathers struggling, struggling, struggling. It's domestic fights. It's women sobbing at Garth's concerts and teens puking at Aerosmith's.

And a little of it, very little, is Grant Avenue.

This is Doctors' and Lawyers' Row. Little Taras, civil war mansions complete with columns and detached barns for garages, surrounded by expansive landscaped yards. It was to the biggest of these houses – a rambling white colonial on four acres – that Tate Collier now drove.

'Who lives here?' Bett asked, cautiously eying the house.

'The man who knows where Megan is.'

'Call Konnie.'

'No time,' he muttered and he rolled up the drive,

past the two Mercedes – neither of them gray, he noticed – and skidded to a stop about five feet from the front door, nearly knocking a limestone lion off its perch beside the walk.

'Tate!'

But he ignored her and leapt from the car.

'Wait here.'

The anger swelled inside him even more powerfully, boiling, and he found himself pounding fiercely on the door with his left hand, his right gripped around the handle of the pistol.

A large man opened the door. He was in his thirties, muscular, wearing chinos and an Izod shirt.

'I want to see him,' Tate growled.

'Who are you?'

'I want to see Sharpe and I want to see him now.'

Pull the gun now? Or wait for a more dramatic moment?

'Mr Sharpe's busy right at the—'

Tate lifted the gun out of his pocket. He displayed it, more than brandished it, to the assistant or bodyguard, or whatever he was. The man lifted his hands and backed up, alarm on his face. 'Jesus Christ!'

'Where is he?'

'Hold on there, mister, I don't know who you are or what you're doing here but—'

'Jimmy, what's going on?' a voice called from the top of the stairs.

'Got a problem here, Mr Sharpe.'

'Tate Collier come a-calling,' Jack Sharpe sang out. He glanced at the gun as if Tate were holding a butterfly net. 'Collier, whatcha got yourself there?' He laughed. Cautious, some. But it was still a laugh.

'Was he driving the white van?' Tate pointed the gun

at the man in the chinos, who lifted his hands. 'Careful, sir. Please!'

'It's okay, Jimmy,' Sharpe called. 'Just let him be. He'll calm down. What van, Collier?'

'You know what van,' Tate said, turning back to Sharpe. 'Was he the asshole driving?'

'Why'n't you put that thing away so's nobody gets hurt. And we'll talk . . . No, Jimmy, it's okay, really.'

'I can shoot him if you want, Mr Sharpe.'

Tate glanced back and found himself looking into the muzzle of a very large pistol, chrome-plated, held steadily in Jimmy's hand. It was an automatic, he noticed – with clips and safeties and all the rest of that *stuff.*

'No, don't do that,' Sharpe said. 'He's not going to shoot anybody. Collier, put it away. It might be better for everybody.'

Jimmy shrugged, kept the gun pointed at Tate's head.

Tate put his own pistol back into his pocket with shaking hands.

'Come on upstairs.'

'Should I come too, Mr Sharpe?'

'No, I don't think we'll needya, Jimmy. Will we, Collier?'

'I don't think so,' Tate said. 'No.'

'Come on up.'

Tate, breathless, after the adrenalin rush, climbed the stairs. He followed Jack Sharpe into a sunlit den. He glanced back and saw that Jimmy was still holding the shiny pistol pointed vaguely in Tate's direction.

Sharpe – wearing navy blue polyester slacks and a red golfing shirt – was now all business. No longer jokey.

'What the fuck's this all about, Collier?'

'Where's my daughter?'

'Your daughter? How should I know?'

'Who's driving the white van?'

'I assume you're saying that somebody's been following you.'

'Yeah, somebody's been following me.' When Tate had seen the Liberty Park sign he'd remembered that his clients in that case had complained to him last week that private eyes had been following them. Tate'd told them not to worry – it was standard practice in big cases, (though he added that they shouldn't do anything they wouldn't want committed to videotape). 'Same as somebody's been following my clients. And probably my wife—'

'Thought you were divorced,' Sharpe interrupted.

'How'd you know that?'

'Seem to remember something.'

'So if you were following us—'

'*Me?*' Sharpe tried for innocence. It didn't take.

'—you've been following my daughter too. Who just happened to disappear today.'

Sharpe slowly lifted a putter from a bag of golf clubs sitting in the corner of his study, addressed one of the dozen balls lying on the floor and sent it across the room. It missed the cup.

'I hire lawyers to fight my battles for me. As *you* well know, having decorated the walls of the courtroom with their hides recently. That's *all* I hire.'

Tate asked, 'No security consultants?'

'Ha, security consultants. That's good. Yeah, that's good. Well, no, Collier. There ain't no private eyes and no see-curity consultants. Not on my part at any rate. Now, what's this shit about your daughter?'

'She's missing and I think you're behind it.'

Another putt. He missed the cup again.

'Me? Why? Oh, I get it. To take you outta the running next Thursday down in Richmond, right?'

'Makes sense to me.'

'Well, it don't make sense to me. I don't need to do that. You know I fired those half-assed shysters you reamed at the trial. I got the big boys involved now. You've seen the briefs. Lambert, Stone & Burns. They're gonna run right over you. Don't flatter yourself. They'll burn you up like Atlanta.'

'Liberty Park, Sharpe. Tell me. How much'll you lose if it doesn't get built?'

'The park? It don't go through? I don't lose a penny.' Then he smiled. 'But the amount I won't *make* is to the tune of eighteen million. Say, ain't it unethical for you to be here without my lawyer being present?'

Tate said, 'Where is she? Tell me.'

'I don't know what you're talking about.'

'Come on, John. You think I don't know about defendants harassing clients and lawyers so they'll drop cases?'

Sharpe ran his hand through his white hair. He sat down, beneath a picture of himself on the eighteenth tee of the Bull Run Country Club, a place that proudly had not a single member who wasn't white and Protestant. Male too – though that went without saying.

'Collier, I don't kidnap people.'

'But how about some of those little roosters that work for you? I wouldn't put it past a couple or three of them. That project manager of yours. Wilkins? He was in Lorton for eighteen months.'

'Passing bad paper, Collier, not kidnapping girls.'

'Who knows who they might've hired? Some psycho who *does* kidnap girls. And maybe likes it.'

'Nobody hired nobody,' Sharpe said, though Tate could see in his eyes that he was considering the possibility that one of his thugs had snatched Megan.

But five seconds on the defensive was too much for Jack Sharpe. 'Running outta patience here, Collier. And whatta I know, I'm just a country boy – but if I'm not mistaken, isn't that slander or libel or some such you're spouting?'

'So file suit, John. But tell me where she is.'

'You're barking up the wrong tree, Collier. You're gonna have to look elsewhere. You're not thinking clear. You know Prince William as good as your grandfather did before you. If you do a deal like Liberty Park you play hardball. That's the way business works in these parts. But for Christ sake, this ain't southeast D.C. I'm not gonna hurt a seventeen-year-old girl. Now it's time for you to leave. I got work to do.'

He sank the next putt into a small cup, which spit the ball back to him.

Tate, chin quivering with rage, stared back at the much calmer face of his opponent.

From the doorway, Jimmy asked calmly, 'You want me to help him outside?'

Sharpe said, 'Naw. Just show him to the door. Hey, so long, Counselor. See you in Richmond next Thursday. I intend to be in the front row. Hope you're rested and comfy. They're going to rub every inch of your skin off. It's gonna be pretty to watch.'

16

Rhetoric, Plato wrote, is the universal art of winning the mind by argument.

Tate Collier, at eleven years of age, listened to the Judge recite that definition as the old man rasped a match to light his fragrant pipe and decided that one day he would 'do rhetoric'.

Whatever that meant.

He had to wait three years for the chance but finally, as a high school freshman, he argued (what else?) his way into debate club, even though it was open only to upperclassmen.

Tournament debating started in colonial America with the Spy Club at Harvard in the early 1700s and opened up to women a hundred years later with the Young Ladies Association at Oberlin, though hundreds of less formal societies, lyceums and bees had always been popular throughout the colonies. By the time Tate was in school intercollegiate debate had become a practiced institution.

He argued in hundreds of National Debate Tournament bouts as well as the alternative-format – Cross Examination Debate Association – tournaments. He was a member of the forensic honorary fraternities – Delta Sigma Rho, Phi Rho Pi and Pi Kappa Delta – and was now as active in the American Forensics Association as he was in the American Bar Association.

In college – when it was fashionable to be anti-military, anti-frat, anti-ROTC – Tate shunned bellbottoms and tie-dye for suits with narrow ties and white shirts. There, he honed his technique, his logic, his reasoning. *If . . . then . . .* Major premise, minor premise, conclusion. Combating straw men, circular logic, *ad hominem* tactics by the opponents. He fought debaters from Georgetown and George Washington, from Duke and North Carolina and Penn and Johns Hopkins, and he beat them all.

With this talent (and, of course, with the Judge for a grandfather) law school was inevitable. At UVA he'd been the state moot court champion his senior year at the Federal Bar Moot Court open in the District. Now he frequently taught well-attended appellate advocate continuing-ed courses and his American Trial Lawyer's tape was a bestseller in the ABA catalog.

When he'd been a senior at UVA and the champion debater on campus the Judge had traveled down to Charlottesville to see him. As predicted, he'd won the debate (it was the infamous pro-Watergate contest). The Judge told him that he'd heard someone in the audience say, 'How's that Collier boy do it? He looks like a farmboy but when he starts to talk he's somebody else. It's like he's speaking in tongues.'

No, there was no one Tate Collier would not match words with. Yet the incident with Sharpe had left him unnerved. He'd let emotions dictate what he'd said. What was happening to him? He was losing his touch.

'I blew it,' he muttered. And told Bett what had happened.

'Did he have anything to do with it?'

'I think he did, yeah. He was slick, too slick. He

was expecting me. But he was also surprised about something.'

'What?'

'I think something happened he hadn't planned on. It's true. I don't think his boys would kidnap Megan themselves. But they may've hired somebody to do it. Oh, and he knew we were divorced and that Megan was seventeen. Why'd he know that?'

'Are you going to tell Konnie?'

'Oh, sure. But people like Sharpe are good. They don't leave loose ends. You follow the trails and they vanish.'

She picked up the pistol, which he'd set on the dashboard. She slipped it in the glove compartment distastefully. 'Aren't we a pair, Tate? Guns, private eyes.'

He said, 'Bett, I'm sorry. About before.'

She shook her head. 'No,' she offered definitively.

They drove in silence for several moments.

She sighed then asked reflectively, 'Do you like your life?'

He glanced at her. Responded: 'Sure.'

'Just sure?'

'How much more can you be than sure?'

'You can be convincing,' she said.

'What's life,' he asked, 'but ups and downs?'

'You ever get lonely?'

Ah. Sometimes the girls would stay the night, sometimes they'd leave. Sometimes they decided to return to their husbands or lovers or leave him for other men, sometimes they'd talk about getting divorced and sometimes they were single, unattached and waiting for a ring. Sometimes they'd introduce Tate to their parents or their cautious-eyed children or, if they had none, talk about how much they wanted some. A boy first, they'd invariably say, and then a girl. Two probably. Maybe three.

They all faded from his life and, yes, most nights he was lonely.

'I keep pretty busy,' he said. 'You?'

She said quickly, 'I'm busy too. Everybody needs interior design.'

'Sure,' he agreed. 'Things working out well with Brad?'

'Oh, Brad's a dear. He's a real gentleman. You don't see many of them. You were one. I mean, you still are.' She laughed. 'You know, I keep expecting to see you on TV,' she said. 'Prosecuting serial killers or terrorists or something. Channel Nine loved you. You gave great interviews.'

'Those were the days.'

'Why'd you quit practice?'

He kept his hands at ten to two on the wheel and his eyes straight ahead.

'Tate?' she repeated.

'Prosecuting's a young man's game,' he said. Thinking he was the epitome of credibility.

But Bett said, 'That's *an* answer. But not *the* answer.'

'I didn't quit practice.'

'You know what I mean. You were the best CA in the state. Remember those rumors that you'd get that job at the Supreme Court?'

Solicitor General – the lawyer who represented the government in cases before the Nine Supremes. The most important forensic orator in the country. Tate's grandfather had always hoped his grandson might get that job. And Tate himself had for years had his sights on that job.

'I wanted to spend more time on the farm.'

'Bullshit.' Well, this was *definitely* a new Bett McCall. The ethereal angel had come to earth with muddy cheeks. 'Why won't you tell me?'

'Okay. I lost my taste for blood,' he explained. 'I prosecuted a capital case. I won. And I wished I hadn't.'

Bett had been deeply ashamed that while they were married Tate had sent six men to die in the commonwealth's death chamber in Jarrett, Virginia. This had always seemed ironic to him, for she believed in the immortality of souls and Tate did not.

'He was innocent?' she asked.

'No, no. It was more complicated than that. He killed the victim. There was no question about that. But he was probably guilty of manslaughter at best. Criminally negligent homicide, most likely. The defense offered a plea – probation and counseling. I rejected it and went for lethal injection. The jury gave him life imprisonment. The first week he was in prison, he was killed by other inmates. Actually . . .' His voice caught. 'He was tortured and then he died.'

'God, Tate.'

What a man hears, he may doubt . . .

'I talked him to death, Bett. I conjured the jurors. I had the *gift* on my side. Not the law. And he's dead when he shouldn't be. If he'd been out of prison, had some help he'd be alive now and probably a fine person.'

But what he does, he cannot doubt.

He waited for her disgust or anger.

But she said only, 'I'm sorry.' He looked at her and saw not pity or remorse but simple regret at his pain. 'They fired you? The CA's office?'

'Oh, no. No. I just quit.'

'I never heard about it.'

'Small case. Not really newsworthy. The story died on the Metro page.'

Staring at the road, Tate confessed, 'You know something?'

He felt Bett's head turn toward him.

He continued, 'I wanted to tell you about what happened. When I heard that he'd died I reached for the phone to call you – before anybody else. Even before Konnie. I hadn't seen you in over a year. Two years maybe. But you were the one I wanted to tell.'

'I wish you had.'

He chuckled. 'But you hated me taking capital cases.'

There was a long pause. She said, 'Seems to me you've served enough time over that one. Most everybody gets a parole hearing, don't they?' As Tate signaled to make the turn for Bett's exit she said, 'Could we just drive a bit? I don't feel like going home.'

His hand wavered over the signal stem. He clicked it off.

17

Tate piloted his Lexus back through Centreville, which some of the redder of the rednecks around these parts disparagingly called New Calcutta and New Seoul – because of the immigrants settling here. He made a long loop around Route 29 and turned down a deserted country road.

The sun was low now but the heat seemed worse. The sour, sickly aroma of rotting leaves from last year's autumn was in the air.

'Tate,' Bett asked slowly, 'what if nothing happened?'

'Nothing happened?'

'What if nobody kidnapped her. What if she really did run off? On her own. Because she hates us.'

He glanced at her.

She continued, 'If we find her—'

'*When* we find her,' he corrected.

'What if she's so mad at us that she won't come home?'

'We'll convince her to,' he told her.

'Could you do it, do you think? Talk her into coming back home?'

Can I? he wondered.

There's a transcendent moment in debate when your

opponent has the overwhelming weight of logic and facts on his side and yet still you can win. By leading him in a certain direction you get him to build his entire argument on what appears to be an irrefutable foundation, the logic of which is flawless. But which you nonetheless destroy at the same time as you accept the perfection of his argument.

It's a moment, Tate tells his classes, just like in fencing, when the red target of a heart is touched with the button of the foil. Not flailing away, no chops or heavy strokes, but a simple, deadly tap the opponent never sees coming.

All cats see in the dark.

Midnight is a cat.

Therefore Midnight can see in the dark.

Irrefutable. The purest of logic.

Unless . . . Midnight is blind.

But what kind of argument could he make to convince Megan to return home?

He thought about the letters she'd written and he didn't have any thoughts at all; he saw only her perfect anger.

'We'll get her back,' he told Bett. 'I'll do that. Don't worry.'

Bett pulled down the makeup mirror in the sunvisor to apply lipstick. Tate was suddenly taken back to the night they met – at that party in Charlottesville. He'd driven her home afterwards and had spent a passionate half-hour in the front seat of a car removing every trace of her pink Revlon.

Five weeks later he'd suggested they move in together.

A two-year romance on campus. He'd granduated from law school the year Bett got her undergraduate degree. They left idyllic Charlottesville for the District of Columbia and his clerkship at Federal district court; Bett got a job managing a new age bookstore. They lived the bland, easy life that Washington offered a young couple just starting out. Tate's consolation was his job and Bett's that she finally was close to her twin sister, who lived in Baltimore and had been too ill to travel to Charlottesville.

Married in May.

His antebellum plantation built the next spring.

Megan born two years later.

And three years after that, he and Bett were divorced.

When he looked back on their relationship his perfect memory was no longer so perfect. What he recalled seemed to be merely sharp peaks of an island rising from a huge undersea mountain range. The wispy, ethereal woman he'd seen at the party, singing a sailor's mournful song of farewell. Walks in the country. Driving through the Blue Ridge into the Massanutten Mountains. Making love in a forest near the Luray Caverns. Tate had always enjoyed being out of doors – the cornfields and back-yard barbecues. But Bett's interest in the outside arose only at dusk. 'When the line between the worlds is at its thinnest,' she'd told him once, sitting on the porch of an inn deep in the Appalachians.

'What worlds?' he asked.

'Shhh, listen,' she'd said, enchanting him even while he knew it was an illusion. Which was, he supposed, irrefutable proof of her ability to cast a spell.

Betty Sue McCall, devoted to her twin sister, with whom she had some mystical link that unnerved even rationalist Tate, reedy folk singer, collector of the unexplained, the arcane, the invisible . . . Tate had never figured out if her sublime mystique magnified their love falsely or obscured it or indeed if it was the essence of their love.

Magic . . .

In the end, of course, it didn't matter, for they separated completely, moved far away from each other emotionally. She became for him what she'd been when he was first captivated by her: the dark woman of his imagination.

Today she prodded her face in the mirror, rubbed at some invisible blemish as he remembered her doing many times. She'd always been terribly vain.

She flipped the mirror back.

'Pull over, Tate.'

He glanced at her. No, it was not an imperfection she'd been examining; she'd been crying again and seemed dismayed at her ruddy eyes.

'What is it?'

'Just pull over.'

He did, into the Parks Service entrance to the Bull Run Battlefield.

Bett climbed from the car and walked up the gentle slope. Tate followed and when they were on level ground they stopped and simultaneously gazed at the tumultuous clouds overhead.

'What is it, Bett?' He watched her stare at the night sky. 'Looking for an angel to help you decide something?'

Suddenly he was worried that she'd take offense at this though he hadn't meant it sardonically.

But she only smiled and lowered her eyes from the sky. 'I was never into that angel stuff. Too Hallmark card, you know. But I wouldn't mind a spirit or two.'

'Well,' he said, 'this'd be the place. General Jackson

came charging out of those trees right over there and stopped the Union boys cold in their tracks. Right here's where he earned himself the name Stonewall.' The low sun glistened off the Union cannons' black barrels in the distance.

Suddenly Bett turned, took his hands and pulled him to her. 'Hold me. Please.'

He put his arms around her – for the first time in years. They stood this way for a long moment. Then found a bench and sat. He kept his arm around her. She took his other hand. And Tate wished suddenly, painfully, that Megan were here with them. The three of them together and all the hard events of the past dead and buried, like the poor, broken bodies of the troops who'd died bloody on this very spot.

Wind in the trees, billowing clouds overhead.

Suddenly a streak of yellow flashed past them.

'Oh, what's that?' Bett said. 'Look.'

He glanced at the bird that alighted near them.

'That'd be, let me see, a common yellowthroat. Nests on the ground and feeds in the tree canopy.'

Her laugh scared it away. 'You know all these *facts*. Where do you learn them?'

A girlfriend, age twenty-three, had been a birdwatcher.

'I read a lot,' he said.

More silence.

'What are you thinking?' she wondered after a moment.

A question women seem to ask whenever they find themselves in close contact with a man.

'Unfinished business?' he suggested. 'You and me?'

She considered this. 'I used to think things were finished between us. But then I started to look at it like doing your will before you get on a plane.'

'How's that?'

191

'If you crash, well, maybe all the loose ends're tied up but wouldn't you still rather hang around for a little while longer?'

'There's a metaphor for you.' He laughed.

She spent a moment examining the sky again. 'When you argued before the Supreme Court five or six years ago. That big civil rights case. And the *Post* did that write-up on you. I told everybody you were my ex-husband. I was proud of you.'

'Really?' He was surprised.

'You know what occurred to me then, reading about you? It seemed that when we were married you were my voice. I didn't have one of my own.'

'You were quiet, that's true,' he said.

'That's what happened to us, I think. Part of it anyway. I had to find mine.'

'And when you went looking . . . so long. No half-measures for you. No compromises. No bargaining.'

The old Bett would have frozen or dipped into her enigmatic silence at these critical words. But she merely nodded in agreement. 'That was me, all right. I was so rigid. I had all the right answers. If something wasn't just perfect I was gone. Jobs, classes . . . husband. Oh, Tate, I'm not proud of it. But I felt so young. When you have a child, things do change. You become more . . .'

'Enduring?'

'That's it. Yes. You always know the right word.'

He said, 'I never had any idea what you were thinking about back then.'

Bett's thoughts might have been on what to make for dinner. On King Arthur. On a footnote in a term paper. She might have been thinking of a recent tarot card reading.

She might even have been thinking about him.

'I was always afraid to say anything around you, Tate. I always felt tongue tied. Like I had nothing to say that interested you.'

'I don't love you for you oratorical abilities.' He paused, struck by the tense of the verb. 'I mean, that's not what attracted me to you.'

Then reflected: Oh, she's so right – what she'd said earlier. . . . We humans have this terrible curse; we alone among the animals believe in the possibility of change – in ourselves and those we love. It can kill us and maybe, just maybe, it can save our doomed hearts. The problem is we never know until it's too late which.

'You know when I missed you the most?' she said finally. 'Not on holidays or picnics. But when I was in Belize—'

'What?' Tate asked suddenly.

She waved lethargically at a yellow jacket. 'You know, you and I always talked about going there.'

They'd read a book about the Mayan language and the linguists who trooped through the jungles in Belize on the Yucatan to examine the ruins and decipher the Indian code. The area had fascinated them both and they planned a trip. But they'd never made the journey. At first they couldn't afford it. Tate had just graduated from law school and started working as a judge's clerk for less money than a good legal secretary could make. Then long, long hours in the Commonwealth's Attorney's office. Then there was the first of the Supreme Court arguments that took months of his life. After that, when they had the money saved up, Bett's sister had a serious relapse and nearly died; Bett couldn't leave home. Then Megan came along. And three years after that they were divorced.

'When did you go?' he asked.

193

'Three years ago. January. Didn't Megan tell you?'

'No.'

'I went with Bill. The lobbyist?'

Tate shook his head. 'Have a good time?'

'Oh, yeah,' she said haltingly. 'Very nice. It was hotter than Hades. Really hot.'

'But you like the heat,' he remembered. 'Did you see the ruins?'

'Well, Bill wasn't into ruins so much. We did see one. We took a day trip. I . . . Well, I was going to say – I wished you'd been with me.'

'Two years ago February,' Tate said.

'What?'

'I was there too.'

'No! Are you serious?' She laughed hard. 'Who'd *you* go with?'

Her face grew wry when it took him a moment to remember the name of his companion.

'Cathy.'

He *believed* it was Cathy.

'Did *you* get to the ruins?'

'Well, we didn't exactly. It was more of a sailboarding trip. I don't believe it. . . . Damn, how 'bout that. We finally got down there. We talked about that vacation for years.'

'Our pilgrimage.'

'Great place,' he said, wondering how dubious his voice sounded. 'Our hotel had a really good restaurant.'

'It was fun,' she said enthusiastically. 'And pretty.'

'Very pretty,' he confirmed. The trip had been agonizingly dull.

Her face was turned toward a distant line of trees. She was thinking probably of Megan now and the Yucatan was far from her thoughts.

'Let me take you home,' he said. 'There's nothing more we can do tonight. We should get some rest. I'll call Konnie, tell him about Sharpe.'

She nodded.

They drove to Fairfax and he pulled up in front of her house. She sat in the front seat in silence for a while.

'You want to come in?' she asked suddenly.

His answer was balanced on the head of a pin and for a long moment he didn't have a clue which way it was going to tilt.

Tate pulled her to him, hugged her, smelled the scent of Opium perfume in her hair. He said, 'Better not.'

18

Crazy Megan reveals her true self.

She isn't crazy at all and never has been. What C.M. is is furious.

He's going down, she mutters. *This asshole Peter is going down hard.*

Megan McCall was angry too but she was much less optimistic than her counterpart as she moved cautiously through the corridors of the hospital, clutching three boxes of plastic utensils under her arm and her glass knife in the other.

Though she was feeling better physically, having eaten half a box of her favorite cereal – Raisin Bran – and drunk two Pepsis.

Listening.

There!

She heard a shuffle, a few steps of Peter's feet. Maybe a whisper of breath.

Another shuffle. A voice.

Her name?

Yes, no?

She couldn't tell.

This could be it! Got a good grip on the knife?

Be quiet! Megan thought.

Megan shivered and felt a burst of nausea from the

fear. Wished she hadn't eaten so fast. If I puke that'll be it . . .

She inhaled slowly.

Then there was silence and she continued on.

A clunk near by. More footsteps. These were nearby. She'd almost turned right down the corridor where he'd been standing.

Megan gasped and closed her eyes, remaining completely still, huddling behind an orange fiberglass chair.

She pressed into the wall and began mentally working her way through Janis Joplin's *Greatest Hits* album line by line. She cried noiselessly throughout 'Me and Bobby McGee', then grew defiant once more when she mind-sang 'Down on Me'.

His footsteps wandered away, back toward his room, and she continued on. Ten endless minutes later she made it to the end of the corridor she'd decided to use for her trap.

She needed a dead end – she had to be sure of the direction he'd come at her from. Crazy Megan points out, though, that it also means she'll have no escape route if the trap doesn't work.

'Who's the pussy now?' Megan asked.

Like, excuse me, C.M. snaps in response. *Just letting you know.*

She rubbed her hand over the wall.

Sheetrock.

Megan had recalled one time she'd been at her father's house. A few years ago. He'd been dating a woman with three children. As usual he'd been thinking about marrying her – he *always* did that, it was *so* weird – and'd gone so far as to actually hire a contractor to divide the downstairs bedroom into two smaller ones for her young twins. He got halfway through the project and they'd broken up; the construction went unfinished but Megan recalled watching the contractors easily slice through the Sheetrock with small saws. The material had seemed as insubstantial as cardboard.

She took a plastic dinner knife from the box. It was like a toy tool. And for a moment the hopelessness of her plan overwhelmed her. But then she started to cut. Yes! In five minutes she'd sliced a good-sized slit into the wall. The blades were sharper than she'd expected.

For about fifteen minutes the cutting went well. Then, almost all at once, the serrated edge of the knife wore smooth and dull. She tossed it aside and took a new one. Started cutting again.

She lowered her head to the plasterboard and inhaled its stony-moist smell. It brought back a memory of Joshua. She'd helped him move into his cheap apartment near George Mason. The workmen were fixing holes in the walls with plasterboard and this smell reminded her of his studio. Tears flooded into her eyes.

What're you doing? an impatient Crazy Megan asks.

I miss him.

Shut up and saw. Time for that later.

Cutting, cutting . . . Blisters formed on the palm of her right hand. She ignored them and kept up the hypnotic motion. Resting her head against the Sheetrock, smelling mold and wet plaster. Hand moving back and forth by itself. Thoughts tumbling . . .

Thinking about her parents.

Thinking about bears . . .

No, bears can't talk. But that didn't mean you couldn't learn something from them.

She thought of the *Whispering Bears* story, the illustration in the book of the two big animals watching the town burn to the ground. Megan thought about the point of the story. She liked her version better than Dr Matthews's; the moral to her was: people fuck up.

But it didn't have to be that way. Somebody in the village could have said right up front, 'Bears can't talk. Forget about 'em.' Then the story would have ended: 'And they lived happily ever after.'

Working with her left hand now, which was growing a crop of its own blisters. Her knees were on fire and her forehead too, which she'd pressed into the wall for leverage. Her back also was in agony. But Megan McCall felt curiously buoyant. Food and caffeine inside her, the simple satisfaction of cutting through the wall, the fact that she was doing *something* to get out of this shithole.

Thinking about what she'd do *when* she got out.

Dr Matthews had tricked her – to get her to write those letters. But the awesome thing was that what she'd written had been true. Oh, she *was* pissed at her parents. And those bad feelings had been bottled up in her forever, it seemed. But now they were out. They weren't gone, no, but they were buzzing around her head, getting smaller, like a blown-up balloon you let go of. And she had a thought: The anger goes away; the love doesn't. Not if it's real. And she thought maybe, just maybe – with Tate and Bett – the love might be real. And once she understood that she could recall other memories.

Thinking of the time she and her father went to Pentagon City on a spur-of-the-moment shopping spree and he'd let her drive the Lexus back home, saying only, 'The speedometer stops at one-forty and you pay any tickets yourself.' They'd opened the sunroof and laughed all the way home.

Or the time she and her mother went to some boring New Age lecture. After fifteen minutes Bett had whispered, 'Let's blow this joint.' They'd snuck out the back door of the school, found a snow saucer in the playground and huddled together on it, whooping all the way to the bottom of the hill. Then they'd raced each other to Starbuck's for hot chocolate and brownies.

And even her sweet sixteen party, the only time in – how long? – five, six years she'd seen her parents together. For a moment they'd stood close to each other, near the buffet table, while her father gave this awesome speech about her. She'd cried like crazy. For a few minutes they seemed like a perfectly normal family.

If I get home, she now thought . . . No, *when* I get home, I'll talk to them. I'll sit down with them. Oh, I'll give 'em fucking hell. I'll do what I should've done a long time ago.

The anger goes away; the love doesn't . . .

A blister burst. Oh, that hurt. Oh, Jesus. She closed her eyes and slipped her hand under her arm and pressed hard. The sting subsided and she continued to cut.

After a half-hour Megan had cut a six-by-three-foot hole in the Sheetrock. She worked the piece out and rested it against the wall. Lay against the wall for a few minutes, catching her breath. She was sweating furiously.

The hole was ragged and there was plaster dust all over the floor. But the window at this end of the corridor was small and covered with grease and dirt; very little light made it through. She doubted that Peter Matthews would ever see the trap until it was too late.

She walked back to where his father had bricked up the entrance to the administration area of the hospital and, quietly, started carting cinder blocks back to the trap, struggling under their weight. When she'd lugged eight bricks back to the corridor she began stacking them in the hole she'd cut, balancing them on top of one another, slightly off center.

Megan then used her glass knife and sliced strips off the tail of her shirt. She knotted them into a ten-foot length of rope and tied one end to the stack of blocks. Finally she placed the piece of Sheetrock back in the opening and examined her work. She'd lead Peter back here and when he walked past the trap she'd pull the rope. A hundred pounds of concrete would crash down on top of him. She'd leap on him with the knife and stab him – she decided she couldn't kill him. But she'd slash for his hands and feet – to make sure he couldn't attack or chase her. Then she'd demand the keys and run like hell.

Megan walked softly down to the main corridor and looked back. Couldn't see anything except the tail of rope.

Now, she just needed some bait.

'Guess that's gonna be us, right?' she asked, speaking out loud, though in a whisper.

Who else? Crazy Megan answers.

Bett McCall poured herself a glass of Chardonnay and kicked her shoes off.

She was so accustomed to the dull thud of the bass and drums leaching through the floor from Megan's room upstairs that the absence of the sound of Stone Temple Pilots or Oasis brought her to tears.

It's so *frustrating*, she thought. People can deal with almost anything if they can *talk* about it. You argue, you make up. You discover differences and you slowly separate into different lives. Or you find you can talk and talk and talk and learn that you're soul mates. But if the person you love is gone – if you *can't* talk –

then you have less than nothing. It's the worst kind of pain.

The house hummed and tapped silently. A motor somewhere clicked, the computer in the next room hummed a pitch slightly higher than the refrigerator's.

The sounds of alone.

Maybe she'd take a bath. No, that would remind her of the soap dish. Maybe—

The phone rang. Heart racing, she leapt for it. Praying that it was Megan. Please . . . Please . . . Let it be her. I want to hear her voice so badly.

Or at least Tate.

But it was neither. Disappointed at first, she listened to the caller, nodding, growing more and more interested in what she heard. 'All right,' she said. 'Sure . . . No, a half-hour would be fine . . . Thank you. Really, thank you.'

After she hung up she dropped heavily into the couch and sipped her wine.

Wonderful, she thought, feeling greatly relieved after just talking to him for three minutes. Megan's other therapist – a colleague of Dr Hanson's, a doctor named Bill Peters – was coming over to speak to her about the girl. He didn't have my specific news but just wanted to talk to her about her daughter's disappearance.

She was curious only about one thing. Why did he want to see her alone? Without Tate there?

III

The Devil's Advocate

19

'When you called,' Bett confessed, 'I was a little uneasy.'

'Of course,' he said, walking into the room. Dr Peters seemed confident, comfortable with himself. He had a handsome face. His eyes latched on to Bett's and radiated sympathy. 'What a terrible, terrible time for you.'

'It's a nightmare.'

'I'm so sorry.' He was a tall man but walked slightly stooped. His arms hung at his side. A benign smile on his face. Bett McCall, short and slight, was continually aware of the power of body stature and posture. Though she was a foot shorter and much lighter, she felt – from his withdrawing stance alone – that he was one of the least imposing men she'd ever met.

He looked approvingly at the house. 'Megan said you were a talented interior designer. I didn't know quite *how* talented, though.'

Talented?

Bett felt a double burst of pleasure. That he liked her painstaking effort to make her house nice. But, much more, that Megan had actually complimented her to a stranger.

Then the memory of the letter came back and her

mood darkened. She asked, 'Have you heard about Dr Hanson? That terrible thing with his mother?'

Dr Peters' face clouded. 'It's got to be a mix-up. I've known him for years.' He glanced at a crystal ball on her bookshelf. 'He's been an advocate for assisted suicide and I think he *did* talk about it with his mother. But I heard she wasn't all that sick. I'm sure it'll get cleared up.' 'Doctor . . .'

'Oh, call me Bill. Please.'

'Is he a good therapist?'

Peters examined a framed tapestry from France, mounted above the couch.

Why was he hesitating to answer?

'He's very good, yes,' Dr Peters said after a moment. 'In certain areas. What was your impression of him?'

'Well,' she said, 'we've never met.'

'You haven't?' He seemed surprised. 'He hasn't talked to you about Megan?'

'No. Should he have?'

'Well, maybe with his mother's accident . . . he's had a lot on his mind.'

'But that just happened this week,' Bett pointed out. 'Megan's been seeing him for nearly two months.'

In his face she could see that he couldn't really defend his friend. 'Well, frankly, I think he *should* have talked to you. I would have. But he and I have very different styles. Mrs McCall—'

'Bett, please.'

'Betty?'

'Betty Sue,' she smiled, and then blushed. Hoped he couldn't see it, thankful for the dimmed lighting. 'All right . . . Deep, dark secret. It's *Beatrice* Susan McCall. My sister—'

'Your twin. Megan told me.'

'That's right. She's Susan Beatrice. We were named dyslexically. I can't tell you how many years we plotted revenge against Mom and Dad for *that* little trick.'

He laughed. 'Say, could I trouble you for a glass of water?'

'Of course.'

She noticed that he examined her briefly – the tight black jeans and black blouse. Wild earrings dangled; crescent moons and shooting stars. She started toward the kitchen. 'Come on in here. Would you rather have a soda? Or wine?'

'No, thanks . . . Oh, look.' He picked up a bottle of Mietz Merlot, which Brad had bought for them last week and they hadn't gotten around to drinking. He glanced at the eighteen-dollar price tag. 'Funny, I just bought a case of this. It's a wonderful wine. Eighteen's a great price. I paid twenty-one a bottle – and that was supposed to be a discount.'

'You know the brand? Brad said it's real hard to find.'

'It is.'

She said, 'Let's open it.'

'You're sure?'

'Yep.' Bett was happy to impress him. She opened and poured the wine. They touched glasses.

'Do you live in the area?' she asked.

'In Fairfax. Near the courthouse. It's a nice place. Only . . . there're a lot of law offices around there and I get these lawyers coming and going at all hours. Drives me crazy sometimes.'

She gave a brief laugh. He lifted an eyebrow. She'd been thinking of all the nights Tate had spent in that very neighborhood, interviewing prisoners and police and getting home at ten or eleven. 'Tate—'

'Your ex.'

'Right. I'm afraid he's one of them. Working late, I mean.'

'Oh, that's right. Megan told me he was an attorney. But he doesn't live in Fairfax, does he? Didn't she tell me he's got a farm somewhere?'

'Prince William. But his office is here.'

Dr Peters smiled and examined the collection of refrigerator magnets that she and Megan collected. It pinched her heart to see them. And she had to look away before the tears started.

He asked her some questions about the interior design business in Virginia. It turned out his mother had been a decorator.

'Where?' she asked.

'Boston.'

'No kidding! That's where the McCalls are from.' She pointed to some pictures of her family in front of Old Ironsides and in their front yard, the Prudential building towering over the skyline in the background.

'Sure,' he said. 'I thought I detected a bit of accent. I'm driving the cah to the pahty . . .'

She laughed.

'You miss it?' he asked.

'No. We moved here when I was ten. The South definitely appeals to me more than New England.'

'To the extent this is the South,' he offered.

'That's true.'

He took her glass and refilled it. He handed it back and leaned against the island, glanced at the expensive, stainless-steel utensils. 'I love to cook,' he said. 'It's a hobby of mine.'

'Me too. It's relaxing to open some wine, come out to the kitchen and start slicing and dicing.'

He lifted the heavy Sabatier butcher knife and tested

the edge carefully with his thumb. Nodded. 'Sharp knives are—'

'—safer than dull ones,' she said. 'My mother taught me that.'

'Mine too,' he said, weighing the knife in his hand for a moment. Then he set it on the table. 'Should we go back in the other room?'

'Sure.'

He nodded toward the door. She preceded him into the living room.

She sat on the couch and he walked over to the bookshelves, looked at the crystals and several boxes of tarot cards.

He chided, 'Didn't you know you're supposed to keep your tarot cards wrapped in silk?'

'You *know* about that?' She laughed.

'Sure do.'

'I was really into the occult a long time ago.' She smiled and realized that she was relaxing for the first time all day. 'I was kind of crazy when I was young.'

'You look embarrassed. You shouldn't be. I think our spiritual side's as important as our physical and our psychic sides. I use a lot of holistic remedies. They have both organic and psychosomatic effects.'

'I try to use them whenever I can,' Bett said.

'If my patients need *something* I'd rather it was St John's wort instead of Prozac.'

He was a *doctor* who felt this way? How often had she explained these things to doctors, or to friends, or to *Tate*, only to be met with a politely wary gaze – at best.

Dr Peters continued. 'It makes a lot of sense to me. Take tarot cards . . . do they predict the future? Well, in a way they do. They make us look at who we are, where we fit in with the godhead or the Oversoul—'

'Oh, you know Emerson?' she asked, pointing to a book of his essays.

Dr Peters walked to it and pulled the volume off the shelf. He flipped through it.

'I've been reading him since college. . . . No, a tarot card reading makes us look at where we fit in with that force, what our relationships are like, makes us question where we're going. That *has* to affect our future.'

'That's true,' she said, feeling warm and comfortable. More wine. 'That's what I've always felt. Most people don't get it. They just make fun of the Madame Zostra's fortune-telling stuff. It's not fair. My ex . . .'

But she decided to let the thought die. And Peters didn't push her to finish.

The doctor was looking at her bookshelf, head cocked sideways. Pointing out volumes. 'Ah, Joseph Campbell. That's very good. Sure, sure . . . You know Jung?'

'Sort of, not really.'

'About the archetypes? There are certain persistent myths we see surfacing in people's lives. The Arthurian legend – you know it?'

Know it? she thought, laughing to herself. I lived it.

'T.H. White, Camelot, the whole thing.' She pointed out an old copy of *The Once and Future King*.

'What a book that is,' he said. 'Oh, and *The Mists of Avalon*—' nodding at the book.

'The best,' she said enthusiastically. Remembering how Tate didn't have time for any of it. She found the old angers and resentments churning up again. Here was a man who understood her. It was so refreshing . . .

Dr Peters tapped his glass to hers and they sipped. Her glass was nearly empty. Yet she didn't feel drunk, she felt elated. He sat down close to her.

'Um, Bett . . . I don't know how much Megan told you about me.'

'Nothing, really. But then she didn't want to talk about her therapy sessions. That's what we were going to do today. Meet her for lunch and find out how it was going.'

He nodded. He was really quite a handsome man, well proportioned. Interior designer Bett McCall thought: Proportions are everything.

'Dr Hanson saw her more frequently than I did. But I wanted to come over tonight and just talk to you about her a little. Try to reassure you.'

Oh, I'll take that. Anything you want to give me in the reassurance department, I'll take.

'Have you heard anything from her?' he asked.

'Not a word. But there are some funny things going on.'

'What sort of things?'

'We think maybe somebody was following her. My husband . . . my ex-husband thinks it might have to do with a case he's working on. He thinks the man he's suing is trying to distract him or something. I don't know.'

'Any . . . what would they say on *NYPD Blue?* Any concrete leads?'

'Not really. But Tate was going to call a friend of his at the police.'

'Oh, is that the detective who called me? He asked me a few questions about Megan. Um, What's his name again?'

'Konstantinatis.'

'Right. Well,' he continued, pouring more wine, 'I think you should know what I told him.'

'What's that?'

'That I don't think she's in any danger.'

'Oh, did she say something to you about running away?' Bett asked quickly. 'You'd tell me if she did.'

'Ordinarily that'd be confidential. But . . . yes, I would tell you. And she didn't say anything specific about it though she was always talking about going to a big city like San Francisco or New York.'

'They found an Amtrak timetable in her car. She'd marked trains to New York.'

He nodded, as if a mystery had been explained. 'I'd guess that's what happened. No, I'd say I'm *positive* that's what happened. I really doubt there are stalkers or bogy-men out to get her.'

'Why're you so sure?'

He didn't answer her. Instead he said, 'I think we need more wine. I'll get it.' Dr Peters vanished into the kitchen, calling, 'Okay?'

'Sure.'

He returned a moment later, sat down and poured. After a moment he asked, 'How does your husband feel about his daughter?'

'Tate's . . .' She groped for words.

He supplied one. 'Indifferent?'

'Yes. He's never been very involved with Megan.'

'I understand that. But why?'

She now looked at the crystal ball. In it was captured the orange glow from a wall lamp. She stared at the distorted trapezoid of light. 'Tate wanted to be his grandfather. He was a famous lawyer and judge in the area. He had a big family. Well, Tate wanted a farm wife.' She lifted her hands and slapped her thighs. 'He got me instead. Big disappointment.'

'No, that's not you. I can see that. That was very unfair to you to expect that.

'To me?' she asked. 'Unfair?'

214

'Of course,' he offered as if it were obvious. 'Your husband had a distorted view of the past and tried to project that on to his family. I'll bet he worked a lot, spent time away from home.'

'He did, yes. But I was busy too. My sister was sick—'

'Her heart condition.'

Oh, she could talk to this man for hours. She'd met him only thirty minutes ago and yet he *knew* her. Knew her cold. Better than Tate had in all those years of marriage.

'That's right.'

'But why are you taking the blame? I can see you're attractive, intelligent, have a mind of your own. If you wanted an independent life, why should you feel bad about that? It seems to me that *he's* the one to blame for all this. He went into the marriage knowing who you were and tried to change you. And probably in some less-than-honest ways.'

'Less than honest?'

'He *appeared* supportive, I'll bet. He probably said, "Honey, do whatever you want to do. I'll be behind it."'

She was stunned. It was as if Dr Peters were looking directly into her memories. 'Yes, that's exactly what he'd say.'

'But in fact, what he was doing was the opposite. Little comments, even body language, that'd whittle away at your spirit. He wanted you barefoot and pregnant and wanted you to give up your life, have dinner on the table for him, give him a brood of kids, ignore your poor sister. And meanwhile he was going to make a name for himself as a prosecutor and to hell with everybody else.' His eyes flickering with pain – *her* pain. 'It was horrible what he did to you. Inexcusable. But I suppose it's understandable. His character, you know.'

'Character.'

'You know the old expression? "A man's character is his fate." That's your ex-husband. He's reaping now what he sowed. With Megan running away.'

I wish I could believe that, Bett thought. Please . . . Tears now. From the wine, from the astonishing comfort she felt, years and years of pain being stripped away. 'I . . .' She caught her breath. 'He'd sit down and talk to me and say that he loved me and what could he do for me—'

'Tricks,' Dr Peters said quickly. 'All tricks.'

'I couldn't argue with him. He had an answer for everything.'

'He's smooth, isn't he? A slick talker. Megan told me that.'

'Oh, you better believe it. I couldn't win against him. Not at words. Never.'

'Bett, most women would've put up with that. They would've stayed and stayed and destroyed themselves. And their children. But you had the courage to do something about it. Strike out on your own.'

'But Megan . . . she's suffered . . .'

'Suffered?' He laughed. 'Because of him, yes. Not because of you. You've done a *miraculous* job with her. Here's to you.'

He handed her the wineglass, filled again, and they drank. The room was swimming. He was very close to her, gazing into her eyes.

'A miraculous job?' Bett shook her head, felt her eyes swimming with tears. 'Oh, I don't think so.'

'Are you serious? Why, if every mother cared for

their children the way you care for Megan I'd be out of business.'

'Do you really think that?' The tears were coming fast now. But she wasn't the least embarrassed. Not in front of this man. She could tell him anything, do anything in front of him. He'd understand, he'd forgive, he'd comfort. She said wistfully, 'Too bad Megan doesn't think so.'

'Oh, but she does.'

'No, no . . . there's a letter . . .' She glanced toward her purse, where the girl's note sat like a puddle of cold blood.

'The detective told me about it. That's the main reason why I wanted to see you. Alone, without your husband here.' He took the wineglass from her and sat forward, took her hands in his. Looked at her until she was gazing hypnotically into his dark eyes. 'Listen to me. Listen carefully. She didn't mean what she wrote you.'

'She—'

'She. Didn't. Mean. It. Do you hear what I'm saying?'

Bett was shaking with sobs. 'But what she wrote, it was so terrible . . .'

'No,' he said in a firm whisper. 'No.' He was completely focused on her. She thought of the other men in her life with whom she'd had serious talks. Tate was often elsewhere – thinking of cases or trying to dissect what she was saying. Brad would smother her with an adoring gaze. But Dr Peters was looking at *her* as a person.

'Here's what you have to understand. Your letter doesn't mean anything.'

Oh, please, she thought, her eyes filling again. Yes, please explain how this happened. Please explain to me why I'm not a witch, please explain how my daughter still loves me. She thought of an expression she'd heard once and believed was true. You'd kill for your mate; but you'd die for your child. Well, I would, she thought. If only Megan knew that she felt that way.

He squeezed her hands. 'Your daughter hates your husband. I don't know what the genesis of that is but it's a very deeply ingrained feeling.'

'So many little things,' Bett began, feeling the impossibility of compressing seventeen years into a few minutes. Her eye went to a board game, Monopoly, sitting dusty on the shelf. 'Megan wanted us to play games together, Tate, her and me. But he never would. And then—'

'It doesn't matter,' he interrupted. 'The fact is that she was a child and he was the adult and failed her. Megan knows it and she hates him. The anger inside her is astonishing. But it's only directed at *him* – I guarantee you that. She loves you so much.'

Shaking with tears. 'But the letter . . .'

'You know the Oedipus and Electra principles? The attractions of sons and mothers and daughters and fathers?'

'A little, I guess.'

'In Megan's subconscious her anger at your husband makes her feel terribly guilty. And directing it *only* at him is intolerable. With the natural attraction between fathers and daughters she either had to write no letter at all or write you both. She was psychically unable to point her anger only at its true source.'

'Oh, if I could believe that . . .'

'During our sessions she did nothing but talk about you. How proud she was of you. How she wants to be like you. How hard you've had it. I promise

you, without a doubt, she regrets writing that letter. She doesn't mean it. She'd give anything to take
it back.'

Bett lowered her head and put her face in her hands. Why
was the room swimming so badly? Well, no sleep. Exhaustion. The wine too. His arm went around her shoulders.

'You okay?'

She nodded.

'Will she be coming back?' Bett asked.

'I don't doubt it for a minute. It might be a while –
your husband's caused some serious damage, But nothing
that's irreparable. Megan knows that she couldn't ask for
a better mother in the world. You've done everything
right. She loves you and misses you.'

Bett leaned against his chest, felt the muscles in his
arms tighten around her. Oh, when was the last time
she'd felt this good, this easy, this comforted? Years.
She felt his hot breath on the top of her head. She
smelled a faint aftershave.

'I feel so light-headed.'

Did she say that or think it?

She wept and she laughed.

The doctor's hand went to her forehead. 'You're so
hot . . .'

He hugged her harder and his hands slid downward,
fingers encircling her neck. An electric chill went through
her and then her arms were snaking around him, pulling
him to her. Her head was up and she pressed her cheek
against his.

No, no, she thought. I can't be doing this . . .

But she was thinking these words from a very different
place, very remote. And it was impossible for her
to release her grip on the man who'd repaired her
torn soul.

He thinks I'm a good mother, he thinks I'm a good mother.

He leaned down and kissed her tears away.

The light touch of his lips felt so good . . .

She was so giddy, so happy . . .

Stretching out, getting comfortable . . . The room was hot, the room was wonderful . . .

And what was this?

He was kissing her on the mouth. Or am I kissing him? She didn't know. All she knew was that she wanted to be close to him. To the man who'd found her single worst fear and killed it dead.

'No,' he protested, 'really.' Whispering.

But she was not letting him go. She knew she should stop but she couldn't. She pulled him down next to her on the couch, refusing to let go, arms fixed forever around his neck. The room spinning, orange lights, yellow lights.

Kissing harder now.

Hands on her belly, then her chest. She glanced down and wasn't surprised to see her blouse was undone. Her bra up, his fingers cupping her breast. This seemed completely natural. A pop, the snap of her jeans opened. Had he done that or had she? It didn't matter. Getting close to him mattered, hearing him whisper what he would whisper in her ear as he lay on top of her. *That* was what she wanted, hearing him speak to her. The sex wasn't important but she'd gladly give him that if only he'd keep speaking . . .

She opened her mouth and kissed him . . .

And then the world ended.

The front door was swinging open.

A familiar voice was crying, 'Bett . . . why, Bett!'

Gasping, she sat up.

Dr Peters backing away, a shocked look on his face.

220

Brad Markham stood in the doorway, his face a horrified mask. His key to her house dropped to the floor with a loud ring. 'What . . .' He was breathless. 'What . . .'

'Brad, I thought . . .'

'I was in Baltimore?' he spat out. He shook his head. 'I was. A policeman called and told me about Megan. Your daughter's missing and you're fucking somebody. You're *cheating* on me?'

'No,' she said, feeling faint and nauseous from the wine and shock. Tears coming again. Tears of horror. 'You don't understand.'

Too much wine, the emotion. She felt drugged . . . 'I didn't mean it. I didn't know what I was doing.'

'I'm sorry.' Dr Peters looked horrified. 'I didn't know you had a boyfriend. You never said anything.'

'Boyfriend?' Brad spat out. 'We're engaged.'

'You're *what*?' The doctor stared at Brad. 'I'm so sorry. She never said anything.'

'How could you?' Brad spat out. 'After everything I've done for you? And Megan? How could you?'

'I don't know what happened . . .'

Leaving the door open, Brad stalked outside.

'No!' Bett cried, sobbing, pulling her bra down and buttoning her blouse as she stumbled toward the door. 'Wait.'

Through her tears she saw Brad's car squeal off down the street.

Leaning against the door jamb, sobbing, sinking to the floor. Close to fainting, wishing to die . . .

'No, no, no . . .'

Then the doctor was standing next to her, crouching down. His mouth close to her ear. When he spoke the voice was so different from the soothing drone of ten minutes ago. It was flint, it was ice water.

221

'What I told you Megan said about you? That wasn't true. I only said it to make you feel better . . . All she told me was that you were a selfish whore. I didn't believe her. But I guess she was right.' He took a final sip of wine. 'What a pitiful excuse for a mother you are.'

The doctor rose, set the glass on the table and stepped over her, out the door. It seemed he was smiling, though Bett was blinded by the tears and couldn't say for certain.

Tate Collier hung up the phone. Sighed.

No, man, Josh still isn't home. I don't know where he is. You called, like, three times already. Maybe we'll give it a rest now? Okay?

Well, where the hell was he – the boy?

Konnie too was still out of the office. And it irked Tate that the detective hadn't returned his page.

He fed the Dalmatian and paced up and down his front porch, looking at the clear early evening skies and the dusting of April growth over his fields.

No more Dead Rebs that he could see.

Again his eye settled on the dilapidated picnic bench in the back yard. Remembering Bett unhooking the Japanese lanterns, feeling the odd heat of that fall fifteen years ago, the residual exhaustion of the funeral. Sweating in November, the way he was sweating now in April, the hot wind pushing crisp, curled leaves over the shaggy grass.

He remembered:

Bett looking down at him. Asking, 'What is it?'

Alarmed, as she gazed at the expression on his face.

What is it, what is it, what is it? . . . A simple question.

Yet simple words can't convey the answer – that two people who were once in love no longer were.

He'd closed his eyes.

'I don't want to be married to you anymore,' he'd said.

Goodbye . . .

Tate now looked impatiently at the cordless phone, sitting on the porch swing. Why wasn't—

It rang. He blinked and snagged it from the cradle.

'Hello?'

Silence for a moment. Then: 'Tate?'

'I'm here, Bett. What's wrong?'

'I'm on my way to Baltimore.'

'You are? Why?'

More silence. 'Brad left me.'

'What? At a time like this?'

'It's not him. I did something stupid. I don't know . . . I don't want to go into it. It's . . . Oh, Jesus, it's a mess.'

'Bett, you sound terrible. Are you crying?'

'I can't talk about it. Not now.'

'When'll you be back? What about Megan?'

'I don't care.'

He heard utter defeat in her voice. 'What do you mean?'

'Oh, Tate. We've blown it. There's nothing we can do. We've ruined her life, she's ruined ours. Maybe she'll come back, maybe she won't. Let's just let her go and hope for the best. I don't care anymore.'

'This doesn't sound like you.'

'Well, it *is* me, all right? It was stupid looking for her, it was stupid getting together like this, you and me. We should have kept our lives on different sides of the universe, Tate. What've we got to show for it? Just pain.'

'We're going to find her.'

'She doesn't *want* to be found. Don't you get that? Let her go and don't worry about it. She's part of the past, Tate. Let her go. The phone's breaking up. I'm coming to a tunnel. Goodbye, Tate . . . Goodbye . . .'

20

Bait.

That's me, yessir. That's me.

He's on to you, Crazy Megan says. *Move, move, move.*

She went to the right and Peter Matthews went to the right.

Left and left, straight and straight.

Getting closer all the time.

Whispering, 'Megan, Megan, Megan.'

Other words too. She wasn't sure but she thought he was muttering, 'I want to fuck you, I want to fuck you.' Or maybe 'cut you'.

She was part of his fantasy now. From those disgusting comic books. The tentacles, the monsters, the purple dicks, the claws and pinchers . . .

And was a game to the boy – if you can call a six-foot, two-hundred-pound *thing* a boy.

As she moved up and down the corridors, gripping the handle of her glass knife in her right hand, stinging fiercely from the blisters, she had all sorts of terrible thoughts.

She suspected why the father had brought her here. As a bride for his son. Maybe Aaron Matthews had wanted grandchildren. Maybe Peter'd been at Jefferson

High – they had a special ed department – and he'd gotten obsessed with her. That might be it. And his father had arranged her to be a present for his son.

Down the corridor toward the kitchen.

No sign of him.

Down the corridor that led past the door to the basement. The lock looked flimsy but not *that* flimsy. Breaking it open would make a hell of a noise. And what was down there anyway?

No, Crazy Megan tells her. *Stick to your plan. He's gotta go down.*

Well, one of us does, thought the less confident half of the duo.

Keep going, keep looking for him. Up and down the dim halls.

It didn't seem that late but the hospital was in a valley and the sun was behind a mountain to the west. The whole place was bathed in cold blue light and she was having trouble seeing.

She stopped. Footsteps getting closer.

This is it, Crazy Megan says. *Just stab the fucker in the back and get it over with.*

But Megan reminded her that she'd thought about it and couldn't do that. As much as she hated him, she couldn't kill.

He wants to fuck you. He wants to pretend he's one of those insect monsters and fuck you till you bleed.

Be quiet! I'm doing the best I can.

Closer. The steps got closer. The sound coming from around the corner. She didn't have time to get into the main corridor – he was too close.

She stepped into a little nook. Trapped.

He stepped closer, paused. Maybe hearing her.

Maybe *smelling* her.

He'd stopped whispering her name. Which scared her more. Because now he didn't want to be heard. He was sneaking up on her. He was playing the invisible monster; she'd seen that story too in one of the comic books. Some creature you couldn't see snuck into girls' locker rooms and raped stragglers after gym class. The comic had been limp. Looked like Peter'd read that one a thousand times.

He moved forward another few cautious steps.

Her hand started to shake.

Should she jump out into the corridor and just run like hell?

But he couldn't be more than ten feet away. And he'd looked so big in the photographs! He could lunge like a snake and grab her by the throat in two steps.

Suddenly a flash of pain went through her hand – from one of the blisters – and she dropped the knife. Gasped involuntarily.

Megan froze, watching the knife tumble to the floor. It can't break! No . . .

Just before the icy glass hit the floor she shoved her foot under it, waiting for the pain as the tip of the blade sliced into the top of her foot.

Thunk. The knife hit her right foot flat and rolled, unbroken, to the floor.

Thank you, thank you . . .

She bent down and picked it up.

Another two footsteps, closer, closer.

No choice. She had to run. He was only three or four feet away.

Megan took a deep breath, another. Jump out, slash with the knife and run like hell toward the trap.

Now!

She leapt out, turned to the right.

Froze. Gasping. Her ears had played tricks on her. No one was there. Then she looked down. The rat – a large one, big as a cat – standing on his haunches, sniffing the air, blinked at her, cowering. Then indignantly it turned away as if angry at being startled.

Megan sagged against the wall, tears welling as the fear dissipated.

But she didn't have much time for recovery.

At the far end of the dim corridor a shadow materialized into the loping form of Peter Matthews, hunched over and moving slowly. He didn't see her and disappeared from view.

Megan paused for only a few seconds before she started after him.

The Shenandoahs and the Massanuten Mountains keep the air in northwest Virginia clean as glass in the spring, and when the sun sets, it's a fierce disk, bright as an orange spotlight.

This radiant light behind Tate, from the sun melting into the horizon, lit every detail in the trees and buildings and oncoming cars. He sped down Route 66 at eighty miles an hour.

He skidded north on the Parkway then east on Route 50, pulled into the County Police station house and climbed out of the car. He practically ran into Dimitri Konstantinatis as he too arrived, carrying two large Kentucky Fried Chicken bags.

'Oh-oh,' the detective muttered.

'What oh-oh?'

'That look on your face.'

'I don't have a look,' Tate protested.

'You had it comin' into my office when you were CA and needed that little bit of extra evidence –

which'd mean I'd lose a weekend. And you've got it now. *That* oh-oh.'

They walked inside the building and into Konnie's small office.

'You didn't call me back,' Tate said.

'Did so. Ten minutes ago. You musta left. What's that?'

Tate set the letter Megan had written him and the knuckle bone he'd found in his house that morning, both in Baggies, on the cop's desk.

'Prints,' Tate said.

'A prince among men, yes I am. So, what's going on?'

'I want you to run the letter through Identification. Something's up. Bett's acting funny.'

'You complained about that when you were married. Crystals, mumbo-jumbo, long-distance calls to people'd been dead a hundred years.'

'That was cute funny. This's weird funny. Witnesses've been disappearing and not calling back and it's just too much of a coincidence. And I think I know who's behind it.'

He also told Konnie about his run-in with Jack Sharpe.

'Ooo, that was bright, Counselor, and you were packing your gun to boot?'

Tate shrugged. 'Was your idea for me to get one.'

'But it *wasn't* my idea to threaten an upstanding member of the Prince William mafia with it. Grant me that at least.'

'I've been on his bad side since I routed his lawyers at the injunction hearing last week.'

'What's wrong with a nice theme park round here, Tate? What'd you rather have, an amphitheater fulla big wheels slugging it out in a mud pit or them fun rides and cotton candy and knock the clown in the water shit?'

'Talk to my clients about it. I'm just telling you that Sharpe would love for me to be out of commission come that argument in Richmond next week. And I think he's had somebody in a van following me. Sorry, no tag, no model.'

Konnie nodded slowly. Then added, 'But he's got boys he'd hire for that. And they could hire other boys. No way could you to trace it back to him. And you think anybody'd snitch on Jack Sharpe?'

'I'm not a prosecutor anymore, Konnie. I don't want to make a case. I want to find Megan. Period. End of story.'

'And kneecap the prick did it.'

'I wouldn't mind that. But it's optional.' He pushed the bags containing the letter and the bone toward Konnie again. 'Please.'

Another mournful glance at his cooling dinner. 'Be right back.'

'Wait.' Tate handed him another Baggie. 'Exemplars of Megan's prints on the keys and mine on that glass. And remember you handled the note too.'

Konnie nodded. 'The prosecutor in you ain't dead, I see.' Carrying the bags, he walked down the hall toward the forensic lab. He returned a moment later.

'Won't be long. I *was* looking forward to supper.'

Tate ignored the red-and-white KFC bag and continued. 'Now, there was a gray Mercedes following her. Can you check that out?'

'Check what out?'

'Registered owners of gray Mercedes.'

'I was asking before: year, model, tag?'

'Still none. Only that it's a Merc.'

Konnie laughed. He typed heavily on his computer keyboard. 'This'll be worth it just to see your expressions.'

As he waited for the results Konnie peeked into the tallest Kentucky Fried bag, kneaded his ample stomach absently. 'You know what the worst is? The worst is when the mashed potatoes get cold. You can eat the chicken when it's cold because everybody does that. On a picnic, say. Same with the beans. But when mashed potatoes get cold you have to throw them out. Which is bad enough but then you think about them all night. How good they would've been. *That's* what I mean by the worst.'

The screen fluttered. Konnie leaned forward.

'Here's what we got. I did Fairfax, Arlington, Alexandria, Prince William and Loudon. Mercedes, all types, all years, gray.'

Tate leaned forward and read: *Your request has resulted in 2,603 responses.*

'Two thousand,' Tate muttered. 'Man.'

'Two thousand *six* hundred.'

Tate knew from his prosecuting days that too much evidence was as useless as too little.

'Forensics're one way to go. But if you're just not buying the runaway stuff—' Konnie sighed. '—we're gonna have to do more thinking. All right, you think Sharpe's a possibility and I don't think he's above snatching a girl. But there anybody else? Think hard now, Tate. Anybody hassling her?'

'Recently?'

'Like last year's weirdos don't count?' Konnie snorted. 'Anytime!'

'Not that I know of. I have to say there was a rumor . . . it was just a rumor . . . she might've been seeing . . . well, having sex with some older men. And maybe there was some money involved. I mean, they were paying her.'

If Konnie felt anything about this he didn't show it. 'You have any idea who? Where?'

'Some kids at this place called the Coffee—'

'—Shop. They been trying to close that piss hole down for a year. Well, I can poke around there. Ask some questions. Now, was she in any cults or anything?'

'No, don't think so.'

'You or Bett in anything like that?'

'*Me?*'

'All right, your wife.'

'Ex,' Tate corrected.

'Whatever. She did that sort of stuff.'

'It was strictly softball with her. No Heaven's Gate or Jonestown or anything like that. Bett wouldn't even put up these Indian posters because they had reverse swastikas on them. Nothing to do with Nazis; she just thought it was bad karma.'

'Karma,' Konnie scoffed. 'Any relationships of yours go south in a big way recent?'

'I—'

''Fore you answer, think back to everyone of them twenty-one-year-olds you promised diamonds to and then run for the hills from.'

'I never proposed to a single one,' Tate said.

'Never proposed to *marry* 'em, maybe.'

'You don't get *Fatal Attraction* after three dates. That's about the longest term I went.'

'Sad, Tate, sad. How 'bout Bett?'

'I don't know. But I don't think so.'

'Any relatives acting squirrely? Might've wanted to take the girl and run?'

'Only relative near by's Bett's sister, Susan. Outside

of Baltimore. She'd never do anything to hurt her. Hell, she was always joking about adopting Megan.'

'You sure she's okay? Maybe she went over the edge, decided to get herself a daughter.'

'Imagine Bett but fifteen pounds lighter. She couldn't kidnap a bird.'

'But she could've *hired* somebody to. She could have a wacko boyfriend.'

'I just can't see it, Konnie.'

'Gimme her name anyway.'

Tate wrote it down.

'Okay, how 'bout any associates of either of y'all? Clients? Or the bad guys? Other than Sharpe.'

'Bett's got this interior design business. But I don't think her clients're the sort for this kind of thing. Me, I've been doing wills, trusts and house closings except for the Liberty Park case.'

Konnie grunted. The detective got a call. Grabbed the phone. Nodded. Slammed it down. 'Interesting . . . That was the lab. Only her prints and yours on the bone and mine, yours and hers on the letter. But . . . there were some smudges on the bone that might've been from latex gloves. Can't say for certain. But that starts me wondering. Think it's about time to do a Title Three.'

'A wiretap?'

'Yours and your wife's phones both.'

'Ex.'

'You keep saying that. Broken record. That's in case you get a ransom call.'

'I thought this wasn't a case.'

'It's becoming one. Tell me again what happened this morning at your place. I mean exact.'

Tate remembered this about Konnie: he was a working dog when it came to hammering on suspects and witnesses. Only exhaustion would slow him down – and even then it never stopped him.

Tate gave another recap of the events.

'So you never actually saw her at your house?'

'No,' Tate said. 'I got back home about ten then got suited up and went to check on a busted pipe.'

'The sharecroppers there?'

'No. Not on Saturday. I never saw anybody at all. Just the lights go out around ten-twenty.'

'All of 'em?'

'Yeah.'

'Didn't you think that was funny?'

'No. Megan doesn't like bright lights. She likes candlelight and dimmers.'

This gave him a burst of pleasure – proving to Konnie that he knew *something* about the girl after all.

'It was dark as pitch this morning,' the detective mused. 'With all that rain. Most people'd want *some* light, you'd think. 'Less they didn't want to be seen from the outside.'

'True.'

'And shit, Tate, wait a minute. Why'd she go to your place at all?'

'To leave the letters and get the backpack.'

'Well, doesn't she have any suitcases or bookbags at your wife's? Sorry, your *ex's?* Your dee-vorced spouse's?'

'Sure she does, you're right! Most of them are there, as a matter of fact. And she had her bookbag with her at Amy's. And a lot more clothes and makeup at Bett's place than mine.'

The cop continued, 'You and Megan hardly ever saw each other.'

'True again.'

234

'So you wouldn't go into her room much, would you?'

'Once a month maybe.'

'So why'd she leave the letters there? Why not at her mother's?'

That would've made more sense, true. The detective added, 'And, hell, why go to the house and leave some letters this morning around the time you were going to meet her? I tell you, if I was going to leave a note to diss my folks and run I'd leave it someplace they *weren't* going to be. Dontcha think?'

'So he made her write 'em and planted them himself. Whoever he is.'

'That's what I think, Counselor. Here's what I'm gonna do. Order some serious forensic work and then have a chat with the captain. Guess what? This's just become a case. And in a big way.'

Tate returned home.

No messages and no one had called; the caller ID box was blank.

Twelve hours ago he had wanted Megan and Bett out of his life again. He'd gotten his wish and he didn't like it one bit.

So Brad had left Bett. He didn't know what to make of that. Why? And why now? He had a feeling that whoever was behind Megan's disappearance was behind their problems too.

Then his thoughts segued to Belize, the trip they'd planned to take. A second honeymoon. Well, a first honeymoon – since they'd never taken one after their wedding.

He looked out over the dark sky, at the spattering of a million stars.

Tate laughed to himself. What a kick if they'd run into each other. He wondered how Bett would have reacted to Karen. No, Cathy. Or was it Kate?

Probably not well.

Not a jealousy thing so much as a matter of approval. She'd never liked his taste in women.

Well, Tate didn't either, now that he looked back over the last ten years.

Belize . . .

Was there actually a possibility that they might take that trip together still, after this thing with Megan got sorted out?

Whatever happened with Brad, the presence of a fiancé didn't seem as insurmountable as simply the concept of Tate and Bett taking a trip together. At one time their joined names had been a common phrase. But that was a long, long time ago.

Yet – this was *feelings* again, not Cartesian logic – yet somehow he believed that they'd get along just fine. The fight today had been as bad as any they'd had fifteen years ago. And what had happened? A reconciliation. This astonished him.

He sighed, sipped his wine, looked out at the Dalmatian nosing about in the tall grass. Thinking now of Megan.

But even if they did get together again, what would the girl come home to? And more important . . . *who* was the person coming home?

Was the drinking and the water tower more than just a one-time fluke? Was that the real Megan McCall? Had she really slept with men for money? Or was there another young woman within her? One Tate didn't know well – or maybe one he hadn't yet met?

Tate Collier felt a sudden desperation to know the girl. To know *who* she was. What excited her, what she hated, what she feared. What foods she liked. What clothes she'd pick and which she'd shun. What bad TV shows she'd want to watch.

What made her laugh. And what weep.

And he was suddenly stung by a terrible thought: that if Megan had *died* this morning, the victim of a deranged killer or an accident, he'd have been distraught, yes, terribly sad. But now, if that had happened or – the most horrifying – if she simply vanished for ever, never to be found at all, he'd be destroyed. It would be one of those tragedies that diminishes you forever. He remembered something he'd told Bett when they'd been married, a case he was working on – prosecuting an arson murder. The victim had run into a burning building to save her child, who'd lived, though the mother had perished. He'd read the facts, looked up to her and said, 'You'll kill for your spouse, but you'll die for your child . . .'

In rhetoric, lawyers use the trick of personification – picking words to make their own clients seem human and their opponents' less so. 'Mary Jones' instead of 'the witness' or 'the victim'. Juries find it far easier to be harsh to inanimate abstractions. The 'defendant'. The 'man sitting at that table there'.

It's a very effective trick, and a very dangerous one.

And it's just how I've treated Megan over the years, Tate now thought. Referring to her usually as 'the girl'. Not by her name.

He walked into the den and spent a long time looking for another picture of her. Was terribly disappointed he couldn't find one. He'd given his only snapshot to Konnie and Beauridge that afternoon.

He sat down in his chair, closed his eyes and tried to create some images now. Images of the girl. Smiling,

looking perplexed, flirtatious, exasperated. . . . A few
came to mind. He tried harder.

And harder still.

Which was why he didn't hear the man come up
behind him.

The cold finger of a pistol touched his temple. 'Don't
move, Mr Collier. No, no. I really mean that. For your
sake. Don't move.'

21

Jimmy, Tate recalled.

His name was Jimmy. The man who'd been far more willing than Tate to engage in some gunplay in Jack Sharpe's immaculate foyer.

Tate glanced at the phone.

Jimmy shook his head. 'No.'

'What do you want?'

'Mr Sharpe sent me.'

'Figured that.'

The gun was really very large. The man's finger was on the outside of the trigger guard. This didn't reassure Tate at all.

'I have something for you to look at.'

'Look at?'

'I'm going to give it to you to look at. Then I'm going to take it back. And neither me or Mr Sharpe'll ever admit we know what you're talking about if you ever mention it. You understand?'

Tate didn't have a clue. But he said, 'Sure. Say, is that loaded?'

Jimmy didn't respond. From the pocket of his leather jacket he took a videocassette. Set it on the table. Backed up. Nodded toward it. Tate walked over, picked it up. 'I should play it?'

Jimmy's face scrunched up impatiently.

Tate put the cassette in the player and fiddled with the controls until the tape started to play. He was looking at a building, some bushes. The date and time stamp showed that it had been made that morning, at 9:42. He didn't recognize where. The tape jumped ahead four minutes and now whoever was making the tape was moving, driving in a car following another car down a suburban street. Tate still didn't recognize the locale but he did the car being followed. It was Megan's Tempo. Because of the rain he couldn't make out who was driving.

'Where did you get this?' Tate demanded.

'Watch, don't talk,' Jimmy muttered. The gun was pointed directly at Tate's back.

Another jump on the tape. To 9:50 that morning. Tate recognized the Vienna Metro station. The man taping – of course, one of the private eyes hired by Sharpe, despite his protests to the contrary – must have been afraid of getting too close to his subject. He was about fifty yards away and shooting through the mist and rain. Megan's car stopped at a row filled with other cars. There was a pause and then motion. After a moment he caught a glimpse of someone. A white man, it seemed, wearing a dark jacket, though he couldn't be sure. Tate could see no distinguishing features. Then there was more motion. Finally a gray Mercedes pulled out of a space and a moment later Megan's car eased into where the Merc had been. At 10:01 the Mercedes sped out of the lot.

The tape went fuzzy. Then black.

Tate stared, his heart pounding. Thinking of the vague motion he'd seen – pixels of light on the screen, distorted to start with, more distorted in the rain and fog. But he believed it might have been the man lifting a heavy object from the trunk of Megan's car and putting it into the Mercedes. An object about the size of a human body.

'That's all,' Jimmy said. 'Could you eject it?'

Tate did. 'Did he see anything else?' he asked.

'Who?' Jimmy asked.

'You know who. The private eye. Can I talk to him? Please?'

Jimmy nodded at the table. 'If you could just set the tape there and back up.'

Tate did. He knew he wouldn't get an answer. This was as far as the old bastard was willing to go. But he asked one more question. 'Why did Sharpe show this to me? He didn't have to.'

Jimmy pocketed the cassette, gun still held steadily at Tate. He backed to the door. 'Mr Sharpe asked me just to mention the old adage that one good deed deserves another. He hopes you'll remember that next Thursday at the argument down in Richmond.'

'Look—'

'He said he didn't think you'd agree. He just asked me to mention it.'

Jimmy walked to the sliding door, through which he'd apparently entered. He paused. 'The answer to your question? I myself would guess it's because he's got two daughters of his own. Goodnight.'

After he'd gone Tate drained his wineglass with a shaking hand and picked up the phone.

When Konnie answered Tate said, 'Gotta lead.'

'Asking or telling?'

'Telling.'

'Go on.'

'Long story. That case with Sharpe?'

'Right.'

'It wasn't just me he had a PI tailing. It was Megan too.'

'Why? Dig up dirt?'

'That's my guess. Lawyer's daughter scores drugs. Sleeps around. Something like that. Anyway a friend of his just showed me a tape.' Tate described it.

'Hot damn. Get it over here—'

'Forget it. It's been atomized. But I think it was Megan he was moving from one trunk to another. She was probably drugged. At least I hope she was just drugged.'

'Tags?'

'Nope. Sorry.'

'Damn, Tate. Why'd you think they put those cute little signs on cars?' After a pause Konnie continued. 'Okay. You don't think it's Sharpe?'

'He didn't have to show me diddly. He didn't even bargain – well, not too hard. Get off the case and I'll tell you what the PI saw. He could've done that.'

'Would you've agreed?'

Tate didn't hesitate for an instant. 'Yes, I would have.'

'Okay, so it's not him. Then let's think. She's got a stalker after her. He's checking out her routine. Following her. When she goes to school, when she goes to pom-pom practice.'

Tate thought of Megan as a cheerleader. 'As if.'

'He knows where she's going to be this morning. He gets her, drugs her, drives her to Vienna, where he's left his own car. He's got switch wheels. The Mercedes.'

'Right.'

'Leaves her car with the timetable. So it looks like she's headed off on Amtrak. . . . He took off to wherever he was going to stash her. Which means what, Counselor?'

Tate couldn't think.

When he said nothing Konnie gave a harsh laugh. 'Damn, I'd forgot how I had to hold your hand when we were putting all those bad guys away. What's sitting right *under* her car at the moment?'

'Tread marks! The Mercedes's tread marks.'

'There's hope for you after all, boy. If you apply yourself and work real hard to make up for all the brain cells you're lacking. Okay, Counselor, this's gonna take some time. Listen, you sit tight and have some nice hot mashed potatoes. And think of me when you eat 'em.'

Konnie Konstantinatis's first lesson in police work was to watch his father run the taxmen like 'coons tricking hounds.

The old Greek immigrant was petty, weak, dangerous, a cross between a squirrel and a ferret. He was a born liar and had an instinct for knowing human nature cold. He put stills next to smokehouses, stills next to factories, stills in ships, disguised them like hen-houses. Hid his income in a hundred small businesses. Once he smooth-talked a revenuer into arresting his innocent brother-in-law instead of him and swore an oath at the trial that cost the bewildered man two years of his life.

So from the age of five or six Konnie learned the art of evasion and deception. And therefore he learned the art of unraveling deceit.

Slowly and tediously. This was the only way to make cases. And this was how he was going to find the man who'd kidnapped Tate Collier's daughter.

Konnie arranged for a small crane to lift Megan's car out of its spot, rather than drive it out and risk obliterating the Merce's tread marks.

He then spent the next two hours taking electrostatic

prints of the twelve tire treads that he could find – ones he determined weren't from Megan's car. He then identified the matching left and right tires and measured wheelbases and lengths of the cars they'd come from. Jotted all this in his lyrical handwriting.

He then went over the entire parking space with a Dustbuster and – in the front seat of his car – looked over all the trace evidence picked up in the paper filter. Most of it was meaningless without a gas chromatograph. But Konnie found one thing helpful. A single fiber he recognized as coming from cheap rope. He recognized it because in one of the three kidnapping cases he'd worked over the past ten years the victim's hands had been bound with rope that shed fibers just like this.

Speeding back to the office, he sat down at his computer and ran the wheel dimensions through the motor vehicle specification database. One set of numbers perfectly fit the dimensions for a Mercedes sedan.

He examined the electrostatic prints carefully. Flipping through Burne's Tire Identifier, he concluded that they were a rare model of Michelin and because they showed virtually no wear he guessed the tires were no more than four months old. Encouraging, on the one hand, because they were unusual tires and it would be easier to track down the purchaser. But troubling too. Because they were expensive, as was the model of the car the man was driving. It was likely that the perp was intelligent. An organized offender. The hardest to find.

And the sort that presented the most danger.

Then he started the canvassing. It was Saturday evening, and although most of the stores were still open – General Tire, Sears, Merchants, Mercedes dealerships – the managers had gone home. But nothing stopped Konnie. He blustered and bullied until he had home phone numbers and the names of night staff managers of data processing departments. He was good at this, though he gave credit to his mentioning that a seventeen-year-old girl had been kidnapped – which opened doors that might otherwise have remained closed until Monday.

He made thirty-eight phone calls and by the time he hung up from speaking with the last parts department manager on his list, faxes of bills of sale were starting to roll in to police headquarters.

But the information wasn't as helpful as he'd hoped. Most of the sales receipts included the manufacturer of the customer's car and the tag number. Some had the model number but virtually none had the color. The list kept growing. After an hour he had copies of 142 records of the sales of that model of Michelin in the last twelve months to people who owned Mercedes.

He looked over the list of names. It was discouraging.

Standard procedure was to run the names through the outstanding warrants/priors database. But a net like that didn't seem to be the sort that would catch this perp – he wasn't a chronic 'jacker or a shooter with a long history of crime. Still, Konnie was a cop who dotted his i's and he handed the stack to Genie.

'You know what to do, darling.'

'It's seven forty-two on a Saturday night, boss.'

'*You* had dinner at least.'

'Lemme tell you something, Konnie,' the huge woman said, nodding at the KFC bags. 'Throw them out. They're starting to stink.'

Dutifully, he did. As he returned to his desk he grabbed his ringing phone.

''Lo?'

'Detective Konstantinatis, please?'

'Yeah.'

'This is Special Agent McComb with the FBI. Missing and Exploited Child Unit.'

'Sure, how you doin'?' Konnie'd worked with the unit occasionally. They were tireless and dedicated and top-notch.

'I'm doing a favor for my boss in Quantico. He asked me to take a look at the Megan McCall case. You're involved in that, right?'

'Yup.'

'It's not an active case for us but you know Tate Collier's the girl's father, right?'

'Know that.'

'Well, he did some pretty good work for us when he was a commonwealth's attorney so I said I'd look into her disappearance. As a favor.'

'Just what I'm doing, more or less. But I'm gonna present it as an active case to my captain tonight.'

'Are you really?'

'Found some interesting forensics.' Konnie was thinking: Man, if he could turn the tire data over to them . . . the FBI had a whole *staff* of people who specialized in tires. That was all they did. In-fucking-credible.

'That's good to know. We ought to coordinate our approaches. Do some proactive thinking.'

'Sure.' Konnie's thinking was: They might be the best cops in the world but feebies talk like assholes.

The agent said, 'I'm up at Ernie's, near the Parkway. You know it?'

'Sure. It's a half-mile from me.'

'I was about to order dinner and was reading the file when I saw your name. Maybe I could come by in an hour or so. Or maybe – this might appeal to you, Officer

– you might want to join me? Let Uncle Sam pick up the dinner tab.'

He paused for a moment. 'Why not? Be there in ten minutes.'

'Good. Bring whatever you've got.'

'Will do.'

They hung up. Konnie stuck his head in Genie's office, where she was looking over the warrants request results. 'Everything's negative, Konnie.'

'Don't worry. We got the feds on the case now.'

'My.'

He took the stack of faxed receipts from her desk, shoved them into his briefcase and headed out the door.

Konnie was feeling pretty good. Ernie's served some great mashed potatoes.

22

Aaron Matthews sat at a booth in a dark corner of the restaurant, looking out the window at a tableau of heavy equipment, bright yellow in the dusk, squatting on a dirt hillside near by.

This was an area that five years ago had been fields and was now rampantly overgrown with townhouses and apartments and strip malls. Starbuck's, Bruegger's Bagels, Linens 'n' Things. Ernie's restaurant fit in perfectly. An upscale franchise. Looked nice on the surface but beneath the veneer it was all formula.

He stirred as the waddling form of Detective Konstantinatis entered the restaurant and maneuvered through the tables.

Good, he thought. Good.

Watching the man's eyes, seeing where they slid – furtively, guiltily.

Always the eyes.

Matthews waved and Konstantinatis nodded and steered toward him. Matthews had no idea what official FBI identification looked like and wouldn't have known how to fake some if he had but he'd dressed in a suit and white shirt – what he always wore when seeing patients – and had brought several dog-eared file folders, on which he'd printed 'FBI PRIVILEGED AND

CONFIDENTIAL' with stencils he'd made from office materials he'd bought at Staples. These sat prominently in front of him.

He hoped for the best.

But after glancing at the files the detective merely scooted into the seat across from Matthews and shook his hand.

They made small talk for a few moments – Matthews using his best government-speak. Stiff, awkward. If the fake files hadn't fooled the cop the stilted language surely would have.

The waitress came and they ordered. Matthews wasn't surprised when the detective ordered milk with dinner. Matthews himself ordered a beer.

He said, 'I'm afraid we don't have many leads. But from what you were telling me you think there's a chance she was kidnapped?'

'First I just thought she ran off. But there's apparently a tape that shows somebody switching her car with this gray Mercedes around the time she vanished.'

'I see,' said Aaron Matthews, who felt fire burn right through him. His battleship-gray 560 sat in the parking lot, fifty feet from them. Resplendent with its stolen license plates. Tape? Who'd taken it? He was furious for a moment but anger was a luxury he had no time for.

'What's this tape?'

'Vanished into thin air. Long story.'

'Oh.'

'Don't envy you that job,' the detective said, revealing a sentimental side Matthews wouldn't have guessed he had. 'Looking for missing kids all day long. Must be hard.'

Matthews said in a soft voice, 'It's where I feel I can make the most difference.'

Their drinks came. They clinked glasses. Matthews spilled some beer on the table. Wiped it up sloppily with a cocktail napkin.

'Detective—'

'Call me Konnie, everybody else does.'

'Okay, Konnie. I hate to ask but I don't know this Collier and the question's come up. Do you think there was anything between him and the girl?'

'Naw. Not Tate. If anything, just the opposite.'

'How's that?'

'Hell, I didn't even know he *had* a daughter until we'd been working together a while. Anyway, naw, naw, it's not that. I do think somebody 'napped her. No motive yet though might be a case Tate's working on. He's decided this local real estate guy didn't do it. But I'm not so sure. I also have some thoughts about the girl's aunt. I was hoping you could help.'

'Of course. What can we do?' Bett's sister, Susan . . . How did Konnie know about *her*?

'I 'statted some tire treads and got a list of a hundred and a half people bought that brand of tire in the past year. Could I give you the list—' He patted the briefcase. '—have your people check 'em out?'

'Be happy to. Have you done anything with them yet?'

'Just run 'em through the outstanding warrants computer. Nothing showed up.'

Planning for the kidnapping, Matthews had bought new tires for the car two months ago; he couldn't afford a flat. At least when he'd taken the car into General Tire he'd given a fake name and paid cash.

'But then I got to thinking,' Konnie continued, 'on the way over here, what I shoulda done – I shoulda looked at the receipts and found out who paid cash. Anybody who did, I figure it'd be a fake name. I mean, those tires cost big money. Nobody pays cash for something like that. So what your folk could do is check the tags and see if the name matches. If not then they're somebody I've gotta talk to.'

Jesus in heaven. Matthews hadn't swapped plates when he'd taken the car in to have the new tires mounted. The tag would reveal his real name and the address of his rental house in Prince William County. Which didn't match the fake information he'd given the clerk at the tire store.

'That's a good idea,' Matthews said. 'A proactive idea.'

He wanted to scream. A dark mood hovered over him.

The food came and Konnie ate hungrily, hunched over his meal.

Matthews picked at his. He'd have to act soon. He flagged the waitress down and ordered another beer.

'You want to give me those receipts?' Matthews nodded at the briefcase.

'Sure, but let's go back to headquarters after. It's right up the street here. You can fax 'em to your office.'

'Okay.'

The second beer came. Konnie glanced at it for a second, returned to his food.

'This Tate Collier,' Matthews said slowly, savoring his microbrew. 'Sounds like a good man.'

'None better. Fucking best lawyer in the common-wealth. I get sick of these shits getting off on technicalities. When Collier was arguing the case they went away and stayed away.'

Matthews held up the beer. 'To your theory of tires.'

The detective hesitated then they tapped glasses.

Matthews drank half the beer, exhaled with satisfaction and set it down. 'Hot for April, don't you think?'

'Is,' the detective grunted.

Matthews asked, 'You on duty now?'

'Naw, I been off for three hours.'

'Then hell, chug down that milk and let me buy you a real drink.' He tapped the beer.

'No thanks.'

'Come on, nothing like a nice beer on a hot day.'

'Fact is, I give up drinking a few years back.'

Matthews looked mortified. 'Oh, I'm sorry.'

'Not at all.'

'I wasn't thinking. A man drinking milk. Shouldn't have ordered this. I *am* sorry.'

The cop held up a calm hand. ''S no problem at all. I don't hold with making other folk change their way of life 'cause of me.'

Matthews lifted the glass of beer. 'You want me to get rid of it or anything?'

As the cop glanced at the beer his eyes flashed – the same as they had when he'd walked through the bar, looking longingly at the row of bottles lined up like prostitutes on a street corner.

'Nope,' the detective said. 'You can't go hiding from it.' He ate some more mashed potatoes then said, 'Where you find most of the runaways go?'

Matthews enjoyed each small sip of the beer. The detective eyed him every third or fourth. The aroma from the liquid he'd spilled – on purpose – filled the booth with a sour malty scent. 'Always the big city. What a lure New York is. They think about getting jobs, becoming Madonna or whoever the girls want to become nowadays. The boys think they'll get laid every night.' Matthews sipped the beer again and looked outside. '*Damn* hot. Imagine that battle.'

'Bull Run?'

'Yep, well, I call it First Manassas but that's because I'm from Pennsylvania.' Matthews enjoyed another sip. 'You married?'

Or did the wife leave the drunk?

'Was. Divorced now.'

'Kids?'

Or did they cut Daddy off cold when they got tired of him passing out during *Jeopardy!* on weeknights and puking to die every Sunday morning?

'Two. Wife's got 'em. See 'em some holidays.'

Matthews poured down another mouthful. 'Must be tough.'

'Can be.' The fat cop took refuge in his potatoes.

After a minute Matthews asked, 'So you a graduate?'

'How's that?'

'Twelve steps.'

'AA? Sure.' The cop glanced down at his beefy hands. 'Been two years, four months.'

'Eight years for me.'

Another flicker in the eyes. The cop glanced at the beer.

Matthews laughed. 'You're where you are, Konnie. And I'm where I am. I was drinking a fifth of fucking bad whisky every day. Hell, at least that. Sometimes I'd crack the revenue of a second bottle just after dinner.' Konnie didn't notice how FBI-speak had turned into buddy talk, with syntax and vocabulary very similar to his.

'"Crack the revenue."' Konnie laughed. 'My daddy used to say that.'

So had some of Matthews's patients.

'Bottle and a half? That's a hell of a lot of drinking.'

'Oh, yes, it was. Yessir. Knew I was going to die. So I gave it up. How bad was it for you?'

The cop shrugged and shoveled peas and potatoes into his mouth.

'Hurt my marriage bad,' he offered. Flicker. Reluctantly the cop added, 'I guess it *killed* my marriage.'

'Sorry to hear that,' Matthews said, thrilling at the sorrow in the man's eyes.

'And it was probably gonna kill me some day.'

'What was your drink?' Matthews asked.

'Scotch. And beer.'

'Ha! Mine too. Dewars and Bud.'

Konnie's eyes softened at this unexpected camaraderie. 'So you . . . what?' The cop nodded at the tall-neck bottle. 'What happened? You fell off, huh?'

Matthews's face went reverential. 'I'll tell you the God's truth, Konnie.' He took a delicious sip of beer. 'I believe in meeting your weaknesses head-on. I won't run from them.'

The cop grunted affirmatively.

'See, it seemed too easy to give up drinking completely. You understand me?'

'Not exactly.'

'It was the coward's way. A lot of people just stop drinking altogether. But that's as much a failure to me . . . sorry, don't take this personal.'

'Not at all, keep going. I'm interested.'

'That's as much a failure to me as somebody who drinks all the time.'

'Guess that makes some sense,' the cop said slowly.

Matthews swirled the beer seductively in his glass.

'Take a man addicted to sex. You know that can be a problem?'

'I've heard. They got a Twelve Step for that too, you know?'

'Right. But he can hardly give up sex altogether, right? That'd be unnatural.'

Konnie nodded.

Oh, he's with me, Matthews thought. Hell, *this* is like sex. He felt so high. 'So,' he continued, 'I just got back to the point where I could control it.'

'And that worked?' Konnie asked. The toady little man seemed awestruck.

'What it was, I stopped cold for two years. Just like I told myself I'd do. This was all planned out. Sometimes it was tough as hell. I'm not gonna sugarcoat it. But God helped me. As soon as I had it under control, two years to the day I stopped, I took my first drink. One shot of Dewars. Drank it down like medicine.'

'What happened?'

'Nothing. Felt good. Enjoyed it. Didn't have another. Didn't have anything for a week. Then I had another shot and a Bud. I let a month go by.'

'A month?' Konnie whispered.

'Right. Then I poured a glass of Scotch. Let it sit in front of me. Looked at it, smelled it, poured it down the drain. Let another month go by.'

The cop shook his head in wonder. 'Sounds like you're one of them masochists or whatever you call 'em.' But there was a desperation in his laugh.

'Sometimes we have to find the one thing that's hardest for us and turn around and stare right at it. Go deep. As deep as we can go. That's what courage is. That's what makes men out of us.'

'I can respect what you're saying.'

'I've been drinking off and on for the past five years. Never been drunk once.' He leaned forward and rested his hand on the cop's hammy forearm. 'Remember that feeling when you were first drinking?'

'I think—'

'It made you relaxed, peaceful, happy? Brought out your good side? That's the way it is now.' Matthews leaned back. 'I'm proud of myself.'

'To you.' The cop swallowed and tipped his milk against the beer glass. His eyes slid over the golden surface of the brew.

Oh, you poor fool, thought Aaron Matthews. You don't have a soul in the world to talk to, do you? 'Sometimes,' he continued pensively, 'when I have a real problem, something eating at me, something making me feel so guilty it's like a fire inside . . . Well, I'll have a shot. That numbs it. It helps me get through.'

The fork probed the diminished pile of potatoes.

Let's go deep.

Touch the most painful part . . .

'If I found myself in a situation where there was somebody I loved and she was drifting away because of the way I'd become – well, I'd want to be able to face whatever had driven her away. I could show her I was in control again, and – who knows? – maybe I could just get her back.'

The cop's face was flushed and it seemed that his throat had swollen closed.

Matthews sipped more beer, looked out the window, at the dusk sky. 'Yessir, I hated living alone. Waking up on those Sunday mornings. Those March Sunday mornings, the sky all gray . . . The holidays by myself . . . God, I *hated* that. My wife gone . . . The one person in the world I needed. The one person I was willing to do anything for . . .'

The detective was paralyzed.

Now, Matthews thought. Now! 'Let me show you something.' He leaned forward, winking. 'Watch this.' He waved to the waitress. 'Shot of Dewars.'

'One?' she called.

'Just one, yeah.'

Numb, the cop watched the glass arrive.

Matthews made a show of reaching down and picking up the brimming glass. He leaned forward, smelled the glass, then took the tiniest sip. He set the glass down on the table and lifted his hands, palm up.

'That's it. The only hard liquor I'll have for two, three weeks.'

'You can do that?' The cop was dumbfounded.

'Easiest thing in the world. Without a single problem.' He returned to his beer and called the waitress over. 'I'm sorry, honey. I'll pay you for it but I changed my mind. I think I better keep a clear head tonight. You can take it.'

'Sure thing, sir.'

The cop's hand made it to the glass before hers. She blinked in surprise at the vehemence of the big man's gesture.

'Oh, you want me to leave that after all?'

The cop looked at Matthews but then turned his dog eyes to the waitress. 'Yeah. And bring my friend here another beer.'

A fraction of a pause. Their eyes met. Matthews said, 'Make it two.'

'Sure thing, gentlemen. Put it on your tab?'

'Oh, no,' Matthews insisted. 'This's on me.'

Matthews, wearing his surgical gloves, drove Konnie's car out of the parking lot of the strip mall and toward the interstate. The cop was in the passenger seat, clutching the bottle of Scotch between his legs like it was the joystick in a biplane. His head rocked against the Taurus's window. Spit and whiskey ran down his chin.

Matthews parked on a side road, not far from Ernie's, lifted the bottle away from Konnie and splashed some on the dashboard and seat of the car, handed it back. Konnie didn't notice. 'How you doing?' Matthews asked him.

The big man gazed morosely at the open mouth of the bottle. A declaration of intent, Aaron Matthews concluded, to his great pride and pleasure.

At the strip mall where they'd bought the Scotch Matthews had pitched a trash bag containing the tire receipts and all the rest of the notes on the Megan McCall investigation into a dumpster.

Matthews now climbed out of the car, pulled Konnie into the driver's seat.

Konnie gulped down two large slugs of liquor. He wiped his sweating, pasty face. 'Where'm I going?'

'You're going home, Konnie.'

'Okay.'

'You go on home now.'

'Okay. I'm going home. Is Carol there?'

'Your wife? Yeah, she's there, Konnie. She's waiting for you to come home. You better hurry.'

'I really miss her.'

'You know where to go, don't you?' Matthews asked.

'I think . . .' His bleary eyes looked around. 'I don't know.'

'That road right there. See it?'

'Sure. There?'

'Right there,' Matthews said. 'Just drive down there. That'll get you home. That'll get you home to Carol.'

'Okay.'

'Goodbye, Konnie.'

'Goodbye. That road there?'

'That's right. Hey, Konnie?'

Matthews looked at the rheumy eyes, wet lips.

'You say hi to Carol for me, won't you?'

The cop nodded.

Matthews flicked the gearshift into drive and stepped back as Konnie accelerated. He was driving more or less down the middle of the road.

Matthews was walking back to Ernie's to pick up the Mercedes when he heard the sudden squealing of brakes and the blares of a dozen horns, signaling to Konnie in his dark blue Taurus that he'd turned on to the exit, not entrance, ramp of I-66 and was driving the wrong way down the interstate. It was no more than thirty seconds later that he heard the pounding crash of what was probably a head-on collision and – though perhaps only in his imagination – a faint scream.

23

Night now.

The corridors of the asylum were murky, illuminated only by the light from two outdoor security lamps, bleeding in through the greasy windows.

Megan McCall, gripping her glass sword, moved silently through the main wing. She couldn't get the comic books out of her mind, the tentacles gripping screaming women, the monsters raping them. In some of the mags, Peter'd circled pictures a dozen times with different colored pens.

Moving toward the boy's room. Closer, closer.

She stepped into the large lobby. In the dim light shadows filled the space. She *believed* he was in his room but he could have been anywhere. She spun around, practically feeling the metal rod he carried swinging toward her head. Gasping.

Nothing.

Was he asleep in there? Reading? Jerking off?

Fantasizing about her.

About what he was going to *do* to her.

The corridors were like a maze. She wasn't sure anymore where his rooms were. She made several false turns and found herself back where she'd started. Feeling desperate now. Afraid that he'd find the trap.

She walked more quickly, listening carefully. But she heard no obscene breathing, no lewd whispering of her name. In a way the silence was *more* frightening; she didn't know where he was.

Then she turned a corner and there it was! She saw light spilling into the corridor from the open door of Peter's room. She was sure the lights had been off when she'd been in there.

The light flickered. A shadow.

He was inside.

Megan, sweating. Megan, scared.

Scared of dying, scared of the monster who lives up the hall, scared of the whispering bears.

Well, you wanted him, Crazy Megan whispers. *What're you waiting for? Go get him.*

She started to tell C.M. to be quiet. But suddenly she stopped. Because a thought hit her with the strength of the cinder blocks piled up in her trap. It was this: that Crazy Megan not only isn't crazy, she's the only one of them that's real.

Crazy Megan is the genuine Megan. The Megan who danced on the scaffolding of the water tower on a dare to make herself known. The Megan who was secretly dreaming of going to San Francisco for a year after high school and then to college in Paris. The Megan who made fierce love with a sexy black boyfriend who – fuck you, Dr Hanson – I *do* love after all! The Megan who wanted to poke her finger into her father's face and scream at him, 'The inconvenient child's back and you've got her whether you like it or not!'

Oh, yeah, Crazy Megan's the sane one. And the other one's just a loser.

'Okay,' she said out loud. 'Okay, prick, come and get me.'

The shadow of Peter Matthews froze on the wall.

The light clicked out.

'Come on, you fucker!' she shouted.

There was a ring of metal – he must have picked up the rod.

She couldn't see clearly but she was suddenly aware of his form lumbering slowly from the doorway. He looked up and down the hall and then turned toward her. 'Megan . . .'

God, he's big.

'*Megan!*' he rasped.

He started toward her. Moving much faster than she'd expected from the shuffling lope she'd heard earlier.

Her courage dissolved. What a fucking stupid idea this is! Hell, it's not going to work. Of course it isn't. He'll get her.

'No!' she screamed in panic.

Get going! Crazy Megan shouts. *Run.*

Stupid, stupid . . . Just like everything else I do. Everything else I get wrong. I'll lead him back to the trap and he'll dodge the cinder blocks, laughing the whole time, and move in slowly, pinning me against the wall and jabbing the rod up into me the way one of his damn monsters would do.

She backed up fast, knowing that she should be watching where she was going but afraid to take her eyes off him for an instant.

Feeling the wall behind her. Nearly tripped on a table. She spun around, pushed it aside.

And when she looked back he was gone.

We're fucked, Crazy Megan says.

He could be anywhere now! Coming up around her from the left or the right.

And, of course, she remembered, he had keys to the

place. He could move from room to room and come up behind her.

There was nothing she could do now except get into the dead end corridor where she'd set up the trap. Get there as fast as she could and wait.

But in her panic she was turned around. Was it back that way? Or to the side? She gazed down two corridors. Which? He could be down either of them. She could hardly see a thing in the darkness.

There, she thought. It's got to be that one. I'm sure.

Almost sure.

She sprinted. She slammed into a fiberglass chair, sending it flying. She stayed upright but the noise of the furniture hitting the wall was very loud.

Megan froze. Had he heard? Had—

Suddenly a huge form stepped from the corridor about two feet away, lunging toward her. 'Megan . . .'

Megan screamed, couldn't get the knife up in time. She closed her eyes, swinging her left fist toward where his face was. She connected hard and must have broken his nose because he wailed in pain and dropped back, around the corner.

She ran.

Turned one corner and paused at the entrance to the hallway that led to the trap.

He followed, moving toward her.

She made sure he got a good look at her, to see which way she was going, then started toward the trap.

But she stopped. Wait! Was it *this* corridor? No, the next. Wait. Was it?

She glanced into the murky shadows and couldn't see the denim rope. Was it there? Yes or no?

Peter was getting closer.

Which fucking corridor? Crazy Megan shouts.

I don't know, I don't know, they all look alike . . .

He was twenty feet away.

Come on, snaps C.M. *Get it together.*

No choice. It better be this one.

Megan ran to the end of the corridor.

Yes! She'd been right. There was the trap. She crouched down and picked up the end of the rope. At the far end of the corridor Peter paused and glanced toward her.

More muttering. Like an animal. She remembered the newspaper picture: his odd mouth, probing tongue, the crazy eyes. The grin of his mother's funeral.

I'm so fucking scared . . .

You're gonna nail him, Crazy Megan says.

In the darkness he didn't even seem to be walking. He just floated closer to her, growing larger and larger, filling the corridor. He stopped right before the trap. She couldn't see his eyes or face in the shadow but she knew he was leering at her.

More muttering.

He stepped closer.

Now!

She pulled the rope.

The denim snapped neatly in half. The cinder blocks shifted slightly but stayed where they were.

Oh, no. Oh, Christ, no! *That's it*, Crazy Megan cries. *It's over with.*

He moved forward another two steps.

She swept the knife from her pocket, looked at his shadowy form.

I'm going to die. This is it. I'm dead. He'll break my arm, take the knife away from he and fuck me till I die . . .

Crazy Megan has gone away. Crazy Megan is dead already.

He stepped forward one more foot. The dim light from outside fell on his face.

No . . .

She was hallucinating.

Megan gasped. 'Josh!'

'Megan,' he mumbled again. Joshua LeFevre's face and neck were bloody messes, his hands, arms and legs too. Large gouges were missing from his skin all over his arms and legs. He dropped to his knees.

Just as the cinder blocks started to tumble toward him.

'No!'

Megan leapt forward and pushed him aside. The blocks crashed into the floor, firing splinters of stone through the air. He fell backwards, hard. She cradled his bloody head.

'Megan,' he said, the name stuttering from his torn throat. Blood sprayed her face. Then he passed out.

Tate Collier's Lexus skidded up to the pay-phone on Route 29.

He leapt out, looking around desperately.

He saw no one.

'Hello?' he called in a harsh whisper. 'Hello!'

He glanced at the old diner – or what was left of it after an arson fire some years ago – and piles of trash. Deserted.

He heard a moan. Then some violent retching.

Tate ran into the bushes. There Konnie sat, bloody and drenched in sweat, vomit on his chin, eyes unfocused. He'd been crying.

'Jesus. What happened?' Tate bent down, put his arm around the man. When Konnie'd called him twenty minutes ago he'd said only to meet him here as soon as possible. Tate knew he was drunk, only half conscious, but had no other clue as to what was going on.

'I'm going down, Tate. I fucked up bad. Oh, Christ . . .'

Bett . . . now Konnie . . . What a day, Tate thought. What a day.

'You're hurt.'

'I'm okay. But I may've killed people, Tate. There was an accident. I left the scene.' He gasped and retched for a minute. 'They're looking for me, my own people're looking for me.' He coughed violently.

'I'll call an ambulance.'

'No, I'm turning myself in. But—'

He rolled over on his side and retched for a few minutes. Then caught his breath and sat up.

A squad car with flashing lights cruised past slowly. The searchlight came on but it missed the bushes where Tate crouched beside the detective.

'They're all over the place, looking for me. But listen to me, you have to get to the office. I couldn't find my briefcase, I don't know where I left it. You need to look at the receipts.'

'Receipts.'

'For the tires. Go to the office, Tate. Genie should've made a copy of them. I'm praying she did. Ask her for them. But move fast 'cause they're going to impound my desk.'

'Genie? That's your assistant?'

'You remember her. The list of receipts, okay?'

'All right.'

'Then look for whoever paid cash for the tires.'

'Cash for the tires. All right.'

'She ran warrants but that's not . . . that's not what I shoulda been looking for. Tate, you listening?'

'I'm listening.'

'Good. Look for the receipts where the customers paid cash. Then run the tag numbers of their cars. If the registered owner doesn't match the name on the receipt that's our boy. The one took your daughter. I got a look at . . .' He caught his breath. 'I got a look at him.'

'You saw him?'

'Oh, yeah. The prick suckered me good. He's white, forties, dark hair. About one seventy. Said he . . . Claimed he was Bureau. He suckered me just like my daddy suckered people. Shit. God, I'm sick.'

'Okay, Konnie. I'll do it. But now I'm getting you to the hospital.'

'No, you're not. You're not wasting another fucking minute. You're going do what the hell I told you. And fuck, be there for my arraignment. I can't believe what I did. I can't believe it.' His voice disappeared in a cascade of retching.

Tate found his old commonwealth's attorney ID badge at home and ran back to his car, hanging the beaded chain around his neck.

The date was four years old but was in small type; he doubted anyone would notice.

In twenty minutes he was walking into the police station. No one paid him any attention. He signed the log-in book and walked into Konnie's office.

A heavy-set woman, red-eyed and crying, looked up.

'Oh, Mr Collier. Did you hear?'

'He's going to be all right, Genie.'

'This's so terrible,' she said, wiping her face. 'So terrible. I can't imagine he'd take to drinking again. I don't know why. I don't know what's going on.'

268

'I'm going to help him. But I've got to do something first. It's very important.'

'He said I should help you when he called. Oh, he sounded so drunk on the phone. I remember he used to call me up and say he wouldn't be coming in today because he had the flu. But it wasn't the flu. He sounded the way he was tonight. Just plain drunk.'

Tate rested his hand on her broad shoulder. 'He's going to be all right. We'll all help him. Did you make a copy of the receipts?'

'I did, yes. He always tells me, "Make a copy of everything I give you. Always, always, always make a copy."'

'That's Konnie.'

'Here they are.'

He took the stack of receipts, owners of Mercedes who'd bought new Michelins. On four receipts the cash/check box was marked. He didn't recognize any of the names.

'Could you run these tag numbers through DMV and get me the names and addresses of the registered owners?'

'Sure.' She sniffed and waddled to her chair, sat heavily. Then she typed furiously.

A moment later she motioned him over.

The first three names matched those on the receipts.

The fourth didn't.

'Oh my God,' Tate muttered.

'What is it, Mr Collier?'

He didn't answer. He stood, numb, staring at the name Aaron Matthews, Sully Fields Drive, Manassas, the letters glowing in jaundice-yellow type on the black screen.

24

The Court: *The prosecution may now present its summation. Mr Collier?*

Mr Collier: *My friends . . . The task of the jury is a difficult and thankless one. You're called on to sift through a haystack of evidence, looking for that single needle of truth. In many cases, that needle is elusive. Practically impossible to find. But in the case before you, the Commonwealth versus Peter Matthews, the needle is lying out in the open, evident for everyone to see.*

There is no question that the defendant killed Joan Keller. He was seen walking with the victim, a sixteen-year-old girl, by Bull Run Marina. He was seen leading her into the woods. He was later seen running from the park five minutes before Joan's body was found, strangled to death. The mud in which her cold corpse lay matched the mud found on the knees of the defendant's jeans. When he was arrested, as you heard from the testimony, he blurted out to the officers, 'She had to die.'

And in the trailer where he lived, the police found hundreds of comic books and horror novels, depicting big, hulking men doing unspeakable things to helpless women victims – victims just like Joan Keller.

The defense can see that shiny needle of truth as clearly as you and I can. There's no doubt in their minds either that the defendant killed that poor girl. And so what do they do? They try to distract us. They raise doubts about Joan's character. They suggest that she had loose morals. That she'd had sex with local boys . . . sometimes for money. Or for liquor or cigarettes. A sixteen-year-old girl! These are vile attempts to distract you from finding the needle.

Oh, they talk about accidental death. 'Just playing around,' they say. The killer was a troubled young man, they say, but harmless.

Well, the facts of the case prove that he wasn't harmless at all.

Harmless men don't strangle innocent young women, seventy pounds lighter than they are.

Harmless men don't act out their sick and twisted fantasies on helpless youngsters like Joanie Sue Keller.

Ladies and gentlemen, don't let the defense hide that needle from you. Don't let them cover it up. This case is simple, extremely simple. The defendant, through his premeditation, his calculation, his knowing, purposeful intent, has taken a life. The life of a young girl. Someone's friend . . . someone's sister . . . someone's daughter. There is no worse crime than that. And he must be held fully responsible for it.

The great poet Dante said that the most righteous requests are answered in the silence of the deed. I'm not asking for hollow words, ladies and gentlemen. No, I'm asking for your courageous deed – finding this dangerous killer sane, finding him guilty and recommending to the court that he pays for young Joan Keller's life with his own. Thank you.

Tate Collier had done everything right in the closing statement. It was short, colloquial, filled with concrete imagery. He'd referred to Peter Matthews as the 'defendant' and to the girl as 'Joan' – depersonalizing the criminal, humanizing the victim. He'd played with shadows and light. The reference to the 'needle' – getting the jury used to the thought of the needle used in lethal injections – was a particularly good touch, he'd thought.

He'd even added the request for the death penalty because that was something they could bargain with in their minds – trading the boy's life for a finding of sanity and a long prison sentence.

And that was exactly what happened.

He won, the boy was found sane and guilty. And was sentenced to life without parole. Which had been Tate's goal all along.

And a week later the young man who'd beaten capital punishment was executed by a far more informal means than lethal injection – a dozen prison inmates, identities unknown, had used broomsticks and sharpened spoons to carry out the sentence. And it took them three hours to do so.

Justice?

After he'd heard of Peter's death, Tate had sat at his desk for a long moment then walked into the commonwealth's attorney's file room and read through evidence in the case once again.

They were the same files and documents he'd read before the trial, of course. But he examined them now untainted by the passionate drive to convict the young man. He looked more carefully at the picture they painted of the boy. Not of 'the defendant'. But of Peter Thomas Matthews. A seventeen-year-old boy, a resident of Fairfax, Virginia.

Yes, Peter had a collection of eerie comics and Japanamation tapes. But many of them, Tate learned, were bestsellers in Japan – where they'd taken on an artsy, cult status and were reviewed seriously and collected by young people and adults alike. What was more, the boy also had a collection of serious science fiction and fantasy writers like Ray Bradbury, Isaac Asimov, William Gibson, C. S. Lewis, J. R. R. Tolkien, Jules Verne, Edgar Rice Burroughs. Peter had spent hours copying long, poetic passages from these books and had tried his hand at illustrating scenes from them. He also wrote pretty good fantasy short stories of his own.

Yes, some psychiatric evaluations called the boy dangerous. But others said he merely had a paranoid personality and was given to panic in stressful situations. He had no history of violence.

Tate had also read about Joan Keller – the victim – who'd been sexually active since age twelve. She'd experimented with 'weird things', possibly erotic asphyxia. She'd seduced older men on several other occasions and would have been the complaining witness in at least one statutory rape case, except that she'd refused to cooperate. She'd been treated for being a borderline personality and had been suspended twice for assaults – against both girls and boys at her school, including one involving a knife.

Peter had abrasions on his face and neck when he was brought to the lockup. He claimed that Joan had struck him with a rock when she got tired of his awkward groping – after she'd taken his hand and slipped it into her panties.

And the statement the boy had made – about how Joan 'had to die' – was disputed by a local fisherman near the scene of the arrest. He claimed the boy might have said, 'She never had to die . . . She shouldn't have hit me.'

But silver-tongued Tate Collier had managed to keep

all of this damning evidence out of the jury's earshot or had shattered the credibility of the witnesses presenting it.

Your honor we will not try the victim in this case your honor a well-written short story has no probative value in this case whatsoever your honor that fact is immaterial and has to be stricken please instruct the witness . . .

The defense lawyers had come to him with a plea bargain. Criminally negligent homicide, suspended sentence, three years' probation and two years' mandatory counseling.

But, no. Peter Matthews had laid his hands upon the neck of a sixteen-year-old girl and had pressed, pressed, pressed until she was lifeless. And so a plea bargain wouldn't do.

The Court: *The defendant will rise. You have heard the verdict of the jury and have been adjudged guilty of murder in the first degree. The jury has not recommended the death penalty and accordingly I hereby sentence you to life in prison . . .*

He went to prison and the last thing anyone remembered about Peter was a giggling fit and his telling a guard he was going to play with his new friends. 'Won't that be way cool?' Peter asked. 'We're going to play ball, a bunch of us. They want me to play ball. Awesome.' Then he disappeared into the laundry room and was found, in several pieces, five hours later.

Why, Tate had wondered then, sitting alone in the musty file room, had he been so vehement about prosecuting the boy? *Why?*

The question he'd asked himself often in the past few years.

The question he asked himself now.

275

What would have been so bad if the defendant . . . if *Peter* had gone into a hospital? Gone to see a counselor.

Wasn't that reasonable? Of course it was. But it hadn't been then, not to the Tate Collier of five years ago. Not to Tate Collier the whiz-kid commonwealth's attorney, the man who spoke in tongues, the Judge's grandson.

Why?

Because the thought of a killer depriving parents of their child was unbearable to him. *That* was the answer. *That was* all he thought. Someone stole away a girl just like Megan. And he had to die. To hell with justice.

Tate had never seen Peter's father at the trial or hadn't paid any attention to him if he'd been there. He was a therapist, Tate remembered from reading the boy's history and evaluations. Lived alone. His wife – a therapist as well, and reportedly more successful than her husband – had committed suicide some years before.

Aaron Matthews . . .

Well, he could give the police a name and address now. They'd find him. He only prayed Megan was still alive.

Now, in Konnie's office, he dialed Bett's home phone. Her voice mail gave her cellphone number and he dialed that. She didn't answer. He left a message about what he'd learned and told her that he was at the county police station.

He started down the hall, striding the way he'd walked when he'd been a commonwealth's attorney and cut up these offices as if he owned them, playing inquisitor to the young officers as he grilled them about their cases and the evidence they'd collected.

He pushed through the door to the Homicide Division and was surprised to see three startled detectives stop in the tracks of their conversations.

He smiled ruefully, remembering only then that he was a trespasser.

One detective looked at another, an astonished gaze on his face.

'I'm sorry to barge in,' Tate began. 'I'm Tate Collier. It's about my daughter. I don't know if you heard but she's disappeared and—'

In less than twenty seconds he was face down on a convenient desk, the handcuffs ratcheting on to his wrists with metallic efficiency, his Miranda rights floating down upon him from a gruff voice several feet above his head.

'What the hell's going on?' he barked.

'You're under arrest, Mr Collier. Do you understand these rights as I've read them to you?'

'For what? What're you arresting me for?'

'Do you understand your rights?'

'Yes, I understand my fucking rights. What for?'

'For murder, Mr Collier. The murder of Amy Walker. If you'll come this way, please.'

25

She cradled him, sobbing.

Megan had eased Joshua LeFevre into the pale light from the outside lamp. He was even more badly injured than she'd thought at first – terribly battered – cut with slashes and bite marks, the wounds covered with dirt and dried blood. A stained scarf was tied around his neck as a bandage. One eye was swollen completely closed. Most of his dreads had been torn off his scalp, which was covered with mud and scabs.

He could speak only in a ghostly, snapping wail. No, it hadn't been Peter Matthew's leering voice, she'd heard; it was Josh's. His throat was split open with a terrible wound. His vocal cords had been cut and she thought, sobbing, of his beautiful baritone. When he breathed, air hissed in through both his mouth and the slash. The bleeding seemed to have stopped but she bound the denim rope around his throat anyway. She could think of nothing else to do.

'I thought it was you,' he gasped. 'I couldn't see. My eyes, my eyes. I thought it was you. But you didn't answer.'

Megan lowered her head to his chest. 'And I thought you were his son. I thought you were going to kill me. Oh, Josh, what happened? Was it the dogs? Outside?'

He nodded, shivered – from the pain, she guessed, as much as the cold.

'That . . . man?' he struggled to ask. 'He kidn—'

She nodded. 'Did you call the police?'

'No,' he gasped. 'I didn't know what was going on. I stopped him but he tricked me . . .' He coughed for a moment. 'Thought you . . . thought you were going with him.'

'What happened?' she asked tearfully.

The stuttering explanation: he'd followed her and Matthews here then the doctor had attacked him and left him for the dogs. But before they could finish him off a young deer had trotted past and they left Josh to pull her down.

His beautiful voice, Megan thought, crying. It's gone. She had to look away from his face.

He'd found a tire iron to use as a cane, he continued, and made his way into the hospital to find a phone. But there weren't any and he found that the doors didn't open outward, that the place was a prison.

She gently touched a terrible wound on his face. Even if they found a doctor soon would he survive?

'Were you . . . you weren't his lover, were you?'

'What?' she blurted.

'He said you were. He said . . . He said you wanted to get rid of me.'

'Oh, Josh, no. It was . . . whatever he said, it was a lie.'

'Who is he?' LeFevre rasped.

'We don't have time now. Can you walk?'

'No.' He breathed heavily and winced. 'Can't do anything. I've about had it.'

She pulled him further into the alcove, hid him from view.

'Wait here.'

'Where . . . you going?'

'Lie still, Josh. Be quiet.'

'I'll get something to use for bandages,' she said, rising.

'But he might be there.'

She showed him the glass knife. 'I really hope he is.'

'I'll tell you whatever you want to know. But for God's sake send somebody after my daughter.'

'Once more from the top, please, sir.' Tate was still stunned from the news that Amy had been found naked and stabbed to death in Tate's north thirty field.

'There's a man named Aaron Matthews. He drives a gray Mercedes. He lives on Sully Field, off Route 29 near Manassas. He's been following my daughter for the past couple weeks. Or months. I don't know. And—'

'We've got our own agenda here, Collier,' the young homicide detective – a dead ringer for the security guard at Megan's high school – said gruffly, his patience gone. 'You don't mind, we got a lotta ground to cover.'

'Is Ted Beauridge around?'

'No. One more time, sir. From the top.'

He was in an interrogation cubicle. At least the cuffs were off.

'Matthews killed Amy. Megan had told her about being followed. He thought she might have some information – Maybe he just killed her to get me out of the picture.'

And *I* gave him her name, Tate thought. He was sure the man who called from the FBI – special agent McComb – was Aaron Matthews, probing to get information. Trying to stop them from looking for her. He forced or tricked Megan into writing those notes and when they kept looking for her anyway, he turned on them.

'How'd you find out about the body?' Tate asked. 'An anonymous call, right?'

The detectives looked at each other. They were slim and in perfect shape. Trimmed hair. Shoes polished, guns tucked neatly away. Law enforcement machines.

'It was *Matthews* who called. Don't you get it?'

'Her mother said you'd been stalking Amy. That Child Protective Service's has been investigating you.'

'What? That's bullshit. Call them.'

'On Saturday night, sir? We'll call on Monday.'

'We don't have until Monday.'

The cop continued lethargically, 'Mrs Walker also said you tried to break into her house today.'

'Amy was going to give us Megan's bookbag. I knocked on the door and tried to open it when no one answered.'

'Uh-huh.'

'There *is* no Child Protective investigation. It's him! It's Matthews. He's trying to stop me from finding Megan. Can't you see?'

'Not exactly, sir. No.'

'Okay. When did this anonymous call come in? Within the last half-hour? Believe me, Matthews killed Amy and dumped the body on my land. I saw somebody watching the house this morning.'

'Did you report it?'

'Well, no, I didn't.'

'Why not?'

Tate remembered thinking, as he stood in the rain-swept field that morning, Hey, looks like the Dead Reb. But it wasn't. It was Aaron Matthews, waiting until I left the house then tossing the dog a bone, planting Megan's letters, shutting the light out, leaving fast.

'I just didn't. Look, he knows I'm after him – Konnie was running a check on the Mercedes. It turned out to be his. That's not a coincidence.'

'How do you account for the fact that this girl was murdered with a kitchen knife that had your finger-prints on it?'

'Because it was probably from *my* kitchen. Talk to Konnie about this morning. He—'

'Detective Konstantinatis is in custody and he's also in no shape to talk to anybody. As I'm sure you know.'

'Beauridge, then. They were out to my house. Matthews broke in, planted some fake letters that Megan supposedly wrote and he must've stolen the knife at the same time. Or stole it tonight. It's an easy house to break into.'

'The cause of death was shock due to blood loss after her throat was slashed and her chest and abdomen punctured thirty-two times. There was some mutila-tion too.'

'Fuck of a way to kill someone,' the other detec-tive added.

Tate's face grew hot. Megan's terrified eyes were the most prominent image in his thoughts.

'We've checked out your house and found you'd packed most of your girl's stuff away. Her bedroom looked about as personal as a storeroom.'

'She lives with her mother.'

'No pictures of her, no clothes, nothing personal. The impression we got was you'd been planning to say adios to Megan for some time. That's making us wonder about this whole kidnapping story.'

'There were some witnesses. There's a teacher . . . Robert Eckhard. He saw—'

But he stopped talking when he saw the expression on their faces.

'You a friend of Eckhard?'

'I don't know him,' Tate said cautiously. 'I just heard that he'd seen the car that was following Megan.'

'Have you ever talked to him?'

'No. I just told you – Why?'

'Robert Eckhard was arrested today on numerous counts of child pornography and endangering the welfare of minors.'

'What?'

'Could you describe your relationship with him?'

'With Eckhard? There *is* no relationship . . . Jesus Christ. I don't know him! Please! Just send somebody out to check out this Matthews!'

A rhetorician never pleads. Tate's talents were deserting him in droves. Think smarter, he raged at himself. He could talk his way out of this. He *knew* he could. There must be some way. What would his grandfather, the Judge have done?

All cats see in the dark . . .

Midnight is a cat . . .

'Officer,' Tate said calmly, offering a casual smile, 'you've got nothing to lose. Absolutely nothing. I'm not going anywhere. If you check him out, if you send a couple officers out to his place then I'll tell you whatever you want to know. Anything. No hassle. We have a deal?'

One of the detectives sighed. He shrugged and stepped out the door.

Therefore Midnight sees in the dark.

Tate pictured Megan, bound and gagged, lying somewhere in a basement. Matthews standing over her. Undressing.

It was a terrible image and, once thought, wouldn't go away.

'Have you ever had sexual relations with Amy Walker?'

He tamped down his anger. 'I've never met her,' he answered.

'Did you send your daughter off somewhere because she knew you were stalking Amy Walker? And fabricate a kidnapping charge?'

'No, I didn't do that.' Struggling now to stay calm, to stay *helpful*. Really struggling. He looked at the doorway through which the other cop had disappeared. Were they sending a hostage rescue team to Matthews's house? Or just patrol officers? Matthews could trick them. He could lull them into complacency – oh, yes, *he* had the gift too, Tate now understood the dicey talent of persuasion.

They can't negotiate with someone like Matthews.

The silence of the deed.

'Did you kill Amy Walker?'

'No, I did not.'

'When was the last time you drove your daughter's car?'

'A month or so ago, I think.'

'Is that how your fingerprints got on the door handle of her car?'

'It would have to be.'

'Could we run through the events just prior to her disappearance once more?'

'Prior?'

'Say, for the week before.'

Tate glanced out the door, squinted. Looked again. The second detective came back into the cubicle. Tate asked, 'Did you send a team to his house? I should have told you to send hostage rescue. Tactical. Don't listen to him. Whatever he says, Megan's there, in the house. Tell whoever's on their way not to listen to him.'

'He wasn't home.'

'What?' Tate asked. He didn't understand. The officers couldn't have gotten there so quickly.

'I called him. He wasn't home.'

'You *called* him?' Tate's heart stuttered.

'Relax, sir, I didn't tell him anything. Just asked him to give us a call about some parking tickets.' The slick young cop seemed proud of his cleverness.

'Jesus Christ, you don't *have* to tell him anything. He's going to know. Are you crazy?'

'Sir, we don't have to pay any attention to your story at all, you know. We're doing you a favor.'

Tate sat back, glanced into the hall again.

After a moment he looked back at the officers again. Closed his eyes and sighed 'You win. Okay, you win.'

'How's that, sir?'

'I'll waive my rights and tell you everything I can think of. No confession but a full statement about my daughter and Amy Walker. But I want some coffee and I've got to use the john.'

They looked at each other and nodded.

'I'm coming with you,' the detective muttered.

Tate laughed. 'I was a commonwealth's attorney for ten years. I'm not going to escape.'

'I'm coming with you.'

Tate gave a disgusted sigh and walked out of the Detective Division into the scuffed halls, which resembled a suburban grade school. He ambled to the men's room and pushed inside. The detective was directly behind him.

He stood at the urinal for an inordinately long time.

When he'd finished and washed his hands he stepped to the door and pushed it open, bumping into the woman who was juggling three large law books and several pads of foolscap, which tumbled to the floor.

'Sorry,' Tate said, bending down to pick up the books.

Bett McCall glanced at him, said, 'No problem.' And slipped the pistol out of her purse and into his hand.

Tate didn't even pause to think – that would've been disastrous. He simply spun around, shoved the Smith & Wesson into the belly of the shocked detective and pushed him back into the men's room as Bett calmly retrieved the books.

In one minute Tate had gagged and cuffed the furious cop and relieved him of his gun. He tossed it in the wastebasket.

'The cuffs too tight?' he asked.

The detective stared angrily.

'Are they too tight?'

A nod.

Tate snapped, 'Good.'

And stepped out into the corridor as a faint rumble arose in the john, like a low-Richter earthquake. The detective was trying to pull down the stall.

When he'd looked into the hallway from the interrogation room he couldn't believe that he'd seen her standing there, motioning with her head down the hall. 'How did you get in here?' he asked as they walked briskly toward the exit.

'Told them I was a lawyer.'

'You cite a case or two?'

'I could have.' She smiled. 'I memorized the names of a couple on your desk. I was going to tell the desk sergeant I had to see my client because these new cases had just been put down.'

'It's "handed down",' Tate corrected.

'Oh. Glad he didn't ask.'

'I don't know if we can get out that way. I came in under my own steam but the desk officer might know I've been arrested.' He looked back down the corridor. 'Five minutes, tops, till they come looking.'

She rearranged the books she was carrying so the cover showed. A school hornbook, *Williston on Contracts.*

He laughed. 'That'll fool 'em.' Then asked, 'You got my message?'

She nodded. 'I called Konnie and his assistant told me you'd been arrested. I couldn't decide whether to get a lawyer or the gun. I figured we didn't have time to wait for public defenders. My car's outside.'

The old Bett McCall might have meditated for days, hoping for guidance. The new one went right for the Smith & Wesson.

They paused just before they turned the corner beside the guard station. He took a breath. 'Ready?'

'I guess.'

'Let's go.'

Mentally crossing his fingers, Tate started forward, Bett at his side. The guard glanced at them but out they strolled without a hitch, signing the 'time departed' line in the log book scrupulously – one a phony prosecutor and one a phony defense lawyer and both of them now fugitives.

Aaron Matthews was driving, seventy, then eighty miles an hour.

Anger had given way to sorrow. To the same piercing hollowness he'd felt in the months after Peter had died in prison.

Sorrow at plans gone wrong, terribly wrong.

Matthews had been at his rental house off Route 29, waiting to see if he'd finally stopped Tate Collier. He believed he had. He'd given up on the subtlety, given up on the words, given up on the delicious art of persuasion. Stiff with anger, he'd dragged the Walker girl, screaming, from the trunk of his car. Said nothing, convinced her of nothing – he'd just slashed and slashed and slashed . . . All of his anger flowing from him as hot and sudden as the blood from her body. And then he'd sped home.

There the phone had rung. He hadn't answered but listened to the message as the officer left it. Some bullshit about the traffic tickets. 'Give us a call when you get home. Thank you.'

It meant of course that they knew. Or suspected, at least.

How had it happened? Why hadn't they just tossed Collier into the lockup and ignored him? Maybe he had actually convinced them that he was innocent and that Matthews had kidnapped the girl. The fucking silver-tongued devil! The mood exploded within Matthews like napalm.

It was only a matter of time now before they found Blue Ridge Hospital. They knew his name, they'd find out his connection there, and they'd find Megan.

In a perfect world, moods don't burn you like torches, juries work pure justice, and revenge befalls sinners in exact proportion to their crimes. In a perfect world Matthews would have kept Megan McCall as his child forever, a replacement for Peter. And Tate Collier would have lived in despair all his life, never knowing where she was – knowing only that she'd fled from him, propelled by undiluted hate.

But there was no chance for such symmetry now. All

289

his hopes had unraveled. And there was only one answer left. To kill the girl and leave. Flee to the West Coast, New England, maybe overseas.

He'd lost his son, Tate Collier would lose his daughter.

A kind of cure, a kind of justice, a kind of revenge . . .

He sped out on to the highway, toward the distant humps of mountains, a sensuous dark line above which no stars became stars and the moon showed as a faint, white crescent of frown.

Cleaning the deep wounds was the hardest part.

She'd found a cheap sewing kit in the bedroom and a bottle of rubbing alcohol in the medicine cabinet.

He took the stitches fine (even though *she* cringed every time the needle pierced his skin). But when Megan poured a capful of alcohol on the wound he shivered frantically at the pain.

'Oh, I'm sorry.'

'No, no,' came his liquid voice. 'Keep at it, Ms Beautiful . . .'

Her eyes teared when she heard the nickname he'd used the night he picked her up.

'Even if you get out, you'll never get past 'em. The dogs. He's got four or five of the big fuckers.'

'You're sure you can't walk?'

'I don't think so,' his voice gurgled. 'No.'

'Okay, you stay here. I saw a door going to the basement. I think I can break it open. I'm going to see if there's a door or window down there. Maybe it'll lead outside.'

He nodded, breathed 'I love . . .' and passed out.

She stacked the cinder blocks around him so that

Matthews, glancing down here from the corridor, wouldn't see him.

She listened for a moment to his low, uneven breathing. Then, knife in one hand, she started down the corridor.

Megan was almost to the intersection of the corridors when she heard the creak of a door opening. Then it slammed. Aaron Matthews had returned.

26

They drove in silence through destitute parts of Prince William County. They passed tilled fields, where the taproots of corn were reaching out silently into the dark, red-tinted earth. Barns long ago abandoned. Decaying tract bungalows, where postwar dreams had withered fast – tiny cubes of vinyl – and aluminum-sided homes. Shacks and cars on blocks.

Through Manassas, where the fearsome Rebel Yell was first heard, then through the outlying farms and past the Confederate Cemetery.

'It was him, Tate,' Bett said finally.

'Who?'

'A man came to see me. He said he was her therapist but he wasn't.'

'It was Matthews?'

'He called himself Peters.'

'His son's name was Peter,' Tate mused. Glanced at her. 'What happened?'

She shook her head. 'He seduced me. Nothing really happened but it was enough . . . Oh, Tate, he looked right into my soul. He knew what I wanted to hear. He said exactly the right things.'

You can talk your way into somebody's heart and get them to do whatever you want. Judge or jury, you've got

*that skill. Words, Tate. Words. You can't see them but
they're the most dangerous weapons on earth. Remember
that. Be careful, son.*

She continued, 'He'd called Brad. I think he pretended
he was a cop and told him to get to my house. We were
together on the couch . . . I was drunk . . . Oh, Tate.'

Tate put his hand on her knee, squeezed lightly. 'There
was nothing you could've done, Bett. He's too good.
Somehow, he's done all of this. Dr Hanson, Konnie
. . . probably Eckhard too, the teacher. Just to get even
with me.' They drove on in silence. Then Tate realized
something. 'You got here too quickly.'

'What?'

'You couldn't have been in Baltimore when you got
my message.'

'No, I got as far as Takoma Park and turned back.'

'Why?'

A long pause.

'Because I decided it had to stop.' Instinctively she
flipped the mirror down and examined her face. Poked
at a wrinkle or two. 'I was running after Brad and I
should have been going after Megan.' She continued, 'I
realized something, Tate. How mad I've been at her.'

'At Megan? Because of what we heard at the Coffee Shop?'

'Oh, Lord, no. That's *my* fault, not hers.' She took
a deep breath, flipped the mirror back up. 'No, Tate.
I've been mad at her for years. She ended up right in
the middle of all our problems. It wasn't her fault. She
was born at the wrong time and the wrong place.'

'Yes, she sure was.'

'I neglected her and didn't do the things I should
have. . . . I dated, I left her alone. I did the basics, sure.
But kids know. They know where your heart is. Here I

was running after Joe or Dave or Brad and leaving my daughter. Time for that to stop. I'm just praying it's not too late.'

'We'll get her.'

The roads were deserted here and the air aromatic with smoke from wood cooking fires. The Volvo streaked through a stop sign. Tate skidded into a turn and then headed down a bad road, surrounded by scrub oak, brush and a rusted wire fence.

'We're in trouble, aren't we?' she asked.

'We sure are. They don't put out all-points bulletins anymore. But if they did we'd be the main attraction in one.'

'They don't know my car,' Bett pointed out.

He laughed. 'Oh, that took all of thirty seconds for 'em to track down. Look, there. That's his place.'

Matthew's small bungalow was visible through a stand of trees some distance away. A rusting heating-oil tank sat in the side yard and the stands of uncut grass were outnumbered by patches of red mud. The house was only two miles away from Tate's farm. Convenient staging point for a break-in and kidnapping, he noted.

'What are we going to do?' Bett asked.

Tate didn't answer her. Instead he took the gun out of his pocket. 'We're going to get our daughter,' he said.

Thirty yards, twenty, fifteen.

Tate paused and listened. Silence from inside Matthews's house.

He smelled the scent of woodsmoke and pictured the kidnapper sitting beside the fireplace with Megan bound and gagged at his feet.

The shabby house chilled his heart. He'd seen places like it often. Too often. When he was a commonwealth's attorney he'd always – unlike most big-city prosecutors – visit the crime scenes himself. This was what detectives dubbed a Section Sixty cottage, referring to the Virginia Penal Code provision for murder. Shotgun killings, domestics, love gone cruel then violent . . . There was a common theme to these houses: small, filthy, silent, brimming with unspoken hate.

The Mercedes wasn't here so it was possible that Matthews hadn't heard the message from the police. Maybe Megan was here now, lying in the bedroom or the basement. Maybe this would be the end of it. But he moved as silently as he could, taking no chances.

He glanced through the window.

The living room was empty, lit only by the glow of embers in the fireplace. He listened for a long moment. Nothing.

The windows were locked but he tested the handle on the door and found it was open. He pushed inside, thinking only as he did so: Why a fire on a warm night?

Oh, no! He lunged for the doorknob but it was too late. The door knocked over the large pail of gasoline.

'God!'

Instinctively Tate grabbed for the bucket as the pink wave of gas flowed on to the floor and into the fireplace.

'What?' Bett cried.

The gas ignited and with a whoosh a huge ball of flame exploded through the living room.

'Megan!' Tate cried, turning away from the flames and falling on to the porch. His sleeve was on fire. He slapped out the flames.

'She's in there? *She's in there?*' Bett shouted in panic and ran to the window.

Scrabbling away from the flowing gasoline, Tate grabbed

Bett and pulled her back. He covered his face with his hand, felt the searing heat take the hairs off the back of his fingers.

'Megan!' Bett cried. She broke the window in with her elbow. She peered inside for a moment but then leapt back as a hand of flame burst through the window at her. If she hadn't leapt aside the fire would have consumed her face and hair.

Tate ran around the back of the cottage, broke in the window in one of the bedrooms, which was already filling with dense smoke.

No sign of the girl.

He ran to the other bedroom – the cottage had only two – and saw that she wasn't there. The flames were already burning through the door, which, with a sudden burst, exploded inward. In the light from the fire Tate could see that Megan wasn't in this room either. He could also see that it wasn't a bedroom but an office. There were stacks of newspaper clippings, magazines, books and folders. Maps, charts and diagrams.

Sirens sounded in the distance.

Bett came up behind him. There was a burn on her arm but she was otherwise okay. 'Tate, I can't find her!' she screamed.

'I don't think she's here. She's not in either of these rooms and there's no basement.'

'Where *is* she?'

'The answer's in there,' he shouted. 'He only set the trap so nobody could find any clues to where he's got her.'

He picked up several bricks and shattered the glass and wooden grid in the window. 'Oh, brother,' he muttered. And climbed inside, feeling the unnerving pain as a shard of glass sliced through his palm.

The heat inside was astonishing, smoke and embers and flecks of burning paper swirling around him, and he realized that the flames weren't the worst problem – it was the heated air and lack of oxygen. He didn't think he could stay here for more than a minute.

He raced to the desk and grabbed all the papers and notebooks he could, ran to the window and flung them outside, crying to Bett, 'Get it all away from the house.' He went back for more. He got two more armfuls before the heat grew too much. He dove out the window and rolled to the ground heavily as the ceiling collapsed and a swell of flame puffed out the window.

He lay, exhausted, gasping, on the ground. Dizzy and hurt. Wondering why on earth Bett was doing a funny little dance around his arm. Then he understood. The file folder he held had been burning and she was stamping out the flames.

The sirens were getting closer.

'Great,' he muttered. 'Now they're gonna add arson to my rap sheet.'

Bett helped him up and they gathered all the notebooks and files he'd flung into the back yard. They ran to the car, started up and skidded out of the drive, passing the first of the fluorescent green fire trucks that were speeding toward the house.

They turned north and drove for ten minutes until Tate figured there was no chance of being spotted. He parked near the quarry in Manassas. A grim, eerie place that looked like it should have been a serial killer's stalking ground though to Tate's knowledge there'd never been any crime committed here worse than pot-smoking and drinking beer and sloe gin from open containers.

Tate in fact had snuck past the gate himself last year, with a date, to park and make out. He shamefully remembered that night briefly now, recalling that he'd been excited that the young woman had wanted to come here for the adventure of it – then realizing soberly that the only reason she'd suggested it was that she couldn't invite him home: she was twenty-one and still lived with her parents.

Tate and Bett pored over the singed files and papers, looking for some clue as to where Matthews might have taken Megan.

The files were mostly articles, psychiatric diagnostic reports, medical evaluations. He also found surveillance photos of Megan. Dozens of them. And of Tate's house and Bett's. Matthews had been planning this for months; some of the pictures had been taken during the winter. In one notebook Megan's daily routine was described in obsessive detail.

More patient reports.

More articles.

More diaries. With shaking hands Tate and Bett read through them all but there was no clue as to any other residences, apartments, houses where he might have taken the girl.

'There's nothing,' Bett barked in frustration. 'We've looked at everything.' Tears on her face.

Tate gazed at the mess of scorched papers and files on their laps. His eye fell on the patient diagnostic report. Then another. He flipped through them quickly. Then read the name and address of the hospital where the patients had been evaluated.

He snatched up his cellphone and, eyes on one of the reports, made a call to directory assistance for Calvert, Virginia. He asked for the number for the Blue Ridge Mental Health Facility.

'Please be out of order,' he whispered.

'Why on earth?' Bett asked.

'Please . . .'

'We're sorry,' the electronic voice reported, 'there is no listing for that name. Do you have another request?'

He clicked the phone off. 'That's where she is. An old mental hospital in the Shenandoahs.' He tapped the reports. 'Matthews was a shrink. I'd guess he was on the staff there a few years ago. It's probably closed and that's where he's taken her.'

'You sure?'

'No. But do we have any other leads?'

'Go, Tate.'

He pulled out on to the highway and steered toward the interstate. Thinking with frustration that they'd have to drive the entire way right on the speed limit. They could hardly afford to be stopped now.

Glass knife in front of her, Megan walked through the hallways.

There was silence, then the shuffling of footsteps. More silence.

I hate the quiet worse than his footsteps.

I'm with you there, Crazy Megan shares.

Then the steps again but from a different place as if the intruder were a ghost materializing at will.

Five minutes passed. Then another noise near by, behind her. A sharp inhalation of breath. Megan gasped and turned quickly. Aaron Matthews was twenty feet away. His eyes widened in surprise. She stumbled backwards and fell over a table, went down hard. Grunted in pain as the edge of the table dug into her kidney.

Despite the pain, though, she leapt to her feet, lifting the knife. She assumed he'd charge at her.

But he didn't. He merely frowned and said, 'Oh, my God, Megan, are you all right?'

In a crouch, eyes fiery, breath hard, gripping the cloth handle of her wicked knife. Staring at his dark eyes, his large shoulders and long arms. Why wasn't he coming at her?

'Wait,' he said with a heart-tugging plea in his voice. 'Please, don't run. *Please.*'

She hesitated.

He sighed. 'Oh, I know you're upset, Megan, honey. I know you're scared, . . . You hate me and you have every right to. But please. Just listen to me.' He held his hands up. 'I don't have a knife or gun or anything. Please, will you listen?'

His eyes were so sincere and his voice so imploring . . .

'Please.'

Megan kept her tight grip on the knife. But she straightened up. 'Go ahead,' she whispered uneasily. 'I'm listening.'

'Good,' he said. And offered her a smile.

27

'I didn't know you'd gotten out of your room,' Aaron Matthews said.

'Cell,' she corrected bluntly.

'Cell,' he conceded, watching her eyes carefully. 'But I should've guessed.' He laughed. 'You're the independent sort. Nobody was going to lock you away. It's one of the things I love about you.'

Matthews noted how she fixed her gaze on his eyes. How her pale lashes stuttered when he'd said the word 'love'.

How had she done it? he wondered. He'd been over the cell so carefully – and the lock was still on the door. Had she gotten through the ceiling? The wall? And she was wearing some of his clothes. So she'd found his living area. What else did she know?

However it had happened, Matthews was surprised. It showed more mettle than he'd expected from the spoiled little whiner.

'Are you all right? Just tell me that.' He looked her up and down.

No answer.

He continued, 'I'm sorry about your clothes. When you passed out from the medicine I gave you . . . well, you had an accident. I'm sorry. I didn't think it would happen. I'm washing your clothes in the laundry room here. They're drying now. They should be ready soon.'

He glanced at the knife in her hand. A long shard. He thought at first that there was something about the glass itself that was particularly unnerving, the sharp, green edge of the triangle. But then he decided that, no, it was her *face* that scared him. She was prepared – no, eager – to use the weapon. And so much in control . . . she'd be a hard one to crack. Harder than in Hanson's office, where her defenses were down and her self-esteem bubbling near empty.

He eased forward. 'Oh, Megan, I'm so sorry.'

The point of the knife tilted toward him and Matthews froze. He said in his best therapist's tone, 'I didn't want it to happen this way.'

He fell silent. And to fill the intolerable gap of silence she asked, 'What way?'

'This . . .' He lifted his arms to the hallways. 'If there'd been anything else I could have done, I would have. I promise you.'

'What do you mean?'

He leaned against the wall, closed his eyes. 'You don't really know me. But I know you. I've known you for a long time.'

She shook her heard, frowning, confused. The tip of the knife was pointed lower.

'My name's Aaron Matthews . . .'

She'd've learned his real name, of course – from looking through the desk in his rooms. But tell someone the truth – no matter how much you've lied to them in the past – and you nudge them closer toward you, if ever so slightly. He continued right away – Matthews had a spell to cast and spells work best when cast quickly. 'I worked with your father on a case last year. He hired me as an expert witness. To evaluate a suspect. We were talking before the trial. Just making conversation. And I asked about children, if he had any, and he said . . .' Matthews paused and his face grew somber. He continued, 'I'm sorry, honey, but he said no, he didn't.'

Megan's beautiful light eyes widened. Shocked for a moment. Then they grew deeply sad, as they had in Hansen's office. A child betrayed, a child alone.

What are the bears whispering to you?

'But I'd heard somebody mention his daughter and I asked him about you. He looked embarrassed and said that, well, yes, he *did* have a daughter. But she lived with her mother. He said you were technically his child but that was all. I told him about my son. Peter. See, he had some problems at birth. Serious mental problems.'

Another flicker of lash. So she knew about him too. He said, looking down, 'But I've always felt that, despite all that, I loved my boy and wanted him to be with me. I mentioned that to your father. But he didn't say anything. I asked him how often he saw you . . . He said virtually never. I asked him about you and he didn't seem to know much at all. And then—' Matthews stopped abruptly, like a man finding himself in a minefield.

'What?'

'Nothing.'

'No, tell me,' she said with faint desperation in her voice.

'He said some things about you.'

'Please.' The knife was pointed straight down. 'I want to know.'

'He said being more involved with a child would be . . . awkward.'

'No he didn't,' she whispered. 'He didn't say that at all, did he?'

'I'm not sure . . .' Matthews stammered, putting a vulnerable look on his face.

She muttered, 'He said being involved with a child would be inconvenient. Right?'

'Yes,' Matthews conceded, sighing. 'I'm so sorry, Megan. But that's what he said. And when I heard it, all I could think of was how I hoped you had a good relationship with your mother. I hoped *someone* cared. I felt so bad for you.'

A faint laugh then her face went still. 'My mother. Yeah, right.'

He cocked his head, offering her another sympathetic glance. And continued, 'Well, I went to see her. When you were in school one day.'

'You did?'

Matthews eased a few inches closer. He decided that anger wouldn't work with Megan, unlike with her boyfriend, Josh. The madder she got the more dangerous she'd be. No, the way to get inside her defenses was to tap into her sorrow and loneliness.

'I lied, Megan. I'll admit it. I told Bett I was a counselor with your school and I wanted to know how you were doing. I was shocked to find that she didn't have much time for you either. She told me she was engaged, trying to make that relationship work, was totally absorbed with Brad, didn't have much time for . . . well, she said, for babysitting.'

'She said *that*?' Megan gasped.

'In fairness she said you were very mature and didn't need a lot of hand-holding.'

'How would she know?' Megan muttered.

Matthews swayed toward her but the coldness returned

to her eyes and she asked, 'But why the fuck did you kidnap me?'

He stopped.

'Because I wanted to give you a second chance, Megan.'

'Kidnapping me? What kind of chance is that?'

He looked down and rocked back and forth on his feet, moving a good six inches closer to her. 'Oh, Megan, yes, I kidnapped you. But I'd never hurt you. That was the last thing on my mind.' If she'd seen the room, she'd probably also seen the kitchen. He said, 'I can prove it. I'll show you the kitchen. It's filled with food that you like. I found out what you liked and I bought a lot of it.'

She nodded. Her defenses slipped a bit more. 'You were the one following me for the past couple weeks.'

'That's right. I followed you. And I talked to people about you too. Teachers, students. And the more I learned about you, the more I couldn't understand your parents. You're creative, you're funny, you're pretty, you have a sense of humor, you were artistic . . . You were everything a teenage girl ought to be. Why didn't they want you? Your parents, I mean?'

Her lip began to tremble. She wiped tears.

'It was so unfair,' he whispered. 'I wanted to give you the love that they never did. Parental love, I'm speaking of. I hope you know that . . . I think you're beautiful but I don't desire you physically.' He nodded toward her padded cell. 'I could have done that when you were unconscious if I'd wanted to.'

Her eyes told him that she understood it. That she'd checked her body for tenderness, for moisture.

But, once again, the eyes hardened. She asked, 'But there's more, isn't there? There's another side to it.'

He smiled. 'Oh, you're smart, Megan. You're very smart. Yes, there's another side. *I* wanted another chance too. I told you about my son. The problems I mentioned? They were pretty serious. My wife . . . she drank and had a Valium habit when she was pregnant. I tried to get her to stop but she wouldn't. Permanent prenatal damage . . . Oh, I wanted a normal child. Someone I could spend time with. Have fun with. Someone I could spoil.' He remembered something Bett had told him a few hours before. 'I wanted someone to play games with, to spend Christmas and Easter with, Thanksgiving. To make oatmeal and pancakes for. To hang out with on Sunday in sweats and sneakers and read the paper and rake leaves.'

From somewhere, he summoned a tear.

'You wanted me to be your daughter,' Megan said.

'Yes! But there was no way you would've agreed on your own. Or even listened to me. You would've thought I was some kind of crank and called the police. So I did what I had to. I waited until I had a chance – Dr Hanson's mother getting sick – and I arranged with him to see you.'

'That part was true?'

'Oh, yes. Of course it's true. We're friends, Hanson and me.' He smiled indulgently. 'Though I think I'm a better therapist than he is. I get right to the core of the problem.'

'Yeah, you sure do.' She offered a faint smile in return.

'You didn't like those letters, I know. But I had to make you see how angry you were with your parents. I had to make you see the truth.'

'That's why you made me write them?'

'Yes.'

'What did you do with them? Did you send them?'

He frowned. 'The letters? No, I threw them out. Writing them was just for you, Megan. I thought maybe, here, we could get to know each other for a while. I'd hoped you'd stay maybe for a few weeks, a month. If it worked out, fine. We could move to San Francisco, you could start college there in the fall.'

He'd moved another few feet closer to her. He was slumped, diminished, looking mournfully at the floor. Matthews had decided how she'd die. He'd strangle her. Her eyes would grow wide and he'd stare at them, drink them in as she died. Pull the glass knife from her hand and get a grip on her neck. Squeeze and squeeze and squeeze until the tip of her protruding tongue stopped quivering. And squeeze some more after that.

It was the way Peter had killed the slut who'd tried to seduce him. Maybe it was the way Peter himself had died. The body was so mutilated the prison doctor hadn't been able to be certain of the cause of death.

Tears flooded the eyes of the inconvenient child.

'Oh, Megan, I'm sorry. I'm so sorry. I just thought that you deserved so much more than you had.'

She was shivering with the sobs.

'A father who wanted to be rid of you. What a terrible thing . . . He wanted to get you out of his life and get back to those ridiculous young women he chased after. And your mother . . . a dear woman but a child herself really. I thought about all sorts of things – how I could adopt you, get you into a foster home . . .'

'You really thought that?' she asked, wiping her face. Her attention was wavering from the glass blade. Her hand was in the shadows at her side. He couldn't tell whether it was pointed downward or at him.

'Yes, I sure did. I talked to a lawyer about adoption.

He said I wouldn't have a chance, not with your natural parents around, however neglectful they were.' His voice was very soft, lulling.

Megan wiped her face again. 'I just wanted to be loved.' Her voice was choked.

'And they didn't love you, did they? They didn't give you any love at all.'

'No.'

'Oh, I would've done things so differently . . . and that's why I took this chance. I'm risking life in prison just to see if something might work out between us. I just wanted you to have a home.' He too was crying now. 'I just wanted a family! That's all *I've* ever wanted too.'

She was sobbing uncontrollably now, hand over her face. 'Yes! That's it. A home. I never had a home. I wanted a father so badly.'

Matthews stepped closer, reached out a tentative hand and touched her cheek, wiped away a tear. He could almost feel her under his hands, peeing and thrashing as she died. He'd leave her out for the dogs. So that Collier would think she'd died as painfully as Peter had.

'I wish I could have done it differently,' he said. 'I mean, this place is so disgusting, Megan. But I didn't have any choice. For both our sakes.'

'I just—'

He reached out his other hand and put his arm around her shoulder. Rubbed her back.

'I just wanted a home . . . only a home.' She struggled to breathe.

'I know you did.' His right hand moved down her face to her neck. His left slipped down her arm until he gripped the glass knife she held.

He gently pulled it out of her hand.

Got you!

But then he glanced down, frowning. It wasn't a knife at all. In his hand was a plastic Bic pen. But he'd seen the blade . . . He looked into her face.

Saw the leering smile.

'Nice try,' Megan whispered.

And with her left hand she jammed the glass blade deep into his side. Once, then again. And again.

A flash of terrible pain shot through him and Matthews howled. He twisted hard away from her and the blade snapped on a rib, leaving a long glass splinter inside of him.

Now Megan screamed – an insane wail – and as her captor groped for the wound she slammed her open palm into his face. A huge pop as his nose broke and blood spurted. He went down on his knees. She kicked him near the knife wound and he coughed as his vision went black.

She came forward but he swam back to consciousness quickly and now it was his fist that connected with her jaw, sending her backwards into the wall. By the time he was on his feet she was disappearing down the dark corridor.

He touched the wound. The pain was astonishing, terrible.

But it was nothing compared with the feeling of shock that raged through him. *She's* the one who fooled me! Suckered me in nice and close, got *my* defenses down. My God, the whole time I thought I was playing her but she led me right into the trap . . .

Her father's daughter, Matthews thought in fury and disgust.

He dropped to his knees and began working the

fragments of glass out of his wound, gasping and savoring the astonishing pain. He wanted to remember it. He wanted to feel what Megan was about to experience.

28

The basement . . .

Megan plunged into the dim corridors of the hospital looking for the basement.

Her jaw ached and the back of her head too – from where she'd slammed it into the wall after he hit her. For just a moment she'd thought about leaping on him again – seeing him lying there, blood filling his shirt, blood dripping from his nose. He'd looked half dead. But no, she wasn't sure that he was hurt as badly as he seemed.

He lied with words, he'd lie with actions.

So she ran – to find the basement door.

She heard Matthews's unearthly scream – it seemed to shake the walls – and then footsteps. Part of it was pain – the breathless sound. But part of it was rage too.

She made slow circles through the corridors until she found the door she'd seen earlier, the one leading to the basement. She grabbed a cinder block and smashed it down on the hasp and lock, which snapped off easily.

Megan flung the door open, looked down into the musty place. For a moment she was paralyzed.

No choice, girl, Crazy Megan the tour guide shouts. *Move, move, move.*

But Josh, she protested silently, I can't leave him.

Hey, you die, he dies. Go!

She clomped down the stairs and found herself in a dimly lit warren of corridors. Trotting slowly from room to room, she took care to avoid the standing water so she wouldn't leave footprints he could follow.

Please, a door, a window . . . Oh, please.

She heard the creak of footsteps from the ceiling above her as Matthews made his way to the door she'd just broken open. She found a door leading outside. It was locked. And the windows too were sealed. Another door. Nailed shut.

Goddamn him! C.M. blurts. *Why'd he padlock the fucking door upstairs if we can't get out this way?*

Megan didn't bother to answer. She couldn't figure it out either. She returned to a room near the base of the stairs and glanced again at one of the windows. The bars on these were wider than the ones on the main floor but she doubted that she could get through.

Fucking hips.

Don't start! Megan started to turn away. Then paused, looked back. Thinking: Okay, maybe I can't get through the bars. But I can make him *think* I did.

She smashed the glass and pushed an overturned plastic bucket beneath it so that it looked like she'd climbed out.

Then she ran back into the warren of dark storerooms to find someplace to hide.

Most of the cardboard boxes piled in the rooms were too small to conceal her. And she didn't have the strength to pull herself up into the pipes that ran along the ceiling.

His steps were approaching the door upstairs. Then he started down.

Megan ran into a cluttered storeroom, the farthest

one from the stairs. It was filled with cartons, small ones again. But over to the side, in the shadows, was a long metal box. It was almost too obvious a choice to hide in but this room was nowhere near the window where she'd faked her escape. And it was pitch dark. Matthews might not even see it.

Could she get it open? And was it empty?

But Megan stopped asking questions. Matthews was now in the basement. A shuffle of footsteps, a moaning wheeze from the pain of the wounds, words muttered to himself.

Now! Crazy Megan prods her. *Go, girl!*

Megan unlatched the trunk.

It took all her strength to lift the thick lid.

And it took all her willpower not to scream as she looked inside.

The blue-white flesh, the limp hair, the closed eyes, a dark, shriveled penis, the long yellow fingernails . . . The terrible Y incision that covered the young man's entire torso. And the cuts and black gouges over his body.

It was Matthews's son, Peter. She recognized the eerie face from the newspaper clipping.

Oh, God . . . My God . . . Tate, Bett . . . Somebody!

The footsteps were closer now. They sounded only thirty or forty feet away.

I can't do it, she thought. No way in hell.

Get inside, Crazy Megan chokes. *You have to.*

Fight him with your fists, she told herself, or you hide in here. Those're your choices.

A moment's pause. The moaning was now right outside the door way, it seemed. Then Megan closed her eyes – as if that would lessen the horror – and climbed into the box, lying down on the corpse, on her back, shivering fiercely.

She let the lid down. The air stank sweetly. Formaldehyde, rotting scents, old skin.

She felt the cold.

Nothing's colder than cold flesh.

Then she heard, faintly, a moan very near. Aaron Matthews was in the room.

Crossing a gap in the Shenandoahs, Tate glanced out the window of Bett's car at the darkened bungalows and ramshackle farmhouses, abandoned barns, the black pits that opened into the network of caverns that laced the earth beneath the Shenandoahs and the Blue Ridge.

They sped past walls of ominous forest – the stark pines, the scrub oak, the sedge, the young kudzu and Virginia creeper. Tate swore he saw eyes peering at them and he thought of the Dead Reb once again.

Ten minutes later, well into the Blue Ridge, Tate pulled Bett's Volvo into an all-night gas station. The elderly attendant glanced at them cautiously when he asked about the Blue Ridge Hospital.

'That old place. Phew.' The man cast a dark look westward.

'Where is it?'

'You get back on the interstate and go one more exit . . .'

'We'd rather stick to back roads, if we can.' The state troopers would be looking for him on the highway, a fact Tate didn't share.

The man cocked his head, shrugged. 'Well, that road there. Route one-seventeen? Take it west ten, twelve miles till you see a Buy-Rite gas station. Then go left on Palmer and just keep going.'

'We'll see the place? The hospital?'

'Oh, you'll see it. Can't miss it. But I'd wait till sunup. You don't wanna go there this time of night, no sir. But you asked for directions, not opinions.'

Tate handed over a twenty and they sped off down the road.

It was a half-hour later that a no-nonsense siren burst to life a quarter-mile behind them. It was a county trooper. The light bar flashed explosively in Tate's rear-view mirror. He accelerated hard.

'You think he knows it's us?' Bett asked.

'Oh, yeah, he knows.' Tate's foot wavered. 'What do I do?'

'Drive like hell,' Bett suggested.

He did.

For about two miles.

The Swedes make a good car but it was no match for the souped-up engine of the pursuing Plymouth. 'Can't make it,' he told her.

He eased up on the gas. 'I'll talk to him. Maybe he'll at least send a car to the hospital.'

'No,' Bett said. 'Pull over.'

'What?' Tate asked, jockeying the skidding car on to the gravel shoulder.

Bett ripped her purse open and dug inside. She paused, took a deep breath, then sat upright, staring in the rear-view mirror at herself, stroking her cheek as Tate had seen her do so often.

What's she up to? he wondered.

'Bett!' he cried as she lifted the nail-file to her face and dragged it hard across her skin.

Blood poured from a gash deep in her cheek.

'Oh,' Bett wheezed. 'It hurts.'

Tate stared at the blood, running more black than red down her neck and falling on to her chest in delicate paisleys.

* * *

'Get out of the car!' reverberated the metallic voice through the rectangular mouth of the PA speaker atop the car.

The young trooper stood beside the open door of his squad car, aiming at Tate's head a blue-black pistol dwarfed by the lawman's huge hand. In his other he held the microphone.

'Get out of that vehicle! Keep your hands up.'

For a moment no one moved.

And then in a blur Bett's door was open – so fast Tate thought that another deputy had snuck up behind them unseen and pulled her out.

She screamed shrilly as she rolled on to the grassy shoulder. The leather strap of her purse was wound around her wrists as if she'd been tied up. Without the use of her hands she fell hard. Dust mixed with the blood covering her face.

'Help me!' she cried. 'He kidnapped me!'

'Don't move. Nobody move!' the trooper called, swinging the muzzle toward Bett. Tate sat perfectly still, hands on the wheel.

Bett scrabbled toward the cop.

'He's got a knife!' she cried. 'Help me, please. He cut me. I'm bleeding. Help me!' She put the harrowing wail of a frightened child into her voice as she stumbled forward. 'He was going to rape me! Get me away from him! Oh, please . . . Oh . . .'

The trooper gave in to his instincts. 'Over here, miss. You'll be all right. He's that fella from Prince William, isn't he? The one killed that girl? Where's the knife?'

'In his belt. He picked me up at a rest stop,' she cried. 'He kidnapped me!'

'Put your hands up!' the trooper called over the

318

microphone. 'And I mean now!'

Tate did.

'What happened?' the cop asked Bett, who was stumbling closer.

'Cut me . . . I need a doctor . . .' The words were lost in the sobbing.

'You in the car. Leave your right hand up and with your left reach out the window and open the door. Don't lower that right hand.'

Tate didn't move.

'I'm not telling you again! I have a—'

'Put it down!' came Bett's raw scream from inches behind his head. Tate's pistol was resting at the cop's throat.

'Oh, shit.'

'Do it!'

'I've got him covered, lady. You do anything to me and he's gone. I'll shoot him. I swear . . .' But he said this out of shame, not resolve, and when Bett screamed, 'We're after my daughter and I'll kill you right now if I have to,' the cop's disgusted grunt was followed by the sound of his large pistol hitting the dirt.

Bett stepped away from the man, who towered over her. He went limp as he saw the ferocity in her face, realizing just how close to death he'd come. He sagged against the car.

'All right,' Bett muttered. 'Lie down on the ground. There. On your stomach.'

Tate was out of the car and jogging toward them.

'There're other troopers coming, lady. They'll be here in minutes.'

'All the more reason to *move*!'

He eased down. Bett handed the cop's pistol to Tate.

319

'Cuff him and let's go,' she said.

But Tate put his hand on her shoulder. 'No. You're staying.'

'No, Tate,' Bett said, holding a wad of Kleenexes up to her bloody chin. 'I want to come.'

What could he say to her? That there wasn't anything she could do and Tate needed to focus on saving Megan – if she could be saved? That it was important for her to stay here and tell the police exactly what had happened, send them out to the hospital? They were both sure-fire arguments. But Tate answered instead from his heart and told her the truth. Simply: 'I don't want to risk losing you.'

'But—'

'No, stay here.'

She looked at the dark blood on the Kleenex and up at Tate once more. She nodded.

'Now, listen to me,' he said gravely, 'when they get here, just set the gun down and put your hands up. They'll be nervous and looking to shoot. Do exactly what they say. You hear me?'

She nodded. He touched her cheek, wiping away some blood.

'A sexy woman with a scar – won't be a man in the county'll keep his hands off you.'

'You'll get her, won't you, Tate?'

'I'll get her.'

He kissed her forehead and ran to the car.

He floored the accelerator, splattering the squad car with gravel and dirt. As he drove over a crest in the road, the tach nosing into the red crescent of the warning zone, he caught a glimpse of Bett in the rear-view mirror, crouching beside the prone trooper, undoubtedly apologizing earnestly. Still, the pistol that was clapped in both her hands was pointed steadily at his face.

She couldn't take it any more.

Crazy Megan was gone, dead and buried or sleeping with the fishes.

The depleted air suffocated her. The smells – the rot and the sweet scent from embalmed skin – wrapped themselves around her throat and squeezed.

Which was bad enough. But then the panic started to sizzle through her body like electricity. The claustrophobia.

'No, no, no,' she said or maybe she just thought it. 'No, no, nonono. Let me out, let me out, let me out . . .'

Not even worried that Matthews was outside, waiting for her. Maybe he was right there, waiting to kill her, maybe not. It didn't matter; she couldn't stay inside a moment longer.

Megan pushed against the lid of the coffin.

It didn't move.

She tried again. Nothing.

'Ah,' she gasped. 'Oh please, God, no . . .'

He'd locked her in! She heard a wild laugh outside. Words she couldn't distinguish. More laughter.

More words, louder: '. . . two having fun together . . . likes you . . . Peter likes you . . .'

'Let me out let me out letmeoutoutoutout!'

Her voice rose to a wild keening, her whole body shivered in violent spasms.

'You fucker you fuck let me outoutoutout!'

She didn't have any idea what words she was saying. It was too much for her.

With both her fists Megan pounded on the lid, banged it with her head, feeling with horror Peter's cold face against her neck, his cold penis against her thigh.

From outside Aaron Matthews beat on the lid too, responding to her pounding. Then more laughter. And finally more tapping, like a drummer, keeping perfect time with the rhythm of her raw screams. Five unbearable minutes later two latches clicked and the lid began to rise.

No subtlety, no nuance . . .

Tate Collier came to the end of Palmer Road and saw the hospital in front of him. He aimed Bett's car directly toward the gate, got his speed up to about forty and bounded over logs and potholes in the neglected surface. He saw the infamous gray Mercedes parked in the staff-only carport. He saw a faint light in one of the windows.

He had no plan other than the obvious and as he skidded around a fallen pine and straightened for the final assault on the gate he pressed the accelerator down harder, sealing his resolve.

Tires spat gravel. He pressed his hands into the steering wheel, pinning himself into the seat. The car plowed through the wrought iron. The air bag popped with an astonishingly loud bang. He'd forgotten about it and hadn't closed his eyes. He was momentarily blinded and lost control of the car. When he could see again he found the vehicle skidding sideways, narrowly missing the Mercedes. The Volvo crashed obliquely into the cinder blocks, stunning him.

Tate leapt out of the car and ran to the first door he could find. Gripping his pistol hard, he flung all his weight against the double panels.

Expecting them to be locked.

But the doors swung open with virtually no resistance and he stumbled head first into a large, dim lobby.

He saw shadows, shapes of furniture, angles of walls, unlit lamps, dust motes circling in the air.

He saw faint shafts of predawn blue light bleeding in through the windows.

But he never saw the bat or tire iron or whatever it was that hummed through the air behind him and caught him with a glancing blow just above the ear.

IV

The Silence of the Deed

29

A hand stroked his hair.

Tate slowly opened his eyes, which stung fiercely from his own sweat. He tried to focus on the face before him. He believed momentarily that the soft fingers were Bett's; she'd been the first person in his thoughts as he came to consciousness.

But he found that the blue eyes he gazed into were Megan's.

'Hey, honey,' he wheezed. 'Fancy meeting you here.'

'Dad.' Her face was pale, hair pasted to her head with sweat, her hands bloody. But she didn't seem too badly hurt.

They were in the lobby of the decrepit hospital. His hands were bound behind him with scratchy rope. His vision was blurry. He tried to sit up and nearly fainted from the pain that roared in his temple. He gasped and collapsed back against a moldy couch.

Aaron Matthews was sitting on a chair near by.

What astonishing black eyes he has, Tate thought. Like dark lasers. They turned to you as if you were the only person in the universe. Why, patients would tell him anything. He understood why Bett had been powerless earlier that night. Konnie too. And Megan.

Then he saw that Matthews was hurt. A large patch of

blood covered the side of his shirt and he was sweating. He glanced at Megan. She gave a weak smile and nodded. He lowered his head to the girl's shoulder. When the pain subsided Tate looked up. 'Hey, you've lost those five pounds you wanted to,' he said to her. 'You're lean and mean.'

'It was ten,' she joked.

Matthews said, 'Well, Tate Collier. Well . . .'

And such a smooth, baritone voice. But not phoney or slick. So natural, so comforting. Patients would cling to every word he uttered.

'I was just doing my job,' Tate finally said to him. 'Peter's trial, I mean. The evidence was there. The jury believed . . .'

Megan frowned and Tate explained about the trial and the boy's murder in prison.

The girl scowled, said to Matthews, 'I knew you'd never worked with him. What a liar.'

Matthews didn't even notice her. He crossed his arms. 'You probably don't know it, Collier, but I used to watch you. After Pete died I'd go to your trials. I'd sit in the back of the gallery for hours and hours. Just watching you. You know what struck me? You reminded me of myself in therapy sessions. Talking to the patients. Leading them where they didn't want to go. You did exactly the same with the witnesses and the juries.'

Tate said nothing.

Matthews smiled briefly. 'And I learned some things about the law. *Mens rea*. The state of a killer's mind – he has to *intend* the death in order to be guilty of murder. Well, that was you, all right, in Pete's trial. You *murdered* Pete. You intended him to die.'

'My job was to prosecute cases as best I could.'

'*If*,' Matthews pounced, 'that was true then why

did you quit prosecuting? Why did you turn tail and run?'

'Because I regretted what happened to your son,' Tate answered.

Matthews lowered his sweaty, stubbly face. 'You looked at my boy and said, "You're dead." You stood up in court and felt the power flowing through you. And you *liked* it. You knew how dangerous it could be.'

Tate looked around the room. 'You did all this? And you went after all the others – Konnie and Hanson and Eckhard? Bett, too.'

'Mom?' Megan whispered.

'No, she's okay,' Tate reassured her.

'I had to stop you,' Matthews said. 'You kept coming. You wouldn't listen to reason. You wouldn't do what you were supposed to.'

'This is where you were committed, right?'

'Him?' Megan asked. 'I thought he'd worked here.'

'I thought so too,' Tate said, 'but then I remembered testimony at Peter's trial. No. He *was* a therapist but *he* was the one committed here.' Nodding at Matthews.

Mr Bogan: *Now, Doctor Rothstein, could you give an opinion of the source and nature of Peter's difficulties?*

Dr Rothstein: *Yessir. Peter displays socialization problems. He is more comfortable with inanimate creations – stories and books and cartoons and the like – than with people. He also suffers from what I call affect deficit. The reason, from reviewing his medical records, appears to be that his father would lock him in his room for long periods of time – weeks, even months – and the only contact the boy would have with anyone was with his father, Aaron. He wouldn't even let the boy's mother see him. Peter withdrew into his books and television.*

Apparently the only time the boy spent with his mother and others was when his father was committed in mental hospitals for bipolar depression and delusional behavior.

Matthews said, 'I was here, let's see, on six intakes. Must have been four years altogether. I was like a jailhouse lawyer, Collier. As soon as the patients heard I was a therapist they started coming to me.'

'So *you* were Patient Matthews,' Megan said, eyes widening.

'That's my Megan,' Matthews said with something that might have been real pride.

She said to Tate, 'They closed this place because of a bunch of suicides. I thought it was Peter who'd killed them. Or talked them into killing themselves.'

'But it was you?' Tate asked Matthews.

'The DSM-III claimed I was sociopathic – well, they call it an antisocial/criminal personality now. How delicate of them. I knew Richmond was looking for an excuse to close down places like this. So I simply helped them. Too understaffed and too incompetent to keep patients from killing themselves. The place was a poster boy for budget cuts. I got transferred to a halfway house and one bright, sunny May morning, I walked out the front door. Moved to Prince William. And started planning how to destroy you.' Matthews winced and pressed his side. The bleeding seemed to have stopped and the wound, unfortunately, didn't look that severe.

Tate recalled something else from the trial and asked, 'What about your wife?'

Matthews said nothing but his eyes responded. And Tate understood. 'She was your first victim, wasn't she? Did you talk her into killing herself? Or maybe just slip some drugs into her wine during dinner?'

330

'She was vulnerable,' Matthews responded. 'Most therapists are.'

Tate asked, 'What was she trying to do? Take Peter away from you?'

'Yes, she was. She wanted to place him in a hospital full-time. She shouldn't have meddled. *I* understood Peter. No one else did.'

'But you made Peter the way he was,' Megan blurted. 'You cut him off from the world.'

The girl was right. Tate recalled the defense's expert witness, Dr Rothstein, testifying that if you arrest development by isolation before the age of eight, social – and communications – skills will never develop. You've basically destroyed the child for ever.

Tate remembered too how he'd handled the expert witness's testimony.

The Court: *The Commonwealth may cross-examine.*

Mr Collier: *Dr Rothstein, thank you for that trip down memory lane about the defendant's sad history. But let me ask you: Psychologically, is the defendant capable of premeditated murder?*

Dr Rothstein: *Peter Matthews is a troubled—*

Mr Collier: *Your honor?*

The Court: *Please answer the question, sir.*

Dr Rothstein: *I—*

Mr Collier: *Is the defendant capable of premeditated murder?*

Dr Rothstein: *Yes, but—*

Mr Collier: *No further questions.*

'All he needed was *me*!' Matthews now raged. 'He didn't need anyone else in his life. We'd spend *hours* together – when my wife wasn't trying to sneak him out the door.'

331

'Did you love him that much?' Tate asked.

'You don't have a clue, do you? Why, you know what we did? Peter and I? We *talked*. About everything. About snakes, about stars, about floods, about explorers, about airplanes, about the mind . . .'

Delusional ramblings, Tate imagined. Poor Peter, baffled and lonely, undoubtedly could do nothing but listen.

Yet . . . with a sorrowful twist deep within him, Tate realized that this was something Megan and he *didn't* do. They didn't talk at all. They never had.

And won't ever, he realized. We've lost that chance forever.

Their captor fell silent, looking into a corner of the hospital lobby, lost in a memory or thought or some confused delusion.

Finally Tate said, 'So, Aaron. Tell me what you want. Tell me exactly.' He closed his eyes, fighting the incredible pain in his head.

After a moment Matthews said, 'I want justice. Pure and simple. I'm going to kill your daughter and you're going to watch. You'll live with that sight for the rest of your life.'

So it's come to this . . .

Tate sighed and thought, as he had so often on the way to the jury box or the podium in a debate, *all right, time to get to work.*

'I don't know how you can have justice, Aaron,' Tate said to him. 'I just don't know. In all my years practicing law—'

Matthews's face writhed in disgust. 'Oh, stop right there.'

'What?' Tate asked innocently.

'I hear it,' the psychiatrist said. 'The glib tongue, the smooth words. You have the gift . . . sure. We know that. But so do I. I'm immune to you.'

'I won't try to talk you into a single thing, Aaron. You don't seem to be the sort I could do that to anyway.'

'It won't work! Not with me. The advocate's tricks. The therapist's tricks. "Personalize the discourse." "Aaron" this and "Aaron" that. Try to get me to think of you as a specific human being, *Tate*. But that won't work, *Tate*. See, it's Tate Collier the human being I despise.'

Undeterred, Tate continued, 'Was he your only child? Peter?'

'Why even try?' Matthews rolled his eyes.

'All I want is to get out of this and save our lives. Is that a surprise?'

'A perfect example of a rhetorical question. Well, no, it's not a surprise. But there's nothing you can say that's going to make any difference.'

'I'm trying to save your life too, Aaron. They know about you. The police. You heard the message from the detective, I assume? On your answering machine?'

'They may figure it out eventually but since you're here by yourself, an escapee, I think I have a bit of time.'

'What does he mean?' Megan asked. 'Escapee?'

He saw no reason to tell her now that her friend Amy was dead. He shook his head and continued, 'Let's talk, Aaron. I'm a wealthy man. You're going to have to leave the country. I'll give you some money if you let us go.'

'Leading with your weakest argument. Doesn't that mean you've just lost the debate? That's what you say on your American Forensics Society tape.'

The faint smile never wavered from Tate's face. 'You saw my house, the land,' he continued. 'You know I've got resources.'

A splinter of disdain in Matthews's eyes.

'How much do you want?'

'You're using a rhetorical fallacy. Appealing to a false need – for diversion.' Matthews smiled. 'I do it all the time. Soften up the patient, get the defenses down. Then, bang, a kick in the head. Come on, I didn't do this for ransom. That's obvious.'

'Well, whatever your motive *was*, Aaron, the circumstances've changed. They know about you now. But you've got a chance to get out of the country. I can get you a half-million in cash. Just like that. More by hocking the house.'

Matthews said nothing but paced slowly, staring at Megan, who gazed back defiantly.

Tate knew of course that money wasn't the issue at all; neither was helping Matthews escape. But his immediate purpose was simply to make the man indecisive, wear down his resistance. Matthews was right, this was a diversion. And even though the man knew it Tate believed the technique was working.

'I can't make you a rich man but I can make you comfortable. I can—'

'Pointless,' Matthews said, as if he were disappointed.

'But you can't change things. You can't make it the way it was. You can't bring Peter back. So will you just let us go?'

'Specific request within the opponent's power to grant, requiring only an affirmative or negative response. Your skills are still in top form, Collier. My answer, however, is negative.'

'You tell me you're after justice.' Tate shrugged. 'But I wonder if it's not really something else.'

Another flicker in the eyes.

'Have you really thought about why you're doing this?' Tate asked.

'Of course.'

'Why?'

'I—'

'It's to take the pain away, isn't it?'

Matthews's lips moved as he carried on a conversation with himself or his dead wife or dead son. Or no one.

What a man hears, he may doubt.

What a man sees . . .

Tate leaned toward him, ignoring the agony in his head. He whispered urgently. 'Think about it, Aaron. *Think.* This is very important. What if you get it wrong? What if killing Megan makes the pain *worse*?'

'Nice try,' Matthews cried. 'Setting up straw men. What you're saying—'

'Or what if it had no effect at all? What if this is your one chance to make the pain go away and it doesn't work? Did you ever *consider* that?'

'You're trying to distract me!'

'You lost someone you loved. You lie on your back for hours, paralyzed with the pain. You wake up at two a.m. and think you're going mad. Right?'

Matthews fell silent. Tate saw he'd touched a nerve.

'I know all about that. It happened to me.' Tate leaned forward and, without feigning, matched the agony he saw in Matthews's face with pain of his own. 'I've been there. *I* lost someone I loved more than life itself. I lost my wife. I can see it in your face. Yes, see! These aren't tricks, Aaron. I *do* know what I'm talking about. That's all you want – the pain to go away. You're not a lust killer, Aaron. You're not an expediency killer. You're not a hired killer. You only kill when there's a reason. To make the pain go away!'

And to Tate's astonishment he heard a woman's voice beside him. A smooth contralto. Megan, gazing into

Matthews's eyes, was saying, 'Even those patients you killed here, Aaron. . . . You didn't *want* to kill them, not really. You just wanted to help them stop hurting.'

Excellent, Tate thought, proud of her.

'The pain,' he took over. 'That's what this is all about. You just want it to go away.'

Matthews's eyes were uncertain, even wild. How we hate the complex, the confusing, the unknown, and how we flock to those who offer us answers simple as a child's drawing.

'I'll tell you, Aaron, that I've lived with your son's death every day since the D of C called and told me what happened. I feel that pain too. I know what you're going through. I—'

In three steps Matthews was on top of Tate, slugging him madly, knocking him to the floor. Megan cried out and stepped toward the madman but he shoved her to the floor again. He screamed at Tate, 'You *know*? You know, do you? You have no fucking idea! The times, weeks and weeks, I haven't been able to do anything but lie on my back and stare at the ceiling, thinking about the trial. You know what I see? I don't see Peter's face. I see your *back*. You, standing in the courtroom with your back to my son. You sent him to die but you didn't even *look* at him! The jury were the only people in that room, weren't they?'

No, Tate thought. They were the only people in the universe. He said, 'I'm so sorry for you.'

'I don't want your fucking pity.' Another wave of fury crossed his face and he lifted Tate in powerful hands and shoved him to the floor again, rolled him on his back. He took a knife from his pocket, opened it with a click and bent down over Tate.

'No!' Megan cried.

Matthews slipped the blade past Tate's lips. Tate tasted metal and felt the chill of the sharp point against his tongue. He didn't move a muscle. Then Matthews's eyes crinkled with what seemed to be humor. His lips moved and he seemed to be speaking to himself. He withdrew the blade.

'No, Collier, no. Not you. I don't want you.'

'But why not?' Tate whispered quickly. 'Why not? Tell me!'

'Because you're going to live a long life without your daughter. Just like I'm going to do without my son.'

'And that'll take the pain away?'

'Yes!'

The lawyer smiled once more. 'Then you have to let her go.' He struggled to keep the triumph from his voice – as he always did in court or at the debate podium. 'Let her go and kill me. It's the only answer for you.'

'Daddy,' Megan whimpered. Tate believed it was the first time he'd heard her say the word in ten years.

'Only answer?' Matthews asked uncertainly.

Tate had known for years it would come to this, he supposed. But what a time, what a place for it to happen.

All cats see in the dark . . .

Therefore Midnight can see in the dark.

He leaned his head against the girl's cheek. 'Oh honey . . .'

Megan asked. 'What is it? *What?*'

Unless Midnight is blind.

Tate began to speak. His voice cracked. He started again. 'Aaron, what you want makes perfect sense. Except that . . .' It was Megan's eyes he gazed into, not their captor's. 'Except that I'm not her father.'

337

30

Matthews had stopped pacing. He seemed to gaze down at them but he was silhouetted by the backlit picture window and Tate couldn't see where his eyes were turned.

Megan, pale in the same oblique light, clasped her injured face. A pink sheen of blood was on her cheeks and breasts. She was frowning.

Matthews laughed but Tate could see that his quick mind was considering facts and drawing tentative conclusions.

'I'm disappointed, Collier. That's obvious and simple-minded. You're lying.'

'How often did you see us together?' Tate asked.

'That doesn't mean anything.'

'You followed us for how long?'

A splinter of doubt. Tate had seen this in the eyes of a thousand witnesses.

Matthews answered, 'Six months.'

'How many weekends was she with me?'

'That doesn't—'

'How many?'

'Two, I think.'

'You broke into my house to plant those letters. How many pictures of her did you see?'

'Dad . . .'

'How many?'

Matthews finally said, 'None.'

'What did her bedroom look like?'

Another hesitation. 'A storeroom.'

'How much affection did you ever see between us? Did I *seem* like a father? I've got dark, curly hair and eyes. Bett's auburn. And Megan's *blonde*, for God's sake. Does she even look like me? Look at the eyes. Look!'

He did. He said uncertainly, 'I still don't believe you.'

'No, Daddy! No!'

'You went to see my wife,' Tate continued to Matthews. The doctor nodded.

'Well, you're a therapist. What did you see in Bett's face when you were talking to her? What was there when she was telling you about us and about Megan?'

Matthews reflected. 'I saw . . . guilt.'

'That's right,' Tate said. 'Guilt.'

Matthews looked from one of his captives to the other.

'Seventeen years ago,' Tate began slowly, speaking to Megan, 'I was prosecuting cases here. Making a name for myself. The *Washington Post* called me the hottest young prosecutor in the commonwealth. I'd take on every assignment that came into the office. I was working eighty hours a week. I got home to your mother on weekends at best. I'd go for three or four days in a row and hardly even call. I was trying to be my grandfather. The lawyer-farmer-patriarch. I'd be a local celebrity. We'd have a huge family. An old manse. Sunday dinners, reunions, holidays . . . the whole nine yards.'

He took a deep breath. 'That was when your Aunt Susan had her first bad heart attack. She was in the hospital for a month and mostly bedridden after that.'

'What are you saying?' Megan whispered coldly.

'Susan was married. Her husband, you remember him.'

'Uncle Harris.'

'You were right in your letter, Megan. Your mother *did* spend a lot of time caring for her sister. Harris and your mother both did.'

'No,' Megan said abruptly, 'I don't believe it.'

'They'd go to the hospital together, Harris and Bett. They'd have lunch, dinner. Go shopping. Sometimes Bett cooked him meals in his studio. Helped him clean. Your aunt felt better knowing he was being looked after. And it was okay with me. I was free to handle my cases.'

'She told you all this?' Megan asked. 'Mom?'

His face was a blank mask as he said slowly, 'No. Harris did. The day of his funeral.'

Tate had been upstairs on that eerily warm November night fifteen years ago. The funeral reception, at the Collier farm, was over.

Standing at a bedroom window, Tate had looked out over the yard. Felt the hot air, filled with leaf dust. Smelled cedar from the closet.

He'd just checked on young Megan, asleep in her room, and he'd come here to open windows to air out the upstairs; several relatives would be spending the night.

He'd looked down at the back yard, gazing at Bett in her long black dress. She hiked up the hem and climbed on to the new picnic table to unhook the Japanese lanterns.

Tate had tried to open the window but it was stuck. He took off his jacket to get a better grip and heard the crinkle of paper in the pocket. At the funeral one of Harris's attorneys had given him an envelope, hand-addressed to him from Harris, marked personal. He'd forgotten about it. He opened the envelope. He read the brief letter inside.

Tate had nodded to himself, folded the note slowly and walked downstairs, then outside.

He remembered hearing a Loretta Lynn song playing on the stereo.

He remembered hearing the rustling of the hot wind over the brown grass and sedge, stirring pumpkin vines and the refuse of the corn harvest.

He remembered watching the serpentine arc of Bett's narrow arm as she reached for an orange lantern. She glanced down at him.

'I have something to tell you,' he'd said.

'What?' she'd whispered. Then, seeing the look in his eyes Bett had asked desperately: 'What, what?'

She'd climbed down from the bench. Tate came up close and, instead of putting his arm around his wife's shoulders, as a husband might do late at night in a house of death, he handed her the letter.

She read it. And nodded.

'Oh.'

Bett didn't deny anything that was contained in the note: Harris's declaration of intense love for her, the affair, his fathering Megan, Bett's refusal to marry him and her threat to take the girl away from him forever if Harris told her sister of the infidelity. At the end the words had degenerated into mad rambling and his chillingly lucid acknowledgment that the pain was simply too much.

Neither of them cried that night as Tate had packed a suitcase and left. They never spent another night under the same roof.

Despite the presence of a madman, holding a knife

a few feet from them, Tate's concentration was wholly on the girl. To his surprise her face blossomed not with horror or shock or anger but with sympathy. She squeezed his leg. 'And you're the one that got hurt so bad. I'm sorry, Daddy. I'm sorry.'

Tate looked at Matthews. He said, 'So that's why your argument doesn't work, Aaron. Taking her away from me won't do what you want.'

Matthews didn't speak. His eyes were turned out the window.

Tate said, 'You know the classic reasons for punishing crimes, Aaron? To condition away bad behavior – doesn't work. A deterrent – useless. To rehabilitate – that's a joke. To protect society – well, only if we execute the bad guys or keep them locked up for ever. No, you know the real reason why we punish? We're ashamed to admit it. It's barbaric. But, oh, how we love it. Good old biblical retribution. Bloody revenge is the only honest motive for punishment. Why? Because its purpose is to take away the pain.

'That's what you want, Aaron, but there's only one way you'll have that. By killing me. It's not perfect but it'll have to do.'

Megan was sobbing.

Matthews leaned his head against the window. He moaned as he gazed outside. The sun was up now and flashed on and off as strips of liver-colored clouds moved quickly east. He seemed diminished and changed. As if he were beyond disappointment or sorrow.

'Let her go. Hell, it doesn't even make sense to kill her because she's a witness. They know about you anyway.'

Matthews crouched beside Megan. Put the back of his hand against her cheek, lifted it away and looked at the glistening streak left by her tears on his skin. He kissed her hair.

'All right. I agree.'

Megan started to protest.

But Tate knew that he'd won. Nothing she could say or do at this point would change his decision.

'I'll call the dogs to the run. I'll be back in five minutes.'

31

'Is it true?' she asked, tears glistening on her cheeks.

'Oh, yes, honey, it's true.'

'You never said anything.'

'Your mother and I decided not to. Until after Susan died. You know how close Bett was to your aunt. She wanted her never to find out – it would have been too hard for her. The doctors only gave her a year or two to live. We were going to wait until she'd passed away.'

'But . . .' Megan whispered.

He smiled wanly. 'Oh, yes. She's still alive. Miracle of modern medicine. That's why we kept up the pretense that you were ours.'

'Why didn't you ever tell *me*? Aunt Susan wouldn't have to know.'

Tate examined wounds on her palms. Pressed his hands against them. He couldn't speak at first. Finally he said, 'The moment passed.'

'All these years,' she cried, 'I thought *I* must've done something.' She laughed, then lowered her head against his shoulder. 'What a terrible thing I must have been for you. What a reminder.'

'Honey, I wish I could tell you different. But I can't. You were half the person I loved most in the world and half the person I most hated.'

'One time I said something,' she said, weeping softly. 'I'd been with you for the weekend and Mom asked how it went. I said I'd had an okay time but what could you expect? You were just an adequate father. I thought she was going to whip me. She freaked out totally. She said you were the best man she'd ever met and I was never, ever supposed to say that again.'

Tate smiled. 'An adequate father for an inconvenient daughter.'

'Why didn't you ever try it again, the two of you?'

He echoed, 'The moment passed.'

'How much you must love her.'

Tate laughed sourly to himself at the irony. The child that drove them apart had now brought them back together – if only for one day.

How scarce love is, he thought. How rarely does it all come together: the pledge, the assurance, the need, the circumstance, the hungry desire to share minutes with someone else. And the dear desperation too. It seems impossible, miraculous, when it works.

He looked her over and decided that the two of them, his exwife and her daughter, would be fine – now that the truth had been dumped between them. A long time coming but better than never. Oh, yes, they'd do fine.

Gritty footsteps approached.

'Now, listen to me,' he said urgently. 'Find a phone and call Ted Beauridge at Fairfax County Police. He's a friend of mine. Tell him your mother's probably in jail in Luray or Front Royal—'

'What?'

'No time to explain. But she's there and tell him to get cops out here.'

The girl looked at him with eyes that reminded him of her mother's. Not the violet shade, of course – those

346

were Bett's and Bett's alone – but the unique mix of the ethereal and the earthy.

Matthews appeared in the doorway.

They turned to look at the gaunt man standing before them, his muscular hand pressed to his bloody belly

'Okay, get going,' Tate said to her. 'Run like hell.'

'Go on,' Matthews said, and reached forward to take her arm.

She spun away from him and hugged Tate hard. He felt her arms around his back. Felt her face against her ear, heard her speaking to him, a torrent of fervid words flowing out, coming from a source other than the heart and mind of a seventeen-year-old high school junior.

'Megan . . .' he began.

But she took his face in both her hands and said, 'Shhh, Daddy. Remember, bears can't talk.'

Matthews grabbed her again and pulled her away. Took her to the door.

He unlocked it and shoved her outside. The door closed with a snap behind her. Through a dirty, barred window Tate saw her sprint down the driveway and disappear through the gate.

'So,' Collier said, glancing up at Matthews.

'So,' he echoed.

'Outside?' the lawyer asked, looking around at the gloomy place. 'Would that be all right? I'd rather.'

Matthews hesitated for a moment. But then decided, why not? 'Yes. That's all right.'

He unlocked the door again and they stepped into the parking area and walked around into the back grounds, past the wild Rottweilers in their cage.

Matthews was thinking back to the times he'd been committed here. The lawns and gardens. They were beautiful. Well, why wouldn't they be? Give five hundred crazy people grounds to tend and, brother, you've got a showplace. He'd sat for hours and hours and hours talking to other patients and – in his imagination – to his dead Peter. Sometimes the boy responded, sometimes not.

The dawn sun was still below the horizon but the sky was bright as they walked side by side lithely through the tall grass and goldenrod and milkweed while dragonflies zipped from their path. Grasshoppers bounced against their legs, leaving dots of brown spit on their clothing.

The dogs were in a frenzy behind them, sniffing the ground and bounding at the wire fence of their run, trying to escape and go after the intruder who walked beside their master.

'Look at this place,' Matthews said conversationally. He waved his arm. 'I remember it like it was yesterday. I remember the strange things people would say. The delusional ones, the paranoid ones, the depressed ones. The ones who were simply nuts – you know, Collier, the mind isn't an exact science, whatever the Diagnostic and Statistical Manual says. Some of the men and women were just plain crazy and that's all you could ever say about them. But I always listened to them. Why, people give themselves away like free samples at a grocery store. Hand themselves to you on platters. And what do they use? Words. Aren't words the most astonishing thing?'

Collier said, 'You bet they are.'

There wasn't much time, Matthews reflected. He supposed he had an hour or two until the police arrived. At best it would take Megan two hours to get to the nearest phone. Enough time to finish here, bury Peter, and get to Dulles for a flight to Los Angeles. Or maybe he should just drive west. Hide in the hills of West Virginia. He took a deep breath. 'Stop here.'

They were beside a shallow ditch. It would make a fine grave for Collier. And he'd decided that he'd kill the lawyer with a single shot to his head. No pain, no torment. And he wouldn't let the dogs have the body. Out of respect for a worthy adversary.

Then the lawyer stunned him by closing his eyes and whispering, 'Our Father, Who art in Heaven . . .' He slowly completed the Lord's Prayer.

Matthews laughed then asked, 'You believe in God?'

Collier nodded. 'Why does that surprise you?'

'When I'd see you in court it seemed that only the judge and jury were your gods.'

'No, no, I believe He exists. That He's merciful and He's just.'

'Just?' Matthews asked skeptically.

'Well, he's the reason I don't send people to death row anymore . . . Do *you*? Believe in God?'

'I'm not sure,' Matthews said.

'You know, I always wanted the chance to prove the existence of God in a debate.'

'How would you do it?' Matthews asked truly curious. 'Prove God existed? Rhetorically, Resolved: God exists. Isn't that how debates start?'

Collier looked up at the purple sky. 'You know Voltaire?'

'Not really. No.'

'I'd make his argument. He said there had to be a God because he couldn't imagine a watch without a watchmaker.'

Matthews nodded. 'Yes, I can see that. That's good. That's compelling.'

'But of course then you run into all of the counter-arguments. The con side.'

'Such as?'

'Incompatible religious sects, interpretations of holy scriptures proven wrong later, no empirical proof of miracles, the Crusades, ethical and secular self-interest, terrorism . . . That's an uphill battle, all right.'

'No answer for that?'

'Oh, sure. I've got an answer.'

Matthews was suddenly fascinated. After Peter's death he'd prayed every night for six months. He believed that the boy had answered some of those communiqués. It gave him clues, but not proof, that Peter's soul floated near by. 'What is it, what's the answer?' he asked hungrily.

'That a watch,' Collier answered slowly, 'no matter how well made, can never *comprehend* its watchmaker. When we claim to, everything breaks down. If God exists then by definition he's unknowable, and souls – yours, mine, Megan's, Peter's – are beyond our understanding. When we create human institutions to represent God they have to be flawed.'

'Yes, it makes sense. How simple, how perfect.'

'You've thought about questions like this, haven't you? Because of Peter?'

'Yes.'

Eyes on Matthews's, Collier said, 'You miss him so much, don't you?'

'Yes, I do.' Matthews stared down at the ground. For all he knew he'd stood on this very spot two or three years ago, studying slugs or dung beetles or ants for hour upon hour, wondering how, in their worldless world, they communicated their passions and fears.

'You can get help, Aaron. It's not too late. You'll be in jail but you can still be content. You can find somebody to help you. Somebody who's as good as you were.'

'Oh, I don't think so. It's too late for that, I'm afraid.

350

One thing I learned – you can't talk somebody out of his nature.'

'"Your character is your fate,"' Collier said.

Matthews laughed. 'Heraclitus.'

He'd learned the aphorism from one of Collier's closing statements. He lifted the gun toward the lawyer.

Then Collier's eyes flickered slightly. He sighed. 'I'm sorry,' he said.

Matthews frowned. 'What do you mean?'

'I'm so sorry.'

He heard the snap behind him.

Matthews spun around. There stood Megan, holding the gun Collier had brought with him. Matthews had left it in the lobby of the hospital and had forgotten about it. The girl was ten feet away and was pointing the black muzzle at Matthews's chest.

Oh yes, Matthews laughed to himself. Oh yes . . . He understood. Remembered her whispering to Tate before he'd escorted her out the door. They'd planned this together. Collier would stall him, Megan would pretend to run but would return for the gun, propping open the door. He remembered Collier protesting as they'd hugged. But she'd had her way.

Maybe she wasn't his blood daughter but they were a family now.

He glanced at her eyes. 'Drop the gun,' she ordered.

But he didn't. He wondered, would she go through with it? She was only seventeen and, yes, she had anger in her heart – enough to attack him with a knife – but not enough to kill, he believed.

Character is fate . . .

He saw compassion, fear, weakness in her eyes. He could stop her. He could get her to put the gun down.

'Megan, listen to me—' he began in a soft voice,

351

gazing into her blue eyes, which *were* so unlike Collier's.
'I know what you're—'

The first bullet tugged at his side, near the knife wound, and he felt a rib snap. He was swinging the gun toward her when another shot struck his shoulder and arm.

Collier dropped to his knees, clear of the line of fire.

Megan stepped closer.

'Peter . . .' Matthews whispered, struggling to lift his pistol.

Yet another shot burned into him striking his chest.

A step closer.

'Please . . .'

She shook her head.

The girl paused a foot away.

He looked into her eyes.

Always the eyes . . .

The gun fired one last time. And for an instant his vision was filled with a thousand suns. And in his ears was a chorus of noise – voices, perhaps.

Peter's among them, perhaps.

And then there was blackness and silence.

Epilogue

The beach at San Cristo del Sol in Belize is one of the finest in Latin America.

Even now, in May, the air is torrid but the steady breezes soothe the hordes of tourists during their endless trips from the air-conditioned bars and seafood joints to the pools to the beach and back again. Windsurfing, paragliding, jet-skis and waterskiing keep the surface of the turquoise water perpetually turbulent, and within the bay itself hundreds of snorklers and resort-course scuba divers engage in their elegantly awkward amphibious activities.

The town is also a well-known staging area for those who wish to see Mayan ruins; there are two beautifully preserved cities within five kilometers of the main drag in San Cristo.

The Caribe Inn is the most luxurious of all the hotels in town, a Spanish colonial hacienda that has four stars from Mobil and accolades from a number of other sources, proudly displayed behind the registration desk, at which Tate Collier now stood, hoping fervently that the clerk spoke English.

The man did, it turned out, and Tate explained that he had reservations, proffering passports and his American Express card.

'That's a party of . . . . ?' the clerk queried.

'Party of two.'

'Ah,' the desk clerk responded. Tate filled out the registration card with ungainly strokes.

'So, you are from Virginia,' the clerk said. 'Near Washington?'

'*Sí*,' Tate responded self-consciously, ready for his pronunciation to throw the conversation off kilter if not insult the clerk personally.

'I have been there several times. I like the Smithsonian especially.'

'*Sí*,' Tate tried again, forgetting even the words that conveyed some meaningless pleasantry – words he'd practiced on the flight. For a man who'd made his way in the world by speaking, Tate's command of foreign languages was abysmal.

He watched the clerk glance down at the reservation form with a momentarily perplexed frown on his dark, handsome face. Tate thought he knew why. The clerk had taken a good look at the attractive woman who'd entered the hotel on Tate's arm a moment before and though surely, in this line of work, the clerk had seen just about everything, he couldn't for the life of him figure out why these two would want separate rooms.

A man is, after all, a man . . . And an age difference of twenty years . . . well, that's nothing.

Megan came out of the lobby phone booth and walked to the desk just as the clerk was showing Tate a diagram of the available rooms. Tate pointed to two, first a smaller inside room, then a corner unit with a view of the beach. 'I'll take this one. My daughter'll have the corner room.'

'No, Dad, you take the nice one.'

'This is your daughter?' the clerk said, his curiosity satisfied. 'Of course, I should have known.'

'I'm sorry?' Tate asked him.

'I mean, the resemblance. The young lady takes after you.'

The man's suspicions crept back when he saw the two guests exchange fast glances and struggle to suppress laughter. Tate thought about pulling out driver's licenses and proving the relationship but then decided: It's none of this guy's business.

Besides, mystery has an appeal that documented fact will always lack.

They settled on the rooms and after Tate's card was imprinted they followed the bellhop through a veranda.

'Josh said his new physical therapist is great,' Megan told him.

'Glad to hear it.'

'But the way he put it was he said "she's" great. Think she's old and fat?'

'We'll be back in six days. You can find out for yourself. When do you say *de nada* again?'

'After somebody thanks you. It means, "It's nothing."'

'They say "*Gracias*" and then I say *"De nada".*' Tate repeated the words several times as if he were a walking Berlitz tape.

'Then I called Bett,' Megan continued. 'She's glad we got in okay. She said to take lots of pictures.'

'I'll call her later.'

'She, um, was going over to Brad's tonight. But she said it in a funny way. Like there was something going on. Is anything going on?'

'I don't have a clue.'

Megan shrugged. 'She said she talked to Konnie and

he's coming to your office on Tuesday at nine to talk about the case.'

The previous week Tate had made his first appearance in a criminal court in nearly five years – Konnie's arraignment. He'd answered the judge's simple query with simpler words. 'Not guilty, your honor.'

He had a novel defense planned. It was called 'induced intoxication', and although he'd promised Megan that they would be spending the week doing nothing but seeing the sights and partying he'd hidden three law books in his suitcase and suspected the last day of the trip would find him with at least a rough draft of his opening statement to the jury – if not a set of deposition questions or two. He knew that as soon as she met a handsome young windsurfer – probably at the cocktail party than night – he would have a few hours free on most of the evenings.

He and Megan arrived at their rooms.

'*Gracias de nada,*' Tate said, and slipped the confused bellhop an outrageously generous tip.

A half-hour later they'd showered and were in khaki shorts, T-shirts and wicker hats. Every inch *los turistas*. They walked down to the lobby and asked about how they might bicycle to the nearest Mayan ruin. The clerk arranged for the bike rental and gave them directions. It was just past the afternoon siesta and most of the guests were headed for the white-sand beach. But Tate and Megan snagged two battered bicycles from the rack in front of the inn and headed away from town.

'Which way?' she called.

He pointed and they mounted up.

Despite the opposing foot traffic and the astonishing heat, they sped along the cracked asphalt path straight into the dense, fragrant jungle, standing on the pedals, hollering and laughing, racing each other, as if every moment counted, as if they had many, many hours of missed exploration to make up for.

JEFFERY DEAVER

THE BONE COLLECTOR

Lincoln Rhyme is one of the world's foremost forensic criminalists. He is also a quadriplegic, paralysed from the neck down. He is strapped in his bed and actually planning his suicide when he gets a call he can't ignore from his old partner on the force.

A single human hand has been found, buried on a deserted railway track on New York's West Side – the hand belonging to a man who got into a cab at the airport and never got out. And the driver was the Bone Collector.

The Bone Collector, a killer and kidnapper obsessed with old New York, leaves clues that only Lincoln Rhyme can decipher. As the minutes count down toward each successive death of an innocent, Rhyme and Amelia Sachs, the female police officer acting as his arms and legs, race to locate the victims by unravelling the Bone Collector's clues.

Slowly the criminalist begins to narrow the noose around the kidnapper. But it appears the Bone Collector has his own plans, and is narrowing his own noose – around Lincoln Rhyme.

HODDER AND STOUGHTON PAPERBACKS

JEFFERY DEAVER

A MAIDEN'S GRAVE

The countdown begins at noon . . .

when two teachers from a school for the deaf and their students stop to help at a car crash on an isolated road . . .

and are immediately captured by three escaped convicts.

Stark against the prairie stands an ancient slaughterhouse that still reeks of decades of spilled blood. It is here that cold killer Lou Handy will bring the hostages.

It is here that he will kill one innocent girl an hour, on the hour, until his demands are met.

HODDER AND STOUGHTON PAPERBACKS

JEFFERY DEAVER

PRAYING FOR SLEEP

Michael Hrubek, a young schizophrenic, has escaped from a hospital for the criminally insane. And he's making his way towards Lis Atcheson, the teacher who testified at his murder trail.

Four people race to intercept him before he reaches her. His psychiatrist; the hostpital director; a professional tracker, and Lis's husband, who must get to Hrubek before the madman reaches his wife.

But Michael's mind – with its delusions of murder and betrayal – is crystal clear about one thing. He knows Lis better than she knows herself. And he carries with him a monstrous secret that will tear apart many lives during the course of this single horrifying night.

'Scary, smart, and compulsively readable' Stephen King

'Seldom have more twists and turns, or more harrowing suspense been packed into a single day – or between the covers of a single book . . . Superior'

James Patterson, bestselling author of *Along Came a Spider*

HODDER AND STOUGHTON PAPERBACKS

JEFFERY DEAVER

THE DEVIL'S TEARDROP

It's Washington, DC; it's the last night of the year, and people are dying . . .

At 9 am on New Year's Eve, 1999, a man gets onto the packed escalator of a metro station and fires a silenced machine gun into the crowd. He escapes without being spotted in the confusion caused by the horror of this vicious attack, which leaves dozens of killed and injured people.

One hour later, a note is delivered to the mayor: 20 milllion dollars, or the writer will instruct the killer to strike again; at 4pm, at 8pm, at midnight . . . Hundreds more will die.

There can be no defence against this plan, not on that day, not in that city. The money has to be found, the ransom will be paid. But then a hit and run victim is identified as the mastermind behind the operation, and suddenly there's no way of stopping the psychotic gunman from killing again, and again, and again . . .

The only clue the FBI has to go on is the note . . . and the only man in the country who might be able to decipher its secrets is Parker Kincaid, forensic document expert, who, along with agent in charge Margaret Lukas, races against the clock to stop the killer before each deadline.

HODDER AND STOUGHTON PAPERBACKS